THE SONS OF DUSTY WALKER

Dylan

JODI REDFORD

Jackson

RANDI ALEXANDER

Killian

DESIREE HOLT

Rogue

SABLE HUNTER

Cover Artist: Diana Carlisle
~~*~*
Cover Model: Scott Nova
~~*~*
"DYLAN: THE SONS OF DUSTY WALKER, BOOK 1"
Copyright © 2015 Jodi Redford
Edited by LR Burnia
"JACKSON: THE SONS OF DUSTY WALKER, BOOK 2"
Copyright © 2015 Randi Alexander
Edited by E Felder
"KILLIAN: THE SONS OF DUSTY WALKER, BOOK 3"
Copyright © 2015 Desiree Holt
Edited by Wizards in Publishing

"ROGUE: THE SONS OF DUSTY WALKER, BOOK 4"
Copyright © 2015 by Sable Hunter
~~*~*

TABLE OF CONTENTS

Dylan

by

JODI REDFORD

This book is dedicated to my Cowboy Club ladies—Sable Hunter, Desiree Holt, and Randi Alexander. Not only are you three incredibly talented authors, your support and friendship is a true blessing.

And although technically not one of the ladies, special thanks goes to the awesome and ever handsome Scott Nova for working with us on this project and bringing our heroes to life on our covers.

Last but never least, to my readers—you make it possible for me to keep doing this job that I love. Thank you!

Prologue

He'd been on the receiving end of some crazy shit in his life, but nothing beat this. No two ways around it.

Swiping his hand across the weeks' worth of stubble overtaking his jaw, Dylan Walker shifted in his seat, feeling like a damn penguin in the tailored black suit his mother had forced him to pack along for the trip to Red Creek, Kansas. She'd insisted it was the respectful thing to do. Mighty ironic, considering the situation. Surely respect was the last thing on his pop's mind when he'd been off banging four women behind his old lady's back.

He winced as he mentally conjured a smack upside his head courtesy of his mom. She'd always been the first to defend Dusty. Just went to show how the smooth-talking sonofabitch managed to pull the wool over her eyes all these years, leading her to believe she was special. She'd clung to the fragile hope that he'd leave his wife for her if he could. No doubt those three other women had thought the same thing.

Hard to say if his ma would have an excuse armed and ready once she found out about all of this. Discovering the man who'd hung the moon and the stars in her eyes was a lowdown liar of the worst kind? Surely no amount of love made any of this forgivable.

Dusty's attorney—Stanley Benner, Esquire—leaned over his desk and plopped a folder of papers in front of Dylan and the three other men who sat on either side of him. Momentarily lifting his attention from that ominous manila folder, Dylan covertly inspected his newly discovered siblings.

Jesus H Christ. Yes, this was definitely some messed up shit.

Benner's gaze skipped from Dylan's face and ping-ponged to each of his brothers. Probably the man was equally thrown by their similarities. The salt-and-pepper-haired lawyer freed the buttons on his suit coat and settled his bulky frame in his upholstered chair, pushing his wire-rimmed glasses up on his nose with a brisk shove of one chubby finger. "Incredible likeness. Your father never mentioned it."

Yeah, well, when it came to leaving out pertinent details—such as the fact that he had four sons scattered across the country—Dusty Walker was a goddamn pro.

The man to the right of Dylan—Killian? Yep, that was it—sat forward in his chair. "Are we quadruplets? Were we separated at birth?"

The attorney shook his head again. "Absolutely not. Each of you is your mother's biological son. You are each about a year apart in age. Mr. Walker...uh...Killian, you're the oldest at twenty-seven." Benner transferred his attention to Dylan. "And you're the youngest. It must be a very strong DNA strand in your father to have produced men who look so similar."

Dylan killed his grunt. That was the understatement of the century. Hell, they were even wearing nearly identical suits. Put 'em up on a stage, and they had their own twisted version of the Blues Brothers.

"When I arrived at your homes last week with the sad news that your father had died, I was under strict instructions not to mention that you had brothers. It was among your father's last wishes that you learn of your siblings' existence by bringing you together." The attorney picked up a sheaf of papers. "I apologize for bringing you to Kansas under these circumstances. As you already know, Dusty and his wife, Theresa, were killed in an auto accident. We were told they died instantly." The lawyer's expression softened on that last part, as if he hoped that provided some relief to them that their father hadn't suffered.

Dylan was still too numb from processing everything to respond. His brothers remained equally quiet. Benner looked from one to the other. "So, if there are no more questions, I'll begin reading the key points in the will." He stalled a few seconds, his gaze mildly hopeful.

"Yeah, I've got one," the one named Rogue spoke up. "How

did he…?" He held up a hand. "Let me rephrase that. Why? Why four families in four different states?"

The lawyer stashed the papers aside and laced his fingers. "Your father wanted to have children, and he confided to me that his wife didn't want them. This broke his heart."

What the hell? Could this get any more fucked up?

"So he went around looking for incubators?" Killian's fiery demand was a mirror to Dylan's angry thoughts.

"That's a little disrespectful," Benner chided.

"You're calling me disrespectful?" Killian snorted. "I'd say your client is the one who was disrespectful."

Amen, brother. More and more, it was becoming clear that the word didn't belong in any definition attached to Dusty. "She knew about all of us? His wife, I mean?" Fucked up wouldn't begin to cover it, if that was the case.

"No, she did not." Benner's cheeks turned redder than a baboon's ass. "And I was sworn to silence under attorney/client privilege. I'm assuming that your mothers made you aware of your father's marital situation?"

His brothers' identical poker faces made it impossible for Dylan to determine if they'd been in the dark about Theresa Walker's existence before their father's death. Even if they'd known, impossible to say if it'd meant a damn to them one way or another. Maybe they'd eventually hardened themselves to the fact that Dusty had a life that they weren't a part of. God knows he'd built up a shell where his dad was concerned. It'd been the only way to get through the endless weeks in between Dusty's monthly visits.

The pathetic part? He'd craved those times spent with his dad. More than he cared to admit to. Didn't matter that he'd been bored to death whenever Dusty insisted on teaching him the insider track on mineral rights, he'd dutifully pretended interest. Whatever it took to keep his dad in his life.

In the beginning it'd worked out fine, despite Dylan's nagging suspicions that everything wasn't copasetic with his parents' odd arrangement. By the time he was twelve he could no longer fool himself that it was perfectly normal to have a dad who only came around once a month. He'd seen through his mom's assurances that Dusty's work kept him constantly on the road. While it'd certainly been true up to a point, it didn't explain why Dusty's life outside of his monthly visits remained a mystery. Then one afternoon Dylan came home from school and overheard his mom crying in her room. In a rare moment of weakness, she'd spilled the beans about her affair with Dusty. In true Georgianna Mayhope style, she hadn't dredged up excuses for what happened. She'd insisted that love made you do stupid things sometimes. Well fuck that shit. If it did, he was never falling in that trap.

In the years that followed, the tension grew between him and Dusty. Dylan had rebelled in every way he could, even going so far as to briefly entertain the idea of forsaking the name Walker. His mother had thrown a conniption fit, insisting that he was a Walker no matter what any might say to the contrary. To Dylan, it'd felt like a lie. A shady cover-up to hide his bastard heritage. In retaliation, he'd gone out of his way to taint his despised surname during his troubled youth and early adulthood. It was a damn miracle he didn't end up in jail.

In the end, the one thing that'd saved him from himself was landing his dream gig as the bass guitarist for Truckstop Pickup. His band members had taken him in, becoming the family he'd desperately craved all those years. Dusty hadn't been much thrilled with Dylan's decision to become a musician. Fair enough. Dylan hadn't been much thrilled to be abandoned the majority of his life. Kinda made them even.

Benner cleared his throat again, jogging Dylan from his private grumblings. "So, in the interest of time, I will read the highlights of the will. The entire document is in the folders I set in front of you." The attorney spouted off a grocery list of assets: a mineral and water rights company that boasted assets near half a billion dollars, including a private ten-person jet, a storefront right there in Red Creek, as well as a big house on the outskirts of town.

Like the rest of his brothers, Dylan remained wrapped in his shocked silence while he took it all in. He'd always known Dusty was loaded, he just hadn't realized to what extent.

"Of course, there are the four houses in four compass points of the US," Benner continued. "In the north, Montana, where Killian resides. Texas, from where Rogue hails. Dylan, of course, from Nashville, and Jackson, from Oregon. These houses are currently company property, but your father notes that you four, as the new owners of D. Walker Mineral, can opt to transfer the homes into your mothers'—"

"Hang on." Dylan stiffened. "You're saying he left the company to us?"

"Yes, of course." Benner looked surprised. "I didn't read that portion of the will because I assumed…" He gusted a sigh. "The company is now legally in your names, exactly one quarter going to each."

Dylan couldn't contain his sarcastic whistle. *Well played, Dusty, you cagey motherfucker. Shake up our lives* and *make it damn near impossible for us to walk away from this bullshit with a stiff middle finger for being such an awesome pops.*

"So, if we sell our quarter?" Jackson finally spoke up, stringing the words out slowly.

"There are repercussions." The attorney flipped pages. "Ah, here. 'Heretofore, the parties to which—'"

"In plain English, please." Killian propped one booted foot on the opposite knee.

"Of course." Benner discarded the papers and leaned back in his chair, his rotund belly making a cozy resting spot for his hand. "The company is essentially frozen as-is for a full year. After that time, if one of you wants to sell, the others have the option of buying you out at half-worth."

"Half-worth?" Rogue balled his fist. Dylan had seen—and

participated in—enough rowdy bar fights to be on high alert. His brother's posture remained rigid. "Meaning they'd buy me out at a fifty-percent discount?"

"Yes, that's correct. Your father wanted to keep the company in the family. Wanted you four boys to run it together." Benner feigned a tepid smile. "However, you are each officially on the payroll, and your first paychecks will be cut the day you successfully complete the one…" He swallowed then cleared his throat. "Stipulation in the will."

This should be interesting. "Stipulation?" Dylan prodded.

"To inherit, you must spend a week in Red Creek, working in your father's office, learning more about the business, sharing with each other what you've learned from your father over the years. You must also reside for that week at your father's house—your house—on Osprey Lake."

Well wasn't that mighty generous of Dusty. Forget the fact that Dylan never stepped one foot in his dad's office or his house while Dusty was alive. Apparently death changed everything.

"A week?" Jackson shook his head. "What's the timeframe here? Anytime in the next year?"

His expression still slightly fierce, Rogue opened his folder and yanked out his copy of the will. "What section is that in?"

"Second from the last page. You'll see that there's a 30 day time limit." The attorney surveyed the calendar propped on his desk. "Today is August second. You'll need to decide which week in August works for all four of you, and plan to be back here then. Or if this week works…" He shrugged, that vaguely hopeful expression once again etched in his features.

Killian tapped his fingertips on his knee. "Dad wants the four of us to live in the same house and work in the same office? For an entire week?"

"Like summer camp for the bastard sons of Dusty Walker." Dylan mumbled a curse. Yeah, he was a bitter dick. Better than being a delusional sap who still believed his dad gave a crap about him.

Jackson rubbed the spot between his eyebrows. "What the fuck was he thinking?"

Good question. It was a complete dick move forcing four complete strangers—and face it, that's what they were, blood related or not—to shack up and work together for a week.

Rogue continued with his mute reading.

Benner's face turned that lovely shade of red baboon ass again. "He loved each one of you. I know that because he took great pains to create provisions to make sure you were taken care of after his death, as you were while he was alive."

"Listen here." Rogue's stare drilled into the sheaf of papers he held. "It says we each have to spend a week, but it doesn't say it has to be the *same* week."

"No, it...uh...what...?" Benner frantically flipped through his paperwork.

"I say we each take a week, get this goddamn stipulation out of the way, and figure out the rest later." Rogue's squint cycled between Dylan, Jackson, and Killian. "Agreed?"

Dylan was pretty damn sure Rogue seldom faced opposition. Fortunately Dylan was in complete accord with his brother when it came to this. He dug his cellphone from his pocket and scanned his schedule. It was all for show. There wasn't a damn thing on it, thanks to his recent falling out with Luke. Motherfucking prima donna singers and their egos. Yeah, he loved the man like, well, a father. But he was damn well impossible to live with at times. "I can stay this week. I got nothin' goin' on." Sad but true. If he didn't get this rift settled with Luke, Dylan might have zero gigs going on for a while.

Jackson snatched his folder. "I can do the week after."

Killian hefted to his feet. "Sure, I'll do the third week."

"That leaves week four for me." Rogue straightened and tucked the folder under his arm.

"Now wait, boys." The springs on Benner's seat squeaking in

protest, the lawyer stood, his focus riveted to his copy of the will as Dylan and Jackson took a cue from their brothers and abandoned their chairs. Benner appeared flustered. "Your father wanted you all to be here together. At the same time. To get to know one another."

Ignoring the frazzled attorney, Dylan stared at the belt buckle situated at Jackson's waist. It was an exact duplicate to the one he wore. The one Dusty had given him long ago, and that Georgianna wanted him to wear today out of respect. Again with the respect. He loved his ma to the depths of his soul, but the poor woman was as delusional as they came. It'd break her heart learning the truth about Dusty. For that reason, he dreaded the necessity of telling her. But if he didn't, she'd possibly find out anyway. And that'd be a million times worse than coming from him.

Tugging his mind from that worrying avenue of thoughts, he glanced at Rogue and Killian, cataloging their matching belt buckles.

"Am I seeing things?" Jackson asked.

Killian dropped his gaze, his eyebrows forming a low V. "Son of a bitch. I can't believe this. They're all alike."

Dylan chuffed under his breath. "That's kinda fucked up, huh? The old man gave us the same belt buckle, like we'd use them to somehow magically find each other." The Bewitched version of The Parent Trap.

And that couldn't be more apropos. Because he'd never felt more fucking trapped in his life.

Almost as if they'd synchronized it, he and his brothers turned toward the door in the same motion. Jesus, they really were taking this similarity to a freak show level. They were one step away from choreographing a Von Trapp number.

"Wait." Benner hustled around his desk and blocked the exit, his expression pole-axed. "Your father's wish was to have you spend this time together."

"Well then…" Killian patted Benner's shoulder as he strode

10

past him. "I guess he should have had his lawyer write that in the will."

Silently giving his brother a finger gun salute for that response, Dylan trailed the others out the door and stalked to the spit-shined limo parked outside. He watched as each of his brothers ducked inside their separate rides before he settled in his cushy seat. It still felt odder than shit thinking of those strangers as his brothers.

On the bright side, nothing could possibly knock him on his ass after this. No damn way. Shaking his head, he grabbed the Stetson he'd tossed aside earlier and tucked it low over his brow. "Let the fun commence."

Chapter One

His head pounding from lack of sleep, Dylan yawned and rubbed the grogginess from his vision before eyeing his opened luggage near the huge oak dresser in the corner of the guest room.

He didn't know what it said about him that almost his entire life's belongings fit in two suitcases. Being on the road more days than not, it didn't make sense getting attached to stuff that'd only take up too much space. That philosophy stood him well in everything. Clothes, furniture, women. Especially that last option.

His band members liked to give him shit for not availing himself of some of their more persistent female groupies. And damn, were those chicks persistent. The instant he'd step into the VIP area backstage, the women would be on him in full accost mode, tucking their panties and hotel keycards into his pockets. But while Luke and the other guys had no qualms hooking up with a different woman in every city, it left a bad taste in Dylan's mouth. Not that he was an angel. He occasionally let his dick overrule his brain. Without warning, his wayward thoughts drifted to the one instance—or more to the point, the one *woman*—responsible for his biggest lapse in that department.

Zoe. He didn't even know her last name. How fucked up was that? They'd shared the hottest twenty-four hours of his life. Granted, they hadn't spent the entire time in bed. There'd also been the backseat of her car, the shower in her hotel room, and even a quickie in the bathroom of the waffle joint they grabbed breakfast at before he caught a flight to Dallas for his next gig. It'd been the first and only occasion he hadn't ridden in the tour bus, and his bandmates had been relentless with their info digging regarding his rare absence. He hadn't caved. His amazing connection with Zoe wouldn't be fodder for those nosy assholes to rib him about.

In the weeks—hell, years—that'd followed his time with her,

he'd never shaken her from his mind. He wished to God he'd gotten her last name. A number. Anything.

Why? So you coulda offered her empty promises you were in no position to keep? He'd seen firsthand the pain that kind of selfishness brought. No way in hell he'd repeat Dusty's legacy.

Melancholy and regret an anvil on his shoulders, he finger-combed his sleep-rumpled hair and pushed up from the bed. Day Three in his father's house, and he still hadn't unpacked. Old habits were partly to blame. He was never anywhere long enough *to* unpack. Hell, if not for his mom fussing over him whenever he was home he'd likely live out of his bags there too. But the big reason he couldn't bring himself to fill the dresser drawers in front of him was it'd feel too permanent. Even a week perpetuating this farce was a week too long. He wasn't cut out for running D. Walker Mineral. He wasn't the prodigal son who'd forgive and forget the tainted heritage he wanted no part of. And he especially didn't want to spend one more minute trapped within these walls that bore memories he held zero connection to.

Tension pressed against his sternum like an angry alien intent on punching its way through his chest. Unable to stand the sound of his own silence for a second longer, he tugged his jeans on and topped the faded denim with a white tee and a short-sleeved blue-and-gray checked shirt. After jamming his feet into his weathered cowboy boots, he jogged downstairs. He bypassed the gargantuan great room. Inviting as that space was, it held too many images of Dusty, and the life he'd built without Dylan and his half-brothers.

His brothers. Still couldn't get used to it. Since the departure from the lawyer's office, Dylan's thoughts had dwelled more than a time or two on Jackson, Rogue, and Killian. As some of the shock had worn loose, a new grievance had settled in place. All these years they'd known zilch about each other. Dusty had deprived them of any brotherly bond. Sure, maybe they wouldn't have been best friends who did everything together. Plenty of siblings weren't that close. But damn it, Dusty had no right to keep that secret from them just so he could continue to perpetuate his lies.

Edginess stiffening his stride, he passed through the entry leading into the kitchen. Marliss, the housekeeper, whistled in greeting somewhere behind the massive center island. He was beginning to think the woman possessed bionic hearing that'd pick up on a footstep the next county over.

Biting the bullet, he stepped around the counter. She flashed him a genuine smile. "Exactly the strapping young fella I was hoping to see. Be a sweetheart, and help an old lady up?"

Concern automatically overriding his need to escape, he hurried to Marliss's side. "What happened? You fall?"

Gripping the arm he offered, she shook her head as he carefully assisted her to her feet. "Gosh darn knees decided to take an early lunch break while I was cleaning out this cupboard. Hate being reminded I'm no spring chicken anymore."

Happy to know she wasn't injured, he tucked his thumbs in his back pockets. "I was thinkin' I'd take a look around town after work today. Anything you need me to pick up?"

She patted him on the cheek. The gesture reminded him so much of his mom, he couldn't help but grin. No sooner did she pop into his head, and his previous gloominess returned. Georgianna was still in the dark about Dylan's half-brothers and the other women. He'd debated breaking the news to her during his brief trip home to collect his things for this week, but one look at the grief lurking in her eyes killed that idea dead in the water. She had enough to deal with right now. He wouldn't add to her pain.

"Now you mention it, Lou forgot to pick up my prescription yesterday. I'd accuse him of getting old and senile, but it'd be like the pot calling the kettle black."

He chuckled. "How can you be senile when you're only thirty?"

"Oh, aren't you just a smooth talkin' fibber." Batting her eyelashes, she smacked his chest with her rubber glove.

"Obviously the apple didn't fall far from the tree."

He immediately stiffened. The sparkle dimmed in Marliss's gaze and she squeezed his arm. "I meant no offense. Your father wasn't perfect, but he was a good man. Just as I know you are."

He stared at the toe of his boot before stepping away from the island. "I'll pick up your prescription. No problem."

Marliss wouldn't be put off topic that effortlessly. Another thing he was quickly learning about the woman. "This can't be easy on you. On any of you boys. Any time you want to talk, I'm always here. Same with Lou. Even if we're off the clock, you come on over to the apartment. Our door is always open."

He appreciated the offer, but it didn't feel right to take her up on it. Didn't matter that she and her husband, the cook, resided on the property, they deserved their privacy. Besides, nothing she'd say would make one damn bit of a difference. Dusty had proved himself to be a bigger bastard than Dylan originally estimated. If nothing else, Marliss hit the nail on the head with the apple comparison. Only in Dylan's case, his bastard lineage was in the literal sense. He cleared his throat. "I should hit the road. Don't need the office sending a search posse after me."

Marliss nodded, her expression sad. Not waiting around for another of her good-intentioned pep talks, he grabbed the keys for the SUV. The only other two options were the Cadillac and the company truck. Normally the truck was more his style, but stubbornness kept him from driving around in a vehicle that blatantly bore the Walker name. He figured every tongue in town was already wagging overtime about him and his brothers. Scandalous gossip like four illegitimate sons sired by the richest dude in the county would be prime grist for the rumor mill. He wasn't about to give them more to chew on, so going low profile was the name of the game.

The ten minute drive to Red Creek proved to be about as uneventful as they came. Tempting as it was to blow off some of his steam by seeing precisely how far he could bury the needle, the last thing he needed was to get popped by one of the local boys in blue. He chose an open parking spot across the street from D. Walker Mineral and grabbed his longhorn trucker cap. Although the odds of town being overrun with die-hard fans were slim to none, the Stetson was his signature wardrobe piece up on the stage, and he was easily recognizable with it on. Tugging the bill of his cap low over his forehead, he moseyed inside the three-story building housing Dusty's offices.

Abby, the receptionist, tossed him a wink while she tapped away at her keyboard. "Sounding good there, handsome."

It took him several beats to catch her meaning *and* the song floating through her Bluetooth speakers. He grunted. "Damn well should. Took us a whole day to lay that track. Luke was on one of his man periods." He shot her a sheepish look. "Sorry, my mouth doesn't come with a filter."

She waved off his apology before plopping her chin in her hand. "So what's he like?"

"Luke?" Plenty used to fielding the question, he shrugged. "Most days I want to shove my boot up his ass, if that gives you any indication."

"In other words, this is a vacation for you then." She chuckled at the side-eye he slid her way. "Come on, maps and charts are way more exciting than screaming, adoring fans rushing the stage."

"You need to get out of the office more often. Clearly being around too many dirt samples has impaired your judgement."

Her eyes twinkled. "Just you wait. Be around them long enough, they'll lure you to the Dark Side too."

Not damn likely. Leaving Abby to her delusions and her computer work, he strode down the hall. He bypassed the other four offices and paused in the doorway to the last one. A familiar hollowness settling in the pit of his belly, he stared at the banged-up wooden monstrosity that insisted on passing for his father's desk. With all the money Dusty had been swimming in, you'd think he woulda upgraded to something that'd been built this century and wouldn't sag if you looked at it cross-eyed. The piece of furniture was so out of keeping with the high-end decor at the lake house. Made him wonder if Theresa wasn't the one who'd called the shots there.

Not too much of a surprise, if that were the case. Especially after what he'd discovered his first day in the office. Or he should say, what someone made damn sure he'd discover by conveniently leaving the black binder for him to find smack dab in the middle of his work space. According to one of the news articles inside the folder, Theresa's father had originally owned the company, and she and Dusty inherited it, eventually turning it into D. Walker Mineral and eventually the flourishing multi-million dollar company it was today.

There was no doubting Dusty's shrewd business acumen, right down to knowing he couldn't rock the boat with Theresa—the woman who'd owned half of his livelihood. But that sure hadn't stopped him from dipping his wick in wells not belonging to his wife. Futile anger rattling at his cage again, Dylan turned his back on his father's office and stalked into the one across the hall. It was smaller and offered no idyllic view of the town's namesake Red Creek, but he wasn't yet ready to sit in Dusty's seat. Maybe he'd never get to that point.

Dropping into the ratty chair, he tore his focus from the doorframe adjacent to him. The surrealism of the moment hit him like a sledgehammer. He felt like an outsider looking in at his own life. What woulda happened if Dusty and Theresa hadn't died in the car accident? Dylan wouldn't be sitting here. He'd remain ignorant of his brothers' existences. All of these lies would have continued unfazed and snuggled in their cocoon of undisturbed deceit. Just knowing that twisted the knife in his gut.

The claustrophobic space closing in on him, he shoved up from his seat. If he didn't shake loose of this suffocating atmosphere he'd do something stupid—like punch his fist through a wall. Praying his expression wasn't as scary as the ragged emotions eating at him, he journeyed out front and nodded to Abby. "Forgot I have to run an errand for Marliss." At least it wasn't a lie. Unlike every other damn thing in his life.

"Sure. Take all the time you need."

The rest of his God-given days wouldn't be enough to get him through this bullshit. Keeping that thought to himself, he ducked outside. Fresh air and the muggy beginnings of an August morning briskly slapped him to his senses. Shoulders relaxing, he sucked in a deep breath and released it slowly. By the time he reached the end of his exhale he was reasonably assured he had his shit together.

Dragging a hand across his nape, he blinked against the blinding glare of the sun, the bill of his cap doing little to shield his eyes. He noticed Walt Forester, one of D. Walker's oil and mineral rights specialists, exiting the front door of Cubby's Creekside Cafe. According to Marliss, her husband's cousin, Cubby, ran the place and offered the best biscuits and gravy in the county, much to Lou's grumbling disagreement. Dylan was also willing to bet Cubby's was the major hub for any gossip in town, hence his strict avoidance of the joint the last couple days. Not about to change that status quo, he loped across the street before Walt could spot him.

Home free from any unwanted run-ins, he ducked into the pharmacy and bee-lined to the counter. A sixty-something year old woman garbed in a powder blue smock that nearly matched her bouffant hairdo peered at him over her spectacles. "You're one of those Walker boys. Spittin' image of Dusty."

Shit. Shoulda known he wouldn't be safe anywhere. "Yes, ma'am, I'm Dylan. Pleased to make your acquaintance—" He took a quick scan of her nametag, "Hazel." He removed his hat and offered his hand.

Hazel nodded approvingly and returned his shake across the counter. "Good to see a young man with manners. Obviously your mama raised you well."

He waited for the inevitable sly questions, but Hazel only adjusted the frame of her glasses. "Now what brings you in today?"

"Marliss asked me to pick up a prescription for her."

Her forehead scrunching with a frown, Hazel shuffled to the wall of cubbies behind her. After a few seconds of inspecting the various packages, she swiveled back toward him. "When did she call it in?"

Feeling like a dimwit, he hitched his shoulders in a shrug. She crossed to a plastic container holding a stack of order slips and rifled through the papers. A harrumphing noise passed her pursed lips. "Gonna have a talk with that Ernestine. Dotty fool keeps putting the unfilled scrips in the wrong box. It'll take me a few minutes to get this ready. You okay with waitin'?"

Not like he was in a rush to get back to the office. "Sure."

"Could always grab a cup of coffee at Cubby's in the meantime."

His brow breaking into a sweat at that suggestion, he shook his head. "Gotta pick up a few things while I'm here anyway. That'll keep me plenty busy."

Hazel eyed him like she was attempting some guesswork at what might be on his shopping list, and he made a mental note not to grab anything he didn't want broadcasted to the rumor mill. Girly mags, Trojans, and jock itch remedies being top on the list. Not that he was in need of any of the above. Though it'd sure be nice to have a purpose for the condoms. Despite his desire to stay untangled and fancy-free, sex was something he could get behind. Especially with the stress of the last several days and the remainder of the week ahead of him. To lose himself for an hour or two in a woman's arms? Goddamn, that'd be sheer bliss.

Only he wouldn't give in to the urge. He couldn't. This town had enough dirt on him. He wouldn't add fuel to the fire by slipping between the sheets with one of the local ladies. He'd ride it out until his stint here was done. Plenty time to find a willing bed partner once he returned to Nashville and his regularly scheduled life. Hell, he'd likely have an excess of free time if Luke still had his head jammed up his ass about settling this rift between them.

Gritting his teeth, Dylan ambled into the periodical aisle and scanned the options. Naturally his favorite—*Guitar World*—was noticeably absent, so he picked up the latest *Time* instead. A nearby fashion rag snagged his attention, mainly because the model on the cover had a smoldering gaze that reeled him in. He stood there like a complete dope, the magazine clutched in his hand, but his mind was a million miles away, steeped in an erotic memory. Gorgeous green eyes locked with his, peering straight into his soul. The sensuous slip-slide of their sweat-slickened bodies. Zoe's nails digging into his ass, refusing to let him go, even when he buried himself so hard and deep within her, he swore he could feel her heartbeat. Or maybe it was the fierce mad rush of his own pulse as she annihilated his defenses. She was a danger to all of his carefully held rules. Don't get close. Offer no promises. Forget her and move on.

The first two had been taken out of his hands with her refusal to give him her last name. But Rule Three was impossible. He'd never forget her. God knows he'd tried.

He thunked the magazine back in the rack and continued his shopping, adding a box of Benadryl to his stash in hopes of it helping him get some shut eye the rest of the week. The sound of a young child's laughter broke through his concentration. Customers must have come in when he wasn't paying attention. Time to get his ass back to Hazel before someone beat him to the front of the line.

Rounding the corner of the aisle, he spotted the petite blonde parked at the counter. *Damn, too slow.*

He checked out the blonde's heart-shaped posterior, his resignation shifting to appreciation. He'd gladly buy a round of beers for whoever was responsible for inventing yoga pants. Hell, he'd purchase them an entire distillery.

The female scraped her hair back and he spotted the hot pink streaks scattered in with the platinum locks. He wouldn't have figured anyone around these parts for adopting an edgier style like that. Maybe she wasn't local.

And didn't that make things potentially interesting?

Hazel scooted up to her side of the counter and beamed a smile, instantly breaking up Dylan's two-second happy parade quicker than a firehose set on full blast. Judging from the older woman's response, the blonde wasn't a stranger in town.

Just his damn luck. First female in a long time who stirred more than a passing fascination in him and he had to keep his mitts to himself.

"Zoe, dear. Perfect timing. I was about to give ya a ring to see about some private lessons for Ginger."

Dylan jolted at the name. *Holy shit.* How damn weird was that? Here he'd been thinking about Zoe, and another one stood a couple feet in front of him. And it wasn't even that common of a—

His thoughts rear-ending each other like a fifty car pileup, he jerked his attention back to the world class butt he'd eagerly admired seconds ago. A tingle of déjà vu tripping through his synapses, he blinked. "Zoe?"

"Hm?" The blonde sent him a distracted look over her shoulder.

Shock punching him square in the solar plexus, he returned the gaze of the woman who'd haunted his dreams for the last four years.

He cataloged the exact moment Zoe registered who he was. Her poleaxed expression hinted that she was equally stunned by their unexpected reunion. He prayed that her silence *was* due to disbelief. They'd left things on good terms, but shit knows women tended to recall events in a wholly different light than most clueless men. And he wasn't too proud to admit that he could be dimwitted as the rest of his gender.

Figuring he better say something rather than continuing to

gape at her like a psycho, he cleared his throat. "Man, it's good to see you."

She opened her mouth, but the only sound that emerged was a wispy, distressed breath. He didn't think it possible, but her coloring turned several shades whiter than Casper the Friendly Ghost. Suddenly alarmed that she might be moments away from passing out, he rushed forward—and collided with the little tike barreling across his path. The kid bounced off Dylan's leg and tumbled onto the ground. Before he could reach for the boy, Zoe snapped out of her daze and hunkered to her knees, her shaking hand smoothing over the tot's stick-straight brown hair. "Hunter, that's why I keep telling you not to run in stores."

"Yes, mama."

The sweet childish voice uttering those two words sent another bolt of shock careening through Dylan. Zoe...was a mom? Desperately trying to process that thought, he slashed his attention to Hunter. As if he'd known he was the subject of deep scrutiny, the little boy popped his thumb in his mouth and peeked up at Dylan.

He stared into Hunter's eyes. Everything surrounding Dylan tilted at a funny angle and a strange prickle of awareness hopscotched across his suddenly flushed skin. The tiny person looking back at him was a mirror of himself at that age. Honest to God, with that kind of resemblance, Hunter could be...

Hot and cold flashes racing inside him, he reluctantly tore his focus from the boy and met Zoe's horrified gaze.

Mother. Fucker.

Chapter Two

There's no way this is happening. Any moment now she'd wake up, drenched in sweat, her heart pounding from yet another nightmare where her past showed up out of the blue to bite her in the ass. Even as she tried to convince herself of that unlikely outcome, Zoe clung to the possibility with everything she had.

Dylan wasn't fading from her vision. No, he remained rooted in place, the shock holding his gorgeous features hostage telling her all she needed to know. Hunter's resemblance to him hadn't gone unnoticed, and Dylan's mind was no doubt spinning.

She should have prepared better for this day. *And exactly how would that have made any of this easier?* It wouldn't have. There was no smooth way to convey the news that Dylan had a son he'd known nothing about.

A rustling noise announced that Hazel had abandoned her station behind the pharmacy counter. Zoe broke gazes with Dylan and glanced up at the older woman hovering over them like a clucking mother hen.

"You know who always cures any boo-boo? Goofy." Hazel stooped and affixed a Band-Aid on Hunter's knee.

Zoe didn't have the heart to tell Hazel that Hunter was perfectly fine. Besides, the Band-Aid seemed to have accomplished the feat of distracting Hunter from the drama brewing around him. She was half tempted to ask for her own Goofy bandage in hopes of it accomplishing the same miracle for her.

Hazel's keen stare bounced between her and Dylan. "You two are acquainted?"

Oh Lord. This definitely wasn't a conversation she wanted to get into with one of the biggest busybodies in Red Creek. Even without the dirty details at her disposal, Hazel would waste no time getting on the phone with her cronies to spill the beans that Zoe had run into a strange man and acted weird. By the end of the day they'd be taking bets on who Dylan was. Old flame? Someone she owed money to? Or maybe even a long lost brother she never told anyone about? It didn't help that she kept her personal life a mystery. No one really knew who she was. They didn't know about her dad. And they never would.

Dylan pushed to his feet and surprised her by helping her up. Well, the good news was he hadn't started yelling at her. Yet. He kept his intense focus trained on her face. "Zoe and I are old friends. Haven't seen each other in nearly four years."

"Ain't that somethin'." Hazel made another of her clucking noises. Her attention drifted down to Hunter, and Zoe could practically hear the woman doing the calculations in her head.

Shit. Desperate to get out of there before Hazel or Dylan launched into their own version of the Spanish Inquisition, Zoe nudged the back of Hunter's head with her hand. "Time to go, Boo Bear. Callie and Josh are waiting for us."

As expected, Hunter's eyes lit up at mention of his best bud. Squealing in excitement, he jumped to his feet and bounced in place like a bunny loaded up on sugar. At least she didn't have to worry about finding a subtle way to drag him out of there. She shot Hazel a frazzled look. "Sorry, I know you wanted to chat about Ginger. Feel free to call me at the house tomorrow and we'll get something set up."

"But what about your prescription?"

"No rush. I can pick it up later." She spun on her heel and grabbed Hunter's waving arm, determinedly steering him toward the exit.

"Zoe." Dylan's whiskey baritone whipped in her direction, attempting to lasso her to a halt. *Damn, damn, damn. Keep moving.* "Sorry, we'll have to catch up another time."

She all but busted through the front door, swinging Hunter in front of her. Ragged breaths scraping her lungs, she frantically scanned the parked vehicles for her beat up Chevy truck before realizing it was right in front of her. *Almost out of the danger zone.* She hauled Hunter into her arms and dashed to the passenger side. Anchoring him against her hip, she swung open the door and shoved the harness to the side of his child seat. Not daring to shoot a look over her shoulder to see if Dylan was headed her way, she plopped Hunter in place and buckled him in. Blissfully ignorant of the fact that his mama was seconds from officially losing her shit, he kicked the back of the seat in front of him. She snatched his sandaled foot before he could wobble the seat again. "No, remember what we talked about?"

Hunter frowned like he'd suddenly acquired a spontaneous case of amnesia.

Fuck it. She had bigger problems on her plate than her son's obsession with karate chopping inanimate objects with his leg. She slammed the door shut and rushed to her side. Sliding behind the wheel, she fumbled the key into the ignition and cranked on the engine. She breathed a sigh of relief that had nothing to do with the cold air blasting from the AC. The passenger door cracked open and she swung her panicked gaze to the right just as Dylan climbed in the truck.

He crooked his arm on the seat back and pinned her with a cool stare. "Did you honestly think I'd let you drive off?"

"Dylan, you have to get out of my truck."

"Why?"

Because she couldn't handle being in this confined space with him. The pharmacy had been one thing. Plus she'd had the benefit of shock addling her brain and her response to him. God, she didn't need to know that he still possessed this overwhelming ability to destroy her equilibrium. Not now. Not when she needed to keep her wits together. What little of them she still had left. She couldn't tell him any of that. So she settled on the other valid reason for kicking him out of her vehicle. "We've given Hazel a mountain of gossip as it is. If she sees you in here there'll be no end to it."

"Trust me, the gossip I'm already feeding this town towers

over whatever puny hill she's building over us, darlin'."

It'd been a lifetime since she'd heard that endearment coming from his too-sinful-for-words mouth. It was enough to momentarily distract her from the rest of what he'd said. "What do you mean? You're not even from around here."

"Yeah, but my old man is." He jutted his chin toward the building behind them.

She didn't need to turn her head to know where he was referring to. D. Walker Mineral Company was practically a historical landmark in Red Creek. *Wait a minute.* She blinked at Dylan. "You're one of *those* Walkers?"

He grimaced. "I see you're familiar with the scandal."

"Everyone within a fifty mile radius is." She rubbed her temples. How insane was it that she'd never once considered the connection? Countless times she'd driven past D. Walker Mineral and it hadn't triggered the slightest thought of Dylan. For Pete's Sake, even the initials were the same! But oh no, the majority of times she stewed in her memories of Dylan it was for an entirely different reason. And usually she was feeling lonely and desperately needed to be held. Then of course she was reminded of him every single time she looked at Hunter.

Reminded of her son's presence, she glanced behind Dylan's seat. Hunter was already sound asleep, his bout of manic excitement apparently putting him down for the count. Thank goodness. At least that was one less thing for her to stress over. She returned her attention to Dylan. "You never mentioned Dusty was your dad."

"Why would I? Not like you two ran in the same circles. Hell, how was I supposed to know you even lived in the same town? You didn't exactly share much in the way of personal details about your life. I don't even know your damn last name."

Guilt sat like a boulder between her shoulder blades. "It's Chapman." It wasn't the surname on her birth certificate, but far as she was concerned, it *was* her name. When she'd turned eighteen she'd filed the necessary documents to have it legally changed, cutting that connection to her old life and ensuring her dad had no way of tracking her down. Not that she thought he would. He hadn't put much effort into being there when she was growing up, so no reason for him to change his MO now she was an adult.

"And is Hunter's last name Chapman?" Dylan's gaze drilled into hers. "Or Walker?"

She swallowed hard, unable to break his stare. Yeah, she'd all but known he'd figured it out, but it was surreal hearing him toss it out there in the open. Especially since it was a secret she'd held inside her for so long. "It's Chapman."

"Good."

His pronouncement and the flatness of his tone surprised her. She'd thought for sure he'd be spitting nails over his family name being left off of Hunter's birth certificate. But then she recalled the circumstances that'd brought him to Red Creek. "I take it you weren't close with Dusty."

"He spent a grand sum of one week a month with me. Not much time there for us to bond."

The total lack of emotion in his voice and expression pinched at her heart. She recognized the wall he'd erected when it came to his father. It was achingly familiar because she'd hand- chiseled her own version from the time she was five years old up until the present. Her dad wasn't exactly a horrible person, but he had no place being a father. He sucked at it. Big time. Only thing he possibly sucked at more was being a husband. Hence the reason her parents split up four months into their marriage. Her mom had insisted it was due to the utter futility of sustaining a relationship with a music man. Zoe didn't doubt she was right, but it probably also had something to do with her dad's reluctance to give up his week-long drunken benders and his dalliances with big-breasted groupies.

Tugging her thoughts from her own familial discord, she picked nervously at the leather stitching on the steering wheel.

"How long are you in town for?"

"A week. It's part of the arrangement of the will." His gaze remained fused to her face. "But I don't want to talk about any of that. Were you ever plannin' to tell me about Hunter?"

Lying would have been the easy route out. And also cowardly. "No."

A dark emotion flashed in his eyes. "Don't you think I deserved to know?"

"Yes. I'm not saying what I did was right. But I didn't want to put that burden on you."

"Goddamn it, Zoe. He's my *son*. In what fucked up world would I consider him a burden?"

Oh, she knew too well how possible it was. She was living proof. Her parents had even been the same age as her and Dylan when Zoe entered the picture as an oopsy. So when she'd seen that positive sign on the pregnancy stick four years ago, all she could think was that the cycle was repeating itself. And when she'd held Hunter in her arms for the first time eight and a half months later, she'd vowed he'd never experience the same fucked up childhood she'd had. He didn't need an absentee dad who occasionally showed up for special occasions, usually wasted off his ass and with a big-boobed bimbo on his arm. No, she'd give Hunter enough love he wouldn't miss having a daddy around.

"You have your career. You're on the road constantly. When would you have time to be a full time dad?" Yes, it hadn't been right to keep their son a secret from him, but she also wouldn't let Dylan disrupt their lives. Hunter needed stability, not someone who'd playact at being a dad and then move on when the novelty wore off.

He stared at her. "You honestly think I'd put my career before my son?"

"It happens."

"You don't know me worth shit if you believe that of me."

"You're right. I don't really know you. We had what, a day

together?" Her flippancy was for show. She couldn't let him know how much he'd meant to her. How much he continued to mean to her. There was no future for them. She couldn't be with a musician. Giving into her weakness for him once had ended up with a three-year old consequence. As much as she loved Hunter and thanked God every day for him, there was no way she was going down that road again with his daddy.

Without warning, Dylan leaned forward and slid his hand behind her head. She jolted. "W-what are you doing?"

"Don't *ever* downplay what we shared." The fierceness of his expression was in direct opposition to the gentle stroke of his fingers through her hair. "Not only did we produce a child from it, it was something that doesn't come around very often. At least not for me. I felt the connection, and I'm willin' to bet you did too."

If he didn't stop touching her soon she was going to scream. Or rip his clothes off and beg him to fuck her until she screamed for an entirely different reason than frustration. Pulse drumming in overtime, she attempted to pull her head back. That only prompted him to follow along with her. The focused way he stared at her mouth made every square inch of her tingle. It was all too easy to recall how effortlessly she melted under his kisses. The man knew how to use his mouth and tongue. Everywhere. Spread out beneath him, her body had been an instrument he'd played with devastating care and ease. And that was before he'd slid inside her, his cock hard, thick, and hot. He'd made love to her with an intensity that'd been sweet, raw, and consuming. With him, the impossible had happened—the aching loneliness that'd been her constant companion had disappeared. There'd been no room for it so long as she was wrapped in Dylan's arms.

"D-don't read too much into it." The words were as much for her as him.

"Yeah? So you're tellin' me that if I kiss you right now, it won't mean a thing to you?"

She swallowed. The desire to encourage his challenge

whispered an enticement through her. Didn't matter that it'd be a dangerously foolish thing to do. With Dylan, her brain had always been on a permanent vacation. "I-it won't."

His eyes darkened, that look of determination on his face sending a thrilling note of anticipation singing through her blood. He leaned across the console, his hand tightening on her nape. The stir of his breath mixing with hers revved her pulse another notch. Eyes drifting shut, she waited for the luscious pressure of his lips sliding over hers. A jarring rap rattled the window behind her, making her jump and she nearly banged her nose into Dylan's. She whipped her head around, fully expecting to see Hazel's hawk gaze trained on them through the pane of glass. Instead she was met with Callie Rogers's grinning curiosity.

Zoe killed a groan. Saved by the bell. Or in this case, the best friend with impeccable timing. Planting her palm on Dylan's chest, she covertly nudged him back a pace. The unfortunate aspect of that maneuver was it gave her the opportunity to feel the solidness of those glorious muscles straining his T-shirt. Good Lord, how could she have forgotten how built he was?

Desperate to steer her wayward thoughts back on track, she jerked her hand away and buzzed the window down. She cleared her throat roughly and tried for a casual expression. "Hey."

Callie's gaze sparkled. "Hey yourself. Was beginning to wonder what was taking you so long, but looks like I'm interrupting something important. Should I catch up with ya later?"

Zoe's emphatic, "No." beat Dylan's equally firm, "Yes.", but only by a millisecond.

Callie chuckled. No doubt she was going to have a field day with this one. "Aren't y'all just too cute for words?" Paying no heed to Zoe's frustrated glare, Callie ducked down and thrust her hand through the window toward Dylan. "Don't believe we've met. I'm Callie."

Dylan removed his cap and returned the handshake with his own introduction. Normally Zoe would have felt unbearably rude for not dispensing the niceties herself but it was a damn miracle her tongue could even function.

Callie's eyes suddenly widened. "Oh my gosh, you're *Dylan Walker*." She slashed an accusing stare to Zoe. "How long have you been keeping this a secret, you traitor?"

Zoe's heart skipped a beat—until she realized that Callie's scolding likely had nothing to do with Dylan being Hunter's daddy. Callie was a big fan of Truckstop Pickup. It was excruciatingly difficult tuning out her best friend's constant gushing whenever one their songs came on the radio. It was even tougher muting her own responses to the hauntingly sweet chords of Dylan's guitar solo on *Summer Rain*. Those notes always seemed like a connection to him, one that broke the boundaries of time and distance. Fanciful but true. "I haven't been keeping anything a secret. Nothing's going on."

Dylan's arm went rigid against her shoulder. She winced, steeling herself for the tongue-lashing sure to be forthcoming. He surprised her by staying silent. His edgy anger spoke volumes though. Steadying her nerves, she sent Callie a pleading look. "Give me ten minutes, okay? I'll meet you at Taylor's."

Callie's attention flickered to Dylan again. Obviously she wasn't thrilled at not getting to properly fan-girl for another hour or two. Her mouth curved with a hopeful smile. "Dylan can always come with you."

"No, he has prior plans."

Callie offered Zoe a hard squint. "Fine. See you in ten."

The moment her best friend stalked out of sight, Zoe fizzled a breath and turned to face Dylan. Judging from his stony expression, he was plenty pissed at her. And she certainly didn't blame him. She was giving him one reason after another to despise her. The knowledge vised her heart. Still, it was better this way. If he hated her, he'd move on. It'd be the best thing for all of them.

A muscle ticced in his strong jaw. "Keeping nothing a secret, huh?"

She rubbed her temple. Yes, she was definitely burying herself up to her neck here. "I know I'm not handling this well. I plan to tell Callie you're Hunter's father. But when *I'm* ready to do it. Okay? I can't just blurt it out."

The granite state of his features softened a fraction, but the hurt lingered in his eyes. "Good. I don't want to be some dirty secret taking up space in your closet, Zoe. I've dealt with enough of that bullshit."

A fierce pressure squeezed against her diaphragm. "I don't think of you that way." She'd heard the not so quiet whispers around town. How Dusty had kept up with four different women and fathered sons with them behind his wife's back. Most folks were willing to look the other way and not speak ill of the man, seeing how Dusty did so much philanthropic good in his life and in the town. There were also those who said they weren't surprised Dusty had sought affection outside of his marriage since apparently things had been rocky between him and Theresa for many years. Coming from a broken household where cheating was a common practice, she tended not to condone the activity, but she knew it sure wasn't unusual.

"I want to spend time with him," Dylan announced, breaking through her thoughts with all the finesse of a battering ram.

She didn't need to ask who he was referring to. She'd been waiting for the inevitable demand. Tried her best to steel for it. But the panic leapfrogging through her refused to cooperate with the necessity for calm. "Please think about what this would do to Hunter. You want to know him better—and I get that. I truly do. But he won't understand a daddy he's never seen before popping into the picture and then leaving him just as abruptly when your week is up here. I won't put him through that."

"Neither will I. Zoe, I have every intention of being a permanent part of our son's life. Whether you like it or not. So you better get used to it." He dug in his back pocket and pulled out a smart phone. "What's your number?" He lifted that dreamy sea-green gaze and pinned her with a patient look when she didn't immediately answer.

She exhaled wearily and recited her number. He punched in the contact information, and an instant later her cellphone buzzed from the confines of her purse. She offered him a peeved frown. "Did you really think I'd give you a fake number?"

"Thought crossed my mind." He pocketed his phone and glanced at her. "Since it appears you have plans for this afternoon, how about you and Hunter come out to the lake house tonight for dinner?"

A renewed surge of panic hit her bloodstream. "I-I thought maybe we could just meet somewhere neutral. Like a park or something."

"Why? You have a problem with us havin' dinner?"

"Dylan, this isn't about you and me."

He offered the grin that'd effortlessly convinced her to drop her panties the second he had her alone four years ago. Superman had an easier time resisting Kryptonite. "Never said it was. But I'm assuming you're not gonna be willin' to leave Hunter with me right away, so the way I see it, that kind of makes all of us a package deal."

She didn't like the way he phrased that. And she particularly didn't trust that gleam in his gaze. But damn it, he was right. No way in hell she'd hand Hunter over unchaperoned. It was as much for Dylan's benefit as their son's. Hunter could be a real handful, and Dylan was ill equipped to jump into the role of Wonder Dad, no matter what he thought to the contrary.

Left with no recourse, she bit back a grumble. "What time?"

Chapter Three

"So what's the story with you and Dylan Hunkalicious Walker?"

Trying her best to hide the grinding of her teeth, Zoe unclicked Hunter's seatbelt and lifted him from the truck. The moment his tiny feet hit the ground, he hollered at the top of his lungs and raced across the yard toward his six-year-old buddy, Josh. Despite the boy being older and bigger than Hunter, Josh was no match for a toddler tornado. Hunter slammed into Josh, sending them both tumbling onto the grass.

Zoe sighed and shifted her attention to Callie. "When are you going to take my advice and pad that child in bubble wrap before we come over?"

Without giving the kids a second glance, Callie waved her hand dismissively. "It's good practice for when he becomes a pro quarterback and makes enough money to set his mama up in the lap of luxury." She plopped her hand on her hip, her expression sassy as her pose. "And don't think you're getting outta answering my question."

"I'm not ready to talk about it yet." She didn't realize she'd shifted her gaze back to Hunter a fraction too soon after that statement until Callie's sharp inhalation drew her attention to the thoughtless mistake. Tempering her wince, she reluctantly panned her focus to her best friend just as Callie's brother, Taylor, stepped out onto the porch. He offered a smile and raised his hand in greeting. Before Zoe could return it, Callie let out a screech.

"Are you tellin' me that Dylan Walker is Hunter's daddy?"

Oh Lord. Why didn't Callie grab a bullhorn and announce it to the entire neighborhood while she was at it? Zoe scowled. "I didn't *tell* you anything. You assumed."

"Well, is he?"

Zoe tweaked the bridge of her nose. The good news was that

Hunter and Josh were too preoccupied with their horseplay to give a patoot what the grownups were discussing. Although the last thing she'd wanted was to get into this with Callie right here and now, not much point in prolonging the inevitable. "Yes."

Callie's eyes threatened to bug from their sockets. "No. Way. Girl, how in the world did that happen?"

She assumed Callie wasn't asking for the specifics. Though anything was possible with her nosy best friend. "It's a long story."

"Do I look like I'm pressed for time?" Callie plopped her rear end on the bottom step of Taylor's porch and patted the vacant spot next to her.

Resignation dragging at her limbs, Zoe shuffled forward. She caught Taylor's eye. Much as she liked Callie's brother, she sure didn't want to have this conversation in front of him.

He cleared his throat. "I'll make up some sweet tea while you ladies chit chat."

Eternally grateful for his consideration—something his sister could take a lesson on—Zoe gave Taylor a wobbly smile. "Thank you."

He ducked inside the house and the screen door banged shut behind him. The second she was reasonably assured he was safely out of earshot, Zoe scooched in next to Callie and buried her face in her hands. The last half hour was finally catching up to her. She trembled, whimpering pitifully.

"Hey now." Callie wrapped her arms around Zoe in a bone-crushing hug. "Whatever's got ya upset, it can't be all that bad."

"It is." The words came out muffled and miserable. Zoe dropped her hands and lifted her tear-clogged gaze to Callie. "He never knew about Hunter. I've kept it to myself all these years."

"Honey, I figured as much." Callie squeezed Zoe's shoulder. "But from what I could see, he didn't look too upset with ya."

"Well, he isn't exactly thrilled by my actions either. And understandably so."

"Can I ask you somethin'?" Callie cocked her head to the side, her expression blatantly curious. "Why didn't you tell him? All this time of going it on your own. He coulda helped ya, at least financially."

Zoe inched her running shoes closer to the edge of the step and clasped her knees. "I do okay for myself."

Callie gave her a narrow look. "Sweetie, you forget who you're talking to here. If you were making loads of cash with the teaching job, you wouldn't have to take on the private voice lessons."

"I do it because I love it." She didn't tack on the part about money not being an issue for her. Because then she'd have to open up about her past.

Zoe averted her gaze and stared at the overgrown patch of wild carrot growing near the upturned wheelbarrow in the middle of the yard. She didn't like having to keep all these secrets under lock and key, but she couldn't risk freeing them into the open. Not after she'd worked damn hard putting that chapter of her life behind her. She lived a simple, drama-free existence now. It's what she'd always craved growing up, and what she'd put her heart and soul into ensuring she provided for her son. She loved the life she'd built here for them. Her farmhouse on the outskirts of town was home in every sense of the word, and they were happy there.

Sure, there were times when she was unbearably lonely. Mostly in the dark of night after Hunter was tucked in bed. Those were the moments when she questioned the wisdom of thinking she needed no one but herself. Yes, she prided herself in being a modern woman who could raise a child on her own. And she did a damn fine job of it. Hunter was healthy and stable. He didn't doubt that his mama loved him with every ounce of her being. And that sweet, wild little boy loved her back just as unconditionally. So she had no doubts that she was a good mom. But she'd be a liar if she didn't admit that there were times she longed for a partner to carry the load once in a while. And on the days when it all felt overwhelming, someone to hold her and tell her it would be all right.

But that person couldn't be Dylan. No matter how much her heart wished it to be different.

"I still think you're crazy." A grumpy noise issued from the back of Callie's throat. "Shoot, if I had a hot package of sin like Dylan Walker interested in me, I woulda never let him off the hook." Devilment flashed in her eyes. "Is he as talented with his fingers as I suspect he is? He gets plenty practice plucking that guitar."

Snorting, she rolled her eyes at Callie. "I figured you'd go there."

"Well, don't hold out on me. You know how long it's been since I've been properly laid."

A grunt preceded the subtle click of the screen door behind them. She and Callie glanced over their shoulders in time to catch Taylor's hasty retreat in the opposite direction.

"That's what you get for snoopin' on conversations," Callie shouted, not the least bit embarrassed. She flicked her gaze to Zoe. "You know Tay is gonna be devastated about Dylan being back in your life."

"Quit matchmaking me with your brother." Although Taylor was undoubtedly easy on the eyes, he was a good friend, nothing more, despite Callie's futile attempts at pushing them together in the past. In every way, it would have made sense to fall for Taylor. He was intelligent, witty, and a gentleman through and through. But there was no real chemistry between them. He didn't fill her with the mad, giddy rush of excitement and love that Dylan did. Frowning, she tamped down that unproductive thought. "As for Dylan, he isn't back in my life. He wants to get to know Hunter, and that's all it amounts to."

"In your eyes, or his?" Callie countered shrewdly.

"What does it matter?" She glared at her best friend. "I'm not intending to start up anything again with him. End of story."

"Uh huh."

She really didn't like that knowing sparkle in Callie's eyes, but she chose to ignore it for the time being. Far more productive than sitting here arguing with her all day. She chewed the corner of her thumbnail, a nervous habit that no amount of willpower seemed capable of cracking. "Hunter and I are going to have dinner with him tonight."

"Holy shit, *tonight*? Why didn't you mention that sooner? Girl, we need to find you something that will make his jockeys spontaneously combust soon as he sees you."

"Oh my God, would you stop it? I already told you nothing's going to happen between us."

Callie offered a one shoulder shrug. "Doesn't mean you can't give that man reason to remember why he got ya knocked up in the first place."

Zoe wrinkled her nose. "You have such a way with words. Miracle Hallmark hasn't come knocking on your door yet." She glanced down at her black stretchy yoga pants. "Besides, what's wrong with what I'm wearing?" She'd throw her black batwing top over her tank and exchange her sneakers for sandals. Surely that'd be dressy enough for something that was definitely not a date.

"Is what you're wearing comfy?"

"As a matter of—"

"Then ditch it." Callie arched one perfectly groomed auburn eyebrow when Zoe opened her mouth to argue her case. "Nope. Whatever you're gonna say is completely invalid. I will not allow you to be seen in public with Dylan Walker wearing clothes that can be described as *comfy*."

"We won't be in public. He invited me to Dusty's lake house."

"Dusty?" Callie's forehead scrunched in confusion before instantly clearing in tandem with her double blink. "Holy hell. Is Dylan one of *those* Walkers?"

It didn't sit well on her that Callie chose to phrase her words that way. Yes, Zoe all but did the same thing herself when Dylan revealed his connection to Dusty. But that was before she knew

38

Dylan was touchy about the scandal. Having that insider information stirred her need to protect him, silly as it was. "Yes, he is. You'd do well to remember your fan girl adoration of him before you go jumping in the rumor pool with all of the other busybodies around here."

Callie grinned. "Look at you being all bitchy. Didn't know you had it in ya, Sassy Britches."

Zoe chuffed under her breath. "There's plenty you don't know about me." *Enough to fill a book.*

"Or maybe Dylan means a little more to you than you're lettin' on."

She turned her focus away from Callie's invasive stare. The roughhousing Hunter and Josh provided the perfect excuse to change the subject. She cupped her hands around her mouth. "Come on boys, snack time." She detected Callie's barely restrained amusement next to her. Let Callie think what she would.

It was better than the alternative—admitting that Callie was right.

Chapter Four

He never thought he'd be this happy to step inside his father's house. But it sure as hell beat spending another second pretending he understood the first thing about reading geological reports. He was beginning to think Dusty's office staff were sadistically inclined, what with their endless enjoyment of thrusting paperwork in front of him that translated as easily as ancient hieroglyphics. Still, the brain-numbing work had offered the occasional distraction from his encounter with Zoe. Occasional being a loose term. If five minutes out of the day counted, well then, he guessed it qualified.

Scratching his jaw, he hooked the SUV's keychain on the proper peg and ambled into the kitchen. He spotted Marliss washing what looked like a bunch of fresh mint in the sink. He glanced at the digital time display on the microwave. "Aren't you supposed to be off the clock?"

She shot him a look over her shoulder. "Figured you might be thirsty after putting in a hard day. Made up a batch of my special mojito mix."

He grunted. "Just happened to make up a batch, huh?"

Chuckling, she flicked the bundle of mint, giving the droplets of water clinging to the foliage a one way ticket down the drain. "I mighta discovered you've got a taste for the cocktail."

"Been doin' a little online reconnaissance on me?" He didn't often do a lot of interviews and such. Usually the folks running the music blogs and whatnot were more interested in landing a one-on-one with Luke. Went with the territory. Being the founding member of Truckstop Pickup and the biggest star power in the band, Luke was definitely the headliner—as he constantly liked to remind Dylan and the rest of the crew. It was annoying as shit, but what could you do? The man did pack in the crowds and helped keep Dylan's bill collectors at bay.

Not that he had to worry about that now. And truthfully, only his stubbornness was to blame for his leaner years in the beginning, before the band really took off and exploded on the scene. Other than the house in Nashville, he'd refused to accept any handouts from Dusty. And the only reason he caved on the house was because Georgianna had fallen in love with the place at first sight. Besides, she lived there a hell of a lot more often than he did, so it didn't feel too much like a compromise. He suspected Dusty had continued to send money to her all these years before his death, but he never asked her about it. What he didn't know wouldn't piss him off.

Only now he was sitting on a huge inheritance that he didn't know what the hell to do with. He couldn't walk away from it. Not when he had Hunter to think of. And Zoe. She might very well snub the idea of taking money from him. Which made it pretty damn ironic, considering his own mule-headedness where that was concerned. But he'd do whatever it took to ensure his son was provided for.

Hm, and who does that remind you of? He shook Georgianna's phantom sing-songy-told-ya-so voice from his head. This was nothing like his and Dusty's situation. More than likely his dad's monetary support had been fueled by guilt. That wasn't the case with Dylan. He wanted to do right by Hunter, and make up for all those years they'd missed. Starting tonight. Clearing his throat, he slid Marliss a worried look. "You, uh, wouldn't happen to know what a three-year-old prefers to eat, would ya?"

She frowned. Not unexpected, given the question. "Well, depends. Sometimes they can be picky. And you also have to take food allergies into consideration."

Aw shit. He shoulda asked Zoe about that. *I'm a fucking horrible father.* Sick inside at his utter ineptitude to get even this tiny aspect of parenting right, he dug his cellphone from his pocket and scrolled through his contact list until Zoe's number was highlighted in the text window. He typed in a quick message asking for her and Hunter's meal request. From now on he wouldn't even attempt to wing it.

A few seconds later her response popped up on the screen. *Hunter loves pizza, and I do too. If it will make things easier, I can stop and grab one at Tivoli's on the way over.*

Damn. No, he was supposed to be the one doing the work here. *Do they deliver?*

She replied back almost instantly. *Why pay the extra charge? I'll be driving right by there.*

He wouldn't be swayed by logic. Screw that noise. *Maybe I wanna support the local economy.*

Her speedy comeback pinged a second later. *I'll leave extra in their tip jar.*

He gritted his teeth. *I'm reimbursing you the money.* All *of it.*

Her final message took longer hitting his inbox. *Fine, you stubborn jackass.*

Grinning, he pumped his fist in victory.

"I take it you got the answer you needed?"

He lifted his gaze to Marliss. "Yep. I'll have a couple guests joining me tonight. We're havin' pizza."

Marliss nodded. "Always a good choice." There was no mistaking the curiosity in her eyes. "Nice to see you're already making some local friends. At least, I'm assuming that's the case."

He recognized a blatant dig for information when he saw one. Didn't bother him though. He liked Marliss, and considering the fact she was looking after him this week—and even made him his favorite drink—he didn't mind providing the details. "Yup, but Zoe and I kinda go back a ways. So we're not exactly strangers." That was putting it lightly. He knew every intimate detail of her anatomy. He just hoped she'd give him the chance to discover even more about her. And not only the sexy stuff. Though he was certainly in favor of that too.

Marliss rolled the mint in a paper towel, soaking up the remaining moisture. "Are you referrin' to Zoe Chapman?"

He shouldn't have been surprised Marliss knew who she was. Red Creek being as small as it was, everyone was bound to be on a first name basis with each other. He also hadn't considered the opportunity small town living provided. He could do a little digging of his own. "Yes, ma'am. Are you acquainted with Zoe?"

Marliss chuckled, confirming his suspicions. "No such thing as a stranger in Red Creek." Stroking her chin, she raked him with her thoughtful gaze. "I can see you two together. What with the musical connection and all."

He blinked. "Musical connection?"

"She teaches chorale at the elementary school. Also does private lessons. Lord knows she's the only reason Cubby's little June Bug can carry a note without causing a howling dog uproar within a twenty-mile radius. Bless that poor tone-deaf child's heart."

Dylan absorbed the shocking information Marliss had given him. Not so much the part about tone-deaf June Bug. While he was sure that was important news for Cubby and the Red Creekian canines, it was of little consequence to Dylan. Learning Zoe was a music teacher, though? Now that was a doozy. Particularly since she'd professed to have little interest in music, whatsoever. He remembered the conversation like it was yesterday. Probably because it'd involved her lying naked on top of him. Memories of her nude, coming, smiling, talking, or pretty much merely breathing within his vicinity tended to adhere to his brain matter like Gorilla Glue. He'd curled one of her long tresses around his fingertip and mentioned something about writing a song that'd commemorate the color of her hair. She'd laughed at that, and then informed him that she wasn't a natural blonde. He'd busted her on that fib by pointing out that the carpet matched the drapes. So unless she dyed downstairs too, she'd have to live with him writing that song. To which she'd stunned him *and* broken his heart by admitting she didn't give a donkey's behind for music.

He'd been at a rare loss for words, the concept of someone not enjoying music more unnatural and disturbing to him than Miracle Whip salad dressing. Eventually she'd soothed his damaged psyche by sliding her pussy over the head of his cock, blowing his mind in an entirely different manner. By the time she'd bottomed out on him, everything had been forgiven. Hell, he'd been lucky to hold a damn thought in his head.

But now his mind was right back to that place of utter befuddlement.

Why had she lied to him? Unlike her flip remark about not being a blonde, she'd seemed so bored when the subject of music came up. She'd given him zero reason to suspect she was being untruthful.

Well, one thing was certain, he'd get to the bottom of this mystery before the night was done.

Reminded that Zoe and Hunter would shortly be on their way with the pizza, he dragged a hand across his jaw, wincing at the overgrowth of stubble. If he didn't do something about that, he'd get mistaken for a mangy coyote soon. "I'm gonna grab a quick shower before they get here."

Leaving Marliss to finish fussing with her mojito makings, he jogged upstairs to his ensuite bathroom. He performed the quickest shower and shave in history and pulled on a fresh pair of Wranglers and the nicest rocker cowboy shirt he owned. After slapping on some aftershave lotion, he ran a comb through his hair and deemed himself presentable as he would get.

Nerves bouncing like they were performing a crazy Mexican Hat Dance, he headed downstairs. He paused in the entry. Should he hang out by the front door? No, that'd appear too anxious. He could turn on the TV in the great room though. Act like he was absorbed with a movie or something.

Studiously ignoring the photos of Dusty and Theresa, he grabbed the remote and clicked the tube on. The overly-loud voice of a news anchor boomed from the surround sound speakers. He lowered the volume several decibels and stretched out in the leather club chair, propping his boots on the adjacent ottoman. Despite his best intentions, his focus drifted to one of the portraits sitting on the built-in shelves across from him. Judging from Dusty and Theresa's fancy duds, they were at some highfalutin shindig. Charity event? Could be. Regardless, his dad looked uncomfortable as shit in his starched shirt and navy suit. He had his arm around Theresa's shoulder, but the gesture almost appeared strained.

Dylan had heard the rumors about the tension in their marriage, and he'd figured his dad deserved what he got. Dusty couldn't have his cake and eat it too. But the longer Dylan stared at that picture, the more uncomfortable it made him. Like he was seeing past the facade of two people putting on their own performance for the camera lens. Dusty looked tired. Weary. As if the weight of the world was resting on his shoulders, and he didn't know how to ease up the burden.

A deep pang pinched Dylan's heart. He sucked in a breath. *Stop it. Stop it right fucking now.* He couldn't think about Dusty. There was enough of Dylan's past sitting on his plate at the moment. In fact, two incredibly important pieces were on their way to see him. That's what he needed to focus on. Because shit knows it was gonna take every ounce of his attention.

The doorbell rang, and his pulse jumped like it'd been kick-started.

"I'll get it, Mr. Walker," Marliss hollered from the kitchen.

It still felt weird having the woman address him that way. He wasn't used to the formality, especially since it was common practice for his band members to call each other endearing pet names, like *Buttweiser* and *Anheuser-Ballsack,* depending on their beer of choice.

"No, I'm right here anyway." He bolted from the chair before Marliss could beat him to the door. Yeah, arriving at the entrance wheezing from his sprint didn't exactly maintain his image of not being anxious. But fuck it. He cracked open the door, his breath snaring in his throat for an entirely different reason than his mad dash across the room as he gaped at Zoe. Hot damn, she was the most beautiful woman on God's green earth.

Much as he'd loved her snug yoga pants, the buttercup yellow sundress she'd exchanged them for made her look like a cotton candy-dipped ray of sunshine. Who knows how long he stared at her? Obviously several beats beyond appropriate because Marliss coughed pointedly from somewhere behind him.

"Mr. Walker, I reckon that pizza has to be hot."

Snapping to his senses, he finally noticed the flat cardboard box resting in Zoe's hands. Smothering a curse at his own bone-headedness, he relieved her of the package. "Come on in."

He led the way inside, keeping his pace leisurely so that he could hang close to Zoe and Hunter as they took in their surroundings. He'd expected Hunter to be shy or wildly rambunctious, similar to how he'd behaved at the pharmacy. The little boy did seem uncertain of how he was supposed to act. Every once in a while Zoe would stroke the top of Hunter's head, which did the trick of putting him at ease. Dylan could see why. Hell, if Zoe insisted on petting him like that he'd curl up in her lap, happier than a puppy dog.

They reached the kitchen and Marliss took the pizza box from Dylan. "Where would y'all like to eat? Dining room? Or it's a gorgeous evening out now it's cooled off. I could light the candles on the patio."

"I wouldn't want you to go to the trouble." One glance at Zoe's face confirmed the trouble she was most worried about was the romantic kind. Apparently candles crossed the line.

Marliss waved off Zoe's concern. "Don't be silly. Y'all get yourselves situated and I'll be out in a sec." She turned her back on Zoe and winked at Dylan before shuffling toward the cupboards.

Making a mental note to suggest a raise for Marliss and Lou to his brothers, Dylan escorted Hunter and his mama outside. Truthfully, he hadn't much thought of what would happen to

Dusty's housekeeper and cook now that his dad was gone. Marliss and Lou were well provided for according to Dusty's will. As they should be. But other than that, he had no idea what their plans were after the end of the month.

Shit, he didn't know what *his* plans were after the end of his week. Originally he'd intended to hustle his ass to Nashville and get back in Luke's good graces in time for their gig in Memphis. But that was before he'd discovered he was a dad. Getting everything straightened out with Zoe and making Hunter a priority in his life, well, they both took precedence over anything else. Now he just had to convince Zoe of that.

She tucked her hair behind her ear and surveyed their surroundings. "Oh wow. This is pretty."

Not nearly as much as you. Wisely deciding to keep that thought to himself while she was still freaked out about the candles, he nodded dumbly. The patio—if you could call it that— was a luxurious oasis consisting of the pool area, cabana, and outdoor kitchen. Other than the lake, it was his favorite feature of the house. He led them to the table and held out a chair for Zoe and Hunter. Rather than take the extra seat, Hunter crawled into Zoe's lap and stuck his thumb in his mouth while he stared Dylan down.

This ain't awkward at all. Not about to be cowed by his own son, Dylan propped the toe of one boot atop the other and pulled the goofiest face he could conjure. A giggle broke around Hunter's thumb. Holy shit, knowing he'd just made his kid laugh? That was some powerful shit right there. Drunk on the *I'm-the-world's-awesomest-dad* rush, he made several more faces, earning a series of hysterical giggles from Hunter and the side eye from Zoe. He didn't even care if she thought he was a moron. Absolutely worth it.

She rolled her lips together, fighting a smile. "Okay, enough. Much more of that and you'll make him pee. Trust me, I won't be amused if that happens."

He dutifully sobered up. Marliss appeared, bearing the pizza box and a pitcher of libations. He automatically jumped up to assist her with her load but she shooed him away and effortlessly settled everything down on the table. She left them for a moment to grab plates, napkins, and glasses from the wet bar beneath the pergola. The efficiency with which she moved boggled his mind. This was definitely not the sixty-something-year-old woman who'd been complaining about her knees this morning. Made him wonder what was in that prescription he'd left on the counter for her. After lighting the candles, she left them to their lonesome.

Not that he was complaining. He was too mesmerized by the way the candlelight created a halo around Zoe's face to pay much attention to Marliss's absence. Zoe tested the temperature of one of the pizza slices before sliding it onto a plate for Hunter. Dylan grunted at his boy's obvious enjoyment of his meal. "Damn, looks like he's into eating as much as his old man is."

A grin tugging at her lips, Zoe ruffled Hunter's hair. "He's a bottomless pit."

"Yep, sounds like me."

She gave him a considering look. "Now you mention it, I do recall how you pigged down three waffles at that diner on the way to the airport."

"Needed my sustenance, since *someone* drained all my energy the night before."

The candlelight turned Zoe's blush into a gorgeous rosy glow. "Now isn't the time to talk about that."

He glanced at Hunter, who appeared to be deeply committed to his pizza slice. "I wouldn't say anything dirty in front of him."

"I know you wouldn't."

Then what the hell had she been referring to? He eyed her more intently, cataloging the smattering of goose pimples across her arms. It was too damn warm out here for her to be cold. And if he wasn't mistaken, that was definitely a flush riding toward her mouthwatering cleavage. The last time he'd witnessed that particular color in that particular area she'd been squirming in his lap in the backseat of her car, rubbing shamelessly against the hand he had buried in her panties.

She was fucking turned on remembering all of the sinful things she did with him that night and the next day. No question about it.

The knowledge fired a heat wave through him, along with a serious case of guilt. Here he was having some raunchy thoughts about Zoe in front of their son—probably that'd disqualify him from Dad of the Year now.

Zoe picked up her glass and took a healthy sip. She licked her lips, the delicate sweep of her tongue stirring up another wave of wicked musings that stiffened his cock against his fly. Tapping the rim of her glass with one pink fingernail, she glanced at him. "This is delicious."

"It's a mojito. Marliss made them special."

"Mm, that's right. They're your favorite."

He stalled in the process of grabbing a slice of pizza. "How did you know that?"

"You told me."

They'd talked about a fair amount of things on the rest breaks during their sexual Olympics. His recently acquired taste for mojitos sure hadn't been on the topic list. Which meant that Marliss wasn't the only female in his life guilty of keeping tabs on him online. Interesting.

Not the least bit perturbed that his grin was undoubtedly obnoxious as all get out, he lifted his pizza and munched on a bite. They remained wrapped in quiet while they ate their meal, but the moment Zoe pushed her plate back he topped off her glass with more of the mojito mix. She shook her head. "If I have any more I'll never be able to drive home."

"So don't."

She offered him a hard squint. "Getting me drunk won't lure me into your bed."

"That's not what I was suggestin'. There are plenty of extra rooms in the house." He couldn't resist teasing her with his best smoky stare. "Then again, mine does have the comfiest bed, Goldilocks."

She pretended an absorbed interest with the stem of her glass. "It's getting late. Hunter and I should probably get going."

"It's barely six."

"I have a lesson I'm giving early in the morning."

The reminder of her livelihood reeled his mind away from erotic delights. He crumpled his napkin and tossed it on the table. "Glad you brought that up. Was meaning to ask why you lied to me."

She jerked her gaze back up to his. "W-what?"

Obviously she hadn't been expecting him to call her out on it. Good. Then maybe she wouldn't have as smooth of a recovery and make up another bullshit story. "You said you had no interest in music. Funny how you're teaching it."

She blinked. "When did I say that?"

So she still wanted to play games. "Same time you told me you weren't a natural blonde and I proved you wrong by—"

She held up her hand. "All right, I remember now. The hair color was me being silly, since I thought you were going to launch into a bunch of dumb blonde jokes. Which I hate, by the way."

"Still waiting on an explanation about the other thing."

Shifting Hunter in her lap, she sent Dylan a pleading look. "Could we please not get into this? It's really not a big deal."

"Nuh huh. I wanna know why you felt the need to lie about it."

"I didn't." An unrecognizable emotion flashed in her eyes. In that brief second a heavy vulnerability descended on her. Every instinct inside him clamored to tug her into his arms and protect her from whatever worries haunted her. But he suspected she wouldn't welcome his comfort right then. She bounced Hunter on her knee, her agitation evident. "I know you won't believe me, but that's the truth. At the time, I was going through an unbearably rough patch in my life. I wanted nothing to do with the music scene."

It was his turn to blink. "Then what the hell possessed you to get involved with me?"

"I didn't intend for it to happen. But when you walked into the gas station...I couldn't move. I couldn't believe you were right there in front of me. So close, I could touch you." She bit the corner of her lip and traced the flower pattern on her place mat. "You were looking at your phone, and didn't notice me. The next instant, our worlds collided."

Literally. He'd knocked into her hard enough, she'd stumbled backward. Thankfully his reflexes kicked in and he grabbed her before she crashed against the display of beef jerky and potato chips. His arms had instinctively hugged her waist tight and she'd leaned upon him, her breath a faint flutter and pupils dilating as she stared at his mouth. Although he'd never hooked up with a woman he'd only known a whole whoppin' two seconds, a dazzling sense of recognition had settled over him. Not only would he know this stranger intimately before the night was done, she'd have a lasting impact on him the rest of his days.

Fuck, did he hit the nail on the head with that premonition. "You knew who I was." He didn't state it as an inquiry. What she was telling him, it left no room for doubt.

"Yes." Her gaze turned beseeching. "I didn't seek you out though. I wasn't some crazy groupie looking to have a one night stand."

He believed her. God knows he'd been around plenty of those types, he knew how to recognize them. And Zoe definitely hadn't been—and wasn't—one. While this new revelation spun in his brain his thoughts kept returning to her earlier admission. "You said you wanted nothing more to do with the music scene. Were you in the biz?"

It would explain why she was now teaching music. He knew a few artists who'd grown weary of the road and found gigs that kept them closer to home.

"No."

Her adamant denial was a little too fast in coming. He'd bet his inheritance she wasn't telling him the whole story. Maybe she hadn't been a musician herself. Didn't mean she hadn't been involved with one. The possibility sat like a two-ton elephant on his chest. Yeah, it was caveman of him, but he didn't like the prospect of Zoe with any lover but him, even if that supposed other man was a ghost of her faraway past. He wanted to ask her more, but he wouldn't push her. Not yet.

He glanced at Hunter, who was yawning now that his tiny belly was full. "How about we all work this pizza off by taking a walk down by the lake?"

Zoe looked like she was on the verge of arguing, but surprised him by nodding instead. "It'll be a good way to wake up before I hit the road."

Damn stubborn woman. Keeping that thought to himself, he stood and helped her scoot back her chair. Hunter climbed down from her lap and peeked toward the pool.

Zoe playfully tugged the cowlick sticking up from his crown. "Don't even think about it, Boo Bear. You're not wearing your swim trunks."

Dylan scratched his jaw. "Sorry, I shoulda suggested you bring them." Yep, that World's Best Dad award was looking slimmer and slimmer.

"It's okay. You would never have gotten us out of the pool if we did."

Didn't sound like a problem to him. In fact, he was enjoying the idea of Zoe and Hunter being around more and more.

That thought kept cycling through his mind during their trip down to the docks. He wanted to spend all the time he could with Hunter. And Zoe. An hour here and there wasn't gonna cut it.

Hunter pointed to the Wave Runner moored at the dock and Zoe chuckled. "That would be a big fat nope, Little Man."

A better opening couldn't have landed in Dylan's hands. "We've got lots of fun toys." Besides the Jet Ski, there were the boats, the pontoon, and just about every other form of water entertainment you could think of. "We can use any of them we want." He feigned deep contemplation. "More I think on it, might make sense to have you stay here so we can avail ourselves of all of this stuff."

Zoe twitched her nose. "That's incredibly generous of you, but like I said, I give lessons out of my home. I can't be making that trip every day."

If she thought he'd be that easily deterred, she had another think comin'. "Okay, then I can hang out at your place and keep Hunter company while you're doin' your lessons."

Zoe worked her mouth, but no words came out. It was damn tough not hootin' in victory. Instead he settled for picking up a stone and skipping it across the placid surface of the lake. Hunter jumped up and down before bopping along the bank, presumably searching for his own perfect rock to throw. Zoe crossed her arms over her chest. "I'm not saying you don't have every right to spend time with your son, but you need to know he requires adjusting time."

He nodded in Hunter's direction. "Yeah, I can see how he's having difficulty coping."

"Damn it, please don't be glib about this."

"I'm not, darlin'. I get it." He scooted closer to her and cupped her cheek. "You're scared spit-less. So am I. But you have the benefit of knowing what the hell you're doing when it comes to raising a kid."

She stared at his lips. The moment felt like it'd been plucked from time. Only instead of standing in a Nashville gas station, they were in Dusty's backyard. Fucking weird.

Her hand drifted to his ribcage. He wasn't sure she was even aware of the way her fingertips brushed him through the knit of his T-shirt. He was damn certain she didn't know the effect she was having on parts of him south of the border. She scored her nails along the ridge of his abs, heading for his navel. "You have to let them know you're the one in charge."

It took several beats for him to realize she was talking about child rearing and not something else. Though considering the tantalizing placement of her hand, she definitely coulda been referrin' to something else. He slid his palm to her nape and followed the delicate arch of her neck. "And what's the best means of doin' that?"

"For starters, Hunter shouldn't be playing unsupervised over there."

He reversed course and slid his fingers through Zoe's silky fine hair and tugged slightly. She shivered, a soft breath catching in her throat.

"Hunter, get up here where we can see you," he called without removing his gaze from Zoe's.

"Okay."

"Good boy." Dylan wrapped Zoe's hair around his fist and coaxed her closer.

A gasp broke from her. "I can't—"

He stopped the remainder of her words with his mouth.

Four years of aching for her went into his kiss. He wished he could say some finesse went in there too, but likely not. Judging from the hungry way she sucked at his tongue, she wasn't complaining. A carnal groan tunneling all the way from his belly, he slid his other arm around her, molding her snug to him. If she hadn't been aware of his erection, she sure as hell was now. No hiding the monster bulge denting his fly.

He re-angled his approach, gliding his tongue deeper into her mouth, exploring every velvety nook and cranny. Through the soft cotton of her dress, he detected the hardened nubs of her nipples poking against his torso, begging for attention. If they'd been anywhere else and without their three-year-old standing by as witness, Dylan would have loosened the pearl buttons keeping him from those gorgeous breasts and worshipped her to his heart's content. Instead he settled for cupping some side-boob.

Zoe pulled away from him with a jolt. Her breathing a staccato accompaniment to his ragged inhalations, she stared at him. "That was *not* supposed to happen."

"You wanting it to be so doesn't make it a reality, darlin'. There's something between us. Always has been. Stop fighting it."

She shook her head furiously. "You're not going to sweet talk and French kiss your way into my bed, Dylan. I'm not some horny twenty-year-old anymore. I have a child and need to be responsible."

He narrowed his eyes. "Hunter is *our* child. And I fully intend to be responsible for him too."

"You're going to be here for a matter of days. This is my *life*. Day in and day out. And I don't regret one moment of it. But don't think that you showing up once in a blue moon when you feel like it is even remotely equal to what Hunter needs. To what *I* need."

Her words were like a punch to his gut. "I would never do that." She was preaching to the choir. He knew too well what it was like having a dad who wasn't around. No way in hell he'd do that to Hunter. And it was mighty unfair of her to lay that shit on his doorstep when he hadn't even known of his son's existence before today. "If you'd come to me back then, I wouldn't have shirked my responsibility. That's not the kind of man I am, Zoe." Damn her for assuming otherwise.

She frowned. "I know that. It's part of the reason I *didn't* say anything to you. I already told you I didn't want to put that burden on you."

He plowed his hands through his hair. She was speaking in circles. "One minute you're reading me the riot act for not being there when you needed me, and the next you're saying you didn't want me there. Which is it, Zoe?"

Judging from her expression, she was just as confused as him. Which made no damn sense. "I didn't—" She halted her rebuttal so fast, it was a miracle her tongue didn't get whiplash. For a brief flash that vulnerability he'd noticed earlier returned. Just as quick as it appeared she locked it down. She glanced at him, her gaze guarded. "That remark didn't have anything to do with you. So don't take it as me giving you grief. Because I wasn't."

Her admission—odd as it was—eased the sting of being wrongfully accused of neglect on his part. "Then what were you referrin' to?"

"Nothing. It's not important to this conversation."

When folks said shit like that, nine times out of ten it was the opposite of the truth. He was beginning to believe there was a whole lotta stuff going on with Zoe that she wasn't telling him about. And that presented a big ass problem in his book. Because as long as she kept hiding herself from him there was no way they could move away from the past.

And into what? A possible future that she seemed dead set on not letting him be a part of with her?

Zoe straightened the front of her dress and walked to the bare patch of lawn where Hunter was poking a small ant hill with a stick he'd found. She snagged his free hand. "Time to go, Boo Bear."

Dylan stepped in the middle of her path, halting her progress toward the house. Tearing his gaze from her shuttered one, he dropped onto his haunches and grinned at Hunter. "I'm gonna come visit ya tomorrow. You a fan of ice cream?"

His eyes lighting up more brilliantly than a sky full of Fourth of July fireworks, Hunter nodded and belted out a "Yeah!" that nearly took out Dylan's hearing.

"Me too." Resisting the urge to shake his head to clear the ringing from his ears, Dylan made a fist. His heart nearly doubled in size when Hunter balled his tiny hand and bumped his knuckles against Dylan's with an exuberant whoop.

Amazing how your life could change in the blink of an eye. He'd thought nothing could flatten him on his ass like learning he had three brothers he'd known nothing about. Now he had a kid. Some guys would probably be running for the hills right about now. The thought wasn't even an option in Dylan's mind.

He straightened and scanned Zoe's face. A fraction of the shield she'd erected had disintegrated but a healthy dose of uncertainty lingered. Letting her continue to build this wall between them? Not an option. Not when he had so much at stake. He'd let her walk away from him once before. Never again.

Chapter Five

The insistent buzz of his cellphone snapped Dylan awake. Blinking away the grogginess swimming in his vision, he stared at the glowing red numbers on the alarm clock. Three in the morning. Who the fuck would be calling him this early? He froze as a possibility hit him. Maybe it was Zoe and something had happened to Hunter.

He whipped the sheets and comforter back and leapt from the bed. Nearly tripping over his own feet, he skidded to his discarded jeans. Damn it, why the hell did he leave his phone in the pocket? What if it'd gone dead and he'd missed this call?

Fingers shaking, he fished the device loose, his heart in the pit of his stomach as he peered anxiously at the caller ID. It wasn't Zoe, but Malcom Flynn, Truckstop Pickup's drummer. Dylan's racing pulse slowly downshifted to normal. Irritation began to replace his adrenalin-fueled panic. He let every ounce of his grumpiness be known as he clicked the Talk button and barked into the receiver. "Do you have any idea what goddamn time it is?"

"Mornin' to you too, Sunshine. If you don't wanna be disturbed there's a little thing called a vibrate setting."

Grumbling under his breath, Dylan stalked back to the bed and climbed beneath the sheets. "Whatever you're calling me about better be damn important."

"What if I just wanted to chitchat?"

"Then I'm hanging up on your ass." He started to do just that, but Malcom's exaggerated exhalation stalled him short.

"This stupid disagreement between you and Luke needs to be put to rest. It's affecting the entire band. I made a comment to Trinity that I'm just not feeling the lyrics for the new song she's working on and she kneed me in the balls."

Dylan snorted. "Well, what'd ya expect would happen, ya dumbass? You know how sensitive Trin can be." Their backup vocalist/occasional song mistress was a force to be reckoned with on and off the stage. Best for the male members of the band to keep their distance when she was in one of her ornery moods. Which was pretty much every day ending in a Y.

"I've been thinkin'...maybe you should be the big one and tell Luke you're sorry."

Dylan glared at the shadowed ceiling. "Why the hell would I do that? I didn't do anything wrong."

"You shoulda signed his birthday card."

"That fucking crybaby can get over it. Jesus. I didn't slight him on purpose. I was outta town. The man needs to learn my life doesn't revolve around him."

A brief silence fell on the other side of the line. "It's hard for Luke to reconcile that fact. We've talked about that."

"Yeah, because he's got an ego that can barely fit on the stage much less in a room populated with us lesser beings," Dylan ground out.

"He is what he is, and you know that. You also know that he's got a soft spot for you that doesn't necessarily extend to the rest of us. It hurt him that your name wasn't on that card."

A tiny niggle of guilt wormed its way through Dylan. He hadn't really looked at it that way. While it was certainly true that he and Luke constantly butted heads, they also shared a strange bond that left him as equally baffled as it did Malcom and the others. Luke was a self-centered prick, but deep down there was another side to him lurking beneath the surface. Every once in a while Dylan would catch a glimpse of it. There was a certain loneliness that clung to Luke, and sometimes it made him feel sorry for the man. But unlike his bandmates, Dylan didn't pussyfoot around Luke and cater to his drama. He suspected that's why Luke sought his company out more than he did the others.

He tweaked the bridge of his nose between his thumb and forefinger. "I don't have time to deal with this right now. You all are just gonna have to figure shit out on your own."

"What could be so important that it preempts mending fences with Luke?"

Dylan filled Malcom in on Dusty's death and the terms of the will keeping Dylan in Red Creek. He left out the part about his reunion with Zoe and discovering he had a son. Some things were better revealed in person. Plus he really didn't want to be on the phone for the next two hours dealing with Malcom's reaction to the news.

"Sorry about your pops, man. Anything I can do?"

"Just hold down the fort back home. And try to keep Trin from nailing any more of our guys in the nads."

"Fuck, that's a full time job in itself."

Chuckling, he exchanged goodbyes with Malcom and hung up. After checking the status of his battery and deeming it fine for the time being, he set his cell on the night stand and folded his arms behind his head. Sleep decided to elude him now that he was keyed up from his conversation with Mal.

Heaving a disgruntled breath, he kicked off the covers and padded downstairs to the kitchen. He cracked open the fridge and surveyed his choices. Too damn early for a beer, though God knows it was tempting after the day he had. Shit, make that the last seventy-two-plus hours. Had it really been that long since he sat in the lawyer's office? It almost seemed like a lifetime ago.

He grabbed the carton of orange juice and fetched a glass. His mom would be proud of him for bypassing the Budweiser *and* getting his daily allotment of vitamin C.

Damn, Georgianna. He still needed to tell her about his half-brothers. And the fact that she was a grandma. That last part would hopefully help ease the pain of the other thing. He'd always noticed the wistful expression on her face whenever someone came into her resale shop pushing a stroller. The majority of the time those babies didn't make it outside without getting their chubby little cheeks pinched by Georgianna. Hunter better be prepared for some serious spoiling.

That thought naturally sparked him wondering about his son's other set of grandparents. Zoe never once mentioned anything about them. Not that it was necessarily weird. He rarely talked about Dusty, and he hadn't really had much chance to bring up Georgianna, seeing how his mind was so damn scattered these days.

Still, he should make a point of asking her. At the very least, he needed to be aware if her dad had a loaded rifle that he intended to use on Dylan for getting his precious daughter knocked up. Steeling himself for that possibility, Dylan returned the carton of OJ to its shelf in the fridge and carried his glass to the panoramic windows overlooking the patio. Marliss had blown out the candles but the pool lights offered a flickering accompaniment to the moon's soft illumination.

Without him encouraging it, his mind wandered to the picture of Dusty and Theresa he'd spied earlier. How many times had his father stood in this very spot at some ungodly hour, feeling that massive weight of responsibility on his shoulders? It was a bizarre musing to have. Unlikely that Dusty's conscience kept him up at nights. A framed snapshot didn't prove anything. For all he knew, his dad had just been exhausted from work that day and that's what the camera captured. Not some sense of regret and deep pining for a relationship with his sons.

His fingers tightening on his glass tumbler, Dylan slammed a hard swallow and pivoted away from the window. He strode down the hall, deliberately avoiding the great room. The distant glow of lamplight drew his attention. He wandered into a dark-paneled room that he assumed was Dusty's office. The masculine touches were in keeping with the common theme throughout the house. Various western art and landscape oils that he'd bet weren't reproductions. The desk was a sight better than the battered hunkajunk Dusty used at D. Walker Mineral. Obviously Theresa had put her foot down when it came to him introducing his questionable design style into their humble abode.

He shifted his attention to the opposite wall and noticed the massive safe with its door wide open. A brief case and stacks of folders occupied the upper shelves. He'd seen enough paperwork the last few days to last him a lifetime. But the big box on the bottom made him curious. Then there was the little fact that safes often served the purpose of keeping information from prying eyes. Given his father's history, the contents sitting in front of Dylan might very well be another curveball he wasn't ready for.

Shit. Maybe his old man had sired a bunch of other children none of them knew about. There could be a whole fucking town of mini-Walkers out there for all they knew. Half afraid of what he'd uncover in the box, he hefted it from the safe and plunked it on Dusty's desk. He popped the lid loose and pulled out the four album-sized books nestled inside. The top one had a big J stamped on the cover. He flipped it open and inspected the 8x10 photo taking up the entire first page. The sole subject was an infant wearing a tiny sailor outfit. Gauging from the resemblance the tyke bore to Dylan, he was looking at one of his brothers.

He ran his thumb down the spines of the three additional books beneath this one, his heart thumping. Did their dad keep baby books of them? It'd explain why they were tucked away in the bottom of a safe that Theresa presumably didn't have access to. Unable to stop himself, he turned the page. The next image was of a trio. Same infant, Dusty, and a woman Dylan didn't recognize. His dad had his arm around the female. The pose was similar to the one with Theresa, only there was no denying the happiness and joy in this picture. It was as if for one second suspended in time, the burden had eased from Dusty's shoulders.

The next dozen or so pages chronicled the passage of years as the baby grew out of his toddler stage. Wanting to confirm his suspicions that he was looking at his brother Jackson—the J on the cover essentially offered this biggest glaring clue—he thumbed to the last several pages in the book. Sure enough, there were some newspaper clippings showing Jackson decked out in chaps and covered in rodeo dust. Apparently his brother was a big hot shot in the arena. That was pretty fucking cool. Maybe he could take Hunter to see Jackson compete sometime. If Killian and Rogue were game, they could all get together and have a guys' weekend. Assuming his brothers wanted to have any kind of relationship with him.

Pushing aside his wistful thinking for the time being, he flipped to the end of the book. He stared at the envelope with Jackson's name on it, written in Dusty's familiar scrawl. Dylan's heart pounded. Had their dad written them a letter? The envelope was sealed. There was no way for him to know without invading Jackson's privacy any more than he already had. Looking at baby pictures and articles was one thing. He could bring himself to cross the line beyond that. Whatever was in that envelope was for Jackson's eyes only.

He set the book aside and grabbed the one with the letter D on it. His hands shook. *Just open the fucking thing.* Maybe he'd finally find some sense of peace inside and forgive his father.

Blood whooshed in his temples, adding to the pressure building in his head. The walls were closing in on him again, like they had in the Red Creek office.

He wasn't ready for this. Wasn't ready to see his past laid out for him in the pages of a book. Pictures proved nothing. They were just one more lie captured by the camera lens.

Pulling his anger around him like the familiar comfort of his favorite blanket, he grabbed the books, tossed them inside the box and slammed the whole kit and caboodle back in the bottom of the safe.

Chapter Six

Zoe's cellphone vibrated in her shorts' pocket midway through Mandy Sweeny running through her vocal chords warm up. She waited for the thirteen-year-old to finish her practice and the first couple of songs before announcing a break. Leaving the girl to enjoy her two minutes of texting free time, Zoe scanned her own inbox. The recent message was from Dylan. *I'm taking off early from work. Benefit of being the boss. What's your address?*

She hesitated before punching in the directions with trembling fingers. It was ridiculous to be this nervous. For Pete's sake, after their initial run in yesterday morning, seeing him again should be a walk in the park.

Only now she had the recent memory of his kiss tormenting her brain. The chemistry between them hadn't lessened with time. If anything, it was stronger than ever. If she wasn't careful she'd be right back where she started from. Letting him kiss the daylights out of her and then feeling her up in the backseat of a car. That'd of course lead to them ripping each other's clothes off and tumbling into bed, a naked, sweaty tangle of limbs.

She couldn't let that happen. No matter how much she ached to feel his mouth sliding over her breasts, teasing her nipples into hard peaks before wandering down her belly, and lower still to her pussy. She didn't have many lovers to base Dylan's talent in the oral department, but even so it was probably safe to say he was a maestro when it came to pleasuring any part of her body. A quiver shot between her legs in testimony of that memory.

This is what she got for abstaining from sex for too long. Granted, she didn't have a ton of opportunities. In addition to most men hitting the road once they found out she had a kid, the pickings were also slim in Red Creek. Plus she didn't want to develop a reputation of sleeping around. A woman in her position had to be careful. That's why she rarely kicked up her heels in any of the hot spots in town. Ha! If you could call them that. Hottest thing you got around these parts was the coffee at Cubby's.

Releasing a weary breath, she pocketed her phone and finished her session with Mandy. The girl fished out her Ipod and looked at Zoe with blatant pleading. Plenty used to her student's persuasive skills, Zoe laughed. "Fine, you get one duet. Which song?"

"Honkytonk First Date."

Zoe killed her groan. Oh Lord. She would have to pick that one. She narrowed her eyes at the girl. "Did Callie put you up to this?"

Her expression perplexed, Mandy shook her head vigorously enough to send her braids flying. Satisfied she was telling the truth, Zoe accepted the Ipod and synched it with the Bluetooth speakers. The guitar intro wailed through the sound system. She shivered, imagining Dylan's fingers racing with lightning speed over the strings, working the same magic with those chords as he'd devastated her body with. She was so wrapped up in the moment she nearly missed her opening lyric. Quickly catching herself, she belted out the line, trying not to giggle along with Mandy when she got to the part about the goat ruining the couple's attempt of a kiss in the petting farm. The song was the silliest thing in creation, you couldn't help but laugh. The chorus kicked in and Mandy's flawless soprano nailed the delivery. Beaming at Zoe's thumbs-up, the girl lifted her fist to her mouth and shimmied to the left. Her eyes suddenly doubled in size and she screamed.

Jolting in response, Zoe swung around to see what had scared the bejeebers out of the girl. Dylan stood in the doorway, looking just as concerned as Zoe.

"Y-you're...*Dylan Walker*!" Mandy's shrill voice hit several octaves above glass-breaking on Dylan's name.

Okay, that explained the scream. He probably dealt with that sort of thing on a regular basis. Sending him an apologetic glance, she leaned over the hood of the piano and turned the Ipod off. Mandy snatched the device and barreled toward Dylan. Zoe had to give him credit for not bolting in the other direction.

Mandy slammed to a halt in front of him. "Can I have your autograph?"

"Sure. You got somethin' for me to write on?"

The girl held out her arm. Well, it could have been worse. Give it a couple more years, and it likely would be. Taking pity on Dylan's obvious discomfort, Zoe grabbed one of her Xeroxed music sheets and a pen and handed both to him. His smile melting her insides, he leaned over the console table near the door and scribbled his name on the blank side of the paper before he passed it to Mandy. The teen held the autograph to her chest like it was one of the Lost Scrolls.

A car horn honked from the vicinity of the driveway, announcing the arrival of Mandy's mom. The girl never removed her gaze from Dylan. "I've gotta go." Her solemn voice conveyed precisely how little she loved that unfortunate necessity. He nodded, and Mandy stumbled out the door, almost running into the porch post since she refused to unglue her stare from Dylan. Somehow she made it down the steps without breaking something vital.

The instant Mandy and her mom rolled out of the drive, Zoe shook her head and chuckled. "I'm so sorry about that."

Dylan grinned. "Don't worry about it." His sparkling gaze swept her in a lazy glide and his expression turned downright smoky. "You look good enough to eat."

Oh God. He would have to use that particular term. Dangerous, considering her raunchy thoughts earlier. "Thank you." Suddenly acutely conscious of the fact that her tank top did a piss poor job of concealing the perky status of her nipples, she cleared her throat and covertly crossed her arms over her chest. "You're looking well yourself." Wow, could she possibly have sounded more stilted and lame?

Without warning, he reached out and fingered a strand of her hair. "I keep meanin' to ask when you got these."

It took forever to concentrate on anything other than the nearness of his face. Particularly that mouth she couldn't get out of her head. If she stood on her tiptoes she could press her lips to his. Bad idea. And yet, oh so tempting. "You mean the pink streaks?"

"Yeah." He trailed his finger lower, following the curve of her jawline.

She swallowed hard, praying he wouldn't notice how his touch made her flush from the inside out. "Callie did them. She's a stylist, and I sometimes let her use me as a guinea pig."

"Hm, I like it. Suits you." His focus dipped to her mouth before cruising upward to lock with her stare. The intense pull punched her equilibrium out of balance. His hand reversed course and slid to her nape. Even the simplest stroke of his fingertips threatened to liquefy her insides.

Feeling as if she was being drawn in by a magnet, she leaned into him.

"Told ya he was here!"

The sound of Callie's bubbly shout acted better than a bucket of ice water sloshed over Zoe's head. She quickly scooted back in time to watch her best friend race into the room two steps behind Hunter. The excitement lighting up Hunter's face made up for having to endure Callie's knowing smirk. Still, she had mixed feelings about her son's growing attachment to Dylan. On the one hand it filled her heart with a special joy seeing the bond beginning to grow between them. But that also meant it would hurt Hunter so much harder if Dylan vanished from the picture.

And what were the odds that it wouldn't happen? Sure, he'd promised he wasn't going anywhere. But words were one thing. Actions always told another story.

His little legs pumping like pistons, Hunter ran across the room. Dylan dropped onto his haunches and their son slammed to a halt a foot away from them, suddenly shy. Completely unruffled by his son's one-eighty in attitude, Dylan held his hand out for a fist bump. A giggle breaking from him, Hunter complied with the request with enough enthusiasm, it was a miracle he didn't flatten Dylan on his ass.

Smothering her smile behind her hand, Zoe glanced at Callie and noticed she was also grinning like a goofball. Steadying himself with a hand propped against the console table, Dylan rifled his fingers through Hunter's hair, leaving it an even wilder mess. Dylan lifted his gaze to hers, the sheer happiness shining on his face just as capable of knocking her off balance as their son's powerhouse fist bump. Butterflies pirouetted in her tummy. Oh man, she was neck-deep in trouble here.

Where were lockable chastity panties when you needed them? Hell, maybe that wouldn't even be enough to keep her safe when it came to Dylan. Her brain kept telling her one thing—there was no sustainable future for them—but her heart and her body refused to listen.

Forcing herself to look away from that beckoning enticement in his eyes, she turned a pleading stare on Callie. "Did you want to join us for ice cream?"

"Sorry, gotta pick up Josh before my mom buys him a pony or something else that will cost me an arm and leg to shelter and feed."

Well damn, that pretty much left no room for argument. Having narrowly escaped her own mom trying to sweet talk her into letting Hunter have a Great Dane puppy, she knew the inherent danger in overextending grandparent visitation. "Give Josh and Louisa a hug from me."

"Will do." After collecting her own hugs for the road, Callie strolled to her minivan.

Dylan leaned in the doorway, looking too delicious for words. "I take it Callie's a single mom too?"

"Yep. It's a big part of why we clicked right away when I moved here. She's a war widow, so her situation is certainly more tragic than mine. But she's one of the strongest women I've ever known."

"Sounds like you're lucky to have met each other."

"I am lucky." Hunter, Callie, and her other good friends Rori, Lexie, and Kit had been her anchors in the storm the last three years. She didn't know what she would have done without them.

Dylan scratched the back of his head. "For some reason I assumed you grew up here. Guess that's not the case."

She cringed, as always happened when her past crept into the picture. It was the last thing she wanted to get into with Dylan. "No, I moved here a few months after I had Hunter." She remembered that trying, terrifying time well.

Scared, uncertain, and feeling more alone than she could ever remember, she'd packed up her meager belongings the minute her lease was up on her tiny cubbyhole of an apartment in Atlanta. Her mom had called her crazy for moving to a strange place with an infant, and no nearby support system to speak of. She'd accused Zoe of being bullheaded and self-centered like her father. For the first couple of months she'd constantly questioned whether her mom was right, at least about the bullheaded part. And true to form, she'd stubbornly held on, determined to prove that she could do it on her own. It hadn't been easy, but she didn't regret her choice to start a life for her and Hunter in Red Creek. The community had welcomed them as one of their own, and this place had become their home.

Dylan's gaze softened. "I'm sorry I wasn't there for Hunter. For you."

His confession brought her thoughts cycling back to their conversation at the lake. For that brief moment she'd flashed back to her childhood, to the constant disappointment of a father who couldn't get his shit together long enough to *be* a father. She fully acknowledged that her daddy issues made it difficult for her to trust that Dylan would be different. That she and Hunter wouldn't be superseded by his love of the stage and the limelight of adoring fans. But she wanted to believe his commitment to them would be stronger. With everything inside her, she wanted to believe it.

Tamping down the fear that ate away at her faith in him, she offered a wavering smile and took the first step at letting him past her defenses. "You're here now. And that's all that matters."

Chapter Seven

Zoe took one look at the sizable queue forming in front of the Dairy Freeze and rethought the wisdom of suggesting the place to Dylan. She should have known better. The ice cream shop was the prime hang out spot for the kids during summer break. "Uh, maybe we should come up with a Plan B."

Dylan tossed her a surprised look. "I thought we were all agreed on ice cream."

She groaned as those two magic words launched Hunter into a rousing chorus of *icecreamicecreamicecream*. Repeat that about million more times—which he did—and it was the makings for an Extra Strength Tylenol moment. She rubbed her temples. "Did you not notice how many kids are parked in front of that place?"

"Yeah," Dylan responded, slowly dragging out the word.

"So that's the equivalent of a whole bunch of Mandys, give or take a few dozen."

Dylan rubbed his jaw. "I see your point." After a brief period of apparently mulling the situation over, he shrugged. "Hell, I don't mind if you don't."

She blinked. "Really?"

"I'll let you in on a secret. The adult fans scare me a helluva lot more than the youngins." He opened up the SUV's center console and snatched a pen. "At least this time I'll be prepared."

Smart man.

For the next half hour he made good use of that pen and autographed every napkin eagerly passed to him by the schoolkids. He fielded their endless questions in easy stride and cracked jokes with them, quickly escalating their fan-crushing to an epic level. Zoe took in his natural rapport with the kids, her heart expanding. Those teens weren't the only ones suffering from a serious case of crushing.

She had it bad for Dylan, with no hope for a cure in sight.

Four years hadn't lessened her feelings for him. If anything, they were growing more uncontrollable.

Jill, one of Zoe's students, flashed a smile that displayed her braces in all their shiny glory. "Ms. Chapman, can Dylan come and teach us all how to play guitar on the first day of school?"

The question, though innocent, instantly carved a hollow chamber in Zoe's belly. Dylan's week would be up long before then. He'd likely be back in Nashville. Maybe even on the road. *This is why you can't hold on to a pipe dream.* Much as she longed to refute the logical thought, she couldn't. She glanced toward Dylan. He was still surrounded by a circle of kids, his head bent toward one of them while he attempted to tune out the cacophony around him. She returned her focus to Jill. "I doubt it, honey."

Jill appeared crestfallen. She wasn't the only one.

Zoe waited until a lull appeared in the constant animated chatter directed toward Dylan. Taking her shot, she anchored Hunter on her hip and wiggled her way to his daddy's side. "Sorry y'all, but it's time for Mr. Walker to get some breathing room."

A series of boos greeted her announcement. Ignoring the heckling, she grasped Dylan's hand and tugged him toward freedom. Unfortunately they didn't get too far before they were stopped by several of the adult townies. Unlike the teens, they didn't pester Dylan for autographs. Zoe wasn't even sure if they were aware of his celebrity status. *There's the generational gap for ya.* Instead they offered condolences on Dusty's recent passing. Dylan somberly accepted each and every one, his bland features giving nothing away regarding his own feelings about his father's death. Once again her heart pinched for him.

She squeezed his fingers, offering silent comfort. His gaze met hers and the heated spark that pinged between them was enough to make her breath catch.

In an instant she was transported to a night many moons ago, when she'd stood in a gas station food aisle, mesmerized and speechless from her overwhelming draw to this man. How was it possible to feel this connected to someone who was entirely wrong for you?

"Zoe."

It took several heartbeats for her to register Taylor calling her name over the sound of her own pulse pounding a chaotic love song. She turned her head to see Tay ambling in their direction. After introducing him to Dylan, the two men shook hands and sized each other up. She resisted the urge to roll her eyes. What was it with those carrying the Y chromosome that they constantly felt the need to do that? And lucky her, she got to look forward to Hunter one day carrying on the tradition. In the meantime, all she could do was raise him to the best of her ability and instill in him the importance of not leaving the toilet seat up when they got to that stage of potty training.

Taylor shifted his focus from Dylan and smiled at Zoe. "I'm throwing a surprise birthday party for Callie on Saturday. Hoping you and Hunter can make it. Dylan too, of course." He tacked on the last part as an almost reluctant afterthought.

She frowned. "But Callie's birthday isn't for another month."

"I know. This is more a means to distract her and Josh from Saturday being the anniversary of Tom's death. Give 'em something positive to focus on."

The gesture was so sweet and caring, it brought a mist to her eyes. Sniffling, she tucked Hunter to her side and offered Tay a one-armed hug. "You're a good brother."

He chuckled. "I try. Gotta make up for sneaking that toad into her bed when I was twelve."

Snorting, she released him. "We'll be there."

Taylor nodded and bid them a farewell before continuing down the sidewalk and ducking inside Heart Starter, Lexie's coffee shop. Nibbling her bottom lip, Zoe turned her attention to Dylan. "Hope you don't think I was accepting on your behalf. You don't have to go."

"No, I'd like to." His expression turned teasing. "One of us has to make sure Taylor doesn't get handsy with ya."

She choked on a cough.

"Mama, no spreading yer germs." Hunter slapped his tiny hand over her mouth. She pried his palm loose and gave him a peck on the cheek.

Smoothing her fingers over Hunter's unruly hair, she glanced at Dylan. The damnable man was still grinning at her. "Taylor and I are only friends."

"Darlin', *you* might think that. I doubt he shares your sentiment."

She squinted. "Are you suggesting that men and women can't be friends?"

"Not at all. But I guarantee ya most single men don't become buddies with a beautiful lady without the intention of finagling for somethin' more."

Hearing him call her beautiful filled her with a radiant glow of happiness. Rolling her lips to keep from displaying her goofy grin, she shifted Hunter in her arms, trying to ease the increasing numbness in her right arm. "So you're saying you and I can't be just friends?"

He surprised her by sliding his hands around Hunter's squirming body and lifting him from her grasp. She was even more shocked by the fact that their son willingly snuggled against Dylan's chest. Hunter rarely allowed anyone to hold him. Even Callie had to threaten him with a tickle fight to get him to stay put in her arms. Taking advantage of her momentary spell of wonderment, Dylan pressed his mouth to her ear. "Oh, we can be friends. But ya damn well better believe I'll finagle for more." He backed up his statement by biting her earlobe.

She shivered, every square inch of her skin flushing.

Hunter poked Dylan in the chest. "No biting or you'll get a spanking."

Oh Lord. Out of the mouth of babes. Clamping her lips together to keep from laughing, she met Dylan's sparkling gaze.

"If your mama delivers it, I might like it."

He probably would, the kinky man. Dropping her arm, she cleared her throat and gestured toward the parked SUV. "We should head out before everyone gets off work."

One corner of Dylan's mouth hitched upward. "What constitutes rush hour traffic in Red Creek? Two vehicles and a squirrel?"

Her lips twitched. "Don't estimate the squirrel. He really creates a snarl."

"Better take your word for it then." He led the way to the vehicle and settled Hunter in the child seat in the back. When she attempted to take over buckling their son in, Dylan waved her off. "I need to learn how to do this stuff."

Unaccustomed to standing by and twiddling her thumbs, she quietly waited for him to figure out the proper placement of the straps. His patience with the task proved fruitful and he got Hunter secured in faster time than it'd initially taken her to figure out. Dutifully impressed, she climbed into the passenger seat and fiddled with her own safety harness. A moment later Dylan slid behind the wheel and she offered him a high five.

His smile warmed her all the way to her toes. "I did okay?"

"Gold star worthy."

"Damn. Go me." He gunned the engine and they were on their way.

The trip to her farmhouse was a pleasant distraction from all the concerns and doubts buzzing in her head. With the windows down, the sticky breeze spiked with the scent of summertime lulled her into a dreamy haze. It was so easy to pretend this fantasy was real—that she and Dylan were normal parents, out for a normal afternoon drive after spending some normal family time together.

It was all so perfectly normal.

"What are ya thinkin' about?"

Snapping from her daydream, she peered at Dylan. "Huh?"

"You had this look on your face just now. Like you were

75

visitin' the happiest place on earth." He chuckled. "Were ya thinkin' about Disneyland?"

She shot a quick glance over her shoulder and gusted a sigh of relief at Hunter's sleep-lax face. Making a tsking sound, she gave Dylan the stink eye. "Mom's rule—you're not allowed to speak that name in front of a three-year-old unless you're prepared to listen to a twenty-four hour continuous loop of said child begging to see Mickey."

"Duly noted." He tore his attention from the road long enough to send her a devilish look. "Is that rule before or after the no biting one?"

Heat spread through her like an eruption of lava. The wicked man was going to be the death of her. "I'll let you figure that one out on your own."

"Oh, I will."

Lord, what monster had she unleashed? Gulping, she wisely kept her mouth shut for the rest of the journey. They parked in the driveway and Dylan once again shooed away her attempts at freeing Hunter from his car seat. He carried their limp, blissfully snoring son all the way to his bedroom and carefully tucked him in bed.

Shaking his head at Hunter's knocked-out state, Dylan scooted the teddy bear with the missing eye underneath Hunter's arm. "Man, wish I could go down for the count like that."

"You and me both."

Dylan straightened and shoved his hands in his pockets. "What do you usually do while he's sleepin'?"

"Take the opportunity to recharge before he's up and Mr. Energizer Bunny again."

He cocked his head to the side. "You mean a nap?"

"Sometimes. If I can sneak one in. My special treat is getting to read a book in the bathtub without Little Man trying to drown his G.I. Joe doll in there with me."

"Should I be jealous that G.I. Joe has been spending quality soaking time with you?"

She batted her eyelashes. "He does tend to get fresh with me."

"Don't blame him one bit."

The butterflies in her stomach whipped into a frenzy at the concentrated way Dylan stared at her. Jitterier than if she'd guzzled two carafes of coffee, she chaffed her arms and inched toward the doorway. "Are you hungry? I could always wrangle together some snacks."

Not giving him room to shoot down that plan, she ducked into the hall and hauled ass into the kitchen. Sucking in a deep, fortifying breath, she yanked open the pantry's accordion doors and blindly canvassed the available options. She grabbed the closest box, not even conscious of what it was, and pivoted— crashing into the solid wall of muscle behind her.

Gasping, she clutched at Dylan, dropping the package in the process. He kicked it away with his boot before pressing her up against the pantry's frame and bracketing her face with his big hands. The next instant that mouth she couldn't stop thinking about slammed over hers. She wished she could say she fought the intensity of the kiss, but that'd be a shameless lie. Her arms encircled his waist, holding on for dear life as the firestorm consumed her. His tongue swept over hers, and then thrust deeper, coaxing a needy whimper from her throat. He cupped the back of her head, his other hand abandoning her cheek to seek out her breast. Devilish fingers squeezed and molded her flesh through the frustrating restriction of her tank top before slipping beneath the fabric.

His first brushing caress over her bare skin nearly made her knees buckle. And that was before his hand closed around her breast. Once that occurred she knew she was a goner. No force on earth would save her now. She needed his mouth on her. Everywhere. Now.

As if he'd read her mind, Dylan whisked her top over her head. Her excitement and the coolness of the AC instantly puckered her nipples beyond the point of bearable. He took advantage of their pebbled state and sucked one between his teeth, laving the distended tip with his tongue. Every wet, sensuous pass of that wicked appendage sent a corresponding ripple of need straight to her pussy. Well aware of the effect he was having on her, he cruised his hand to her mound and massaged her through her shorts, earning her whimper.

He tore his mouth from hers, his gaze dark and stormy. "Gotta taste you, Zoe. Before I fucking combust."

"Then what the hell are ya waiting for?" she gasped in return. "Git to it."

His laugh sending shivers skating across her skin, he pinned her to his chest and back-walked her to the built-in breakfast nook in the corner of the room. He hoisted her onto the table, his expression ravenous. She swerved her focus to the kitchen entry. "Push one of the chairs against the door." A typical nap for Hunter usually meant he'd be sawing logs for a minimum of ninety minutes. They should be safe, but she wouldn't risk their son waking up and wandering in to bust them in the act.

Dylan went to do her bidding and she quickly shimmied out of her shorts and panties. He turned back in her direction and wheezed out a breath. Self-conscious and acutely aware of the extra padding she'd accumulated since the last time he saw her naked, she hugged her chest. "W-what is it?"

"*Goddamn*, you are beautiful. I know I said it before, but it bears repeatin' at least a thousand more times."

Happiness rushed through her, banishing her lingering insecurities. It wasn't so much the words that did it—though Lord knows they were lovely to hear. No, it was the way Dylan looked at her. Like she truly was the most beautiful woman he'd ever seen. She didn't like to think of herself as a vain person. If anything, she tended to neglect her appearance, deeming makeup and such a pain in the rear end most days. But she wanted to be pretty in Dylan's eyes. She wasn't ashamed to admit that.

She held out her arms to him and he responded to the summons by crossing the room with a purposeful gleam igniting his gaze. Even the way he moved reminded her of a big jungle cat stalking its prey. Only *she* was the meal he planned on savoring.

Skin hot and prickly, she waited for him to pounce. Infinitely more graceful than that, he insinuated himself between her legs and combed his fingers through her hair before twisting the strands with one hand, forcing her neck to arch. The possessive dominance in the maneuver turned her insides to mush. Quivering, she bowed her back, desperately trying to press her lips to his. He teased her relentlessly, offering her the tiniest brush of his mouth. A slight graze of the tip of his tongue on hers. She begged him with her eyes, and he pulled her hair with a firmer grip, the sting shooting right to her core. His head dipped and he slid a kiss along her neck, his teeth scraping ever so lightly.

The sensory overload proved too much to take. Nails digging into his biceps, she shuddered and gasped, the inescapable orgasm spiraling through her in rippling waves.

Dylan lifted his head, disbelief in his hazel eyes. "Baby, did you just—"

"Y-yes." She buried her face in his shirt to hide her embarrassment. "It's been a while. You overwhelmed me is all."

He released her hair and caressed her cheeks. "You are the hottest fucking thing alive. Don't ever be ashamed of grasping that pleasure."

"I'm not. I just wish I'd held out a while longer."

"Why? Hungry to feel my big ole cock inside you, ya insatiable hussy?" He grunted in response to rightfully getting his nipple tweaked over his impertinence. "Would that be a yes or a no?"

Rather than answer, she unbuckled his belt and toggled his zipper down. Holding his transfixed stare, she slipped her hand past the waistband of his jockeys and caressed his rigid length. He pulsed, thickening in her grasp. A quiver ran through his belly, his washboard abs tensing. Breathing shaky, he closed his eyes and groaned. "I've missed the way you touch me."

No more than she'd missed getting to explore every hard inch of him. And God, was he hard. The contrast of his velvet-soft smoothness was a marvelous thing. How could a man be made of silk and steel? It really was a wonder. She peeled his briefs down, freeing his gorgeous cock so she could properly appreciate the generous gift she was holding. And that's precisely what it was—a glorious package perfectly designed for her pleasure. Stroking his fat shaft, she wiggled sideways, fully intending to plant a kiss right on that glossy crown.

He gripped her upper arms, halting her progress. "Nu huh, darlin'. No way you're getting a taste before I've gotten mine."

His features set in determination, he pushed her flat on the table and snagged the nearby ladder-back chair with his boot. Sitting his butt on the rush-woven seat, he draped her legs over his shoulders and slid his hands to her hips. The first swirl of his tongue on her clit had her white-knuckling the edge of the table. The man had moved beyond maestro. There wasn't even a title fitting for the level of his prowess now. He shifted the placement of his right hand and used his thumb to hold back the hood protecting the bundle of nerves he was devastating. Over and over he swabbed her with his tongue, until she was panting and writhing. She reflexively squeezed her legs together, the tantalizing scruff of his beard stubble abrading her inner thighs pushing her closer to the peak. "D-Dylan, I'm g-gonna come again."

His heated gaze met hers while he continued eating her pussy, and the intimacy of the moment lit the final fuse to her climax. A choked cry clogging in her throat, she broke apart on his tongue, his ceaseless lapping triggering endless aftershocks. Just when she thought she couldn't take it anymore, he wrenched his mouth free and fumbled with his jeans, rucking them down enough that no vital parts would get snagged in the zipper. He dug his wallet from his pocket and fetched a foiled packet from one of the compartments.

She stared at the condom, her mind returning to the last one that'd failed to prevent Hunter's conception.

Dylan must have read something in her eyes that gave away her thoughts because he stalled in the act of ripping the packet open with his teeth. "I can double up if you're worried about it breaking."

She shook her head. "My gynecologist put me on birth control after Hunter finished breast feeding."

"You're still on it?"

She released a wobbly breath. "Yeah. I've had no need for it, but I like the sense of security it gives me anyways."

Dylan lowered the packet. "I can still wear the condom if it'll make you more comfortable."

She had to ask the question. It would be irresponsible not to. "Are you good about wearing them?"

"I've never not worn one. But I'd like to forgo it—with you—if you're okay with that."

She scooted from the table and straddled his lap. Stroking the planes of his cheeks, she nodded. He leaned forward to kiss her, and she wrapped her arms around his neck. As his tongue played over the tip of hers she reached between them and lifted herself up slightly. Guiding the engorged head of his cock, she rubbed the tumescent gland along the slickened folds of her labia. Their mutual groans blended as one. Slipping her free hand to his nape, she eased herself over his shaft and slowly sank down on his thick girth. That initial penetration sent a shudder through both of them.

Tearing his mouth from hers, Dylan swallowed hard, his Adam's apple bobbing. "You feel fuckin' amazing." His gaze full of wonder, he flexed his hips, retreating slightly before sinking in another inch. "So wet, warm, and tight. Like your pussy is giving me an incredible blow job."

She chuckled. "I can see why they don't let you write the songs."

His grin making her about a hundred times wetter, he pulled her closer and growled against her neck. "I'm good at other things."

He showed her that firsthand by pumping inside her with one powerful, smooth glide that lodged him to the hilt. Gasping, she gripped the back of the chair and tried to chase down her breath. Refusing to give her time to recover, he slid his hands underneath her ass and rolled his hips, driving into her with a steady, rocking rhythm that slowly annihilated her senses. Biting her lip, she ground into his thrusts, each corkscrew motion of her hips creating a decadent friction between the base of his cock and her clit. His fingers tightened on her flesh. "Yes, baby, ride me just like that. I want you to fuckin' lose it on my cock."

She whimpered, all too ready to give into his desire. Releasing the chair, she dug her fingers into the meat of his shoulders and bounced on him harder, faster, until she was practically slamming her pussy down onto the fat, rigid shaft providing her so much ecstasy. Judging from Dylan's strained, sweat-sheened features, he was right there in the zone with her. But she wanted to give him the pinnacle of pleasure. She wanted him to fall through that wall of rapture alongside her. She squeezed her inner muscles, milking him for all she was worth.

A curse hissing between his teeth, he pumped one last time and lodged deep inside her, the pulse of his release beckoning her into the eye of the storm. She flew higher and higher into the brilliant light before shattering into a million pieces of bliss.

Shivering through the aftershocks, she slumped in Dylan's arms. He held her close, gently easing her back to a state of clear-headedness with soothing strokes along her spine. His muffled chuckle hummed across her scalp. "What in the tarnation are you exercising your kegels with? The Kegelator?"

She snorted. "I'm impressed you know what they're called."

"Hell, I aced anatomy."

Oh Lord. There was something that didn't surprise her in the least.

Chapter Eight

He could get used to this. Spending the evening with Zoe and Hunter—the two people quickly becoming the center of his universe—yeah, it felt like he was right where he needed to be.

Tucking his son closer to his side on the couch, Dylan slid a look over his shoulder to see what Zoe was up to. "Hey, you're missing Scooby Doo."

"Trust me, I've seen that video a million and one times," she called back from the vicinity of the kitchen. "Besides, you can't watch the main feature without popcorn, you silly man."

He grinned. "Yeah, I am kinda hungry from someone wearing me out earlier."

Her snort was easily detectible even with the wall separating them. "Guess you won't be up for *napping* with me later then, huh?"

Oh hell. No way he was getting deprived of nap time. He just hoped that was innuendo for hot bath time fun. Minus G.I. Joe. "I'm always *up* for any occasion with you, darlin'."

"So I've noticed." The sound of her shuffling around in the kitchen preceded the ding of the microwave timer. A few minutes later she stepped into the living room carrying a big bowl of the fragrant popcorn.

He was suddenly ravenous. And not necessarily for food. She was so damn scrumptious, it was a miracle he wasn't a constant walking boner advertisement. It didn't help that every time he looked at her he was reminded of her sweet pussy clinging to him tighter than one of those Chinese finger puzzles. And getting to feel her bare? *Damn.* Talk about mind blowing.

Okay, he needed to put a pause on those thoughts if he didn't want to be dealing with blue balls until *nap* time.

Zoe curled up on the other side of Dylan and placed the bowl of popcorn in his lap. She leaned sideways and snatched a handful of the salty snack, her movements squishing her breasts right to his chest. Gauging from the way her lips twitched, she knew full well how much she was tormenting him right then. "What's the matter? You look a little flustered."

"What time does the little guy usually go to bed?"

She snickered. "Someone sounds like they're ready for an early nap."

Fuck yeah. He gave her a pleading puppy dog stare and she shook her head, instantly dashing any hope of that happening sooner rather than later. Resigning himself to his sad fate, he scooped up his own handful of popcorn and munched along with the cheery soundtrack to the cartoon on the boob tube.

The next three hours were the best agonizing three hours of his life. His overwhelming desire for Zoe was a constant presence, but getting to spend the evening with her and Hunter next to his side was something he'd never take for granted.

Against his will, his thoughts drifted to the scrapbooks he'd found in his dad's safe last night. How many times had Dusty sat in his office alone and thumbed through those pages, wishing for a simpler life where he didn't have to settle for faded memories?

His mind traversed his own mental snapshots from his childhood until a particular one stood out brighter than the others. He'd been about six, and it was a couple weeks following Christmas—just one of the many holidays he hadn't been able to spend with Dusty. But that particular Christmas had seemed harder to bear than the others for some reason he couldn't recall. Even the coveted Schwinn that'd awaited him under the tree hadn't pulled him from his moodiness. Georgianna had been worried sick about his quiet withdrawal. The next day he woke up to his dad sitting next to him on the twin bed. Despite being jetlagged from his red-eye, Dusty had spent the entire day teaching Dylan how to ride his new bike. The next morning they'd watched cartoons together exactly like Dylan had with Hunter. Hell, it'd probably been Scooby Doo. That one had been his favorite growing up too. Dusty left two days later, but not before giving Dylan a fierce bear hug that'd brought them both to tears.

Shit. Blinking against the phantom wetness dampening his eyes, he stretched his arms over his head and covertly brushed his sleeve across his face. That should take care of any embarrassing offenders sneaking loose on him.

"Everything okay?"

"Yeah," he replied, not liking the huskiness in his voice.

Zoe stroked his arm, her expression concerned. "I'll put Hunter in bed and be right back."

"I can do it." Not giving her the chance to beat him to the task, he scooped his son up and carried him down the hall to his bedroom. He tucked him in tight and kissed him on the cheek. "I'm never settling for scrapbook pictures." Whispering that plea as much for his benefit as Hunter's, he straightened and pivoted. He hesitated at the sight of Zoe watching him from the doorway.

Swallowing past the thick emotion in his throat, he stepped to her and took her hand in his. "I could really use that naptime now."

Nodding, she led him upstairs to her bedroom. The space upstairs had been converted into an entire master suite. He took in the massive sleigh bed and deemed it mighty cozy looking with its piles of pillows and fluffy comforter. A door stood across from them. More than likely the bathroom. Twining her fingers with his, she escorted him in that direction. They stepped inside and his suspicions were confirmed. She dropped his hand and sashayed to the claw foot tub big enough for two. He stared at the delicate curve of her spine as she bent over to flick on the faucets. Dropping his gaze to her heart-shaped ass, he licked his lips.

She glanced over her shoulder and caught him ogling her. Her smile saucy, she hooked her thumbs in her shorts and inched them down like she was the leading star of his private peep show. She stepped out of the frayed denim and employed the same slower than molasses removal of her panties. By the time the lacy scrap of fabric dropped to the braided rug in front of the tub his mouth was dry and his cock was giving a stiff salute against his zipper. She peeled her top off and tossed it aside. Sliding her hands along the enticing swell of her hips, she turned to face him fully. His tongue stuck to the roof of his mouth.

He'd never in a million years get tired of looking at her luscious body. He'd always preferred a woman with some curves, and *goddam*, she had them in spades. In addition to that booty that made him sweat, her breasts were a generous handful, with ripe, firm nipples that were just begging to be kissed. The gentle bump of her tummy led down to the treasure trove that awaited him between her legs. Her neatly trimmed landing strip of pale blonde fuzz brought a grin to his lips. *Not a natural blonde, my ass.* Shame on him for falling for that for even one second.

She twisted the bath faucets off. Perching her fanny on the lip of the tub, she tossed him a challenging stare. "Your turn, cowboy."

"Yeah, you want me to strip for you?" He was probably gonna suck so hard at this, but who cared. He was Zoe's willing slave. He'd do anything she wanted.

"Yup. So git to it."

He unbuckled his belt and eased his zipper down, freeing up some much needed space. He opted not to remove his jeans yet. While it'd been sexy as hell watching Zoe leave her top for last, he had a feeling he'd look dopey trying that tactic. He tugged his T-shirt off and was rewarded for his decision to go that route when Zoe bit her lip. Her gaze eating him alive, she stared at his chest. A fluttery sigh passed her lips. Encouraged by her response, he shucked his jeans down. Thank Christ he'd had the foresight to remove his boots earlier. Nothing ruined the mood faster than trying to look sexy and *not* falling on his ass in the process of shucking his footwear.

The only article of clothing left was his jockeys. Given the fact his dick was pretty much busting out of them, not much point in delaying the prison break. He dragged the garment off and kicked it toward his discarded jeans.

Zoe's focused glued to his cock. "Oh. My."

"I take it you like?"

"Very." Her breath tighter than her nipples, she crooked her finger and beckoned him closer.

Gladly accepting the invitation, he moseyed toward her. When he was roughly a foot in front of her she halted his progress with a hand pressed against his belly. Even that simple touch was enough to curl his toes. She looked up at him, her expression sultry. "I do believe I'm owed a taste."

He shuddered in anticipation. She dropped onto her knees and boldly caressed his length before ducking her head. Her tongue flattened against the base of his cock and slowly cruised upward, following the main vein all the way to the grooved indent beneath the crown. Encircling his shaft with her fingers, she licked his swollen gland, her saliva quickly blending with the precome pearling from his slit. She opened wider and slid her entire mouth around him. He groaned, his fingers sifting through her hair. Jacking him with her hand, she swallowed him deeper, her hungry moan vibrating along his flesh. If she kept that up he'd never last long enough to give her a dozen or more orgasms.

And God knows that's what he wanted to do. More than anything.

He gently pulled her off of him and coaxed her to stand. Tunneling his fingers through her hair, he explored her mouth with a lazy kiss, the taste of himself on her tongue stoking his hunger. She wiggled against him, the brush of her nipples on his overheated skin driving him crazy. Her hand ghosted below his navel but he caught it before it could close around his cock. He nipped her bottom lip in warning and kissed the sting away. Squeezing her fingers, he helped her into the tub and climbed in behind her. A groan fell from him at the muscle-relaxing warmth surrounding him. That sensation was usurped by Zoe settling in his lap, her lush bottom grazing his super-sensitized cockhead.

Sliding his arms around her, he cupped her breasts, his fingertips feathering over her nipples. She arched into him and he kissed her neck, basking in the shiver that trembled through her. He slipped his hand between her legs, seeking out the tiny nub that provided such a powerhouse to her pleasure. Easing back the hood of her clit, he swirled a light figure-eight over the swollen bud. Her fingers curled around the edge of the tub, her breath quickening.

"Feel good, darlin'?"

"Oh God, you have no idea."

"Mm, not necessarily. Your mouth and your pussy gives me that same kind of heaven when they're wrapped around me."

"I-I want to give that to you. Right now."

The cramped quarters of the tub made her suggestion challenging, but not impossible. Lifting her slightly, he positioned her on the tip of his cock. She scooted up higher and hung her legs over the side of the tub. That freed up plenty of room and he was able to glide inside her effortlessly. Continuing to caress her clit, he pumped into her slowly, wanting the hot, sensuous moment to last forever. He was strung out on bliss, lost in the warm, wet, delicious snugness of her pussy rippling around him.

"S-so good, Dylan."

"I know, baby. For me too."

He was desperate to string the sensations to the max, but already he could detect the looming presence of his release waiting in the wings. There was no way he was coming without her. No damn way. Increasing his thrusts until the water sloshed around them, he stroked her clit firmer, faster, until he hit the chord he'd been chasing. She arched with a strangled cry, her pussy cinching him tight. Her climax was enough to trigger his. Groaning her name against her steam-dampened shoulder, he throbbed and thickened inside her, blood rushing through his head as his orgasm slammed into him.

Gasping for breath, they both slowly surfaced from the afterglow. He hugged her to him, his heart stuttering. He couldn't deny it anymore. He was head over boot heels in love with her. She'd stolen a piece of his heart four years ago. He hadn't fully comprehended the depths of his emotional connection and the deep void inside him until he'd seen her again at the pharmacy. It was patently clear now.

She laced her fingers with his and kissed his knuckles. "I could stay like this forever."

"Me too." Holding her in his arms for a lifetime? Nothing would complete him more.

Tucking the back of her head against his collar bone, she sighed. "Of course, we'd get awfully pruny and folks would eventually mistake us for weird water aliens."

"Yeah. Damn pruny skin ruining everything."

She scooched forward and pulled the plug on the drain, sending the water on its merry way. He folded his arms behind his head, enjoying the view she provided as she stood up in the tub and snatched a towel from the nearby peg. Wrapping the terry cloth around her, she glanced down at him and snorted. "Does that thing ever shut off?"

He eyed the stiffening status of his cock. "Nope. Not where you're concerned."

"Let me at least have a nap first. A *real* one."

Chuckling, he waited for her to vacate the tub before hefting to his feet and accepting the spare towel she tossed to him. He briskly dried himself off and trailed her to the bed. They climbed in and he snuggled her against his chest again. He stroked her hair, content to just touch her in this simple way.

A soft exhale floated from her. "This is nice. I've missed being held."

He traced the gentle slope of her shoulder with his knuckles, regret a crushing weight on his sternum. "I'm sorry I wasn't here when you needed me."

"You keep saying that. You don't have to. There's nothing to apologize for."

"It's not so much that as me wishing I coulda been around."

She twisted in his arms to face him. Her fingertips ghosted along his jaw. "That was my fault. I should never have deprived you of Hunter. I...I just didn't see any other choice at the time."

"And now?"

"I won't keep you from getting to know him. It wouldn't be fair to you. Or him." She swallowed roughly, vulnerability evident in her eyes. "I just ask that you don't half-ass this. If you don't think you can be there for the long run please don't give him—me—false hope."

He returned her haunted gaze and a strong awareness splintered through him. The vulnerability was recognizable now, because it echoed the familiar ache he'd kept buried inside him for so long. "Which is it—your mom or your dad?"

She blinked. "What?"

"One of them checked out on you."

Her fingers slipped from his face, but not before he caught their trembling state. He'd definitely hit the nail on the head. He cupped her nape, refusing to let her retreat from him. "Baby, I know. I understand. Believe me. For too many years I hated Dusty for doing that to me."

A tear rolled down her cheek. "Have you forgiven him?"

"I'm workin' on it. I know I have to in order to find peace. But it's damn hard lettin' go of a strong emotion that's sustained you for the majority of your life. Even if it's a negative one that slowly erodes your soul." He smoothed his thumb across her skin, wiping away the tear. "Talkin' about it helps me. Maybe it will for you too."

Her gaze flickered away from his. His heart squeezed. He wanted her to open up to him. Share the things that hurt her deepest. If she couldn't do that, couldn't entrust him with her hidden pain, then what hope did they have of building a foundation for their future?

She released a broken breath. "When I was eight my school

threw one of those daddy/daughter dances. I remember my mom bought me a pink dress. It was so pretty, like something Cinderella would wear. I even had these shiny patent shoes that matched. Probably the only outfit I've owned that was color coordinated."

He smiled, imagining a pint-sized Zoe all dolled up. "Bet ya looked like a fairy princess."

"My mom has a picture." She chewed her bottom lip and trailed her finger across his breast bone. "She wanted me to have it."

He smoothed a lock of hair behind her ear. "Why didn't you take it?"

"Would you want a constant reminder of the night your dad was too wasted to show up for a dance you'd anxiously waited a whole month for?" A thin laugh escaped her. "I know that doesn't seem like long, but for a kid that's forever."

Emotion balled in his chest. "Yeah, it is." He pressed his forehead to hers. "I'm so sorry, baby."

"It wasn't the first time he did something like that to me. And it wasn't the last. Eventually I hardened myself to the fact that he just didn't have it in him to be the father I needed him to be." She took a deep breath and looked up at him. "I haven't seen him in six years. I cut him out completely. Because it was the only way I'd stop hating him."

He understood. Too well. "Does he know about Hunter?"

"Not unless my mom told him. And I seriously doubt it." She grunted. "Gasoline and fire mix better than my parents. They don't talk much if they can help it."

"Take it they're divorced?"

"Four months into their marriage."

He winced. "That has to be a record."

"If not, pretty close." She continued tracing an abstract pattern across his skin.

Shit, no wonder she had a hard time trusting in promises of forever.

He tucked her to him and she wrapped her arms around his waist. A strong wave of love and protectiveness swept over him. Whatever it took, he'd convince her that he was in it for the long haul. She'd never have to deal with being abandoned by a man again.

Chapter Nine

"Girl, you are positively glowing."

Wrinkling her nose, Zoe lifted her gaze to Callie. "Probably shoulda put my sun hat on." That's what she got for gardening without the proper protection. Lord knows she likely resembled a lobster now.

"I don't mean *that* kinda glow. Ya look like you've been gettin' properly fucked. About damn time too."

Zoe slashed a quick peek sideways and breathed a sigh of relief that Hunter and Josh were occupied with burying their Ninja Turtle action figurines in the sandbox near Hunter's swing set. She returned her squint to Callie. "If my child drops an F bomb his first day in preschool I'll know who to blame."

"Oh phooey. I haven't damaged Josh yet so your boy is likely to come out unscathed."

"Thank God for small miracles." Using both hands, Zoe wrestled with a particularly stubborn weed, nearly dislocating her shoulder in the process. Finally she defeated the evil offender. Holding it up by its foliage, she stared at the mutant-length root system. "I think it was working its way to China."

Callie plopped her butt down on the parched patch of lawn. "You intendin' to spill the beans?"

"On what?"

Her best friend snorted. "Don't even play innocent with me, missy. Town's buzzin' with the news that a certain SUV has been seen parked overnight in your driveway the last two days."

Zoe groaned. "Do folks have nothing better to talk about?"

"Around here? Nope. Doesn't help that you're canoodlin' with one of the infamous Walker boys. That's like two scrumdiddlyumptious platters of gossip for the price of one."

A particularly aggravating fly landed on Zoe's arm. She swatted at the troublemaker but it zipped off before she could send it to its maker. Grumbling, she scrubbed at the flecks of dirt left by her garden glove, creating a bigger mess than she'd started out with. "I feel sorry for Dylan's half- brothers. They have no idea what's waiting for them when they get their week."

Her pronouncement was an instant reminder of the approaching weekend. According to Dylan, Sunday was his last required day in Red Creek. He'd made a point of saying he'd be back after taking care of business in Nashville. And she wanted to believe him. God, did she ever. The sincerity in his eyes when he'd delivered that promise had been impossible to ignore.

So why did her stomach twist whenever she pondered his departure? Was she really that cynical that taking a man on his word seemed an impossible feat?

Yes. No matter how much she wished it weren't the case, assuming a man would eventually leave her had become the norm. The presumption had burrowed deep into her psyche and made a comfortable nest out of her fears and insecurities. She might never be able to rid herself of its corrupting presence.

"I wonder what they're like?"

She snapped out of her worried musings and blinked at Callie. "Who?"

"Dylan's brothers."

She shook her head and smiled. "They're Walker boys. That means they're bound to be charming, too handsome for their own good, and professional heartbreakers."

"Says the hussy lucky enough to be sleeping with one of 'em."

"Not my fault. He charmed the panties right off of me."

Callie broke into a huge grin. "Aha!"

Aw damn it. She glared at her best friend. "You little sneak. I'm never fallin' for your bait again."

"Well now ya did, no point hoardin' the dirty bits to yerself." Callie scooted closer. "Is he hung like I think he is?"

"You really need to get a boyfriend."

"Why? You offerin' yours for a night?"

"You wish."

"Hell yeah I do." Callie leaned back on her elbows and waggled her eyebrows. "We could tag team him. Give him a night he'd never forget."

Well used to Callie's outrageous comments, Zoe rolled her eyes. "I'm not sharing him with you, ya pervert. Besides, you have bigger boobs than me."

Callie glanced down at her chest. "Yeah, the girls are fuckin' outstandin'. Kinda gives me an unfair advantage."

Rolling her lips together to keep from laughing at her friend's banter, Zoe wiggled the forked end of her weeder beneath a clump of dandelions. Wiping her forehead with her free hand, she sent a look in Hunter's direction. Satisfied he wasn't eating sand or something worse, she concentrated on loosening up the root.

"Oh, that reminds me, my mom was wonderin' if you'd be interested in takin' in a kitten."

She frowned at Callie. "How in the world could your boobs remind you of a kitten?"

"Boobs, pussies, kittens. It's a natural progression."

"Only in your mind." She narrowed her eyes at Callie. "Wait a sec. Is this the same kitten that your mom tried to give Josh?"

Callie's expression morphed from sheepish to pleading. "Help me out here. The woman's already suckered me into enough kittens that I'm a recognized member of the Crazy Cat Lady Club."

"Damn it, I don't need a kitten."

"But Hunter does. Think how happy it'd make him having an adorable bundle of fluff to play with. Why, I'm certain he'd love you for life for being such a caring, considerate mom who'd do anything for her child and her best friend."

She pointed the weeder at Callie. "You are a vile, despicable beast."

"Does that mean you'll do it?"

Sighing, she speared her garden tool into the ground. "Fine."

Letting out a whoop, Callie tackled her to the lawn with a hug.

"I owe you."

"Yeah, for life." Swatting her friend off of her in a similar fashion as she'd done with the fly, Zoe scooted up onto her knees. Recalling the dwindling time she had before Dylan left for Nashville, she gazed at Callie consideringly. "But we can call it even if you babysit Hunter tonight."

"Ah, got a hot date planned with your stud man?"

Not yet. But hopefully—with the assistance of Callie—that would be rectified soon. "We haven't really had time for just the two of us." Guilt immediately washed over her for that admission. "God, that makes me sound like a horrible mom."

"No, honey, it makes you human. Parents need that reconnection once in a while. No kids around. Time for you and your man, with just some whipped cream, roller blades, and handcuffs for entertainment." Callie exhaled wistfully. "Lord, I miss Tom somethin' fierce."

Despite really not wanting to know what the deal was with the roller blades and handcuffs, Zoe's heart pinched for her friend's loss. Tay's party for her tomorrow couldn't come at a better time. "I wish I'd gotten to meet your Tom."

"You would have loved him. Everybody did." Sniffling, Callie smiled through her tears. "But enough sadness. This is supposed to be a joyous time. With lots of sex for you. I tell ya what, how about if I take Hunter and Josh to an early matinee in Richfield and then the boys can have a sleepover? That'll give you the whole day with plenty of time left over for some hot morning nookie."

She squeezed Callie tight. "You're the best."

"Just remember that the first time that kitten coughs up a fur ball on your brand spankin' new quilt." Callie pushed to her feet with a groan. Hooking her fingers in her mouth, she whistled loud enough dogs were probably barking in response the next county over. "Boys, train's a leavin'."

Hunter and Josh reluctantly dragged themselves from the sandbox. The instant they discovered they were going to see a movie they morphed from sloth creatures to whirling tornados of energy. Acknowledging that the kitten was likely the lighter of the two punishments here, Zoe assisted with getting the kids packed into Callie's minivan. Waving, she watched the vehicle cruise down the drive and make a left onto the dirt road.

The sound of birds chirping in the nearby cottonwood tree provided an idyllic soundtrack to her solitude. It felt odd having the place to herself, no screaming kids or noisy cartoons disturbing the peace. It was kinda...too quiet. Shaking her head at her own craziness, she hurried up the porch steps. After leaving her dirt-caked gloves and shoves on the mat, she rushed inside the house and upstairs to the bathroom. She didn't linger over her bath. She was too anxious to set things in motion for her date night with Dylan. Besides, bathing wasn't nearly as much fun without him there to scrub her back.

She rifled through her dresser drawer until she located the pretty pink bra and panty set she'd been saving for a special occasion. Once she'd slipped into her undergarments, she inspected her wardrobe for something that'd fall somewhere in the middle of respectable and *fuck-me-right-this-instant*. Her denim miniskirt and off-the-shoulder white peasant top should fit the bill.

Properly attired, she skipped downstairs and pulled on her cowgirl boots. Perfect. She snatched her cellphone and typed a quick message to Dylan. *Callie's on babysitting duty. We have until tomorrow afternoon.*

His replied winged back almost instantly. *Be there in ten minutes.*

Giggling like a fool, she slapped her cellphone down on the console and went to grab a bottle of lemonade from the fridge before returning to the living room. Giddy anticipation stirring her restlessness, she journeyed from the couch, the chair, a speedy trek to the screen door to see if she could spot any dust cloud signaling an approaching vehicle, then back to the couch again.

Just when she thought she'd jump out of her skin with

impatience, muffled music from a car radio drifted from outside. Forcing herself to stay put, she twiddled her thumbs and waited for the slam of Dylan's SUV door. A moment later, the *clomp, clomp, clomp* of his boots on the porch steps, and then there he was, breath-stealingly gorgeous in his faded Wranglers and snug black T-shirt. God, she wanted to lick him from head to toe.

Judging from the focused way he was staring at her, similar thoughts cycled through his mind. He strode to her and pulled her up from the couch. She opened her mouth to greet him and he took the opportunity to turn her knees to putty by kissing her senseless. Squeezing her ass, he hiked her up into his arms. She wrapped her legs around his waist and he sucked her tongue into his mouth, his fingers splaying across her bottom.

Coming up for air, she nibbled his lip. "So whatcha wanna do?"

He started to glide his hand down the back of her panties and she gave him another warning nip. "No way, Bubba. First ya gotta woo me."

"Darlin', I was plannin' on spending a minimum of an hour goin' down on ya."

Her pussy clenched at his admission. "Nice as that sounds— and I fully intend to hold you to it—I was thinking more along the lines of an early dinner someplace cozy and intimate."

"Your bed?" His hopeful expression almost made her cave.

Instead she pinched him through his shirt. "I've wanted to check out the new restaurant in Mayweather for a while now. There's also some really cute antique shops that'd be fun to poke through."

"Know what else would be fun to poke?"

Fighting back a laugh, she smacked his chest. "Behave yerself."

He settled her on her feet and rubbed his chin. "This sounds suspiciously like a date to me."

A hint of doubt crept in. "We don't have to call it that."

"Why not?" He grinned. "I happen to like the sound of it."

Relief swept through her. "Then you're okay with us doing that? I wasn't trying to be pushy or call the shots. It's been a while since I've been out with a man, and I...kinda don't know what I'm doing."

He brushed the hair away from her cheek. "I'd love nothing more than to spend the day with you, baby. I truly don't care what we do. I'm just happy to be with you and see you smilin'."

Well damn. Emotion tightening her chest, she hugged him. "Thank you."

He draped his arm around her shoulder. "You ready, princess? Your chariot awaits."

Chapter Ten

The Chateaubriand that she and Dylan shared at the Wooden Nickel was the most romantic treat she'd ever experienced. Of course, any meal with Dylan beside her was an instant recipe for romance. Rubbing her full belly, she groaned. "I'm glad I didn't opt for my midriff-baring top. I'd walk out of here looking like an overstuffed Care Bear."

"You'd never look anything less than beautiful, darlin'." He caressed her nape and reached for the dessert menu."

She gave him the side-eye. "You're kidding, right?"

"Hell, no. In fact, if we didn't have an audience I'd take advantage of how close you're sittin' to me right now." His hand slid from her knee and coasted upward along her thigh.

Desperately trying to ignore the tingling in her clit, she halted his hand before it could torment her any further. "I was referring to you wanting dessert."

"I'm always *up* for some sweet stuff."

She snorted and pointed to the menu. "I mean *that* dessert."

"Ah. I thought maybe you'd want something to finish off that amazin' meal."

"Ugh. No room." As it was she might have to covertly pop a button on her skirt in order to breath. "We could always stop at that farm stand we passed on the way here and pick up some fresh fruit to take home."

He looked unimpressed with that scenario so she decided to go for the big guns. "I already have whipped cream and chocolate."

"Where was that stand again?"

"Figured that'd get your stamp of approval."

He signaled for the check. Less than five minutes later they were cruising down the interstate toward Friskie's Farm Fresh Produce. The name threatened to give her giggles, particularly considering what they had planned for the fruit.

Armed with a mental shopping list, she dragged Dylan inside the large, open-sided shed housing the produce stand. Truthfully, he wasn't all that reluctant. Probably because he was too busy visualizing what he'd do with the strawberries piled in the little woven baskets across from them. She snagged one of the containers, along with some plums and nectarines.

Dylan held up a huge cucumber and she gave him the stink eye. He offered the vegetable a consolation pat before tossing it back in the heap. "Maybe next time, buddy."

Hauling him away from there before they got arrested by the food fetish police, she plopped their goodies on the checkout counter and dug in her purse. Dylan whipped out his wallet and handed over a twenty before she could stop him. He collected his change and the bags and offered his free arm. Sighing, she accepted it. "You didn't have to do that."

"I wanted to. Besides, paying gives me dibs on choosing where to lick the whip cream off ya first."

"Oh, is that how it works?"

"Yes, ma'am."

They ducked back into the SUV and headed on their way again. He surprised her by pulling into the parking lot of the tiny antique store she'd spied earlier. She sent him a mystified look. "I thought you wanted to get home."

"I promised you a date. This is part of it."

"But—"

He leaned over and caressed her cheek. "Don't get me wrong, I'm dyin' to lap you up like a Zoe sundae. It can wait though. Giving you this is way more important."

She blinked against the tears accumulating in her eyes. "You are so getting lucky tonight."

"Baby, I already am. Having you with me makes me the luckiest bastard on earth."

The intensity shining in his eyes did her in. Pushing aside every other thought in her head, she grabbed a hold of his face and kissed him hard. He groaned and delved his tongue past her lips. She eagerly accepted him, lightly scraping the tip with her teeth. Coasting her hand along the front of his shirt, she slipped past his belt and rubbed him through the denim of his jeans.

He tore his mouth away from hers, his breaths ragged. "If we keep this up, I'll never be able to walk through that store without knocking everything over with my dick."

That made her laugh. Nipping his whiskered jaw, she stroked him again. She moved her mouth lower and licked his neck. His warm, masculine scent left her woozy. "I don't feel like shopping anymore."

"No? What do you feel like?"

"Having you take me home and eat me like a big ole sundae."

He required no more encouragement. The second she was safely buckled in her seat, he gunned the engine and sped out of the lot. They reached the farmhouse in record time. Likely due to the fact that he broke every speed law in existence. He carried the bags into the house for her and set them next to the kitchen sink. Giving her a light swat on the butt, he nipped her earlobe. "I'll get things situated in the living room."

She couldn't think of the last time she did anything more scandalous than read a naughty book in that particular room. *This is going to be fun.* Excitement accelerating her pulse, she washed up the fruit and sliced the plums and nectarines into manageable pieces. She carefully arranged everything in a pretty rainbow shape and placed the can of spray whipped cream and the bottle of chocolate syrup in the center. Hugging the platter to her chest, she shuffled into the living room.

She blinked at the amazing sight greeting her. Dylan had moved the coffee table against the wall, making room for the twin-sized air mattress. A heart made out of rose petals decorated the sheet covering it. Flickering tea lights scattered across every available surface completed the tableau. Overwhelmed by the romantic touches, she settled the platter down and caught her breath. "How—*when* did you have time to do this?"

"The mattress is self-inflating, so that took no work. The petals I snagged outside from your rose bush." He looked momentarily sheepish. "Hope you don't mind I took the liberty. And the candles are LED. Flip a switch, and presto."

"But that still doesn't explain where you got the mattress and candles."

"I stashed them in the back of the SUV the other day. Was gonna surprise you with a little romance under the stars after Little Man went to bed."

She crossed to the mattress and smoothed her thumb over the velvety surface of one of the rose petals. Uncertainty shadowed Dylan's eyes. "Do you like it? It's not lame, is it?"

"It's the sweetest thing anyone's ever done for me." Twining her arms around his neck, she offered him a tremulous smile. "Thank you."

He coasted his hands to the small of her back and hugged her to him. "You're welcome, baby." He kissed her tenderly, his tongue a soft, exploring promise of hotter pleasures to come.

Her insides turning liquid, she untangled her arms from his shoulders and scored her fingertips along the firm plane of his chest. She needed to feel his bare skin. Touch and taste him until she was intoxicated on his head-rushing pheromones. With his assistance she shoved his T-shirt up over his head. He whipped the garment to the rug and divested her of her top and miniskirt.

He raked his fiery gaze over her, lingering on her itsy bitsy pink panties. "You are the sexiest thing alive."

Flushing with pleasure, she sat on the mattress and reached for her boot. He shook his head. "No, leave those. I've always had this fantasy of you riding me like a true cowgirl."

She giggled. Grinning, he stretched over her, forcing her flat to the airbed. He aligned his body over hers, settling between the cradle of her thighs. Lacing his fingers with hers, he lifted her hands and pinned them above her head. It felt naughty and oh so wanton being spread-eagled beneath him, only her skimpy bra and panties shielding her from his wicked ways.

Ha! Like she wasn't eager for him to defile her in every filthy way imaginable.

He rolled his hips, deliberately grinding her pussy with that luscious hardness straining at his zipper. She wrapped her legs around his waist, moving along with him. He kissed her lightly on the lips, his tongue teasing. A whimper broke from her and his mouth moved lower, teeth scraping her chin. Shifting his head, he dipped his tongue in the hollow of her collarbone. "How wet are you for me, darlin'?"

Her mouth was too dry for her to form a coherent response. Fortunately he didn't seem to require one, because he released one of her hands and eased up enough to slide his fingers inside her panties. A carnal gleam flashing in his eyes, he slicked over her drenched labia. "Mm, juicy and sweet as any peach. And even better to eat."

Mesmerized by his dirty bedroom talk, she bit her lip and rubbed shamelessly on his hand. Just when she thought he couldn't possibly drive her crazier with need, he slipped out of her panties and licked his fingers.

"Oh Lord," she whispered. "You're killing me."

His devilish smirk confirming that he was mighty proud of that turn of events, he freed the clasp on her bra and peeled back the cups. He massaged the globes of her breasts, his touch sensuous and confident. He worked his way inward and upward, feathering over her areolas without making direct contact with her nipples. The taunting absence of his touch there triggered her frustrated moan.

The glint in his eyes hinting that he was well aware of the torment he was inflicting on her, he reversed course, abandoning her breasts completely. He ghosted his hand along her belly, the tantalizing brushstrokes of his fingertips making her quiver. Tracing the elastic band of her panties, he inched the fabric down slightly before hooking the side strings with his thumbs and dragging the scrap of lace down her legs. He worked the elastic down and over her boots and dropped the undergarment onto the floor.

Leaning sideways, he grabbed the can of whipped cream. He primed it with several hard shakes and squirted a healthy dollop on both of her nipples, the cold sugary foam instantly puckering the peaks of her breasts. Next he painted a stripe straight down her abdomen and bisected it with a triangle on her mound, the whole thing forming an arrow. He tossed her a wink. "Just in case I get lost along the way."

"Insightful of ya."

He set the whipped cream aside and flipped open the cap on the chocolate syrup. A fine drizzle trickling from the tip, he retraced the path he'd already marked. Smacking his lips in a way that made her smile, he plunked the bottle down and leaned over her. He licked her cream-covered left nipple first. Once it was squeaky clean, he sucked the swollen nub, the heat of his mouth a decadent contrast to the chilled foam. He treated the other nipple to the same oral devotion, the pull and tug of his lips and tongue shooting corresponding tremors deep in her core. She gripped his hair, arching her back for more of his feasting pleasure.

Flattening his tongue, he cruised down the lane of cream and chocolate traversing her stomach and the top of her mound. He dropped between her legs, his broad shoulders providing the perfect resting spot for her thighs. Sliding her labia open with his thumbs, he licked her from her slit all the way up to the throbbing nubbin that'd been aching for his tongue for the last ten minutes. Finally having him where she most needed him brought a blissful sigh to her lips.

"I wanna hear you do that again, only this time usin' my name."

She honored the request and he growled into her flesh, the sound and the carnal friction of his tongue shooting stars in her vision. Her hips bucked and he caught them with his hands, holding her steady as she shattered into a million brilliant shards of blinding light. While she was still gasping for breath, he shoved to his feet and shucked his boots before stripping off his jeans and jockeys. He dropped onto the mattress and hooked her behind the knees with his arms, pulling her to him. A firm nudge of his cockhead, and then he thrust to the hilt with one smooth, breath-stealing stroke.

They stared into each other's eyes, the connection miles beyond the mere physical. He rolled his hips, stoking the embers of pleasure still burning in her cells. She bowed her back, matching him thrust for thrust. Groaning, he pulled out of her and rolled onto his back, taking her with him. With her straddling him now, he eased back inside of her pussy and coaxed her to sit up on his cock. He laced his fingers behind his head. "I wanna see you work it, cowgirl."

"Oh yeah? Think I can't last eight seconds in your saddle?"

He chuckled. "Think we both know I'm the one most at risk of not lasting the bell."

"Damn straight." And just in case he was still unconvinced, she started undulating her hips in a slow, steady grind, riding the rock-hard length of his shaft until his gaze turned glassy and sweat beaded his brow and pecs. Sliding her hands to her breasts, she squeezed them and pinched her nipples.

"*Fuck me.*" His gaze glued to her motions, he licked his lips. "Play with your clit for me, darlin'."

She obediently released one of her breasts and caressed the bundle of nerves, a gasp springing from her at the languorous spiral of pleasure that coalesced into a wild burst of ecstasy. Shuddering, she rode out the intense sensations. She was acutely aware of Dylan soaking up every detail of her climax. Sharing the intimacy with him only suspended her higher on the cloud of bliss.

Before she fell back to Earth, he eased her off of him and rolled her onto her stomach. Assuming he wanted her on her knees, she began to lift up, but he stretched over her, hugging her between his arms and bracketing her legs with his. He kissed her neck and slid his cock inside her, the angle hitting her G spot in precisely the right way. She bit her lip, unable to suppress the wanton moans that purled from her as his engorged head pumped deeper, retreated, stroked again, ceaselessly working that over-sensitized patch of tissues, over and over. She trembled. "Dylan, I'm c-com—"

"Yes, baby, I'm right with ya."

Hearing him say it was all the permission she needed to fly off the edge, her rapturous cries blending with his strangled shout. Her heart thumping like mad, she groaned weakly, too spent to move a muscle. Good thing, considering Dylan was still slumped on top of her.

Unable to help herself, she laughed. He nuzzled her neck, his arms tightening around her. "That better not be due to my performance or my ego will be wilted."

"No, it's due to mine. I don't think I lasted the full eight seconds."

"Don't worry. That was only a practice round."

Practice round? Lord have mercy.

Chapter Eleven

Spending the morning making slow, sweet love to Zoe made up for having to leave her at ten to make the trip into Red Creek. After tomorrow he wouldn't have to step foot in that office again.

Rather than a huge wave of relief swamping him, he was met with an odd twinge of sadness. Truth be told, that place started to grow on him a bit the last couple of days. Maybe Abby had been onto something about dirt samples and their mystical abilities to lure you to the Dark Side.

Shaking his head at that fanciful thought, he parked the SUV and detoured to the coffee shop aptly named Heart Starter. He'd discovered the place the other day and deemed it a nice alternative to the longer wait at Cubby's. Not to mention he was starting to get a tad addicted to Lexie's pastries.

The owner of the shop gifted him a smile. "Let me guess, your usual?"

Damn, he had a usual? Pondering the coolness of that, he watched Lexie select a giant bear claw danish with her tongs and slip it in a cellophane to-go wrap. His stomach rumbled in anticipation. Zoe would likely give him hell for snacking after the generous breakfast of bacon and eggs she fixed. All this hot lovin' was taking a toll on his appetite. "Why don't you throw in extras for Abby and the gang?"

"Sure."

Lexie boxed up a variety of the mouth-watering goodies. He accepted the package and passed her a twenty. "Keep the change."

She nodded her thanks. "No coffee this morning?"

"Already half a pot past my daily allotment."

Her eyes twinkled. "Sounds like someone's been burning the midnight oil."

Sure did. And damn if it hadn't been the hottest, most wonderful night of his life. After taking a bath together, he and Zoe had dragged the airbed into the backyard. He'd pitched the pup tent he'd bought along with the mattress, giving them some safety from the buzzing insects. They'd fed each other the succulent slices of fruit and made love under the twinkling canvas of stars visible through the overhead tent flap. Afterwards he'd held her in his arms, the gentle beating of her heart a lullaby that rocked him into blissful slumber.

Lexie chuckled. "Judging from the look on your face, I'm guessing you're not complaining."

"Nope." He pinched off a corner of his pastry and snuck a bite. "Oh, Zoe wanted me to ask if you're able to make it to Callie's surprise party this evening."

"I'll try my best. I have to make a trip out to Richfield after I close up shop. If I don't get back in time, give the girls a big hug from me, okay?"

"Will do."

He ducked out the door and made his way to his dad's office. *No, not Dusty's anymore. Mine and my brothers'.* Assuming they didn't sell off their shares. Initially that'd been the route he'd planned to take. But now that option didn't call to him as much. Crazy notion, considering how dead set he'd been against involving himself in anything attached to the Walker name.

Abby's gaze lit up when he strode through the entry with the bakery box. "Aw, you shouldn't have."

"Didn't. They're all for me." Tossing her a wink, he strolled toward the kitchenette. He stashed the box on the counter and situated a stack of Styrofoam plates for easy access.

Abby snickered behind him. "Look at you being all generous."

"Shh. Don't let that nasty rumor past these walls."

She inspected the contents of the box. "In the spirit of your largesse, I'll leave the honeybun for Elaine."

"Damn, I was hopin' my largesse wasn't showin'." He patted his belly. "Probably should cut back on the pastries."

"Silly man." Giggling, Abby grabbed her plate and returned to her station.

Dylan strode down the hall. Walt and Vic were in their respective offices. He lifted a hand in greeting to both men before heading to his own workspace. His attention shifted to Dusty's doorway, and he hesitated. The familiar ache settled in his belly, only minus its usual sharpness. Maybe his emotional scars were finally starting to scab over. Intent to test his theory, he ambled into the room and sat in his father's chair. Running his fingers along the upholstered arms, he stared at the worn surface of the desk.

He waited for the hurt and rage to sink their claws in. The photo of Dusty and Theresa flashed through his mind—his father's weary acceptance triggering that strange twinge of empathy in Dylan's chest. His dad was a cheating asshole—nothing would redeem or change that—but it couldn't have been easy juggling five families and knowing he'd have to take that secret to the grave with him. Who would willingly take on that kind of burden?

A chirp beeped from the vicinity of his pocket. Figuring it was Zoe texting him, he dug his cellphone out and glanced at the display. Not his sweet cowgirl, but Georgianna.

Hi, honey. Just checking in to see how you're doing. Call me when you have a chance.

Shit. He'd completely forgotten to touch base with her the last few days. Dread percolated in his stomach. No more putting this off. He needed to tell her about his brothers and the other women. Steeling himself, he punched in her number.

She picked up on the first ring. "I didn't mean you had to call me right this second," she laughed.

Relief crashed through him. She sounded so much better than the last time they spoke. Hopefully that meant she'd worked through the toughest stage of her grieving. "I know, but I've missed hearing your voice."

"You're such a sweetheart. I've missed you too. Are you taking care of yourself? I hope you're not eating fast food every night."

Her typical momma bear worrying brought a smile to his lips. "I'm not. Marliss and Zoe are watchin' out for my arteries."

"Who are Marliss and Zoe?" There was no mistaking the curiosity in Georgianna's tone.

"Marliss is Dusty's housekeeper. She and her husband, Lou, live at the house. And Zoe, well, she's just the prettiest angel sent to Earth, and..." He sucked in a deep breath and expelled it slowly. "She's the mama of your grandson."

A lengthy pause drifted through the receiver. Dylan swallowed. "Mom, are you there?"

"Dylan Mitchell Walker, you have a son and you're just now telling me about it?"

He gulped. Georgianna only busted out his middle name when he was in some serious shit. He quickly recounted the situation to her, praying that his ignorance of Hunter's existence would let him off the hook. Didn't matter that it made perfect sense to him that it should. Women could be mysterious creatures who viewed rational explanations in an entirely different light.

Fortunately Georgianna took the additional details in stride and her strident tone immediately softened. "I can't wait to meet Zoe and our little Hunter."

"I can't wait for you to meet them either." He frowned. "You're not pissy that she kept him a secret?"

"I'm sure she had her reasons."

He grunted. Here his mom had been ready to whop him with a frying pan when he returned home, but Zoe got the reasonable treatment. *Women.* He gripped the phone tighter, his stomach pitching in anticipation of the second part of this conversation. "I need to tell ya somethin', and I don't want ya to get upset." *Though I know you will.* How could she not?

"You and Zoe are expecting twins? Sweetie, that doesn't upset me at all. After all, Hunter needs a little baby brother and sister."

"You're an evil woman. Now stop your grandbaby

daydreaming because this is important." He blew out a heavy breath. "Dusty has three other sons—my half-brothers. Each from a different woman."

Dead silence greeted him. *Fuck.* "If you need me to come home early, I will." He wouldn't risk Georgianna falling into a deep pit of depression and possibly doing something harmful to herself. No inheritance was worth that.

"No, hon. I don't want you to do that. I-I'm just...processing."

"I understand. Believe me. When I first saw them at the lawyer's, and found out who they were, it about knocked me on my ass."

"How are you doing? How are they? Your brothers, I mean? It has to be difficult for all of you."

Leave it to Georgianna to focus on everyone else—including three strangers she'd never even met. The woman was a miracle. "I can't speak for them since I haven't seen them after we left the lawyer's office, but I'm doin' okay."

"Are you?"

His mind traveled to the box of scrapbooks, and the one that he hadn't been able to bring himself to open yet. "I'm gettin' there."

"He loved you. And I'm sure he loved your brothers. Family was so important to Dusty."

"Even though he couldn't be there for ours?" Yeah, guess he still had some work to do on that bitterness.

"He was there as much as he could be. He was there when he *needed* to be."

A memory flashed across his mental big screen. His childish whoops of happiness while his little legs pumped away, trying to keep his Schwinn bike upright as he flew down the sidewalk. Dusty jogging beside him, his shouts of encouragement alternating with his radiant smiles.

He coughed gruffly, clearing the emotion clogging his throat. "Gotta go, mom. There's an emergency up front."

"Okay, honey." The gentleness in Georgianna's voice hinted that she'd seen through his excuse to get off the line before he embarrassed himself in front of her. "I'll see you soon. And please think about what I said. Holding onto the pain and anger only scars your soul. I don't want that for you."

He swallowed roughly. "I love you, Mom."

"Love you too, sweetie."

They said their goodbyes and hung up. He placed his phone on the desk and laced his fingers, pressing his forehead against the steeple they'd formed. She was right. He needed to get past this. Needed to heal, once and for all. Not just for himself, but Zoe and Hunter too. Because he could never build a future with them without first forgiving his past.

Chapter Twelve

If he hadn't seen the spectacle with his own eyes, he never would have believed forty-plus people could fit inside a postage-stamp-sized backyard. Squeezing Zoe's shoulder and tucking Hunter close to his side, he followed his beautiful angel into the congested throng. "I didn't think this many folks lived in Red Creek."

She laughed. "Oh, they don't. Tay trucked half of them in from the next county."

He wasn't sure if she was kidding or not.

"Oh, there's Tay." Zoe started hustling them in that direction. She released Dylan's hand for a moment to hug the other man. "I'm so glad you got a good turnout for the party."

He noticed the flash of appreciation in Taylor's eyes as the man took in Zoe's eyelet camisole and denim skirt. *Yeah, only wants to be friends, my ass.* He shook Taylor's hand when it was extended his way, putting a little something extra in the forceful squeeze. Judging from Tay's smirk, he'd gotten the message loud and clear.

"Glad you three could make it." Taylor scratched his jaw. "I'm just wondering the wisdom in keeping this a complete surprise from Callie. We know how fond she is of F bombs, and that's when she's *not* dealing with a bunch of people startling the bejeebers outta her. Who knows what'll pop out of her mouth?"

"We'll pray for the least terrifying outcome." She patted Taylor's arm reassuringly.

They spoke for a few more minutes before Taylor excused himself to go call Callie with the excuse that Josh was ready to be picked up. Abby approached them, a man that Dylan assumed to be her husband next to her side. "Hey y'all, quite a turnout, huh? Mr. Walker, I'd like you to meet my hubby, Elbert."

He exchanged handshakes with the man. "Great to meet you.

And please, no Mr. Walker business. It's Dylan."

Abby's expression turned hopeful. "Any chance you're going to grace us with some entertainment tonight?"

He chuckled. "I would, but my guitar and amps are back in Nashville." He'd debated bringing his old Rogue acoustic guitar along. It might not be as flashy and sexy as his Gibson Stratocaster, but it offered the same security blanket his music always provided during tough times. In the end he'd left it behind, figuring he'd be too busy to get the use out of it.

"Taylor would probably be fine with you borrowing his guitar."

Elbert rubbed Abby's nape. "Hon, you're being pushy."

She blushed. "I am. Please forgive me."

"Nothing to forgive." Dylan cocked an eyebrow. "I just didn't realize that Taylor played guitar."

"Not professionally, like you." The man in question stepped next to Dylan and inclined his head. "You're more than welcome to use my Rogue. I know it'd mean a lot to Callie hearing you play."

"No shit, you have a Rogue? That's what I practiced on."

"Same here."

Zoe sighed. "And so the male bonding begins."

Abby clapped her hands. "You should perform with Dylan."

Panic flashed across Zoe's face. "What? No. I only teach singing."

"Oh, baloney." Abby grinned. "According to Sue Sweeny, you have a gorgeous voice. Time to show it off, girl."

Dylan rubbed Zoe's stiffened spine. "It's totally up to you, baby, but I would love to accompany you. I'd even let you pick the song."

She gritted her teeth. "How generous of you."

"Yeah, everyone's been pointing out my magnanimous nature lately." He winked at Abby. "So what do ya say?"

"I'll think about it."

Taylor's cellphone beeped, immediately putting a halt to the conversation. He scanned the incoming text and waved his arm in the air. "Everyone, Callie's minivan was spotted down the block. We need absolute silence from here on out."

A hush fell over the crowd. Dylan leaned forward to whisper in Zoe's ear. "I haven't been this excited since getting to see you in only panties and cowgirl boots." She pinched his arm, earning his low chuckle.

The minutes ticked by in excruciatingly slow increments. Just when he was worried folks would grow restless and start chatting again, muffled voices drifted from the inside of the house. A moment later the sliding glass door opened, revealing Callie's profile as she said something to her son. She tossed up one arm. "I'm not climbing no tree to get that kite. We'll buy you—"

Forty-something voices shouted "Surprise!" in unison.

Callie jolted. "Holy fuck!"

Taylor grunted. "Coulda been worse."

Josh dragged his befuddled mom down the deck steps. Callie was immediately engulfed in a sea of hugs and Happy Birthday wishes.

Her forehead scrunching, Callie stared at the balloons tied to the crabapple in the corner of the yard. "But it's not my fuckin' birthday."

Taylor pinched the bridge of his nose. "We know. Now could ya stop using that word?"

Zoe squeezed her friend's arm, gaining Callie's distracted attention. "Tay wanted to get your mind off of today and create a happy memory instead."

The confusion cleared from Callie's face. Her eyes filming over with tears, she gaped at her brother. "Y-you did this for me?"

"And Josh," Taylor added, ruffling his nephew's spiky ginger hair.

"Aw damn." Sniffling, Callie wrapped her arms around her brother and son.

The emotional scene got to Dylan a bit and he hugged Zoe to his side and kissed Hunter's temple. The love and connection this community shared was amazing. Or, more appropriately, and in Callie's immortal favorite word—fucking amazing.

A cake was wheeled outside and Callie cut a slice before smashing it against Josh's mouth. Giggling and sputtering white frosting and chocolate cake, he chased her into the crowd. A second later Callie faced her sad fate, laughing and cursing a storm at the kids who tackled her and held her in place for Josh's retaliatory cake smash.

While everyone was preoccupied with the kids' antics, Dylan grabbed three plates of the decadent dessert and passed one to Hunter and Zoe. He took a bite of the cake and hummed around his mouthful of sugary goodness.

Zoe watched his lusty appreciation with a twinkle in her eye. "Lord, you do have a sweet tooth."

"Especially when chocolate is involved." He waggled his brows. "Only thing missing is the whipped cream."

She blushed all the way to her platinum roots.

Callie jogged up to them, breathless and covered in cake. "Abby says you both are gonna perform a special song for me. Do I get to pick it?"

Zoe groaned. "I didn't say for sure I would do it."

"You have to." Callie's gaze turned pleading. "It'd mean the world to me. And knowing my Tom is listening in from Heaven, it makes it even more special."

Zoe snuffled. "Damn you. No way I can say no to that."

Callie pumped her fist in the air before cupping her hands around her mouth like a megaphone. Considering the volume her voice carried, not like she needed it. "Listen up, folks. We're getting a live concert from our very own Zoe Chapman and Dylan Hunter, so gather 'round and get ready to shake what ya mama gave ya."

Taylor clapped Dylan on the back. "I'll grab my Rogue."

"Thanks, man." Dylan glanced at Callie. "What's your first pick?"

"Honkytonk First Date."

Zoe sighed. "What is it with everyone and that stinkin' song?"

He grinned. "It's a classic."

Taylor approached with the Rogue acoustic and Dylan accepted it with a nod. He swung the strap around his neck and settled his butt against the deck post. Positioning the soundboard, he open tuned the guitar by running through the notes in the D major chord. The familiar vibrato of the box and the strings between his fingertips sent a rush of exhilaration through him. How the hell had he gone an entire week without immersing himself in that sensation?

Well, you had a mighty fine substitute every time you were balls-deep in that special little lady eating you up with her gaze over there. He returned Zoe's smoldering stare and acknowledged his inner voice had a most excellent point.

Zoe cleared her throat, preparing for the opening line of the song. He could see her knees shaking slightly. *Aw, sweet baby, don't be nervous. You're gonna kill it.* She must have somehow intuited his mental encouragement because she relaxed her shoulders. Nodding, he led her in with a strum of the C chord. She opened her mouth—and nearly knocked him on his ass with the powerhouse voice that emitted from her vocal chords.

Where the hell has she been hiding that? Dazzled and impressed as shit, he quickly got his groove back and finger-plucked the perfect chords to harmonize with her melody. When they reached the chorus he joined in with his own baritone and Zoe smiled at him, her vivid green eyes sparkling like the brightest emeralds. The crowd was hooting and clapping, several of the youngins creating their own dance steps. It was a blast to watch, but the best part was Zoe tiptoeing her fingers along his shoulder and swaying along with him, their voices blending in duet. In that moment they were having their own little honkytonk first date. In front of forty some people, but it only added to the joy.

The song ended too soon and several Bic lighters waved in the air, signaling the desire for an encore. He glanced at Zoe. "One more?"

"Sure. Why not."

Callie high-fived Josh. "We want Moonshine On My Mind."

Zoe stiffened. "Could you please pick another song than that?"

"I know it's completely inappropriate." Callie waved her arm. "Why do you think I chose it?"

He strummed the opening bars, but Zoe didn't immediately join in. A glance in her direction confirmed that she was still glaring at Callie. He coughed pointedly and ran through the intro again. She picked up the chorus, her inflection flatter than the Sahara. Getting through her joyless performance of the song proved to be a trial. He breathed a sigh of relief when he closed on the ending note without either one of them getting pelted by rotten tomatoes. He swung the guitar strap from his neck and passed the instrument to Taylor.

Scratching the back of his neck, he approached Zoe. "Take it you're not a fan of that song."

"No." Her face tight, she glanced up at him. "My father was a drinker. Guess what his favorite poison of choice was?"

Aw shit. "Baby, I didn't know. You shoulda said something. We coulda picked a different song."

Her features slowly softened. "No. It's what Callie wanted." She rubbed her eyes, but not before he caught the gleam of moisture sheening their surface. "God, I ruined her song because of my stupid issues."

His heart aching for her, he hugged her close. "You did fine. And don't ever think the way you feel is stupid. Sometimes old hurts take a long time to heal." Fuck, did he know that better than anybody.

She clung to him, her tears forming a wet spot on his T-shirt. "C-could we maybe go home?"

He massaged her nape. "If that's what you want to do, absolutely."

"I do." She knuckled her cheek, wiping at the dampness. "I don't want to be a wet blanket on Callie's party."

"She's not gonna think that."

"I know. But I do. Plus I could really use the quiet right now."

He nodded. "Should we say our goodbyes to Callie, Taylor, and Josh?"

Securing her approval of that plan, they made their way to their host and guests of honor. After convincing Callie that they were leaving due to Zoe's sudden migraine, Dylan scooped Hunter into his arms and led the way to the exit. They'd parked by the downtown office in order not to give any clues to Callie earlier, so the short walk into town gave them all a moment to wind down. He slid a sideways glance to Zoe and noticed that she seemed to be relaxing with each step she took. Good.

He had a million questions tumbling in his brain, but he didn't dare voice any of them. Not until she was in a better frame of mind.

D. Walker Mineral popped into view, its upstairs bank of windows reflecting the orange ball of the setting sun. He dropped his focus to Dusty's SUV and the large black conversion van parked next to it. He frowned. Not because he hadn't seen the vehicle in town before, but rather because it looked awfully familiar. He blinked. *No, it can't be.*

Tightening his grip on Hunter, he picked up his pace. Zoe grumbled next to him. "Why are you walking so fast?"

He was close enough now he could make out the license plate. He broke into a grin. "I can't believe it."

"What?"

Instead of answering, he snagged her hand and hauled her along with him. He skidded to a stop behind the van and set Hunter down before kicking the rear door with his boot. Zoe groaned. "Now I know where our child gets it from."

Giggling, Hunter got into the act by pounding his little hand on the metal. Dylan offered his son a proud fist bump.

Grumbling sounds issued from inside the vehicle. The door swung open, revealing a scowling Trin. "Jeez Louise. Some of us are trying to meditate back here." She squinted at Dylan. "You don't look like you're contemplatin' hangin' yerself."

"Uh, why would I be?"

Malcom popped his head out, his expression sheepish. "I mighta told everyone that to get them here."

Dylan scratched the back of his head. "Why? What's going on?"

"Man, we've *got* to get this rift straightened out. So since you couldn't come to Nashville..."

Disbelief crept through Dylan. "Are you tellin' me—?"

The driver's side door opened, and the last person Dylan ever expected to log nine hours on the road just to see him climbed down from the van. His boot heels ringing on the pavement, Luke Pendergrass stepped into view. The worry in the man's gaze instantly morphed into suspicion. "You don't look suicidal." His attention drifted beyond Dylan and moved to Zoe. A strange stillness settled over him. He moved his lips, but no sound immediately vacated his mouth. Finally he choked out one word. "Moonshine."

A distressed noise came from Zoe. Dylan slashed his attention to her just as she took a stumbling step backwards. She steadied herself before he could reach her. The way she was staring at Luke sent prickles of foreboding down Dylan's spine. For a brief moment he got that weird sensation again, like he was standing outside of himself, looking in at a scene he didn't fully comprehend but probably should. "Zoe?"

"No." The single syllable flew from Luke's tongue like a bullet. "My daughter's name is Moonshine."

Chapter Thirteen

This was a nightmare. It had to be. She'd wake up any minute and these figments of her past would dissolve into the ether.

Before she could blink him out of existence, her father clomped in her direction and cupped her face. "Moonshine." He whispered the despised name like he half expected to wake up any second now too.

"Stop calling me that." She swiped at the useless flood of tears, breaking Luke's tenuous hold on her. "I hate it."

Who the hell scribbled the word moonshine on their daughter's birth certificate anyway? Oh, that's right. A drunk who showed up several hours after his child's delivery because he'd been sleeping off the effects of a three day bender. Her mom had eventually gotten the hospital to correct the name to Zoe on her birth certificate, but her father had—and apparently still—refused to use it.

Luke rifled his fingers through his thick, graying blond hair, looking eons older than his forty-eight years. Zoe's heart cramped. Her entire life she'd worked hard at numbing herself, and in one fell swoop she was right back where she started. A desperately lonely little girl who cycled between hating her daddy and loving him so much it hurt.

It was always the ones you loved who hurt you the deepest. She'd been shown that truth, time after time.

The tense quiet surrounding them was thick enough to take a steak knife to. Wiping her eyes again, she stared dispassionately at their audience. She couldn't bring herself to look at Dylan yet. She felt too raw, too exposed. Like the painful scars of her past were oozing out there in the open for everyone to see.

"Moon—" Luke sighed when she gave him a hard look. "Zoe."

She almost keeled over in shock. It was the first time she'd ever heard him use her real name. Probably he thought that'd win her over. Well he had another think coming. She bent over and picked up Hunter. Luke stared at her son, his features frozen in disbelief. "Is...he your boy?"

"Yes. You're a grandfather. Congratulations. I'm sorry I didn't have the nurse call you while I was in labor so you could commemorate the moment with a fifth of Jim Beam."

Luke winced. "I've cleaned up my act. Haven't touched a drop of alcohol in over a year."

She wanted to believe him. But after a lifetime of similar lies and empty promises it was hard to trust anything that came out of his mouth. Hugging Hunter to her chest, she finally glanced at Dylan. He appeared shell-shocked. Guilt and regret churned her stomach. She didn't like that she'd had to keep this secret from him, but there'd been no other choice. If she'd revealed who her dad was it would have put Dylan in the middle of her and Luke. That's something she'd wanted to avoid at all costs.

But he'd found out anyway, and now he'd probably hate her for keeping this from him.

Stomach queasy and her heart heavy, she strode to Dylan and touched his arm. "Can you take us home now?"

Before Dylan could respond, Luke stepped forward. His hawk-like stare cycled between Zoe's hand on Dylan's arm, Hunter, and then up to Dylan's face. Her dad's eyes narrowed. "What in the *hell* is going on here?"

She glared at Luke. "That's absolutely none of your business. Or concern." She nudged Dylan toward the SUV.

Luke stalked directly in Dylan's path. "Have you been messing around with my daughter?" He slammed his hand on Dylan's chest, knocking him back a step. "Did you knock her up, you sonofabitch?" Luke roared that last part and swung at Dylan's face, connecting with his jaw.

"Aw shit." The guy with the neon blue mohawk leapt on Luke before he could take another swing. Her dad growled and elbowed the kid in the ribs. Luke whipped around, his fist flying, ready to hit its target. Before her dad's punch could make contact, mohawk kid's female partner cold-cocked Luke, sending him down for the count. The woman un-balled her fist and cursed. "There goes my damn manicure."

Mohawk glanced at Dylan. "This isn't exactly how I pictured this reconciliation going."

Dylan worked his jaw. Apparently satisfied nothing was broken, he exhaled heavily. "It coulda been worse."

The kid nodded. "A media crew could have been around and captured that for the ten o'clock news. Then Luke would never live down getting his lights knocked out by a girl."

Reminded that they were standing in the middle of town, Zoe slashed a look over her shoulder. Thankfully Red Creek had rolled up its sidewalk for the night. The few cars around likely belonged to the folks still at Callie's party. Who knew when that would break up? People could walk down the street any moment now.

Sighing, she shifted Hunter in her arms and stroked her hand over his hair. He'd been unusually quiet the last few minutes. Probably he was confused and scared after the scuffle with Luke. Just one more reason to be furious with her dad. She turned her attention to Mohawk. "Can you get my father in your van? You can follow us to my house."

Dylan frowned at her. "If you're not comfortable with that I can always take them to my dad's place."

Tempting as it was, she needed to stop hiding from her past. If she didn't take care of this now it would haunt her the rest of her days. "No, it's okay."

His expression unreadable, Dylan strode to Luke's side. He squatted and gripped Luke beneath his lax arms, hefting him into a sprawled sitting position. The kid hustled behind Luke, and with Dylan's assistance, they hoisted her dad upright and dragged him to the opened door in the back of the van. With little ceremony and plenty of grunts and curses on their part, they managed to get him onto the floor of the vehicle. Dylan hopped down from the tail gate and slammed the door shut. He pulled his keys from his pocket. After clicking the lock release button, he took Hunter from her and buckled him into his child seat, all without saying a word to her.

Her belly a noxious pit of swirling unease, she ducked into her own seat and fastened her safety belt. Dylan climbed behind the wheel and started the engine, a fierce energy radiating from him. He backed out of the parking space with a squeal of the SUV tires and pointed them in the direction of home.

She swallowed hard, desperately wishing he'd say something. "Is your jaw feeling better?"

"It's fine. Were you ever intendin' to tell me he's your father?"

Of course he'd have to lead with the one question that he wouldn't like the answer to. "No."

He slashed a look her way, the pain and fury in his eyes cutting straight through her. "You trust me that little, huh?"

"It has nothing to do with that, Dylan." Feeling like the entire world was pressing down on her shoulders, she hugged her chest, the straps of the seatbelt digging into her. It seemed a fitting metaphor to her life. She was a constant prisoner to her past, unable to completely break the bonds. Hell, she'd fallen in love with a man who was a tangible link to the one person she'd fought so hard to sever ties with. If that wasn't living proof that she couldn't escape her past, nothing was. "I couldn't tell you because it'd put you in the middle."

"It's still the same thing, Zoe. A total lack of trust in me that I would stand by you no matter what."

She blinked against the tears threatening to well into existence. "You're telling me you could have kept that secret from him? Because that's what it would have come down to. I wouldn't have let you tell him about me and Hunter."

Dylan tore his focus from the windshield again. "You honestly think he wouldn't have eventually found out about us? My band is a part of my life. *Luke* is a part of my life. Your paths would have eventually crossed."

She averted her gaze. A thick silence shrouded the vehicle. When Dylan finally spoke a noticeable edge serrated his tone. "You weren't plannin' to be a permanent part of my life, were ya?"

The tears broke their dam. He had it all wrong. "When your week here is up, I figured..."

"What, Zoe? What assumption did you make?" The hurt etching his features hinted that he'd already put the pieces together. "That I would check out on you like Luke did? Do you think that little of me? I'm *nothing* like your father. Or mine. I wouldn't abandon my family."

Guilt seared her to the bone. "I'm sorry." Those two words sounded too feeble for repairing the hurt she'd inflicted on him. "And I don't think those things about you."

"But you do," he bit out. "If you didn't, we wouldn't be having this conversation right now."

She needed him to understand exactly how fucked up she was. Then he'd know what he was dealing with. He'd know the uphill struggle she faced every day of her life. "It's not easy for me to trust, Dylan. Sometimes I think it's impossible. Yes, I assumed you would leave. It was easier than building my hopes and waiting for the day you wouldn't come home to me and Hunter. Because that's the only existence I've known—daddies who can't be there for their families."

He remained silent, the tension still sparking from him. Finally he dragged his fingers through his hair, a weary exhale slipping free. "I went through the same thing with Dusty. I get that trust can be a hard thing to grasp onto when you expect the worst from a person. We build walls. So thick that sometimes we can't even break past them. But we have to, Zoe. There's no future for us if we don't."

The finality of his words shot a tremor through her. If she didn't shake loose of her demons he'd leave her. In the back of her mind she realized that wasn't really what he was saying, but her fears eagerly grasped onto that interpretation with zealous glee. *Give them an excuse to check out and they will. The only one you can depend on in this life is you.*

They pulled into the driveway leading up to the farmhouse. Dylan parked. Before he could get to Hunter she freed their son from the car seat and hiked him into her arms.

Dark clouds of emotion shadowing his gaze, Dylan shoved his hands in his pockets. The van pulled in next to the SUV, giving her something else to focus on than the wounds her fucked up issues were inflicting on her and the man she loved.

Mohawk kid jumped down from the driver's seat and sent Dylan a wary look. "He's conscious. And pissy as a bear with a toothache."

The side door opened and Luke climbed out, his scowl complimenting the description that'd been slapped on him. He glared at Dylan. "I oughta bust your damn kneecaps. Sneaking around behind my back with my daughter like a fucking weasel. After everything I did for you. Taking you into the band and treating you like a son."

His choice of words triggered a humorless laugh from her. "And what exactly did that amount to? Paying him off with a car to make up for disappearing from his life for eighteen months straight?"

A flush crept over Luke's face. "I'm not proud of the way I failed you, Moonshine." His apology was slightly ruined by the stubborn slant of his chin. She knew where this was leading. Her dad could never take the entire blame for anything. He jabbed a finger, swiping the air between them. "But you walked out on me too."

And there it was. "Because I had to. If I didn't cut the tie it would have strangled me with its bitterness."

"So you washed your hands of me? Decided I wasn't even worth giving another chance?" Genuine hurt lined her father's haggard features.

She trembled, despising that he could still make her feel anything other than a cold emptiness against him. "How many chances am I expected to give you?" *How many more times am I supposed to let you in so you'll crush my heart once and for all?*

"I'm beggin' for one more, baby girl. That's all. If you can't forgive me enough to start over—" Luke's voice broke, preventing him from finishing his speech.

Don't fall for it, you fool. Fear spackled the chink forming in her wall. "You can stay tonight, but I want you gone tomorrow. For good."

Forcing herself to turn her back on Luke's visible pain, she carried Hunter up the porch steps and disappeared inside the house.

Chapter Fourteen

Heaviness wedged against his chest, Dylan watched Zoe walk away with their son, her walls a fortress stretching to the sky. He ached for her, even while he recognized that same quality within himself. That protective need to shut out those who held the key to hurting you the most.

He shifted his focus to Luke. The man looked like he'd aged ten years in the last five minutes. He wanted to despise him for Zoe's sake—for *their* sake—not feel this pity that stirred inside him. But it was impossible to ignore when the man looked like his world was crumbling around his feet. Clearing his throat, Dylan caught Malcom's eye and nodded toward the house.

Fortunately the kid caught on quick. "Hey, Trin, want to give me a hand taking the bags in?"

"Why not?" Trinity grimaced. "My nails are busted anyway."

Deciding to risk a possible busted kneecap, Dylan clapped Luke on the shoulder. "How about you and I take a stroll?"

"Do I look like I'm in the mood for a fucking stroll?"

Dylan increased the pressure of the fingers digging into Luke's muscle. "No, you look like a man who needs to get his shit together."

Stubbornness flared in Luke's eyes for a moment before dimming. The tension drained from his body and he hunched his shoulders inward. "Been working on that for near forty-eight years, and still haven't gotten it right."

He nudged Luke toward the back of the house. They approached Hunter's swing set and Luke propped his boot on the plastic slide. "I'm sorry for punching ya. Guess I don't exactly have a right to defend my daughter's honor considering what a shitty father I've been."

Dylan rubbed his jaw. "Don't worry about it. Not the first time someone's taken a swing at me and probably won't be the last."

"Did she tell you not to say anything to me about where she's been livin' all this time?" Luke dropped his gaze. "Never mind. I'm sure she did. Can't say I blame her."

"I didn't know she was your daughter until half an hour ago."

Luke's head jerked up. Another hint of that pain twisted his features. "Does she hate me that much?"

"That's for her to answer, not me." Dylan flicked his thumb along the chain suspending one of the swings. "These six years I've known you, you've never once talked about your daughter." He'd been aware of her existence, in a vague, ghostly sort of a way. Everyone in the band knew there was some kind of estrangement there between Luke and *Moonshine*. Considering the foulness of Luke's moods on most occasions, everyone wisely steered clear of any topic that could potentially set Luke off. But considering Dylan was in love with that very woman Luke had refused to speak of, he'd gladly take the risk of poking the hornet's nest. "Some would say you were the one holding a grudge."

"Anyone thinks that needs to pop their head outta their ass." Luke's eyebrows snapped into a V. "You think a man wants to speak of his failures?"

"So instead you pretended she didn't exist?"

"Damn it, it wasn't like that!" Luke balled his fist and stared at it for a moment before unclenching his fingers. His entire hand shook in the aftermath of his outburst. "I love my daughter with everything I am. But what I am is a man who doesn't know how to control his drinkin'. I can finally admit that." He shook his head. "Only took me a lifetime and some serious soul searching in rehab to get to that point. Still, a day doesn't pass that I don't worry I'll fall off the wagon."

Luke expelled a weary breath. "Moonshine—Zoe—needed more from me. Even back then I saw it. And every time I'd miss one of her birthdays or some important event in her life, it hammered home what a failure I was at being a father. Hell, a human being. So I'd drink more, deadening that sick feeling in my gut." His knuckles whitened on the edge of the slide. "Only thing I've ever been good at is singing. Up on that stage, I was something. No one had to know what a mess I was off of it. But every time I looked at my little girl, I knew. That tiny perfect angel I helped create—she was a constant reminder of my failure."

"That is seriously fucked up."

"You think I don't know that?" Luke tossed up his arms. "I told ya I'm one huge fucked up mess. Get the wax outta yer ears."

Dylan grunted. "Nice to see you're back to being the dick we all know and love." Despite his sarcasm, his mood remained pensive. The rift between Zoe and her dad might very well be an unconquerable divide. So much hurt and damage had been done, it was a wonder that Zoe had even allowed her dad to step foot on her property. But the fact that he *was* here, well, that gave them an opening to start repairing some of the hurts between them.

And, God willing, pave the way for Dylan to build his future with Zoe and Hunter.

He inclined his head toward the house. "Ready to go inside?"

"She doesn't really want me here. I could sleep in the van."

"Stop being a stubborn jackass." Jesus, he was gonna have his work cut out with these two. "Now git your ass movin' before I stick my foot up it. Though that might do ya some good."

Luke snorted. "Don't think you're completely in the clear of not getting your kneecaps busted. Especially if you don't do right by my grandson and marry his mama."

Whoa. That came outta left field. Though truthfully he liked the sound of that plan. A lot. Now he just had to convince Zoe of it.

They ambled up the back porch steps together. He lifted his gaze to Zoe's bedroom and noticed the open window and the shadow behind the curtain. Zoe. How long had she been listening in? And more importantly, had it made a difference in her mindset?

He opened the door and ushered Luke inside the mudroom. After leaving their boots on the mat, they journeyed into the living room. Malcom was already stretched out on the couch with a sleeping bag tossed over him. Dylan hitched his chin. "Where's Trin?"

"Guest bedroom," Malcom grumbled. "She wouldn't share the bed even though I said we could lay pillows between us."

"Wouldn't let ya sleep near me either. Ya snore like a chainsaw," Luke pointed out.

Malcom snuggled into his downy cocoon, his smile beatific. "Guess you'll have a hard time sleeping tonight then since you're bunking with me."

Leaving Luke to curse over that turn of events, Dylan jogged up the stairway. Zoe was sitting on the foot of the bed, her expression closed. Weariness settled on Dylan's shoulders like a horsehair blanket. "I take it nothing's changed. Even with what you overheard."

"Why should it?"

He sat beside her and caressed her cheek. "Do you love your dad?"

She lowered her gaze. "Yes. But there are also times I hate him, Dylan."

"I understand that, baby. I truly do. But sometimes you've got to let go of the hate. Before it cripples your soul. Pushing him away is hurting you just as much as it is him." He swallowed against the thick emotion threatening to strangle him. "You can't change the past, but you have a chance here to rewrite a different future for yourself."

He dropped his hand and laced their fingers. "My dad kept a box of scrapbooks of me and my brothers. I haven't been able to bring myself to look at mine, but I did peek at Jackson's. There's all kinds of memories in there, but guess what? They all ended too soon. There's a bunch of empty pages that Dusty was never able to fill. Baby, I don't want that for you and Luke. I don't want that for Hunter. Seize onto the chance to make new memories—better ones—before fate steps in and takes that choice away from you."

Zoe's lips trembled and her eyes clouded with tears. "Damn it."

"I know, darlin'. It's not gonna be easy. But I'm here for ya. No matter what." He pulled her to him and hugged her tight.

After he rocked her in his arms for several minutes, she sniffled and leaned away from him. "I'll be right back."

"Do you need me to go with you?"

"No, but thank you. It means a lot to me just knowing you're here for me." She gave him a tender kiss and headed for the stairs. He detected her deep breath before she took the step. That first one toward forgiveness was always the hardest.

His chest tight, he listened to the muffled sound of voices downstairs and then the creak of floor boards. A moment later the backdoor opened and closed. If Luke somehow fucked this up with his jackassery, Dylan would be the one doing some kneecap busting.

He waited for shouts and accusations to begin flying outside. When he was met with nothing but silence his senses prickled with warning. Maybe Luke had stormed off. Or Zoe.

Unable to take the uncertainty a second longer, Dylan shoved up from the bed and crossed to the window. He eased the curtain aside.

Luke had one arm wrapped around Zoe while he stroked her hair. She was clinging to her father, tears streaming down her face. Luke bent to kiss the crown of her head, and that's when Dylan noticed the tears in the man's eyes. Even without words, the touching scene spoke volumes.

His eyes also a little misty, Dylan closed the drape, allowing them their privacy. The heaviness eased from his shoulders, leaving him lighter than he could recall being in a long time. Seeing Zoe heal her wounds had at last healed his.

He was ready to forgive his own past.

Chapter Fifteen

"Are you sure you want me to be here for this?"

His fingers hovering on the box lid, he glanced up at Zoe. "Absolutely."

She still looked uncertain, despite his assertion. "Okay. It just seems like it should be a private moment."

His thoughts trekked to the prior evening and the brief glimpse he'd had of her and Luke hugging. Sharing this with her would put them on even ground. He knew she'd understand better than anyone. "No, I want you here. Both of you." Hunter squirmed in his lap and he ruffled his son's curly mop of hair.

He set aside the lid and pulled out the top scrapbook with the big D on it. A big 8x10 of him wearing a tiny cowboy outfit, complete with a miniature version of his favorite Stetson, took up the first page. "Damn, I was a good lookin' baby."

Hunter tapped the plastic covering the photo. "Me!"

"Wow, you guys really do look alike," Zoe mused, moving in for a closer look. "No wonder you about passed out at the pharmacy."

He shot her the stink eye. "Men do *not* pass out."

"Oh yeah? Then what do you call it?"

"A very short-lived nap on the floor." He flipped to the next page. It held his baby announcement and baptism photo.

"Is that your mom?"

"Yup."

"She's beautiful. And she and Dusty look so happy."

He studied the image. The joy he saw was similar to those in his brothers' books. Rather than feel any jealousy over that fact, or feel a little less special that his dad's happiness hadn't been reserved exclusively for him, it lightened his heart to know that Dusty *had* indeed loved them. He'd stubbornly resisted that notion for a long time, but acknowledging it now freed another layer of the scab eroding his soul.

The next several pages chronicled his younger years. There was even a picture of him on his Schwinn and proudly showing off his missing middle tooth.

"Uh, did that happen while you were riding your bike?"

"No, it was loose and I tied a rock to it."

Zoe shuddered. "Didn't that hurt?"

"What do I look like, a sissy?"

"In other words, it hurt."

"Yeah," he mumbled, turning the page. He blinked at the photo of him up on the stage with the band. Mystified, he leaned closer, scanning for the copyright symbol that all publicity shots were marked with. He couldn't find out. His pulse giving a funny little upswing, he peeled back the plastic and lifted the image. As he did so, a concert stub fell from the back. He picked it up and stared at the date. It was exactly five years ago—his official first gig with Truckstop Pickup. "Dusty was there."

"You didn't know?"

"No. He was always against me joining the band."

"Did he tell you that?"

He shook his head. "It was just a feeling I had."

Zoe squeezed his shoulder. "Well, whatever his feelings were, he put them aside to see you perform. That's pretty big."

"Yeah." He cleared the gruffness from his voice. "It is."

He thumbed through the remaining pages, all of them showcasing his music. There were several more photos Dusty had taken at different concert venues, along with the accompanying ticket stubs. There was even an image someone had snapped of Dusty. He wore one of the band's T-shirts and the biggest grin Dylan had ever seen.

The photo threatening to do him in, he dropped his head into his hands, struggling to keep his shit together. Hunter wrapped his arms around him, sniffling. Little Man's empathy getting to him just as much as the picture, Dylan hugged his boy. He looked up at

Zoe as she rubbed his back. "I wish I'd known he was there. I wish—" His voice cracked.

Tears rolling down her cheeks, she nodded and leaned down to kiss him. "I know."

He caressed her cheek and returned his focus to the scrapbook. Sucking in a shaky breath, he turned to the very end and stared at the envelope with his name written on it.

"Is that from—?"

"Yeah." He glanced at her. "Can you open it? I...don't know if I'm ready for whatever's inside."

She nodded and picked up the envelope. Using her thumbnail, she broke the seal and fished out the paper inside. She unfolded the sheet and gave him an uncertain look.

"Go ahead and read it."

Zoe returned her focus to the letter, her hand trembling slightly. "Dear Dylan—"

"I've changed my mind. I-I think I need to read it for myself. See his handwriting."

She handed the sheet to him and stroked his hair as he read the words his father had written to him.

Dear Dylan,

I'm writing the things I didn't tell you in life. Maybe it's the coward's way out, but I hope you can see past that and forgive me.

I know we didn't always see eye to eye. I know too that you've probably spent a good deal of your life hating me. I can't say I don't deserve it. But know this son, I've always loved you. Even when I couldn't be there for you, you were never out of my mind. Not you or your brothers. You boys were my world. My reason for putting in the hours I did and building D. Walker Mineral into the company it is today. I know that your music is your life, and I don't expect you to give that up. But consider being a part of the company too. My fondest dream is for you boys to become the family that you were meant to be. It won't rectify the sins I've committed, but it will give you the foundation each one of you

136

deserves.

Anyway, I hope you consider it. I have passed on to you the only heritage I have, and I hope you'll find a place in your heart for it.

I love you, Son.

Your dad,

Dusty Walker

Dylan folded the sheet and tucked it back in the envelope. He gazed at his name scribbled on the front. Once he felt reasonably collected, he stashed the letter inside the scrapbook and returned everything to the box.

"Are you okay?"

He lifted his focus to Zoe. "Yeah." And he was. Better than he'd been in a long time. He scooted back his dad's chair and hefted Hunter into his arms before heading into the hall. A figure ducked behind a doorway. Frowning, he headed in that direction. He stepped into the billiards room and met Marliss's sheepish smile.

"Ya busted me."

He gave her a considering look. "You're the one who left the safe open."

She nodded. "Sometimes hearing the words from others doesn't have the same impact as uncovering the facts on your own."

"You're a helluva smart woman, Marliss. My dad was lucky to have you in his employ."

"No, he was lucky to have you boys. Dusty told me that himself." She tickled Hunter's arm, making him giggle. "Looks like you're well on your way to carrying on the tradition of fine Walker men."

"That I am." He offered Marliss a one-armed hug. "Thank you. For everything."

"Oh pooh! Weren't no trouble at all. And you better not be a stranger, you hear?"

"I won't. Take good care of my brothers when they're here." After bussing her cheek with a kiss, he led the way out to the stretch limo waiting in the drive. Zoe's truck sat on the other side of the vehicle, along with Malcom's van. The kid and Trin would be driving minus one passenger. Dylan had talked Luke into flying back with him in Dusty's private jet. It'd give them a chance to bond without threat of breaking someone's kneecap. He hoped.

He hesitated next to the passenger door of Zoe's truck, stalling. Emotion welling inside him, he hugged Hunter tight. His son squirmed before allowing Dylan to situate him in his car seat and kiss him goodbye. His chest heavy, he straightened and faced Zoe. He smoothed a glossy pink-tipped lock of hair behind her ear.

This was going to be the toughest part to get through. He needed her to have faith in him that this trip to Nashville was temporary. He'd be back to her before she even started to miss him. But damn it, he was going to miss her the second he got in that limo. Hell, he was already missing her. "Come with me."

"I have to report to the school on Tuesday. You know that."

He sighed. "Yeah."

She stroked his cheek. "You'll see us next weekend. No getting rid of us that easily, Dylan Mitchell Walker."

He grimaced. "You and my mom are gonna get along like two peas in a pod."

"Scared?"

"Hell yeah." He leaned in and kissed her fiercely. Cupping the back of her head, he pressed his forehead to hers. "And for your information, I don't wanna be rid of you guys. Not ever."

"Good. Because we don't wanna git rid of you either." Smiling tremulously, she stepped back. "Now I've gotta scat. Before I embarrass myself weeping all over you."

Every inch of him aching for her, he watched her climb behind the wheel and speed off.

His feet like blocks of cement, he trudged to the limo. He ducked inside and slid across from Luke as the driver shut the door.

Luke cocked an eyebrow. "You look like shit."

"I feel like it."

A silence fell over them. The driver rolled down the partition separating the back seating area from the front cab. "Ready, Mr. Walker?"

"No, he's not. Give us a moment, would ya?"

"Of course." The driver rolled the partition back up.

"Here's where you need to decide what you want to do, son." Luke propped his arm on the seatback. "Be on the road for the next eighteen months, exhausting yourself and barely seeing your woman and child? Or playing gigs closer to home and doing something worthwhile while you're at it?"

Dylan frowned. "I'm not entirely following ya."

"I think you should take this tour off. But don't worry, I've got an idea that will prevent you from becoming a lazy man of leisure in the meantime. For a while I've been wanting to put together a year-round band camp for underprivileged kids." Luke grunted, presumably in response to Dylan's disbelieving stare. "Yeah, I know y'all think I'm a selfish prick who don't care about nobody but himself. Little do ya know I got more layers than an onion."

"That's really deep of ya, Buttweiser."

Luke grunted. "Anyway, I think you and Zoe are the ideal candidates for overseeing this project for me."

Dylan stroked his chin. "Only if we can be full partners in the whole operation. And if Zoe agrees, of course."

Luke held out his hand. "Deal."

Dylan accepted the shake on it. Holy hell. Was this really happening? He wouldn't have to be away from Zoe and Hunter. And they'd be working together, doing something that they both loved. He stared at Luke, still trying to process it all.

Luke dropped his hand, and thumped on the partition. "Jeeves, follow that truck."

***

The deluge of tears started before she hit the town limits. Why was she being so silly about this? She knew Dylan was coming back to her. She trusted him implicitly. Even the ghosts of her old fears were no match for that love and conviction of his. He'd managed to slay her demons, and the future she envisioned for them shined so bright, it was blinding. But in the best possible way.

She sniffled and dug in her side pocket for a tissue just as a scary hissing noise came from the engine. An ominous clunking noise preceded a billow of smoke.

Aw damn it. Not the stupid radiator again. Of course it'd have to choose to act up when she was in the middle of having a meltdown. Resisting the urge to weep harder, she wiped the moisture from her eyes. The service station was just down the street. At least she had that on her side. The damn truck could have broken down miles from town and then she would have had to worry about calling for a tow.

Nursing the vehicle along at a snail pace, she finally rolled into the gas station. She parked and grabbed Hunter out of his seat. Clutching him to her, she hurried into the building. Al, the owner, was working the counter. He smiled as she approached. "Afternoon, Zoe. What can I do for ya?"

She explained the situation with the truck and he promised to have his mechanic look at it first thing in the morning. Not exactly the news she'd been hoping for. Battling the frustration adding to her sense of hopelessness, she nodded glumly and reached for her cellphone. She'd have to call Callie and ask if she could come pick her and Hunter up.

"Mama."

She fumbled with the phone.

"Mama."

Finally she got her contact list open. A warning ding sounded, announcing a low battery. An instant later the screen went black.

No, no, no.

"Mama."

Distracted and desperately trying not to give into the tears stinging her eyes, she stroked Hunter's head. "What Boo Bear?"

"Lan."

Hearing her son use his shortened version of Dylan's name was the final straw breaking the camel's back. A shuddery whimper broke from her throat.

"Zoe."

She blinked, certain she was so far gone in her pathetic misery that she'd conjured Dylan's voice. But when she turned around he was standing right there. Too blessedly real to be a figment of her imagination. "Dylan?"

He stepped toward her the same instant she moved in his direction. They stalled for a moment, staring at each other. Then she was in his arms, kissing him in between her sobbing fits. Mindful that she was crushing their child between them, she set Hunter down and tongue kissed Dylan hard again before caressing his dear face. "What are you doing here? You're supposed to be on your way to the airport."

"I'm not leaving you guys."

"I know that." Oh God, he came back because he thought she didn't believe him. "I'm sorry my issues made me ever doubt you."

He cupped her nape and looked her in the eyes. "No, baby. You have nothing to be sorry about. And I meant that I'm staying. For good. Other than us going to Nashville so you can meet my mom, I have no reason to go back there. Luke made me an offer that's impossible to refuse."

She stared at him. "I don't understand."

"We can talk about it later." He brushed a lock of hair out of her eye. "Do you love me?"

"Yes." She closed her eyes and let out a wispy breath before meeting his gaze again. "Oh God, yes. I have from the very first moment I saw you."

"Me too, darlin'. The day I crashed into you, my world tipped off its axis. I knew you would have my heart forever." He took a deep exhale. "That's why your answer to this next question is vitally important."

A mixture of nervousness and determination etched into his handsome features, he got down on one knee. Her pulse danced a Macarena. He took her hand in his, his fingers shaking slightly. "I was gonna wait until I had a ring to do this, but I think fate keeps telling us something here."

She was befuddled by his statement, until she followed his gaze to the row of chips and beef jerky next to them. Her mind flashed to the first time they met, and a blubbery laugh bubbled from her. "Yeah, I think it is."

"So what do you say, Zoe Chapman? Will you marry me?"

"Yes." She pulled him to his feet and wrapped her arms around him. "A million times yes."

Hunter bounced around in a circle near their feet, wanting to join the happy-fest. Laughing, Dylan swung his son up with one arm. His face shining with joy, Dylan pressed his lips to hers, kissing her senseless. He pulled back and grinned at her. "Ready to spend a lifetime making sweet memories together?"

She hugged both of her guys, her heart swelling with an overabundance of love. "You better believe it."

Epilogue

Damn hard to believe it was the thirty-first of August already. It seemed a lifetime ago that he'd sat in the lawyer's office, unable to believe he'd just inherited a fourth of his dad's company *and* three new brothers. A lot had changed since then. Him, for starters. For the better.

He glanced around the interior of Cubby's. He hadn't been in the joint since his first week in Red Creek, but he swore those old timers over in the corner booth had been there last time he was in. Probably they never left. The men nodded at Dylan and his brothers. It felt good having roots in this place, where folks welcomed ya as one of their own if you hung around long enough. Granted, he'd been too busy setting things in motion for the Walker Pendergrass Band Camp project to spend much time in town. Plus with him, Zoe, and Hunter just getting back from visiting his mom in Nashville, he was woefully ignorant of any of the juicy gossip going round. Reckon he was in the perfect place to get caught up. *Man, I really am becoming a Red Creekian.* The realization sounded pretty damn good to him.

His attention drifted to the champagne-colored land barge parked at the curb. "You're driving Dad's Caddy?" He grinned at Rogue, who'd spent the last week in Kansas.

"Damn right. The thing is smooth as sin."

Jackson fiddled with the fork that sat on a napkin in front of him. "You know, Dylan, when I got your email after that first week, I thought you'd gone crazy."

Rogue and Killian nodded.

Hell, if anyone told him the beginning of that first week that he'd be extoling the virtues of small town living, he woulda called *them* crazy. "I was under the influence, I guess." He scratched his cheek as he pondered the reasons why. "But damned if I don't feel exactly the same way being back here today."

"I figured that." Rogue crooked one arm over the back of his chair. "Figured you'd found yourself a gal." A smirk curved his lips. "But I agree, this place grows on a man."

Killian rested his forearms on the table. "Sure does. I mean, who knew this dustbowl in the middle of fucking nowhere would leave an impression."

They were interrupted by the appearance of the waitress and they took a minute to place their orders. Jackson looked around the table after the waitress walked away. "So we're all agreed? We're going to do this thing?"

Dylan and his brothers exchanged conspiratorial glances. No doubt that'd get the regulars wondering what the Walker boys had up their sleeves. *Gotta give 'em something to talk about.* "I'm in." Recalling his words from the lawyer's office, he grinned and adopted a shrug. "Got nothin' else going on."

Rogue nodded.

"We'll stay the week, the four of us gettin' to know each other, just like the old man wanted?" Jackson frowned. "Get the business sorted out between the four of us?"

"That's the plan." Killian curled his upper-lip in a sneer. "Live in the house for a whole week and bond with each other." He snorted.

They all laughed, but Rogue pointed at Killian. "From what I hear around town, you found yourself someone to help pass the time."

"Sure did."

Dylan took in Killian's grin. *No shit.* Must be something in the water.

Rogue looked at Jackson and Dylan. "And rumors are spreading about you two. You both fell for a local gal?"

Jackson nodded. "Afraid so." His smile hinted that he wasn't much upset by that turn of events.

Well this was just getting plain crazy. Dylan scratched his nape. *Definitely somethin' in the water.* "Yep. Happy as a puppy with two tails." That was putting it mildly. Every day he was falling more and more in love with his little angel. Both of them. He couldn't wait for Zoe to make an honest man outta him. Seeing her walk down the aisle toward him, damn, he was already getting emotional thinking about it.

"What about you, little brother?" Killian asked Rogue, breaking through Dylan's mental wedding planning. "Don't tell us you're the only Walker boy without a happy ending?"

Rogue sat quietly for a few seconds. "Well, I wouldn't want to be the one to ruin a perfect record." The man tried to keep from grinning, but his brothers smacked him on the back, laughing, and he let go with a smile.

They all looked at each other, matching pleased expressions on their faces.

Killian tapped his belt buckle. "Damn if I don't feel now that we're part of an exclusive club of some kind."

"We are," Jackson said. "The Walker brothers club."

Dylan grinned at his brothers. He could almost sense their dad smiling down on them, nodding in approval.

"Old Dusty must have known what he was doing," Killian added, "even if we didn't think so four weeks ago."

The waitress arrived with their burgers, fries, and pie a' la mode, and they ate and talked about their new lady loves. Dylan decided to keep the news about them being uncles for another day. They had enough to absorb for the time being. Not like he wouldn't have plenty time to hit them with that bombshell over the next week.

Cubby's wife brought their bill to the table. "Well, you four are quite a sight, sittin' here all lookin' like peas in a pod." Sherry cocked her ample hip. "You all decide if you're stayin' or goin'?"

They all four smiled.

"Hard to believe, but it looks like we'll be stayin'." Jackson pulled out his wallet.

"Yeah, but you three cowboys forgot about that damn

bonding." Dylan grabbed the bill and handed it back to Sherry with a couple twenties. "Come back and ask us that same question again in a week."

That earned everyone's laugh.

Outside they all shook hands and said they'd see each other back at the house later to start their week living and working together. Dylan couldn't remember the last time he'd felt this excited.

Oh yeah, might have been last night, when a certain sweet angel rode him cowgirl style underneath the stars. Grinning, he jumped in his truck and hightailed it for home.

Home.

Yeah, he liked the sound of that. And there was no place he'd rather be.

About the Author

At the ripe age of seven, Jodi Redford penned her first epic,
complete with stick-figure illustrations. Sadly, her drawing
skills haven't improved much, but her love of fantasy worlds
never went away. These days she writes about fairies, ghosts
and other supernatural creatures, only with considerably more
heat.

She has won numerous contests, including The Golden Pen and
Launching a Star.

When not writing or working the day job, she enjoys gardening
and way too many reality-television shows.

She loves to hear from readers. You can email her at
jodiredford@jodiredford.com and visit her online at
http://www.jodiredford.com

Jodi is also on Facebook https://www.facebook.com/jodi.redford.3
and Twitter https://twitter.com/jodiredford

Please follow her Amazon Author page at
http://www.amazon.com/Jodi-Redford/e/B002YUEZ0U

Other Books by Jodi Redford

Now Available:

Double Dare
Hurricanes and Handcuffs
Kinky Claus
Perfect Chemistry
Kissin' Hell
Naughty Girls Do
Taking Liberty
Light My Fire
Vanessa Unveiled
The Naughty List
Checking It Twice
Cat Scratch Fever
Breaking Bad

That Old Black Magic
That Voodoo You Do
The Seven Year Witch
Maximum Witch
Getting Familiar With Your Demon

Thieves of Aurion
Lover Enslaved
Lover Enraptured

Coming Soon:

Bad Boys Do It Better

Triple Knockout

Jackson

by

RANDI ALEXANDER

Prologue

The attorney for the late Dusty Walker leaned over his desk and set a folder of papers in front of each of the four young men who sat like a row of penguins in their dark suits and white shirts.

Jackson Walker, one of the four, adjusted the gray tie his mother had strongly suggested he wear. Shock had him speechless—for the first time in his life.

The lawyer's gaze rested on each face. Was he taking in their similarities? Even though the four brothers had never laid eyes on each other until five minutes ago, they sat silently, letting the man have his fill of staring.

His three half-brothers had to be as gobsmacked as Jackson was. He kept his gaze forward, not ready to look at the three faces that proved his dad had been a rat bastard.

The gray-haired lawyer unbuttoned his suit coat and sat, pushing his wire-rimmed glasses up on his nose. "Incredible likeness. Your father never mentioned it."

Their father, Dusty Walker, hadn't mentioned a whole hell of a lot of things, like the fact that he had four sons, each of whom had no idea there were three more just like him in other parts of the country.

Killian sat forward in his chair. "Are we quadruplets? Were we separated at birth?"

The attorney shook his head again. "Absolutely not. "Each of you is your mother's biological son. You are each about a year apart in age. Mr. Walker…uh…Killian."

Jackson almost laughed. Since they were all four *Mr. Walker*, the man must have realized he needed to take a different approach.

"Killian, you're the oldest at twenty-seven, and Dylan, you're the youngest. It must be a very strong DNA strand in your father to have produced men who look so similar."

Besides different eye and hair color, their faces and bodies could have been stamped from the same mold.

"When I arrived at your homes last week with the news that your father had died, I was under strict instructions not to mention that you had brothers. It was among your father's last wishes that you learn of your siblings' existence by bringing you together." The attorney picked up a sheaf of papers. "I apologize for bringing you to Kansas under these circumstances."

Jackson had spent the week since learning of his father's death with his mother, then had made use of the first-class flight from the Pacific Northwest and the limo transportation provided for him by the law firm. When he'd arrived at the lawyer's office, he'd been shown into a separate office until the attorney, Stanley Benner, Esquire, had asked the four of them to come into his office.

The shock when they'd seen each other kept them all silent, warily watching each other.

The attorney rattled the papers in his hand. "As I told you, Dusty and his wife Theresa were killed in an auto accident. We were told they died instantly." He looked from one to the other. "So, if there are no more questions, I'll begin reading the key points in the will." He waited a few seconds, meeting each of their gazes.

"Yeah, I've got one." Rogue looked at his brothers. "How did he…?" He held up a hand. "Let me rephrase that. Why? Why four families in four different states?"

The lawyer tossed the papers on the desk and laced his fingers together. "Your father wanted to have children, and he confided to me that his wife didn't want them. This broke his heart."

"So he went around looking for incubators?" Killian spat out.

"That's a little disrespectful." Benner frowned.

"You're calling me disrespectful?" Killian made a rude noise. "I'd say your client is the one who was disrespectful."

"She knew about all of us?" Dylan held his hands out, palm up. "His wife, I mean?"

"No, she did not." Benner's cheeks turned ruddy. "And I was

sworn to silence under attorney/client privilege. I'm assuming that your mothers made you aware of your father's marital situation?"

One of the men cleared his throat, but no one spoke.

Jackson's father had spent very few weeks with him every year, and now he—they all—knew why. The man not only had a wife, but four families. The time his dad did spend with Jackson was dedicated to grooming his son to one day run the family business; poring over contracts for regional mineral rights, surveying land, and interpreting tests to determine if the acreage had value.

Jackson stared at the law degree on the wall, but his mind spun back ten years to when he'd just turned fifteen and his mother had let Dusty's secret escape: Dad had a wife in Kansas. Worse, despite knowing Dusty was married, Sapphire, Jackson's mother, was Dusty's lover, which made Jackson a... Shaking away the memory, he focused his attention away from Oregon and back to Kansas.

"So, in the interest of time, I will read the highlights of the will. The entire document is in the folders I set in front of you." The attorney cleared his throat and read for a quarter of an hour. The details included a grocery list of assets: a mineral and water rights company that boasted assets near five-hundred million dollars, including a private ten-person jet, a storefront in the small town of Red Creek, Kansas, as well as a big house on the outskirts of town.

The brothers sat silent.

"Of course, there are the four houses in four compass points of the US. In the north, Montana, where Killian resides. Texas, from where Rogue hails. Dylan, of course, from Nashville, and Jackson, from Oregon." Jackson's gaze flicked to each of his brothers as they glanced at each other, then back at the lawyer. "These houses are currently company property, but your father notes that you four, as the new owners of D. Walker Mineral, can opt to transfer the homes into your mothers'—"

"Hang on." Dylan stiffened. "You're saying he left the company to us?"

"Yes, of course." Benner looked surprised. "I didn't read that portion of the will because I assumed…" He hefted out a sigh. "The company is now legally in your names, exactly one quarter going to each."

Dylan let go with a long, low whistle.

Jackson closed his gaping mouth and swallowed. He owned a fourth of a half-billion dollar company? Hell, he'd always figured Dusty had plenty of money. Their house, which sat a block from the ocean in Bandon, had an unobstructed view of the Pacific from the rooftop deck, and stood within walking distance of his mother's pottery shop downtown. But half a billion? Man, what he could do with a fourth of that. "So, if we sell our quarter?" Jackson said the words slowly, figuring the other three had to be pondering the same question.

"There are repercussions." The attorney flipped pages. "Ah, here. 'Heretofore, the parties to which—'"

"In plain English, please." Killian put one booted foot on the opposite knee.

"Of course." The man set down the papers and leaned back in his chair, placing one hand on his round belly. "The company is essentially frozen as-is for a full year. After that time, if one of you wants to sell, the others have the option of buying you out at half-worth."

"Half-worth?" Rogue fisted his hand. "Meaning they'd buy me out at a fifty-percent discount?" The guy looked pissed.

"Yes, that's correct. Your father wanted to keep the company in the family. Wanted you four boys to run it together."

Jackson could wait a year. He had a sizeable savings account. All he needed was money to get him to rodeos and pay his entry fees. But hell, no matter what his father wanted, there was no room in his life for small-town Kansas and an eight-to-five job. He'd be the first to sell his quarter of the company.

153

Benner attempted a smile. "However, you are each officially on the payroll, and your first paychecks will be cut the day you successfully complete the one…" He swallowed then cleared his throat. "Stipulation in the will."

All four of them leaned an inch closer.

"Stipulation?" Dylan prodded.

"To inherit, you must spend a week in Red Creek, working in your father's office, learning more about the business, sharing with each other what you've learned from your father over the years. You must also reside for that week at your father's house—your house—on Osprey Lake."

"A week?" Jackson shook his head. He'd be damned if he'd be forced to work and live with three strangers, even if they were blood relatives. "What's the timeframe here? Anytime in the next year?"

Rogue slapped open his folder and pulled out his copy of the will. "What section is that in?" His words came out clipped.

"Second from the last page. You'll see that there's a thirty day time limit." The attorney checked his calendar. "Today is August second. You'll need to decide which week in August works for all four of you, and plan to be back here then. Or if this week works…" He shrugged.

Killian tapped his fingertips on his knee. "Dad wants the four of us to live in the same house and work in the same office? For an entire week?"

"Like summer camp for the bastard sons of Dusty Walker." Dylan mumbled a curse.

Jackson rubbed the spot between his eyebrows. Good. At least he wasn't the only one who found this situation bizarre. "What the fuck was he thinking?"

Rogue kept reading silently.

Benner's face turned a dark shade of red. "He loved each one of you, I know that because he took great pains to create provisions to make sure you were taken care of after his death, as you were while he was alive."

"Listen here." Rogue stared at the will. "It says we each have to spend a week, but it doesn't say it has to be the same week."

"No, it…uh…what…?" The attorney sat forward and frantically flipped through his paperwork.

"I say we each take a week, get this goddamn stipulation out of the way, and figure out the rest later." Rogue looked at his brothers. "Agreed?"

"Yeah. Okay." Dylan accessed his phone. "I can stay this week. I got nothin' goin' on."

Jackson grabbed his folder. "I can do the week after." The sooner he got this bullshit out of the way, the sooner he could get back to his real life. A burst of unease gripped him. Rodeo was his real life? Traveling solo around the country, one-nighters with buckle bunnies, broken bones and torn ligaments. One hell of a life he'd chosen.

Killian rose. "Sure, I'll do the third week."

"That leaves week four for me." Rogue stood and tucked the folder under his arm.

"Now wait, boys." The lawyer stood, still staring at his copy of the will as Jackson and Dylan got to their feet. "Your father wanted you all to be here together. At the same time. To get to know one another."

The brothers stood in a half-circle. Jackson's gaze dropped to the belt buckle Killian wore, then to the other two brothers' belts. The exact same belt buckle on all four of them. The one given to Jackson by his father.

"Am I seeing things?" Jackson caught Killian's surprised gaze.

Killian looked down at his own waist. "Son of a bitch. I can't believe this. They're all alike."

"Kinda fucked up, huh?" One side of Dylan's mouth curved up. "The old man gave us the same belt buckle, like we'd use them to somehow magically find each other."

Jackson wanted to fling the buckle into the nearest lake and watch it sink. So much for imagining his father thought he was special. Special, like one of a matched set of four.

The room went silent, then, as if on cue, they all turned toward the door.

"Wait." The attorney raced around his desk and stood in front of the men, his brow wrinkled, his breath coming fast. "Your father's wish was to have you spend this time together." His hands fluttered like he didn't know what to do next.

"Well then…" Killian patted Benner's shoulder as he strode past him. "I guess he should have had his *lawyer* write that in the will."

Jackson bit back a grin. That Killian was a smart-ass, but thank heavens Rogue had the brains to read the contract and get the four of them out of the bunking-together clusterfuck. Dylan—he couldn't read the kid, but he appreciated how the youngest blurted out whatever came into his head. He almost wished…naw. Fuck, they were complete strangers. Best to keep it that way.

The four brothers left the office, walked to their separate limousines, and left the parking lot.

Then, the fun began.

Chapter One

Jackson Walker stood on the white line running down the middle of Main Street, Red Creek, Kansas as the sun rose behind him. His shadow grew shorter by the second, merging with his body. As if his deceased father, Dusty Walker, was casting a reminder that his third-oldest son would be walking in his boots that week.

He glanced along the right side of the street where the town stretched out for a few blocks before hitting the open space of the farm implement dealer. Gazing at the left side of the street, he watched the activity inside Cubby's, where the metal *Open* sign hung on the restaurant door in this time-warp of a town. He'd eaten breakfast at his father's…no…*his and his three brothers'* massive house out on the lake, but with his cowboy metabolism, he'd be hungry again before the sun hit a forty-five degree angle.

Next to Cubby's, and directly to Jackson's left, lights gleamed from the big main level windows of the three-story building bearing the name D. Walker Mineral Company. Although barely past seven in the morning, the employees were already busy at work, like they'd been struck with gold fever. He wandered that way, ready to start another long day. Today was only Tuesday, and he'd signed on to stay the week, but yesterday, learning the business from the three people who had worked for Jackson's father, had exhausted him. The massive amount of information he needed to assimilate made him dizzier than riding a world-class bucking bronc.

He pushed open the glass door and greeted Abby, the receptionist/bookkeeper. She winked at him from behind her tall counter, and pointed toward the little kitchenette hidden around a corner. "Coffee's fresh." Her short, blonde curls bounced as she adjusted her chair. Jackson guessed her to be in her mid-forties, working to supplement her and her husband's income from their small farm outside of town. Although the company used an accounting firm in Kansas City, Abby managed to keep everything at the office running smoothly.

"Thanks." He trudged back toward the big office at the end of the hall. Along the way, he passed the four open doors of the other offices, but only one desk was occupied. The specialists worked odd hours, depending on what time zone their current project landed in, and today, Vic typed as he spoke Spanish into his earpiece.

Would Jackson ever get used to this incredible venture he'd ended up owning a quarter share in?

His father's banged-up wooden desk didn't look like it belonged to a multi-millionaire. Nor did the worn leather chair. But then, his old man had traveled more than he officed, especially seeing as how he'd been juggling five families around the country.

Kicking the rolling chair back with a little too much aggression, he grabbed at it before it hit the bookshelf. Who the hell did Dusty Walker think he was, starting families wherever he pleased? And when the hell had his dad planned to introduce the brothers? At his retirement party? "Shit." Jackson would probably never find the answers he was looking for. The attorney, Stanley Benner, didn't have any clue, or at least he wasn't talking.

With a long exhale, Jackson unbuttoned the cuffs of his white and blue plaid cotton shirt and rolled up the sleeves, staring out the window at Red Creek, which wound its way along the backs of the buildings on this side of the street. How often had his dad looked out at this view? Had he ever thought of Jackson, wishing he could be out west with his son?

He frowned. With one of his *many* sons.

A twinge of loneliness hit him. Dad was gone.

Jackson looked in the direction of the cemetery where Dusty and his wife, Theresa, were buried. Or at least, what was left of them after the car crash that killed them both instantly. A good plan would be for Jackson to go visit the graves, forgive his dad, make his peace. But the anger residing inside him at the man's screwed-up idea of "the perfect family" grated like an old rusty gate swinging in the wind.

He scratched the side of his head, pulling on his too-long hair. He'd always taken pride in having the same dark-brown hair as Dusty. But now, Jackson wished he'd gotten it cut in Oregon before he'd left to come here Sunday night. He'd spotted a barber pole somewhere down a side street. If the August humidity got any heavier and made his hair curl, he'd go get it chopped clean off.

Jackson pulled his phone from his pocket and accessed his email. The one with the flag on it, from his younger half-brother Dylan who'd been here in town the week before, caught his eye again.

He shook his head. He had a younger brother? And two older brothers? "Strange world."

Crazy Dylan had suggested they all meet back in Red Creek on the last day of the month, at noon at Cubby's Restaurant. He'd written something about the town having a lot to offer, the family business keeping his interest, and the people here accepting him like a born-and-raised Red Creekian.

His younger brother had actually used the term *Red Creekian* in a sentence. Even so, Jackson had no plans to ever revisit this town after his week's incarceration was up.

No new emails, so he tucked his phone away and took a look at the files sitting on the desk. With a deep breath, he prepared his brain for another day of massive info dump.

Jackson sat in his dad's chair and opened the top file. *West Virginia coal and gas plant production specification codes...* The words didn't even register as English. "Hell." Jackson didn't have enough fuel in him yet for this tedious shit. He stood, hiked up his jeans, and walked back down the hall to the small kitchen. Pouring a cup, he spotted a black ringed-binder on top of the refrigerator.

He pulled down the book and flipped it open. The first page had a newspaper article about Dusty Walker's first day as owner of the newly re-incorporated company he and his wife had inherited from his father-in-law. "Huh." So Dad had changed the company name. And his wife owned half, which probably explained why Dusty had stayed with her, the greedy asshole.

Jackson felt the heat of anger surface again, and shook his head. The guy was gone. Wasn't it time to shove past this pissed-off phase and move on to…moving on?

He scanned through dozens of pages of news articles, the first half from actual newspapers, the later ones printed from online sites, all of them chronicling the rapid growth of the company under his father's leadership. He had to admit, Dad had a crap-load of business sense.

"Hi there." The receptionist's voice reached him from her desk.

"Hi. Is he here?" A deep female voice had Jackson cocking his head.

"He is. Let me—"

"Wait, which one is this, now?" That sultry voice again.

"It's Jackson, the third son. He's twenty-five. From Oregon." Abby didn't bother to lower her voice. She must not realize he was just around the corner. Or did she know he was there, and just didn't care if she appeared professional or not? "Did you hear about what went on with Dylan last week? You know Zoe Chapman, right?" Abby's voice went quieter.

"I know Zoe. What happened?" The sultry one sounded curious.

Abby's voice dropped down to a mumble and the two spoke for a minute.

Jackson strained to hear, but couldn't catch anything.

"That's quite a coincidence." The sexy voice spoke.

"Yes, I thought so, too." Abby tsked. "So, would you like me to let Jackson know you're here to see him?"

"Wait, is this the rodeo cowboy?" Ms. Sensual Voice sounded disappointed.

"Yes. That's him." A giggle. "Is that a problem?"

Jackson set down his cup and moved a few inches to peek around the wall. His jaw dropped.

Tall, maybe just a few inches shorter than his six-feet, two-inches, even in her flat...red *high-tops*? Different. Her jet-black hair shone in the bright light as it swung thick and straight, cut just at her shoulders. Her jeans clung to her curvy hips and she had a booty that made him forget to breathe. The graphic printed T-shirt strained at the press of her full breasts against the front of the material.

He ducked back into the kitchen and swallowed, recognizing the heat rushing through his body as blood racing from his head to his groin. Holy hell, she was the best thing he'd seen in this town, by a long shot.

"I was hoping..." Her sexy voice switched to a long sigh. "For one of the business-type brothers, but I was in Kansas City for two weeks setting up new servers for a startup company, and I really need to talk to one of Dusty's heirs."

Jackson took another quick look at her. Yeah, she definitely put a rocket in his pocket.

"You should talk to Jackson. He's a nice guy."

Ms. Sensual Voice pressed two fingers between her eyebrows. "It can probably wait until next week. Talk to that one, instead."

Abby shrugged. "Why?"

Jackson knew he had to make his presence known before the hottie said something that'd make her too embarrassed to go out with him. He grinned. And he would sorely like to take her out. Then take her back home, and spend the night with her.

"Because..." Stepping out of the kitchen, he strode toward her, using his sure-hit cowboy gait.

She turned to look at him. Her sky-blue eyes widened and her cheeks pinked up to a sexy shade of embarrassment.

"Our guest thinks this dumb ol' cowboy don't have enough gray matter upstairs to understand what she needs." And what she needed was to have those red lips of hers kissed. Hard.

"I'm sorry, Mr. Walker." Her sensual voice rolled quietly from her as her gaze dropped to take him all in, then shot back to his face.

He held out his hand. "Jackson Walker."

She took his hand and the surge of electricity that ran up his arm and through his nerves blotted out all thoughts except bedroom ideas.

"Aurora Hughes." She pulled her hand back a little too quickly, and sucked in an uneven breath. Did she feel it, too? That zip and ping of lust?

"Is that your real name, Rori?" Abby smiled like she was enjoying every minute of this meeting.

"Yes." Rori's blue gaze met his. "My friends call me Rori." She shook her head as if to pull her thoughts back from wherever they'd shot off to. "May I speak with you for a few minutes, Mr. Walker?"

"Sure thing, and it's Jackson." He gestured for her to precede him down the hallway. "Abby, hold my calls please." Of course, he hadn't received one call since he'd arrived here, but it sounded good anyway.

"Yes, Mr. Walker." She sing-songed with a smirk as she went back to her keyboard.

In front of him, Ms. Aurora "Rori" Hughes walked stiffly, but that nicely-rounded bottom of hers moved and swayed in an amazingly seductive way. They stepped into the big office and he shut the door. When he turned, she stood right there.

Those blue eyes stared into his, and when he inhaled, her light patchouli scent wrapped itself around inside his head. She opened her mouth.

He swallowed and leaned a centimeter closer, ready to kiss her perfect lips if she gave one more sign that she wanted him as much as he craved her.

"I want to apologize for what I said out there." Rori nodded toward the front of the building. "I meant no offense, but I have a bad history with rodeo cowboys."

Her words cooled his jets as effectively as a shovel-full of snow dumped inside the front of his pants.

****

Rori bit her tongue when Jackson jerked back as if she'd thrown a rotten tomato at his forehead. She hadn't meant to blurt it out, but oh boy, was he a barrel full of sexiness. Those inky blue eyes surrounded by long, thick lashes. That mouth, full and curved in a teasing smile. A jaw that looked strong enough to withstand anything a rodeo horse could throw at him. She fisted her hands, wanting to run them through his shaggy, slightly curling hair.

She'd almost imagined he wanted to kiss her. Right here in Dusty's office. Blinking, she backed up a few steps but bumped into the edge of the desk. "Sorry. I'm a little..." Rori glanced at the desktop. What was she? Incredibly turned on by a guy she'd met less than a minute ago? A shiver raced through her, tightening her nipples and sending a sweet ache to her belly.

"A little...?" He reached around her and pulled one of the guest chairs nearer. Leaning over her a bit too close.

He gave off the purely masculine scent of soap and outdoors and she held her breath, keeping her gaze fixed on the desk to fight back that naughty temptation. Rori had to remember the pitiful existence her cousin lived because of a rodeo junkie. She refused to end up the same way.

When Jackson finally moved away from her, she sank into the chair, glad her knees held out as long as they had, and watched him stroll around the desk and take a seat in Dusty's chair. Dang, she had more than one reason to be uninterested in this man. Besides rodeo cowboys being poison, this one was her benefactor's son, to whom she was indebted. So why did the idea of shoving all those files off the desk and spreading herself on the flat surface for his pleasure keep intruding on her thoughts?

"Ms. Hughes?" He leaned back in the chair, watching her with those too-seductive eyes. "What can I help you with?"

"It's Rori. Please." Her gaze darted around as she recalled the points she'd come here to make. "First…" She blurted the word too loudly, and his eyebrows rose. "First, I wanted to tell you how sorry I am about your father. He was a kind man, a good businessman, and everyone in town is feeling the loss."

Jackson nodded once, his lips thinning.

Yep, she could imagine how he felt, learning he had three brothers he hadn't known about. She'd be angry as a hornet, too. Maybe she could help him by showing him the good his father had done. "Second, I want to talk about Cyber Wise."

Glancing at her T-shirt then at the powered-down computer on the desk—both of which bore her company's logo—he nodded once. "I'm guessing you're Cyber Wise?" Those beautiful eyes of his shifted to look at her.

"I am." Rori scooted to the edge of her chair. "Two years ago, Dusty recruited me from the University of Kansas. I'd just completed my MSCoE and was…"

His gaze dropped when she'd thrown out her credentials. Was he uninterested? He wasn't a college man, from the rumors floating around. Did she just lose him?

She waved one hand to dismiss what she'd just said and started over. "I finished my Master's in computers, and he asked me to come to Red Creek and work for him."

Jackson met her gaze. "But you're not on the payroll."

"We worked out a deal. I started my own business in town, but made D. Walker Mineral my number one priority." Dusty's business sense combined with her need to work on her own terms had clashed then melded into a win-win arrangement. "He leases the old five-and-dime building to me free of charge, for as long as I remain in town and stay available to his company."

His jaw shifted and he narrowed his eyes. "You just told Abby you were in Kansas City for two weeks."

Shit, he'd caught that? Rori took a deep breath. "I want

to…someday…open another office in KC." Hopefully with the help of Dusty's company. "And getting my name associated with corporations in that area is imperative." There. She didn't exactly lie, but she didn't confess everything either. Now, just how sharp was this rodeo cowboy?

His lips curved in a smirk. "So, after Dusty died, you figured you'd just go do whatever you wanted, and damn the contract?"

She clamped her jaw closed. The man did not play fair. "The job in KC was a last-minute thing. The company they'd hired to do their startup went belly-up, and they urgently needed help."

Jackson just stared at her.

Loosening her facial muscles, she gave a sad smile. "Dusty was…gone already, the company shut down for the week after, and I was only a three-hour drive away from Red Creek if an emergency arose. One hour by Dusty's private jet, if needed." Shifting in her seat, she let go of the guilt she felt for missing the funeral and for semi-breaking her contract with the company.

The man in Dusty's chair did not look impressed.

She needed to hit this cowboy with more facts.

"The contract specifies that I can take jobs outside the region. And I have, many times, with Dusty's okay." She gestured out the window. "I mean, you've seen Red Creek. How much computer work do you think this town needs?" Her voice rose as her panic grew. This man could terminate her contract and leave her without a storefront, and with a truckload of electronics to move. She should probably have been nicer to him from the start.

He watched her for long moments, then placed his hand flat on the desk and stood. "Let's go see this building of yours." A shaft of sunlight coming through the window highlighted his face.

She stared, unmoving. He was handsome, rugged, but those eyes were too compelling, too sharp.

"Rori?"

His hair fell in disarray, and in the sunlight, gleamed with a dozen shades of brown. "Huh?" He'd said something…

With a grin, he walked around the desk and opened the door. "Your building? The old five-and-dime? Let's go take a look at it, then we'll have breakfast at Cubby's, and talk business."

With her butt still stuck to the chair, she shifted her gaze, trying to figure out his plan of attack. "Sure." She got to her feet and wandered past him and out the door. How had a quick confirmation of contract validity become a personal tour and breakfast? She glanced down at her old *Get Cyber Wise* T-shirt. And why hadn't she worn something a little sexier?

Chapter Two

Jackson followed Rori down the hallway and out the front door, nodding at Abby who gave him a wave and a smile. He'd be sure to question her later, since she seemed to know Rori. Well enough to share gossip with her, anyway.

The sun had climbed in the sky and the breeze carried the scents of heating asphalt and grass. It would be a hot, humid day again today, and visions of him lying on a cushioned chair next to the pool at the lake house all day reading a rodeo magazine kept sneaking into his head.

They stood at the curb and waited for a slowly passing pickup truck to go by before stepping out to cross the street.

"You said two years?" He liked that he had something on this woman, since she had something against him already—his rodeo career. Whatever the hell that was about. The anger in her eyes when she'd shot him down earlier looked fresh, as if whatever had happened to her—rodeo-related—was still going on.

She stepped up onto the opposite curb. "What?" Turning to walk down the street, she left room for him to walk next to her. On the inside.

Placing his hand on her lower back, he guided her toward the buildings, leaving space for him to walk on the outside, along the curb. Just as his father had taught him. Old-fashioned, but that's what a gentleman did, according to Dusty Walker. And the feeling of her firm body against his palm proved too much to resist.

Balking a little, she glanced up at him. Pink colored her cheeks.

Firm and warm… He dropped his hand away as revolutions of sexy ideas spun wildly in his head. "Two years ago you came here?"

She nodded and looked down the street. "I'll be forever grateful to him. He was more than generous. It was such a stroke of luck that we met, and both happened to be—"

"Oh, hell." A horrific thought flashed into his brain, making Jackson trip over his own feet, nearly tumbling into her. Holy shit, could she be another one? He stared at her face, looking for any similarities to Dusty.

"What is it?" She waited a second, and when he stayed silent, she pulled her keys out of her pocket and slid them into the lock on the reinforced glass door of an old glass-front, brick, two-story building bearing a round sign proclaiming *Cyber Wise Inc.*

"I was wondering about your family." His voice came out wobbly. Damn him, if he had the hots for his half-sister… A chill of disgust raced through him and his stomach turned.

"My family?" She walked into the building and lights flickered on overhead. "Why?" Turning to face him, she crossed her arms.

Jackson set aside his suspicions for the moment and scoped out the room. Ten tables, each with computer stuff on them and chairs on one side of them. Like a showroom, where she'd give her customers hands-on demonstrations. "This is really smart." He walked to one setup and looked at the monitor, keyboard, box that made computer things happen, and mouse.

"I've found that actually letting people get in elbows-deep is the way to avoid any dissatisfaction with my products." She'd uncrossed her arms but hadn't moved.

"Give me your sales pitch." He didn't really care about computers, he just liked hearing her voice.

She squinted at him, then proceeded to give him a quick lesson in the different options of computers…and she lost him. His phone served as his only connection with the world, otherwise he stayed as far away from technology as he could get.

"You'd be able to teach me?" He thought of the setup back at the office on Dusty's desk. That monster, Jackson didn't even know how to turn on.

"Teach you…" She tipped her head, and that flow of sexy hair brushed her shoulder.

He looked away, silently reminding himself that he needed to get her paternity sorted out first.

"Computering." He shrugged. "Haven't had much need for one, but the people in the office are telling me to open documents and spreadsheets and internet and powerpoints, and I only know what one of them things is." He pulled a frown.

She smiled. "You do that 'good ol' boy' thing pretty darn well."

Glancing at his boots, he shuffled one foot. "Aw shucks, ma'am. Wish it was just an act." He played it off as a joke, but it was a sore point with him. He didn't have the book learning his mother had wanted him to have, but Dusty had been on his side. Dad hadn't gone to college, and he hadn't tried to pressure Jackson into going. But now that he'd met someone as smart and accomplished as Rori, he felt a hundred steps behind her.

"Sure." She shot the word at him.

He glanced into her soft, blue eyes. "Yeah?"

"Yeah. I'll teach you what you need to know. But not this morning." She pointed toward the back of the building. "I've got a few projects I need to finish." She started walking that way. "Let me show you the work area in the back and the storage area in the basement."

He nodded and followed her into the back room, past the tables bearing the bits and pieces of unfinished computers, laptops, tablets, and a dozen boxes with cables and plug-ins that he had no clue about. She opened a wide door and headed down the steps.

He followed, although it sounded like a hell of a lot of boring awaiting him down there. He'd go along, seeing as he owned this building. And he had some important information to get out of her. "So, your family?"

At the bottom of the steps, she faced him. "Just Mom and Dad. They're high school teachers in KC, and spend the summer traveling." Her gaze didn't leave his. "Why do you want to know about them?"

How did he handle this…without asking for a paternity test? "Just curious."

It took her a few seconds to process that before she gave him a blessedly brief tour of the rows of racks holding electronics, and explained the temperature and humidity control system she'd installed.

"Impressive." He followed her back upstairs, resolutely keeping his eyes off her derriere. Back on the ground level, he pointed to the ceiling. "What's upstairs?"

"Living quarters." She glanced away. "Mine."

She lived and worked here. Dedication, for sure. He'd bet any money that if he drove through town at midnight on any random night, he'd see the lights on and her bent over one of the tables. "Let's see it."

She wrinkled her brow at him. "Why?"

He laughed. "Darlin', if you want to go on ahead and straighten the place up a bit first, that's fine."

"No, it's not messy..." She groaned. "It's just…it's my private space."

"I understand that, but I'd like to take a quick look at the setup." And search for clues about her father. He leaned forward, his mouth quirking up a bit. "You're not hiding anything up there, are you?"

She rolled her eyes and huffed out a breath. "Besides nuclear weapons and a kilo of cocaine? No." Spinning on the rubber-soled heel of her red high-tops, she trudged past a small coffee area, set up for guests, he'd bet, and opened the door to a flight of stairs. He followed her up to a bright, sunny space. The blue couch and two matching chairs sat around a low table holding a few game controllers, all facing a big-ass television. An impressive array of game consoles resided on the shelves under the TV.

He opened his mouth to make an obvious comment, then snapped it shut and looked at her.

Her face looked shuttered, closed down, as if she was embarrassed that anyone saw her hobby.

Jackson didn't spot any photos sitting around, so he walked past the couch and into the small kitchen. "This is nice." He enjoyed cooking some, a talent his mother shared with him from an early age. "This gas stovetop is state of the art."

"Um. Sure." She walked up to it. "Never been used." She grinned. "But I've gone through three microwaves in two years."

He laughed. "I'll have to cook you up my..." He shook his head. First things first. "Show me the rest?"

She blinked a few times, then turned and wandered toward the back of the building. "Bathroom." She pointed toward the left. "Bedroom." Her finger moved toward the right.

Jackson peeked his head into the bathroom. Tub, separate shower, and all the rest. He strode right into her bedroom and glanced at the bare walls, then looked at the top of the dresser. There it was. A photo of Rori in a cap and gown, her parents on either side of her. Pointing to the picture, he glanced at her. "May I?"

She nodded slowly. "Okay." Her voice rose on the last syllable. She was confused, but he wasn't about to explain.

Picking up the eight-by-ten frame, he walked past the yellow-quilted bed to the window and held the photo in the sunlight. Her mother's brown hair and brown eyes, then her father's... Jackson breathed a sigh of relief. Her father had a full head of black hair, and eyes the color of the noon sky. "Nice family."

"Wait." She stomped toward him. "Are you fucking kidding me?" Her eyes shot blue lasers at him.

His brows shot up and he considered backing away from the shitstorm headed his way. "What?"

She grabbed the picture from him, staring him down. "You thought I was one of Dusty's..." Breathing fast, she shook her head. "You thought..." She backed away a step and set the photo on the dresser, face down.

He hung his head, not that he was ashamed…much…but it was a trick that always worked with his mom. "Can you blame me?"

"Damn it." She leaned against the end of the bed. "I don't know what to say."

"Darlin', I owe you an apology." He faced her head-on. "But if you'd lived in my boots for the last few weeks, you'd be looking for more of Dusty's surprises in the faces of folks you met, too."

Her fingers played with the cotton bedspread. "Especially here in town, right?" She looked up at him, her eyes blue and sad.

All he wanted to do was tug her into his arms, kiss away the sadness and leap with her in his arms onto the mattress. But he knew it wasn't the moment. Taking her arm, he gestured toward the main room. "Breakfast?"

She had to know he was changing the subject, but she went along willingly. "Breakfast and business talk, right?"

"Right." He followed her down the steps and out through the front of the building.

She locked up.

"Security?" He looked for wires or boxes or cameras, but saw none.

"The best." Turning, she ended up just inches in front of him. "Just try to get to my bedroom again, cowboy."

He leaned a fraction closer and smirked. "Is that a challenge?"

Her eyes widened as the double-meaning of her words struck her. When her cheeks turned pink, he took pity on her, placed his hand on her back, and led her across the street to the town's restaurant. *Challenge accepted.*

****

Rori sat on the opposite side of the booth from Jackson as a parade of townsfolk stopped by to pay their respects and welcome him to Red Creek. Women boldly flirted with him, and some people actually asked for his autograph. Evidently, he was some big hoo-ga-doo in the rodeo world.

172

Which served as a good reminder to her to stay the heck out of situations where she'd be alone with him. Like, for instance, in his office teaching him "computering," as he'd so colloquially put it. She'd like to take back that agreement, but working with his company was her primary job.

Cubby's wife, Sherry, stopped at their table and refilled their coffee cups as the last gawker shook Jackson's hand and wandered away. "Met your brother Dylan last week, you know." The older woman stared at Jackson for a few seconds. "You look a lot alike. 'Cept he has green eyes. Lighter-colored hair."

After a pause, Jackson lifted his hand toward the woman. "Jackson Walker."

Sherry set down the coffee pot and grasped his hand. "Sherry. My husband and I own this place." She picked up the pot again. "So what's all this talk about Dylan and Zoe Chapman? Is it true?"

Jackson blinked a few times. "Uh, I don't know. Haven't communicated with Dylan."

Rori frowned at Sherry, who nodded her understanding. Jackson could barely cope with his new family situation. And if the rumor Abby had just shared that morning was true, Jackson sure as heck didn't need to find out about another family member.

Sherry swung her gaze back to Jackson. "You plannin' on staying?"

With a glance at Rori, he smiled up at Sherry. "For at least five more days."

Sherry snorted and walked away. "Full of that same Walker B.S., that's for sure."

He coughed out a laugh. "Where do you go in this town for privacy?"

Their breakfasts arrived, and Jackson buttered his stack of pancakes. The side plate of scrambled eggs, bacon and ham sat between them, and he gestured for her to help herself.

The smell of the bacon sent her mouth watering like crazy, but she sipped her coffee and stirred her bowl of fruit, granola, and yogurt. Sitting all day didn't allow room for fried pork in her diet, not if she didn't want to spread out like a melting snowman.

"There's nowhere that people aren't watching you. It's like living in a fishbowl." She didn't know why she said that. She liked Red Creek, mostly, but her love life had taken a direct hit in the two years since she'd moved here. Red Creekians liked to make everything their business, and she didn't want *her* business to suffer because of gossip.

Shoving a pie-shaped stack of three pancakes into his mouth, Jackson groaned.

Her stomach rumbled, and she scooped a big spoon of her sorry breakfast into her mouth. Maybe if she jogged more? Bought a treadmill? Did yoga?

"Is that all you're having?" Jackson gestured with his coffee cup toward her bowl.

"I usually skip breakfast." She poked at a strawberry hiding in yogurt.

"Most important meal of the day?" He went back to cutting his pancakes. "Why's that?"

She shrugged. "Most days, I don't get out of bed until later."

He smiled. "I like hearing that."

A wave of desire roared through her. "It's because I stay up until near dawn working."

"Ah, a night owl."

"Whoo, me?" She batted her eyes at him.

He laughed, a slow, low rumble that tingled into her ears and made her ridiculously happy.

Sherry came back with her coffee pot. "Your food okay?"

"Great." Jackson's gaze never left Rori. "Thanks." He crunched into a piece of bacon.

The waitress hummed for a second, then moved on.

Rori stuck her spoon into the unappealing breakfast and shoved the bowl to the side. "Should we talk about the contract while we have a few minutes between admirers?"

"Sure, you start."

"First…" She took a second to gather her points. "The contract is with the company, not Dusty personally."

"Makes sense." He cut a sausage in half and put it in his mouth, chewing slowly as he watched her.

"Then, there's the fact that I'm still needed. The company is going to continue its work." For at least another year, if what Dusty's attorney told her was true.

"Good enough for me. I see no reason to make any changes." He poured more syrup on the cakes then reached across the table and picked up her fork. "If Dad negotiated it for the company, even though he's gone now…" He stuck her fork in the short stack, cut a wedge of pancake, and held the dripping mess out for her to take. "I'd bet my best boots it's a valid contract."

The smell of real maple syrup mixing with the carb scent of the pancakes weakened her beyond redemption. Grabbing the fork from him, she shoved the whole pile into her mouth and chewed. Bliss floated inside her mouth and mellowed all the way down to her soul.

He pushed the plate of cakes closer to her and spread more of the whipped butter on the top layer.

Rori should talk to Jackson about her expansion ideas now that he was all…buttered up, but it could wait until they weren't in such a public place. Giving up all pretenses of interest in her own breakfast, she dug into the pancakes, eggs, and breakfast meats. Damn him for making her run five extra miles today.

Her phone beeped and she pulled it from her pocket. "Sorry, my customer is at the shop early." She reached into her back pocket, but he held up a hand. "My treat."

"Thanks." She stood and he wrapped his big, calloused hand around her wrist.

"Sorry about the…photo thing earlier." His blue eyes softened. "I didn't mean any offense."

Rori nodded, letting the warmth of his touch slide along her bloodstream like a river of lava. "I understand. And sorry for..." She glanced around, seeing every eye in the place on them. "My overreaction." Whispering the words, she slid her arm out of his grasp.

"Not a problem." His hand went right to his coffee cup. "So I'll see you this afternoon?"

"What?" How was she so easily distracted by this cowboy's touch?

"Computering lessons?" His lips curved up into a delicious smile. "You are free this afternoon, correct?"

It shouldn't be a problem, the two of them in the office with the other employees present. "Sure. I'll call before—"

"No need." He leaned closer to her as he pulled his wallet out of his back pocket. "I'll be there reading through files. But..." His brows drew down. "You may have to wake me up."

The giggle that escaped her throat sounded louder than church bells as they echoed through the restaurant. Damn. She tucked her head down and bee-lined it to the door. What the heck was wrong with her?

Chapter Three

Jackson got the hell out of Cubby's before more of the town came by to introduce themselves. As he walked the few yards to the office, he replayed his conversation with Rori. She wanted to open another Cyber Wise in KC? Did that mean she'd be leaving town?

He pushed open the door to D. Walker Mineral Co. and stepped inside. Elaine Dennis, one of the oil and mineral specialists, stood talking with Abby.

"Morning, boss." Her pretty face bore little makeup, and for a woman old enough to be his mother, she had few wrinkles, and even fewer grays in her brown hair. "I saw you met Ms. Rori."

"I did." He leaned against the tall reception desk, his elbow on the counter. "She wanted to check on her contract with us." Jackson should probably have okayed it with Elaine, Vic, or the other specialist, Walt, but that bronc had already left the chute.

"Everything taken care of?" Elaine and Abby watched him.

"It is. She's coming in this afternoon to help me with Dad's computer."

Abby puckered her face up. "Is something wrong with it?"

"Nope." He held back a smile. "But I want her help so as to make sure it stays that way once I get my paws on it."

The women laughed and Elaine wandered away. "I'll be in my office if you need anything."

"Thanks." He waited a few seconds then bent closer to Abby. "What's the story on Ms. Hughes?"

Abby's green eyes perked up. "Well, it's Miss, never married, doesn't date much at all, and is one of the smartest people you'll ever meet."

He knew she was smart. "Doesn't date much?"

She shook her head. "Not that she doesn't get asked. I heard one time, three bachelor farmers ended up at her store at the exact

177

same time when she opened Monday morning." She glanced around, then up into his eyes with a grin. "Guess they got to talking about her at Saturday night poker, and ended up all scratchin' at her door at once." Abby laughed. "Can you just picture it?"

"Yeah." He strolled past her desk. "I sure can." Rori was one special woman, and he wanted to explore every single one of her secrets.

Hours later, after staring at graphs and charts and reports from the company's professional geologist, who had an office in the building, but was on jobsites most every day, Jackson needed air. He knocked on Vic's open office door. "You wanna grab something to eat?"

"Sure." The guy picked up his cell phone and came around his desk. "It'll just be us. Elaine's got a lunch meeting." They walked down the hall. "Walt was supposed to be back today, but he's stuck in Arkansas waiting for some geo tests to come back before offering them a contract."

Abby sat at her desk eating potato chips, a spreadsheet open on her computer.

"And Ms. Abby, here, works through lunch, so she can get home to her honey." Vic smiled at the receptionist, his appreciation of the woman clear in his expression.

"Jackson hasn't met my honey yet, so he doesn't know what a lucky lady I am to have him a waitin' on me to come home at night." She wiggled her eyebrows.

Jackson laughed. "Sounds like you've got it made."

"Juuuust the right amount of separation to make a marriage work." Abby went back to her computer.

Vic held open the door and the two of them walked outside. "She's a good worker, a strong woman."

"You've only been here a few months?" Jackson held open the door to Cubby's, their only choice for lunch.

"Yes, and despite that, I felt like part of the family." Vic looked up at Jackson. "Still do, if you'll pardon my familiarity."

"Not at all." Jackson wasn't sure what the guy meant, but there was no way he'd make Vic feel his job was at risk. Especially from Jackson, who was impatient to shake the dust of this town off his boots come Sunday morning.

They took a table in a corner and ordered the special: a meatloaf sandwich with gravy and mashed potatoes, green beans, and a home-baked roll.

"What made you come to Red Creek?" Jackson took a cold gulp of his strong sweet tea.

"A couple things." Vic narrowed his dark eyes. "I got tired of California, and the Walker Company has one of the best reputations in the business."

Jackson hadn't been aware of the company's status in the industry. The hours he'd spent with Elaine and Abby the day before had filled him in on what was going on with the company, but besides the way the women spoke highly of his father, they didn't go into much detail. "He's done pretty well financially."

"That, and his honesty, integrity, business sense..." Vic shrugged. "I would tell you that it'll be a pretty big hat to fill, but I get the feeling you're not planning on filling Dusty's hat."

At that last part, the wind went out of Jackson's sails. He'd been questioning the honesty/integrity piece, recalling the illegitimacy of the sons of Dusty Walker. "How do you figure that?" Vic was right about Jackson's future plans, of course, but he'd tried to keep that fact hidden.

Their lunches arrived, and Vic got busy turning his sandwich black with pepper from the shaker. "Just a hunch." He gestured out the window. "This town doesn't hold much appeal for a young guy like you."

Jackson laughed. "You're what, five years older than me?"

"Ten." Vic took a big forkful and chewed, swallowing it down with coke. "But I'm an office kind of guy. You? Rodeo, buckle bunnies, seeing the country."

Running away, as Sapphire had always said when Jackson had gone out on the circuit. "I guess."

"You don't have to sit behind Dusty's desk for the rest of your life." Vic set down his utensils. "You can always travel the country doing what your dad loved best."

What Dad loved best? Besides his four mistresses and their bastard sons? "It's all up for grabs right now." He said the words, but they were a deflection. His brothers could do what they wanted with the company for the next year. Jackson was looking forward to that big payout come next August.

"I understand." Vic ate for a while. "Just so you know, your dad's done some really good things for this town. The Walker name is highly respected here."

"I'm sure it is." Jackson had heard about his dad bailing out businesses, but that could have been just self-preservation. If the town went under, the company wouldn't have a place to call home.

Elaine walked up to their table. "Mind if I join you? My lunch meeting just ended."

The guys stood and Jackson pulled out a chair for her. "Please do."

"Oh, such gentlemen. The town of Red Creek is blessed to have you two bachelors gracing our streets."

Jackson met Vic's gaze, sending the man a silent request for confidentiality.

Vic turned toward Elaine. "So, who did you meet with?"

Tucking back into his meal, Jackson let them talk business while he considered his options. Dusty's death threw a whole lot of new ones in front of him, and he couldn't overlook the fact that his old way of life would change no matter how hard he tried to keep it the same.

****

Later that afternoon, Rori stepped into Heart Starter, Lexie Choate's quirky coffee shop, glad to see the place was empty.

"Hey, girl." Lexie had her sketch pad out and was drawing

180

something. The woman's artistic talent was insane, and the shop walls were filled with her artwork.

"Hi. Can I get an iced mocha? Large, please."

"Sure." Lexie started the big, scary espresso machine. "Need to stay awake this evening?"

Rori sat on a stool at the counter. "No. I'm just procrastinating. I promised Dusty's son, Jackson, I'd show him how to use the computer."

"Oooh. He's a cute one." Lexie pulled out another cup. "I'll make one for him, too. Keep you both awake this afternoon."

Cussing under her breath, Rori stuck her tongue out at her friend. "He's the rodeo cowboy. You know how I feel about that."

She shrugged. "Whatever prejudices get you through the day."

Rori frowned. "What's that supposed to mean?"

"Nothing." Lexi set the chocolate-infused iced coffees in front of Rori. "I'll put this on your tab."

"Thanks." Rori stood. May as well go and get it over with. "We need to get Kit and Zoe and do a girls' night out."

"Okay. I'm in."

Rori waited to see if Lexi would mention anything about the gossip surrounding Zoe, but Lexi just picked up her pad and started drawing, looking from it to Rori's face and back again.

"Jeez, you know I hate it when you sketch me." Rori crossed her eyes and contorted her lips.

Lexi laughed. "I'm going to paint your portrait that way one day."

Rori chuckled and left the store, strolling down the street to D. Walker Mineral Company and an afternoon of computering and too-closeness with that dang rodeo cowboy. She walked past the empty reception desk. Abby worked a seven-to-three shift, and since it was already three-thirty, the woman would be long gone. Heading down the hall, she looked into the four offices along the way to Dusty's…Jackson's…to find them empty. So much for her plan to get here early enough to not be alone with the cowboy.

At his office door, she peeked in and found him staring at papers in an open file folder. She rapped her knuckles softly on the doorframe. "Am I too late?"

His head jerked up. "To keep me from falling asleep?" He sat back. "Yeah. It's happened four times already this afternoon."

"This'll help." She stepped into the room and set the cups on the desk. "Thought you could use this." The red cotton shirt she'd changed into after she'd showered and put on sexier lingerie evidently caught his attention because his gaze dropped to her cleavage and stayed for a long while. "I bet you had the Tuesday special at Cubby's." She walked around the far side of the desk and pressed the buttons to turn on the computer and monitor. "His meatloaf sandwich has put me out cold more than once."

"Thanks for the coffee." Jackson stood and offered her his chair, sipping on the coffee. "That meatloaf and these reports nearly put me into a coma."

She slid into the seat, the residual warmth from his body heating her bottom, sending a sexy shiver along her skin. "Well, this won't take too long." She clicked the mouse a few times.

"Miss Rori, you're overestimating my skills." He grabbed a guest chair and hauled it around the back of the desk and set it next to the big leather one. "Like, for instance, what did you do to turn these on?" He sat, picked up a pencil, and held it poised over a small notepad.

"Seriously?" Was he teasing her? The look on his face told her he was serious.

"My mom has a tablet thing which I've used, but all this…" He gestured to the computer. "It's been since high school, the last time I used one. And I don't want to break anything.

She held back a smile at how solemn he looked, his eyes intent, his lips thinned into a straight, sexy line. "Okay, sorry." She went over the power-up, gave him the login and password she'd set up for him before heading over here, and showed him the different folders and files, printing out a sort of map for him and making notes on it in red.

"Good." Jackson compared the printout to the screen. "I'm following this."

She spent another hour showing him Dusty's private files, the ones saved to only his computer, which included payroll and banking information.

He had her open files so he could see details, and as the evening sun turned everything orangey, he pointed to a folder. "What's that?"

Dusty had called it *Theresa*.

"That looks like something personal." She stood and motioned for them to switch chairs. "If you want to look at it now, I'll go down the hall."

"No." He sat in the big chair and used the mouse. "Sit. I'll take a look."

She turned her back to him, facing the coatrack in the corner where Dusty's old white straw cowboy hat hung next to his denim jacket with the company logo embroidered on the left chest. Poor Dusty. He didn't deserve to die the way he did.

"What the heck is this?" Jackson tapped her arm with the back of his hand.

She swung around and looked at the columns of numbers and dates. "I don't know." Standing, she leaned over him and looked at the screen. The first column was dates, a month apart each, which began eight years ago. "Scroll down."

He did, a little slower than she'd like, but he was getting better. The last date was just days before Dusty died. "Huh."

"Yeah. Strange." She pointed to the screen. "The second and third column look suspiciously like bank routing and account numbers. The bank routing numbers repeat themselves on a regular basis." She counted. "Every eighteen months, it's the same routing number."

"You're saying whatever they're doing, they use just eighteen banks on a rotating basis."

She nodded. "What could be the significance of eighteen?"

Jackson snorted. "Knowing Dusty…" He bit off the words. Was he going to make a snide comment about Dusty and his harem? "So that makes the fourth column…dollar amounts?" Jackson scrolled back up slowly. "This year it's thirteen thousand, and a thousand less every year going back."

"I have no idea what it is." She sat in her chair. "I can pull up a list of Walker Co.'s bank accounts, but I know that's not Red Creek Bank's routing number."

He looked at her. "Can we search the world wide web for these banks?"

She bit back a smile. "Most of us call it *the internet* now, and yes, I'll show you how to do it."

After a few minutes of trial and error, they found a site that gave the information.

"These are all over the country." He scratched his cheek. "What do you think this is?"

To her, it looked sketchy.

"You're thinking the same thing I am, right?" He stared into her eyes. "Some kind of payoff or blackmail or gambling debt?"

She snorted. "Do you read a lot of international intrigue novels?" But she wouldn't rule out any of Jackson's suspicions.

"You can scoff, but I'll bet you a million bucks there's something strange going on." He pressed print and walked over to the printer on a shelf in the corner.

"I don't know, Jackson. I don't mean to minimalize this, but is it worth your time digging into it further?"

He swung around and smiled. "Compared to the boring-ass files sitting on that desk? Hell, yeah!"

She couldn't keep the smile from curving her lips. "Okay. But I don't know how you're going to get any further than—"

"You can hack computers, right?" He gestured for her to take the big chair again. "Can you do that from here or do we need to go to your store?"

She sucked in a breath. "I don't hack." Standing, she backed away from the computer. "That's illegal, immoral, unscrupulous—"

"Okay." He held up a hand. "Sorry. But you know someone who does, right?" His brows rose as he stalked toward her. "You have to. Somebody from college?"

"Why would you think that?" She backed up a step and bumped up against a file cabinet.

He stood feet from her, staring at her. "I can see it in your eyes. You do know someone. I'll pay them."

She could stand there and deny it, but she had no poker face. "Okay, but let me keep your name out of it." Holding her hand out, she waited for him to place the papers in her hand. "I'm doing this under protest."

"Protest acknowledged. Remember, you're a contract employee of D. Walker Mineral Company, and therefore you're protected by said contract from any legal whatevers."

She closed her eyes for a second so he wouldn't see her rolling them. "That's just shy of being convincing, but let me text my contact." Taking a photo of the top sheet, she cropped it to show only eighteen of the bank routing numbers and bank accounts, then texted them to Kiwi with a request for information. "Done." She gave him a glare. "But you can never mention this to anyone."

"Understood." He nodded. "How long? What now?"

She read Kiwi's reply text. "He says, 'Give me an hour'. Now, we could search Dusty's emails." She scrunched up her nose. "If that's okay with you."

"Yeah, that's okay." He let her take the big chair and access the emails. After a half hour of searching emails, files, and photos, she sat back. "Nothing."

"What about his personal emails? He has a laptop and a computer at his house." Jackson stood.

"Your house?" She closed down all the files and software.

"Yeah. The house I own a fourth of." It still sounded odd to him. He gestured. "C'mon. Marliss will have supper ready and you can help me get into those computers."

"I don't know." She got up and walked around the far side of the desk. "I don't want to just show up for supper at Dusty's house and—"

"My house. Remember?" Jackson folded the papers and stuffed them into his back pocket, then held out his hand to Rori. "And since you're under contract..." He grinned then laughed. "You can't say no."

She giggled as she took his hand and let him pull her down the hall toward the front door. "I feel like Nancy Drew all of a sudden."

"Who?" He pulled open the door and glanced back at her.

She should have known. With a mother named Sapphire, and growing up in a quirky Pacific Northwestern town... "Just a favorite book character of mine."

"Oh, right." He pulled the door shut and used his key to lock it. "Your parents are teachers."

She laughed as he hauled her around the side of the building to where the red company truck sat. Jackson and her—they each saw the world through very different filters.

Chapter Four

Jackson helped Rori into the company truck, almost surprised that she didn't insist on taking her own car. But the house…his house…was only a ten minute drive from town. As he walked around the front of the truck, he dialed the home number.

"Good evening, Mr. Walker." Marliss' voice, almost too perky for a woman in her sixties, carried from his phone.

"Hey, Marliss, I'm heading that way, and if it's okay, I'm bringing someone for supper."

"Well, of course. Lou makes enough food for a dozen." Her husband, Lou, had cooked since he was old enough to work outside the home. "Will this be a formal meal in the dining room?"

He looked through the truck window at Rori. "Sort of more of a…date?"

Rori lifted her brows at him.

"Uh huh. Not too sure, then?" Marliss hummed for a couple seconds. "A nice breeze has come up. How about a few candles on the table out by the pool?"

He smiled. "Perfect. Thank you."

"My pleasure. Now, drive safe." She'd told him that this morning, too. A warning based on his father's demise?

"Will do. Be there in ten."

"We'll be ready."

Jackson opened the driver's door and slid in. "I called the house to see if there was enough for two, or if we needed to stop at Cubby's for a to-go order."

Rori laughed. "Oh man, your dad used to talk about the battalion-sized meals Lou cooked. When Dusty was home, he'd bring in the leftovers for lunch the next day and feed the whole office."

Turning onto Main Street, Jackson tried to wrap his head around Dusty bringing chow in for a crowd. Most likely his frugal need to not waste anything.

They rode silently until the house came into view. Up on a hill facing Osprey Lake, surrounded by acres of land, the long, two-story modern-looking place loomed like a giant country mansion. Glass windows along the front of the house reflected the sun. There'd be a beautiful sunset tonight. He'd be sure to watch the time and take Rori down to the lake to enjoy it with him.

Of course, right now, his groin tightened with anticipation of pulling Rori into his arms, a kiss, then another, then a quick walk back to the house and up to the bedroom he'd chosen to use. Jackson had to shift to make room in his jeans for the hardening behind his fly.

"I'm excited to see the house. I've heard so much about it." Rori fidgeted and pulled down the visor, checking her face in the mirror.

"You've never been in the place?"

"No." From her pocket, she pulled a tube of something pink and shimmery, opened it, and smoothed some on her lips.

Why did he want to kiss it off her right there, halfway up the driveway?

"Your dad was a stickler for separating business and personal." She scrunched up her face as she looked at him. "I think it was Theresa's way of keeping us common folk out of her life."

He'd guessed that Dusty's wife was a socialite-type. Born into money, the best schools and college out east. "Well, since I'm about as common as they come…" He should have a party at the house, invite the whole company and their families.

"You're a Walker." She flipped up the visor. "Around these parts, that's akin to royalty."

He laughed. Even when he'd won on the rodeo circuit, he was treated as just plain folk. "If I find a crown hidden in the storage space, I'll be sure to start wearing it to the office."

Her smile did wild things to him, and as he pulled up to the side of the house, outside the garage, he winked at her. "Here it is.

It ain't much, but it's home. For this week."

She let herself out and they walked around the back to where the pool, cabana, and outdoor kitchen took up a half-acre of land.

"Yep." She looked around, taking it all in. "Ain't much."

Jackson took her hand and led her to the wet bar under the shady pergola. "Can I make you a drink? Beer? Wine?"

He opened the refrigerator. "Looks like Marliss made a pitcher of margaritas." He pulled out the glass container and showed Rori. "If you're brave."

"Mmmm." She nodded. "I'll have a little one. We still have some work to do this evening, so I don't want to get too goofy."

He selected two tall glasses, filled them with ice, and poured the green concoction into them. Handing one to her, he raised his. "To a long evening, and getting to know each other."

She tipped her head. "How about, to a productive evening getting to the bottom of things."

He'd nearly forgotten about the computer searching they had to do. "To a little of both of those?"

Tapping her glass against his, she nodded once. "Perfect." She sipped. "Oh my gosh, this is delicious."

"Thank you." Marliss' voice came from the French doors that led into the kitchen. "A recipe I've perfected over the years." The older woman, her short hair curly and jet-black, carried a festive Mexican platter with a variety of appetizers on it. She set them on the counter next to Rori and Jackson. "Dinner in fifteen minutes."

"Thank you, Marliss." He gestured to Rori. "I'd like you to meet Rori Hughes. She's on contract with the company."

Marliss nodded, but Rori held out her hand for a shake, and the housekeeper took it. "Glad to meet you, Marliss. I'm sure we've seen each other in town a few times."

The woman smiled. "I think we were on the Founder's Day cleanup crew together last year."

"We were." Rori smiled. "It's nice to officially meet you."

"Ditto." Marliss gestured to a round table with four

comfortable-looking chairs that sat under a huge sun umbrella by the pool. "I hope dining al fresco is agreeable with you, Ms. Hughes."

"It's Rori, please, and yes, I'd love to stay outside now that it's cooled off a little." Rori turned to look at the table. Behind her back, Marliss winked at Jackson and gave him a thumbs-up.

He shook his head and picked up the platter. "C'mon Ms. Hughes. Let's get comfortable and enjoy the best cookin' in the tri-state area."

They sat and picked at the amazing, spicy, southwestern-themed appetizers until Marliss carried out two covered plates, set them in front of them, and removed the covers to reveal a meal as delicious as any he'd had in expensive Mexican restaurants. They dug in.

"Wow, Lou is really good." Rori set down her fork, patted her belly, then sipped at her second refill of margarita.

"Last night, he made me this steak…" Jackson had been amazed at the welcome he'd received from Marliss and Lou. They'd treated him like he was family, gave him the full tour, the codes for the doors and the keys for the vehicles. After they'd shown him which bedroom his half-brother, Dylan, had used the week before, he'd chosen the one next to it, with a view of the lake. Marliss had even brought his supper to his room, where he sat at the table watching TV for a while until he gave it up and began counting the stars as they appeared over the lake.

"That good, huh?" Rori's smile warmed him deep inside.

"Sorry, this is all a lot to take in." He blinked down at the food on his plate. And it would be so easy to get used to. He looked toward the hillside behind the house. The orange glow told him the sun was getting close to the horizon. "C'mon." He stood. "Let's go watch the sunset."

She jumped up and reached for her plate.

"No. Don't touch that." He glanced toward the kitchen. "I learned the hard way that we don't bus our own dishes. That's

Marliss's job."

"Oh, that's too funny." Rori lifted her hands as if in surrender. "Wouldn't want to get into any trouble."

He took her hand and led her around the side of the house and down the gradual sloping walkway to the sandy lakeshore. Three docks jutted into the water, two of them holding boats and a pontoon, the other longer, with personal watercraft, both motorized and paddle-driven. A gazebo sat at the end of the dock.

"This is pretty impressive." Rori held tight to his hand, and it felt too right to Jackson. Like she was someone he'd known for a long time.

Outside the gazebo stood a swinging seat just big enough for two, and he gestured for her to sit.

She didn't move, just looked up at him, the orange glow of the sun shimmering in her hair, sparkling in her eyes. "Jackson."

"Darlin'." He stepped closer, his belt buckle brushing against her stomach. "I've been wanting to do this all day."

After glancing at the water, she blinked her pretty eyes up at him. "Throw me in?"

"Not hardly." He slid his hands along her arms to her shoulders, slowly, gently, giving her plenty of room to say no. When she tipped her head, he had to take. Pressing his lips to hers, he let a wash of desire flood him, hardening him in his jeans, and sending his thoughts to the two of them in his bedroom.

His tongue slid along the seam of her lips, tasting sweet and sour margarita, before he pressed it inside her mouth, tasting the deep, warm spices of their supper mixed with the addictive flavor of her.

Her arms wrapped around his neck as she pulled herself closer to him, deepening the kiss.

Against his shirt, burning through layers of fabric, her nipples rubbed, hard and hot against his chest. She let out a little moan that made him far too wild.

Sliding one hand down her back, he cupped her ass, squeezing the firm, ripe roundness as his tongue played with hers. Then it hit him. Rori was okay with this? He ended the kiss but stayed just an inch from her lips. "You know, I'm still a rodeo cowboy."

Her eyes, unfocused and darker blue than the evening sky, shifted left, then right. "I know, but I've made peace with it."

Backing away another inch, he narrowed his eyes. "How so?"

****

Rori shrugged. "First..." She thought for a few seconds.

"That's how you like to get your points across, Ms. Hughes. Logically, and in perfect order."

With a smile, she closed her eyes. "You noticed that in me?"

"Yeah. First..." He laughed. "It's because it's different from anyone else I know."

"Is that why you like me?" She felt her face heat. Had she really just asked him that? And sounded like a teenager with her first crush?

"Oh, no you don't. You're not changing the subject. You finish telling me your list." He guided her to the swing and sat them hip-to-hip, his arm around her shoulders. "First..." he prodded.

"First, I know you'll be leaving this town, probably never returning." It killed her to realize she might never see him again, but facts were facts. "So the whole rodeo problem ends Sunday when you fly out of Kansas."

He stared at her, but his lips thinned slightly.

"Second, people have seen us together, so gossip has more than likely spread to about half the population of Red Creek, and by tomorrow, we should have total saturation."

A corner of his mouth quirked.

"You know they're assuming we're getting cozy, so we may as well do it."

Jackson let out a laugh. "Those are your reasons? I'm short-term and we're assumed guilty already?"

She turned in to him, pressing her hand on his chest. His hard, well-developed chest, where his heart beat strong and fast. Warm tugs pulled at her core, and she barely refrained from pressing her thighs together and wiggling with the pleasure. "Um…" What had she been about to say? "No. Yes. No." She shook her head a few times to clear it. "I feel this pull toward you, like a chemical reaction, or a magnetic force." She needed to admit it, to him and to herself. "From the moment you walked up to me at your company, and then in your office, I thought I might just kiss you. For no reason." Recalling those moments, her heart beat faster, too.

Jackson cupped her cheek and leaned closer. "Don't need a reason." He slanted his mouth on hers, opening his lips and sweetly running his tongue along her teeth, then tasting her mouth and teasing her tongue with his.

She laced her fingers through the back of his hair, thick and silky, she loved how it curled just a little around her fingers. With a tug, she ended the kiss and touched the tip of her nose on his. "Your turn." Her voice came low and breathy, sounding too far gone for her own good.

"That voice of yours. The second I heard it, I got ideas." His fingertip traced along her collarbone to the base of her neck, then moved slowly downward as his eyes followed the movement. "But when I looked around the corner and saw you…" His hand flattened under her breast, wrapping his fingers around her ribcage. He looked into her eyes. "I knew you wanted to kiss me."

She laughed. "I think you started it. In your office, you leaned—" Her phone chimed. She pulled it from her pocket. "It's my contact. He's going to need a couple more hours to try to get the info we need."

"Perfect." He stood, holding out his hand to her. "I know how we're going to spend those hours."

Laying her palm on his, that magic jolt rolled through her again. She stood. "Not on a computer?" Her knees wobbled a bit and she held tighter.

"Doesn't sound like the most comfortable of positions, but if

193

you're into that kind of kinky…" He wagged his brows at her.

She giggled. Again. Something she hadn't done for years, until she met Jackson Walker.

He tugged her closer and guided her along the dock. Lights set into the edges of the boards guided the way back to shore. "There's a side door with stairs up to the bedrooms."

They moved quickly along the walkway, and between her desire and her anxiousness, she had a hard time catching her breath.

Wrapping his arm around her, he jostled her a little. "You okay? You look like you're walking into a police lineup."

How did she tell him it'd been a while since the last time? "I'm good."

"Hm. Those are not exactly the words a guy wants to hear." He stopped, set his hands on her shoulders, and turned her toward him. "If you're not sure about this…"

She couldn't remember ever wanting a man the way she craved this cowboy. Was it the bad boy aspect of his rodeo life? The fact that she'd never started a relationship with a man who she knew would be gone in a few days? Or just the big, sexy muscles and blue eyes that turned her tummy to jiggling jelly? "I'm sure, Jackson." She took his hands in hers and backed toward the house. "Now stop your stalling."

He grinned. "Yes, ma'am."

In minutes they'd gotten in the house and up the stairs, and stood in Jackson's bedroom with the door closed behind them, the small lamp on the bedside table casting a romantic glow. The place was more rustic than she'd imagined after seeing the outside, but it fit Dusty's personality. The log-framed king-size bed took up half the room. Across from it, a couch and two chairs faced a flat-stone fireplace. The dressers and nightstand matched the bed, and a thick red rug covered most of the hardwood floor.

Rori pointed to a door. "Bathroom?"

"Yeah." He dimmed the light. "Help yourself."

She didn't have any birth control, didn't take anything. "Do you have…protection?" She gripped her hands in front of her.

His head shot up, his gaze locking with hers. "I do. But don't think that just because we're up here, I've gone past the point of no return."

Damn, how had he gotten to be such a gentleman? She'd love to meet his mother someday. Giving herself a mental head slap, she reminded herself that this was temporary. *Temporary!* Rori walked to where Jackson stood by the window. "It's gone past that point for me already." Attempting a seductive smile, she felt her lips quiver. She really liked this guy. Liked everything about him so far.

He wrapped his arms around her and pulled her tight against him. "Good, 'cause I've just about worn out my restraint."

"Good." Rori went up on tiptoes and kissed him.

Chapter Five

Rori let go of all her restraint too, her lips taking what she wanted from Jackson, her tongue doing its own exploration of his mouth. How was it that he tasted like spices and sex all at the same time?

She pulled back and slid her fingers to the button at his chest. "I'm ready to see what I'm gettin' myself into." Unbuttoning each one slowly, she trailed her fingertips along his chest, loving the few hairs that curled around her fingers on her path downward.

Tugging his shirt from his jeans, she slid it back, down his big arms, and let him toss it aside. Defined pecs, nice six-pack abs, and a narrow, tight waist. "Yummy." She leaned forward and kissed the spot next to one of his tight, flat nipples.

He growled. "My turn to unwrap my dessert." Jackson pulled the bottom of her shirt up, she lifted her arms, and he dragged the thing off and threw it. His breath left him in a rush as he stared at the red lace demi-bra that showed more of her breasts than it covered. "Beautiful." He cupped the sides of her breasts and ran his thumbs across the tight points of her nipples.

Rori's eyes rolled back for a few seconds and sweet chills shimmied across her skin. Licking her lips, she looked into his eyes as she reached for his belt buckle. It took a few seconds to unhook it, then she flipped open the button on his jeans and slowly dragged his zipper down.

His eyes turned a darker blue and his breath came faster, moving his chest up and down in a primal rhythm that matched her breathing.

Pressing her fingers to the bulge at his open zipper, Rori felt a power fill her, the ability to make this strong, irresistible man desire her this much could become very addictive. "You're hard."

His lips curved upward as his hands slid down her sides to her waistband. "And I bet you're soft." Jackson poked the tip of his tongue between his front teeth. "And I bet you're sweet and wet."

Between her legs, she became just that, wet and hot and aching with the need to be touched by him, tasted until she came for him. "Guess you'll just have to find out." Wherever this uncharacteristic boldness came from, she'd make it work for her. And him.

He unbuttoned and unzipped her pants, then with the speed of a cobra, he picked her up in his arms and deposited her on the bed, catching one of her feet as she bounced up. "What's with these shoes, darlin'?"

Her red, high-top, canvas tennies always gave guys pause. "The rubber soles." She watched as he unlaced her. "They don't conduct any static electricity."

Lifting one brow, he glanced at her face, then back to her foot. "Practical, yet quirky." He pulled off her shoe, revealing her striped socks. "I wouldn't have expected anything less." He peeled off her socks and gazed at the coat of pink polish she'd slapped on her toenails this afternoon before heading over to his office.

She'd been called weird before, so his assessment of her wasn't any kind of a shock. Rori was also tall, so even cowgirl boots sometimes made her inches taller than men she wanted to flirt with. But with Jackson, she could wear stilettos and still be eye-to-eye with him.

With his gaze locked with hers, he kissed each one of her toes. And she giggled.

He laughed, made quick work of her other shoe and sock, then got down to business, pulling off her jeans and throwing them across the room.

The matching red lace panties felt soaked and warm between her legs. They grew even wetter as his gaze traveled along her legs to fasten on the spot where she needed his lips. "You're beautiful, Rori. Desirable, sexy, smart, funny, interesting." His gaze shot to her eyes. "After I taste you and make you scream my name…"

Her hips jerked up and her vision flickered between darkness and light as sparks ignited in her belly.

"Then I'm going to try to figure out if you're as perfect as you seem to be." He slid his hands up her thighs and grasped her panties, pulling them down slowly. "Oh god, yes." His voice quavered.

She'd spent a good hour in the shower this afternoon, buffing and shaving.

"So pretty. Bare naked and dripping honey to lure me in." He tossed her panties in a different direction than her jeans, toed off his boots, then knelt between her legs, staring at her pussy.

Unable to stop it, her hips circled slowly, little movements that pumped up her desire, her uncontrollable need for him. Only him. Nothing, no one else, ever mattered the way he did right this second.

Jackson eased her legs open and lay between them, on his side, his soft hair brushing her thigh, his firm lips kissing his way up, slowly, staring at her, teasing as he moved closer.

"Your scent, patchouli, right?"

"Uh…" She didn't remember which body scrub she'd used today, didn't give a damn if she ever did, as long as he kept drawing closer, closer. Then he was there, his lips on her, touching and kissing every inch of her, down lower, lower, then up to the top of her mound where his tongue flicked inside to find her tight little bud.

She jerked and cried out.

"Easy, darlin'." He kissed lower again, then spread her legs even further and stared at the quivering lips between her thighs. "If I thought you were beautiful before, holy hell, you're like breath for a drowning man."

So poetic, so sensual. She almost hated for him to stop talking, but she needed more from him. Letting out a little whine, she tipped her hips up toward him.

"Ah, let me guess. Telling me without words to get busy?" He pressed his tongue deep inside her canal, swirling it around and around as he sucked at her juices.

So close to climax already, buzzing started in her head, swirling and swelling until she felt nothing but his mouth on her.

Moving his tongue from her core to her clit, he used his thumbs to part her, looked closely at her, then dove in, taking her bud between his lips and sucking, rubbing his lips on her, touching her every... "Oh Jackson, yes!" The words blasted out of her as she stiffened and blew apart, her mind shattering in a million different directions as her body flooded with heat, her core contracted tighter with each heartbeat. "Jackson." The second wave hit her, making her shake and squeeze her eyes tight, flashing colors popping and shooting off in her head.

Slowly her body relaxed, her thoughts came back from their journey around the universe, and her eyes opened to see him smiling, kissing her pussy lips, and lapping up her cream. "Jackson. Wow. Like, double happiness."

He laughed. "Even your bedroom talk is uniquely Rori."

Feeling her cheeks heat, she gave him a slow smile. "I don't want you to..." She almost said *forget me,* but that would throw a cold, wet blanket over the night. "...get bored."

"Bored." His expression shifted, darkening, his brows dropped and his mouth turned down into a frown.

Had she made him angry?"

****

Jackson froze with the mixture of regret and loss that hit him like a freight train. How could she think he'd be bored with her? She was like no one he'd ever met. Not even like a new chapter in his life, but more like a whole new book he'd never seen before. Unique and quirky, absolutely, but also fresh and honest and smart as anyone he'd ever known.

He crawled up next to Rori and rearranged her so she lay tucked into him, her warm body reminding him how cold his nights were when he slept alone. Which was most always. He'd accept the favors offered from buckle bunnies on the rodeo circuit, but after their hours were up, he'd drive them home, or leave their place, always returning alone to his empty bed.

It was his way of protecting them. He didn't want to become like his father.

"Now, haven't we forgotten something?" Rori's hand brushed the front of his jeans where inside his briefs, his erection prodded through his unzipped fly, thrumming even fuller with her touch.

"I think you might be right." He shifted his hips, letting her tug his jeans down.

Her face in the soft light gave his heart a lurch. Pretty, honest, natural. Not practiced in the art of seduction like the women who went after rodeo cowboys.

Her fingers traced his hard cock through the soft fabric of his briefs. "I think you're ready."

"Darlin', *ready* barely covers it." If he didn't rein himself in, he could pop off at just the touch of her hand. Easing the elastic over the bulge of his shaft, she exposed him, watching with wide eyes as he bobbed free, blood pulsing through his veins, hardening and lengthening him so quickly, his brain fuzzed for a few seconds.

"Oh, wow." She quickly pulled off his remaining clothes and let them drop to the floor. Kneeling near his feet, she bit her lower lip, and slid her hands along his shinbones.

Her gentle touch warmed him, shattered his calm, made him want her fingers brushing along every inch of his skin.

She moved slowly upward, circling, caressing, tracing scars and rubbing the pads of her fingers in divots. "What do you like, Jackson?' Her gaze moved to his and she blinked a few times. Was she nervous?

His usual dirty talk didn't fit the moment, and he hesitated, thinking of the right way to phrase his request. A lazy guy, he enjoyed watching his women ride him, reverse or forward, sometimes both.

"Speechless?" She grinned and leaned forward, taking the

head of his cock into her mouth.

The sight made him jerk and grab fistfuls of the quilt. Her beautiful lips on his shaft, her hair framing her face, her breasts about to spill out of her bra…which he should have removed by now, but unwrapping Rori a little at a time seemed to be his newest hobby.

"Darlin'. So good." He ran his fingers through her thick, silky hair as she teased him in slow motion, her tongue doing wild things, her mouth sucking strong and sure. The temptation to come in her hot mouth nearly did him in. "Ride me." He couldn't wait another minute to be inside her, and he opened the drawer on the bedside table.

Her head popped up and her lips slid off him as he handed her a condom. She opened the packet and slid the thing on him, carefully and accurately. His breath caught for a second. She handled everything like her work ethic in the other pieces of her life. He'd take pleasure in watching her fall apart on top of him.

Crawling up his body, she kissed his ribs, his chest, his chin, then lapped her tongue on his lips. "You'd best hang on, cowboy, 'cause this is gonna be wilder than any eight second ride."

He almost laughed at the cliché, but her eyes told him she was dead serious. Lifting his head, he kissed her, fast and wild, their tongues tangling, their breaths mingling. She ended the kiss, and he let her take charge, let her do what she wanted to him. He was content to lay back and enjoy the fuck out of whatever happened tonight. Why that didn't bother him, he didn't know, but he'd embrace it, let it be okay for him not to need to be in charge.

Lifting herself, she settled back, his cock brushing her soft inner thigh, blood heating his groin in anticipation. She grasped his shaft in her hand, moaning as she eased up, rubbed his blunt head along the hot, slick passage between her legs.

Jackson's eyes rolled back as her warmth promised him heaven. *Hold it together, cowboy.* He couldn't embarrass himself and shoot off the second she—

Rori dropped down onto him, her tight core fisting around him so snug and hot, he almost did what he'd sworn not to. Sucking in a breath, he lifted his head and stared at the perfection of his cock sliding deep inside her pussy. A picture he'd keep in his mind forever.

Dropping her head back, she shuddered and licked her lips.

"Damn, woman. You're perfection." He wanted to say more, let her know he could do this with her for the next hundred years and still be just as turned on, but neither of them wanted long-term. Right?

Her gaze met his, her eyes dark-blue as sunset now, her pupils enormous. "You're so big." She eased up then back down, taking more of him inside her, welcoming him into her body.

"Take it slow, Rori. Take it any fucking way you want it."

That put a naughty smile on her face, and she leaned forward a few inches, placing her palms on his chest, capturing his nipples between her fingers. "I want it crazy, Jackson." Squeezing her fingers together, she pinched his nipples, causing ripples of lust to spread through his body.

With a groan, he sat forward and reached behind her, unhooking her bra and slowly pulling it from her. Her breasts popped free, showing off her cherry red nipples, the same color as her beautiful pussy, hardened and puckered. Cupping her breasts, he stared for long moments before moving in and sucking one into his mouth.

Her taste was sweet, the scent of her filling his nostrils as she puffed breaths in and out, then threaded her fingers into his hair. He moved his lips to her other breast, taking it in, teasing and nibbling on it.

"Oh, yes." She lifted her body, sliding her pussy along his cock until only the head remained inside her. "This will work."

He chuckled, his lips still locked on her nipple. The way she always said what was on her mind amazed him.

She dropped her body back onto his cock, impaling herself.

He gasped a breath, releasing her nipple, and she pushed against his shoulders until he lay on the bed. Her gaze locked with his. "I need this. Right now."

Damn, that sexy voice of hers nearly made him shoot off. He played with her nipples as she used her thigh muscles to ride him, slowly and thoroughly at first, then faster, gaining speed and pushing herself toward climax with the power of desperation.

She sat up, grasping his wrists to keep his hands on her breasts, using that to give her leverage as she bounced up and down quickly, her head dropping to the side as her breath came in rhythmic gasps. "Uh, Jackson." She whispered the words, but to him, it was like a shouted order.

Moving his hand to the apex of her legs, he brushed his thumb against her mound, burrowing it in to find her hard little button. Her hands still clasped both wrists, the sexiest touch he'd ever experienced as her motion let her ride along his thumb.

Within seconds, she shook and cried out, a high-pitched scream that ramped up his desire until he nearly followed her over into climax. At the last second, he pulled himself in, holding his orgasm at bay.

She slowed her manic ride, her body flushing pink, her hands loosening her grip on his wrists, her head dropping forward, until with one last shudder, she went limp.

He caught her and eased her flat on top of him, her face nestled at his neck, her body hot, burning onto his. Sliding his rock-hard shaft from her, he wrapped his arms around her, letting her pant and shiver with the aftershocks of her orgasm.

"I've seriously never experienced anything that intense." She whispered the words against his neck. "I can't explain it. Just...so frickin' weird."

He chuckled, kissing her head between his bursts of laughter. Did this woman know how perfect her words sounded to him? How new and sincere? Something warm wrapped itself around his heart, filling his chest. Who was he holding in his arms?

Rori lifted her head, her eyes glazed, her cheeks bright pink. "But you're still hard as steel." She wiggled her hips, proving his erection still lay full and nearly painful with need. "And it's my turn to tell you what I want."

His hips jerked with the burst of lust her words evoked. "Anything you want, Rori, darlin'. Just name it, and I'm your servant."

Chapter Six

Rori couldn't stop shocking herself with the things she blurted out. It was her turn to tell him what she wanted? Where had that come from? It felt as if her two outrageous orgasms had drained all her normal thought processes away and left her without a filter between her brain and mouth. Well, worse than usual.

Lying flat on top of him, both of them bare naked, she pressed her hips softly toward his hard, sheathed erection. "Something I've always liked." Looking around his bedroom in Dusty's big house on the lake, she hoped he'd locked the door, because she'd be doing some screaming when she got Jackson where she wanted him.

He smacked her butt. "You gonna tell me, or do I have to waste time guessin'?" His sexy smile belied his coaxing words.

"I like to be…" A flush of heat rose to her face. "On my hands and knees." It felt so empowering to say what she wanted.

He froze for a second, then with a growl, he turned them to their sides, knelt beside her, and picked her up as if she weighed nothing. Placing her on her hands and knees in front of him, he massaged her butt cheeks, his hands firm and his callouses abrading lightly, sending lovely aching contractions to her core, moistening her pussy lips.

With a moan, Rori arched her back downward, turned to look at him, and stared into the midnight blue of his eyes. "Do you like this position, too?"

His breath left him audibly as his eyes rolled back and his body shook. "Fuck yeah, darlin'. This is what you want, it's what I love."

His words crept into her soul and made her heart thump an extra beat. Love. How had a wild night of sex turned into love? She dropped her head, shaking it. No, this wasn't love. This was—

In one slick motion, Jackson pushed his cock deep inside her waiting canal, pumping in and out, going deeper with each forward press, faster with each withdrawal. His fingers played along her back door, touching her anal opening softly, pulsing, pressing.

The combination of his thick cock inside her, his decadent play on her rosebud back there, and his fast, loud breaths, turned her belly, her core, into hot, needy, quivering bliss. His pumping, his balls slapping hard against her bare pussy, sent electric currents up her spine to short-circuit her brain. "Jackson, can't hold on." She wanted to come with him, wanted them both to connect in those moments.

"Not yet, Rori. Hold on." He slid his hand upward along her spine. Everywhere he touched, tingles radiated outward, pebbling her skin, ending at her nipples where the pressure tightened her breasts.

Rori's arms quivered, and she fought to keep herself up, struggled to hold back the climax that threatened to hack into her mind and send her soaring.

Jackson gripped her hips, moving her forward with each withdrawal, then slamming her back against him with each pump into her. The motion, the fullness, the feeling of his big cock reaching every hot spot inside her filled her brain with snapping static.

He roared and reached around her hip to her pussy and found her clit, rubbing fast and wild as his hips worked like a jackhammer, pumping his shaft into her faster and harder.

She shouted a laugh as her tension broke and raced out of her, twisting her reality and streaking like pieces of the sun through a black velvet sky. The keening cry of her own voice echoed in her ears, combining with his cries, his shout of, "Rori, darlin'. Oh hell, what have you done to me?"

Rori stayed suspended, floating in silent ecstasy for long moments until her shuddering body regained feeling, realizing she was hanging in midair, then laid down on soft sheets, covered with sweet-smelling blankets, and pulled tight in masculine arms.

Without opening her eyes, she snuggled into Jackson, his chest rising and falling quickly with his breaths, his heart thudding under her palm, his skin moist with a musky coating of manly sweat. She loved every second of this. Kissing him, she licked her lips, tasting the salty, spicy perfection of him.

"That was insane, amazing." His voice rumbled from his chest where her ear pressed to his hot skin.

It was more intense than she'd ever experienced, but she'd already blurted out far too much with this cowboy. "Mmm hmm." A cowboy who would be leaving town in a few days. The thought set her stomach aching in a hollow sorrow. There could never be anything between them. In her mind she knew that for a fact. But her heart beat out a different message.

Brushing back her hair from her face, he tipped his head and looked at her. "That's all you got to say?"

"I wouldn't know where to start." And she didn't want to make a blubbery fool of herself by worshiping at the feet of this sex god.

He laughed. "You usually start with, 'First…'"

A smile curled her lips. "First…let me close my eyes for ten minutes and see if I have any strength left to talk."

He kissed her forehead, reached for the lamp, and shut it off. "Fair enough."

Rori didn't know how long she slept, but her phone's ringing woke her. She lay in the same spot, but now half her body rested on top of Jackson's, her head on his chest.

His chest rose as he yawned. "You need to get that?"

Her mind wouldn't quite connect… "Kiwi." She sat up, listening for the location of her phone in the pocket of her jeans.

Stroking her back, he cleared his throat. "Like the fruit?" He turned on the lamp.

She slid out of bed and located her jeans, pulling out her phone just as it stopped ringing. "No. Like the hacker." Turning her head to face Jackson, she smiled at him, then took a glance down his long torso, narrow hips, semi-hard, beautiful erection, then down his legs, one that was bent, his knee pointing toward the ceiling. "Uh, what was I…"

He stacked his hands under his head and smirked at her, his eyes half closed. "I'm enjoying my view as much as you're enjoying yours."

Rori blinked, then as her phone rang again, she looked at it and pressed answer. How did it get to be three in the morning already? "What did you find?"

Jackson motioned her over and she pressed speaker as she wandered to the bed and sat on the edge of the mattress.

"Some crazy shit going on there in bumfuck Kansas, girl." Kiwi's monotone male voice came from her phone.

She bit back a smile. "I've got my boss here listening. Go ahead."

Kiwi paused. "Sorry about the location dis, man."

Jackson rolled closer, ending on his side with his head propped up on a bent arm. "No problem, brother. I feel the same way about the place."

Rori didn't. She loved almost everything about the town, except for the dating situation, but nobody was asking her opinion. "So what is it?"

Jackson's finger trailed from her shoulder down to her elbow, making her shiver with delight and her nipples perk and tighten. She had to force back the urge to turn off her phone and pounce on the cowboy.

"These accounts? They're being opened and closed in a short span of time, like less than a week."

She frowned at Jackson, and he shrugged, so she asked, "What does that usually mean?"

Kiwi snorted. "Money laundering, drugs, terrorist activity, blackmail, asset hiding, tax evasion. You name it, it could be happening."

"Who's opening the accounts?" Jackson's brows drew down.

Did he suspect his father of illegal activity? Rori couldn't imagine Dusty doing anything illegal. Immoral—like having four illegitimate sons by four separate women—yes, but that was a far shot from breaking the law.

"A holding company out of Kansas City." Typing noises came from the phone. "I haven't isolated the owner yet, but I've called in a favor from the Federal…uh." Kiwi sniffed. "From a friend."

Jackson looked at her, shaking his head.

"He's good," Rori whispered.

"Damn right I am, girl." Kiwi was typing again. "I'll stay on it and get back to you."

"Thanks, buddy. You're the best." She loved this guy like a brother.

"Stay out of trouble, Rori." He hung up.

Jackson pointed to the phone. "*He's* telling *you* to stay out of trouble? That's a laugh."

Setting her phone on the bedside table, she turned to fully face Jackson. "I won't be able to sleep. Can we do some poking at your dad's computers?"

"Can't think of anything else I'd rather do right now." He brushed his knuckles along the side of her breast. "I'm naked, hard as a fencepost, and I have the sexiest woman in the world in my bed. She's just as naked, too." He lifted a brow, his gaze shifting to her face. "So yeah, let's go do a bunch of boring computer shit."

She laughed as she pushed him onto his back and lay on his chest. "What if I promise that every minute we spend on computers, we'll spend twice that long in bed afterward?"

He threaded his fingers in her hair and pulled her down for a kiss. "I need a down payment, darlin'." That one kiss led to a second, then to an hour of the hottest missionary position sex she'd ever had.

****

After they showered and dressed, Jackson held Rori's hand and led her down the front stairs. Lights popped on automatically, and she gasped at the two-story magnificence of the great room that spanned nearly the entire first floor.

Heavy, dark wood, a two-story flat-stone fireplace, lots of leather furniture, and thick rugs covering the hardwood floors added to the rustic elegance.

"This is beautiful." She stood in the middle of the room and turned slowly, her gaze trailing from the original western artwork to family photos. There were no photos of Jackson or his brothers or their mothers, only ones of Dusty, Theresa, and people he guessed were Dusty's in-laws, since he had no parents or siblings left alive.

"Yeah. It's something, I guess." The house sat on acres surrounding half the lake. If he ever wanted to build his own place, there'd be room… He grunted. Why in the flying fuck would he ever build here? He glanced at Rori. She didn't want a rodeo cowboy, and he had no intention of changing his ways.

"What's wrong?" She walked up to him and stared into his eyes. "You look like a hungry bear right now."

"Just wondering what's going to happen to this place." Would they sell it? Turn it into a museum? Would one of his brothers decide to stay here in bumfuck Kansas?

"Turn it into a bed and breakfast. Hire somebody to run it for you."

He nodded. "A possibility."

"It's a little out of the way, but some folks like a quiet place to vacation."

This wasn't his problem. He just wanted to do his time here and get the hell out. And if the beautiful Rori Hughes wanted to help him pass the time—solving a computer mystery and sharing his bed—he'd be the happiest inmate in the history of probate incarceration.

"C'mon, let's get something to eat first." He took her hand and led her through the huge dark dining room into the big kitchen.

"This is like heaven." She ran her fingers over the golden

marble countertops, peeked in the double-wide refrigerator, then sat on one of the chairs at the counter.

"Like heaven? You said you don't cook." He leaned on the counter across from her.

"That doesn't mean I can't appreciate a room this awesome." She swung her gaze back and forth. "Look, you can see out both sides of the house."

He hadn't noticed that before. Big windows framed the lake on one side, and on the other, French doors opened onto the pool deck that glowed with the blue of the pool lights. "Yeah. It's a showplace." He opened the refrigerator. "What're you hungry for?"

A half-hour later, full of reheated leftover Mexican food, they waddled down the hall toward Dusty and Theresa's offices. "I haven't checked out his computers. Or his office." He felt a sorrowful tightening in his chest. His dad was dead, and no matter how angry Jackson was at him for his deceit, he'd loved the guy. He'd miss him.

As if she could sense his mood, Rori ran her hand up and down his arm. "I'm sorry. If this is too much too soon, we can wait."

"No. I'm good. It just didn't seem right before, but now that we have a purpose, I think it'd be wise to get this figured out before I leave." He glanced at her.

Was that a wince? Had Rori winced when he mentioned leaving town? Or was it a little smile of relief? Hell. He had to get his shit straight. Just because she was the most interesting woman he'd met in as long as he could remember, and just because sex with her was friggin' outstanding didn't mean it would be that way forever. Did it?

He stopped outside Dusty's office and snapped on the overhead light. Rori walked in, moving around the desk then tapping on the keyboard. The monitor came to life and she rolled Dusty's modern leather chair closer and sat. The desk looked like it could have come from an old cowboy movie, and the room's dark paneling gleamed like it'd been in place for a hundred years.

She kept typing as he wandered around the room, looking at the western and landscape paintings that looked original, a framed one-dollar bill, a tall bookcase filled with books on geology, and finally the refrigerator-size safe that stood open. Had Dad's attorney opened it? Or had Dylan last week?

"Nothing." Rori shook her head, her nose less than a foot from the monitor. "I don't find anything with the same name, and nothing unusual." She turned in the chair. "Do you know where his laptop is?"

They spent a few minutes searching until he found it in a briefcase in the safe. Rori took it and got busy while Jackson looked through the safe. Papers, legal stuff dealing with the company, the house and land, the airplane, and other holdings. A thin black leather box containing paperwork for Dusty's four houses around the country was hidden among other similar boxes.

Evidently his dad hadn't let his wife see inside the safe. On the bottom, a big box with a cover on it sat at an odd angle. Jackson pulled it out and set it on a side table. He lifted the cover and found a stack of big scrapbooks, the top one with a *D* on it. He pulled it out and flipped open the cover.

A baby picture, an announcement with Dylan's name on it, a picture of a baptism with a minister, his dad, a blonde woman holding a blond baby. "Holy shit."

"What is it?" Behind him, the desk chair squeaked.

He turned and held up a hand to stop her. "Nothing." The word came out too sharp.

Rori stopped halfway-standing, then plopped down again. "Okay." She swallowed before going back to the laptop.

He'd offended her, but he sure as hell wasn't ready to share this. With anyone. The next book in the pile had an *R* on it. Rogue? He'd like to look through that one, see what kind of woman named their kid that. But he wasn't ready to see one with a *J* on it. Not

212

tonight.

Sliding Dylan's book back into the box, he reset the cover and tucked the box back into the safe. He strolled over and sat on the desk next to Dusty's laptop. "Find anything?"

"Just the same file he had on his work computer." She touched the screen a few times and the screen went black. Closing the laptop, she handed it to him. "Would you feel comfortable looking at Theresa's computer?"

He took the laptop from her and walked to the safe, setting the computer back into the briefcase. Although he didn't know Dusty's wife, it felt odd to look at her personal stuff. But if it would help solve the mystery of the bank accounts... "We should, since Dusty had named that file *Theresa*." He gestured for her to go ahead of him, and they walked down the hall to the next room.

Theresa's office was done in light oak, more modern than Dusty's by about a century. Her desk looked delicate, and her pink floral chair matched the curtains. Rori slid right in and fired up the computer while Jackson looked for a safe, but found none. He opened the desk drawers to see if she had a laptop, but didn't find one. He'd ask Marliss about it in the morning.

"Got that printout?" Rori held out her hand to him.

He tugged the folded papers from his pocket and handed it to her, and she spread them flat on the desk and started typing again.

Jackson would love to go back into his dad's office and do more snooping, but it could wait until tomorrow. He glanced at Rori. Unless she didn't have work, and wanted to stay here with him for the day.

"Okay, she doesn't have that same file." Rori practically buzzed with excitement. "But I searched documents around the date of the first entry on Dusty's list." She turned the monitor toward him. "See this document? It's an invoice. From a private detective."

Chapter Seven

Rori watched Jackson's face as he read the invoice on Theresa's monitor.

Then he read it again. His brows dropped. "What does this mean?"

She pointed to the date on the monitor. "Eight years ago." Rori turned and shuffled through the papers Jackson had printed at this dad's office, then she pointed to the first date. "A week after the first payment Dusty made."

"Or received?" Jackson sat on his heels next to her chair. "We didn't think of that. Could he have been the one getting this money? Not paying it?"

"It's possible." She caught Jackson's gaze. "But he has a heck of a lot of money in the bank. Liquid assets that total millions." She pressed her lips together for a second. "Chances are better that he's paying this, rather than receiving it."

"You're right."

"But it's a possibility he was getting this money. Taking it out of the bank in cash." Which smacked of money laundering.

Jackson pulled out his phone and typed. "I'm gonna have Abby pull bank records for a few months and look for these amounts."

"Good idea." She opened another window. "Let me search on this guy's name and see what else comes up." Typing in *Harold Logan*, she clicked search and found only an e-business card. "He's from KC. Want me to print this stuff out? Or email it to you to save a part of a tree?"

He grinned. "You and your new-age cloud crap." Getting to his feet, he leaned over the desk and turned on the small printer. "Best keep my email out of this computer."

She pressed print. "Now you're thinking like a true detective."

After reading the papers, he folded them with the rest and

stuck it back in his pocket. "Until we hear back from your hacker, I guess we're done detecting?" He set his hand on her shoulder and twirled his thumb in a sensual circle on her collar bone.

A blast of arousal rallied deep inside her, spreading to her breasts and all the way down to the needy lips between her thighs. He was diverting her from her curiosity about what they'd found on Theresa's computer, but she could understand his need to keep it private.

She shut down the computer and stood, sidling in and getting right in his space. "We're done computering and detecting. We've already eaten, and I don't like watching TV." She licked her lips and set her hands on his hips.

"There's a gaming console or ten in the billiards room." Jackson tugged her close, his hands sliding to her lower back, his hips working against hers, pushing the hard flesh behind his zipper into her belly. "You wanna do that?"

"I don't wanna do anything in the billiards room." She leaned forward, brushing the hard points of her nipples against his chest, the layers of cloth between them practically nonexistent, the way her body responded.

"Skinny dip?" He leaned in and kissed the corner of her mouth.

"Maybe another time. You've got to get me home before sunrise, you know. Else we give the whole town even more fuel for the gossip fire." Not that he cared, but she did. She had to live here.

"So you're saying, all my efforts to entertain you are just a waste of time?"

Rori nodded.

He grabbed her ass and pulled her up along his body. "Good." He kissed her, quick and thoroughly.

She nearly melted into a soft blob as his tongue took what he wanted, gave her everything she needed. In minutes, they were upstairs in his bedroom, peeling off each other's clothes. She grinned. "This is all the entertainment I was hoping for, Jackson." She grasped his cock in both her hands and knelt. "And consider this…my favorite version of recreation."

****

Jackson sat in his father's chair in the home office, the box of scrapbooks on the desk, front and center. The sun poked above the horizon, shining through the window right onto the box, as if a sign from above.

He'd gotten Rori back to her building and safely inside an hour ago, but when he'd arrived back at the lake house, he couldn't rest. The box kept calling to him, but he wasn't motivated to dive in yet, so he'd been sitting and staring.

Which was less appealing? Looking through his own book, or those of his brothers? Jackson wasn't in a place where he was ready to forgive his dad yet, and he sure as hell wasn't prepared to get to know every damn detail of his half-brothers' lives.

Footsteps padded along the hardwood floor outside the door. Marliss walked past, then backed up and looked at him. The blue of her cotton top and pants was broken up only by her white apron. "Good morning." Her gaze shifted to the box on the desk. "Or is it?" She pulled a sorrowful face.

"I don't know, ma'am." He should call his mother, get some guidance from her, but as long as Marliss was right here and seemed to know what was in the box… "What's the story behind these?" He gestured to the scrapbooks.

She walked in and perched on the arm of one of the guest chairs. "Your dad had a PO box in Kansas City."

A secret PO box. "That was how he had his baby mommas contact him?" The words snapped out of him before he could temper them some.

She fiddled with the hem of her apron. "If that's how you want to put it, yes." Her gaze met his. "But if I were a bettin' woman, I'd wager they were more than that to him. That *you* were more than that to him. Especially with the care he took with those

216

scrapbooks."

This woman and her husband had been with Dusty and Theresa since the beginning, since Dusty married Theresa and took over her family's company. "You knew about us."

With a nod, she let out a breath. "We did." She pulled her phone out of her pocket and texted.

He waited, a little irritated that the conversation they were having was less important to her than whatever she needed to communicate through her phone.

Tucking the phone away, she sat in the chair. "What questions do you have for me?"

Jackson opened his mouth, then closed it. What kind of questions did he want to ask a complete stranger about things his father had shared with her?

"What was Theresa like?" That was safe.

Marliss talked about the woman, about how she'd changed over the years from a quiet, determined woman to a very proper, cool, well-mannered socialite, connecting with other wealthy women in the area, and traveling often to Kansas City for events. Jackson could understand it happening, especially when Theresa realized that Dusty would be gone ninety percent of the time.

"Jackson." Marliss' eyes looked moist. "Ms. Theresa didn't want children."

He felt the blood drain from his face. That's what Benner had said, too, but it just didn't make sense. Why marry a woman who didn't want kids, when Dusty evidently did? Desperately enough to father four.

She shifted in her chair. "Lou and I knew this from hearing them shouting at each other. Ms. Theresa didn't tell him until after they were married, after they'd built this big house, and Mr. Walker was running the company. I think it made your dad a little crazy." She waved one hand. "Not in a bad way, but that's when he started traveling a lot. Staying away from home most of the time."

Jackson could almost commiserate with his dad. Almost. Not

217

to the point of forgiving him for deceiving five women the way he had done.

Footsteps sounded, then Marliss' husband, Lou, stood in the doorway holding a heavy-laden tray.

So that was who Marliss had texted.

"Heard there was a party in here?" Lou gave a crooked smirk and stepped inside, his long, fit body and handsome face—even for a sixty-year-old—giving him the appearance of a movie star. Especially with that full head of gray hair.

Jackson picked up the box and set it on the floor so Lou could set down the tray.

Lou poured three cups of coffee, handed one to his wife, set one on a coaster for Jackson, then took his and sat in the chair next to Marliss.

The scent of cinnamon and freshly-baked sweet dough hit Jackson, and he automatically reached for one of the rolls, the warm frosting coating his fingers. He stuffed about half of it in his mouth and couldn't help the groan that escaped him.

Marliss patted her husband's forearm. "Another satisfied customer."

Lou sat quietly. The man didn't say much, but he didn't have to when his wife was around.

"Jackson was just wondering about the scrapbooks." She crossed her legs. "We found out about you boys when you were just a few years old. Your father seemed almost glad that someone knew his secret. He talked with us about you...all of you." Leaning forward, she stared into Jackson's eyes. "He really did care about you."

Jackson scratched his head. "The one thing I can't figure out was why he didn't let us know we had brothers." The faces of his three siblings popped into his head. Killian, taller than the others, that black hair and black eyes matching the anger Jackson sensed rolling off his brother. The guy was a smartass, though, and Jackson had appreciated the way Killian had handled the attorney at the reading of the will.

Rogue's hair had looked nearly the same color as Jackson's, but the guy had those clear green eyes. Smart as all shit, Rogue had a cool aura around him, like nothing bothered him. And the youngest, Dylan, his hair almost blond, with that amusement in his hazel eyes. He'd blurted out a whole lot of the stuff Jackson had wanted to say, but couldn't find words in his state of shock.

"Can't rightly answer that." Lou frowned. "While we were happy to listen, it wasn't our place to question your father's decisions."

Jackson looked down at the box on the floor. These scrapbooks would let him get to know his brothers. But there was nothing that'd help him understand Dusty. Why he'd kept four women in different parts of the country, and why he'd kept his sons ignorant of each other.

Marliss stood. "Why don't we give you some space, and if you have questions, just text us and we'll come back."

He looked up at the woman. She would have been an amazing grandmother to have around while he was growing up. "Thanks."

Lou stood. "I'll bring your breakfast in here."

Jackson nodded. He'd confessed to Lou the morning before that he ate the same thing every morning: scrambled eggs, breakfast meats, and pancakes. Some days, like yesterday, twice a day. "Thanks, Lou. I'd appreciate that."

The couple left, taking their cups with them. Jackson slid the computer over to one corner and pulled out the scrapbooks, laying them side-by-side according to the age of each Walker boy.

He set his jaw. It'd be Killian first, then Rogue. He'd skip his own and look at Dylan's next. Save his own for last. He had the feeling it would be less traumatic reading his own after getting a look at the others. Or maybe he was just chicken-shit, and wanted to put it off as long as possible.

Refilling his coffee cup, Jackson shoveled down another one of Lou's amazing cinnamon rolls, then settled back, sliding

Killian's scrapbook in front of him. He opened the front cover, and there was his dad, the woman who must be Killian's mother, with her black hair and eyes, and baby Killian, maybe just a few days old with a shock of black hair. And the homeliest face Jackson had ever seen on a baby. Laughing, he sent a text to Abby at the office, telling her he'd be working from home for a few hours.

Flipping the page, he settled in to learn what he could about the three men he'd been thrust into brotherhood with. The thought didn't upset him as much as it once had.

****

After a huge breakfast, a few more rolls at around ten, and a fantastic lunch of cheese-stuffed hamburgers and homemade fries, Jackson chose to set aside his own scrapbook and look at it later. He had enough to take in with the life history of his three brothers.

He stepped out of the house into the heat of the early afternoon. After the chill of the air conditioner, it almost felt good. As he walked across the grass, he pulled his phone out of his pocket and pressed his mother's number.

"Hello, honey." Sapphire's soft voice carried across the miles. "How are things there?" She'd seemed hesitant when he told her about his week in Kansas, but she'd agreed with him when he said he felt obligated to do it.

"Going well. People are nice."

His mom laughed. "Thanks for the detailed update."

He grinned. "I'll fill you in when I get home Sunday. I'm taking lots of pictures, like you asked."

"Thanks. I'm just…curious. You can understand that." Her voice came out sad and breathy.

"I do, Mom." He didn't know how to bring up the subject of the scrapbook.

"Any surprises?"

Jackson thought of the document with the bank account numbers, but his mother wouldn't be interested in that. "The house is on a lake. I didn't expect that."

"You know how much your dad loved to be out on the ocean." Her voice caught on the last words. "I always pictured him living near the water somewhere."

Jackson scraped the toe of his boot in a dry patch of the lawn. "Yeah. He sure has it here." Would his mother ever want to come to Red Creek? See the business and house that Jackson now owned a stake in? He gazed out over the lake. Lots of lakefront here. If he could take a portion for himself, build a little house... Hell, what was he thinking? Setting down roots was not in the future for him.

"Mom?" He had to ask her about the scrapbook.

"Yes, honey?"

"Did you know about the post office box in Kansas City?"

She stayed silent for a while. "I did. I'm guessing you found your dad's stash?"

"Yeah, he put it all in a scrapbook."

"Really? He never mentioned that."

Jackson snorted. Probably the only way the old man could keep his four boys' lives straight. "I haven't looked at it yet."

"You should." Sapphire hummed softly. "He was still your dad, no matter who else called him dad, too."

Her words hit a nerve deep in his heart while they generated thoughts in his head.

"Honey, I'm sorry, I have to go. I'm in the middle of a class of fourth graders, and you can imagine..."

He laughed. "I sure can. Love you, Mom. See you soon."

"I love you too, honey. Call anytime. Take care of yourself." She ended the call.

Jackson slipped into the driver's seat of the company pickup. How the hell did he know if he was taking care of himself or not?

Walking through the front door of the office, he nodded to Abby and headed down the hall.

"Mr. Walker." Her sing-song voice stopped him.

"Yes, Mrs. Hollister?" He turned, giving her a smirk. She was one of his favorite people in town. Her and Vic and Elaine and

Cubby and his wife Sherry, and Marliss and Lou. And jeez, Rori. Last night…holy hell. The woman had already become an obsession.

"I have those bank reports you wanted." She stood and spread papers along the high counter. "I printed them out because I know how you hate that computering stuff." She winked.

He nodded. "Much appreciated, ma'am."

Abby blushed a little, then pointed to a number. "This amount was deducted from the general fund account." Moving to the next paper, she pointed to the same amount. "And again the next month." She pointed to the next paper. "Here again." Frowning, she looked up at him. "I checked back a few years, and the same day every month, this amount, or one just a bit smaller, went out every month. Dusty categorized it as General Miscellaneous Reserve." After glancing behind her, she turned and leaned toward Jackson. "Which means jack shit."

He laughed, surprised at her honesty. "That's what I was thinking, too." He didn't want Abby to continue to look into this, or to say anything to anyone. "I know what it was for, so we're good." Jackson gathered up all the papers, folded them, and shoved them in his back pocket, along with the other papers Rori had printed out for him. Pretty soon, he'd be carrying around a frickin' briefcase full of them. That visual made him half nauseous.

"Okay." She didn't sound completely certain. "But if you want me to do more looking, I'll be glad to."

"Thanks. I got this. We're all set."

"You're welcome." She held up a small pink paper. "And guess what? You've had your first phone call." Handing it over, she smiled. "Rori has that information you were looking for, but didn't want me to call and interrupt you at home."

He looked at the note. *Data on those numbers has come in. Call or stop by.* Spinning on his heel, he strode to the door. "Thanks. I'll be back."

"Take your time." Another sing-song answer.

Was the whole town talking about them? He stepped out into the hot midafternoon sun, the humid air making his dark green cotton button-down hot as an oven as he checked for traffic and cut across the street. If there was a rush hour here, he'd bet it consisted of seven, maybe eight, cars at the most.

He pushed open the glass door of Cyber Wise and the cool air hit him as a buzzer went off overhead.

"Be right there." Rori's voice carried from the back of the building.

Wandering past the rows of computers, he shook his head. How did he and Rori, two such opposite people, end up having sexual chemistry that exploded like rodeo fireworks?

She stepped into the room, and all Jackson could see was that beautiful face lit with a glowing smile. The little makeup she'd drawn on made him more than half-hard down below, and her usual jeans, logo T-shirt, and high-top tennis shoes gave him wild ideas about locking up the store and taking her upstairs.

He advanced on her and she shook her head. "Oh, no you don't." She held up one finger. "It's business hours. We can't just—"

Jackson pulled her against him, nibbled on the tip of that one tempting finger, and pressed his lips on hers, swallowing her last words, tasting coffee on her tongue. He could kiss her for hours. "Don't you have a *Closed* sign?" He licked a path along her lips.

She sighed and rubbed closer to him. "I do, but I have a customer coming in this afternoon."

"I'd offer to make it a fast one, but that's not what a woman wants to hear."

She raised her brows and smiled.

"Or does she?" He cupped the side of her breast.

"Let me show you what Kiwi found first." She backed away a step, gestured for him to follow, then turned and walked to the back of the store.

"I always picture him green and fuzzy." He followed, walking a little crooked due to the swelling cock pressing hard against his jeans.

She sat at a chair next to a huge table full of electronics and typed on a laptop. "The guy is pretty fuzzy, but definitely not green." She turned the computer toward him.

He leaned both hands on the table, looking at the monitor. "What is this?" The same name appeared over and over.

"This is the person who opened and closed these accounts." She pulled a face.

Shaking his head, he straightened, his hands fisting at his sides. "This has got to be some kind of a mistake."

Chapter Eight

Rori turned the laptop back toward her, scrolling through the file her friend Kiwi had sent that morning. Each one of the accounts on Dusty's list had been created by his attorney, the town's attorney, Stanley Benner.

Jackson's face grew pale. "What the fuck does that mean?"

She sat back in her chair. "I don't know. You'll have to ask Benner." She'd been working on that question all morning. Another thing that seemed too convenient to be a coincidence was the close proximity of the date of Theresa's private investigator's invoice and the fact that Dusty had named the file after his wife. Was that part of this mystery? It had to be. "But Benner's out of town until Friday."

His gaze shot to hers.

"I checked when I got this list." If Benner had been in town this morning, she would have gotten in touch with Jackson even if she'd had to drive out to his house and barge her way in. They hadn't exchanged phone numbers. The thought gave Rori an empty feeling in her stomach.

He paced the room, back and forth a few times, then pulled out his phone. "I could call him, but I want to see his face when I confront him with this." His words came out clipped, his jaw tight. Dialing, he looked at her then put the phone to his ear. "This is Jackson Walker. I'd like to make an appointment with Mr. Benner." He paused. "Yes, this is urgent, but no, I don't want to do this over the phone."

A few minutes later, he hung up. "Friday, one in the afternoon. He flies in that morning." Jackson paced again. "It's going to drive me crazy, imagining what Benner and Dusty were doing." He pulled out a stack of folded papers from his back pocket and sat on the corner of the table. "Here's what Abby found." Jackson showed her the money going out of Dusty's account, then frowned

225

at her. "What was this? Were they into something illegal together? Was Benner scamming Dad?"

"Be sure to show Benner Theresa's private eye invoice, see if—"

"Uh uh." He folded the papers and stuck them in his pocket. "You're comin' with me."

"To see Benner?" She hadn't expected that.

He took her hands and pulled her out of the chair. "Yeah, to see Benner." He nodded toward the front door. "But first to turn that *Closed* sign, then to get hauled upstairs for a few hours."

Rori couldn't resist those sweet eyes, those full, sensual lips that she could almost feel on her nipples and on the soft spots between her legs. Pulses of heat beat down low, spiraling a muzzy compliance through her whole body. Glancing at the time on the laptop, she nodded. "I've got an hour and a half before—"

Jackson tugged her with him to the front door, flipped the sign while she set the locks and turned off the lights.

"You're gonna get me in trouble, cowboy." This time, she pulled him along with her to the back of the building and up the steps to her apartment.

"I didn't mention it, but trouble is my middle name." He said it so seriously, she stopped mid-stairway and turned to look at him.

The grin on his face needed kissing so badly, she ran the rest of the way up the steps, hauling her willing bronc rider with her.

****

Four hours later, Rori stood at the front door of Cyber Wise and said goodbye to her customers, an older farm couple who were looking for a new computer system. She'd had lunch with the wife, Grace, a few times, and they'd bonded quickly.

The woman waited inside until her husband walked out the front door. "Rori, please don't take this the wrong way, but you look tired. Is everything okay?"

Rori wasn't so much tired as she was afterglowing. The last hours had been torturous, trying to concentrate on computers when all her mind could focus on was the wild, amazing sex she and Jackson had had up in her bedroom. And on the couch. And in the kitchen.

"I haven't been getting enough sleep." Two hours earlier, when Grace had called from outside the locked front door, Rori had wrestled into her clothes while showing Jackson where the back door and outside exit were. Now, she was ready for a nap. Up all night with him the night before, worn out by their afternoon delight.

"I've heard you're getting to know Jackson Walker." Grace smiled, but Rori knew she was looking for some inside information.

Rori could feel her face heat. "I work for his company."

"That's not really an answer." She looked outside where her husband waited patiently for her in the hot sun. "I've got to run, but don't you worry about me spreading gossip." Grace winked at her. "I'm just happy you're having some fun, finally."

"Thanks." She liked the woman, but dreaded the weeks and months after Jackson left Red Creek when Grace and everyone else in town would be looking at Rori with pity in their eyes. "I'll call you when the computers are ready to be installed."

Grace left the building and walked down the street with her husband.

Rori missed her own folks. They'd be back from vacation soon to start getting prepared for the school year, and she'd make a trip to KC to visit them. Her stomach rumbled. She hadn't eaten since breakfast and as she reached to lock the door, she spotted Jackson jogging across the street.

Where the hell did that man get his energy? She quickly flipped the *Closed* sign and turned off the lights, laughing when his jog turned into a full-out run.

She stepped back out of the way as he pushed in through the door. "You wouldn't lock me out, would ya, darlin'?"

Rori scanned the street to make sure they weren't being

watched, then stepped up to him for a kiss. Short and sweet, it still made her want to haul him upstairs with her. They hadn't tried out her shower yet...

"Grab your swimsuit. Let's go to my place and get out on the lake." The sparkle in his eyes had her envisioning a younger, less cynical Jackson."

"You know how to drive a boat?" She set her hands on her hips and raised one eyebrow.

"I grew up a block from the ocean. Yes, I know how to 'drive' a boat." He opened the door. "I'll get the truck and pick you up—"

"Out back." She shuffled him out of the building. "Pick me up out back in five minutes."

He looked confused, then nodded. Rori locked up and ran up the stairs, trying to remember where she'd stored her swimsuits. Had she offended Jackson, asking to be picked up out back? Better that than out front, where half the town would witness it. She and Jackson would already be a hot topic around the bars and the restaurant. No sense adding more gasoline to that conflagration of gossip.

She pulled her one-piece out of the closet, then grabbed the two-piece too, and stuffed them, with shorts and a tank top plus flip-flops, into a big Cyber Wise branded tote bag.

Checking the back of the building, she didn't spot any cars or pedestrians. Since when did she care who knew she and Jackson were together? Wasn't that her reason for hooking up with him? Everyone was already talking. May as well make the best of the short time they had together.

That reminder hit her like a brick to the chest, and she rubbed the spot over her heart. "It's not because of Jackson leaving." Talking to herself always helped her sort out her thoughts. She grabbed her sunglasses and trudged down the steps to the back door, stepped outside, and hid herself behind her big white Cyber Wise van. "It's because you do care what people think of you, silly girl. No matter what you tell yourself."

She'd repeat that every time she ached thinking about him leaving. Something that'd been happening far too often for her own good.

****

Jackson gunned the double inboards on the big-ass pontoon, propelling them out onto Osprey Lake and put his arm around Rori, who sat next to him in shorts and a skimpy pink bikini top, her giant, round sunglasses covering half her face.

She rubbed her hand along his bare abs, causing lust to clench low in his gut. He took a breath. Tonight wasn't about finding new sex positions and exploring each other's sensual triggers. He wanted to have fun with her, show her he wasn't in this just for the sex.

But wasn't this week with her just about sex? True, it was, but he'd needed somebody to have fun with, to spend time with, and not just spend every minute together naked and intertwined. Although, the thought of that made him hard as a hammer.

Rori pointed to a big white bird flying across the lake. Osprey Lake was figure-eight shaped, and he'd learned that he and his brothers now owned over half the shoreline. Convenient for privacy.

His stomach rumbled. "Okay if we eat first?" He spoke into her ear as the cool air off the lake rushed by them.

"First?" She kissed his shoulder. "What do you have planned for seconds?"

He laughed. Damn, she was naughty, and he loved it. "Seconds we'll have to figure out on the fly." And not the one on his swimming trunks. They'd changed in the house then walked down to the docks where two pontoons, three power boats, a sailboat, and kayaks, canoes, and wave runners stood lined up and ready to go. He eased back the throttle and turned them in a slow half-circle until they faced his dad's big house on the hill. "Quite the impressive shack."

"Yep." She shrugged. "To me, it almost seems like Theresa

needed the biggest house in the county." She looked up at him. "Dusty just wasn't the type. You know what I mean?"

"I do." He cut the engine and let them drift. The place had rustic touches, which had to be Dusty's doing, but from the outside, it looked like a house that could have been built for any rich family anywhere around the country. "He got the inside, she got the outside."

"Exactly." They floated silently, the only sound coming from birds on the shore. When the pontoon stopped moving completely, Jackson got up. "Lou said the boat is completely stocked." He opened a small aft refrigerator. "Yeah. Beer, white wine, margaritas." He looked at the plastic bottles on top of the fridge. "Red wine, vodka, gin, whiskey. This must be the party barge."

"I guess so. Wow." She stood beside him. "One of Marliss' margaritas would taste like heaven right now."

He poured the slushy drink from the plastic pitcher into a tall cup, then selected a can of beer for himself. "I'll get the grill started."

"Grill?" She sipped her drink, looking around at the seating areas and the pop-up changing room/head at the back. "With a potty on board, too? I could live on this boat."

He lifted the stainless steel grill from inside one of the bench seats and hung it over the edge of the railing, clicking the ignite button until the propane caught. "If you could figure a way to get a power cord out here for those machines of yours, you'd be all set."

"Yep." She settled on a seat across the deck from the grill. "Add internet and cell service, and I could be Cyber Wise Ahoy."

Jackson groaned, winking at her.

"Sorry. I'm bad at puns."

He sat next to her and held up his beer can. "Bad at puns, good at everything else."

She shook her head but tapped her cup to his. "I don't know about everything, but I have been surprising myself with how good I feel when I'm with you." Her eyes widened and her face turned red. "I meant in bed." Puffing out a breath, she looked away. "Awkward."

Jackson took her chin between his thumb and finger and turned her face back to his. "Darlin', I'm a big fan of you saying what's on your mind without holdin' back."

She smiled a little. "It's one of those bad habits I may never get over."

Staring into her eyes for long moments, he gave in to the urge to open up to her some. "Don't try to. It's what makes you special." He kissed her, tasting the tang and sugar of her drink, then letting his tongue tickle the roof of her mouth.

When he ended the kiss, she breathed rapidly for a few moments.

He liked making this amazing woman lose her breath. Jackson slid an arm around her, watching the sun settle behind clouds on the horizon. "It's gonna be a nice sunset." He kissed her temple. "Fitting, since I saw the sunrise after driving you home this morning."

"You're going to wear me out, cowboy."

"I'm doin' my best, darlin'." He took a long pull on his beer.

"What kept you at home this morning?" She liked to be direct, that was for sure.

"I found a box in Dusty's safe." Jackson knew he could trust her with the information, but did he trust himself not to get emotional about what he'd found?

Rori just looked at him, didn't push.

"It seems my dad kept a scrapbook on each of his sons." Once it was out, it didn't seem so monumental.

"That's great." She licked her lips. "You looked at them?"

He nodded. "I looked at my brothers' books. They started with baby pictures and went all the way up to current."

"Hm." She sipped her drink.

Throughout the day, Jackson's thoughts had drifted back to those books, remembering small details about Dylan's band, orKillian's expertise with ropes, or Rogue's skills at the poker table. All three were guys he'd like to know, under normal circumstances, but having to accept them as family still just didn't set right.

"You haven't looked at yours yet?" Her voice sounded small, tentative.

"Not yet." He didn't know when he'd be ready for that stroll down memory lane. Maybe not this trip to Red Creek. Or even the one after that. But maybe someday. Or maybe not. His dad's death pulled his mood in one direction, while Dusty's betrayal and his intentional isolation of his four sons shoved Jackson's anger to the forefront of his ragged emotions.

"If you'd like, and I won't be upset at all if you say no…" She swallowed. "I'd be glad to look at it with you." Her brows knitted together.

He barely breathed. Her offer was so kind and sincere, he didn't know how to answer, how to even decide.

"I mean…" She took a sip of her drink. "It'd make it more like you were showing a new friend the scrapbook of your life, instead of thinking of it as your father's collection." She tipped her head, her eyes looking worried. "Does that make any sense at all?"

He forced a small smile, then let it grow bigger as her idea grew on him, made a hell of a lot of sense, then felt so right that it surprised him. "Yeah, it does make sense, Rori. Thank you for thinking of it. I'm gonna take you up on that offer."

Amazing woman. How was he going to stick to his plan and leave Red Creek Sunday morning without a backward glance?

Chapter Nine

Rori sat on the big leather couch in the two-story living room of Dusty Walker's house, staring at the flat-stone fireplace that rose to the ceiling, the many-pointed buck head hanging above the mantel, the balcony that ran the length of the second floor, and the grand wooden staircase that connected the levels. The place was big and roomy, but cold and silent.

They'd eaten the killer cheese-stuffed hamburgers that Lou had prepped and Jackson had cooked on the little grill hanging over the edge of the pontoon. They'd watched the sunset, then headed back to the dock where, as if by magic, Lou and Marliss stood waiting to clean the pontoon, and had shooed away Jackson and Rori when they'd tried to help.

At the pool in back of the house, Rori had peeled off her shorts, accompanied by much whistling and suggestive language from Jackson, then they'd swum and floated on their backs, holding hands and looking at the stars until Jackson announced he was ready to tackle the scrapbook.

After showering off in the pool house, they came inside, and Jackson had gone to get the scrapbook and drinks.

Rori had almost rescinded her offer to look at the book with Jackson. She felt too invested in him already, especially for a five-day fling, which was all he was. Nothing more.

And if she kept telling herself that, she'd believe it sooner or later.

He padded into the room, barefoot, in sweatpants and a T-shirt, carrying a bottle of red wine and two glasses and the big scrapbook under one arm. "Wine okay? Otherwise Marliss has more of her margarita concoction in the refrigerator."

"Wine sounds lovely." She shivered. In the air conditioning, with her hair wet and just her shorts and tank top on, her skin goosebumped.

233

Jackson sat next to her and grabbed a remote. "Watch this." He pointed it at the fireplace and flames filled the big opening. "Decadence is air conditioning and a fire on an eighty-degree night."

She laughed. "We deserve it, just this once."

"Agreed." Pouring wine, he handed her a tall, stemmed glass and held his up. "Here's to reliving the past and enjoying the hell out of the present."

Rori tapped her glass on his and sipped, wishing there was a future, but knowing that was impossible.

He set down his glass and picked up the scrapbook, laying it on his thighs. "You ready?" His fingers traced the *J* embossed in the cover.

"Are *you* ready?" For him to share this with her had to be incredibly difficult.

He took a deep breath and opened the cover, letting it lay on her lap. A big eight-by-ten-inch picture of tiny Jackson filled the first page.

"Oh my gosh!" She laughed through the moisture that filled her eyes. "Look at you." A full head of inch-long brown hair, serious blue eyes, and the strong jaw she'd come to adore kissing.

"Yeah, jeez, the damn picture is nearly life-size." His voice was soft though, and his mouth curved up a tiny bit.

The outfit they'd put him in looked like a tiny sailor suit, leaving his chubby arms and legs bare.

"Big feet." She snuggled closer to him, loving the closeness, the intimacy of this moment.

"You know what they say about guys with big feet." He glanced at her, his eyes narrow.

A surge of desire raced through her. "I can vouch for the truth in that one." She wagged her brows at him.

He chuckled, and turned the page. It was a picture of the three of them, baby Jackson in his mom's arms and Dusty with his arm around her, the ocean in the background.

"She's beautiful." Petite and devoid of makeup, his mother's long, curling brown hair shone in the sunshine, her deep blue eyes sparkled just like Jackson's, and her smile could easily be seen from space. "She looks happy."

"She was. She is. She misses him, though."

"What does your mother think…" Rori tugged at her earlobe. "Never mind." Thankfully, she was able to choke back that question before it flew from her mouth.

"No, ask me. It's good to get stuff talked about."

"Okay, but tell me if it's too personal." She sucked in a breath. "What does she think of Dusty having three other sons by three other women?"

He stared at the fire. "She didn't seem all that surprised when I told her." He worked his jaw. "I had to wonder if Dusty slipped up some, calling her by another name, or me by another name, maybe." He shrugged. "She might have hired a private eye. I don't know. It was good that she had a week between finding out about Dusty passing and learning about his other families."

Rori couldn't imagine loving someone and knowing they were legally bound to another. Even worse, finding out that she wasn't the only extramarital family he had. Jackson's mother had to have been pretty deep in love with Dusty, and pretty darn strong.

He tapped the bottom of the picture. "Dad bought us this house just a block from the ocean, and it has this rooftop deck."

"Oh wow, that's your house?" She'd love to have a view like that from her place.

"Yeah. Dad met Mom—her name is Sapphire—when he came into her pottery shop in the downtown section of Bandon." Jackson looked like his thoughts drifted west for a few moments.

"Is she still a potter?"

"She is, teaches classes and employs five people full-time now. But back then, it was just her in the shop, doing it all and living in an apartment above it." He glanced at Rori. "Just like you."

A snort escaped her. "Me, but with creativity." Rori wished she had an ounce of artistic talent.

"You're creative, darlin'. Don't doubt it for a moment. The things you do with hardware and software, man, I'm so frickin' impressed, I want to kneel at your feet and worship you." He winked.

His words filled her with pride, but the vision of him down there clenched a sexy ache in her core. "Maybe later?"

"Definitely later." He gave her a soft, quick kiss, then went back to the book.

Rori touched the corner of the page. "Dusty looks happy." The man had a big grin, standing nearly a foot taller than Sapphire, his brown hair was cut short, but his brown eyes had the same happy gleam as Sapphire's. "You resemble him when he was younger."

Jackson just looked at the picture. On the next page, a dozen more baby pictures chronicled his growth, his rolling over, and finally, his sitting up. All of them showed him smiling.

He flipped pages, commenting on the boat rides pictured, swimming at the beach, catching his first crab, and his first day of preschool.

She held back her ooohs and awwws as much as she could, but her chest filled to capacity with the sweetness of the little man with the combed-back hair and shiny-clean face. "You were just an angel."

"Ha." He turned the page. "I was happy, mostly, and I dealt with the fact that the other kids had dads around all the time, but I didn't."

"I can't imagine." Her parents were her foundation, her father was her greatest supporter.

Jackson sat back, drinking his wine. "You see your parents a lot?"

"I do, when I'm in KC, and once in a while they make the trip to Red Creek." She rolled her eyes. "The sightseeing here isn't that great, so they don't stay long, but I appreciate that they make the effort."

"You said they're teachers?"

"Yep. Mom teaches calculus and Dad biology at a private high school." Rori shrugged. "They've been offered positions at colleges, but they're not interested in making money. Instead, they feel kids at that age need a lot of guidance and encouragement, and they've both got minors in psychology."

"Holy hell, that's how you turned out so well."

A laugh blasted out of her. "I was a social mess in high school, as you can imagine, with my propensity to say whatever thoughts pop into my mind." She thought about her teen years, her awkwardness and book smarts, valedictorian, teachers' pet. "I was a virgin until I was…" Oh hell, had she just said that aloud?

****

Jackson's head jerked back of its own power and laughter roared out of him. This woman. What the heck kind of treasure had he stumbled upon? "Oh darlin', you can't just blurt out half of that sentence." He laughed, setting down his wine glass to keep it from sloshing out.

Red flooded her cheeks and she sighed. "I'm not much of a mystery, am I." She glanced at him, then away. "I was a sophomore in college before I had a boyfriend."

Cupping his hand at the back of her neck, he massaged her warm, soft skin. "I like that you were old enough to make the right decision."

She nodded. "You know me. I had to have all the facts and data lined up perfectly first."

He laughed again, and when she didn't say more, and sipped her wine a little quicker, he gave her a break and went back to flipping pages in the scrapbook.

"Is that you at a rodeo?" She pointed to a picture of Jackson looking downright giddy at age ten.

"Yeah, Dad would take me to the rodeo in Myrtle Creek every year, starting when I was about six. It was our thing, and I looked forward to it for months before the event." His roomy bedroom had posters on the wall from each of the rodeos, and signatures of the cowboys and cowgirls procured for him by Dusty filled each poster.

The memories flooded him and a burning feeling collected behind his eyes, moistening them. "I'd sit on the front porch all morning in my boots and jeans and cowboy hat just waiting for Dad to pull up in his rental car." Jackson could almost smell the salty spindrift from the ocean waves, and feel the warm June sun on his shoulders. "I saved up my allowance, did extra chores, so I'd have enough to buy Dad and me a hotdog and coke." He'd been so proud to be able to pay, and Dad's chest had always swelled when he'd told the hot dog vendor, "My son's treating me today."

The moisture swelled and he had to look away and blink, had to turn his memories from those sweet times to the year he turned fifteen. The anger flowed in, then. "It ended when I was fifteen. I woke that morning and Mom was sitting at the kitchen table, her eyes red as if she'd been crying.

Rori took his hand. He hadn't realized his whole body had gone stiff as new rope.

Looking into her eyes, he saw real compassion, true interest.

"Dad wasn't coming that weekend. He couldn't get away." Jackson had felt disappointed that day, but it wasn't worth tears. "I sat and rubbed Sapphire's arm, told her it was fine. But then she got angry, blurted that it wasn't fair, that just because his *wife* wanted him to accompany her…"

At first, the word had gone in Jackson's ear and directly out the other, as if she hadn't just revealed a secret that would change his life.

"Then Mom's eyes widened, and she froze."

"I asked, her, 'Wife? What are you talking about?'"

Rori's hand tightened in his and her breathing sped up.

"Mom started crying and she covered her face with her hands. I remember her words as if she said them yesterday. 'Oh honey,

I'm so sorry. I didn't mean for you to find out this way'."

"Jackson, I'm sorry." Rori's eyes shone with moisture.

His chest hurt just reliving that day. "I remember standing up, but my head was spinning like I'd just gotten off a ride at the fair." His world had changed with each passing second, with each recollection of the days, weeks, months that Dusty had spent away from them.

"I ran out of the house, in my boots and jeans and cowboy hat and belt buckle." He glanced down, but he wasn't wearing the one Dusty had given him when he'd turned ten. The same buckle his dad had given his three other sons. That wasn't something he was ready to talk about. Not even with Rori.

She sniffed and wiped tears off her cheek with the back of her hand.

Jackson swallowed down his own emotion. "I ran and ran, just kept running. I ended up on the highway, and realized I was heading toward the rodeo."

"Your mom must have been frantic." Her voice shook.

"She was. I found out later she called Dad, and he got on his plane and flew out right then." Jackson took in a few breaths, the drama of that day raising his blood pressure. "I hitched a ride that got me halfway there, then hitched again and got in a truck full of rodeo cowboys who were going to Myrtle Creek."

"And so it began." She smiled through her tears.

"Exactly. The hour I rode with them in that truck convinced me that it was the life I wanted to live." No responsibilities except for getting to the rodeo on time, no emotional attachments, no roots.

"How much of that do you think was because of finding out about Dusty's wife?" Rori looked too serious.

"There's that psychologists' daughter coming out." He almost smiled, but knew he was deflecting her question. He'd asked himself the same thing a hundred times. "I'm just glad it wasn't a circus Dad took me to every year. Can you imagine me in clown makeup?"

She chuckled, even though she looked upset. "I'm sorry, that was not something I should have said aloud." When she tried to release his hand, he grasped hers a little tighter.

"No, it needed to be said. I've given it thought over the years, but it'd take a hell of a shrink and about ten thousand hours to figure out what went wrong with me."

"There's nothing wrong with you." Rori's declaration came out firm and sure. "You've lived your life the way you wanted. Not many people can honestly say that."

She was right, he had done exactly what he'd wanted all these years, but was it still working for him? Or was he finally outgrowing his "running away to join the rodeo" phase?

"How did you get home?" She poured each of them a little more wine, then sipped hers, tucking her legs up under her and relaxing back into the cushions.

"Dad showed up about an hour into the rodeo. Just sat down next to me and handed me a hot dog and a coke." Jackson remembered how his hands shook as he took them from Dusty, anger, disappointment, fear, all ricocheting around inside him, not knowing where to go, what to do.

"Dad said, 'Son, we'll talk on the way home,' and for the first time, Dusty had looked old and frightened."

Jackson flipped pages of the scrapbook, reading the headlines on articles about him winning a saddle at a rodeo, or visiting a children's hospital, or wearing pink in October to support breast cancer research.

Rori sat silently, pressed against his side and looking at the book with him. Her silence was exactly what Jackson needed.

That talk, between Dad and him on the way home from the rodeo, had made him realize how fragile people were. How susceptible to being hurt by others. Like the way his mother had been hurt by Dusty. Jackson had vowed that day that he'd be nothing like his father. Instead, he'd find his happiness where he could, then move on before he got the chance to hurt anyone. The plan had worked for him, but it sure as fuck felt lonely.

The end of the scrapbook contained recent photos and a few articles, then Jackson was staring at an envelope. With his name printed on it. In his father's handwriting. He couldn't move for a few seconds. "Ah, shit." He slammed the book closed and dropped it on the coffee table.

Her eyes wide, Rori set down her wine glass and wrapped herself around him, squeezing tight.

Jackson melted into her. What was in that envelope? What words could Dusty have written that Jackson would need to read? "I can't..." He'd read that letter someday. Not now. He couldn't take any more memories tonight. "Come upstairs with me, Rori. Please."

She cupped his cheeks, her nose nearly touching his. "Of course, Jackson. Anything you need."

Chapter Ten

The next morning, Rori screwed up a software install twice before shoving away from the table at the back of Cyber Wise and wandering to the front door of the shop. Last night... She sighed. Jackson had been tender and slow, their lovemaking innovative, but thoughtful, as if the emotion flowing from both of them cocooned them in... Wait, had she just thought *lovemaking*? Damn, that was a dangerous road to go down.

They'd had sex. Hot, perfect sex, but it'd been different than the times before. Long looks into each other's eyes, whispered words, deep kisses. And she'd fallen for it like a girl who'd never been in love before. Which, she had to admit today, she probably hadn't ever been. If what she'd felt before was a kilobyte of affection for a man, what she felt now was at least a terabyte, maybe more. For Jackson.

She stormed away from the door and back to her work. "It's not happening, Rori. He's rodeo poison, and to him, you're a few days' distraction. Done." She closed off all thoughts of him and tried to concentrate on work. But every few minutes she checked the clock.

Rori knew Jackson needed to be in the office all day. His three specialists were in town and they were going to hit it hard today and tomorrow, get Jackson up to speed with everything, even if it killed the poor guy. She grinned as she thought of him sitting there surrounded by Elaine, Vic, and Walt as they peppered him with information, and he stared blankly. Not that Jackson wasn't smart. No, the man was just a little on the lazy side, and a technology Luddite, but if he wanted to, he could run the company easily.

But he didn't want to. She sat back in her chair. What would it take to get him to stay?

"Uhhhh." She shouted the groan and banished the thought from her head. "Jackson is leaving. Get used to it."

Instead of finishing the install, she went online and printed out a recipe for baked potatoes. She'd invited him for supper tonight. And she didn't cook. The steaks were in her refrigerator upstairs, the potatoes on the counter, and the rest of the meal, including dessert, lined up next to them. She'd give it her best effort, but he might have to jump in and help.

How was he today? When he'd told the story of finding out about Dusty's wife, she didn't think she could hold back her sobs. Her heart just broke for him. Tall and lanky at age fifteen, those big eyes of his in a skinny kid's face, lord, she'd wanted to take him home with her and keep him safe from the big ugly world forever.

She'd never had that kind of instinct before. Maybe she was moving into that part of her life where she'd start nesting, looking for a man to settle down and have babies with. Her mother warned her it would be coming, but she'd assured her mom that all she needed was a fast operating system and a new video game every month to keep her happy.

Boy, had she been wrong.

****

The next afternoon they had the appointment to confront the attorney, and Rori couldn't wait. She had a lot of questions for the man.

The dinner the night before had gone as she'd expected— she'd begged his help halfway through cooking, and he'd easily taken over and finished preparing a fabulous meal for them. They'd only eaten half, though, before they'd tumbled onto her couch for a hot hour of oral delight. They'd finally gotten back to the meal, but had left the dishes on the table and spent the rest of the night working their way through a box of condoms in her bedroom.

Rori smiled and tested the pleasant ache of every muscle in her body. Jackson had stamina, that was a proven fact.

The buzzer sounded at the front door of Cyber Wise and she

checked the time. Twenty minutes before Jackson's appointment with Stanley Benner, Esquire. The cowboy was punctual, that was certain. She saved her work and headed toward the front of the store. When she walked into the room, she stopped cold. "Marliss?"

The older woman tipped her head. "You have a fabulous store here, Ms. Hughes." In her floral dress and sandals, she bore no resemblance to the woman who worked at Dusty's house in serviceable cotton clothes.

"It's Rori, please." She wandered slowly toward her. "Are you in the market for a computer?" The woman had never set foot in Cyber Wise before, and her visit on a Friday afternoon, when she was technically supposed to be working at the house, didn't bode well.

"Oh no, I'm happy with letting Lou do all the web-searching things."

Another Luddite. "What can I help you with?"

The woman set her bright orange purse on a table. "May I talk to you about Jackson?"

Rori glanced out the front window. "That's fine, but he's going to be here any minute."

"Oh." Her hands fluttered a bit before she clasped them in front of her. "Then I'll make this brief."

"Unless you'd rather talk later?" Rori wanted to hear what Marliss had to say. Every word of it.

"No, this will take just a moment." She pursed her lips and blinked a few times. "Mr. Walker—Dusty—spoke with Lou and me about…the boys." She shrugged. "We were the only people, besides their mothers, who he could talk to, so I know a little bit about Dusty's concerns with Jackson."

This was a lot deeper than Rori had imagined Marliss would go. "I don't know that I could—"

"Please." Marliss stepped forward. "Just let me say this, then I'll go, and we won't mention this conversation again." She pressed her fist to her mouth. "I'm afraid that if he leaves Sunday, he won't come back."

Rori could lie to save the woman the anguish she was evidently going through. But that wasn't her way. "I think you're right."

She dropped her hand. "Dusty worried that Jackson avoided relationships because he feared he'd become just like him. Like Dusty. See, Dusty thought Jackson saw his mother as a martyr. Living on the fringe of Dusty's life, having a family with him without the benefit of marriage."

Rori just nodded, anxious to have Marliss get to the point before Jackson came across the street.

"I know he and you looked through the scrapbook together. I saw it when I was cleaning up this morning, so you don't need to worry that I was spying on you."

With a laugh, Rori shook her head. "I didn't think that at all."

"Well, thank you. But I needed to talk to you to know if you got to the end of the scrapbook. Did he see the envelope?"

"He did." Rori had seen the fear on Jackson's face as he stared at it. She'd actually worried that he'd toss the thing in the fire.

"Well, that's half the battle."

Rori caught a movement across the street and took a step closer to the window.

Marliss turned and looked out in the direction of D. Walker Mineral. She swung around, grabbing her purse. "He's coming." Her voice went up an octave.

"I have a back door." Rori gestured for her to follow, and they stopped at the back entrance, close together, face-to-face.

"Ms. Rori, if you have any way to reach him, could you please encourage him to open that letter?" Marliss' gaze locked with Rori's. "I wouldn't normally ask something like this, but I think you might be his only hope."

The buzzer went off, announcing the front door opening.

Rori wanted to help, but she couldn't make any promises. "I'll try, Marliss." She whispered the words. "I promise to do my best."

"Thank you, dear." Marliss smiled and skittered out the back way and down the alley.

"Rori?" Jackson's voice carried through the building as she locked the back door and hurried toward the storefront.

"Coming." She nearly ran smack into him, and he caught her, pulling her into his arms.

"Whoa, where're you going in such a rush?" He looked at her, his brows down over his blue eyes.

"Um, aren't we going to Benner's office?" She was a little breathless, a little shaky, but about as turned on as a girl could be when her man held her tight against him.

"We are." His hands roamed along her back. "But I came a few minutes early so we could do this." He tipped her sideways and gave her a kiss she'd never forget. A kiss that would have to last her a lifetime—if Jackson never showed his face in Red Creek again after Sunday.

****

Benner escorted Rori and Jackson into his office. "This is a surprise, Ms. Hughes. Jackson didn't mention you would be here, too." The man looked decidedly nervous.

Jackson helped her into a chair, then sat, waiting for Benner to take his seat behind the big desk.

"I'm here as a witness." Rori blurted out the words.

The attorney froze halfway down to his chair, then plopped into it, tipping back a ways before catching his balance. "Is that right?"

Jackson held in a laugh. Nothing like putting a guy on the defensive. "I found these on Dusty's computer." He spread out the printouts containing the dates, amounts, and account numbers in front of Benner. "Do these account numbers look familiar to you?"

Benner's cheeks turned ruddy. He adjusted his glasses and picked up one of the papers, holding it up between himself and Jackson. "They just look like a bunch of numbers to me. Not necessarily account numbers."

Rori sniffed and gave Jackson a look. "Check again, Mr. Benner. Are you sure nothing on that page triggers a memory?"

Jackson could kiss her right there. She would be a fantastic courtroom attorney.

Benner laid the paper down, giving Rori a glare, then fastening his gaze on Jackson. "Is this something you'd like me to look into further for you?"

Pulling the next wad of folded papers from his pocket, Jackson spread them out on top of the other papers. "Here's what Abby found when I had her look through the bank accounts for these amounts. Payments were made from D. Walker Mineral's general account to these account numbers." Jackson pointed to one of the first papers. "What is happening here?" Jackson would give the man the opportunity to admit his involvement.

"Hmmm." Benner studied the papers. Each one of them. For much longer than necessary. "I can have one of my staff—"

"Not necessary." Jackson sat back in his chair and set his booted foot on the opposite knee. "We know who opened and closed these accounts."

Benner's lips tightened as his gaze ping-ponged from Rori's to his, then fastened on Jackson. "This is not something that should be discussed with anyone outside your family."

Jackson sat completely still, staring down the attorney. "Ms. Hughes is, as she mentioned, my witness. Do you want to tell us everything, or do we take this information to the county attorney's office?"

Benner shuffled all the papers together into a ncat pile and set them in front of Jackson. "This may be embarrassing for you to hear in front of your..." He glanced at Rori. "Friend."

"Ms. Hughes is a contract employee of D. Walker Mineral." Jackson could slug the man for making Rori seem less than important. He glanced at her. She'd pursed her lips tight together, and her eyes sparkled. This wild, wonderful woman was enjoying this, trying not to laugh. Damn. Her sense of humor…

Benner let out a long breath, seeming to deflate. "Mrs. Walker—Theresa—hired a private detective."

Rori sat forward in her chair, glanced at Jackson, then back at Benner. "Through you?"

He waved his hands in front of him. "No, no, no. She went to KC and hired him. She knew I wouldn't help her with anything like this."

"Let me guess." Jackson gripped the chair arms. "He followed Dusty and found out about his extra families."

"That's exactly right." Benner stood and stepped to the large safe behind him, dialing in the code to open it. "This detective found out about three of the four of you." The safe door opened with a squeak as the lawyer looked at Jackson. "He realized he could make more money blackmailing Dusty than he could with just the one-time payment from Theresa." Benner shuffled through his safe.

"Harold Logan." Rori said the detective's name, and Benner paused for a few seconds.

"That's right. You're quite a bit more accomplished than I've given you credit for, Ms. Hughes." He turned and smirked at her. "Perhaps there's a place for you in my firm." He went back to digging through the safe.

She laughed once, then cleared her throat. "I'm always open to offers, Mr. Benner." She winked at Jackson.

He smiled and nodded, but sobered as Benner pulled a thick brown envelope from the safe and set it on his desk. From it, he pulled a one-inch stack of papers and photos.

Jackson sat forward as Benner leaned over and set the items on the desk between Jackson and Rori.

"This Logan character followed your father and took these pictures." One after another, they looked at photos of Dusty with women who looked familiar from the scrapbooks—his brothers' mothers. Benner revealed pictures of Dusty with Sapphire, then photos of Dad with Dylan, Killian, and even a few with Jackson, which sent a chill up his spine.

"Wow." Rori eased her leg closer and touched it against Jackson's.

He appreciated the gesture, and squeezed her knee. "So Logan went to Dusty with this? Or to you?"

"To Dusty." Benner sat, resting his hand on his stomach. "Who came to me. From there, the three of us reached an agreement. Monthly payments for life…and in this case, Dusty's life…increasing annually, and sent through anonymous accounts." Benner tapped the stack of papers Jackson had brought in. "But you know all that."

"And Logan told Theresa…?" Rori put her hand on top of Jackson's.

"He got some pictures of Dusty eating alone in restaurants, heading to his hotel room early, and alone, working long hours, etc." Benner shook his head. "I encouraged Dusty to be forthcoming with his wife, but he became angry and told me it was none of my business." He gathered the photos and slid them back into the envelope. "Which it wasn't." He held the envelope out to Jackson. "Would you like to dispose of these?"

He tipped his head down. "No, why don't you keep them. Just in case." He looked at Rori. "I'll have our contract employee copy off then remove the files from Dusty's computers, and I'll hang on to this secret for a while."

Rori smiled and nodded. "Good plan, boss."

"I agree, Jackson." Benner placed the envelope back into the safe, closed the door, and spun the lock.

"Why the different bank accounts?" Jackson looked at Rori.

She frowned. "And why open and close them? Why not leave them open?"

Benner snorted. "That's how this Logan character wanted it done. I think he believed he could escape legal and tax ramifications by withdrawing the funds from banks in different counties."

"What about legal action?" Jackson wanted revenge. "Can we do anything to put this Logan guy out of business?"

The attorney shook his head. "The agreement was that Logan would not reveal any of this to Theresa or publicly, provided there was never any legal action brought against him." Benner looked between Rori and him. "If we were to contact the authorities, or in any way try to discredit Logan, he could go public with it, release the photos, write a book, make a movie based on—"

"Okay, I get it." Jackson glanced at Rori. His family's privacy, or what was left of it, was the main concern.

Benner's professional smile had returned. "Now, is there anything else I can help you with?"

Jackson stood and shook the man's hand. "No. I think this is just about all I can manage for today."

Benner nodded for a few seconds. "Understandable. But don't hesitate to call or come in if there's anything in the future."

Jackson narrowed his eyes. "Hopefully, there's nothing else in that safe of yours that I need to be concerned with?"

Benner laughed, loud and long, then held up his hand, his three middle fingers pointing upward. "Scout's honor, there's nothing else in there that could bite either of us in the ass." He nodded to Rori. "Excuse the language, ma'am."

She stood and grinned. "I've heard worse." She shook Benner's hand. "Thanks again."

Jackson took her arm and guided her toward the door.

"I'll be in touch, Ms. Hughes." Benner called from behind them. "I can think of three or four cases you can help us with just off the cuff."

"Looking forward to it, sir." She preceded Jackson out the door and into the heat of a late Kansas afternoon. Turning to face Jackson, she lifted her brows. "Did you have any idea?"

"Nope." He looked into her eyes, shaking his head. "I wouldn't have guessed. But I can see Dusty pulling that one off.

Can't you?"

"I can. He had a lot to lose."

Jackson walked next to Rori along the sidewalk toward her building. He couldn't imagine a man so intent on keeping secrets that he'd go through all that work and expense to hide them. Was that a good sign? Maybe Jackson wasn't destined to be just like Dusty. But he wasn't ready to risk finding out. "You got customers this afternoon?"

"Nope." She looked up at him with a sexy smile. "You got work to do this afternoon?"

He gave her a naughty grin. "Nope. Let's flip the *Closed* sign."

"Already done." She looked around the deserted street, grabbed his wrist, and tugged him between two buildings and down the alley to the back entry to her apartment. "I'm officially off the clock, and on the hunt."

He laughed. "Take me to your lair, darlin'. I'm officially your afternoon snack."

Chapter Eleven

Sunday morning, just after midnight, Rori lay in Jackson's bed staring at the ceiling. He'd be leaving in a few hours. All she could think of was how difficult it would be to say goodbye to him.

Friday afternoon, and most of the night, they'd stayed in her apartment, making love, cooking, playing video games, then making love some more. It had been magical, and she'd kept praying for time to slow down.

After sleeping in Saturday morning, she'd driven to Jackson's house, at his invitation, for lunch and an afternoon of using every water toy he and his brothers owned. By the time they came back to the house, they were both starving and exhausted. They ate at the kitchen counter while Lou and Marliss entertained them with stories of Dusty's attempts at the jet skis, then headed upstairs for their last hours together.

The sex had started out fast and wild, but changed to slow and easy as both of them silently said goodbye.

Rori had brought up Dusty's letter earlier when they'd been sitting on the dock, but Jackson hadn't responded. She'd like to talk about it again, with more enthusiasm, and she hated to leave without another try, but he was sound asleep, and she had a bunch of tears in her eyes. Those tears would turn into a waterfall if she had to kiss him goodbye and walk out of his life forever.

Sliding out of bed, she pulled her clothes on and blew him a kiss from the doorway. She would never forget him.

The waterfall started halfway down the steps and she could barely find her bag through the blur of tears, let alone get her key out, and slip out the door. In her van, she let it go, bawling like a baby for long minutes before grabbing her composure and driving home.

Home? Was this home? Her parents, her family, lived in KC. Maybe she'd just close up shop and move everything there? Start from scratch in her parents' basement, or maybe even take out a business loan and rent a storefront.

She pulled into her parking spot in back of the Cyber Wise and trudged up the steps to her apartment. After they'd made love, she hadn't showered, wanted to keep the soapy, masculine scent of Jackson with her as long as possible. Tossing and turning, she watched the clock. Now he'd be leaving the house. Now he'd be driving through town toward KC.

For a half-hour, she listened, hoping she'd hear the engine of his company truck stop out back, hear a knock at her door. Nothing.

Now he'd be at the airport, and now…his plane had lifted off.

It felt like someone had taken a knife and sliced a jagged hole in her heart. Why had she just let him go? "Because you don't do rodeo cowboys." Why hadn't she at least told him how she felt about him? "Because he's not looking for anything longer than this past week."

She closed her eyes and let herself drift into a dream of being in his arms. She woke with the sun blazing through the window. Checking the clock, she sighed. He'd be home by now with his mother, making plans for the rest of his life.

A noise outside caught her attention. Was that a car door? She didn't have customers scheduled today. Banging sounded at the back door of her apartment. Still dressed in her shorts and tank top, she trudged down the steps. Only one person would be here this damn early. Lexie from the coffee shop. And she'd better have brought scones, too.

Rori yanked open the back door.

"Hi." Jackson stared at her, sober as Sunday morning.

"Hi." Her heart skipped a few beats. "You missed your flight?"

"On purpose." He gestured up the steps. "Mind if I come in?"

Her heart restarted, thumping loud enough to be heard in Missouri. "Don't mind at all." She turned and padded up the steps

253

with him clomping right behind her. She couldn't let herself hope. Couldn't dream that this meant anything more than him stopping by to say goodbye.

In her kitchen, she turned to face him. "What's up?" Trying to make her voice sound cool nearly choked her.

He smiled and shook his head. "Really? That's all I get?"

Grabbing the edge of the countertop, she swallowed. "Did you come to say goodbye?"

"No. I came to talk to you." He leaned his hip on the counter.

"Okay." How much could she read into that statement?

"You don't look excited to see me, Rori."

She'd be honest. "Until I hear what you have on your mind, I'm going to hold tight to my emotions."

He raised a brow. "Fair enough."

Jackson slid the envelope with his name on it from his back pocket. "You said I shouldn't forget about this letter from my dad."

She nodded.

"I opened it after you snuck out this morning." He dropped his eyes, frowning a little.

"You heard me leave?" And he'd let her go? Damn it. Not good.

"I figured if you'd wanted to say goodbye, you would have woke me. I didn't want to mess with your escape."

Huffing out a breath, she shrugged. She had no response to that one.

"Yeah, that's what I thought." He smirked. "Dusty's letter said a few things that made sense to me. He explained a lot, and I can see things differently right now. A lot differently." His eyes narrowed as he looked at her.

"Such as?"

"First..." He smiled.

She didn't return it.

"First, I have to ask you, what do you have against rodeo

cowboys?"

Rori opened her mouth, then closed it again. "Huh?"

"What's your problem with us?"

"Well, just my cousin." That sounded stupid. "She's married to a bull rider. "Her kids are essentially growing up without a dad. He only comes home when he's busted. Physically or financially."

Jackson nodded. "Okay. What else?"

"What else?" She tipped her head.

"What else has made you distrust rodeo men?"

"Well...nothing. That's it. And that's enough, isn't it?" Now that she said it aloud, it sounded even more stupid.

"And you know of no other men who exhibit that sort of behavior?" He widened his eyes. "It's only rodeo cowboys who behave that way?"

She coughed out a laugh. "I see your point." And felt like a fool. "So I might have been a little judgmental."

"Just a little?" He held up a hand. "Second..." He pointed downstairs. "You said there weren't eligible bachelors in town, but I have it on completely reliable gossip that one Monday morning, after discussing you at a Saturday night poker game, three guys showed up here looking to ask you out."

"Oh for fuc...for heaven's sake. Who the hell told you that?" She couldn't believe that piece of nostalgia was still rolling around town.

"True? You could have had your pick of any of those men, and you chose none of them. And none of them were rodeo cowboys, right?"

"I'm not following your logic." She hoped he was leading to what she wanted to hear, but she wasn't taking any chances, and kept her heart on lockdown.

"Darlin'." He took a step toward her.

She took one step back.

"When you left this morning, I knew I had to see you again." He reached for her arm and she wasn't quick enough—or emotionally tough enough—to stay away from him.

"Jackson." Her body reacted to his touch, quivering and heating. She stepped toward him and laced her fingers in the back of his hair, pulling him closer. "I want this." Even if it was the last time. Even though she knew better.

He bent and picked her up in his arms, carrying her through the bedroom door and laying them both on the bed. "I *need* this." Sliding his hand under her tank top, his rough skin played sexily on her softness. He pulled her bra up, tugged her shirt up too, and bent to kiss her nipple.

Shockwaves flowed from her breast to her core, loosening and swelling her down low, heating and creaming between her legs.

In seconds, he'd unfastened her bra and pulled it and her shirt off her, ripped off his shirt, and rubbed his chest along hers as he moved up to kiss her.

"Darlin'." He took her mouth with his, his tongue tracing along her cheeks, sucking at her tongue until she pushed into his mouth and tasted his spicy flavor mixed with coffee. He slowed the kiss, breathing heavily against her lips. "I want you now, riding me, looking into my eyes as we come together."

Rori's hips jerked up, her thighs tightening against the sweet pressure between her legs. "Yes, Jackson, anything you want." She'd give this man one last ride, even if it broke her heart irreparably.

He eased downward, kissing from her neck to her belly, nibbling and sucking. Removing her shorts, he kept his lips pressed to her mound, his tongue flicking inward, finding her little button and shocking her entire body with each pass. Jackson spread her legs and pressed his face into her pussy, his tongue lapping, his lips sucking, his nose pressing on her clit. Her brain began to flicker into blackness.

"No." She grabbed a fistful of his hair and pulled his face from her core.

He looked at her, his eyes deep blue, his breath panting

through his parted lips.

"I want you…" She had to suck in a breath. "Want your hard cock inside me when I come."

One corner of his mouth crooked up as his eyes narrowed.

The sexiest look she'd ever seen on any man. A look she'd never forget. Ever.

"My pleasure, darlin'." He stood and ripped at the button on his jeans, tugged down his zipper.

She sat up and helped him shove the fabric down his thighs, watched as he hopped a one-legged circle taking off his boots, and throwing them and his clothes into the corner. He paused to look at her. "You sure now, Rori?"

Her belly flipped, sexy flames roaring to her pussy, tightening her nipples as she stared at his big shaft. "Yes, Jackson. I want this." When she licked her lips, he strode to her, grabbed her hair and eased her face to his cock.

She took it all, deep-throating the long, salty staff, cupping his balls with one hand, teasing just behind them with her fingers.

"Gonna make me come." He pulled her hair back, easing her mouth off him. "And I want to be inside you, like you ordered."

She smiled. "I like giving the orders."

"Just this once, darlin'." He handed her the condom.

Sliding it on him, she pressed kisses to his belly, his hips.

"Pile up the pillows on the headboard." Jackson helped her, then sat on the bed and reclined on them, his knees bent. "Come and sit on me here, Rori." He grasped his cock, his teeth clenching.

"I'm gonna ride you, cowboy. So you'll never forget…" Her voice broke as she knelt beside him and threw a leg over him, her bottom sliding down his thighs until her pussy touched the hot head of his shaft.

Jackson stared at the spot where her lips touched his cock. "Damn, that's beautiful." He ran his finger along her pussy and drew back his hand. "Look how wet you are for me." He stared into her eyes and sucked his finger.

"Ahhh." Rori's legs went weak and she slid downward, slowly taking him into her sensitive core. "So big…and…hot, Jackson." Her head rolled around on her neck, her eyes closing as sparks of pleasure rode up her spine.

"Look at me, darlin'." His voice rolled low and fierce.

She forced open her eyes.

"Ride your cowboy." He grasped her under her thighs, his fingers cupping her ass cheeks, pushing her up and off him, then letting her drop down onto his shaft.

Finding muscles in her legs that had gone nearly lifeless with pleasure, she worked her body on his, taking him deep and holding, then pushing off and pulsing on and off quickly a dozen times, then so deep, she could feel him in her belly.

"You make me wild, cowgirl." Jackson took over then, guiding her hard and fast, lifting his hips to meet her downward drop, pulsing himself inside her quicker with each thrust. "Play with your nipples. Show me how hot I make you."

She squealed, staring into his eyes as she plucked at her nipples, twisting and tugging them.

He bared his teeth, his gaze locked with hers, groaning with each plunge into her. Her core tightened around him, shooting flames to her brain, and bringing tears to her eyes.

She loved this man. He could have been her everything. She sobbed and dropped her head.

Jackson pumped harder as he moved his hand to her mound, finding her clit and rubbing it with his thumb. "That's it, Rori. Don't hold back. Let me see all of you."

She cried out and let herself fly out of her body, out of the room, soar through clouds wet with tears.

Through the fog, Jackson's voice came from miles away, shouting her name.

Gasping for breath, Rori let out her heartbreak, shuddering and spinning as earth came back much too quickly.

Jackson moaned as his thrusts slowed, his hands on her thighs shook and sweat sparkled on his chest. "Darlin', that was epic." He puffed breaths, his eyes barely slits.

Another wave of tears surfaced and she swallowed back the cries, covering her face with her hands as the drops leaked through her fingers and fell onto her belly.

"Rori." He lifted her, shifting himself out of her, and lay her on top of his body, covering them with the sheet. "Rori, tell me those are tears of happiness." Low and full of worry, his voice shook her soul.

"I thought I could…do this." She couldn't catch her breath. "I thought I could hang on through this last time, say goodbye to you with dignity and…grace." The last word rose like a shriek as tears came again. "I don't cry, damn it." An octave higher than her normal voice, she pushed out all her emotion with those words.

Sucking in a deep breath, she pushed up, her hands on his chest, keeping her head down so her hair covered her mucky face.

A half-dozen tissues appeared between her hands.

"Thank you." She wiped up as best as she could then tried to roll off him.

He guided her onto her side, with him laying right next to her. "What happened there, darlin'?" Jackson smoothed her hair away from her face.

She'd already made a complete fool of herself. Time to rebuild a little dignity.

"I'm just overtired." She attempted a smile, but it felt more like a scowl.

"You rest." He pulled a pillow and tucked it under her head. "I'll talk."

"What is there to talk about? You have a plane to catch. Don't you?" She didn't dare let herself believe he wasn't disappearing from her life forever the moment his boots hit the pavement. She couldn't let herself visualize it any other way, or when he did leave, it might just kill her.

259

Chapter Twelve

Jackson had resurfaced from the blast furnace of an orgasm to see Rori crying. Now, laying side-by-side with her, looking into those sky-blue, red-veined eyes, he knew he'd made the right decision that morning. But now, he had to convince her.

"Darlin', when you left the house, I wasn't sure what to do with myself. Run after you, or let you go and shut you out of my life completely." Tracing her cheekbone with his finger, her vulnerability hit him hard. "So I did nothing, but I took your advice."

"The letter?" She settled into the pillow, staring at him like she was getting her fill of him one last time.

"Yeah. Dad talked about what drove his decisions." He needed to share this with someone he trusted. "Theresa didn't want children."

Rori's eyebrows shot up. "Really?"

Should he ask her now if she wanted kids? Of course, that'd probably have her kicking him out the door and wishing him good luck with his life. "Dad said he didn't know how to handle it. He wanted a family, and his need for immortality drove him from woman to woman, not caring about who he hurt or the damage he did to his own soul. By the time he could see the mistakes he'd made, it was too late. He had created four lives, and he had to live up to his responsibilities."

"That's pretty deep."

Jackson huffed out a laugh. "For Dusty, yeah, it sure is." He took Rori's hand, lacing their fingers together. "Dad saw that my running away to the rodeo was done out of fear. The fear that I'd end up like him. But he said in the letter, I'm not like him. I'm my mother's boy, and although she consented to be with a married man, she did it for life. She was faithful."

He almost snorted at that, considering how *un*faithful Dusty was.

"From what you tell me about your mom, and what I know of Dusty, I think your dad's words were insightful."

"I knew you'd see it that way." He'd gotten that out of the way. "Oh, and ironically, Dusty didn't mention why he hadn't gotten us brothers together, or if he ever planned to do it. So that looks like it'll remain a mystery."

"Strange." Rori's eyes shifted. "I thought that was going to be the entire content of the letter."

"Nope. I think the old man wants us boys to figure it out ourselves." As if any of them cared any more. After reading all the scrapbooks, and going over Dusty's letter five times, Jackson was of a different outlook about things. But change would come slowly, and he had to focus on the most important one.

He'd fallen hard for one outspoken, geeky, sexy, beautiful, tear-stained woman, and he had to convince her he was more than just a rodeo cowboy. He had to make her see that he was the right cowboy for her. "There's something I didn't tell you, and I want to get your opinion."

"Okay." She didn't sound too certain.

"Dusty gave each of his sons a belt buckle. The exact same one."

"Like the one he always wore? With the steer head in the middle?"

Jackson hadn't realized Dusty wore it around Red Creek, too. "That's the one. Dad wore it all the time when he came west, too. So, since you're so smart at figurin' out mysteries, why do you think he did it? Gave us each one, I mean."

Rori propped herself up on her elbow. "The only reason I can think of is to show that while you were growing up, you were part of him. And now that he's gone, and you've found your brothers, it's his way of saying you're all part of each other." She shrugged one shoulder. "Too sappy?"

"Not at all." He leaned over and kissed her. "I think you're right. Dusty was a good dad. A really good dad. I think he wanted us four to see the belt buckles as our connection to each other."

She smiled. "Now that's deep, cowboy."

If she thought that was deep, this next part would have her believing Jackson was a friggin' intellectual. He cupped her face in his hand. "I've got somethin' more to say."

"Okay." She tightened her jaw, as if getting ready for a blow.

"I've changed my mind about things."

"Things like what?" She kissed his palm and pulled his hand to the warm spot between her breasts, where her heart beat strong and steady.

"First…" He grinned at her.

She nodded. "Make your list, stick to it."

"Yes, ma'am. You've taught me well." He took a breath. "So first, I wasn't looking for someone to be with for longer than this week."

Rori glanced away, blinking rapidly.

"But now I am."

Her blue gaze shot to his. "You are…?"

"I want to try this for a while, Rori, if you'll have me."

She opened her mouth and he pressed a finger to her lips for a second.

"I know you've got a vendetta against rodeo men, and I'm not ready to give up rodeoing. I've got an event next weekend in Georgia." He watched her face.

Her eyes widened a bit.

"I want you to come with me." He put his finger to her lips again. "I'll pay for the airfare, I'll fly in to KC, and we can hop on a plane for Georgia together. I have a nice hotel room reserved, so none of the crappy motels you hear about rodeo men crashing in."

She kissed his finger and tugged his hand down, her smile breaking slowly across her face. "Are you askin' me out on a date? To a rodeo?"

He chuckled. "I guess I am, Ms. Rori." He took a breath. "And if things work out, we can discuss…more." Jackson wasn't going to tell her about the email from Dylan, inviting him back to Red Creek on the last day of the month. Whether he came back or not would depend on what this woman said right now.

"More." Closing her eyes, she scrunched her face for a second before looking deep into his eyes. "I misjudged you, Jackson Walker. You're exactly right for me."

Punching a fist into the air, he shouted, "Yee-haw!" Jackson rolled on top of Rori, kissing her quick and hard. "And you are exactly the perfect place..." He swallowed back emotion. "The perfect place for me to stop runnin'."

Epilogue

On the thirty-first of August, Jackson arrived at the small airport outside Red Creek in the small plane he'd chartered. Two more planes sat parked along the hanger. Dylan's, and Killian's, probably, if they'd decided to come back for this bonding week. And Rogue would still be here, unless he'd skipped out. The red company truck Jackson had used sat next to the planes, and he found the keys in the ignition. "Small towns."

A few minutes later, he sat around a table in Cubby's Restaurant with the other three Walker offspring.

"You're driving Dad's Caddy?" Dylan grinned at Rogue, who'd spent the last week in Kansas, and gestured to the champagne-colored land barge parked at the curb.

"Damn right. The thing is smooth as sin."

Jackson fiddled with the fork that sat on a napkin in front of him. "You know, Dylan, when I got your email after that first week, I thought you'd gone crazy." From the first minute he'd set foot here, Jackson had wanted nothing more than to shake the dust of this town off him and leave. But a letter from a deceased man, a town full of characters, and most importantly, an amazing woman, had changed his mind.

Rogue and Killian nodded, and Jackson recognized Dusty's same mannerism in his half-brothers.

The note had told the others that the town had a lot to offer, the business was surprisingly interesting, and the people of Red Creek had accepted him like a born-and-raised Red Creekian.

"I was under the influence, I guess." Dylan scratched his cheek. "But damned if I don't feel exactly the same way being back here today."

"I figured that." Rogue hung one arm over the back of his chair. "Figured you'd also found yourself a gal." A smirk curved his lips. "But I agree, this place grows on a man."

Killian set his forearms on the table. "Sure does. I mean, who knew this dustbowl in the middle of fucking nowhere would leave an impression."

They were interrupted by the appearance of the waitress and they took a minute to place their orders.

After the waitress walked away, Jackson looked around the table. "So we're all agreed? We're going to do this thing?" Since getting to know them through the scrapbooks, Jackson felt invested in this new family, and in this new company structure.

The men looked at each other.

"I'm in." Dylan shrugged. "Got nothin' else going on."

Rogue nodded.

"We'll stay the week, gettin' to know each other, just like the old man wanted?" Jackson frowned. "Get the business sorted out between the four of us?" A few weeks ago, the idea of traveling the country like Dad did had appealed to him, but now, with Rori grounded in Red Creek, he wasn't so excited about that idea.

"That's the plan." Killian curled his upper-lip in a sneer. "Live in the house for a whole week and *bond* with each other." He snorted.

The guys laughed, but Rogue pointed at Killian. "From what I hear around town, you found yourself someone to help pass the time."

Killian grinned. "Sure did."

Rogue looked at Jackson and Dylan. "And rumors are spreading about you two. You each fell for a local gal?"

Jackson nodded. *Fell for* was an understatement. After spending the previous weekend with Rori in Georgia, he kept picturing the two of them in all sorts of strange situations: in front of a church in wedding gear, carrying her over the threshold of their new house, at a hospital with a brand new baby between them. "Afraid so." He smiled to soften the words.

The brothers laughed, then looked at Dylan.

"Yep. Happy as a puppy with two tails." Dylan stared off,

looking lost in thought.

In Georgia, Jackson had tried to pry the secret of Dylan's week in Red Creek out of Rori, but she'd firmly shook her head and told him it was Dylan's secret to tell. Jackson figured the guy would open up about it sooner or later, and with the fully-stocked bar back at the lake house, it'd probably be tonight.

"What about you, little brother?" Killian winked at Rogue. "Don't tell us you're the only Walker boy without a happy ending?"

Rogue sat quietly for a few seconds. "Well, I wouldn't want to be the one to ruin a perfect record." He tried to keep from grinning, but his brothers smacked him on the back, laughing, and he let go with a smile.

They all looked at each other, unexpectedly pleased expressions on their faces.

Killian tapped his belt buckle. "Damn if I don't feel that these tell people we're part of an exclusive club of some kind."

"We are," Jackson said. "The Walker Brothers Club." He'd worn his buckle today, too, same as his brothers. This next week would be interesting, complicated, confusing. But Jackson vowed to give it everything he had, to make these men…family.

They all grinned at each other.

"Old Dusty must have known what he was doing," Killian added. "Even if we didn't think so four weeks ago."

The waitress arrived with their burgers, fries, and pie á la mode, and they ate and talked about the ladies they'd found and claimed in Red Creek. They discussed the company and pondered out loud their prospects for the future.

Cubby's wife brought their bill to the table. "Well, you four are quite a sight, sittin' here all lookin' like peas in a pod." Sherry cocked her ample hip. "You all decide if you're stayin' or goin'?"

The brothers smiled.

"Hard to believe, but it looks like we'll be stayin'." Jackson pulled out his wallet, looking down to hide the burst of emotion that crowded in on him.

"Yeah, but you three cowboys forgot about that damn bonding." Dylan grabbed the bill and handed it back to Sherry with a couple twenties. "Come back and ask us that same question again in a week."

They all laughed.

Outside they all shook hands and said they'd see each other back at the house later to start their week living and working together.

Jackson headed across the street to Cyber Wise. He hadn't seen Rori in a week, and he missed the hell out of her. Opening the door, he let the buzzer announce his arrival.

She peeked around the wall from the back room, squealed, and ran toward him, her red high-tops eating up the distance.

He braced himself and caught her, spinning them around a few times before setting her down and kissing her soundly. "Darlin', you miss me?"

She cupped his cheeks and kissed his chin, ran her fingers through his hair and kissed his cheeks, then wrapped her arms around his neck and just stared at him, her beautiful blue eyes shining with moisture. "More than I should admit."

"Me too, Rori." His chest filled with that strange emotion reserved only for her. "I've got a few hours to kill." He looked up to where her bed sat a floor above. "What are you up to?"

She laughed and released him, but he didn't release her. "So much for romance, huh cowboy?"

Jackson tugged her close again. "I just missed being with you, darlin'. That's romantic, ain't it?"

Shaking her head, she sighed. "It shouldn't be, but for some reason, yes it is." Her hands ran along his ribs. "Still sore from last weekend? You took some hard falls."

He'd gotten bucked off more than he stayed on. "Hey, I made the buzzer once."

Rori's brows dropped. "Made the buzzer? So you were trying

to stay *on* the horse for eight seconds? Dang, I kept cheering when you were able to get *off* the horse before the buzzer."

He swatted her sweet round ass. "You're gonna need a few more lessons in rodeo, Rori darlin'."

"Any time, cowboy. I had fun, except for those few seconds when you were on the horse, or flying through the air getting off it."

Jackson almost admitted that the thrill of being on a bucking bronc had become less appealing than spending time with this woman of his. And she was his, now. Whether or not either of them was ready to admit it. Before he'd left Red Creek that Sunday morning at the end of his official week, he'd asked her for her phone and had punched his number into her contacts list. And…she'd started to cry again.

She looked out the window. "How was your lunch?"

"Our first time together for more than ten minutes, and it went well. We're going to meet at the house later for supper, sit and talk and drink the rest of the night. Tomorrow we're going out on the lake and do some water skiing and jet skiing. Stuff like that."

Her smile looked so sweet. "All the things brothers do together. You've got a lot of years to catch up on."

Equal parts anticipation and anxiety rolled through him at the thought. There were bound to be some moments of disagreement, but he hoped that for the most part they'd all get along. "We're spending one day at the office with Benner to talk about the company structure. That'll be interesting."

She nodded. "Are you still thinking about traveling?" Swallowing, she seemed to hold her breath.

"Right now, I'm leaning more toward a job as a desk jockey." Relief flowed through him at his admission. He'd been traveling—running—for too long.

Her smile lit the room. "Really?"

"Uh huh. And I chartered a plane so when I do need to travel, it'll be easy to get where I'm goin' and back." He kissed her. "I want you to use it to go visit your parents whenever you want."

Shaking her head, she frowned. "Would that be misappropriation of company funds?"

"The company isn't paying for it. I am." He'd never told her he had money, and with his paycheck from the company, and a quarter ownership of the half-billion-dollar company falling into his pocket in less than a year, he had more than he knew what to do with.

"Thanks, I'll take you up on that." Rori cocked her head. "Wow, your own plane? I sure picked the right rodeo cowboy to fall in…" Her eyes popped wide, and she looked away. "To fall for."

Had she been ready to say, fall in love? Jackson had the same feeling, but it was still too soon to say it out loud. But it would be real damn soon when he'd blurt it out. It grew too strong inside him to hold on to for long.

"I'd like to take you west, darlin'. Meet my mother."

Her lips formed a little O. "I…I'd love to. And if you want, you can meet my parents."

With a chuckle, he ran his fingers through her silky hair. "You don't sound too sure."

"They're great, you'll love them, and they'll love you." She smiled softly, and his heart swelled.

"My brothers talked about getting all of us and our ladies together this week, too. Supper out at the lake house, maybe a sunset pontoon cruise around the lake." It sounded so domestic, it should be making him nervous, but instead, he couldn't wait.

"I'd like that a lot." With a sigh, Rori hugged him closer.

"Let's plan some family weekends in the next month." He couldn't wait to show her Bandon. Take her sailing out on the ocean, crabbing off the pier, out in the woods to see the redwood trees.

"Done." She glanced up at the ceiling, then winked at him. "So, what do we do in the meanwhile to keep busy?"

He grinned, letting the blood rush from his head down low to where he wanted her so badly, it hurt. But he had a few things to talk about with her first.

"How about walking the shore of Osprey Lake with me?"

Her smile weakened. "Sure. That would be fun." She didn't sound too certain.

"The brothers and I were talking about the big house. We don't want to live together there, and it doesn't sound like any of us want to live there." Jackson sure didn't. The memories of his dad, the good and the not good, would haunt the place forever.

"I can understand that." She waited, staring into his eyes.

"I'll bring up your idea of making it into a bed and breakfast at our meeting with Benner."

She nodded. "I think Marliss and Lou would love that."

Here was the difficult part. He didn't know how she would react to his idea. "We're going to divide the lakeshore in fourths, and each build houses on our share."

Her mouth opened in a surprised smile. "That's great. It's such a beautiful spot."

Jackson set his hand on the side of her neck. "Rori, I want you to help me pick out a section. I want you to help me design the house and decorate it and fill it with stuff."

She blinked rapidly, a sheen in her eyes. "Jackson. Are you sure?"

He nodded, not able to talk around the lump in his throat.

"I'd love to." Pressing up on tiptoes, she kissed him. "Really, really love to."

"Darlin', I'd really, really love to…take you up on your offer now." He glanced at the ceiling.

She laughed, then sobered. "Thank you, Jackson, for showing me what I was missing in my life."

"Aw, Rori. Thank you for giving me a place to put down roots." He kissed her. "A place where I can be me, and not just one of the sons of Dusty Walker."

~~*~*

270

Connect With Me

Thank you for reading Jackson and Rori's book. I loved writing a rodeo cowboy who considered himself "lazy." Of course, Rori found a way to love him just as he was, despite his resistance to *computering*. I hope you're enjoying all the other books in The Sons of Dusty Walker Series. Subscribe to my Newsletter so you can hear all the latest on my upcoming projects.

I'd love to hear from you. I've listed all the places I hang out, and I hope you'll connect with me at one or more of them.

All my best,

Randi

"Rode Hard and Put Up Satisfied"

http://randialexander.com/

http://randialexander.com/subscribe-to-my-mailing-list/

https://www.facebook.com/RandiAlexanderAuthor

https://www.facebook.com/RandiAlexanderBooks/

https://twitter.com/Randi_Alexander

http://www.goodreads.com/author/show/4885056.Randi_Alexander

http://randialexander.com/blog-3/

http://wildandwickedcowboys.wordpress.com/

http://69shadesofsmut.com/

About the Author

New York Times and USA Today Bestselling Author Randi Alexander knows a modern woman dreams of an alpha cowboy who takes the reins, and guarantees they're rode hard and put up satisfied.

Published with Cleis Press, Wild Rose Press, and self-published, Randi writes smokin' hot romance with heroes who'll have you begging to ride off into the sunset with them. When she's not dreaming of, or writing about, rugged cowboys, Randi is biking trails along remote rivers, snorkeling the Gulf of Mexico, or practicing her drumming in hopes of someday forming a tropical rock-band.

Forever an adventurous spirit with a naughty imagination, Randi is also family oriented and married to the best guy in the world, her own cowboy, Kick. Give in to the allure of erotic passion, strong but vulnerable heroines, and irresistibly seductive cowboys, as Randi's emotional love stories sweep you off your feet and leave you breathless with passion.

Saddle up! And prepare yourself for the sexier side of happily ever after.

Other Books by Randi Alexander

Read the book blurbs and first chapters at my website
  http://randialexander.com/

Legend Awakening Book 1 of the Diaries of a Casanova Series
All Hat No Cattle Book 1 of the All Cowboy Series
All Flash No Cash Book 2 of the All Cowboy Series
All Smoke No Fire Book 3 of the All Cowboy Series
Double Her Fantasy Book 1 of the Double Seduction Series
Double Her Pleasure Book 2 of the Double Seduction Series
Double Her Temptation Book 3 of the Double Seduction Series
Double Her Destiny Book 4 of the Double Seduction Series
Chase and Seduction Book 1 of the Hot Country Series
Heart of Steele Book 2 of the Hot Country Series
Rough Ryder Book 3 of the Hot Country Series
Cowboy Jackpot: Christmas
Cowboy Jackpot: Valentine's Day
Cowboy Jackpot: St. Patrick's Day
Redneck Romeo: Red Hot Valentine
Her Cowboy Stud
Turn Up the Heat
Cowboy Bad Boys
Skin Deep (short story in the Cowboy Heat Anthology)
Banging the Cowboy (short story in the Cowboy Lust Anthology)
FREE READ A Gentleman and a Cowboy

Killian

by

DESIREE HOLT

Prologue

The office could have been straight out of another century, with its massive desk, huge carved furniture, and lingering scent of cigar smoke. The most modern things were the four men seated across from the desk big enough to sail a battleship on.

Killian Walker shifted in his chair and wished, not for the first time, he had his familiar length of rope to play with. Maybe the comforting feel of the twisted strands in his hands would calm his jumpy nerves and ease his anger. This was definitely a what-the-fuck situation, and he wasn't one bit happy about it. If wishing worked, he'd be back in Montana riding fence instead of sitting here with three strangers who looked like him and an old man who had facilitated this situation.

Stanley Benner, Esquire, attorney for the late Dusty Walker—his father, of all the fucked-up things—leaned over his desk and plopped a folder of papers in front of Killian and the three other men sitting in a row with him. Killian slid a glance at them, not for the first time, and swallowed a chuckle. There they sat, like four penguins in their suits and ties, all appearing as if they'd rather be any place but here.

And that was another thing. The damn suit was driving him nuts. Or maybe it was what it implied that he resented. If not for his mother's insistence, he wouldn't be wearing it. If not for his mother's insistence, he'd have shown up in his jeans and work shirt and been a damn sight more comfortable.

Brothers! Damn! Who the fuck would have thought he had three brothers, anyway?

The one introduced as Jackson Walker adjusted the gray tie he wore as if it was choking him. Killian held back a snort. It probably was. He wondered if they were all as uncomfortable in them as he was.

The lawyer's gaze rested on each face in turn. Was he taking in their similarities? Even though the four brothers had never laid eyes on each other until five minutes ago, they sat silently, letting the man have his fill of staring. His three half-brothers had to be as gobsmacked as Killian was. He kept his gaze forward, not ready to take in the three faces proving his dad was a rat bastard.

The gray-haired lawyer unbuttoned his suit coat and sat, pushing his wire-rimmed glasses up on his nose. "Incredible likeness. Your father never mentioned it."

Their father sure hadn't mentioned a whole hell of a lot of things, like the fact he had four sons, each of whom had no idea there were three more just like him in other parts of the country.

Killian sat forward in his chair. "Are we quadruplets? Were we separated at birth?"

The attorney shook his head again. "Absolutely not. Each of you is your individual mother's biological son. You are each about a year apart in age. Mr. Walker...uh...Killian."

Jackson gave a rough laugh. "Since we're were all four *Mr. Walker,* the man must have realized he needed to take a different approach."

"Killian," Benner continued, "you're the oldest at twenty-seven, and Dylan, you're youngest. It must be a very strong DNA strain in your father to have produced men who look so similar."

Besides different eye and hair color, their faces and bodies could have been stamped from the same mold.

"When I arrived at your homes last week with the news your father had died, I was under strict instructions not to mention you had brothers. It was among your father's last wishes you learn of your siblings' existence in person." The attorney picked up a sheaf of papers. "I apologize for bringing you to Kansas under these circumstances."

Killian had spent the past week peppering his mother with questions about how and what and where and every other damn thing. To say he was shocked was the understatement of the year. And at his mother when he discovered she had been way less than forthcoming. She had known the situation from Day One. While Killian had thought his parents had been married, his mother finally confessed to him she'd known Dusty had a wife back in Kansas and she'd also known the state of his marriage. But she loved him desperately, and it had given her real pleasure to bear him a son. She took his name to avoid gossip in town. Killian felt betrayed by both of them. His father had spent very few weeks with him every year, and now he—all the sons—knew why.

How he'd anticipated those infrequent visits, cherished every minute of them. The man not only had a wife, but three other families. The time their dad did spend with him he said was to prepare him to one day run the family business. They poured over contracts for regional mineral rights, surveyed land, and interpreted tests to determine if there was value in the acreage. When he was younger, he hadn't been all that interested, but he'd do anything to be with Dusty.

Killian treasured the time his father had spent taking him on trips to mineral leases and meetings with geologists. While it didn't replace horses, the business still fascinated him, and he felt honored Dusty wanted to share it with him. He'd believed the bastard when he'd said Killian was so very special to him and he wished he could spend more time with him. Maybe if he hadn't been so busy screwing every single female he hooked up with, that might have been possible.

His mother had been much less concerned with the legitimacy of the situation than she was with how he now viewed his late father. She'd hauled out photo albums, pointing to the pictures of him and Dusty and telling him how much his daddy loved him. And her. Her! Yeah, what a laugh. Her and at least four other women, including his wife. All the pictures in the world wouldn't ease the hurt he felt now. Or soften the fact she'd known about Dusty's wife and the situation all the time. Had the business he'd set her up in and the beautiful house he bought for them been enough to buy her silence? He wasn't sure he could ever forgive her for that.

He did feel sorry for her on one count. It was obvious from the questions she'd asked the lawyer she'd thought she was the only "other woman" in Dusty's life. Although she hadn't voiced her feelings, Killian had seen the shock and dismay as well as the sense of betrayal evident in her eyes. But she'd kept her feelings to herself, urging Killian not to let it affect how he viewed his father.

He hadn't even wanted to come today, but his mother had insisted.

"Dusty wanted you to have his name," she kept repeating. "He was proud of you, and he acknowledged you in his will. Substantially. If nothing else, you'll get closure."

Closure. Yeah. Six feet under. Oh, wait. The old man is already there.

Very reluctantly, he'd made use of the first-class ticket the attorney had left and flown here to Red Creek, Kansas. Where he'd received the next biggest shock of his life, meeting his half-brothers. When he and his half-brothers had seen each other for the first time, they were stunned into silence, warily watching each other.

The attorney rattled the papers in his hand. "As I told you, Dusty and his wife Theresa were killed in an auto accident. We're told they died instantly. It was a very sad day." He looked from one to the other. "So, if there are no more questions, I'll begin reading the key points in the will." He waited a few seconds, meeting each of their gazes.

"Yeah, I've got one." Rogue looked at his brothers. "How did he…?" He held up a hand. "Let me rephrase that. Why? Why four families in four different states?"

The lawyer set down his papers and laced his fingers together. "Your father wanted to have children, and his wife was not able to produce heirs for him."

"So he went around hunting for incubators?" Killian spat out.

"That's a little disrespectful," Benner chided.

"You're calling me disrespectful?" Killian made a rude noise. "I'd say your client is the one who was disrespectful."

"She knew about all of us?" Dylan interrupted. "His wife, I mean?"

"No, she did not." Benner's cheeks turned ruddy. "And I was sworn to silence under attorney-client privilege. I'm assuming your mothers made you aware of your father's marital situation?"

Killian wanted to shout, *Mine damn sure didn't.*

One of the men cleared his throat, but no one spoke. Out of the corner of his eye, Killian saw Jackson stare at the law degree on the wall. What was going through his mind? Any of their minds? Had any of them known about Dusty's wife or the fact this made all of them.... No, he wouldn't go there. Instead, he focused his attention away from Montana and back to Kansas.

"So, in the interest of time, I will read the highlights of the will. Copies of the entire document are in the folders I set in front of you." The attorney cleared his throat and read for a quarter of an hour. The details included a grocery list of assets: a mineral and water rights company boasting assets near five hundred million dollars, including a private ten-person jet, a storefront in the small town of Red Creek, Kansas, as well as a big house on the outskirts of town.

The brothers sat silent.

"Of course, there are the four houses in four compass points of the US. In the north, Montana, where Killian resides. Texas, from where Rogue hails. Dylan, of course, from Nashville, and Jackson, from Oregon."

Killian's gaze flicked to each of his brothers as they glanced at each other then back at the lawyer.

"These houses are currently company property," Benner went on. "But your father notes you four, as the new owners of D. Walker Mineral, can opt to transfer the homes into your mothers'—"

"Hang on." Beside him, Killian sensed Dylan stiffen. "You're saying he left the company to us?"

"Yes, of course." Benner's eyes widened. "I didn't read that portion of the will because I assumed...." He hefted out a sigh. "The company is now legally in your names, exactly one quarter going to each."

Dylan let go with a long, low whistle.

Killian was dumbfounded. *Holy fucking shit!* He owned a fourth of a half-billion dollar company? Hell, he'd always figured Dusty had plenty of money. Their house in Montana, where Dusty had set up Killian's mother, Mairi, was practically a goddamn mansion. It sure cost more than a pretty penny.

But half a billion? Man, what he could do with a fourth of that. Although he wasn't sure money would take away enough of the pain of betrayal.

"So, if we sell our quarter?" Jackson said the words slowly, figuring the other three had to be pondering the same question.

"There are repercussions."

Repercussions? What the fuck?

The attorney flipped pages. "Ah, here. 'Heretofore, the parties to which—'"

"In plain English, please." Killian put one booted foot on the opposite knee.

"Of course." The man set down the papers and leaned back in his chair, placing one hand on his round belly. "The company is essentially frozen as is for a full year. After that time, if one of you wants to sell, the others have the option of buying you out at half-worth."

"Half-worth?" Rogue fisted his hand. "Meaning they'd buy me out at a 50 percent discount?" The guy glowered.

"Yes, that's correct. Your father wanted to keep the company in the family. Wanted you four boys to run it together."

"I can wait a year," Jackson drawled. "I've got savings, money to get me to rodeos and pay my entry fees. I expect to win some during the season, too. But, hell, no matter what Dusty wanted, there's no room in my life for small-town Kansas and an eight-to-five job. I'll probably be the first to sell my quarter of the company."

Benner cleared his throat. "However, you are each officially on the payroll, and your first paychecks will be cut the day you successfully complete the one…." He swallowed then cleared his throat. "Stipulation in the will."

All four of them leaned an inch closer.

"Stipulation?" Dylan prodded.

"To inherit, you must spend a week in Red Creek, working in your father's office, learning more about the business, sharing with each other what you've learned from your father over the years. You must also reside for that week at your father's house—your house—on Osprey Lake."

"A week?" Jackson shook his head. "What's the time frame here? Anytime in the next year?"

Rogue slapped open his folder and pulled out his copy of the will. "What section is that in?" His words came out clipped.

"Second from the last page. You'll see there's a thirty-day time limit." The attorney checked his calendar. "Today is August second. You'll need to decide which week in August works for all four of you and plan to be back here then. Or if this week works…?" He shrugged.

Killian tapped his fingertips on his knee. "Dad wanted the four of us to live in the same house and work in the same office? For an entire week?" He had things to do and places to go. He saw this windfall as the means to realize a long-held dream, and he wanted to do some investigating.

"Like summer camp for the bastard sons of Dusty Walker." Dylan mumbled a curse.

Jackson rubbed the spot between his eyebrows. Good. At least, Killian wasn't the only one who found this situation bizarre. "What the fuck was he thinking?"

Rogue kept reading silently.

Benner's face turned a dark shade of red. "He loved each one of you. I know because he took great pains to create provisions to make sure you were taken care of after his death. Just as he did while he was alive."

Yeah, real good. The jackass obviously thought money could buy anything and everything, including his kids.

"Listen here." Rogue stared at the will. "It says we each have to spend a week, but it doesn't say it has to be the same week."

"No, it, uh…. What?" The attorney sat forward and frantically flipped through his paperwork.

"I say we each take a week, get this goddamn stipulation out of the way, and figure out the rest later." Rogue looked at his brothers. "Agreed?"

"Yeah. Okay." Dylan accessed his phone. "I can stay this week. I got nothin' goin' on."

Jackson grabbed his folder. "I can do the week after. Get this bullshit out of the way."

Killian rose. "Sounds good. I'll do the third week."

"That leaves week four for me." Rogue stood and tucked the folder under his arm.

"Now wait, boys." The lawyer stood, still staring at his copy of the will as Jackson and Dylan got to their feet. "Your father wanted you all to be here together. At the same time. To get to know one another."

The brothers stood in a half-circle. Killian saw Jackson's gaze drop suddenly to the belt buckle he wore then the others. The exact same belt buckle on all four of them. The one given to them by their father.

"Am I seeing things?" he asked.

Killian looked down at his waist. "Son of a bitch. I can't believe this. They're all alike."

"That's kinda fucked up, huh?" One side of Dylan's mouth curved up. "The old man gave us the same belt buckle, like we'd use them to somehow magically find each other."

Jackson frowned as if he wanted to fling the buckle into the nearest lake and watch it sink.

Killian sympathized. So much for imagining his father thought he was special. Special, like one of a matched set of four.

The room went silent, and, as if on cue, they all turned toward the door.

"Wait." The attorney raced around his desk and stood in front of the men, his brow wrinkled, his breath coming fast. "Your father's wish was to have you spend this time together." His hands fluttered like he didn't know what to do next."

"Well, then…." Killian patted Benner's shoulder as he strode past him. "I guess he should have had his lawyer write that in the will."

He noticed Jackson bite back a grin.

They were complete strangers. Best to keep it that way.

Dylan gave the others a trigger finger salute and headed out the door, the others right behind him.

Killian watched as each of his brothers—half-brothers, you idiot—entered their separate limousines and left the parking lot. He climbed into the one still waiting for him and leaned back, eyes closed, as the vehicle began to move.

Now, the fun begins.

Chapter One

Killian pushed back from his desk where he'd been working all morning and stretched. He'd spent the last two weeks catching up on what he had to do at Hart Brothers Ranch and making sure Larry Hart was okay with him taking off. After all, in a couple more weeks, all this bullshit would be over and he could get on with his life.

"I like to think of you as a friend as well as a hand here," the man told him. "I'd never stand in the way of you doing something like this. Anyway, my brothers and I know you've wanted to have your own place for a long time. While we'll hate to lose you, if this makes it possible, we wish you well." Then he clapped Killian on the shoulder. "And we'll help you any way we can."

Killian had had to turn away at that, choked up at the kindness of the man.

The money, however much he ended up with, would help him realize his lifelong dream of raising Appaloosas. He'd kept his dream to himself. He hadn't even told the Hart brothers. But in all the years he'd been working for them, he'd made it his business to learn everything about the company, from buying to breeding to training. Apparently, they knew him better than he thought.

As he got older, he'd brought it up to Dusty when they were together. The man, however, had never seen the value in it, and, after a while, Killian stopped talking to him about it.

Yesterday, the Walker company plane had picked him up in Montana. His mother had insisted on driving him to the small airport, where the plane landed, and seeing him off. Things were still unsettled between them, and he didn't know how he could fix it. He was still hurt she'd kept such vital information from him, and he felt betrayed. The shit with Dusty—he had stopped thinking of him as his father—was bad enough, but he'd always loved and respected his mother. He just couldn't seem to get past this.

At the moment, he wasn't feeling too kindly toward either of his parents.

This morning, Lou, the cook, had insisted on feeding him a full breakfast then told him to take whatever ride he wanted from the garage. What an eye-popping experience. After picking up his jaw at the sight of the boat of a Cadillac and a tricked-out Ford F-159 truck, he'd settled on a silver SUV. Less obvious, he hoped. Marliss, the housekeeper, handed him a piece of paper with directions to the office of D. Walker Minerals, and off he went.

When he got there, only two people were in the office. According to the information the attorney had given him, they were Abby Hollister, the receptionist/secretary, and Elaine Dennis, one of the mineral and oil rights specialists. It was obvious they'd been prepared for him.

"Welcome," Abby said. "We're glad to meet you."

"We've got Dusty's office all set up for you," Elaine told him, urging him toward the office door.

"You're the king for a week," Abby teased. "You get to sit where the king does."

Killian shook his head. He was no king, and he sure didn't think of Dusty as one.

"Just give me a closet," he said. "All I need is a desk and a place to set my coffee mug."

Muttering under her breath, Elaine ushered him into a small office next to hers. He gave a short laugh when he saw it really wasn't much more than a large closet.

"This is what you asked for," she pointed out, a smile twitching at her lips.

"Where did my…brothers…work when they were here?" The descriptive word stuck in his mouth like bad whiskey.

Elaine nodded at the tiny office. "Right here. Seems none of you want to sit where Dusty did." She lifted a shoulder and dropped it. "It's a damn shame. He really wanted you boys to step into his shoes."

Killian snapped back before he had a chance to think. "We're not 'boys,' and if we had a choice, we'd really have nothing to do with all of this."

Abby eased back to her desk as the smile disappeared from Elaine's face.

"I'm sorry you all are making such snap judgments about the man. Maybe while you're here you can force yourself to find out a little more about him."

"I doubt it." He hauled in a deep breath and let it out slowly. "I'm sorry. I need to mind my manners better."

She studied him for a long moment. "Out of curiosity, if all of you are so angry with Dusty, why did you agree to the terms of the will?"

He thought about it for a moment. "I think none of us wanted to be the one to screw it up for the others."

She gave a brief nod. "Okay. Well, I'd better get you started here while the place is still quiet."

Now, after a full morning of studying reports and maps and more shit like that, he needed a break. He lifted his Stetson from the hat tree, clapped it on his head, and walked into the front office.

Abby glanced up from her computer. "Going out?"

"For a minute. Just need to stretch my legs. Maybe get a bite to eat. Where do you all go, anyway? Is there someplace close by?"

Elaine walked out of her tiny office to place a folder on Abby's desk and chuckled.

"I think I dropped too much stuff on him today," she teased. "He needs to refill the well."

"Whatever you've got," Killian said, looking from one to the other, "bring it on. You don't scare this country boy. So, where's a good place to eat?"

"You could try Cubby's Creekside Café right next door," Elaine suggested. "He's a cousin to Lou, your cook."

Killian thought about the breakfast he'd consumed.

"If he's half as good as Lou, it sounds like a winner. But I think I just want a bite of something. And to walk a little."

She smiled at him, warming him with its genuineness. According to the information in the folder each of the brothers had received, Elaine had been with Dusty for a long time, longer than either of the two men on staff, and probably knew more about the business of D. Walker Mineral Company than anyone. Her light-brown hair was streaked with touches of silver, but her face was smooth and unlined. He had no idea how old she was. Somewhere between forty and sixty, he guessed. But she was spoon-feeding him the business and made him feel comfortable. He was grateful for that.

"Well, give yourself a look at Red Creek. There's a great coffee shop down the street you could try, also. It's called Heart Starter."

"Yeah?" Killian gave a short laugh. "That's some name."

"Lexie's coffee is indeed that. And her pastries taste from heaven."

"Lexie?" He lifted an eyebrow.

"Lexie Choate. She owns the place."

Killian stared at Elaine who exchanged a glance with Abby and tried to conceal a smile. "Is there a joke here I don't know about?"

Abby shook her head. "Not at all. However, if you do stop there and you're so inclined, I'd love one of her honey buns."

"Consider it done."

He walked out the door, wondering if he was walking into yet another trap. His life seemed to be full of them.

It was just after noon, and the sidewalks were busy. Killian glanced into Cubby's Creekside Café, studying the place through one of the windows. It seemed very homey inside and nearly full. Probably a good place to pick up local gossip. He'd bet a dime today's was all about him and his brothers. Half-brothers, he reminded himself, and the familiar bitterness washed through him.

Benner had called this morning. He wanted Killian to stop by later today, so he could catch him up on how the first two weeks had gone, but Killian wasn't even sure he wanted to hear. He wanted out of this disaster as soon as possible. Still, he'd have to talk to the man sooner or later. Might be best to get it over with.

He had made it to the end of the block, in front of Heart Starter. Was her coffee like battery acid, or just strong with a rich flavor? Whatever, he needed something to clear his brain, so he pushed the door open and walked in. A bell tinkled overhead.

"Be right with you," a voice called.

Killian stopped in his tracks. The voice had the lyrical quality of an angel's, plucking at his heartstrings as well as other parts of his body. When she rushed out from the back of the shop and he caught sight of her, he was sure he'd need some of the strongest coffee, because his heart stopped. Just. Stopped.

Lexie Choate was his actual dream come true, the best package Killian had ever seen. *Holy shit!* The top of her head just came to below his shoulder, a head full of streaky blonde curls. Gold-flecked hazel eyes surveyed him from beneath a fringe of thick lashes sweeping over creamy cheeks with a light dusting of freckles. She was busily tying a clean apron over a pink tee shirt and skinny jeans and smiling an apology to him with plump, kissable lips.

Kissable?

What the fuck, Killian? First of all, he wasn't here in this bumfuck town to have fun. Secondly, with the damnable truth about Dusty and the whole situation, was he even good relationship material anymore? What kind of genes did he carry, anyway? Could he be faithful to one woman? He needed to get his head out of his ass before it got permanently stuck there.

Yeah? The little voice in his head remarked. He should tell that to his cock which was suddenly begging to be let loose to have fun.

"Sorry." Her voice danced over his skin like a teasing wind. "I got a little tied up in the back."

At the words "tied up," Killian's fingers curled up over his absent length of rope. A picture burst into his mind of the very tasty barista naked except for his rope tied around her in an indicate pattern.

Down, boy!

The bell jingled again, interrupting his erotic reverie. He glanced behind him to see three people walk in. He stepped aside and motioned them to the counter.

"You were here first," the hot angel pointed out.

"I'm in no rush. Take care of your customers."

"Well, okay." Her smile made his errant cock jump. "But don't leave."

"I won't." Not even if someone paid him.

"Good morning, Billy." She smiled at a tall, stocky man, with graying hair, wearing a plaid shirt, and jeans. "Your usual?"

"Of course." He nodded. "I swear you make the best pastries in Kansas, Lexie."

Okay, so this was the owner, Lexie Choate. Somehow the name fit her, sparkly fun with a subtle sexy overlay. He had to stop himself from licking his lips.

He took the opportunity to scan the interior of Heart Starter. The owner had put together a very attractive place. Cafe tables and chairs occupied much of the polished wood plank floor. Framed colorful artwork hung on the walls, giving the place a warm feeling. A counter ran the length of the wall opposite the door, with all the equipment and supplies for coffee on shelves behind it. One end of the counter topped a glass display case with an assortment of pastries. Adjacent to all that was a small refrigerator case with sandwiches.

Apparently, she had just stocked a fresh batch of goodies because the aroma of cinnamon and sugar filled the room, mingling with the scent of fresh-roasted coffee and making his mouth water.

The tempting little blonde expertly filled the orders, smiling and chatting as she did so.

"Thanks for stopping in," she said as she rang up the purchases. "It's always good to see you. And, Risa, tell your sister if she's still interested in something part-time to come by and see me."

"I will," the woman named Risa said. "She'll be so excited. With her youngest in day care, she really wants to get out and do something."

"I'd love to have her." Lexie smiled as she handed the woman her change. Then she turned her hundred-watt smile on Killian. "Have you decided what you'd like?"

Yes. You.

"I'd like to have dinner with you."

Had he asked her out? He could hardly believe the words had dropped out of his stupid mouth. He wanted to smack himself. God, was he a dumbass or what?

Lexie stared at him. "Excuse me?"

"Uh, black with a shot of espresso, please. And I'll take a couple of those cinnamon rolls." Then, he couldn't help himself. "And I still want to take you to dinner."

She didn't say anything while she fixed his coffee and slid a couple of rolls onto a small plate for him. He waited while she processed his payment, wondering if she'd even respond to his invitation.

"Take any of the tables." She laughed. "We're not busy at the moment. You just beat the noon rush."

But he stood there at the counter, stubbornly, unable to believe what he was doing. This was so not like him. He'd met his share of women both in his hometown and when he travelled to Great Falls, and he hadn't been tongue-tied with any of them. Or with any of those he'd had a more extended relationship with. So, why was he suddenly acting like a teenager?

"Well?" he finally prompted.

She cocked her head and studied him for long moments. "You're new here," she said at last. "You're one of the Walker boys. Is this week your turn?"

Fuck. Was the whole sordid story common news here?

"I'm Killian." He held out his hand.

She took it, her warm, soft skin igniting the blood in his veins. Or maybe it was the intense irritation at being the object of common gossip.

"Lexie Choate. Welcome to Red Creek and Heart Starter."

"So, does everyone in Red Creek know all the grimy details?" he asked.

She gave a slight shrug. "Dusty lived here forever and was always larger than life. When the four of you came for the meeting with the attorney, everyone's curiosity jumped about a hundred points. Word got out and, yes, you can't blame people for talking about it. The story is a little unusual."

"To say the very least." He couldn't keep the edge of bitterness from his voice.

A tiny frown creased her forehead. "You all aren't happy about the money?"

The money. Right.

"It's all the rest of the baggage that's hard to swallow. It's tough to learn at our age that we're all bastards."

Shock washed over her face. "Oh, Killian. No one in this town thinks of all of you that way. We loved Dusty. He shared his success with Red Creek and did a lot for this town."

Killian picked up his cup and took a healthy swallow, even as hot as it was. "That so?"

"Yes, it is. You should take the time to learn about him while you're here this week."

"Maybe you could tell me about it over dinner."

She laughed, a wonderful silvery sound. "You don't give up, do you?"

"No, ma'am." He grinned. "Not when it's something worth having."

"But you don't even know me," she protested.

"That's what the dinner is for." He waited with barely controlled impatience for her answer. "You could take the opportunity to tell me about Red Creek."

Finally she gave a quick nod. "Okay, but only because you're Dusty's kin, so I can count on you to be trustworthy."

His cock sent him an urgent message. *Not on your life.* He willed it into submission. One thing at a time.

"I'll take it any way I can get it," he assured her. "What time is good for you?"

"Seven? I close the shop at five thirty. I need some time to get ready."

He wanted to tell her she looked ready now. Instead, he said, "Seven is good. You'll need to give me your address."

"Not very far. I live upstairs."

"Nice and convenient. Okay, works for me."

The bell rang again, and a fairly large group of people crowded inside. Her lunch rush was about to start.

Killian took his plate and half-filled cup to one of the tables and ate slowly, watching Lexie at work. She was cheerful, smiling, joking with people, exchanging personal comments. It was obvious this was a popular place, and everyone in Red Creek loved the owner. *And why not?* he asked himself. *What's not to love?*

He almost hoped she had a hidden personality disorder or was running from the law. Anything to discourage and put a lid on his sudden attack of raging hormones. He might as well have been sixteen again. What the fuck was wrong with him? He was here on serious business, with no time for this stuff. Besides, he had carefully guarded himself all this time from any kind of meaningful situation. Now, it was even more important, knowing he had Dusty Walker's genes. What kind of husband would he be, when cheating was in his DNA?

Husband? Jesus, Killian. Stupid much?

He gave himself a mental shake, bussed his table, and got in line again.

"Hungry for more?" She grinned.

"Two honey buns to go."

Now she gave a full-out laugh. "I see Abby's got you trained your first day on the job."

"I have to take good care of her. Otherwise, I have no idea what I'm doing."

"She's the one to show you. We all believe she's the one who keeps that office together."

A sudden, unpleasant thought struck him, one he wasn't sure he had the nerve to ask.

"Uh, so she worked for Dusty for a long time?"

"Yes, and get your mind out of the gutter." The frown was back. "They never had anything more than a working relationship."

He held up his hands. "Sorry. Didn't mean too imply otherwise." He took the little box she handed him. "See you at seven."

"Seven o'clock."

On his walk back to the office, he mulled the whole thing over, stunned at what had happened. This was so far out of his wheelhouse he couldn't begin to understand why he'd done it. Since he'd hit puberty, there had been no shortage of women. Ever. He wasn't a pussy hound, but he knew all he had to do was wink at a female when he was out with the guys and things got going. Maybe he'd taken too much for granted and didn't appreciate the women who came his way. But Lexie was from a whole different world, and, for her, he needed to clean up his act.

No, what he really needed to do was shut the whole thing down before he got into trouble. He'd suddenly realized when the reality of his heritage came out, he might not be such a bargain for a woman, the money aside. What if he turned out to be a cheater just like Dusty? Besides, he wasn't going to be around here long. He had no intention of making Red Creek his home, now or ever.

Shit, shit, shit. His hands itched to grab the piece of rope he always fiddled with when his thoughts got out of hand. It was his pacifier, his comfort toy, and a lot more. He'd stuck it in a drawer in his desk when he got to the office, keeping it out of sight. Now, he couldn't wait to get his hands on it. It always helped him think, among other things. Sort out his thoughts and feelings.

Abby grinned at him when he walked back into the office. "Did you get lunch?"

He shook his head. "Wasn't that hungry. But I had some great pastries. And here." He handed her the box. "This is for you."

She chuckled. "You remembered. You get definite points for this. So I guess you met Lexie. Isn't she a sweetheart?"

"I asked her out to dinner." The words fell out of his mouth like stones. *Great. Just great.*

Elaine stared, her eyes nearly drilling holes through him. "Isn't that a little fast, cowboy?"

Irritation scratched at him. "Is there a problem?"

She lifted her hands, palms up. "Don't know. But you're only here for a week. What happens then?"

Killian didn't want to make an enemy of this woman whose help he needed so badly, but he also didn't need a nursemaid or hall monitor.

"It's dinner, you know. Besides, she seems smart enough to make up her own mind about a date. And that's all it is, a dinner date."

Elaine studied him again. "Just watching out for my town."

"Well, your town seems to know every damn detail of this situation. It didn't seem to scare Lexie off." He was starting to get really pissed off. "I should think you'd be glad I'm making friends in this town."

Elaine finally gave him a smile. "I am. I'm telling you to be straight with her. Don't promise something you won't deliver. You don't even expect to be here after this week."

"Why don't we wait and see what happens? If I screw up, you can beat my ass."

"And you can bet I will." She sat back in her chair and opened the little box on her desk. "Of course, these honey buns will go a long way toward sweetening me up."

"One more thing," he said. "How is it everyone knows all the details about this?"

Elaine shrugged. "Word gets around."

That apparently was all he was going get for the moment.

"Fine, but I'm not done asking."

"Meanwhile, how about tackling the latest pile I put on your desk?" She bit into one of the buns, a sure signal the conversation was over.

Chapter Two

Lexie didn't think Killian Walker had been around long enough to scope out the restaurant scene, so she decided she'd suggest a couple of places to him. Casual places. Everyone knew he, like his brothers, was required to stay for one week. The others had made it plain when they got to Red Creek the week was all they'd commit to. She figured Killian was probably just looking for some female companionship to pass the time. She still couldn't believe she'd accepted his dinner invitation. Since she'd come back to Red Creek, trailing the disaster her personal life had become, she'd refused to date any of the men in town who kept asking her. No more relationships. Been there, done that, had the T-shirt to prove it. Seemingly, her judgment where men were concerned was seriously flawed.

But the minute she'd clapped eyes on him at Heart Starter, every female hormone stood up and saluted while all her girl parts began planning a celebration. She was tempted for the first time since she'd run home to Red Creek, pulling the tatters of her life around her. She wanted to think it was because she'd been on sexual hiatus for a long time while she sorted out her life. She ignored the internal warning he was big trouble for her. The impact he made on her evidently froze all her brain cells. Maybe she was overdue for a fling. And if he was leaving, not staying here, she didn't have to worry about the messy aftermath.

Right. You just keep saying that.

If she was honest with herself, though, it really had to do with the appeal surrounding Killian like a cloud of electricity. His black shirt and jeans had emphasized his lean, rangy yet muscular body and made his eyes as dark as ebony. The square jaw and high cheekbones framed a face accented by thick brows and lashes. There was a tiny scar at one corner of his mouth and another faint one running down his left cheekbone. She knew via the grapevine he worked on a ranch outside the town where he lived in Montana. Had he gotten them there, or was he a brawler, wearing his badges of war?

Whatever the answer, her palms itched to smooth over the hard wall of his chest and the taut muscles of his ass. His ass? Holy crap! Where was her mind? She might be a sensuous creature—if she remembered that was—but she didn't have those kinds of random thoughts about men. Certainly not one she'd met for five minutes.

She took one last check in the bathroom mirror, fluffed her hair slightly, and decided this was as good as it was going to get. She was crazy. She should have worn her least-flattering clothes and made herself dull as dishwater. But she was so ready for something new in her life. If it was only for one week, so be it. And Killian Walker was exactly what she needed. She just had to convince him.

Instead, she'd changed into a new pair of skinny jeans with rhinestone studs, a deep-purple tank, and a gauzy white blouse over it, tied at the waist. Sandals with medium heels and dangly earrings completed the outfit. She wanted to knock his socks off, so when he left, he'd carry a good memory of her with him. Excitement coursed through her as she thought about the evening ahead and all the possibilities.

She heard the sound of booted feet on the outside stairs, followed by a knock on the door. Taking a deep breath, she let it out slowly, wiped her palms on her jeans, and opened the door. And literally had to haul her tongue back into her mouth.

Killian Walker was dressed all in black again, this time in an embroidered Western shirt and dress jeans, spit-shined black leather boots, and yet another black Stetson. Heat blazed in those onyx eyes. Between her thighs, an insistent throbbing let her know she was just as affected as he was.

Damn!

His eyes took a leisurely tour of her body, from her neck over her breasts and hips to her polished toenails and back up again. With every pass, her skin felt scorched, as if he'd actually touched a match to it. She swept her tongue over her suddenly dry lips and swallowed, hard. For some reason, her gaze automatically dropped to his fly, her eyes widening at the sight of a significant bulge. Maybe going out to dinner wasn't such a good idea. But staying in might be a whole lot worse.

This was *so* not her style.

"Lookin' real good." The husky quality of his voice sent shivers racing down her spine.

"Thank you." She wet her lips again. "You, too."

He drank her in once more then held out his hand. "We'd better get out of here before I do something to get us in trouble. Shall we?"

"Yes. I'm ready."

She grabbed her slim purse from the little table by the door, slid the thin strap over her shoulder, and stepped out into the little landing. Pulling the door shut behind her, she double- checked that it was locked.

"Okay." She smiled up at him. "Let's go."

He handed her into the silver SUV and leaned in to buckle her seat belt.

"I can do this myself, you know." He was so close she could inhale the clean, male scent of him, earthy and outdoorsy.

"Just being a gentleman."

He snapped the buckle into place, his face so close to her she could almost count his eyelashes. For a second, they were frozen, his mouth barely an inch from hers. Time stood still for an interminable moment. Then he backed out and closed her door.

"So," he said when he was buckled into the driver's seat. "This is your town. How about picking a place for us."

She had thought about Bib's Ribs then discarded it as too messy. She didn't want to spend half the evening with barbecue sauce all over her face and hands. Steak. Kansas was known for steaks, and The Roadhouse had excellent meals at reasonable prices in a very informal atmosphere. She mentioned it, and Killian nodded.

"I can always eat a good steak. Just point me in the right direction."

"It's on the other side of town," she told him. "I thought we'd take the long way so you can see some more of Red Creek."

"Such as?"

"You'll see."

He slid her a quick glance. "Okay. You're calling the shots."

She was a little nervous as she gave him directions. How would he react when she took him past some of Dusty's accomplishments. She knew how all the sons felt about the man. Lordy, the whole town knew. But if Killian was really Dusty Walker's son, then he should know the man was someone other than a guy who didn't marry Killian's mother. She pointed out the playground at the little park in the middle of a residential section. The new wing he'd paid for at the small retirement home. The high school where he'd paid for computers.

"There's evidence of his giving nature everywhere," Lexie told him. "He's bought businesses going under, propped them up, and let the owners stay there rent-free until they got on their feet. Helped folks with their mortgages, and he saved more than one or two farms around here."

"Okay, okay, okay," Killian said at last. "I get it. The man was a goddamn saint. A fucking angel. Wonderful. I'll get him a halo."

"He wasn't a saint at all, but he was more than you believe him to be." She shifted in her seat. "That's all I'm saying, for now. Take the next right, and we'll head to The Roadhouse."

Since it was a weeknight, the restaurant was barely half-full. Still, Killian requested a booth rather than a table. People watched, curious, as the hostess led them to their spot. Lexie smiled at some of them and dipped her head in a casual nod.

"Will the gossips be working overtime tomorrow?" Killian

asked.

She laughed that light musical sound. "Probably, but not to worry. The next day, they'll be chewing on someone else."

The hostess seated them and told them their waiter would be right with them. Lexie saw Killian taking a long look around the place, at the planking on the walls, the high-back booths, the long bar with its old-fashioned mirror. A tiny stage in one corner was currently empty.

"Weekends a band plays here," she explained. "They aren't half bad."

He turned those incredible onyx eyes on her. "That so? You like to dance?"

She lifted one shoulder. "Same as anyone else, I guess."

"You do your dancing with anyone special?"

Before she could answer him, the waiter in jeans and a Roadhouse polo shirt showed up with their menus.

"Something to drink?" he asked.

"Lexie?" Killian deferred to her.

"Um, a glass of white wine, please."

"Beer for me," he told the waiter. They discussed brands until Killian settled on one he liked. Then he turned his attention back to Lexie. "So, do you?"

"Do I what?" She'd hoped he'd forget the question.

"Dance with someone special," he reminded her.

"Let's say no one special at the moment." Or for a long time. "Otherwise, I wouldn't be here with you."

"Good to know."

The long, slow grin he gave her sizzled her nerve endings. She hardly knew what to do with the chemistry exploding between them. She didn't remember any other man having this effect on her. Danger, she told herself, yet she didn't seem to be able to control her reaction to him.

Lexie had never realized exactly how erotic eating a meal could be until tonight. She was fascinated at the play of muscles in

Killian's face as he chewed and in his throat as he swallowed. Whenever he lifted the bottle of beer to drink, she couldn't tear her eyes away from the way his lips closed around the neck, imagining how they'd feel pressed against hers. Or wondering how his long fingers clutching the bottle would feel on her body.

Good lord, Lexie! Get it together!

"You okay?" Killian's voice broke the spell.

"I'm fine. Why?"

"You've hardly touched your steak, and you had a weird expression on your face."

What she had on her face was a flush of heat. *Damn it.*

"No, I'm fine. The steak is fine. Excellent, in fact." To demonstrate, she cut off a piece, popped it into her mouth, and chewed.

Killian laughed, a nice, husky sound. "Lexie, if you aren't having a good time, we can leave. I hate to see a woman forced to pretend something she doesn't feel. I really was hoping we could have a good time. I'm only here for a week, and I'd like to spend some of it with you."

"A week?" She wrinkled her forehead. "So, you aren't staying, either?"

"Either?"

"Well, your brothers made it plain to everyone they were out of here as soon as possible. I guess you feel the same way."

He nodded. "Sorry. My life doesn't include Red Creek." He paused. "I don't want to mislead you, Lexie. I felt a connection with you the minute I walked into Heart Starter and thought it would be nice to spend some time with you. It doesn't matter that we just met. I like what I see, and I want to know you better. Nothing more than that. I'm sorry if you got the wrong idea."

Embarrassment surged through her. "I didn't get any idea, Killian. If you think—"

He held up a hand. "I didn't think anything. Except, as I said, I'd enjoy spending time with you. Can we do that? Just enjoy the evening? No pressure?"

At his words, she suddenly found herself relaxing. She wanted that, too, didn't she? Maybe a fling for a week to prove to herself she was still a desirable woman? Especially to a man as hot and sexy as Killian Walker. She had never been a fling sort of person, but hadn't she told herself just tonight it was time to break out of her shell? And who better to do it with than a man who would only be around for a week?

She looked across at Killian and saw him watching her carefully.

"Um, yes, we can do that. I'd like that. Absolutely."

The smile he gave her curled her toes. "Great."

The atmosphere for the rest of the dinner was much more relaxed. Killian told her about growing up in Montana, how he'd been in love with ranching all his life, and how his love for it had continued to grow. She talked about Red Creek, about her parents who owned a wheat farm outside of town, and her brother who was a Marine stationed in Afghanistan.

"And you run Heart Starter," he commented. "Did you always want to be a shopkeeper? A barista?"

Now it was her turn to laugh. "Barista," she repeated. "That's a fancy word for Red Creek. Maybe not my childhood dream, but I enjoy it."

"So what *was* your dream growing up?"

She hesitated. Should she tell him about that dream, the one she was still chasing? No, not yet. Most people who knew about it chalked it up to a hobby, and unless something spectacular happened, that was probably what it would remain. Especially after her one disastrous relationship had tanked partly because of it and sent her back to Red Creek. She didn't like to dwell on either and was grateful people didn't ask her questions.

"Oh, just this and that," she said as casually as she could. "I'm not very interesting. I'd rather hear about you."

"And I'd rather her about you," he insisted.

"I told you. I'm really very boring."

He had finished eating his dinner. Now, he reached across the table and took one of her hands in his. "I don't think there's a boring bone in your body, darlin'."

She was determined to bring the focus back to him. "Tell me about those scars on your face." To soften the remark, she added, "They're very sexy." Damn! She shouldn't have said that, either.

"Sexy? Really?" He winked. "Glad to hear it."

"So, where did you get them?" she repeated, determined to keep their conversation out of dangerous territory.

He shrugged. "Paying more attention to myself than the horse. We had a little battle over which one of us was boss."

She laughed. "And the horse won?"

One corner of his mouth, the one with the scar, kicked up in a tiny grin. "Only one time."

"Tell me more about your work on the ranch. I want to know everything about you."

His face sobered. "One thing you should know, Lexie, is when my week is over, I don't intend to hang around. I have plans."

One week and he'd be gone. Didn't that make him a safe bet for her little fling, or whatever she chose to call it? So, why the sudden pang of disappointment?

"I'm a big girl, Killian. Right now, I'm out for dinner with a very hot cowboy. Let's do this one day at a time. No promises, no commitments."

"I have plans," he persisted, as if he wanted to be positive she understood where he was coming from. "Dusty's money will let me follow them."

"That's good. So, let's just spend some time together." A thought stabbed at her. "Unless this is your way of telling me we're done after tonight."

His eyebrows jerked upwards. "Hell, no. I always like to be up front about things."

"Duly noted." She finished the last swallow of her wine. "So, tell me about your work back in Montana."

Lexie listened with fascination to his stories about working on the Hart Brothers Ranch. About the shop Dusty had bought for his mother. About growing up in Montana. Before she realized it, only a handful of people remained in the restaurant.

"Guess I need to get the check," Killian commented. "Don't want to wear out my welcome. I sure plan to eat here again."

"I'm glad you enjoyed it."

Killian paid the check then stood up and waited for her to slide from the booth. While they walked to the SUV, he kept his hand on her arm. He moved to open the door, and Lexie missed the warmth of the contact at once. He again helped her into the seat and buckled her belt for her. When his face was so close to hers she could feel his breath on her cheeks, he leaned forward that last little bit. She held her breath, waiting to see if he'd move away again. But no, he pressed his lips gently against hers in the briefest of kisses. Still, even with light contact, the heat it created set her blood to boiling, and the pulse in her pussy was beating with long-suppressed need.

Without thinking, she opened her mouth slightly, and Killian's tongue swept in like a sword of flames. The kiss was so intense it stole her breath, but she never thought to break away. At last he lifted his head and looked at her with ravenous hunger blazing in his eyes. And mixed with that, a look of stunned surprise that matched her own, shock at the connection they made.

Oh, lordy!

He stared for another long minute before closing her door and jogging around to the driver's side. They were both silent on the drive back to her place. When he walked her up the stairs to her door, he kept his hand on her as if needing to maintain contact. On the landing, he turned her to face him.

"I'm not coming in, Lexie. I'd like to think I'm too much of a gentleman to act on what I want to do with you on our first date. But, trust me, there will be others. So, if you want me to stay away, now would be the time to tell me."

Her heart pounded so loud she was sure he could hear it. "I want to see you again." The words were a whisper.

"All right, then."

He pulled her into his arms and cupped her head with one large hand. His scent surrounded her as did the strength of his body. When he pressed her to him, she could feel the unmistakable bulge of his cock through the thick denim. It pressed hard against her mound, the contact causing a flood of moisture to her panties. Could he smell the fragrance of her arousal?

This kiss was deeper than the other, more intimate. He licked every inch of the inner surface of her mouth, brushing his tongue over hers in an erotic dance that made her weak with wanting. She clutched his arms, fingers tightening on ropes of hard muscle, the heat of his body scorching her hands. She had an insane desire to rip off his clothes so she could run her hands all over his naked body. At the point where she had forgotten to breathe, he lifted his head. The shimmer in his eyes told her he was as affected as she was.

"See you tomorrow." His voice was thick with desire. "Keep my cinnamon buns warm."

"Of course." But she wasn't thinking of pastry then. "See you."

He waited until she was inside and had turned the lock. When she heard him jogging down the stairs, she leaned against the closed door and exhaled. *Well!* One evening with Killian Walker and she knew the man should come with a Danger sign. She touched her fingertips to her lips, remembering the pressure of his mouth, the hot sweep of his tongue. She hugged herself, pretending she could still feel his body pressed to hers.

For a brief moment, she had thought of inviting him inside, especially after those incendiary kisses. Then one of her frozen brain cells kicked in, and she forced the thought back. Not after one date, her inner voice shouted.

Tomorrow night, she told herself. The week would go by too fast, and she didn't want to waste a minute of it. She desperately needed affirmation from this man that she was desirable and appealing. That she appealed to *him*. Oh, she was ready to go wild, all right. For one week she could let loose. At least she'd have the memories. Afterward? Who knew what would happen.

Chapter Three

Killian wished he could get rid of the itchy anxious feeling holding him in its grip since he'd gotten up that morning. No, since he'd arrived home the night before. No, no, no. Since he'd taken Lexie home the night before and walked away with unsatisfied desire and a raging hard-on. If it was just the physical attraction, he could deal with it and move on. After all, he intended to get his ass out of this town as soon as he could.

Unfortunately he had to face the fact it was way more. How had she captivated him so fast and so easily? What he was feeling for Lexie Choate had struck him with the force of runaway horses, and he had no idea what to do with it. She wasn't a woman he could take his pleasure with and walk away. There was a lot more to her than the women he usually bedded. In less than twenty-four hours, he'd already figured that out.

Could he do what had in mind, spend the week enjoying her company, and then head off to the rest of his life? It couldn't be anything else. First of all, he had a plan, and now he'd have the resources to make it happen, just as soon as he fulfilled the terms of the will. And then, of course, there was his sudden re-examination of the kind of person he was. He carried the genes of a man who'd cheated on not one but five different women.

So, what did he do? Stay away from her? Hell, no. He might as well stop breathing.

Damn, Killian. You've really fucked up this time.

Okay. He'd do what he's talked to her about last night. Spend time with her while he was here and leave with some damn good memories. She seemed on board with the idea, so what was his problem? By the time he pulled into the parking place behind D. Walker Minerals, he had worked himself up into such a lather, he wondered how he'd ever be able to concentrate on the complexities of mineral and oil rights and the delicate structures of royalties.

"Somebody bite your ear?" Abby asked as he walked in.

"No, why?"

"You look like you've been wrestling wild animals," she told him.

"Must be trying to absorb all the info Elaine shoved at me yesterday." He grinned

"I heard that," the woman called from her office. "Better get in here, Killian. I've got another folder full for you today."

He smothered a groan, sailed his hat onto his desk, and stepped into Elaine's office.

"You trying to torture me? I thought you liked me."

She smiled. "I do. And I have every confidence you can learn this stuff easily."

He dropped into the chair in front of her desk. "Can I ask you a question and get an honest answer?"

"Uh-oh." She lifted an eyebrow. "Sounds like I'm not going to like it."

"You were with Dusty longer than anyone around here. Did you ever think he was the kind of guy to do what he did?"

Her brows pinched together. "What kind of *guy* do you mean?"

He shrugged. "You know. One who would cheat on his wife, collect a bunch of mistresses, and sire some bastard kids?"

"Wow. A pretty harsh description, isn't it?"

"How would you describe it?"

She was silent for a moment, as if gathering her thoughts. "I'd say he was a man who desperately wanted children to carry on his name, who loved four women equally, and who would have married any and all of them in a hot minute."

"Yeah? And how do you suppose those women feel? Don't you suppose they feel betrayed?" he demanded. "And what about his wife? How did she fit into all of this?"

Elaine sighed. "Quite a dicey story, Killian. I'm going to try and make you understand."

"Please. It would be a big help."

"Dusty's wife knew he wasn't in love with her from the beginning. He wanted into the oil and mineral business, and she wanted Dusty for a husband under any circumstances."

"Just a business decision." He snorted.

Elaine nodded. "And it would have worked out well if they'd had children. But poor Dusty found out after the fact that she didn't want kids at all. It was a freal blow to him."

"But he stayed with her anyway?"

Elaine nodded. "That was Dusty. It went against his grain to divorce her. He'd made a commitment and he was going to honor it."

"Which is how he ended up creating a family with four other women." Killian didn't know whether to be disgusted or feel sorry for the guy.

"It wasn't that he did it deliberately. It just sort of happened with each woman."

"And his wife?" he asked again. "Did she know?"

"I think she knew he was attached to other women. But she was desperate to keep her marriage together, so she overlooked all the signs another woman would have made a fuss over." She paused. "But you should know he took very good care of her and, when he was home, he was faithful as the sun coming up."

Killian twisted his lips. "Saint Dusty."

"No." Elaine's voice was quiet. "He was no saint by any means. But he loved all four mothers, and he loved each of you boys. He took care of everyone financially, which is more than a lot of other men would do."

"So, I should overlook all the crap?"

"What you should do is spend some time thinking about everything. Talk to Marliss and Lou. They knew him better than anyone. But, meanwhile, get your ass back to work." She handed him a thick folder, smiling to soften her words. "Now, cowboy."

But, when he went into his office, his mind was still in turmoil, over both Dusty Walker and Lexie Choate. Reaching into his briefcase, he pulled out his favorite length of rope and sat there, sliding it through his fingers while his mind raced like a stallion chasing a mare in heat. How the hell was he supposed to concentrate on complicated contracts under these circumstances? Later this week, one of the guys in the office was going to take him out overnight to visit some of the sites already leased and explain the process to him. Then he had the weekend and he'd be gone. Could he possibly resolve everything in his mind by then?

Especially the situation with Lexie. Already he was itching to see her again. If he did, however, he'd get good and tangled up, and what would happen when he left? Because, at least from where he sat now, he couldn't wait to shake the dust of Red Creek from his boots. His entire future was focused on getting his ranch.

How had he gotten himself in this situation after less than forty-eight hours in town? He hadn't planned on finding someone like Lexie for damn sure. Sighing, he stuck the rope back in its place and went to work.

He spent a good portion of the morning studying the contents of the folder Elaine had given him, the rest of it being quizzed by her on what he'd absorbed so far. He surprised himself—and probably her—with the amount of information he'd absorbed and understood.

"You could be a natural at this, you know," she told him.

"Thanks, but...." He flapped a hand helplessly, not wanting to give voice to his thoughts.

"But you don't plan to make this your life's work," she guessed. "Or Red Creek your permanent home."

He shrugged. "It isn't who I am."

She watched him silently for a long moment. "You know, Dusty really loved all you boys, and your mamas." She gave a short laugh. "Although boys hardly describes the men you've become. He was proud of each and every one of you."

"And did he realize what a mess he'd created?" Killian demanded.

"Of course he did." She stared off over his shoulder. "He agonized over it all the time. Thing was, he loved each of the women equally. He knew what he did was wrong, but he did his best to make amends. He wasn't all bad, Killian. I hope while you're here you can learn about the other side of him."

"People seem to want to keep cramming it down my throat, so it's not as if I can exactly get away from it."

"Oh?" She raised an eyebrow in a gesture he was learning meant *Tell me everything.* "You've only been here since Sunday night, so who else has been pounding your ear? Marliss and Lou?"

"Not yet." He winked. "But I'm sure they're working up to it."

"Hmm." Her lips twitched. "So, who else could you have been talking to?"

His cue to end this conversation. He pushed himself out of the chair. "I think I'll take a break. Maybe wander down the street for some pastry."

Elaine burst out laughing. "You are about as subtle as a sledge hammer, Killian. Say hello to Lexie for me. Don't forget to get Abby's honey buns." He was almost out of her office when her voice stopped him. "And Killian?"

He turned. "Yeah?"

"Take care with that young lady. Everyone thinks the world of her."

He nodded. "Duly noted."

All the way down the street, Elaine's words echoed in his head. *You could be a natural at this.* Not if he was raising horses. *Dusty really loved all you boys, and your mamas.* Bullshit! And the worst: *Take care of that young lady. Everyone thinks the world of her.*

So did he, and that was the trouble. More than the world, as a matter of fact. How was it possible? He'd known her less than twenty-four hours, yet he found himself on some kind of emotional roller coaster he was totally unprepared for. The memory of those scorching kisses were imprinted on his body. He'd had a hard time not dragging her into her apartment and tearing her clothes off, but he respected women, treated them well, even if the connection was only for one night. His mother had hammered it into his head.

Respect women, Killian. They deserve that.

Had she been trying to tell him something? Had Dusty not respected her? Well, fucking damn, consorting with three other women besides her while he had a wife at home? Did he not respect any of them?

Shit, shit, shit.

His head was so fucked up he should go home and dunk it in a bucket of cold water. Except, he was already at Heart Starter. As if it had a mind of its own, his hand grabbed the handle and pulled the door open. Since it was closer to noon than his visit yesterday, the place was pretty full, but Lexie looked up from handing over two coffee cups and gave him a million-watt smile. Then she held up one finger.

"One minute," she mouthed.

He made an okay sign with his thumb and forefinger and hung back while she waited on her customers. At least half of the tables were filled today, and the people seated there stared at him with curiosity. Probably studying the latest Walker offspring to hit town. What did they all think about this circus? Leaning in a corner while he waited for Lexie, he nodded at everyone and gave them a casual smile. Several people actually smiled back at him. He had to admit this place wasn't as bad as he'd expected.

He let his gaze wander around the shop, taking in things he hadn't really noticed yesterday. The artwork on the walls, for instance. Yesterday, they had been blurs of color. Today, he realized they were great examples of contemporary Western art. The style was very distinctive and arresting. Someone had lovingly painted a magnificent stallion, a small herd of horses galloping across a pasture, a tired cowboy at the end of a long day, and other similar scenes. Whoever this was might have come from Montana like he had, because the essence of the cowboy had been captured perfectly.

He was still admiring them when someone touched his arm and he saw Lexie holding out a mug of coffee to him. He inhaled, and her jasmine scent filled his senses.

"I'm still in the middle of a late-morning rush," she told him, smiling, "and lunch rush is coming in. I didn't want to leave you without your coffee, though."

Her smile lit up every one of his nerve endings and sent heat cascading through him. Jesus! If he got this way from looking at her in a roomful of people, what was he going to do when they were alone again?

"Listen." He took a sip of the smooth liquid in the mug. "Why don't I get my stuff to go, and I'll see you later."

She raised her eyebrows. "Later?"

"For dinner?" He held his breath, waiting for her answer.

Her easy smile unknotted his muscles. "Sure. Same time?"

"Yes, if that works for you. And, Lexie? I'd like to take you someplace really nice, if there's one where we won't be caught up in everyone's radar."

"I think I have just the place," she told him. "It's a little more expensive than The Roadhouse."

"No problem. Any place you'd like to go is fine with me."

"Okay." She brushed a stand of hair back from her face. "Let me box up your pastries for you."

He noticed the crowd gathering at her counter again. "I can wait."

"Oh, no. This won't stop for at least another half hour. Let me get your stuff." She gave him a tiny wink. "On the house."

"I can't—"

"My pleasure. Don't argue with the owner." She was back in seconds with two small boxes in a plastic bag with the Heart Starter logo on it. "Enjoy. I'll be ready at seven."

Then he was back on the street, slightly dazed, the little bag in his hand. When he glanced at his watch, he realized it was barely noon. Seven hours until he could see her again. How would he ever last?

*****

Lexie had changed her clothes five times by the time the clock showed almost straight up seven.

You'd think I'd never been on a date before.

But all her tingly girl parts as well as the functioning portion of her brain kept sending her messages this was more than just a date. Killian Walker had blown into her life by an accident of fate. She'd probably never see him again when this week was over. There was no guarantee he—or any of the brothers—would hang around little Red Creek when their time was up. They all had places in the larger universe, and she was pretty sure they'd go back to them. Oh, wait. She'd heard a rumor that Dylan, the first to stay the week in Red Creek, may be hanging around.

In any event, it had nothing to do with Killian. He'd probably be on a fast plane back to his real life after this. She'd never met a man quite like him, all quiet, solid strength, intense masculinity, and sex appeal off the charts. She'd laid awake a long time last night, thinking about their kiss and wondering what it would feel like to be naked against him, lying close to his equally naked body. What his hands might feel like roaming over her, teasing all her erogenous zones. How his mouth would feel on her, placing those kisses on her breasts and her—

Heat flushed over the entire surface of her skin. The pulse low in her pussy that had leaped to life last night with their kiss hadn't abated one bit. Nor had the tingling in her breasts or the ache in her nipples. Or the yearning to feel his hard length inside her. Normally, she had much better control of herself. But, normally, she didn't have a man as hot and sexy as Killian walk into her life. Or one who touched her soul and her heart as well as her body.

And, in his eyes, she saw signs of a similar reaction, irises that darkened with heat, hunger, and desire. He might be leaving, but he'd take the memory of her with him. She was determined. So, tonight she would be more daring than she'd ever been in her life. Do something completely out of character. If she only had one week with him, she intended to make the most of it. Starting with inviting him into her apartment when he took her home. The romance novels she devoured painted erotic scenes in her mind and a longing for the kind of romantic adventures the authors wrote about.

And she didn't need to have her bedroom looking like a suitcase threw up all over it. Finally settling on a red skirt that swirled around her legs, a silk-print blouse that showed off her breasts to best advantage, and a pair of strappy, high-heeled red sandals, she swept everything else into a pile and shoved it into her closet.

Taking a deep breath and letting it out slowly, she made a final pass at her hair and makeup and sprayed on a little more jasmine cologne.

Just in time for the knock on her door.

Don't leap on him the minute you see him.

She opened the door and went weak in the knees. Tonight he wore black dress pants, a black silk shirt, and his Stetson. Lordy, but the man looked like sex on wheels in black. His clothes enhanced his lean muscular frame, his wide shoulders, and his long legs. But what really got her was the expression in his eyes, as if he was mentally undressing her and licking every inch of her body.

She shivered with suppressed delight.

"Ready?" His lips curved in a smile lethal in its intensity.

"I am." She stepped out onto the platform, pulled the door shut, and locked it. Then she glanced up at him and smiled. "More than."

His eyes darkened. "Me, too." Then, as if pulling himself back to reality, he offered his arm. "Shall we go?"

"Absolutely."

She was glad she'd decided on Maximilian's. It had a warm, old-world charm, an elegant feel with the crystal chandeliers, white linen tablecloths, and crystal goblets. The thick carpet silenced footsteps, and classical music played faintly in the background. But the best part was it was located in the next county, and it was a weeknight, so they were not too likely to run into people they knew.

"Not exactly what I was expecting out here in—" He stopped. "Out here."

"Go on," she teased. "Out here in Hicksville, right?"

He laughed; the rich full sound made her panties dampen and her nipples tingle. Lord, it seemed everything this man did had an erotic effect on her. She just hoped she hadn't misread him and he was as anxious for this as she was. He certainly was giving off those signals. But she also knew he was a man who respected women. Whatever he might want, he'd wait for a signal from her.

Tonight, she would give it loud and clear.

"Actually," he told her, "even in Montana we have really nice restaurants, even in small towns. My mother made sure I learned to eat properly in public and not pick my teeth at the table."

Lexie giggled. "I'll bet you did that as a kid."

"I did a lot of things as a kid I got my hide tanned for. I think my mother was afraid I'd grow up to be a heathen and a bum."

She tilted her head. "What's your mother like? And I'm asking not because of her relationship with Dusty, but because I really want to know. I want to know about *you*."

"Well, let's see." He waited while the waiter placed their drinks on the table—wine for her, bourbon and water for him—before he went on. "Her family came over from Ireland. I guess you could figure it was in the blood somewhere when you heard the name Killian."

"What's her name?"

"Mairi. It means of the sea. Which is a little odd, considering her family lived in the mountains of Montana."

"How did she get there?"

"Her ancestors came over in the nineteenth century, from what she told me. I'm not even sure of the entire story, but she was fourth generation." He laughed. "Her great-grandfather liked to call himself an Irish cowboy."

"They really liked the West?"

He nodded. "They did. As if they were born to it, from what I know."

"And Killian? What does your name mean?"

"Well," he drawled, "the Urban Dictionary says it means 'a kid who doesn't take shit from anyone.'"

"And is it accurate?" She looked at him over the rim of her wineglass.

He shrugged. "Maybe not as aggressively as when I was a lot younger, but I still hold my ground when I need to."

"I don't know if this will please you or not, but I see some of Dusty in you. He held his ground, too. When he was right, he didn't let anyone push him around."

"When he was right." Killian took another sip of bourbon. "Let's make a bargain. Tonight, we leave Dusty out of the conversation. That okay with you?"

Anything he wanted was okay with her.

She lifted her wine and waited until he touched his highball glass to hers. "To a pleasant evening."

His eyes ate her up. "The most pleasant," he agreed and took another swallow of his drink. "So as long as we're on names, what does Lexie mean? Is it short for something?"

"For Alexandra." She brushed her curls back from her face. "No one's called me that for years, though. In either form, it means defender of man. So I guess when you're out with me, you're safe from attack."

He chuckled. "You can defend me anytime, darlin'."

Then he had questions about her family, how long they'd lived in Kansas—three generations—and what she wanted to do with her life, if anything, besides run Heart Starter.

She fiddled with her wine glass as she tried to give him answers without revealing anything to him. Few people were aware what they thought of as her hobby was really her secret passion. And she wasn't quite ready to expose herself to Killian. So, she glossed over the fact she'd gone away to school, without saying where, mentioned she'd come home while she figured out what to do with the rest of her life, and shared how the opportunity for Heart Starter had jumped into her lap.

The conversation flowed smoothly and easily,

For dessert, they shared a piece of Decadent Chocolate Cake. Every time his lips slid over the tines of the dessert fork, she imagined them closing over one of her nipples. When he licked the frosting from his lips, she imagined his tongue sliding over her body and into her tight channel. It was all she could do to sit there and act as if nothing was happening to her.

Finally, *finally*, Killian paid the check and ushered her out of the restaurant.

"Enjoyed it, darlin'." His voice slid over her like warm molasses.

"Me, too." She hoped she enjoyed the rest of the evening as much. If only she could get rid of the butterflies dancing the jitterbug in her tummy.

Chapter Four

Killian had barely been able to concentrate on his food, as tasty as it was. His entire attention had been focused on the woman who sat across from him all evening. From the moment she opened her door and he saw her in the silky blouse draped so easily over her breasts to the flirty red skirt that emphasized and teased at her shapely legs, to the sexy sandals showing off her feet to best advantage, she was a package made to tempt the most stoic man. Watching the delicate way she chewed her food, sipped her wine, blotted her lips made him want to drag her into his arms. The way she flipped her streaky blonde curls back from her shoulders and lowered her eyelashes over those warm hazel eyes when she looked down had him harder than cement.

He had to restrain himself from grabbing her when he helped her out of the SUV. He wanted her more than he wanted to breathe. He rested his hand at the small of her back as he guided her up the stairs to her place, the heat of her body scorching his palm through the thin fabric of her blouse. When they reached the top of the stairs, she fished her key from her purse and turned to face him.

"This was a wonderful evening, Killian. Thank you so much." She ran her tongue lightly over her bottom lip.

His cock nearly pushed its way out of his pants. He cleared his throat and tried to figure out how to get himself invited inside.

"The pleasure was all mine, believe me."

She stood there, watching him, making no move to open her door.

Say something, he told himself. *Don't stand there like a big jackass.*

"Uh, Killian?"

He kick-started his brain. "Yes?"

"Would you, uh, like to come in?" She licked her lip again.

"Inside?"

Holy shit! She had opened the gates of heaven for him.

Don't jump her bones the minute the door is closed. Try to restrain yourself. Make her feel special.

Because she was. She most definitely was.

He managed to unstick his tongue from the roof of his mouth. "Yes, Lexie. I'd like to very much."

When she placed the key in the lock and turned it, her hands were trembling slightly. He hoped it was caused by anticipation and not a sudden attack of nerves. He was nervous enough for both of them, a completely unfamiliar state of affairs. He was always confident and self-assured with women. He prided himself on knowing how to please a woman and satisfy her, to always put her needs first. Tonight, his confidence and skill would be more important than ever before, yet here he was, shaking in his boots like a horny teenager.

He waited while Lexie put her key and her purse on the little table by the door, wondering how to make his first move. He didn't have to wonder long. She turned to him, did the little thing with her tongue on her lip that made him hard as rocks, and stepped right into him. With a flip of her hand, she swept his Stetson off his head and placed it on the table beside her things. Then she stepped up close to him.

"Got any more of those hot kisses, cowboy?" Her voice had a tiny quaver in it, and he was glad to realize she was as nervous as he was. As if they both sensed they were on the verge of something more important than casual sex.

"As many as you want," he told her, his voice low and raspy. Then his conscience stuck a pin in him. "Lexie, I need to tell you I don't expect to be moving to Red Creek. When my week is over, except for the wrap-up—"

"Ssh." She touched his mouth with the tips of her fingers. "I know. And you should know I don't usually jump into things like this. But Killian? I want to enjoy this—us—while you're here. If that's not—"

"It's what I want," he interrupted her. "I don't want you to think—"

"I'm not thinking." She gave him a smile, half-shy, half-vixen. "I'm just waiting for more of those kisses."

He banded one arm around her, pulling her tight to his body, and thrust the fingers of one hand through her thick curls. Cupping her head, he tilted it back enough to take her lips in a slow, smooth kiss. They were as soft as he remembered, delicious with the taste of strawberry gloss. He licked the seam, teased at the corners until she opened for him then swept his tongue inside. He tangled with her small tongue, coaxing it into an erotic dance setting every nerve in his body on fire.

A tiny moan vibrated through him, and he realized it was Lexie making the sound. He deepened the kiss, sliding his hand up and down her back, drawing her more tightly against him. Her breasts were soft mounds pressing into his chest, making his nipples harden beneath his shirt. He lifted his head, breathing hard, and saw in her eyes a hunger to match his own.

Taking a step back, he trailed kisses down the line of her jaw and the slender column of her neck before reaching for the buttons on her blouse. One by one, he popped them through the tiny buttonholes, peeling the silk of her blouse away an inch at a time. Lexie stood immobile while he slid the sleeves down her arms and pulled the garment away.

Holy shit!

She was a living wet dream, right in front of him. The swell of her breasts rose above the lace-edged cups of the low-cut bra, and the sheer fabric did little to conceal the darkness of her nipples. Unable to restrain himself, he cupped one luscious mound, lowered his head, and pulled the taut bud into his mouth, fabric and all. She gave her sensual little moan again and arched into him, silently urging him to suck harder, pull her deeper into his mouth. He obliged, biting down gently and tugging with his teeth, feeling the tip swell even more against his tongue. He had to force himself to lift his head or he'd stand here doing this all night.

For one hot moment, he wished he had his length of rope with him. He'd wrap it around her wrists, anchor it to the bedpost, and feast on her splayed helplessly before him. But that quickly reminded him of the fleeting nature of the situation. What if he tried it and it frightened her away? Then he wouldn't have even these few days with her. Deliberately, he pushed it from his mind and got back to the very delicious business of the moment.

Dropping to his knees, he unfastened the skirt, easing the material down her thighs to the floor. Lexie braced her hands on his shoulders as she stepped out of it and kicked it aside. Now she stood before him in those fuck-me sandals and her miniscule peach-colored bra and thong. Holding her hips, he pressed his face to her mound and inhaled deeply.

Jesus!

Her fragrance drove him nuts, swirling through his body to his cock and his balls, making everything tighten with need. Giving in to temptation, he drew his tongue through the line of her slit, pressing the fabric into it and tasting her juices. Her exotic flavor burst in his mouth, so he did it again and again. She trembled in his grip, thrusting herself closer to him. The little sounds of pleasure drifting from her throat only made him hungrier for her.

Unexpectedly, she gave a tiny shove and stepped away from him.

"One of us still has too many clothes on," she told him in a shaky voice.

"Is that so?"

"It is." She stroked his cheeks.

"Then maybe you should do something about it."

She inhaled slowly, the action thrusting her breasts forward. Killian couldn't stop staring. He curled his fingers into his palms to keep himself from cupping those very tempting breasts. With tremendous effort, he forced himself to stand still as she placed her hands on his chest. Popping the buttons on his shirt, she tugged the tails from his slacks and shoved the sleeves down his arms. One corner of her mouth edged up in a tiny smile as she let her gaze roam over his naked chest.

"Yum," she murmured, gliding her hands over him, brushing her fingertips over the curls of dark hair. With a wicked grin, she scraped her fingernails over his fat nipples, already hard and aching, and tweaked them lightly.

"Tease," he said, his voice thick.

She gave him a heated look and leaned forward to run the flat of her tongue over each nipple. Killian sucked in his breath, electricity streaking straight down to his shaft.

She glanced down at his feet then back up again.

"Boots," she told him.

For a moment, he couldn't think what she meant. Then he realized she wanted him to take off his boots. He leaned on one arm of the couch for balance and yanked his footwear off as fast as he could.

The moment he stood before her again, she undid the button on his slacks and slowly lowered his zipper. His eager cock tried to push out to freedom, bumping against her fingers. She smiled that sexy little smile again and shoved his slacks down his legs. Hooking her fingers in his boxer briefs, she stopped and watched at him for a moment, as if waiting for permission to continue.

"Don't stop now." He heard the strain of restraint in his voice.

"Okay." The word came out on a soft puff of air.

She slid the briefs down his thighs, stopping for a moment when his cock burst into freedom. Her eyes widened at the sight of it. Killian knew from the time he became a horny teenager he had more than his share of this this particular body part. Now, he was glad he was endowed more than the average man. Whatever happened after this week, he'd definitely leave her with something to remember.

"There's…a lot there," she finally said. "I think you got more than your share."

"And I'll make sure you get every bit of it." *And damn quick, please.*

Completely divesting him of all items of clothing, she knelt between his legs, took his shaft in her hand, and very gently ran her tongue over the head. Shivers of need skated over him, and he had all he could do to stand still. Lexie wrapped her slim fingers around his thick shaft and glided them slowly up and down, adding slow licks with her tongue for emphasis.

An ache built slowly in his balls, and he closed his eyes for a moment. Enough. He was only human, after all. Placing his hands beneath her elbows, he urged her to her feet, swept Lexie into his arms, and looked around the living room. The apartment wasn't very large, so it was easy to spot the entrance to the bedroom. He strode through the door and reached out to flip on the bedside lamp. Then he placed her carefully on the bed.

Kneeling between her thighs, he used his teeth to grasp the lacy top of her thong and dragged it slowly down her body, inhaling her spicy essence as he did so before tossing the little scrap of nothing to the floor. Then he eased her legs apart and licked his lips at the feast spread before him. For a long moment, he could only stare, drinking in the sight of her neatly trimmed pussy, the curls slightly darker than those on her head.

A natural blonde! Damn! He'd died and gone to heaven.

Holding her hips in place, he ran his tongue over the fluffy little curls. Then, because he couldn't wait another moment, he used his thumbs to press open her pussy lips and drew a long, slow trail with his tongue. God, had he ever tasted anything so delicious? He had to stop himself from licking his lips.

"Mmm." Lexie moaned and arched her hips up to him.

"Easy, darlin'. I want to take my time here."

He loved up her body until he reached her lips. Cradling her head in his hands, he took her mouth in a gentle kiss, brushing the surface of her lips as he'd done earlier before delving inside again. She tasted so damn fine. He didn't know which tasted better, her mouth or her exquisite pussy. He lapped every inch of the wet surface, tasting her tongue and her gums.

Breaking the kiss, he trailed his mouth over her cheekbones, along the length of her jaw, and down the graceful line of her neck. He nibbled at the spot behind her ear and bit gently on the sweet lobe. She wriggled against him, and his demanding cock jerked against her. Slowly and with great deliberation, he placed kisses along her collarbone and down the valley between her breasts.

Then he was at her mouth again, nipping her plump lower lip, sliding his tongue over it, lightly peppering her neck again. All soft touches, gentle but erotic kisses, meant to ignite her nerve endings and heat her blood. From the way she writhed and moaned beneath him, he was accomplishing his objective. He wanted her begging for her climax, straining for it, exploding in his arms. She was aflame now, twisting in his grasp, his own body on fire from it.

Her nipples were like ripe berries, swollen and taut with need. He sucked and licked and pulled them into his mouth, nibbling at their pebbled surface. Lexie gripped his shoulders, her fingernails digging into him as he coaxed stronger and stronger responses from her.

Shifting, he trailed his mouth down to her sweet little cunt. With great care, he peeled back her lips as if opening a flower, sucking in his breath at the sight of the slick pink flesh. Unable to help himself, he buried his face in her cunt and inhaled her essence, drunk with the scent of it.

Then he got busy, lapping and licking, pulling her swollen clit into his mouth and tormenting it with his teeth and his tongue. As he sucked and nipped Lexie gripped his hair, holding on for dear life. He loved the sexy little sounds she made and the way her body responded to him. She tasted better than the finest drink he'd ever had, and he lapped every wet inch of her.

When he sensed her climax was near, he eased two fingers inside her hot channel, then three, sliding them in and out while he continued to torment her clit. And then she exploded, pushing herself up to him, crying out her pleasure. The walls of her pussy gripped his fingers and spasmed around them as she drenched them with her juices. When he sensed the release slowing, he drove her up again, once more taking her over the top, relishing her shouts of satisfaction. He kept his fingers inside her, stroking her inner walls, until the last spasm finally subsided and she went limp beneath his touch.

He scattered kisses over her inner thighs, the top of her mound, her belly, working his way up to taking her mouth again.

"Taste yourself on me, sweet girl," he murmured. "Best juice in the entire world."

He brushed her hair away from her forehead and placed his lips on hers, rubbing them lightly back and forth. When she opened her mouth slightly, he slipped his tongue inside and slid it lazily around. He wanted to capture this moment forever, this unexpected feeling conjuring through him. What they had done—what they were about to do—would permanently impact his life in some way.

But no way was he going to stop. Not when he wanted his cock inside her more than he wanted his next breath.

"You doing okay, darlin'?" he asked.

"Mm hmm." Her sweet lips curved in a little smile. "But we aren't done yet, are we?"

His laugh was low and hungry. "Not by a long shot. Hold on a sec."

He'd meant to take the condoms out of his wallet and put them on the nightstand within easy reach. That was before they ended up stark naked in the living room and he'd carried her away to the bed.

"Where are you going?" She frowned as he strode toward the other room.

"Just taking care of a little business. But don't worry, I'll be right back."

He was as good as his word, dropping two foil packets on the nightstand, ripping open a third, and swiftly sheathing himself.

Lexie looked from the nightstand to him, a grin teasing her lips. "You plan on being that busy tonight?"

"I like to be prepared."

Then he was over her again, back kneeling between her thighs. When he lifted her legs and bent them at the knee to spread them wide, he gave a small grunt of satisfaction to see she was still so wet. She'd need it to take the full size of him.

Gripping his thick shaft in the fingers of one hand, he nudged her opening with the inflamed head. Her slickness eased his way as he pushed gently into her, pausing every few seconds. He knew he was stretching her, hoped he'd prepared her so her passage was relaxed enough to absorb the width of him. Slowly, slowly he eased in more, watching her face for signs of distress, feeling her body's response. When he was fully seated inside her, he stopped to take a breath, closing his eyes to reach for control. With her inner walls gripping him in a hot, viselike clutch, it took every bit of self-restraint not to pound into her.

Bracing himself on his knees, he began the familiar, steady in-and-out movement, thrust and retreat, each slide easier than the last as her body opened to him more and more. Lexie wrapped her legs around his waist, digging her heels into the small of his back as she locked herself to him.

"Look at me, darlin'." Killian spoke in a thick, hoarse voice. "I plan to take you on the ride of your life."

That was exactly what he did, driving in and out of her in a steady rhythm that rocked them both. Faster, he went, and harder, plunging deeper and deeper as Lexie kept them locked together. He gritted his teeth, hanging on by a thread, until he felt her body tighten around him, her cries grow louder, her heels press harder into his back.

"Now, darlin'." He barely got the words out, holding onto himself until he felt her body give in to its release.

The explosion was intense, the climax gripping him and shaking him like a leaf in the wind. Beneath him, plastered to his body, Lexie took the wild ride with him. They shuddered together as spasms racked them, spinning out into a black-velvet void, cartwheeling in an explosion of fireworks until the very last of the tremors had died away. Little by little, Killian came back to himself, his breathing evening out. The silence in the room was broken only by the raspy sounds as they both drew air into their lungs.

He braced himself on his forearms, loving the flush of pleasure on her face and the gleam of satisfaction in her heavy-lidded eyes. He gave her a soft, gentle kiss, and when he was sure he could move again, he slowly eased himself from her body.

"Be right back," he told her, brushing his mouth over hers.

In her small bathroom, he disposed of the condom and washed his hands. He looked at himself in the mirror, staring at the flush of pleasure still darkening his face. At the glow of sexual satisfaction in his eyes. The orgasm was more than just the most stupendous he could ever remember. It had satisfied something, touched something deep inside him, and he knew, whatever happened, he would never be the same again.

A week, he told himself. One week. He still had no idea what would happen then. He still had no intention of staying in Red Creek. He had plans. Would he feel guilty leaving? Could he walk away from Lexie Choate as he'd walked away from other women? Lexie was way beyond other women.

Would she come with him back to Montana? Would she—

Stop it, cowboy. Don't get ahead of yourself here. He splashed water on his face, dried it on one of her fancy little towels, and headed back into the bedroom. Lexie was lying there exactly as he'd left her, her mouth curved in a tiny smile of satisfaction. He climbed in beside her and pulled her into his arms, lazily stroking his hand up and down her spine, loving the silky feel of her skin.

She sighed and nestled her head against his shoulder. "That was…beyond wonderful."

He gave a low chuckle. "Just so you know, we're not done yet."

She cuddled closer to hm. "Just so you know, I didn't think we were."

Chapter Five

"You're pretty chipper for someone out carousing all night." Marliss picked up the full mug of coffee Lou had poured, set it on the table in front of Killian, and gave him a narrow-eyed look.

He smiled. He'd tried to be as quiet as possible when he came home, but nothing escaped Marliss and Lou.

"Watching out the window, were you?" He took a fortifying sip of the dark brew.

"I'm a light sleeper." Without asking, she pulled out a chair and sat down at the table with him. "Lou and me can never sleep until all the chicks are in the barn."

Killian laughed. "I think you're mixing your metaphors a little, Marliss. And I hardly think I could be classified as a chick."

"You're Dusty's chick. That's what counts."

"Yeah? Didn't count for much for a long time, did it?"

Marliss slammed her hand down on the table. "I won't let you speak ill of the man. He loved all you boys, and your mamas."

Killian quirked an eyebrow. "And his wife, too?"

Lou set a plate of bacon and eggs in front of Killian, along with a basket of biscuits. "Dusty and the missus made a good marriage out of what they had. They knew what they was getting from the gitgo, and they forged ahead."

Killian swallowed a bite of egg and bit off a piece of bacon. "I don't understand how they could stay together if they didn't love each other. What kind of marriage is that?"

"The kind they could both live with," Marliss told him. "She wanted Dusty at any price, and he wanted in on the oil and minerals. He was always respectful of her."

"Respectful." Killian snorted. He took a moment to butter a biscuit. "You call it respectful for a man to have four women on the side like he did?"

Marliss leaned toward him. "He loved every one of those

331

women, including your mama, and he did right by them, and you boys."

Killian ate more egg, more bacon, a little biscuit, taking his time so he didn't blurt out something in anger.

"Well?" she prodded. "Nothing to say?"

He chewed slowly, sipped a little more coffee. "What I have to say is, my mother is one of the most gracious women on the face of the earth. I cannot begin to imagine what she saw in Dusty or how she put up with his bullshit all these years, and that was before she knew there were three more women just like her."

"He took good care of her," Marliss insisted.

"With visits every few weeks, a few crumbs of his presence, a few smooth words now and then? You call that taking care of someone?"

Lou refilled his coffee mug. "He loved your mother," he told Killian. "He talked about her all the time. And you."

"And all the others, I'll bet."

"You were the oldest," Marliss reminded him. "The first born. You and your mama held a special place in his heart."

"Not special enough to keep him away from three more situations like mine."

"Okay, enough." Lou brought his own cup of coffee and sat down at the table. "Dusty Walker made a lot of mistakes. He was the first one to admit it. But there was a lot of good in the man, too. And a lot of love."

"He sure was good at spreading it around," Killian said stubbornly.

"He was a man with a big heart," the cook insisted. "He wanted kids something fierce. It was a sad thing his wife couldn't have them, and it gave both of them a lot of sorrow. I'm not saying the way he chose was the right one, but he lived up to his obligations with everyone. And he did it willingly."

"I'm gonna show you something." Marliss pushed her chair back from the table. "You sit right there."

"Where's she going, Lou?" Killian asked.

The big man shrugged. "Probably to get something."

"Well, that tells me a whole hell of a lot."

He ate in silence for a few minutes until Marliss came scurrying back into the room. She carried a big book and slammed it on the table next to Killian.

"Go on," she told him. "Take a look."

The book was covered in heavy, embossed leather and in the center, in script, was the letter K. What the hell was this? A scrapbook? What kind of scrapbook could Dusty have been keeping? He continued eating in silence, preparing himself for whatever he was going to see, while Marliss and Lou gave him what he called the deadeye stare. Finally, he pushed his plate away, wiped his mouth, and opened the book.

And stared. His jaw actually dropped as he turned the pages slowly, stunned at what he was seeing. His mother must have sent every picture of him she'd ever taken to Dusty, along with all the articles in the local paper about his awards in school. Academic honors. Athletic awards. Even pictures of him working at Hart Brothers Ranch. *What the fuck?* He stared at Lou and Marliss.

"What the hell is this?"

"He had one for each of you boys," Marliss explained. "He knew it was impossible for him to be as much of a constant in your lives as he wanted to, but he didn't want to miss out on everything, either."

"One of these for each of us?" he repeated. He was having a lot of trouble absorbing this.

"He made sure each of you boys and your mamas were well taken care of," Lou reminded him. "Bought good homes for y'all. Made sure each of you had everything you needed, though he couldn't be there all the time. *Especially* since he couldn't be there all the time."

Killian went back to the beginning of the book. This time, when he turned over the first page, he saw a small sheet of paper had been folded lengthwise and tucked into the crease. His hands shaking slightly, he unfolded it and smoothed it out.

Dear Killian,

If you are reading this, it means I am gone to whatever reward God has chosen for me. There are so many things I wanted to say to you whenever we were together, but the time was never right.

By now, you and your brothers have all the details of the story. I'm sorry this was a big shock to you. It's important for you to know, however, I loved your mother unconditionally and you always held a special place in my heart. I know you have grown up to be a fine young man and do me very proud.

I hope you and your brothers will decide to give D. Walker Minerals a chance in your lives, as well as the town of Red Creek. There are many great rewards to be had, and I'm not just discussing money.

Anyway, the last thing I want to say is I love you, son. I have passed on to you the only heritage I have, and I hope you'll find a place in your heart for it.

I love you, Son.
Your dad,
Dusty Walker

Killian stared at the note then he turned the pages again, this time more slowly. There were many pictures of him with his mother. Dusty had devoted special pages to those particular shots. It astounded him his mother looked so happy in each of them. Had she really been so satisfied with her part-time relationship with Dusty Walker? What was he missing here?

And did a few pictures and a wad of cash really make up for the mess of a situation Dusty had created. Again Killian worried those genes had passed down to him, leaving him unable to give any woman the kind of relationship she wanted and deserved.

"He used to talk about you all the time," Lou said, breaking into his thoughts. "All of you. I sometimes thought if he could have found a way, he'd have brought all of you, boys and mamas, here to live with him."

Killian actually laughed. "That would have been an interesting situation. Would have given the town a lot of fodder for gossip."

"This town loved Dusty," Marliss said, ignoring what Killian implied. "He gave back to it at every opportunity."

"When someone lost a job," Lou added, "Dusty always stepped in to make sure they had a roof over their head, food to eat, and walking around money until they got hired again. He was a big sponsor for the school district carnival every year, raising money for extracurricular and after-school programs."

"And," Marliss picked up, "there's hardly a person in the county he hasn't touched in some way."

"He worked his ass off, building his company up to the multimillion dollar business it is so he could provide security for everyone." Killian frowned. "I thought the gas and mineral business was his lifelong dream."

"It was." Lou nodded. "But then, beyond the excitement of finding those mineral deposits and negotiating those leases and royalty payments, he found a way to be able to take care of people. He liked doing it. Seemed like he made the whole town his family."

Marliss nodded. "I'd say Lou's right. He was very family oriented. That's kinda how he got into the situation he did."

"You know," Lou said in his slow drawl, "he really wanted you boys to get to know each other. To bond with each other. Really be the brothers you were. Be connected."

Killian made a rude noise. "I'm sure. Is that why he gave us all the same buckle? Like we're in some kind of special club?" He swallowed the bitter taste surging in his mouth. "Did he think that was going to make us all hug and kiss?"

"Or maybe take some pride in being his sons."

"Pride? Ha! After what he's done, to all of us?"

Marliss gave a half-smile. "I know you feel all kinds of bitter and betrayed, but talk to the folks in town, Killian. Get their take on him. They'll give you a real feel for the kind of person he was. It might change your opinion."

"She's right," Lou agreed. "While you're learning the business, maybe you could learn about your daddy, too."

"And speaking of people in town," Marliss put in, "am I right in figuring you were out with Lexie Choate again last night?"

Killian couldn't decide if she was glad he was spending time with Lexie or about to chew him out and ask his intentions. He fiddled with his coffee mug, choosing his words carefully.

"I took her to dinner." He shrugged. "A very nice dinner, by the way."

"And the night before," Lou put in. He winked. "Right in front of everyone in Red Creek."

"Damn!" Killian sat up straight. "I don't think quite everyone was there, Lou. But don't people have anything else to talk about around here?"

"'Course they do. But everyone knows Dusty's story, and they loved him despite his flaws. Now they're all taking the measure of his sons. Not to mention their curiosity's at an all-time high."

"That Lexie's a real sweet girl," the housekeeper told him.

"She is damn sure that."

"So, Killian." Lou's skewering look made him squirm. "We know you're only here for a week."

"And one more at the end of the month," he reminded them.

"Still, I expect you'll be kicking the dust of Red Creek from your heels when you're done here."

"For more reasons than you know." Even if he was tempted, how could he enter into a long-term relationship with a woman like Lexie Choate when his heritage was a philanderer like Dusty Walker? What if it was in his genes to be unfaithful? They'd start off with one big strike against them, and he'd never do that to her.

"Those look like some big heavy thoughts," Lou commented.

Killian rubbed his cheek. "If only you knew."

"Maybe not as heavy as you think if you haul them out in the daylight." Marliss frowned. "Too bad we can't convince one of you yahoos to stay around and run the company, the way Dusty wanted."

Killian studied them both. "What did my…the others say?"

"I think y'all will find out at the end of the month. But I want to get back to Lexie." She glared at him the way his mother had when he screwed something up. "I'd hate for someone to do that young lady wrong."

Killian forced himself not to squirm in his seat, feeling his neck redden. "Lexie knows I'm only here for a week," he assured them. "We've talked about it and decided there's no reason why we can't enjoy each other's company for the short haul."

"Short haul?" Marliss sniffed. "Don't you dally with her emotions, Killian Walker. She's had enough grief."

He wrinkled his forehead. "Grief? What kind of grief?"

"That's for me to know and her to tell you if she wants. Just keep this in mind. Lou and me will be looking over your shoulder."

He shook his head. "You sound like you're my mother."

"Just watching out for everyone." She rose from the table. "Hadn't you best be getting on to work?"

He grinned. "Yes, Mom. I'm on my way."

"You might want to carve out a little time to check out this piece of property," Lou suggested. "It's got the best view in the county, not to mention a lot of plusses you ain't discovered yet."

"I'll do that. Thanks for pointing it out."

"I mean, if this got to be my piece of property, I'd want to know about every blade of grass."

"I hear you," he called as he hurried out of the kitchen.

Grabbing his Stetson from the peg in the front hall, he headed out to the garage. He was anxious to get out of there before the old couple found a few more things to throw at him. But as he headed down the driveway in the silver SUV, he drove slowly, glancing left and right. Osprey Lake sparkled in the morning sunlight and, beyond, the property stretched in both directions. Completely unbidden, a question popped into his brain.

I wonder if you can raise horses out here?

*****

Despite how little sleep she'd gotten, Lexie was up at her usual predawn hour to begin her baking. Killian kept her company for a little while, but then he insisted on leaving. He told her he didn't want to subject her to the gossip if people saw him leaving in the daylight hours.

"I don't care," she kept telling him.

"But I do." He'd kissed her on the tip of her nose. "There'll be enough tongues wagging as it is. Hell, I'd stand in your window nude with a sign saying *Lexie Rocks* if I didn't know what the fallout would be. I'm thinking of you, darlin'."

She wanted to tell him she was tired of being such a good girl. It was boring. Maybe boring was what she'd wanted when she first came home and opened the coffee shop, but she was ready for a little spice. And Killian Walker was definitely her choice from the spice rack, even if he would be gone by the end of the week.

But what if I can get him to change his mind?

She gave herself a mental smack. Trying to nail him to Red Creek was a sure path to disaster. She could tell, not just from what he said but from the things he didn't say. At least, this way, when he left, it would be with great memories of her and, hopefully, a desire for more. Sometime. Someplace.

She'd had a feeling last night Killian had been holding something back, and not just an inner part of himself. The sex had been way off the charts, yet she sensed a darkness in him he'd managed to put a leash on. Could she find the key to opening that door? If so, when he left she'd have some darkly erotic memories to keep her very warm on the long nights afterwards.

As she pulled the last of the pans from the oven, however, she contented herself with knowing there were traces of his on her linens, a sharp earthy scent that made her hormones dance and shout. She paused and wrapped her arms around her body, imagining they were his arms and remembering the feel of them holding her close to him. She closed her eyes, remembering the warmth of him, the feel of the hard planes of his chest against her breasts. The soft, scratchy sensation of the curls of his chest hair on her skin. His thick cock slowly sliding into the wet clasp of her body, stretching her, filling her completely.

And orgasms so explosive, she still felt the tremors from when she came completely apart.

There was something else wrapping around her, too. Something too dangerous for her to think about. Killian was leaving when his stint at D. Walker Minerals was up. He'd been pretty open that his future plans did not include the company or Red Creek. She needed to put a lid on the intense emotions she felt for him or she'd really be hurting when he left.

She glanced at the clock and realized she was a little ahead of schedule, so she headed back upstairs. In her bedroom, she pulled on a pair of shorts and a long ratty sleep shirt she used when she immersed herself in her secret. Well, sort of secret. People knew about it, but they had no idea she still harbored secret dreams, or that they were her medicine when she needed comfort.

She took a moment to fix herself a cup of coffee then carried it with her to the closed door in the wall opposite the front of the apartment. When she opened it, she took a moment to look around the room. Sunlight poured in through the big window, bathing the room in natural light and kissing the canvases stacked against the wall. Two unfinished ones stood on easels, angled to take maximum benefit of the natural light. They were uncovered because, for one thing, hardly anyone ever came up to her apartment and, for another, she never brought a guest into this room.

Holding her mug and sipping from it, she considered the painting she'd started yesterday morning before opening Heart Starter. In seconds, she was holding her brush and palette and filling in the portrait of Killian Walker with bold strokes. At least, after he left, she'd have an image of him to keep her heart warm. She stopped a moment to set the little alarm clock she kept on a low table. If she didn't, she'd be up here absorbed in her painting while the hordes knocked down the door of Heart Starter.

She was thankful her parents hadn't asked many questions about the blowup with Rick, its effect on her career, and her abrupt return to Red Creek. After two years, she still wasn't ready to discuss it. But getting back to her art was proving to be great therapy for her. Maybe one of these days—

The ringing of the telephone interrupted her thoughts. She looked at the number on the screen and sighed. The town gossips had probably been at it again.

"Hi, Mom."

"I know you're always up early," Sarah Choate said. "So I don't think I'm waking you."

"No, I was up. How are you?"

"I'm fine. I'm calling to see how you are? I haven't heard from you since last weekend."

"I've been—" Been what? Busy with the sexiest man she'd ever met?

"I hear another of Dusty Walker's sons is in town," her mother went on. "Rumor has it he's become a regular customer at Heart Starter."

"Mom." Lexie sighed. "He likes my cinnamon rolls."

"And a lot more, the way I hear it." Her mother chuckled. Then, in a more serious voice, she said, "Honey, I don't want to see you get hurt again."

"Because I had dinner twice with a good-looking man?" She ground her teeth then reminded herself her mother was just really concerned for her. "It's okay, really. He's here for a week and then gone. I'm having a little fun for a change. Isn't that what you've been telling me to do?"

"Of course. You can't blame me for being a mother, though, right?" Then, as if knowing it was time to stop pushing, she said, "How about coming out for dinner Sunday? Your brother is going to Skype from Afghanistan, and I know he'd love to talk to you, too."

"Sure. That would be great." She worried about her brother all the time, his being in such a dangerous place. Talking to him this way would make her feel better, as it always did. And take her mind off the fact that by then Killian would be gone.

"Okay. Good. Make it around noon."

"See you then."

Hanging up, she glanced at the clock. Time to get dressed and open up for business. With a sigh of reluctance, she cleaned her brushes, closed the door to the room, and headed for the shower.

Despite the early rush of business and a steady stream of customers after that, the morning passed so slowly, Lexie wondered if someone had tied cement on the movement of time. She had glanced at the clock for maybe the hundredth time when the jangling bell signaled the door opening again. She turned away from the back counter where she'd been restocking the machines in time to see Killian walk into the shop.

She felt as if the sun had come out, casting its golden glow on everything and surrounding them with a shimmering heat. The same heat she felt when she and Killian made love.

"Morning." The scar at the corner of his mouth dimpled when he grinned at her.

"Morning to you. The usual?"

He laughed. "Am I getting predictable?"

"You know what they say," she told him. "Predictability is a good foundation."

"They also say there is pleasure in the unexpected." He winked. "Maybe the best thing is a mixture of both."

"Maybe. So on that note, would you like a couple of slices of coffee cake instead of cinnamon rolls today?"

He laughed again, the sound rolling through her like sunshine. "Sure. I'll live dangerously. But don't mess with Abby's sticky buns."

"I wouldn't dream of it."

"I think I'll eat mine here today. And how about straight espresso instead of my usual plain old dull coffee with a shot?"

Lexie had a feeling they were discussing something way more intimate than food and drink here.

"Something to give you a jolt?" she teased, and was rewarded with a darkening of his irises and a flash of light in the deep obsidian.

"If you think I can handle it."

"I'll make sure of that."

As she put the order together, she glanced around the shop and noted almost every person staring at them with open curiosity. Killian lifted his head in a gesture of greeting, nodded, and said, "Howdy, everyone."

Several people murmured greetings to him, and many of them smiled. Did he see how friendly people were in this town, or was he putting on a show until his week was over? She gave herself a mental shake; she needed to quit thinking of those things. He'd be leaving soon. Too soon. She just needed to stick the hope he might stay in the back of her mind.

Lexie was very conscious of him watching her as he took a seat at a little corner table and slowly ate his coffee cake and drank his coffee. She had to keep dragging her eyes away from him because the sight of him made her nipples peak and moisture dampen her panties. The pulse in her pussy could have given competition to a jungle drum. She hoped nobody in the shop had any idea she was so turned on.

Finally, she went into the back room and splashed cold water on her face and hands at the sink. When she returned to the front,

Killian was dumping his trash in the big barrel next to the sugar and cream area. He waited until she filled an order for a walk-in before moving up to the counter.

"I have to go out of town later today," he told her in a low voice. "That means dinner is out tonight."

Disappointment slivered through her, but she forced herself to smile. "I understand."

"It's the damn office. Walt Forester wants me to fly to Georgia with him to meet a geologist we work with. Apparently, he's finished with a study we requested on land near Stone Mountain, and he thinks it's worth offering leases for. Plus we'll visit some sites already under contract, so I can get a real feel for things in the field."

"Really?" Her eyebrows flew up. "But that's great, right?"

He gave her a rueful grin. "Yeah, for the people who own the land. For me, it means a night away from you."

She glanced self-consciously at her customers. "Um—"

"They can't hear me," he assured her. "I'm talking too low. I wouldn't embarrass you." Now, he looked around. "At least any more than these people already do. I'm the latest topic of conversation, right?"

"Small towns," she pointed out.

"I know. I grew up in one. So, we're taking one of Dusty's planes—"

"Wow. High cotton," she interrupted.

"Doesn't make up for missing you. But I'll be back by noon tomorrow, so don't make plans for tomorrow night. Got it?"

"Pretty confident, are you?" she teased.

"No, just don't want to waste whatever time is left."

At the reminder their situation had an end time, sadness washed through her, but she deliberately pushed it away.

"Um, how about if I make dinner for us tomorrow night? We can eat in."

Heat simmered in his eyes again at her words. "In more ways

than one, darlin'. In more ways than one."

It took all her self-discipline to maintain a casual appearance when he waved and headed out the door. Then, in order to avoid the gossips ready to bombard her with questions, she hurried into the back room and busied herself straightening things up back there. She hadn't wanted to tell him how disappointed she was at his announcement, but the thought of a night without him took the shine off the day.

The portrait. She'd work on his portrait tonight. When he was gone, she'd hang it in her bedroom so she could look at him every night. And while she worked, she'd plan their evening together. Maybe if she pulled out all the stops, she could find out if Killian Walker really did have a dark side, and if he'd take her with him on a walk down its erotic path.

Chapter Six

Killian slept little, and he knew it was more than just a strange bed. Hell, he'd slept in line shacks and on the ground in a bedroll. No, it was the image blasting into his brain every time he closed his eyes. The image of a sexy, tempting blonde with curls he wanted to run his fingers through and hazel eyes with intriguing gold flecks in them. It was the body that even in semi-sleep his hands kept reaching for, molding the shape of mouthwatering breasts. And the sweet, sweet pussy with its neatly trimmed adornment of dark-blonde hair. He could still feel her tongue in his mouth and the grasp of her inner walls around his cock, the intense shudders of the most powerful climax he'd ever had. It was a smile both innocent and sultry, and the easy manner surrounding it all.

He woke from a very erotic dream, embarrassed to find his fingers wrapped around his cock, stroking the swollen shaft. Groaning, he finished himself off in the shower, resisting the temptation to bang his head against the wall. One week, you idiot. One week and you're gone. And even if he wasn't, he still wasn't fit for any kind of relationship with Lexie or her kind of woman.

He realized with shocking clarity he was falling in love with Lexie Choate. He, the man who had just decided he'd never have a permanent relationship with a woman, had fallen in love. His mother would tell him Fate was playing tricks on him.

His mother. Oh god! What would she say about the mess he was making? He didn't really want to find out.

He had to get his head back on straight. He had to put his feelings for Lexie to rest when he came back for the one week with the others. He'd been pretty specific the first night, and they both agreed a week of fun would be just right for both of them. But would that really work? This had nothing to do with Lexie and everything to do with him, with his screwed-up head, and his plans for the future. He thought of what Lou and Marliss had said and knew they'd think him all kinds of a shit for what he'd be doing where Lexie was concerned.

How could he screw things up so badly? The worst part was he could hardly wait to see her again tonight. Knowing everything, didn't that make him as bad as Dusty?

I rest my case.

It was late morning when Dusty's plane landed in Kansas. Killian had left his ride at the small airfield, so he and Walt drove directly to the office. He followed Walt inside, knowing if he headed to Heart Starter he wouldn't be able to tear himself away. He had a report to write, per Walt, and Elaine would have a ton of questions. He did, however, take a minute to call Lexie, tell her he was back, and ask her what time he should be at her place. Maybe tonight he could find the strength to tell her how bad he had it for her.

"Seven," she told him. "And bring your appetite."

"For you *and* the food," he told her in a low voice he hoped conveyed his simmering hunger for her. Then he ended the call before he forgot his good intentions not to race down the street and see her.

Abby came into his office to place two folders on his desk. "Homework from Elaine," she told him, then looked at his empty hands. "No sticky buns today?"

He almost told her he had another kind of sticky bun in mind, but he bit his tongue. "You'll just have to suffer for one day, I'm afraid. Sorry."

"I may have to give you a demerit," she joked.

"I'll bring you extra tomorrow," he assured her. "Meanwhile, I'd better get busy writing up my report, or I'll be in big trouble here."

"At the very least."

Elaine waited in his doorway. "You giving me demerits, too?"

She shook her head. "No, as a matter of fact, if I had gold stars, I'd be giving you some of those."

"Oh?" He quirked an eyebrow. "What brings that on?"

She came into the office and dropped into a chair in front of his desk. "Walt gave an excellent report on you. He says you're a natural at this business. Understood everything the geologist had to say. Asked the right questions. Even helped seal the deal on the leases."

"I appreciate the good words from him."

She tilted her head and studied him, eyes filled with curiosity. "I don't suppose you've given a real thought to staying after this is all over, have you?"

"Not a real one," he joked.

"I'm sure you must have plans, like your brothers. But this is an exciting business, Killian. New challenges all the time."

"My brothers?" He studied her. "Well, you've had the pleasure of meeting two of my *half*-brothers so far. What did you think of them?"

She laughed and shook her finger at him. "Uh-uh. You aren't getting anything out of me. Right now, I'm concentrating on you."

"Well, next week you can concentrate on the last of my *half*-brothers."

She flipped her hand in the air. "Half or whole, they're still your brothers. I really believe you have more in common besides Dusty, if you guys would take time to really get to know each other."

"I appreciate your intentions," he said slowly, unwilling to offend this woman who was nothing but nice to him. "But I think emotions run too high as far as the four of us are concerned."

"How can they run high? You've only just met each other."

He picked up a rubber band and stretched it with two fingers. "And I think we've learned all we want to. Wouldn't you resent it if you found out your mother wasn't really married to your father? And there were three other women in the same situation? So you're a bastard whose father didn't even respect his mother."

Elaine leaned forward, bracing her arms on the desk, all

humor gone from her face. "You listen to me, Killian Walker. Your daddy loved you boys, and he loved your mamas. Yes, it was an unusual situation, but he did right by all of you. The will was structured to give you a way to bond together. That was very important to him."

Killian just shook his head. "This is a no-win conversation, Elaine, and I like you too much to get in a fight with you about it."

"Then what about Lexie?"

He drew his brows together. "What about her?"

"Couldn't she be enough to convince you to hang around here?"

He snapped the rubber band. "You think I'd make good husband material, Elaine? How long before I'd be off cheating on her, and maybe with more than one woman?"

She pinned him with her dark-brown eyes. "First of all, I'll say again Dusty's situation was unique. Second of all, if you were able to love a woman half as good as he did, try to be a father as hard as he did, I'd say any woman—especially Lexie—would be tickled to have you."

"You must be drinking some kind of crazy juice." He snorted. "I'm doing her a favor by leaving."

Elaine leaned back in her chair and held up her hands. "You're as hardheaded as your daddy was."

"See? I told you I was just like him."

She rose, pushing back the chair. "I give up. But you're passing up what could be the two best things in your life. Think about that." She paused on the way out of the office. "Just make sure whatever you do, you're full honest with the girl. I'd hate to see her get slammed twice."

Killian's insides twisted into a knot. "Twice? What's that supposed to mean?"

She flapped a hand at him. "Not my story to tell. Just putting it out there for you."

He sat in his chair, staring at the wall, for several minutes after she was gone. What on earth had she meant? First Lou and Marliss, now Elaine mentioning something had happened to Lexie. Had someone hurt her? Badly? Was he about to do it again? That might be a good indication he was right about his genes and relationships with women. Maybe he should rethink going over there tonight, but he knew he'd never be able to stay away from her. If his time here was almost up, he wanted this one last night with her. He'd make it totally memorable for her then explain why, under any circumstances, it couldn't work between them.

Forcing himself to tuck those thoughts into a corner of his mind, he turned on his computer, pulled up a blank document, and began writing his report on the trip to Georgia. He'd focus on work today then run home to shower and change and stop to get flowers for Lexie before he got to her apartment. At least his mama had taught him good manners.

His mama.

He owed her a phone call. She'd left text messages and voice messages on his cell, and he felt real guilty about not returning any of them. He realized now she must have loved Dusty very much to do what she did, bear him a son and be a part of his life, knowing he couldn't marry her. Maybe he should try looking at this from her point of view. He wasn't a child anymore, so he should try acting like an adult.

Damn!

He had so many fucked-up thoughts running around in his mind.

Okay, get to work. Sort the rest out later.

The day dragged interminably. He finally managed to get his report written to Walt's and Elaine's satisfaction, but it wasn't a labor of love. He had to admit, grudgingly, he'd really enjoyed being in the field, seeing the leases, negotiating new ones. It took him back to the short trips he'd taken with Dusty. He had to ruthlessly suppress the memory. He didn't want to enjoy any part of this business, not one tiny bit of it.

Then he tackled the new folders Elaine had set on his desk, with notes as to what she wanted him to absorb. He felt like he was back in school again, preparing for a test. He wanted to say the hell with Dusty and this fucked up situation and the damn business, but he'd given his word to his brothers.

Brothers? He realized this was the first time he hadn't actually thought of them as half-brothers. What the hell was up with that? Maybe he was getting soft in the head.

Or maybe you're taking a second look at things?

At last, the day ended. He was glad he'd brought a little travel bag with another change of clothes and toiletries. Dusty had built a private bathroom off his office, and today Killian was grateful for it. He took a long, hot shower, shaved carefully so he'd minimize the whisker burn on Lexie's delicate skin, and splashed on his aftershave. He pulled on clean clothes and his boots, and settled his Stetson on his head. Finally, to calm himself because he had no idea how this night would turn out, he grabbed his length of rope, curled it into a coil, and shoved it into his pocket. He might end up not using it the way he wanted to, but the feel of it would calm his nerves.

He was glad everyone had left by the time he was ready. He didn't feel like answering a bunch of questions tonight, especially since he had no answers, not even for himself. He thought about leaving the SUV in the office parking lot, but he wasn't sure how late he'd be at Lexie's, especially after he spilled his guts to her. And if he stayed all night, he'd rather pull out of the space behind Heart Starter than do the walk of shame down the block to D. Walker Minerals. Anyway, he remembered he'd thought about bringing her flowers.

The florist shop was only a couple of blocks away. He appreciated the fact the woman who waited on him didn't make any comments, although she had a knowing smile the whole time she put his bouquet together.

"I hope these do the trick," she said, when she took his money.

"Whoever she is."

Yeah, Killian thought, *like you don't know*. When he bailed on Lexie, the town would probably get out a mob to lynch him. Good thing he didn't plan to stay here permanently.

Parking the SUV behind Lexie's building, he took the stairs two at a time. When he reached the landing, he stopped for a moment to settle himself before he knocked on the door. When it opened, for a moment, he was struck so dumb he couldn't breathe. He was sure his heart had stopped beating. Every intention he'd lectured himself on for tonight melted like butter on a hot biscuit. Lexie was barefoot, her graceful toes decorated with purple nail polish. Instead of a dress or jeans, she wore a pair of short jeans shorts and a halter top offering a great view of her cleavage. Her familiar jasmine scent made his hormones sit up and beg, and his cock was already yelling for attention.

Her eyes widened when she saw the bouquet. "For me? Wow! You sure do know how to sweep a girl off her feet." She held out her hand for them.

Killian blinked and remembered to give them to her.

"Would you like to come in? I don't think I can serve dinner out here on the landing." Mischief sparkled in her eyes. "And I want to put these in water."

He somehow managed to unstick his tongue from the roof of his mouth. "Yes, of course. And I'm glad you like the, um, the flowers."

"They're beautiful."

He watched her stand on tiptoe to retrieve a vase from a cabinet then fill it with water and place the flowers in it. He couldn't tear his eyes away from the way the muscles of her ass flexed as she moved, or how the shorts rode up just enough to give the view of a tasty crescent of flesh beneath the cuffs.

"You, uh, dressed more…." More what. *Idiot*. "More casual tonight."

When she turned around, her lips were curved in a teasing grin.

"I thought it would be better since we weren't actually going out." She tilted her head. "I can change, if you prefer."

"What? Oh, no, no, no. You look just fine. I mean really fine." He swallowed. "Excellent, as a matter of fact."

He shoved his hand into the pocket where he'd stashed the rope, rubbing his fingers over the familiar surface. He'd been doing this since he got his first lariat from Larry Hart. It calmed his nerves when he learned roping and when he was out chasing mavericks on the range. As he grew older, he found other uses for it, the thought of which made his cock throb demandingly. How would Lexie react if—

Naw. Don't go there, cowboy. Just because she's dressed more provocatively doesn't mean she's into the kind of games you want to suggest. This is Lexie. Red Creek Lexie. Mind your manners.

But that was very hard to do when he wanted to fuck her six ways from Sunday, tied up or not, plundering every inch of her body.

Especially when he'd come here to tell her how things had to be. Sure she had said they'd have the one week and make good memories, but he really needed to confirm she understood that.

She placed the flowers on the small table beside the couch then hurried back to stir something at the stove in the tiny kitchen area. He suddenly realized the most delicious smells filled the air. He had been so besotted with Lexie's appearance it overrode everything else. Now, he took a sniff, and his mouth watered.

"Wow! Gorgeous woman and what smells like great food. Have I died and gone to heaven?"

"Hope you like it. I made roast chicken with a beer glaze, a corn casserole, and hot rolls. Work for you?"

"More than you know." He nearly licked his lips. "It sounds like ambrosia. When do we eat?"

She laughed, that silvery musical sound he loved, and winked at him. "In a few." She danced back to the counter, fixed a drink, and handed it to him. "Jack Daniel's, right? Have a seat on the couch while I finish getting things ready."

From the corner of the couch where he plopped himself, legs stretched out in front of him, he could sip the smooth whiskey and watch Lexie as she tended to the business of the meal. Every movement she made was so graceful. But it was also tantalizing. The halter barely restrained her breasts, especially when she opened the oven door and bent down to baste the chicken. As she stirred and mixed, the muscles of her arms flexed gracefully. He couldn't take his eyes off her. Every part of his body waved the *Go* sign.

Finally, unable to restrain himself any longer, he set his drink on the coffee table, uncoiled himself from the couch, and eased up behind her where she stood at the stove. Moving the fall of curls to the side to expose her neck he placed a soft kiss at the nape, licking the area with a swipe of his tongue. He didn't miss the shiver skating over her body. He had to have her, right this minute.

He pressed his lips to the side of her neck. "Will the dinner be okay if you turn the stove off for a few minutes?"

She drew in a breath as if knowing what he had in mind. "I think I can put everything on low."

"Do it," he ordered. "I can't wait another minute to get my hands on you."

Obediently, she turned the oven to warm and shut the burner off completely. The basket of rolls she covered with a folded towel. Then she turned in his arms.

"What did you have in mind, cowboy?"

"This, for starters."

He threaded his fingers through her hair to cup her head, tilted her face up to his, and lowered his mouth to hers. Her lips had the flavor of the strawberry gloss she was wearing, and he licked every inch of the surface before pressing the tip of his tongue against the seam of her mouth. When she opened for him, he slid his tongue inside, licking the soft inner surfaces, coaxing her tongue to dance with his. He slanted his mouth, first one way then another, using every angle to deepen the kiss more and more. She tasted hot and sweet, her flavor permeating his body and sizzling his nerves. Only when he ran out of breath did he lift his head and stare into her eyes.

"Minx," he said softly. "You dressed this way on purpose tonight."

"And if I did?"

He nipped her lower lip. "It's working. That's all I can say."

Lowering his head, he scattered kisses along her collarbone and down between her breasts. He laved the upper swell of her breasts then followed the damp trail with more kisses. Unable to stop himself, he lifted his hands to cup her breasts, brushing his thumbs over the now-beaded nipples. He swallowed a sound of satisfaction when she gave one of those breathy little moans he loved so much.

"We're not doing this standing in the kitchen," he told her, his mouth against her jaw. "I want you where I can spread you out before my eyes and feast on every naked inch of you."

"Promises, promises," she goaded, standing on her tiptoes to nip at his chin.

"And I follow through," he told her.

Lifting her in his arms, he carried her into the bedroom, plastering his mouth to hers as he set her gently on her feet beside the bed. But she pushed away from him, climbed up onto the bed, and sat with her legs curled beside her.

"Uh-uh. Tonight, you get naked first, and I get to watch."

She was much bolder, causing him to wonder what prompted the change. Maybe, like him, she was trying to cram as much into this week as she could. They'd agreed, right? A week of fun. What if he introduced her to his kind of fun? Would she throw him out the door? Would the week end too soon? But just thinking about what he wanted to do with her made his balls ache.

"You mean like a strip tease?"

She put a finger to her chin and tilted her head, giving him another of her minx looks. "Ooh, that would be wonderful. I've never been to a strip club."

"This is a private showing." God, the woman was turning out to be full of surprises. Her bold attitude was doing bad things to his self-control, even as he began to unbutton his shirt. "A performance for one."

Her eyes flashed with hunger at his words. "Then let's get it on."

He had no idea where this bold Lexie had come from. Not that she'd held anything back the other night, but this woman? Hot damn. She was making him more conflicted than ever.

But not enough to call a halt to things, selfish bastard that he was.

He finished unbuttoning his shirt, slipped it off, and tossed it to the little chair next to the bed. Next, his hands went to the button on his slacks, but he stopped when he had it open. Tonight, he'd be better prepared. He reached in one pocket for the condoms he'd slipped in there, only to come out with the familiar length of rope. Before he could shove it back out of sight, Lexie spotted it, and her eyes widened.

"I won't ask what that is because it's obvious," she said. "But what are you planning to do with it?" She rose to her knees and held out her wrists. "Are you planning to tie me up, Killian?"

He caught his breath. "And if I am?"

Her eyes darkened, the gold flecks like little sparks of flame. "Maybe I'll like it. What do you think?"

Jesus! "What do I think? I think it would be a dream come true for me. But what about you, Lexie?"

She still held her wrists out to him. She caught her lower lip between her teeth. "I think I, um, want to try it." She looked up at him. "You'll stop if I don't like it?"

He reached out to cup her chin. "You don't have to do

anything you don't like, darlin'. Ever."

"Then I think, first, you should finish taking off your clothes."

Killian dropped the length of rope at the foot of the bed, dumped the condoms on the nightstand, unzipped his fly, and shoved both his slacks and his boxers down his legs. He'd forgotten for a moment he still had his boots on, creating a brief awkward moment. But then he was totally nude, standing before her, his hands on his hips.

"Well?" His nostrils flared. "Like what you see?"

She ran her tongue over her lower lip in the motion that always spiked a fever in him, and his cock twitched automatically.

"Yes. Very much." She reached over and picked up the rope, running it through her hands.

The sight of her with the rope was so arousing, it took all his self-control not to grab her, rip her clothes off, and fuck her with no preliminaries.

"Your turn," he ordered, his mouth dry.

Still on her knees, she reached behind her to unfasten the ties at the top of her halter, letting it fall forward and release her breasts. His hands tightened into fists as he quelled the urge to reach out and squeeze them. The tip of her tongue peeped out between her full lips, and she bit down on it lightly as she finished undoing the halter and pulled it away from her body. Finally, she rose to her feet, balancing herself on the bed, and shimmied out of those teeny, tiny shorts. She kicked them away and stood with her legs spread, feet braced, hands on hips, waiting for his next move.

If he hadn't been watching closely, he never would have noticed the slight tremble in her frame or the look of uncertainty washing quickly over her face. It reinforced his feeling this was not her normal method of operation. That while she was a very sexy woman, a treat in bed, for whatever reason she was not normally this forward or deliberately tempting. He felt honored she had chosen to expose this side of herself to him. Whatever happened, he'd make sure to let her know how he cherished her sharing it.

Letting out a slow breath, he moved forward until he was right at the side of the bed, close enough to reach for her.

Lexie's heart pounded so loud, she was sure Killian could hear it. She wasn't a novice sexually, nor was she timid, but this was the boldest thing she'd ever done. Killian Walker called to a darker side of her sexuality she'd never even known she had. She might never want this with any other man, but she wanted it with him.

Careful to keep her balance, she walked across the mattress to where he stood at the side of the bed. Kneeling, she leaned forward and ran her tongue over his lips. When he groaned, she did it again then pushed her tongue inside to give him a full, openmouthed kiss. He tasted delicious. She thought she could drink from him forever. Shoving her fingers into his, thick midnight silk hair to anchor herself, she took the kiss as deep as she could, licking every inner surface.

Killian spread his fingers on her hips, steadying her, holding her in place. When he pulled her closer, the rigid thickness of his magnificent cock impressed itself on her. It was hot and hard, and suddenly she was overcome with a need to take him in her mouth. Breaking the kiss, she sat so her legs dangled over the bed, situating her so his swollen shaft was just at the right height for her. With her fingers curled around it, she slowly licked up one side and down the other, dragging her tongue against the soft skin over hard steel.

"Jesus!" he breathed. "You're killing me, Lexie."

She smiled as she pressed a kiss to the dark, velvet-soft head. "Good. That's what I intended."

Oh, yes, she was definitely being bold tonight. Killian Walker only had to look at her to blow away any lingering inhibitions and bring out her erotic dark side.

When she had licked her way up one side and down the other of his rigid shaft, she swiped her tongue across the velvet-soft head, probing the slit with the tip before closing her mouth over it and sliding her lips down the length of him. He gripped her head with fingers of steel, holding it in place as she sucked from root to tip and back again. Scraping her teeth lightly against the velvety skin, she slid one hand between his thighs and cupped his balls, squeezing gently.

"Holy fuck, Lexie." His grip tightened on her. "You're killing me here."

She hummed in satisfaction as she brought her other hand into play, gripping his cock and sliding those fingers up and down in rhythm with her lips. With her other hand, she played with his balls, rolling them with her fingers and lightly pinching the softly furred skin. He was so big she had to work hard to take him all the way into her mouth, finally tilting her head back so she could take him deep. When the head hit the back of her throat, he groaned again and tried to pull away.

"I'm gonna come, Lexie, if you keep doing that."

She slid her lips back until his shaft was free. "But that's what I want."

"And I want to come in your sweet pussy."

"Are you telling me you can't do both?" She gave him a wicked smile. "I know for a fact you've got good recovery time."

His laugh was hoarse and unsteady. "You're gonna kill me, aren't you?"

She licked her lips. "Only with pleasure."

She took him in her mouth again, fingers curled around the root of his stalk, and went to work on him. The blood in the vein wrapped around his shaft throbbed in response to her ministrations. Taking in a deep breath, she increased her pace, lips and tongue and fingers working together.

She knew the minute he was on the verge of orgasm. His fingers dug even harder into her scalp, and his entire body tensed. She tilted her head back a shade more, squeezed his balls, and sucked real hard. He exploded into her mouth, his cum hitting the roof of her mouth and sliding down the back of her throat. He jerked his hips as each spasm shook his big body, a harsh cry erupting from his throat. Lexie stroked up and down his cock as shudder after shudder rocked him, squeezing gently, still rubbing his balls.

Finally, the last of the tremors died away. He eased from her mouth, gripping her wrists to pull her hands away, and dropped forward on the bed, taking her with him, wrapping her in his arms. Against her body, she could feel the heavy thudding of his heart, feel his breath against her cheek as he struggled for air. He sprinkled kisses over her cheeks and forehead and brushed his mouth lightly over hers. With his warm hand, he stroked up and down her back, gently, softly, tracing the length of her spine and molding the curve of her ass. At one point, he eased his middle finger into the hot cleft and left it there as he let his body recover from the explosive release.

"You have the mouth of an angel," he said, at last, when he could speak again.

She giggled. "I didn't think angels did those kinds of things."

He kissed her forehead. "My kind of angel does." He rolled until she was beneath him. "My turn."

"You just had your turn," she teased.

"Not the kind I'm thinking of."

"Oh?" They were almost nose-to-nose. "And exactly what kind do you mean?"

"Let me ask you a question." His gaze locked with hers. "Are you up for a little adventure?"

Now, her heart pounded. She kept thinking of the length of rope lying on the bed and the erotic things she'd read in the romance novels she was addicted to. Well, she'd wanted an adventure, a little walk on the wild side, so what was she waiting for?

"Yes." She touched his full lips, ran her finger along the square line of his jaw. "Yes, I definitely am."

She felt the darkly sexual blaze in his eyes clear through every place in her body.

"Good." The kiss he gave her was hot and intense, scorching her nerve endings. Urging her lips to part, he circled every inch of her delectable mouth with his tongue, licking and tasting. She sucked on it, pulling hard and closing her lips around it, wanting to drag every bit of him deep inside her. He kissed her until she had no air left in her lungs and her body was begging for him to touch her everywhere. When he lifted his head at last, she felt dazed and totally at his mercy. A not unpleasant feeling at all.

"Let's play a little game," he said, his voice hoarse and rough.

"Like what?" Hers was breathless.

"You'll see."

He arranged her on the pillows at the headboard, placing her body just so. Then he grabbed the length of rope lying on the bed and dragged it across her breasts.

"You know one of the things I thought of when I saw you?"

She shook her head wordlessly.

"I got a picture in my mind of that luscious body naked with one of my ropes wound around you in a special design." He wound the rope around one breast then pulled it away. "Do you know anything about shibari?"

Again, she shook her head.

"It's the practice of creating intricate designs on a body with knots at special pressure points to bring about the most exquisite pleasure." He brushed his mouth over hers. "You'd be surprised at the things you learn about in Montana."

She finally found her voice. "I don't think anything about you would surprise me, cowboy."

"And there you have it. You know how good cowboys are with ropes." He tugged her arms over her head and braceleted both wrists with the fingers of one hand. His eyes glittered with hunger as he studied her face. "Think you'd like being tied up, Lexie? Totally at my mercy? Spread out before me for whatever I want to do?"

She swallowed and wet her lips. *Now or never, Lexie.*

"Y-Yes. I would."

"You sound a little uncertain there, darlin'. I want you to be sure." His mouth was nearly touching hers now, his breath mingling with hers. "Ab-so-lute-ly sure."

She nodded. "I am. Really, really sure."

"Okay, then."

Anticipation raced through her as Killian wound the rope around her wrists and pulled it tight. She couldn't see what he was doing behind her head, but she assumed he was fastening it to one of the spokes in her headboard. At that particular moment, she was glad she had one of those old-fashioned spindle headboards and not a smooth plane of wood.

"All set." He traced the line of her jaw with his tongue, a whisper of a caress. "You lie back and enjoy this, although I think I might enjoy it more than you."

He proceeded to work on every erogenous zone of her body—behind her ears, the crook of her elbows, the hollow of her throat. He took his time with her breasts, sucking and nipping at the nipples until they were on fire with need. Easing slightly down her body, he closed his hands around her breasts, kneading them as he gave further attention to the taut buds crowning them. She tried to arch beneath him, to thrust herself up to him more, but the way he had her arms stretched out and the rope fastened gave her little room to adjust her body.

More, she silently urged. *Touch me everywhere.* And everything was more intensified because she was helpless, at his mercy to do with as he wished.

It seemed forever until he moved farther down her body, trailing kisses everywhere. Maybe it was being restrained and knowing she was totally at his mercy, that he could do whatever he wanted to her. Maybe it was the erotic, sensual stream of kisses he placed everywhere on her body, his hot lips branding her. Whatever it was, by the time he touched the inside of her thighs, she was shivering with anticipation and shaking with need.

He spread her legs wider, placed a hot, open-mouthed kiss on the lips of her pussy then proceeded to string more kisses along the inside of her labia, punctuating them with little bites that made the throbbing in her pussy increase in tempo and strength. She twisted on the bed, silently urging him to move his hands and his tongue to where she wanted them the most, but he gave a low laugh, the sound vibrating against her thigh.

"Remember who's in charge, darlin'," he reminded her in his deep voice. "I know what you want, and I'll sure give it to you, but not until I'm good and ready."

"Please," she begged.

"Please what?" he teased. "Tell me what you want."

"I want you to put your mouth…there."

"Uh-uh-uh. Better be more specific, or I might not get there at all." As if to emphasize she was at his mercy, he flicked the tip of his tongue against her clit, her body jerking in response to the exciting caress.

Lexie wasn't good with verbalizing during sex, but, at the moment, she was so aroused she'd make herself say anything. "Put your mouth on my…on my…pussy." She nearly spit the word out.

"There you go." There was his dark laugh again. "Ask and you'll get your wish."

He pressed open her labia, blew a stream of warm air on the sensitized skin, and drew a long line the length of her slit.

Oh god!

She must have shouted it because Killian placed an open-mouthed kiss on her exposed sex, licking her juices and sucking her skin. He took his time, lapping and licking and swirling his tongue, punctuating it with little nips of her clit. Every touch of his tongue and his mouth pushed her closer and closer to release, yet he kept her right on the brink, ready to fly into black-velvet space, yet not…quite…there.

Oh god, he had her teetering on such a fine edge here.

Everything was open to him, even, she thought with sudden clarity, her soul.

"Please, Killian." She cried out her plea, arching her hips up to him as best she could. Between the restraint on her arms and Killian lying between her legs, keeping them wide apart, she was going crazy. She didn't remember the last time she'd been so on edge, so close to climax without release.

When she was sure she would really lose her mind if he didn't let her come, he thrust three fingers inside her, sucked her clit into his mouth, and took her over the edge. She jerked and shuddered, quaking with the force of the orgasm, which seemed to go on and on and on. She was just coming down, slowly, body still quivering, when he abruptly eased his fingers from her, reached for a condom, and rolled it on quickly.

"Don't think I can wait any longer, darlin'."

Placing his hands beneath her buttocks, he lifted her body to him and, with one swift movement, drove inside her.

Lexie sucked in a breath at the sudden intrusion of the thick cock filling every inch of her.

Ohmigod!

Killian rose over her, locked his gaze with hers, and took her on the ride of her life. In and out, harder and harder, the restraints of the rope enhancing the eroticism and driving her right up that steep cliff again. In moments, she forgot everything except being in Killian's control and his cock pounding into her. Everything faded away, the only thing that mattered, the climax hanging just out of reach while her body cried out for it.

Then Killian thrust once more, twice more, and took them both over the edge, his body stiffening as he pulsed inside her and her walls spasmed around him. They shuddered together as if they were one person, and, in that instant, she had the sensation they were. She clung to him as the tremors eased to aftershocks and the aftershocks finally subsided.

This time, when she came down, she was totally spent, limp,

unable to move an eyelid. She could barely breathe, and her heart thudded so hard it echoed in her ears. What had happened here? In giving him total control of her body, she'd somehow given him total control of her heart. He'd touched the place deep inside her she'd kept protected for so very long. It thrilled and frightened her at the same time.

Killian gave her a gentle kiss. "That was amazing, darlin'. I hope it was for you, too."

She wanted to tell him it was more than amazing. That she now felt this deep connection with him, a bonding. She could even see it in his eyes, despite the fact he'd never admit it. So, instead, she adopted a lighter attitude.

"Are you kidding me? Oh my god!"

His eyes darkened to obsidian. "Having your hands tied made it a little spicier, didn't it?"

"Yes, it did. I never knew…. Never imagined…."

"I wasn't sure you'd want it," he told her. Then he gave her a slow wink. "Maybe we'll do it again sometime."

"I'd like that." She sighed. "But not tonight, okay?"

"Definitely not tonight."

"I'm not sure I could even move an eyelash now." She grinned.

His gaze bored directly into hers, flames dancing in those obsidian eyes. "Next time, darlin', I might show you a few tricks with that rope. Let you see how you feel when I have those knots placed just so on your nipples and your clit, and in the cleft of that hot ass."

Lexie trembled at the images his words conjured up. She wanted it all with him, everything. Could they cram it all in over the next couple of nights?

"Damn, I'm going to hate leaving you," he murmured.

Then don't, she wanted to shout, but she pressed her lips firmly together.

She had no idea where Killian found the energy to crawl up

her body and release the rope.

"Be right back," he told her. "Don't move."

That was no challenge. She wasn't sure, as she lay there waiting for him to dispose of the condom, if she'd ever be able to move again.

"I think those sore muscles of yours could use a good massage," Killian said as he came back into the room. "He placed a soft kiss on her lips, sliding his own back and forth like the whisper of a breeze.

"Oh, that sounds like heaven. I'm ready"

She was surprised when he lifted her from the bed. "Wait. What—?"

"It's better in the shower. All the hot water is good for your body." He gave her a soft kiss. "I want to take good care of you."

The shower was beyond heavenly, especially when Killian slowly soaped every inch of her body, rubbed in the rich lather, and massaged every sore area. By the time they had dried off, she felt she could at least serve them dinner before she collapsed on the bed again. She told him as much.

"You sure?" He lifted an eyebrow. "I'm pretty handy around the kitchen. I can probably figure it out."

"Nope. Uh-uh. I invited you to dinner, and I'm going to serve it."

"Okay, then." He winked at her. "But the towel is all I'm going to allow you to wear."

She had the food on the table in no time, the hot rolls and butter in the center. She poured a beer for Killian and wine for herself before she sat down. Dinner was relaxed and conversation between them easy and fun. She had never felt so fulfilled, so cherished, so at ease.

If only this could go on forever. You can't have such great sex with someone if it's just short term. Right?

Damn! How had that thought popped into her head? That wasn't on the agenda, right?

She was about to take a sip of her wine when she realized Killian was staring at her, a tight expression on his face.

"What?" She frowned. "What's wrong?" Then she realized she must have voiced her wish out loud. Oh god. Oh holy god. "Killian, I—"

"You knew the situation from the beginning," he told her in an expressionless voice. "You knew I wasn't planning on staying. I can't believe you said that."

"Killian, I'm sorry, but…. What would be so wrong if you changed your mind and decided to stay in Red Creek? Would it be the worst thing in the world? Would staying with *me* be so terrible?" God, she hated sounding so much like she was pleading. But oh, how she'd love it if he'd change his mind.

He downed a long swallow of his beer. "You know I have plans that don't include this town. I told you so from the gitgo. We agreed the first night we'd enjoy ourselves for this one week, remember?"

"I do, but who says things can't change? And they did. You can't deny it."

"Say they did. There's still that other thing. You know how I feel about a long-term relationship. I'm a bad bet for any woman, but especially one who has as much to offer as you. I'm trying to save you from disaster."

"Save me? *Save me?*" Anger washed over her. She was so tired of him putting himself down that way, especially over something that did not have to be true.

"Yes. You should thank me. I'm thinking of you."

"What a crock of shit." She slammed her napkin down on the table. "You are your own person, Killian. It's not as if you have some dread hereditary disease, for heaven's sake."

He glared at her. "It *is* hereditary. Or at least I feel like it might be." He drained his beer and stood up to get another from the fridge.

Even in the midst of her anger, Lexie couldn't help admiring the fine shape of his ass beneath the towel or the broad muscular back. What a waste of an incredible man if he let his opinion of his heritage destroy his life.

"So, you're never going to fall in love?" she demanded. "Never get married? Do you know how stupid that sounds?"

"It's not stupid at all. It's the truth." He uncapped the beer and took a long drink straight from the bottle. "What if I took a chance, and I was right? Someone like you can't imagine what it would be like to make a mistake in a personal relationship."

Enough.

"Is that so? Someone like me? Well, I made a monumental mistake, and I've regretted it ever since."

"Like what?" he challenged.

"I went to art school in Savannah. Yes, art school," she repeated, when she saw his expression of skepticism. "Even people in Red Creek can love the arts."

"I didn't mean—"

"Oh, yes, you did. I saw it on your face. See? See what happens when you make assumptions?" She swallowed some of her wine. "So I met someone in art school, a very talented painter. His name was Rick."

"Let me guess." His mouth twisted in a grimace. "The two of you fell in love."

"At least one of us did," she snapped. "But he had an ulterior motive. I was in line for a prestigious award and the possibility of my own show. He made me feel so special about it, encouraged me, told me he was so happy for me." She snorted. It had been a big fat lie.

"What happened?"

"Rick came from a very wealthy family. I learned afterwards he bought off two of the judges, including the gallery owner. My two closest friends, the ones who told me to dump him from the beginning, told me to fight for myself, but I didn't have the heart."

He scowled. "And Rick? What did he do or say?"

"Oh, he was all consoling and everything. Said he knew I really deserved it. But I knew he was lying. And it didn't take more than a couple of days before he wasn't even hanging around anymore." She dashed a hand at her eyes again. "Can you imagine what a fool I felt like?"

He stared at her. "So, you packed up and came home? Why didn't you stay and fight for yourself?"

"Why aren't you staying and fighting for the person I know you are?" She drained her wine. "I know we haven't been together very long, but you can't deny there's something special between us. You know, you can raise horses anywhere. Even here in Red Creek."

His mouth tightened in anger. "Who told you? I only said I had no plans to stay."

"That's not important. Just someone concerned maybe you were going to throw your life away. Horses aren't much company on a cold night. Don't you want to find out what we've really got?"

"I know what we've got. At least what I've got. A bad family history. Anyway, speak for yourself. You ran home and left your art behind. Why aren't you still painting if you've got that kind of talent?"

She jumped up from her seat and grabbed his hand. "Come with me."

"What's going on? Come with you where?"

"Shut up." She was going to be sorry, but she was too angry to let it go. She opened the door to her studio room and threw up her arm in a sweeping gesture. "Here. Come take a look. I haven't walked away from it. I'm trying to reclaim it." She flipped on the light.

He walked into the room, looked around, and stopped, a stunned expression on his face.

Uh-oh. She had totally forgotten the portrait on the easel. She should have covered it, but she hadn't planned to bring anyone in here.

"That's me." His voice was filled with awe and amazement. "You painted me."

Lexie blew out a breath. Okay, in for a penny, in for a pound.

"Yes, I painted you. I painted the man I saw. The one I see right now. Look at him. Does he seem like someone who would cheat on his wife? Who'd be the kind of person you think you're going to turn into? I'll bet if I asked people who know you, maybe even your mama, they'd tell me they see the same person I do. Someone who's good and kind and smart and faithful."

Killian kept staring.

"Maybe you were brought here for a reason, however you got here. Maybe we were supposed to meet. And maybe this is the best place for you to raise your horses. Why can't you give it a chance?"

Still, he said nothing.

"I painted you as I see you, Killian, strong and caring, and brave and honest. I saw you with an artist's eyes. Why can't you see the same things in yourself and get rid of this ridiculous notion about genes?"

"You painted all the artwork in Heart Starter." Shock was evident in his voice. "You should try for another gallery showing."

"I paint now for myself," she told him. "That's all I need to be happy. What about you? Have you figured out yet what will make you happy?"

She waited, holding her breath, to see what he'd do. When he walked out of the room and headed to the bedroom where he picked up his clothes, she knew she'd lost.

"Damn you," she said. "Just damn you to hell. Go on. Live your miserable life. Hide away with your horses so you don't have to be with people. Be sure to tell your mother you aren't the son she thought she raised." She waved her arm at the front door. "Go on, go. Get the hell out of here. Next time, I'll find someone who really appreciates me."

He stood in the bedroom, dressed except for his shirt. "Lexie."

He looked at her helplessly. "I never wanted to hurt you. You have to know that."

"I know you're a spineless coward, so maybe I don't want you after all. Go on. Out. Right now."

He was still struggling into his shirt when she pushed him out the door. Looking around the room, she spotted the flowers sitting on the little table where she'd placed them. Impulsively, she picked up the vase, opened the door and threw them, vase and all, down the stairs. They landed in the alley with a satisfying crash. Then she sat on the landing, still dressed only in a towel, and let the tears come.

Chapter Seven

Killian didn't remember the last time he'd been so miserable. When he'd left Lexie's, he'd felt worse than garbage, so upset with himself he didn't think he'd feel better any time soon. He drove around for a long time, not thinking, just trying to get his head on straight. Lexie's excellent dinner sat like lead in his stomach, much as the whole situation lodged like a rifle bullet in his brain.

How had he let this happen? All he'd wanted was to get into Red Creek, do his week of servitude, and get the hell out. There was nothing here for him, he'd told himself. And certainly it was no place for him to pursue his dream.

But then he'd walked into Heart Starter, and his brain took a vacation. Lexie Choate slammed into him with the force of a tornado. He felt like Dorothy must have in the classic movie, *The Wizard of Oz*. Unfortunately, he didn't have red boots, and when he clicked his heels, all that happened was the sound of the heels hitting each other. He'd done his best to keep in mind the object of this charade—getting the money to start his ranch to raise Appaloosas. Red Creek wasn't even on his personal map.

Then, of course, there was his belief Dusty's genes made him an unsuitable partner for any woman. He couldn't seem to get his mind around the whole situation. How could this man have said he loved four women? How could he keep them all secret from each other and his wife? Out and out lie to everyone? What did he think his sons would think when the cat was finally out of the bag and they all met for the first time? Did he have any idea of the shock it would cause?

Killian hadn't been prepared for Lexie Choate, either. If he was real honest with himself—and he figured it was finally time he was—he'd probably fallen in love with her the minute he'd laid eyes on her. She'd not only taken his breath away, she'd captured his heart. All the bullshit about enjoying each other for a week, having a good time until he left, and then good-bye with no hard feelings? That was exactly what it was—bullshit. He hadn't been fooling anyone but himself.

Still, she'd agreed to it, right? He had laid it all out for her, and she'd been fine with it. She'd said so. If tonight hadn't been so intense, if what she really felt hadn't slipped out of her mouth unintentionally, would he have enjoyed her for the rest of the week then headed off—even though now he was sure he'd have a hole in his heart? So which way was he worse off—taking a chance on something sure to end in disaster or running away from it and playing it safe, never knowing what he might have had?

An image of Lexie flashed across his brain, naked beneath him, bound and pliant, offering herself to him without restraint. When they'd climaxed together tonight, even an idiot would have realized it was more than just sex. They'd touched each other deep inside, a feeling he could only describe as…love. Could you fall in love with someone so quickly? She had already been badly hurt once. Could he take the chance he'd do the same thing to her?

He thought about the portrait she was painting of him, the way she'd captured him. She'd painted him with strength in his face and compassion in his eyes. He was stunned she saw him that way when he didn't see himself like that. She had obviously found things deep in his soul he didn't know were there.

She had painted them in all her work. As he recalled the ones he'd seen, he realized she had an incredible talent going to waste because of some idiot. If he, Killian, was stronger and smarter, he could help her move beyond her anguish and feeling of betrayal and share her talent with the world. Of course, he couldn't coax her to take a chance when he was such a coward himself.

The more he drove and tumbled his thoughts, the more confused he became. When he realized the sun was peeking over the horizon, he finally headed back to the house. Lou and Marliss would be up, ready to put him through an interrogation. What in hell could he tell them? That he and Lexie had agreed to play house for the week and then part as friends?

Dumbass!

He realized now how he'd felt about her from the minute he'd laid eyes on her. It had been too fucking stupid of him to think that could work.

He smacked the steering wheel hard.

Jackass!

He never should have come to Red Creek to begin with. Should have told his mother he wanted nothing from someone like Dusty, left it all to the other three sons, and stayed in Montana still dreaming about raising his own horses.

He crested a small hill, pulled over to the side, and stopped, just staring at everything. For the first time since he'd arrived, he took a real good look at the sight. The house, a massive structure of stone and wood, stood on a small rise surrounded by acres of hills and pastures, with an unimpeded view of Osprey Lake. It was easy to imagine cattle roaming over the fertile land, or a herd of horses.

Could he ever see himself living here instead of Montana? Would he be haunted by Dusty's ghost and the things he'd done? But, damn, this was gorgeous land. Truth to tell, Red Creek was about the size of his hometown in Montana. He liked the closeness of the people, the friendly and familiar environment.

Then there was the question of whether he could work at all for D. Walker Minerals. He'd loved his side trips with Dusty, and the overnight to Georgia had gotten his blood flowing again. Maybe it was possible to do both—raise horses and hunt for mineral leases. The company had good specialists and worked with top geologists. It wasn't as if he had to live in the office. A good balance could give him everything, including his horses.

Of course, he might have already blown the whole thing, as idiotic as he was.

He should drive on up to the house, go in and shower and change his clothes, and hope Lou would fix one of his special breakfasts—after he and Marliss finished giving Killian the third degree, of course. Then they might ask him to pack up his gear and get his ass out of town for good.

He groaned and banged his hand on the steering wheel again. It really should be his head.

He wished his mama was there for him to talk to. She'd slap him upside the head then give him words of wisdom that would set him on the right path. He looked at his watch. In Montana, it was only five o'clock. He'd probably be in trouble, but he had to make this call. Not even Lou and Marliss could give him the words he needed right now.

He punched the speed dial for his mother then tapped his fingers on his thigh while he waited for the call to be answered.

"Killian?" His mother's voice sounded as if she'd just woken from a dead sleep, which she probably had "This better be some kind of emergency."

"Hey, Mama." He pulled out his best soothing tone.

"Don't you hey Mama me. You don't answer any of my calls then you wake me up at dawn? What's going on there in Kansas? Are you in a jam?

He sighed heavily. "You might could say that. Yes, I am in a spot of trouble." He swallowed. "Actually, more than a spot. Maybe a whole river."

"Oh, Killian." Her sigh was even louder than his. Let me get a cup of coffee so I can wake up my brain. Then you can tell me how you've made a mess of things."

He waited impatiently until she picked up the phone again and told him she was ready. It took him a while, and he wasn't sure he was coherent at all times. His mother listened without interrupting until he got it all out. When he finished, he blew out a breath and waited for her to tell him he was full of shit. What she said hurt him even more.

"Killian." Her voice actually sounded sad. "I can't tell you how disappointed in you I am."

"Oh, Mama, you know I hate hearing that."

"Too bad," she said. "It's the truth. I thought I gave you a good picture of the kind of man Dusty was, of his good qualities and why I fell in love with him. I tried to get you to remember what a good dad he was when he was with you."

"Yeah," he said bitterly, "when he was with me. I was one of many."

"You stop that," she snapped. "He may not have gone about things the right way, but he took good care of all of us. Now that he's gone, he's left you all a legacy and the means to bond as a family."

"You really think it's possible?" he asked, skeptical about the idea.

"You managed to agree on how to meet the terms of the will, didn't you?"

That was certainly true, although the meeting hadn't exactly been friendly.

"And thinking flawed genes will make you a bad lover or husband is plain idiotic," she went on. "If you turned out to be half the man he was, I'd be prouder than proud. Take a look at the real man, Killian. Get off your high horse."

Well. This was certainly not what he'd expected.

"Look at the mess you've made of things with the woman you've met there. Do you think Dusty would be proud of the way you handled that? He'd tan your hide, big as you are. Forget about everything else. Dusty respected his women and wasn't afraid to take chances with us." She gave a soft laugh. "He made all our lives richer and fuller."

Killian tried to get his mind around the idea that if his mother could feel the way she did about Dusty, how could he do any less? Mairi Walker wasn't an idiot. She knew the reality of the situation. Still, she loved and defended the man, so maybe he was ignoring all the good. Letting his anger take center stage. Could he get past that?

"Tell me more about your beautiful young lady, son. It sounds like you've screwed things up pretty bad there."

Killian closed his eyes as he talked about Lexie, again seeing her naked beneath him, skin flushed rosy, eyes flashing, body soft and wet and ready for him. He thought about her across from him at dinner, relaxed and laughing and talking. He thought about the first time he saw her and the way the earth had stood still. And he thought about the painting of him she was doing, and the way she'd seen right into the heart of him.

What a fool he was. What an asshole. An idiot. And a few other names he could call himself. His mother was right. He'd been looking at things all wrong, letting his own selfish anger take over. If he could do it, he'd kick himself in the ass with both feet. Fortunately for him, his mother was doing it for him.

"Did you get all that?" Her soft voice broke into his mental chastisement.

"Yes, Mama, I sure did."

"Answer me this. Do you love her? Really love her, the way a woman deserves to be loved?"

"I do," he answered, and knew it was the truth the minute he said it.

"Then you get your act together, wait at least until the sun is fully up, and go throw yourself on her mercy." Her tone softened. "She's lucky to get a man like you, son."

"Let's hope she feels the same way. And pray she listens to me."

"And Killian?"

"Yeah, Mama?"

"I know you'll be home next week before you go back to meet the others and wind things up. If you get this fixed, bring her with you."

He smiled, knowing she was itching to get her eyes on the woman who had stolen his heart.

"I'll do my best."

"One more thing," she said before he could hang up. "You don't need to be in Montana to raise your Appaloosas. Keep an open mind."

He sat in the truck for long minutes after he disconnected the call. Every single thing his mother had said to him was true. Maybe Dusty hadn't gone about things right, but he had loved each of the women and his sons and done his best to do right by them. Wasn't that all you could really ask of a man? And when he thought about it, searched deep inside himself, he knew if Lexie agreed to give him a chance, he'd never want anyone but her. Ever.

Finally, he cranked the ignition and headed down to the house, dreading the confrontation with Marliss and Lou.

They sure didn't disappoint him. As early as it was, they both sat in the kitchen, drinking coffee, when he walked in from the garage.

"You want to tell us why someone driving by Heart Starter last night saw Lexie Choate sitting on the landing in nothing but a towel and crying her eyes out?" Marliss attacked him with a fierce frown on her face.

Killian held up both hands. "The truth? No, I don't want to. But rest assured that's the last time anyone will see that. I'm about to try and make it right."

"So, we don't get to give you a tongue lashing?" Lou looked almost sorrowful, his mouth turned downward, a sad expression in his eyes.

"My mama already did, and she's the champion, so save your words." He headed out of the kitchen. "I'm gonna go clean myself up and throw myself on her mercy. You may be pissed off at me, but I hope you'll wish me luck."

*****

Lexie poured fresh coffee into the mug on the counter and took a sip. She'd been drinking coffee since Killian left and by now probably had a caffeine high she'd never come down from. But at least she wasn't crying any more. She'd pulled on shorts and an old shirt five sizes too big for her, pulled her hair into a ponytail, and cleaned up the kitchen. Later, before she opened the shop, she'd clean up the mess from the flowers, but at the moment, she hadn't been able to tackle it. Then, with her first cup of coffee, she'd gone to work on Killian's portrait.

Maybe it was a form of self-punishment for deluding herself into thinking they had something together. She probably would have been a lot better off finishing the painting of the stallion she'd started, but working on Killian was a form of self-flagellation. Now, hours later, the portrait was almost done, and the sight of it made her heart hurt and tears come to her eyes.

Why was he so damn stubborn? So stupid about this Dusty thing? If she really looked deep inside herself, she'd have to admit when she agreed to the one-week-of-fun thing, she'd known it wouldn't work. The very instant he'd walked into Heart Starter she was lost, and so was her heart. She could only hope he'd be respectful enough to stay out of Heart Starter for the next couple of days. Then he'd be gone, and she could begin to heal.

She was through with men. No more after this. Apparently, her judgment was completely flawed.

She'd started back to her studio room when she heard footsteps on the stairs outside followed by pounding on the door.

"Lexie"

Oh my god! Killian!

"Lexie, open the door. Please, please, please." More pounding. "I'm begging you."

She backed up to the kitchen counter, clutching her mug. *Go away. Please.*

"Lexie, I'm not leaving. If you don't open the door, when all your customers get here, they'll see me making a fool of myself. But it will be worth it to get you to listen to me."

Bam! Bam! Bam!

She wondered if he could actually break it down.

"Lexie, please," he shouted again.

Sighing, she set her mug down and walked over to unlock the door. Killian loomed over her, hands braced on the door jamb. He had obviously showered again and put on clean clothes, but lines grooved his face, and his bloodshot eyes held a world of pain.

What on earth? *She* was the one hurting here.

"Lexie, I...."

He shook his head, picked her up in his arms, walked into the apartment with her, and proceeded to give her a kiss she felt clear to her toes. His mouth fused to hers, he eased his tongue inside and licked every surface as if he was dying for a taste of her. At first, she tried to push him away, but he held her too tightly against his chest, and his kiss was too fierce, too possessive. About the time she thought she might stop breathing completely, he broke the kiss but kept his mouth a hairs breadth from her lips.

"I'm an ass. A jerk. A jackass. And a whole bunch of other things. Whatever you want to call me, I deserve every bit of it."

Lexie was so stunned she could only stare at him from the cradle of his arms. Before she could get one word out, Killian kissed her again, just as ferociously and possessively. Maybe more so. He only stopped when they both ran out of air.

"Put me down," she said breathlessly. "Killian, what on earth is going on?"

"I'll put you down, but I'm not letting go of you."

He set her on her feet, but then he knelt in front of her, grasping her hands in his as if frightened she would get away.

"I'm sorry, Lexie. Sorry, sorry, sorry." He pressed his head to her breasts, knocking his Stetson to the floor. "I am such an idiot."

Lexie forced herself to take a deep, calming breath. She had no idea what had triggered this, but she wasn't about to get caught up in it only to be tossed aside again. She wanted answers, and she wanted them now.

"Killian." She wet her lips. "What is this all about? Why are you here?"

He bracketed her hips with his hands and looked up at her, a mixture of pain and fear and—yes, love—in his eyes. Where on earth had that come from?

"Listen to me." He swallowed hard. "I was so pissed off at what Dusty had done I saw everything all wrong. I ignored all the good things people, including my own mother, tried to tell me about him, and focused on one stupid, idiotic, unreasoning thought." He locked his gaze with hers. "I'm not a cheater, Lexie. And maybe, in his skewed way, Dusty wasn't either. But I promise you, if you just give me a chance to show you, I'll be faithful to you forever. Forever," he repeated. "I love you."

Then, as if he'd run out of breath for the moment, he closed his eyes and pressed his forehead to her breasts again, clutching her to him as if he'd never let her go.

She wanted to hug him tightly, to run her fingers through his thick, silky hair and stroke his troubled face. But she had to make sure he really meant what he said. That this wasn't just some temporary glitch of conscience.

"Look at me, Killian. Please."

He tilted his face up. "Please believe me, Lexie. I mean every word."

"What brought about this big revelation?" she asked. "How do I know you really mean it?"

"I believe I fell in love with you the first moment I laid eyes on you," he told her. "I came up with the stupid one-week-fling idea more to protect myself than you, and I am totally ashamed. I love you," he said again. "With everything I am, however messed up that is. Please tell me you'll give me another chance."

It wasn't the words so much the sincerity in his voice that really made her believe him. And his expression of abject need as well as the deep love in his eyes. Still, she had questions.

"I thought you were going to be done with Red Creek after the one week wrap up with your brothers. How do you plan to handle that—us—if you're leaving?"

He rose to his feet and cupped her chin, tipping her face up so he could gaze into her eyes.

"You know, it's a funny thing. My mama pointed out to me you don't have to live in Montana to raise horses. In fact, I might see if the land adjoining Dusty's house would work."

Her heart beat faster at his words. "Really? You'd stay here? For me?"

"For us," he corrected. Then he frowned. "Unless you want to leave. I want to live wherever you do."

"No matter where it is?"

He nodded. "No matter. And I want you to do more with your painting. Listen, when the will is finally settled, I'll have a bunch of cash. I can take you wherever you want to go, hit up any gallery owners you want, whatever will work. You have a rare talent, Lexie, and I want you to use it and follow your dream."

Her hands shook so badly now, she had to clasp them together to steady them.

"Say it again," she told him.

He frowned. "Say what?"

"You know."

A slow grin spread over his face. "I love you, Lexie Choate. You are the woman of my dreams and all my hopes come true."

She pulled his head down so she could plant her lips on his, giving him as intense a kiss as he'd given her before.

"I love you, too, Killian Walker. Don't think you'll get away this time."

"Darlin', I don't want to get away. Not now, not ever." He wrapped his arms around her, pulling her into the heat of his body.

Lexie relaxed and, for the first time in longer than she could remember, she actually felt she belonged. She giggled against his chest.

"Think I can get you to help me clean up the flowers and vase at the bottom of the stairs?"

He yanked lightly on her ponytail. "Sure thing. I'm just glad it wasn't my head they landed on. By the way, my mama wants me to bring you to Montana with me next week when I go back. Can you get someone to run the shop for you?"

"I can ask Cubby to spare one of his people," she told him. "He's helped me a little before."

"Great. Excellent. Perfect, in fact." Relief smoothed out the lines of uncertainty that had been carved into his face. "We can come back while the others and I wrap up the last details of the will. Meanwhile we can talk about details like where we'll live and how we wrap my horse ranch, Heart Starter, and your art all in together."

"I can't believe you'd do that for me."

"Darlin', I'd do anything for you. So, will you come to Montana with me?"

She nodded. "But, first, I want to take you out to the farm to meet my family."

"Your dad won't be greeting me with a shotgun, will he?"

Lexie grinned. "Not unless I tell him to."

"Good, because I want to do this right and ask for his permission to marry you." He cupped her chin. "How about saying it to me again?"

"Say what?" she teased.

"You know what, you little minx. Come on. I don't think I'll ever get tired of hearing the words."

She smiled up at him. "I love you, Killian Walker."

"And I love you, Lexie Choate. Always and forever."

"Always and forever," she agreed.

He lifted his wrist to check his watch. "We've got a couple of hours until you have to open up downstairs."

She gave him a sly smile. "Why, whatever will we do with all that time?"

"I think I have a real good suggestion." He laughed and swept her up into his arms, carrying her into the bedroom.

Yes, this is going to work out just fine.

Epilogue

Killian looked out the cabin window as the D. Walker Minerals jet he flew in landed on the tarmac. Here he was, back at the little airport Dusty had built outside Red Creek. Through the window he could see two similar planes already parked. Jackson and Dylan. Of course. Rogue was already here, having worked the fourth week of their schedule. Today was the thirty-first of August, and they were right on target for their final meeting.

"Nervous, honey?" Lexie stirred in the seat beside him.

"No." He took her hand and linked his fingers with hers. "For the very first time since this whole mess exploded, I actually feel calm. I know where I'm going and what I'm going to do." He lifted her hand and kissed her knuckles. "I have you to thank for most of it."

She laughed softly, the musical sound that made his heart and cock both jump.

"I wish I could take all the credit, but I'd say a good share of it belongs to your mother."

"She's really something, isn't she?"

"She sure is," Lexie agreed. "She made me feel so very welcome. It was like we'd known each other forever."

"That's my mama all right." He rubbed his thumb over her hand. "But a lot of the credit goes to you, too, darlin'. You both made me see Dusty through her eyes—and yours—and create a new image of him in my mind."

"I'm glad we worked through all of that. It will make things a lot better for the future."

"I'm glad we settled where we're going to be living, too." He grinned and shook his head. "Who'd a thunk it four weeks ago?"

"Are you going to tell your brothers when you meet today?"

"Uh-huh. I hope they'll think it's okay." He was a little nervous about this meeting, although he'd tried to hide it from

Lexie and his mother. Dylan had emailed his thoughts to each of them, so he had a pretty good idea what they were going to discuss. Still, he wanted to get it all set in stone so they could move forward.

"They will. I have faith in you and them."

The silver SUV Killian drove when he was here before waited for him by the little building, the keys in the visor. He dropped Lexie at Heart Starter, giving her a quick kiss before she scooted out of the vehicle.

"You come right back here when you're done," she told him,

"I will. Not to worry." He lowered his voice when he leaned across the seat. "I brought a longer rope back from Montana with me, darlin'. Snuck it into my suitcase." He winked. "Think you're ready for the full treatment?"

"Bring it on, cowboy. Whatever you can dish out."

Killian was glad they'd be back alone tonight, without other ears to hear what they did. Being at his mother's had put a real damper on their sex life.

"Don't forget to call your mama," he reminded her. "I'll see you right after the meeting."

It was straight up noon. He parked in the street in front of Cubby's. Taking a deep breath and letting it out slowly, he walked inside to find the other three Walker offspring already there and waiting for him at a table.

"You're driving Dad's Caddy?" Dylan grinned at Rogue, who'd spent the last week in Kansas, and gestured to the champagne-colored land barge parked at the curb.

"Damn right." Rogue winked. "The thing is smooth as sin."

Jackson fiddled nervously with the fork on a napkin in front of him. "You know, Dylan, when I got your email after that first week, I thought you'd gone crazy."

Rogue nodded. So did Killian, who'd thought the same thing.

The note had told the others the town had a lot to offer, the business was surprisingly interesting, and the people of Red Creek had accepted him like a born-and-raised Red Creekian.

"I was under the influence, I guess." Dylan scratched his cheek. "But damned if I don't feel exactly the same way being back here today."

"I figured that." Rogue hung one arm over the back of his chair. "Figured you'd also found yourself a gal." A smirk curved his lips. "But, I agree, this place grows on a man."

Killian set his forearms on the table. "Sure does. I mean, who knew this dustbowl in the middle of fucking nowhere would leave an impression."

They were interrupted by the appearance of the waitress, and they took a minute to place their orders. Then it was back to the conversation. Killian was anxious to get to it, so he could learn their definite plans and tell them about his own.

Jackson studied each of them after the waitress walked away. "So, we're all agreed? We're going to do this thing?"

The men looked at each other.

"I'm in." Dylan shrugged. "Got nothin' else going on."

Rogue nodded.

"We'll stay the week, gettin' to know each other, like the old man wanted?" Jackson frowned. "Get the business sorted out between the four of us?"

"That's the plan." Killian curled his upper lip in a sneer. "Live in the house for a whole week and *bond* with each other." He snorted.

The guys laughed, but Rogue pointed at Killian. "From what I hear around town, you found yourself someone to help pass the time."

Killian grinned. "Sure did. I'm sure you all know Lexie Choate. She owns Heart Starter."

"Lexie?" they all said in unison.

"Uh-huh. And we've got great plans." He looked at Jackson and Dylan. "And rumors are spreading about you two. You both fell for local gals?"

Jackson nodded, smiling. "Afraid so."

"Yep. Happy as a puppy with two tails." Dylan stared off, looking lost in thought.

"What about you, little brother?" Killian winked at Rogue. "Don't tell us you're the only Walker boy without a happy ending?"

Rogue sat quietly for a few seconds. "Well, I wouldn't want to be the one to ruin a perfect record." He tried to keep from grinning, but his brothers smacked him on the back, laughing, and he let go with a smile.

Killian tapped his belt buckle. "Damn if I don't feel now that these tell people we're part of an exclusive club of some kind."

"We are," Jackson said. "The Walker Brothers Club."

They all grinned at each other.

"Old Dusty must have known what he was doing," Killian added, "even if we didn't think so four weeks ago."

The waitress arrived with their burgers, fries, and pie a la mode. They happily chowed down while they told each other about the ladies they'd found and claimed in Red Creek. Killian listened as each of his brothers—yes, *brothers*—discussed their plans. Then it was his turn.

He cleared his throat. "Lexie and I have plans, too."

"Well," Jackson said, "spit it all out."

He told them about her art and the plans he had to help her with it. She would keep Heart Starter for the immediate future until her art really took off. But their jaws dropped when he told them what he was going to do.

"Buy land adjacent to Dusty's?" Dylan asked.

"You might ought to take a parcel of Dusty's land, too," Rogue said. "It's gonna be ours to do with as we wish, so share and share alike, right?"

The others nodded.

"But raising Appaloosas." Dylan shook his head. "Mighty ambitious." Then he grinned. "Be sure to have one for me to ride, though."

They discussed the company and the prospects for its future as well as the role each of them would take, some more than others.

Cubby's wife brought their bill to the table.

"Well, you four are quite a sight, sittin' here peas in a pod." Sherry cocked her ample hip. "You all decide if you're stayin' or goin'?"

The brothers smiled.

"Hard to believe, but it looks like we'll be stayin'." Jackson pulled out his wallet.

"Yeah, but you three cowboys forgot about that damn bonding." Dylan grabbed the bill and handed it back to Sherry with a couple twenties. "Come back and ask us the same question again in a week."

They all laughed.

Outside, they all shook hands and said they'd see each other back at the house later to start their week living and working together. Killian wasn't positive he could stand a week not sleeping next to Lexie, but it was all for a good cause. Besides, he wanted to make sure it would work out for the two of them to live in the house while their own was being built. Then he strolled down the block to Heart Starter. It pleased him the people recognized him and greeted him along the way.

Lexie's place was almost empty when he got there, thank goodness. He walked behind the counter and, ignoring the few people sitting at tables, lifted Lexie off her feet and gave her a big kiss.

"I take it things went well," she commented when he put her down.

"Better than," he told her. "Tomorrow, I'm gonna have Elaine fix me up with a real estate agent so I can see about buying some of the land next to the house, but the guys—"

"Your brothers," she interrupted. He grinned because she never missed an opportunity to remind him.

"Okay, you're right. My brothers. Anyway, they're all being real great about sharing and insist we take some of Dusty's land, too."

"Wow!" She touched his cheek. "I'm so happy for you, Killian."

"For us," he corrected. "Think we can manage in your little apartment while our house is being built?"

"As long as we're together, I can handle anything."

"Wait." He held up a hand. "I think that's my line."

"Okay, then let's hear it."

"As long as we're together, I can handle anything. Because I love you."

"Love you, too, cowboy."

He cupped her cheeks and touched his mouth to hers, increasing the pressure of his lips until she opened and he took the kiss deep. He meant what he said. With her, anything was possible. She'd already proved that. They had plans for the new life they were going to build, and he could hardly wait to get started.

~~*~*

Check Out These Titles by Desiree Holt

Stark Naked

Buck Naked

Striped Naked

Bare Naked

Naked Desire

Naked Flame

Crack the Whip

Slapping Leather

Bite the Bullet

Buckskin, Boots and Bondage

Hard to Handle

Soul Dreams

Knockin' Boots

Dark Secrets

Cajun Spice

Eyes of the Wolf

Firecracker

Quarterback Sneak

Learn More About Me and Read About My Novels Here:

http://www.amazon.com/Desiree-Holt/books
www.desireeholt.com
www.desiremeonly.com
www.facebook.com/desireeholtauthor
www.facebook.com/desireeholt
Twitter @desireeholt
Pinterest: desiree02holt
Google: www.desiree02holt
LinkedIn: www.LinkedIn.com/desiree01holt

Rogue

by

SABLE HUNTER

A loner by choice and a renegade by nature.

Rogue is living up to his name. He's lived life on his own terms, doing everything from team-roping in college, Texas Hold 'em champion to founding his own company, Lone Wolf Oil.

Everything he's accomplished has been in spite of Dusty Walker, a man who sired four sons by four women – none of them his wife. Rogue might be following in his father's footsteps, but he is nothing like his father.

And he never will be if he can help it.

When he flies to Kansas for the reading of Dusty's will, three brothers and a quarter interest in a half-billion dollar business aren't all he finds...Rogue feels like he's been hit by a tornado after he walks into a room and finds a woman in his bed. Not just any woman, either...

The last time he saw Kit Ross, she was racing off in her truck leaving him naked and hard by the side of the road. Of course, he deserved it; he'd hurt her. To say she wasn't happy to see him was an understatement. And when he wins her ranch with a good poker hand, the game is on.

It's not just poker that's being played. They can't keep their hands off one another. Rogue doesn't know if he has room in his life for family and love. He doesn't know if he can be trusted with people's hearts and happiness. What if he's more like Dusty Walker than he ever knew?

The Sons of Dusty Walker. Four brothers – one tainted legacy and a wild, wild ride.

Prologue

Rogue Walker stood outside the attorney's office in Red Creek, Kansas and debated the wisdom of going in. Sometimes leaving a door closed was the smartest thing to do.

"Excuse me." A deep, somewhat familiar voice sounded behind him.

Rogue stepped aside. "Sorry." When his gaze fell on the man reaching for the same doorknob he'd been staring at, he almost dropped his dress Stetson. WTF? Their eyes met and it was like looking in a mirror.

The two men stopped and stared at one another for a moment. His doppelgänger had the same befuddled expression Rogue knew he wore on his own face. "You look like some really handsome guy I've seen before," the stranger drawled with a smirk.

Rogue chuckled. "No shit."

For him, the plot thickened. This whole trip was a mystery. His counterpart went on in, being greeted by someone Rogue couldn't see from where he stood. Curiosity got the better of him. He took a deep breath and crossed the threshold, feeling like he was stepping through the looking glass.

"Rogue, welcome!" An older bespectacled gentleman stepped forward and offered his hand. "We were waiting for the two of you. Come in and have a seat."

Stanley Benner was the attorney for his father, the late Dusty Walker. Just thinking Dusty's name made Rogue angry. This whole thing was fucked-up as far as he was concerned. Apparently his look-alike was a cousin of some sort here for the reading of the will. Rogue expected to have relatives he'd never had the chance to meet, but this was surreal.

As he walked into the inner office, Rogue felt like he was stepping back in time. A big dark mahogany desk dominated the room and a wall of bookshelves provided a backdrop. He waved away a cloud of smoke wafting from a cigar smoldering in a crystal ashtray. When his vision adjusted Rogue froze, not believing what his eyes were seeing.

Three men sat in front of Benner's carved desk. Three identical men—identical to Rogue except for eye and hair color. "I can't wait to hear this story," Rogue muttered under his breath.

Taking his chair, Rogue placed one booted foot on his knee and waited - impatiently. Something told him his life would never be the same.

"Thank you all for coming, your father was very specific in his instructions."

It took a second for the words to sink in. Brothers? He had brothers? Obviously the others were as dumbstruck as Rogue. They sat there like four penguins in their similar dark suits and striped ties, waiting for the other shoe to drop.

The gray-haired lawyer unbuttoned his black suit coat, leaned forward and pushed his gold wire-rimmed glasses up on his hawk nose and shook his head. "Incredible likeness. Your father never mentioned it."

Rogue thought Dusty had failed to mention quite a few things. He ran a finger under his tight collar, wishing he was in a poker game or back in Texas—anywhere but where he was at the moment. Picking up the manila folder, Rogue began leafing through it and what he saw confounded him. These men were indeed his brothers, each from a different part of the country. As the knowledge sank in, his stomach rolled. Dusty was as bad as those polygamists he'd seen on television, only he hadn't possessed the decency to marry his mother or any of the other three women. And to think his sweet mother had loved the son-of-a-bitch.

The elderly lawyer began to talk and Rogue half-listened, the facts Benner laid out were practically unbelievable.

"Are we quadruplets? Were we separated at birth?" The one named Killian sat forward in his chair.

The attorney shook his head again. "Absolutely not. Each of you is your mother's biological son. You are each about a year apart in age. Mr. Walker...uh...Killian."

Another of the bothers, Jackson, barked out a laugh. Since they were all four Mr. Walker, the man had to take a different approach.

"Killian, you're the oldest at twenty-seven, and Dylan, you're the youngest. Your father must have a very strong DNA strand to have produced four men who look so similar."

Besides different eye and hair color, their faces and bodies could have been stamped from the same mold.

"When I arrived at each of your homes last week with the bad news that your father had passed away, I was under strict instructions not to mention that you had brothers. It was among your father's last wishes that you learn of your siblings' existence in person." The attorney picked up another sheaf of papers. "I apologize for bringing you to Kansas under these circumstances."

Rogue sat silent, taking it all in. Now, everything made sense. His mind flashed back to the moment when Benner had broken the news of Dusty's death, how he'd held his mother while she cried. She'd begged to come to his funeral, only to be told it had already taken place—just one more thing Dusty had robbed her of. He'd agreed to come, making use of the private plane from Austin and the limo that had picked him up and brought him here to this podunk law firm in central Kansas. But now that he was here, he was angrier than he'd been before.

The attorney shook the papers in his hand. "So, if there are no further questions, I'll begin." He waited a few seconds, meeting each of their gazes.

"Yeah, I've got one." Rogue looked at his brothers, wondering what in the hell they were all thinking. "How did he...?" He held up a hand. "Let me rephrase that. Why? Why four families in four different states?"

The lawyer tossed the papers on the desk and laced his fingers together. "Your father wanted to have children, and he confided to me that his wife didn't want them. This broke his heart."

"So he went around looking for incubators?" Killian spat out.

"That's a little disrespectful," Benner chided.

"You're calling me disrespectful?" Killian made a rude noise. "I'd say your client is the one lacking in social graces."

"She knew about all of us?" Dylan frowned. "His wife, I mean?"

"No, she did not." Benner's cheeks turned ruddy. "And I was sworn to silence under attorney/client privilege. I'm assuming your mothers made you aware of your father's marital situation?"

Rogue sneered. His mother had protected him or that's what she thought she'd been doing. But he kept his thoughts to himself. One of the other men cleared his throat, but no one spoke. Running the tips of his fingers over the rim of his black cowboy hat, Rogue tried to make sense of the situation. Brothers? Just the idea that he had family was alien to him. Like his name implied, he preferred to work alone. Dusty hadn't been around enough to earn the title of father as far as he was concerned. His mother should've let go of her dream and moved on years ago. At least now he knew why his father had spent very few weeks with them every year. The man not only had had a wife, but four other families to split his life with.

When he'd been around, Dusty had done his best to teach Rogue what he called the family business. Rogue had watched his father pore over contracts for regional mineral rights, rode with him while he surveyed land and listened as he interpreted tests to determine if there was value in the acreage he was considering. Rogue had taken the lessons to heart and later used them to his advantage in the oil business, acquiring some land and sinking a few exploratory wells. One of these days it was going to pay off— big time. Hopefully sooner than later.

The attorney rattled the papers in his hand. "Dusty and his wife, Theresa, were killed in an auto accident. We were told they died instantly." He looked from one to the other. "So in the interest of time, I'll read the highlights of the will. The entire document is in the folders I placed in front of you." The attorney cleared his throat and read for a quarter of an hour. The details included a grocery list of assets: a mineral and water rights company that boasted assets near five-hundred million dollars, including a private ten-person jet, a storefront in the small town of Red Creek, Kansas, as well as a big house on the outskirts of town.

The brothers sat in silence, listening.

"Of course, there are also the houses in the four compass points of the US. In the north, Montana, where Killian resides. Texas, from where Rogue hails. Dylan, of course, from Nashville and Jackson, from Oregon." The brothers looked at each other, then back at the lawyer. "These houses are currently company property, but your father notes that you four, as the new owners of D. Walker Mineral, can opt to transfer the homes into your mothers'—"

"Hang on." Dylan stiffened. "You're saying he left the company to us?"

"Yes, of course." Benner looked surprised. "I didn't read that portion of the will because I assumed…" He hefted out a sigh. "The company is now legally in your names, exactly one quarter going to each."

Dylan let out a long, low whistle.

Rogue sat forward. Had he heard right? Five hundred million dollars divided by four…was a shit load of money. Thinking back on how he'd spent his childhood and what his mother had gone through… Instead of making him happy, the news just pissed him off. He didn't know if he wanted to be associated with anything belonging to the late Dusty Walker.

Apparently, he wasn't the only one.

"So, if we sell our quarter?" Jackson said the words slowly.

"There are repercussions." The attorney flipped pages. "Ah, here. 'Heretofore, the parties to which—"

"In plain English, please," Killian spat out.

"Of course." The man set down the papers again and reclined back in his chair, placing one hand on his round belly. "The company is essentially frozen as-is for a full year. After that time, if one of you wants to sell, the others have the option of buying you out at half-worth."

"Half-worth?" Rogue fisted his hand, not liking the idea. There was always a catch. "Meaning they'd buy me out at a fifty-percent discount?"

"Yes, that's correct. Your father wanted to keep the company in the family. Wanted you four boys to run it together."

"I can wait a year," Jackson drawled. "I've got savings, money to get me to rodeos and pay my entry fees. I expect to win some during the season too. But hell, no matter what Dusty wanted, there's no room in my life for small-town Kansas and an eight-to-five job. I'll probably be the first to sell my quarter of the company."

Benner attempted a smile. "However, you are each officially on the payroll and your first paychecks will be cut the day you successfully complete the one..." He swallowed, then cleared his throat. "Stipulation in the will."

All four of them leaned an inch closer.

"Stipulation?" Dylan prodded.

"To inherit, you must spend a week in Red Creek, working in your father's office, learning more about the business, sharing with each other what you've learned from your father over the years. You must also reside for that week at your father's house—your house—on Osprey Lake."

"A week?" Jackson shook his head. "What's the timeframe here? Anytime in the next year?"

Rogue slapped open his folder and pulled out his copy of the will. "What section is that in?" He had his own business to run, he didn't know if he had time for this shit.

"Second from the last page. You'll see that there's a thirty day time limit." The attorney checked his calendar. "Today is August second. You'll need to decide which week in August works for all four of you, and plan to be back here then. Or if this week works…" He shrugged.

Killian tapped his fingertips on his knee. "Dad wants the four of us to live in the same house and work in the same office for an entire week?"

"Like summer camp for the bastard sons of Dusty Walker." Dylan mumbled a curse.

Jackson rubbed the spot between his eyebrows. "What the fuck was he thinking?"

Rogue kept reading silently. He was ready to get out of here. Turning a page, he glanced at the clock on the wall. The game was at six and he didn't want to be late. When the lawyer informed him he needed to come to Kansas for the reading of the will, he'd called his friend in Wichita and told him to set something up close by. No use wasting an opportunity to play poker when there were fools ready for him to take money off their hands.

Benner's face turned a dark shade of red. "He loved each one of you, I know that because he took great pains to create provisions to make sure you were taken care of after his death, as you were while he was alive."

Sure, Rogue thought, he felt about as loved as a stray dog. "Listen here." Rogue stared at the will. "It says we each have to spend a week, but it doesn't say it has to be the same week."

"No, it…uh…what…?" The attorney sat forward and flipped through his paperwork.

"I say we each take a week, get this goddamn stipulation out of the way and figure out the rest later." Rogue looked at his brothers. "Agreed?"

"Yeah. Okay." Dylan accessed his phone. "I can stay this week. I got nothin' goin' on."

Jackson grabbed his folder. "I can do the week after."

Killian rose. "Sure, I'll do the third week."

"That leaves week four for me." Rogue stood and tucked the folder under his arm.

"Now wait, boys." The lawyer stood, still staring at his copy of the will as Jackson and Dylan got to their feet. "Your father wanted you all to be here together. At the same time. To get to know one another."

Rogue hid a sneer. Yea, he'd get to know them. He planned on asking Zane to look into his so-called brothers. Trusting people wasn't his strong-suit.

The brothers stood in a half-circle, their eyes dropping to the belt buckle each of them wore. The exact same Western belt buckle.

"Am I seeing things?" Jackson asked.

Killian looked down at his waist. "Son-of-a-bitch. I can't believe this. They're all alike."

"That's kinda fucked-up, huh?" One side of Dylan's mouth curved up. "The old man gave us the same belt buckle, like we'd use them to somehow magically find each other."

Jackson looked as if he wanted to fling the buckle into the nearest lake and watch it sink – Rogue understood the feeling. The room went silent and in a few seconds, almost as one, they all turned toward the door.

"Wait." The attorney raced around his desk and stood in front of the men. "Your father's wish was to have you spend this time together." His hands fluttered like he didn't know what to do next.

"Well then…" Killian patted Benner's shoulder as he strode past him. "I guess he should've had his lawyer write that into the will."

Jackson bit back a grin.

As far as Rogue was concerned, they were strangers—and he, for one, would prefer it to stay that way.

Dylan gave the others a trigger finger salute and headed out the door.

Rogue wasn't far behind. All he could think about was how

fucked-up this was—four brothers, one tainted legacy.

Let the games begin.

Chapter One

"To the airport, sir?" the middle-aged limo driver asked perfunctorily, his eye on the road.

Rogue stared out at the small town street, so different from what he was used to seeing. His mind was still blown with the bombshell news he'd received—he had three half-brothers and together they'd inherited a business worth half a billion located in this sleepy little hamlet in the middle of nowhere Kansas. "No, I'm staying an extra day, not going back to Texas till tomorrow. I need you to take me to the White-Wing Ranch, if that's possible. I've rented one of their cabins for the night. Do you know how to get there?"

"Why, certainly, no problem, sir. Let me cool you off, this August is turning out to be a scorcher." The chauffeur turned up the air conditioner and headed north out of town. As the big black limo eased through Red Creek, Rogue noticed every eye was on it. He stared back, knowing he was practically invisible through the heavily tinted windows. That was fine with him, anonymity worked well with his plan. In passing, he gazed at the small shops, the people meandering down the sidewalk, and the tubs of fall flowers sitting by the parking meters. A typical Midwestern small town, as different from Austin, Texas, as night was from day.

"How far is it?" Rogue asked, pouring himself a Scotch in a crystal glass from the small wet bar to his left. He needed something to calm him down. The whole idea that Dusty had treated his mother like she was some nobody trollop just pissed the hell out of him. He'd known they weren't married. Even though he bore the Walker name, his mother hadn't. What he wasn't aware of was that Dusty had not only a wife, but four other women he supposedly loved as much as he'd claimed to love his mother, Marian Lofton. For all of his life, she'd never spoken one ill word against Dusty and it hurt her when Rogue did. So, he'd mostly suffered in silence. Doing that, like he did most things—alone. Even his name infuriated him. Who the hell names their kid Rogue? His mother had said it was a good name, a name of his father's choice. She'd said it wasn't a built-in insult, rather a testimony that he could accomplish anything he wanted all on his own. So he'd tried to think of himself as a rogue wave, a rogue stallion or a rogue wolf.

A loner.

"Just a few miles, sir. You'll enjoy it out there, the Parkers are fine people. I can remember when White-Wing raised the best cattle in this part of Kansas." The older man pushed his felt hat up on his head, peering at Rogue through the rearview mirror. "Drought and the bottlenecking of the beef market have put a lot of mom and pop ranches out of business. Dave and Sheila are just lucky they have that daughter of theirs. Katherine is doing everything she can to save their land. I just hope they can make a go of it, takes a lot of money to renovate a working ranch into a tourist destination."

Rogue was barely following the conversation. Instead, he was recalling what he'd read about the ranch: the pheasant hunts, fishing on the placid lake and the accommodations for weddings, reunions, corporate retreats and receptions—until he heard the name Katherine.

He'd known a Katherine once…who was from Kansas. Rogue shook his head, dispelling the uncomfortable memory. Not possible. Besides, Kit's last name had been Ross, not Parker. For a while, Rogue lost himself in the past. When he finally came out of his daze, he realized he'd never responded to the driver. "I've heard a lot of good things about White-Wing. I look forward to seeing it."

"Well, you don't have to wait long. We're here." The chauffeur smiled as he pulled up to a beautiful rambling stone and cedar structure. "What time shall I call for you, sir?" He got out and opened Rogue's door, then retrieved his leather bag from the trunk.

"Tomorrow at this time should be good. I've arranged for a late flight."

"Thanks, Mr. Walker." The man tipped his hat after Rogue handed him a folded bill. "I'll be here when you're ready. This is my card in case you need anything."

Rogue accepted the business card and pocketed it. Once the stretch had departed, he looked around curiously before entering the big double doors with the heavy wrought iron knockers. On every hand were sweeping pastures covered in waving grass, bordered by stands of mature trees. A few placid blue ponds dotted the pleasing landscape and there were smaller rustic cabins built in a half-moon shape around the central building. If he had more time, he would've enjoyed taking a ride and looking around.

But not today. He had a date with four queens and a pitcher of beer.

As soon as he stepped foot onto the cool terra cotta Spanish tile, Rogue felt a sense of tranquility wash over him like a spring rain. Dark Spanish-style furniture and rich jewel tones blended graciously with the wood paneling and stone accents. "May I help you, sir?" A pleasant female voice greeted him.

Rogue passed by a round table with scrolled wrought iron legs bearing a huge bouquet of golden sunflowers to get to the check-in desk where a pretty older woman with salt and pepper hair waited for him. "Yes, ma'am, I'm Rogue Walker and I called about a room a couple of days ago. I'm here for the poker game."

An uncomfortable look came over her attractive face. "I see. Yes, that game…" Her voice trailed off, and she cleared her throat. "May I see your credit card?" He handed it to her, and she filled out some information on a laptop. "You're a few hours early, but the cabin should be ready now. Here's the key. I'm Sheila Parker and if there's anything I can help you with, let me know." She pushed an entry card across the counter to him. "Go out the side door and it's one of the cabins on the south side, #9." Sheila pointed across the room to the exit. "Enjoy your stay. I won't say I hope you win, because my fool husband is playing and I'll save my 'good lucks' for him." Turning away, she mumbled, "Because he's probably going to need them."

Women who muttered under their breath made Rogue nervous, so he moved on, passing by what had to be a restaurant or a dining room. He was assailed by the most wonderful aroma ever to greet his sense of smell. "Homemade wheat bread," he groaned, a special weakness of his. He glanced into the dimly lit, comfortable looking eating area. Tables were set, but there was no one about. In fact, there was no one about anywhere. Rogue seemed to be alone.

Stepping back out into the sunshine, he pulled his hat down to shade his eyes. Making his way across the yard, he wondered where the poker game would be held. Probably in the building he'd just left. He smiled, seeing that the accommodations were small log cabins. Whoever had designed the place hit the nail on the head with rustic appeal. Coming to his door, he started to put the key in – and noticed it was unlocked, ajar a couple of inches. With a gentle shove, he pushed it open and stepped into the generous sized suite. His eyes roved the room, taking in the big recliner, the heavy desk – but when he came to the focus of the room, he froze. "There's somebody in my bed," he mused under his breath.

Walking quietly toward the big oak four-poster, Rogue felt like one of the three bears from the fairy tale. The only difference was the riot of luscious curls lying on his pillow were sable brown locks instead of golden ones. A brown velvet bedspread was thrown back to the foot, the only cover over the curvy female body was a thin baby blue sheet. He could see every dip and curve and the outline of a very intriguing heart-shaped bottom.

Glancing down at his keycard, he noted the number nine, stepped backward and verified that he indeed was in the right cabin. "Well, this beats a mint on my pillow any damn day."

A sweet female sigh came from across the room, and Rogue

returned to it like a rope had been dropped around his shoulders—
the tug was strong. Heaven was smiling on him, because when he
drew near, Sleeping Beauty rolled over and it became apparent she
was sleeping in the nude. A pair of scrumptious round breasts with
rosy pink nipples were winking at him like cherries topping an ice
cream sundae. A delicate creamy arm was thrown over his little
bedmate's face, but Rogue didn't mind, there was plenty of other
good stuff to see. His cock rose to the occasion, and he had to
reach down and adjust his package for comfort. With a cute little
kick, she pushed the sheet farther down and now he was seeing a
flat tummy and a narrow waist. If he didn't do something fast he'd
be treated to a centerfold peek at her feminine treasure.

Should he awaken the fair maiden with a kiss?

Probably not a good idea. Damn, sometimes he wished he
wasn't so gallant.

Turning his back, he crossed his arms with a smirk. All of a
sudden, he was feeling better. The worry of Dusty and his brothers
seemed far away. Clearing his throat, Rogue announced, "Excuse
me, I didn't mean to barge in, but the door was standing open. I do
believe, however, that you're in my bed." His bit his lip and smiled
when he heard a gasp, the snap of a sheet and small bare feet
padding on the floor, coming across the room toward him. Bowing
his head, Rogue closed his eyes. Counting under his breath, he
prepared himself for a blushing kissable vision voicing her abject
apologies. Five, four, three, two…

Not what he got.

Wham! A fairly substantial pillow came crashing down on his
very expensive beaver-skin cowboy hat.

"What do you think you're doing in my cabin, you pervert?"

Rogue held his hands up, attempting to defend himself from
the crashing satin covered weapon she was wielding quite ably.

"Give me your key!" she demanded with a hiss.

He held the plastic card out like a peace offering, keeping his
eyes tightly shut. When he heard his small attacker moving away,

he carefully opened one eye and had to laugh at the sight. Long dark hair hung down in corkscrew curls to butt level and the sheet trailed behind her like the long train of a bridal gown.

"Follow me!" Miss Priss marched out the door and across the yard, gesturing grandly to another cabin. "This is #9! Mine is #6, the damn numeral must have spun upside down on the screw."

Rogue followed the sexy husky-from-sleep voice. Why was he feeling an odd sense of déjà vu? "I'm certain I can't be held accountable for malfunctioning hardware and like I said before, your door was standing open." His argument sounded good to him. "My name is Rogue Walker and I'd like to apologize for waking you from your cat nap."

A horrified gasp met his ears. "Rogue Walker?"

Rogue had never heard his name said with that same degree of distaste before – but when he finally got close enough to lay eyes on the face that went along with the incredible body he'd ravished with his eyes – he understood.

Standing before him in all of her glory was Kit Ross, the woman who'd been his partner in what had to have been the worst blind date in the history of mankind.

Both of them stared at one another, their own memories crashing down on them like an unwelcome downpour...

...back to the Texas Hill Country College Rodeo Finals six years before.

"Just look at him, Beth." Kit stared at Rogue Walker, unable to look away. He walked by her, completely unaware of her presence. He wore that ever present leather vest, but this time there was no shirt underneath and the muscles of his chest rippled, moving with the effort of carrying the saddle over his shoulder. Drops of perspiration glistened on his golden skin, running down between his pecs and over his chiseled abs. "Lord have mercy," she whispered. Unconsciously Kit licked her lips, wishing she had the courage to go up and talk to him.

"Quit lusting after our rival." Beth teased. "You're going

to lose your competitive edge."

"I can't help it." Kit sighed, following his progress as he ambled toward the livestock chutes. "He's perfect. I don't know if I'm roping for the scholarship, the thrill, or just the chance of seeing him." She kept her eyes on Rogue till he disappeared in the crowd. "Besides, you're one to talk. You could eat Elijah Bowman up with a spoon."

"Here, hold your horse." Beth handed Kit Hotshot's reins. "There is a difference between me and you, though, my friend. After we ride, I'm going to go flirt shamelessly with Elijah and if I have my way, I'll be saving a horse and riding a cowboy tonight."

Kit adjusted her goggles. She wished she didn't have to wear them. But she was blind as a bat and if the dust from the arena got under her contacts during the ride, she would instantly be unable to function. "Come on. Let's go watch. Rogue and Elijah ride second, we're sixth tonight."

They found a spot on the fence out of the way but near enough to see the action. As she waited for her heartthrob to appear, she gazed around the arena. There were at least a thousand people crowded into the stands and it seemed they were all yelling or cheering as two cowboys raced behind a steer, bringing it to a halt in less than ten seconds. She hoped her team did far better than that. Smiling, she acknowledged how much she loved this sport. There was nothing as high energy as a rodeo, nor one that had as many hot men—especially one like Rogue Walker.

Standing up on a lower rail so she could get a good look, Kit leaned over the top and folded her hands together. They were shaking a bit, but that was normal. Her adrenaline always ran high before a ride. A dozen cowboys milled around behind them. Some called out their names and others hurried to get ready for one event or another. The bronc riders had already finished but the bull riders would compete after team roping.

The sound of feminine laughter wafted over the other noise. Kit looked back over her shoulder and saw one of the barrel racers clinging to a handsome cowboy. He had his fingers hooked into one of her belt loops as if he was afraid she'd get away. Kit sighed. Barrel racers were a different breed, she and Beth chose to compete with the guys and some welcomed them, some resented them—and others, like Rogue, ignored her for the most part. And why wouldn't he? He could have any woman here. Why would he be interested in a no-frills tomboy when he could have a rodeo queen or a buckle bunny on his arm?

"There they are," Beth said, pointing toward the boxes. Kit could see Elijah and Rogue astride their mounts, waiting tensely for the moment to arrive. "Go!" Elijah called and the steer ran. As soon as the barrier was released, Elijah who was the header, tossed his rope around the steer's horns. Once the four-hundred pound animal was under control, he turned his horse slightly to the side so Rogue, the heeler, had a clear view of the steer's hind legs. Kit held her breath. "Go, Rogue!" she whispered, her eyes devouring him. She was a heeler too, so she knew how critical the next step was. Rogue threw his rope under the steer's feet, pulling up to secure both legs inside the loop. Stopping his horse, he backed it up and the horn blew. Kit's eyes flew to the score board. Five point six seconds. "Good score." She looked over her shoulder at Beth. "Think we can beat that?"

"Hell yeah," Beth answered. "Let's do it."

* * *

Rogue Walker and Elijah Bowman slapped the rodeo dust off their jeans, arguing over what went wrong—again. The Aggie roping team had kicked their butts for the third time in a row and frankly, they were sick of it.

"How in the hell are those two scrawny little women out

roping us?" Rogue wiped his sweaty face on his shirt sleeve.

Elijah let out a long whistling sigh. "I don't know, Rogue. Kit Ross is damn good and her header is no slouch. Their timing is uncanny."

"That's what they used to say about us." Rogue led his horse up the ramp and into the gooseneck trailer. "Rest, girl. We'll get back on the road tomorrow." He checked Mariah's hay and water before joining Elijah at the truck. "I need a drink. How about you?"

Elijah was digging in the glove compartment. "Shit. I thought I had some condoms put back."

Laughing, Rogue watched his friend's somewhat panicked search. "Do you have a sexual emergency?" He pulled his wallet from his back pocket. "If you do, I can let you borrow one."

Elijah turned, grinning, holding out his hand. "Thanks, I didn't want to have to drive to town."

"I hear you, we are out in the boondocks." The arena where they were competing was housed in a rural exhibition hall between Bryan-College Station and Brenham. The nearest convenience store was probably ten or fifteen miles away. "They don't exactly stock these in the restrooms in this Bible-belt community. So, you gotta hot date, huh?"

Elijah grinned. "Actually, I do."

Rogue grunted. "I don't know how you get as much action as you do. What am I doing wrong?" He looked at his friend. Elijah wasn't a bad-looking dude with his dirty blond hair and wide smile.

"Well, where do I begin?" Elijah drawled. "You have a full class load at Texas, you try to take care of your mother since your absentee father is a no-count son-of-a-bitch, and you're starting your own wildcatting business on the side. Rogue, you don't have the time or the energy to chase women."

"Just because I'm busy doesn't mean I don't need to get

laid occasionally," Rogue muttered, feeling horny at the thought.

Elijah paused, started to walk, stopped, then turned around. "Look, I'm going to get a motel room. I need a shower. Why don't you come with me, clean up and I'll call my date. She has a friend, I can probably fix you up."

Shaking his head, Rogue stepped up to Elijah. "I'll go in half on the room, I could use a shower too. But I don't have much luck with double dates, especially a blind one."

"You're welcome to the shower, bud, but you'll have to get your own room if you don't want to sleep with the horses. I'm planning on needing some privacy." With that, he went around to the driver's side. "You with me or are you gonna hang out here?"

They'd spent many nights in the cramped quarters of the gooseneck, and he had no problem in doing it again tonight. Right now, a shower sounded too good to pass up. "I'm coming with you." He piled in and rolled the window down, leaning back against the headrest. "Is she hot?"

"Mine or yours?"

Rogue snorted. "Both." Was he considering this? His cock twitched at the thought. How long had it been since a woman had gone down on him?

"We won't have to put a bag over their heads." Elijah pulled his hat down over his eyes. "I'm not picking out china, Rogue. I just need pussy."

The frank talk did it. "Me too. Count me in."

As Elijah pulled up in front of the motel, he smiled. "I'll make the phone call. Your date is named Katherine."

* * *

"Hurry up, Walker!" Elijah hollered. "We're gonna be late."

Rogue zipped up his jeans and fastened his belt buckle. He patted his fly, giving his Johnson a lick and a promise. "Hold your damn horses. Is it all arranged? Katherine okay with it?"

Elijah looked at himself in the dresser mirror that sat in front of the big king-size bed. "He's gonna kill you," Elijah muttered to himself. Louder, he answered, "Everything's a go. Elizabeth said Katherine is looking forward to going out with you."

"Great." Rogue grabbed his wallet off the dresser. "I'm ready and glad I carry extra rubbers."

"All right, we've got to stop by the announcer's booth. I lost my insurance card somewhere and someone turned it in. I just got a text." Elijah explained as they went out the door. "Oh, and this isn't a double date. We're on our own, Elizabeth will be riding with me and you'll ride with Katherine."

"Fine with me," Rogue agreed. "I work better without an audience."

On the ride over, he tried to pry information out of Elijah about Katherine. It didn't work. "Where are we meeting the girls?"

"At the arena, over by the concession stand. Just let me get my card and we'll head over." They bounded out of the truck and climbed the stands to reach the booth, their boots causing the black metal bleacher seats to clank and groan. Elijah opened the door. "The guy must've stepped out, there's no one here."

"Do you see your card? Maybe it's just lying around here somewhere." Rogue helped him look. While he peered under papers and on the floor, curiosity got the best of him. "Why are we meeting the girls here? Are they buckle bunnies from out of town?"

"Uhhh…" Elijah delayed answering. "Here it is!" He held the Blue Cross/Blue Shield card up triumphantly. Seeing Walker was waiting for an answer, he huffed and just laid it out. "No, they ride the NIRA circuit like we do."

An uneasy feeling came over Rogue. He sidled up to Elijah,

who was staring down into the arena, watching some cowboys load a stock trailer. "Katherine and Elizabeth. Nah, you wouldn't do that to me, would you? This isn't Beth McGee and Kit Ross, is it?"

"Yea." Elijah actually dodged when he said it, halfway expecting Rogue to throw a punch. "Beth is fun and she says Kit's been dying to really meet you."

Rogue thought he would choke. "Goddammit, Eli! Kit Ross? You've got to be fuckin' with me! She's my blind date?"

Elijah held up his hands. "She cleans up nice, Walker. I've seen her."

"She'd have to! You can't even look at her and tell she's a woman. Hair slicked back into a bun, no makeup, men's clothes. Hell, she's always got dirt streaked across her face. Nobody in the world would ever believe I'd willingly date a woman who looks like her. That woman is nowhere near my type and I'm surprised she agreed, I bet her type has tits and a pussy." Rogue was so pissed he was yelling. "Horse-face Kit Ross! Shit!"

"Now, Rogue..." Elijah held up his hands. "Calm down."

"There's no way I'm taking her out in public. I should just cancel."

"No, don't do that. Elizabeth, she—"

About that time, the door was slung open and a red-faced man came barreling in. With a snarl, he walked up and flipped a switch. "The microphone was on, assholes. Your voices were carrying all over the countryside."

Down by the stock pens, Kit Ross stepped backward, deeper into the shadows. Her face was flaming, she was fighting hard not to cry. How could she have been so stupid? For the last year and half, she'd had this huge crush on Rogue Walker. The few times they'd spoken to one another, he'd been nice. Polite. She always enjoyed competing against him, he was as talented as he was handsome.

413

Apparently, he was also a huge dick.

Finding out her idol had clay feet hurt. She didn't know why she'd wound so many of her girlish daydreams around him. Probably because his name was Rogue, it was such an unusual name and what her father had said was burned deep into her mind and heart. It just seemed meant to be—she was wrong.

Part of her wanted to run and keep on running, never see him again. Another part of her had the urge to get even, make him feel just a little bit of the humiliation that had taken her breath away. Could she do it? Dare she do it? Remembering what Rogue had said about how she looked, Kit glanced down at what she was wearing. He'd been right. She wasn't much to look at. But maybe she could wear something that would take his mind off her plain face. The denim skirt and western blouse would never do—not for what she had in mind.

Frantically, she racked her brain. Then she remembered the red dress she'd thrown behind the front seat. Yes, that would do.

Get ready, Rogue Asshole Walker. The Kit Ross he was expecting was not the Kit Ross he was going to get.

About a half hour later, Rogue's face was sore from frowning so hard. He was going to go through with this but it had cost Elijah Bowman dearly—to the tune of a brand new pair of handmade boots from Texas Traditions. By the time Eli slapped down a grand or more for the custom footwear, he'd be less inclined to pull a fool stunt like this one again.

"She wears thick glasses when she rides, for fuck's sake, they almost look like goggles." Rogue fumed. "A date with gawky Kit Ross, I won't survive this."

"Yes, you will. You must've been studying her pretty close to notice all that detail." Eli chuckled. "Those are safety glasses, not goggles. We stir up a lot of dust out there if you haven't noticed. Some people have to wear them." When

Rogue began cussing again, Eli held up his hand. "Smile. Here they come."

Eli and Rogue had driven over to the concession area where Rogue spotted Ross's utilitarian white truck with the maroon Texas A&M sticker on the bumper. "Sheesh, I'll lose my Longhorn card for socializing with an Aggie." Squinting his eyes as if the view was going to hurt, he glanced over to see where the women were waiting. He recognized Beth McGee, her long red hair gave her away immediately. But he didn't see Kit Ross.

But then he wasn't looking that hard, something else worth looking at had caught his eye.

All he could see was a smoking hot honey with bouncy curls hanging past her waist, a bright red dress hugging every curve from her generous breasts to a perfect ass. Why was she with Elizabeth and where was… "Oh my God," he muttered.

"I told you she cleaned up nice."

Rogue heard Eli, but he didn't react. He was out of the truck and standing in front of an impossible vision of beauty. "Katherine." Rogue held his hat in his hand. Why she looked so different wasn't a point of concern. Besides, he couldn't think rationally anyway. All the blood in his brain had flowed down to harden his cock.

Kit calmly met his gaze, betraying absolutely nothing of how she was really feeling. Lifting her lips in the most sweet, seductive smile she could manage, Kit spoke to her roping partner. "Elizabeth, I was wrong. He doesn't just take off his hat for one thing."

Elizabeth snickered and it took Rogue a second or two to realize Kit was making a sexual reference—about him. He could hear Elijah laughing, but he wouldn't take his eyes off Kit for the amount of time necessary to shoot him the finger because he didn't want to flip him the bird without aiming it properly. "Thank you for agreeing to spend the evening with me, Katherine." He let his eyes rove her gorgeous body from her toes to her little turned up nose. "You look…amazing."

Katherine bit her tongue to keep from saying what she was thinking out loud. Idiot, she thought. "Thank you, Rogue. I'm looking forward to it." Which was certainly the truth.

Elizabeth grabbed her arm, and as Rogue and Elijah watched, they hugged and giggled, speaking the incomprehensible girl-talk that men can't begin to grasp. Rogue's mind was boggled because these two ultra-feminine women, so unlike their gutsy cowgirl alter egos, were exuding pheromones, making his cock like stone and blowing all of his preconceived theories of what makes a woman desirable right out the window.

When they returned to their dates, Katherine gave him a wink. "I'm ready. Shall we?" She pointed to her truck. Inflating his ego, she held out her hand with a pair of keys dangling from the tip end of one pale pink painted fingernail. "Wanna drive?"

"Yea, sure, great." He took the keys and escorted her to the passenger side, gently helping her into her seat. The shape of her body and the scent of the delicate perfume cloud surrounding her mesmerized him. "Where do you want to eat? Eastwood's?" Rogue named a nice steakhouse in the area where a lot of the cowboys went to celebrate.

Katherine crossed her long smooth tanned legs, sliding one over the other as if she enjoyed how velvety soft they were. Rogue felt his cock rise and he licked his mouth, wishing he could kiss those soft red lips. He hit a bump in the road and had to drag his eyes away to make sure he kept her ride between the ditches. When he had control again, he glanced back only to find her staring at him. Mimicking his earlier action, she slowly licked her top lip with her tongue.

"If you don't mind, Rogue. I'd rather skip dinner and go right for dessert." There was no way in hell she would go out in public with him knowing what he'd said. "I'd rather go somewhere we could be alone."

Rogue swallowed hard. Hot Damn! "Sounds good to me." He lifted his hand. "You tell me where to go and I'm your man."

Katherine rolled her eyes in the half-shadows. "Why don't we pick up a six-pack of beer and go parking?" She paused. "Or is that too juvenile for a sophisticated lady's man like you?" Yea, she was putting on a show. But Kit Ross had no illusions. She was a tomboy country girl from Red Creek, Kansas, who loved horses, the outdoors and only owned this sexy red dress because she'd been asked to be her cousin's bridesmaid at a Valentine's Day wedding earlier in the year. She'd run out of the church and driven right to a rodeo competition, and that was the only reason the dress was with her.

"Nothing I'd rather do, beautiful." Rogue whipped into a drive-through Beverage Barn and bought a six pack of locally brewed Shiner beer. "Now, where can we have some alone time?"

He hoped wherever they were going had a bright security light because he wanted a better look at the wet dream sitting next to him. Man, he'd have to eat crow over this situation and he didn't mind at all. He'd pour on the Jardine's hot sauce and chow down. He had been wrong, dead wrong about Katherine Ross, and Rogue would have no trouble admitting it to anybody.

"Go another mile and turn down the dirt road to your left. It leads to a little park on a small lake. We'll have all the privacy we need. A few people live on the road but there's not much traffic and both sides are banked by underbrush thick with poison ivy. No one will bother us there." Parents of a college friend lived down this way and let Kit and Beth practice on their property occasionally.

Rogue's heart was pounding. Her suggestion wasn't the most romantic sounding locale, but this outing wasn't about romance. As Katherine moved her hand to his leg and kneaded his leg above the knee, Rogue admitted it—tonight was all about S-E-X. His breath was coming hard as he found the dirt road and exited, the worn truck bouncing on the uneven gravel surface. "How far do I go?"

"All the way, baby," she whispered sexily.

Fuck, fuck fuck…Rogue muttered to himself. "I meant how far do I drive?"

She laughed. "Oh, I know what you meant, I was just teasing." She squeezed his muscular thigh. "All the way to the end, we'll be there before you know it."

"I can't wait, baby." He covered her hand with his, rubbing his thumb over the silky skin.

All of a sudden Kit wasn't in that much of a hurry. She was nervous. Could she pull this off? Could she be a temptress long enough to give Rogue Walker exactly what he deserved? "There's some tables and benches on the shore, a pretty place."

Rogue flashed her a grin. "The only thing I'm going to be looking at is you."

Sadness flowed over Kit. She'd been so desperately hung up on this guy. True hero-worship. She'd adored him with her eyes, dreaming of what it would be like to actually be noticed by him. If she'd been sitting here unaware of the ugly things he'd said over the loudspeaker about her, Kit would've thought she was the luckiest woman on the face of the earth.

But she did hear.

Oh well, he wasn't her Rogue Angel—he was just a conceited horn-dog. Looking out the window and down the narrow lane canopied by trees, she pointed. "We're here." Her voice was husky with unshed tears.

Rogue slowed down and pulled the truck up to a picnic table. The moon glinted on the still dark waters of the small lake. "Let me come help you." He grabbed the beer, jerked open the door and hurried around, anxious to get his arms around her.

Kit steeled herself. She had zero experience, but she had won best actress in high school. She'd seen enough rom-com movies to pull this off. When Rogue opened the door, she gave him her hand and the heat of his body made her tremble. This whole thing confused her. How could he have been so disgusted with her one moment and so infatuated the next? All she'd done was let her hair down, put on a little lipstick and wear something provocative. Except for the thin veil of physical enhancement, she was exactly the same nondescript woman. Rogue's male gullibility made her doubt the evolutionary standing of the whole species.

She let him lead her to a table and gasped when he picked her up and sat her gently on the hard wooden surface. Taking a can, he popped the top and handed it to her. Doing the same, he relished the way her mouth fit over the rim. Thanks to the moonlight and the park lighting, he could see her quite clearly—and God, she was incredible. He was so jealous of that Shiner beer can he could die. "Were you thirsty? It's been so hot."

When he spoke, she tilted the beer back a bit too far and the fizz got up her nose. She coughed and giggled, so nervous she needed to pee. Raising her beer, she toasted him. "Here's to team roping in Texas in the month of August."

Wow. Rogue felt like he'd stepped through the looking glass. He felt completely disconnected from what had happened earlier. Kit Ross was so different than what he'd expected. He was having a hard reconciling that this totally desirable vixen was the same rough-riding, steer-roping, boot wearing horsewoman who trounced him in the rodeo arena at every opportunity.

She was gazing up at him, eyes liquid with desire. Her

mouth was parted and the low-cut neckline of her blouse showcased the creamy mounds of her breasts. Her cleavage begged for his tongue, her lips called like a siren for his kiss and when she leaned forward, her eyes darting to his mouth, he could no longer resist. "I'm going to kiss you now. If you don't want me, speak up because I'm dying to know what you taste like."

Katherine knew the feeling. "Come get me, Rogue Angel." For a moment, she laid aside her vendetta and surrendered, lifting her head and holding her breath until…until he layered his mouth across hers. Softly. Gently. The touch of his firm lips sent an amazing arc of heat blazing through her. Kit shivered. It wasn't fair, an asshole shouldn't be able to kiss like a dream.

Rogue didn't get the Angel part, but he didn't care. He'd be her angel if that meant he'd get lucky. Katherine felt perfect in his arms. He feathered kisses over her pillowy lips, lingered, then rubbed harder, tempting her to respond. She was accepting his kiss, her fingers digging into his shoulders, but what he wanted was for her to kiss him back. Desire overwhelmed him. With a groan, he pressed harder, licking a path across her lower lip. When she whimpered, letting him know she wanted more, arousal sizzled through his blood like lava.

Katherine was losing the battle. She didn't want to enjoy this, she didn't want to crave his kiss. She parted her lips to protest and when she did…his tongue darted in to tease hers and she was lost. Rogue took her in his arms and pulled her close, his kiss becoming voracious, his mouth taking hers, tongue licking, teasing, making her press against him. Her stiff nipples were tingling and her sex was throbbing.

This had to stop.

Placing her hands on his chest, she pushed and he gave, dragging his mouth from hers with a growl. "What's wrong?"

"Nothing," she muttered. "I just need to do this." She had

to continue on with her plan before she lost the will to do so. With shaking hands, she began to undo the buttons of his western shirt, pushing that sexy as hell vest aside.

"God, yes." He began to help her.

As she got down to the middle of his chest, Kit gave in to her fantasies and planted a kiss on his warm skin. Unable to resist, she palmed his pecs, then scraped her fingernails over his nipples, loving that he growled at her touch. God, he smelled so good. She inhaled, her own breath hitching with a combination of nerves and desire. "Can I?" She tugged the hem of his shirt from his jeans.

"Just tell me how you want me," Rogue panted.

"Naked."

She only had to say the word and he was pushing his boots off, toe to heel. Kit worked on his belt buckle, a heavy silver one with a longhorn's head emblazoned across it. She'd stared at that particular spot—and lower—a hundred times. "Help me," she whispered.

"Here, let me." Before she knew it, he had stepped out of his pants, shucked his briefs and even peeled off his socks. He'd taken her naked literally—perfect. He had to be in the buff for her plan to work.

"Mmmm." She ran a hand down his chest. "You look as good as I knew you would." With a hard swallow, she let her gaze drop lower. "Damn," she whispered, and the sentiment was genuine. He was hung! All of her secret fantasies came flooding back, she longed to reach out and touch him. If this was a real date, she'd take him in her hand, rub her thumb along the very thick, long shaft—she'd make him beg. Kit pressed her legs together, clenching her pussy. She could feel her own juices starting to flow.

"Now you." Rogue picked up her red blouse and his fingers grazed the sensitive skin of her side.

Flinching, Kit managed to stop his roaming fingers before

they eased their way to her breasts. "Later. I can't wait." In explanation, she sank to her knees until she was eye level with his cock.

"God, yes." He threaded his fingers into her long, dark hair, tightening until she could feel the pull against her sensitive scalp.

Kit licked her lips, placed one hand on his thigh and leaned in close.

"Oh, yea, take me in your mouth. Suck me, baby." Rogue threw his head back and bucked his hips in erotic anticipation.

Katherine's eyes widened. This was nothing like she expected. Part of her wanted to think she'd be turned off, disgusted by the idea—but she wasn't. Shaking, she leaned forward and placed a chaste kiss on his right thigh.

"Fuuccck," Rogue moaned. "Don't make me wait, you're killing me."

That was the idea.

For a moment she let her fingers pet his skin, her mouth caressing his abs, moving a little lower, teasing him – making him wait. Hopefully, driving him certifiably insane.

Until she stopped, hissing in fake pain.

"What's wrong?"

Katherine knew she had to quit, this was all about revenge. It embarrassed her to know what she really wanted—and that was to climb on top of the table, open her legs wide and beg him to fuck her hard. Playing out her role, she grasped her eye. "My contacts, something's in my eye. I need to take them out so I can enjoy going down on you."

"Oh, okay," he said, his whole body shaking, needing her to finish.

"Lie back on the table and wait." She placed a hand on his middle and pushed. "Relax. I'll be right back."

"Hurry," he groaned, settling down.

"Oh, I'll go fast. Promise." Katherine stood up and while

he was staring at the stars fisting his cock, she picked up his clothes, every scrap—boots and hat included—and high-tailed it to her truck. Quickly she crawled in and before he knew it, she'd started the engine.

"What the hell?" he called, raising his head up from the table. "Kit? Where are you going?"

"Away from you." She held her hand out the window and shot him the finger. "I heard what you said about me, every NIRA member from four counties heard what you said. You think I'm ugly. I disgust you."

"No, baby." He rose up. "I think you're beautiful. Perfect. So sexy. What I said in the booth was just my first impression, you know how wrong those can be."

"Yea, I do," she said, quickly putting the truck in gear because he was moving toward her. "My first impression of you was that you were a nice guy. I was wrong. Have fun walking out."

It was at that moment, Rogue realized she was leaving him. Nude. Buck-ass-naked. "Where's my clothes?"

"I have them. Have fun hitching a ride in your birthday suit, asshole."

"Hey! At least leave my hat so I can hold it in front of my dick!" He made one last desperate entreaty. "Or my phone!"

Katherine rolled her window up and gassed the truck, leaving a very pissed, very naked, very vulnerable Rogue Walker to walk or hitchhike back to the rodeo arena.

"Well, shit." Rogue stood with his hands on his hips, staring after Kit Ross in utter disbelief. With a sigh, he set off, his naked skin gleaming like a ghost in the moonlight, his now very flaccid cock waggling low between his legs. He kept to the shadows when he could, cussing and wishing every conceivable ill down on the head of his nemesis. That she'd been gorgeous, sexy-as-hell and a generous lover before she'd turned on him was something he had to push out of his mind. When he arrived near the end of the road, vehicle lights made him hit the ditch. And when they slowed down, he didn't know what he was going to do. Until…

"Rogue?"

Rogue breathed a sigh of relief. It was Elijah. A laughing hoo-rawing knee-slapping Elijah. "Having problems?"

"Yea, Kit Ross fucked me over."

Elijah threw him some clothes when Rogue opened the door, quickly putting them on.

"I guess you'll be nicer to her next time."

"I hope I never lay eyes on that Jezebel ever again."

And he didn't…

Until today.

Chapter Two

"Get out!" Kit raised one elegant small arm and pointed to the door. "Get off our property! Now!" She glanced around, making sure the coast was clear. This was one time she was glad there were so few paying guests.

"Katherine Ross? Kit?" Rogue was fifty kinds of shocked and more than a little turned on. Because he was so stunned, feeling things he didn't know how to deal with, Rogue decided to antagonize her. Why that seemed the right thing to do, he didn't stop to analyze. "I haven't seen you in forever." He held out his hand. "How have you been?"

Ignoring his hand, she narrowed her eyes, pursed her lips, picked up her sheet and proceeded to stomp toward him, wagging her finger in his face. "You are the last lily-livered polecat I'd ever want as my guest. Just turn around and head your ornery ass out of town. Your money's no good here."

Rogue's lips twitched with humor. This was one reunion he'd fantasized about over the years. After their date from hell, he'd been angry at first. Later he'd mellowed, seeing the whole fiasco from her point of view. But now – standing face to face, Rogue didn't feel like he thought he would. He'd long since gotten over it. In fact, he'd looked for her so he could apologize, even called Beth McGee to no avail. The only information she'd given Rogue was that Kit didn't want to see him again. And that was a shame, because he hadn't met a woman before or since that excited him quite as much. In fact, she'd starred in many of his fantasies in the last six years, he'd awakened from more than one dream with her name on his lips.

"I wish you'd reconsider," he cajoled, enjoying watching her face. She had huge wide-set blue eyes fringed with dark lashes. Her small nose was gently turned up and her lips were generous— suckable—just like he remembered. Her hair was long, lush and curly. The blush tingeing her high cheekbones made him want to rub his face against hers to see if she was as warm and soft as he remembered. "I'd love to catch up on old times, Kit. Exchange stories, compare our sex lives." Rogue had enough sense to realize he was skating on thin ice—but then he'd always liked to live dangerously.

"No. Hell no," she fumed. A blush matching her cheeks was rising from the intriguing area beneath the sheet, giving an enchanting rosy hue to her creamy skin. "Leave!"

"You haven't aged a day, beautiful." Rogue stood his ground, crossing his arms over his chest. "Was that your mother who checked me in?"

Kit sputtered, ignoring his compliment. The infuriating cowpoke was making her completely crazy. "Yes, that was my mother. She had no idea you were a creep or she would've turned you away herself."

Was she relenting? He hoped so, he had no intention of leaving no matter how many hissy fits she threw. "What have you been up to?" He leaned back against a tree, crossing one booted foot over the other. Glancing down at his feet, he almost choked to realize he had on the boots that their night out together had cost Elijah Bowman. He decided not to share that info with Kit, she probably wouldn't appreciate the irony. Besides, she had inflicted more damage on him than she'd known. When he'd jumped into the ditch to hide from the truck that had turned out to be Elijah, he'd landed in some of the poison ivy she'd warned him about. He'd been laid up scratching for a week, swathed head to toe in calamine lotion. "I looked for you, you know. I wanted to thank you for such a wonderful evening, but you vanished into thin air. I hope that wasn't because of me." He was talking, but he was also looking. The way the sun was shining, he could see right through that sheet to the intriguing gap between her legs. Man, he'd like to get his fingers in that pussy. The woman was seriously stacked.

Kit made herself stare into those stormy eyes of his. She could smell his familiar scent, a mix of freshly mown grass and leather. "No, of course not. I would never run away just because you hurled some petty insults into the air." She paused, then added, not sure why she was sharing. "My father died the next day. I came home to help my mother."

A wave of contrition hit him. "I'm so sorry," he said sincerely. "Dave Parker must be your stepfather." Now, he understood the difference in the last names.

Kit didn't get a chance to answer.

"Yes, as a matter of fact, I am." A disapproving voice spoke up from behind her. Kit jumped. "Katherine, what are you doing outdoors in such a disheveled, inappropriate state? You should be more mindful of our guests and have a little bit more pride in your appearance!"

Katherine felt her cheeks burn. Another man making more snide remarks about her appearance. God, sometimes she hated half of the world's population. "I'm busy and this is none of your business, Dave." She despised the ground her stepfather walked on. He was up to no good, she didn't really understand how beyond the fact that he manipulated her poor mother at every opportunity, but she didn't trust him an inch. It was hard for her to believe that he used to be her father's best friend.

Rogue turned his head to find a middle-aged man, not as tall as he was, with a weathered face and pale blue eyes. "Hello, I'm Rogue Walker."

Dave's face brightened. "And I'm Dave Parker, glad to meet you. You're here for the card game! We've heard so much about you. Barnaby speaks highly of you and we have a fourth coming, a man you'll enjoy meeting, Troy Keller, a businessman from Wichita. He owns a string of car dealership. When Gordon told us you were coming and wanted a game with Barnaby, we couldn't resist. You're a legend in these parts among card players."

Kit, who was still standing there, clutching the sheet over a set of generous breasts, snorted. "Legend. More like a lizard, a scaly coldblooded reptile with no heart and no scruples."

"That's enough, Katherine!" Dave held out a hand, infuriating Kit worse than Rogue had. They'd been at odds from the time he'd moved into her family home and immediately started trying to change things. Dave hadn't been satisfied until he'd pulled up every floorboard and relocated every wall. His involvement in every aspect of her life unsettled Kit. A portion of White-Wing, not the homestead, but the acreage where her horses ran and her little house set was even owner financed with him. That was bad enough, but when he'd stepped in just months after her father was killed and began courting her mother, Kit knew he would end up bankrupting them. His reputation as a reckless gambler was well known.

Anger began to boil in her blood. One day she was completely gobsmacked by the chaos her stepfather had brought into her world, and the next the former object of her desire/nightmare stole her ability to breathe. Rogue had encroached upon her space, barging into her life and looming over her like some kind of chocolate éclair laced with cyanide—she'd love a bite but it would kill her.

Her gaze moved from one irritating man to another. Despite her adolescent yearnings for romance and a family, she'd learned there weren't many men one could depend upon—from her mother's weak second husband who didn't have enough sense to come out of the rain, to Rogue Walker who had eviscerated her foolish tender feelings as effectively as if he'd stomped a small ladybug beneath his boot. "Dave, this man—"

"Is our guest and will be staying here, whether you like it or not." With that, Dave put a hand on Rogue's shoulder and led him off to the lodge where she knew a card table would be set up so he could squander even more of White-Wing's diminishing returns.

* * *

Rogue accepted a cup of strong coffee from Dave Parker. He was half listening to Dave's recollections of the 2003 World Series of poker where legendary player Chris Moneymaker turned forty dollars into two and a half million.

In 2003, Rogue had been fourteen years old—lost, lonely and hating his father. Dusty Walker had waltzed in and out of his life, spending only a meager amount of time with a sad teenager who hung on every word he uttered. Hell, the truth was, back then he hadn't hated him, he'd worshipped the man. As a small boy he'd often wondered why Dusty was gone more often than not, and once he'd asked him. Rogue could still remember his answer. He'd said, "I have responsibilities, Rogue. One day you'll understand. But know this; it's not the quantity of time we spend together, it's the quality." The worn cliché had satisfied him at that tender age, but now he couldn't imagine the gall of the man whose urge to leave heirs to carry on his name overrode his ability and desire to be a father.

Dave kept talking, pouring drinks while Rogue reminisced. His unexpected encounter with Kit had made him nostalgic for the past. He'd grown up in West Texas, his mother still lived in the same small town. After he'd graduated from UT, like many alumni, he'd stayed in Austin. No matter. You might take the boy out of the Permian Basin, but you didn't take the Permian Basin out of the boy. Now, after meeting his so-called brothers and finding out what Dusty had spent his lifetime building, his father's presence in that part of the world where Rogue had spent his formative years made sense.

Rogue's youth had been untamed, surrounded by mesquite-choked fields dotted with hundreds of pump-jacks, as common a sight as tumbleweed in that part of the world, giant metal sculptures, rhythmically lowering their heads to the ground like horses taking a drink of water. When night fell, the gas flares from the derricks burned bright orange and yellow, shimmering through the darkness.

In the hill country of Texas, one might catch a whiff of mountain laurel or lavender, but in the part of West Texas where

Rogue grew up, it was the sour stench of gas that filled the air. Rogue hadn't known the phrase then, but he knew it now—the smell of crude oil, gas and cow shit doesn't stink – it smells like money.

The oil fields had been where he'd played, shooting pop bottles, chunking dried dirt clods at snakes, riding bikes and swimming in fiberglass stock ponds. When Dusty had sprung for him an old secondhand pick-up, he'd prayed for rain so he could mud-hog, a game teenage boys played plowing their trucks through mud to see who could slide and who got stuck.

Since college, he'd started out as a smalltime speculator, traveling all over the country acquiring small oilfields or property where he thought there might be oil. Before he worked for himself, he worked for others, building a reputation as a man who could locate crude when no one else could. He'd been known to get tingles or itch when there was oil beneath the ground. Hell, he'd even been known to get an erection, but Rogue didn't know if it was from excitement or some chemical awareness. Unlike the old-timers phrase about having a nose for oil, Rogue had a dick—a dick that just seemed to sense black gold beneath the ground like a dousing rod.

The one thing he'd learned was that when he traveled out of Texas, he missed it. He missed everything being chicken-fried, the absolute obsession with high school football, and pickups with a gun rack on the back window. That's why he couldn't see himself moving to Kansas full time, no matter what Dusty Walker's will offered.

Rogue had paid his dues on work-over rigs. Instead of high rises, his world was dominated by one hundred foot derricks, jutting into the air like oversize rusty Legos with huge metal blocks falling and rising, carrying pipe from the bottom to the top. He'd worked as a roughneck, a floorhand, a derrick-man, and a hotshot. No job was too small or too insignificant. Rogue had learned the craft, developed the skill and became what he'd always wanted to be—a Texas oilman.

But oil wasn't his only passion, Rogue also loved sex and he loved poker, especially Texas Hold 'em.

There was just something about taking a gamble that appealed to him. The oil business was a constant gamble as was dealing with women. What appealed to him about Texas Hold 'em was that it wasn't just a game of chance, Texas Hold 'em was a thinking man's game. Strategy played a huge role. Unlike draw poker, where the player can only bet twice per hand, in hold 'em, two cards are dealt that play along with up to three of the five that are free for all to play on and there are four bets instead of two.

"Since you're the star, we're letting you pick. Pot-limit, fixed-limit or—"

Rogue didn't let the older man finish. "No limit, of course." He smiled and saw Dave wipe his mouth nervously. "How long before the others get here?"

Dave checked his watch. "Another couple of hours. I just thought you might need a respite from my stepdaughter. What was all that about anyway? I take it you two know one another?"

Rogue was careful. "We knew one another in our college days. We both team-roped on the college circuit. Kit was damn good, she beat my team and we were nobody's slouch."

"Yea, so I hear." Dave pulled out a chair and sat down at a big round table where cards and chips rested waiting. "So, Gordon said you were here on business?"

Gordon seemed to talk too much. Rogue saw no harm in telling the truth, it wasn't like it could remain a secret. "Dusty Walker was my father."

Dave looked thunderstruck. "Well, I'll be damned. Never put two and two together. Walker is a fairly common name. Your father and I used to be good friends, years ago. Before he got rich. In fact, he and I ran around with Will Ross, Kit's father. We used to do everything together."

"Well, it's good to meet you." Rogue reiterated. "It was a

surprise to meet back up with Kit."

"Yea, her mother dotes on her. She's smart, I guess. It was her idea to stock pheasant and add the cabins. Katherine spends too much time with those horses of hers. She needs to find a husband and move away. Her mother and I would do better on our own." He fanned his hand in the air. "She's got a little house down closer to the lake that's being fumigated. That's why she's staying in the cabin for a day or two, and I, for one, will be glad when she's outta here. We don't exactly get along."

"I know the feeling," Rogue agreed.

"And whose fault is that?"

Rogue jerked around at the female voice and saw Kit standing in the door, hands on her hips, glaring at first one of them and then the other. He was somewhat disappointed to see she'd dressed, leaving behind the make-shift toga for more reputable attire.

"I want to talk to you." She pointed at Rogue, crooked her finger and started off, expecting him to follow.

Rogue tipped his hat at Dave and followed. What else was he to do? This was a woman who'd once had him naked with his cock straining to get in her mouth. "Yes, dear."

Dave choked back a laugh. "Good luck."

"You didn't have to get dressed on my account," he muttered, checking out the sway of her hips lovingly molded by a lucky pair of blue jeans. He could also see a leather belt with her name 'KIT' stamped on the back. Above that she wore some type of lacy pink camisole which had see-through places in it. Lord help, he'd go blind trying to peek through those intriguing little openings.

"I needed to put on clothes so I could walk you to your car," she snarled over her shoulder.

"I'm not leaving," he reiterated.

He expected her to head for the front door, instead she led him into the dining room where the enticing smells were still as strong. His stomach grumbled loud enough for her to hear it.

"Yes, you're leaving. Sit down." She pointed at a table graced with a white linen cloth and a bouquet of wildflowers.

He did, noticing again that he was the only one around. "We're going to have to hone our communication skills. You have an inordinately hard time comprehending what I'm saying today."

"Sorry, it's hard for me to dumb-down." She placed a small plate in front of him with a thick slice of homemade bread smeared with butter. "There, I don't want you spreading false rumors that I'm not hospitable."

Rogue couldn't have been more surprised if she'd slapped him in the face with a wet mackerel. "Wow, thanks." He didn't even hesitate but picked up the bread and took a big bite. "Damn, this is good."

Kit sat across from him, her hands folded in front of her. She had to do something to keep from touching him. He looked like a fuckin' dream. He'd said she hadn't changed a bit…well, he certainly as hell had. She would never have thought it possible, but the man was better looking than she remembered—and she remembered it all – every last damn detail. He wore tight jeans, a white western shirt rolled up to reveal strong forearms dusted with dark hair, a leather vest and a pair of custom made boots with longhorns on them to match that belt buckle she so well remembered unhooking on the night of her greatest shame. "You're welcome. I like to bake."

Rogue smiled around the ambrosia he was chewing. She was still mad and Kit Ross was damn sexy when she was pissed. "From everything I've heard about White-Wing, it looks like it could be a huge success. Why am I the only one here?"

Kit debated whether to carry on a conversation with him, her ingrained sense of decency won. "We're located in the middle of nowhere and I have no money left for advertising. But I do have a few guests scheduled, there's even a group coming in tomorrow to see about making a big reservation—not that it's any of your business." She reached into her pocket and withdrew cash. "Here, I insist on giving your money back. When you get through with your card game, I want you out of here." She leveled a look at him that would've melted asphalt.

Rogue laid the remainder of his slice of bread down, ignoring the bills folded on the table in front of him.

He had hurt her.

For the first time it really hit him. He'd known he pissed her off, made her angry. Perhaps even embarrassed her. But obviously it had been more. Rogue looked into her beautiful face and saw remnants of pain still residing in her eyes years after he'd so stupidly inflicted it. "Katherine, I can't take your money and let me stop right here and say something I should've said that night. I'm sorry. I was wrong. What I did was idiotic and worse, it wasn't true. I was a self-centered wet-behind-the-ears kid who didn't know a good thing when he saw one. Will you forgive me?"

Katherine stopped. She just stopped—moving, thinking, breathing. Their eyes were locked as he waited. Slowly her mind started to weigh the idea. What would it hurt? A fresh start. Wipe the slate clean. Let bygones be bygones. Let him off the hook.

"No, I don't think so." She stood. "Please feel free to use the cabin to freshen up, but I'd appreciate it if you'd leave when it's over. I can make you a reservation at the motel near the airport if you'd like. The sooner you're out of Kansas and back in Texas, the happier I'll be."

Rogue glanced at her right hand. He was somewhat relieved to see it was ringless. "I hate to break it to you, but I'm sorta considering moving here part-time." Up until that moment, he'd been weighing his options on how he could break Dusty's will or sell his interest to his brothers. Well, he'd changed his mind.

Kit had changed his mind. He was going to think long and hard about it before he decided.

"What do you mean?" Horrified was a good word for how she was feeling.

"As it happens, Dusty Walker was my father. Walker Minerals belongs to me and my brothers."

Rogue

Katherine opened her mouth, then shut it, opened it again and all that came out was a squeak. Throwing up her hands she stomped off and Rogue leaned way out in his chair so he'd have a good view of her leaving—cause she looked damn good.

* * *

Rogue took a sip of Jack Daniel's. Jack was his go-to drink while he played. He sat fairly still, letting his eyes rove around the room. He had pocket aces and there were two more on the table. Of the three men playing with him, Dave Parker was the one most out of his league. So far, he'd identified Kit's stepfather's tells right away. He whistled when he had a good hand and stared at his cards when he had a bad hand.

Troy Keller wasn't consistent. So far, he covered part of his face with a good hand and frowned with a fair one. Some player's transparency almost made playing against them a crime. Barnaby, on the other hand, was a challenge. He, like Rogue, had no tell.

The only thing proving to be a distraction for him was the beautiful woman who sat at the back of the room, silent and still. He didn't know why Kit was there, she wasn't encouraging or even offering them refreshments. Perhaps she was there to make sure he left as soon as the game was over.

"I raise," Barnaby muttered and pushed another pile of chips toward the center of the table.

"I fold." Troy sighed.

"I raise again." Dave added more chips.

Rogue checked out each man's face before he raised again. When the time came to show their hands, Dave threw his cards down and cussed, "Goddammit," as Rogue raked in the chips. Kit looked nervous, Rogue noticed. Barnaby didn't react, he was one cool SOB.

When it was Barnaby's turn to deal, he did so with no show of emotion. Dave was sweating. Rogue smiled to himself. He never played any game he couldn't afford to lose—be it with cards or people.

435

After that, the hands became more and more intense. Keller encouraged Dave from the side. Once, Barnaby told him to shut up. Rogue didn't let on either way. When Gordon, a fellow poker fanatic who owned a trucking company arranged this gig, Rogue had known about Barnaby. He had a rep for not fearing big bets or big risks. Rogue had a hit list of players he wanted to beat and Barnaby Miller was on it.

Yet as the game wore on, Barnaby began to make mistakes and Rogue soon realized he'd overestimated him. Maybe he was having an off day, it happened. The man was a surgeon from Kansas City and Rogue was sure that was a nerve-wracking profession. Soon Barnaby folded for the last time and it was just Rogue and Dave left to play. The amount of money that had passed over the table so far was over a hundred grand and most of it would be going into his pocket.

Finally, Rogue sat with a six and a seven of hearts in his hand. An eight, nine and ten of hearts lay on the table. A straight flush. Dave was whistling Dixie—literally. Rogue had no crystal ball, but something told him this was it. He raised. Dave wiped sweat, he didn't have enough chips to make the bet. "Whatcha gonna do?" Rogue asked him.

Dave glanced nervously at Kit, then blew out a long breath. He reached into his coat pocket and brought out a notepad. "I hold the lien on several properties."

This wasn't what Rogue was expecting. "Yes?"

"Is this even legal?" Keller asked.

Rogue shrugged. "This is a private, unsanctioned game. We can do whatever the hell we want to." He addressed Dave. "Are you sure you want to risk it? I have a pretty good hand." Yes, he was cocky.

"I'm sure." He began to write. "I have better cards."

"So, what you got?" Rogue asked, curious as to what the man would risk and what hand would give him so much confidence.

Dave placed a scrap of paper on the table, a description of the property, an amateur IOU. "I wouldn't risk this if I wasn't sure."

"What's happening?" Kit moved forward.

Rogue picked up the offering and he couldn't believe what he was reading: Transferable Lien against White-Wing Ranch, Red Creek, Kansas.

Kit snatched it out of his hand. "No! You can't do this." She looked at all of them, obviously flabbergasted. "My mother or my father never missed a note and now she's your wife!"

Dave held up his hand. "Stay out of this. This isn't the homestead, it's the grazing acreage. The note's still in my name and I haven't taken any money from the till for three months, there just hasn't been any extra. Besides, I'm not going to lose. This is a sure thing!"

In college, Rogue hadn't made the best grades, but he'd done fair. In some areas, he'd excelled and one of those areas was analytical thinking. He prided himself on being able to study all of the facts, see all the angles and make the best decision. Here, he was faced with a quandary. On one hand, he wasn't in the habit of taking people's land away from them. On the other, it was apparent Dave Parker had a gambling problem. If he would risk White-Wing this time, he'd do it again.

Rogue met Kit's gaze, she looked as if she were about to cry. Undoubtedly the financial situation of White-Wing was a bone of contention between her and her stepfather. Whatever she knew about the note, he was sure that she considered Rogue's obtaining it to be going from bad to worse.

"Are you sure you want to do this?" he addressed Dave.

To his surprise, Dave laughed. "What? Are you a coward? I match your bet and raise you by the current amount left owing on this property, fifty thousand dollars."

Rogue held his gaze. "A coward I'm not. Let's do it."

"Rogue, I swear to God!" Kit yelled behind him. "Men!" She threw her hands in the air. "Every man I've ever met seems intent on fuckin' up my life!"

"Four kings," Dave announced proudly.

Rogue slowly laid down his cards. "Straight flush."

"Shit." Dave laid his head in his hands.

Rogue turned to Kit Ross. "I guess I'll be staying here tonight, since I have this." He picked up the paper and put it in his pocket.

* * *

Cabin nine suited his needs just fine. He was in dire need of a shower, the game hadn't been heated but what happened next had been a scorcher. There had been a scene between Kit and Dave. He'd stayed only long enough to get the legal papers that made his win official, but from what he'd heard, Kit had reason to be angry. She'd reminded Dave of every hurtful detail. When her father passed, things had gone downhill. Like the driver had said, small cattle ranches were a difficult proposition, hard to keep profitable. It hadn't really been Kit or her mother's fault. A few years before Will Ross died, the price of beef had gone down, a drought had come, the price of hay had risen and the big corporations used the circumstances to force small ranches out of business. White-Wing had eventually been one of the casualties. Kit had made a difficult decision. To preserve the land, she'd sold the last of the cattle and had turned their focus toward training horses and hosting hunters. All of this cost money, so maintaining their home and paying for the improvements was a cost in addition to paying the long standing mortgage on the acreage purchased from Dave Parker, a mortgage Dave had held himself.

He'd listened as she reminded Dave that she'd poured her personal savings into the note and sold off some of her prized horses to pay cash for the improvements, so the ranch could one day be self-supporting again. "My house is on that acreage you so casually wagered, my horses are kept here. Everything is there except the original homestead. You've literally placed the future of my home in the hands of a man who despises me!"

Rogue had known Kit blamed him, but he hadn't realized she thought he despised her. Something had to be done. He wasn't the bad guy, not in this situation anyway. Yea, he'd once mouthed off when he had no business to—all because he had a huge ego and zero tact. He didn't have all the facts yet, but she'd learn soon enough that she didn't have anything to fear from him. Compared to her stepfather, Rogue felt like he was a safe bet.

Rogue undressed by his bed. It had been a long day. He'd flown out of Austin before dawn, arriving in Kansas for the reading of his father's will. Met three men who looked so much like him that they could have been cloned in some mad scientist's laboratory. Learned that he was now part owner of a business, while profitable, was going to eat into the time he used to manage his own company, a company he loved and had built from the ground up with his own two hands.

And lastly, he'd come face to face with a woman with whom he shared memories that haunted him to this day. Her face. Her kiss. Her touch.

Once he was naked, he strode to the bathroom, flipped on the shower and leaned on the wall while the water came up to temperature. He needed to do some thinking, decide what would be the wisest thing to do. First he needed to call Elijah and see what was going on with his company. His former team roping partner/schoolmate worked for him. They'd stayed friends and Rogue was as close to him as he was anyone, which wasn't saying much. He'd read scholarly articles about how your relationship with your father could impact your whole life, and Rogue feared it was safe to say he was impacted, in some ways fucked. But checking on his business interests with Elijah was something he could put off till tomorrow. Tonight, he needed a shower, some room service and a good night's sleep.

As he soaped his body, his hands roving over his skin as he washed away the dirt and grime of the day, his mind wandered to Kit. If he closed his eyes, he could still feel her hands on him, her lips on his body. He groaned as his hand rubbed over his cock and balls. Rogue was just about two heartbeats away from jacking off when he heard it...a noise from the other side of the door. Someone was in his bedroom—again.

Shutting off the water, he grabbed a towel, dashing the water from his face and chest before hastily wrapping it around his hips. Throwing open the door, he smirked as he stalked into his room to see who had intruded on his privacy...as if he didn't know...

Kit Ross sat on Rogue's bed. She'd known he was taking a shower, but she at least hoped the man would have the decency to get dressed before barging out to where she was waiting. But decent wasn't a word that could be applied to Rogue Walker. Especially when he was wearing nothing but a scrap of cotton that wasn't big enough to wrap up a decent size pan of biscuits.

"I need to invest in bigger towels," she drawled.

"Not on my account." He almost jerked it off, almost. But he was striving to be the gentleman he should have been six years ago. Facetiously, he asked, "As lien holder, will I get a master key to all the rooms?"

She gave him a cold hard stare. "The note isn't on the homestead."

"Right. It's what's in your house that I have...an interest in." He gave her a smile. "We need to stop meeting like this. To what do I owe the pleasure of your company?"

"I want to talk."

"All right." He leaned back on the dresser, not bothering to worry if the towel was fully meeting where he had it tied. "Shoot."

"Don't tempt me." She huffed. "Would you please put some clothes on?"

"Once you were very anxious to get my clothes off." When she nailed him with another glare, he smiled and turned to go dress. With a mischievous grin, he jerked off the towel and flashed his bare ass at her as he sauntered off. Her enraged gasp satisfied him. As soon as he'd finished, he returned. "Better?"

It wasn't. Covering up his gorgeous body was a sin, she just wouldn't admit that to him. "Yes, thank you." Kit cleared her throat. "I want you to give it back."

"The note?" He'd known this conversation was coming.

"Yes, pretend that stupid bet didn't happen and just return the note for White-Wing to my stepfather."

Rogue sat, one leg halfway on the dresser, his forearm resting on his thigh. "I'm sorry, I can't do that. I won it fair and square."

Kit jumped up, furious. "Why are you doing this to me? Do you hate me that much? I sent your friend back to pick you up that night, you know."

"Yea, but when I saw the lights from the vehicle coming, I jumped into the ditch filled with poison ivy and scratched for a week."

She didn't want to laugh, but she did.

Rogue softened his voice. "I don't hate you or despise you. At all."

"Then give the note back. Don't do this."

She gave him such a look of desperation that Rogue dry-scrubbed his face, wishing he could make this easier. "I'm not out to get you, Kit. You're just going to have to trust me."

Kit looked as if she were about to cry. "You know that's impossible."

"Your note is safe with me," Rogue spoke slowly, gently, then grinned. "A lot safer than you are right now."

She stepped right up into his face. "I'm not afraid of you." And she wasn't—she was excited.

"Maybe you should be." Rogue curled his fingers around her neck.

Her heart pounding, Kit knew she should push him away. But those incredible green eyes of his were delving deep into hers and if she didn't know better, she'd say he really wanted her. Shaking her head, she tried to pull from his grasp. No, she wouldn't put herself through that again. She wasn't a sex-starved twenty-year-old anymore. Ha! She was a sex-starved twenty-six-year-old.

"Stay put," he growled. "I'm not going to hurt you and you

know it."

"I don't know any such thing," she hissed back. "You humiliated me at that rodeo, and for what? What was my crime? Having the audacity to have a crush on you?"

Rogue said nothing for a long heartbeat, just rubbed his thumb slowly along the velvet flesh of her throat, staring down into her face. "Guess what?"

"What?" she asked automatically, magnetized, unable to look away.

"Now I have a crush on you." With a low moan, he lowered his head and crashed his lips to hers. Not gentle. Not tender. He consumed her mouth with heat and hunger, his tongue prowling inside, claiming possession. Rogue kissed her as if had every right to do so.

And she let him. For a few crazy, precious moments, she kissed him back, dizzy with desire. Her whole body trembled, responding to the blatant male who held her tight. Passion flared and all coherent thought fled. She'd wanted this man so much and despite the pain he'd inflicted, her Rogue Angel had never left her dreams. Never.

What was he doing? Rogue wondered. If he wasn't careful he was going to make this worse. "I'm sorry," he said, putting an inch or two between them, just enough so he couldn't feel her nipples poking against his chest.

Sorry? He was sorry? Suddenly, she was cold. Kit rubbed her arms, chafing her skin against the chill. "I didn't ask for that kiss."

"No, but I couldn't help myself. You're irresistible," he whispered in her ear, his warm breath making her tingle.

Kit felt her breasts swell. He was torturing her. "Then don't resist me, do as I ask, return the loan to Dave Parker."

Rogue knew she'd never believe he had her best interest at heart. Well, he'd just have to convince her. "I can't do that. But I'd appreciate if you showed me around tomorrow. I'd like to inspect the property. Maybe I could make some suggestions. We could start over."

Despair and desperation flashed through Kit. This was a nightmare. "I don't want your suggestions and I don't want to start over. Just stay out of my way and out of my sight and we'll get along just fine."

With that, she slammed out of his room, knocking a picture of a ring-neck pheasant off the wall.

Rogue smiled. This could be fun.

Chapter Three

"I will not let him get to me. I will not let him get to me." Kit chanted as she ran. Rogue Walker was playing havoc with her life—again. After a restless night she had gotten up early and set out on a run around White-Wing. Usually the sight of her beautiful home raised her spirits. Today, all she could think about was that she might lose it. Every inch of it reminded her of her father. She turned and ran down the hill to where he was buried beneath a big elm. The horse he'd valued so much, the one he'd tied their hopes and dreams up in, lay buried a few feet away from him. She stopped, resting her hands on her knees. The stallion, Rogue Angel, had been in the trailer Will Ross was pulling behind him when his brakes had failed and he'd lost control on a curve, crashing into a tree. She'd shared her father's love for the big quarter horse, but he'd been more than a pet or an investment, he'd been the future of White-Wing. While they'd owned him, he'd sired a whole herd of champions and would have continued for years if he'd survived.

She couldn't help but smile. What would Rogue say if he realized he shared a name with a horse? When she'd first laid eyes on Rogue Walker, the coincidence had struck her, especially since her father always said—if he'd said it once, he'd repeated it a thousand times. "Rogue Angel will take care of you. You never have to worry." The last present he'd given her had been a statue of the animal with a bronze plaque on the base inscribed with the name. He'd placed his hand on it and repeated that Rogue Angel would always be there for her. She didn't know if he was talking about the live animal or the statue…later, Rogue Walker had gotten intertwined in her thoughts with her father's promise—but that was silly. He wasn't her protector, he had been one of the few people in the world who made her cry.

But her father had died and so had his horse and Kit learned to care for herself.

While she stood, feeling lonely, two of the horses noticed her and trotted over. She pushed her hair off her forehead and smiled. As her mother would say, she was glistening. Perspiration dampened her hairline. This summer was turning out to be brutal. "Hey, boy." She caressed Hotshot's muzzle. He was a beautiful roan with a blaze face and white stocking feet. Not to be outdone, Diva, a gorgeous red quarter horse, pushed her way to the forefront to be petted. Both were sired by Rogue Angel and both were prize winners. "Are you two ready to be put through your paces?"

Working with her horses was how Kit wanted to make a living. She'd never had any intention of getting involved in ranch business. If her father had lived or if her mother had married someone who didn't seem determined to drive the place into the ground, Kit would have concentrated on raising and training quality roping horses. If she hadn't been forced to sell off most of her prime stock, she'd be sitting pretty now.

"Come on, run with me." She invited the pair and as she took off, they galloped alongside her, tails up in the air like flags. When she topped the hill behind her house, she noticed the exterminators were gone. They'd finished. What a fiasco yesterday had been, Rogue walking in on her in her sleep. The maid who'd left the cabin door open had been soundly reprimanded, but Kit hadn't had the heart to let her go. Sally had two small children and needed the job.

A car horn had her speeding up, a smile coming over her face. A group of ladies were coming in today to check out the place for a college sorority reunion. If she could sell White-Wing as a full service facility that catered not only to their needs of a place to sleep, meet and eat but also as a locale that could provide things to do such as a dance, a trail-ride, swimming, and hunting, she'd be well on her way to solving her mother's financial problems. The only thing standing in her way was money and Rogue Walker.

Sure enough, when she got close, she could see it was

Maureen Finch and her group. This was their ten year reunion.
"Hi!" She jogged up to them, feeling decidedly underdressed.
From the look of their car, a black spotless Lexus, and their
designer clothing this was the cream of the society crop that
Wichita had to offer. "I'm so glad you're here. Did you have any
trouble?"

"No, not a bit." Maureen took her hand and smiled, turning to
her friends. "Kit, this is Charlotte Bradshaw and Nina Grady. Girls,
this is Kit Ross, our hostess."

"I hope to impress you today. Let me walk you in, introduce
you to my mother and take you to the dining room. There's a
delicious brunch waiting for you. While you eat, I'll change
clothes and meet you for mimosas."

"Sounds wonderful." Maureen leaned closer. "And if you're
worrying about impressing us, don't. If that luscious man we just
passed is a sample of the man-candy we can expect around this
place, you're booked."

Man-candy? Kit turned to see where the ladies were pointing.

Dammit! Rogue Walker was strolling up like he owned the
place.

"Hello, ladies. I'm Rogue Walker." He tipped his hand and
flashed one of those thousand watt smiles. Kit could have
cheerfully kicked him, but the three women were tittering and
blushing, clearly smitten.

"Hello, Mr. Walker." Charlotte beamed. "You have a beautiful
place here."

Kit fumed. To correct her guests would appear petty, so she
just pasted a smile on her face and kept quiet.

Rogue was amused, he could tell Kit was fit to be tied.
"White-Wing is gorgeous. I've been enjoying a morning walk."

"We're thinking about renting the facility for our ten year
reunion." Maureen chimed in.

"Ten year reunion? From Junior High maybe, you're certainly
not old enough for anything else." Yea, he knew how to charm

women. He winked at Kit for good measure.

"Oh, you're good," Nina muttered. When she reached out to feel his muscular bicep, Kit almost choked.

"I think White-Wing is an excellent choice." Rogue added with a smile as he held his arm out for the other women to test.

"Miss Ross has promised us a tour. Some of our men attendees will be interested in hunting and fishing. Will you be joining us?" Maureen batted her eyelashes at him. "I'm not married, by the way."

"Neither am I," the other two said at the same time.

Suddenly Rogue realized he'd stepped into a feminine trap. Exiting quickly was the only antidote. "Oh, well…"

Inspiration hit Kit with a resounding ring. This was the answer. If she could make Rogue miserable while he was here, perhaps he would relinquish claim on the note and let it go back to Dave. She was used to dealing with her stepfather—the old 'devil you know is better than the devil you don't' routine. She'd talked to her stepfather late last night and he finally agreed to try and work other arrangements out with Rogue, on the condition that she cease interfering between him and her mother. She'd agreed to his terms, although Kit didn't know what those arrangements would be and she didn't care, just as long as it didn't put her mother's livelihood and her legacy in jeopardy. "Mr. Walker will definitely be joining us. He has an interest in the property and he's been wanting to check out some of the finer points himself. Right?"

Rogue narrowed his eyes at Kit. What was she up to? No good, he was sure of it. If she wasn't so damn sexy, he could tell her no. "Of course. Wouldn't miss it. I have some things to discuss with Miss Ross and this outing can lead right into lunch."

"That's right," Kit answered smoothly. "I'm sure we'll have plenty to discuss." She had an idea. While Rogue had begun the flirtatious exchange, it had apparently heated up past the point he was comfortable. He was handsome enough to have any woman he wanted. He'd said once that she wasn't his type. She doubted very seriously if any of these three were his cup of tea either. But when she got through with him, they'd be convinced he was more than interested in them. He'd be running out of White-Wing like a scared rabbit and she'd close the gate behind him. "If you'll excuse us, we'll be on our way."

"Won't Mr. Walker be joining us?" Charlotte asked, obviously dismayed at the thought of losing the view she was so admiring.

"I've already eaten, thank you." He smiled again and this time his dimples came into play. "I have a couple of phone calls to make."

"Perhaps Rogue will join us for drinks before we set off."

Rogue was pleasantly surprised at Kit's invitation. "I like the sound of that. I'll be there."

"Oh, good." The women clapped effusively and Kit's stomach turned over.

"Shall we?" She motioned for them to follow her into the lodge. Rogue hurried and opened the door for them. When she walked past him, Kit gave him the evil eye, but all he did was chuckle.

As soon as she had the women settled and the cook personally seeing to their needs, she ran to take a shower—with only one detour. With an evil smirk, she headed to the main house to raid her parents' medicine cabinet. Dave was out of pocket, attending a Rotary Club luncheon and her mother was busy at the front desk. In a classic e-w-w-w moment when hunting something for a headache, she'd stumbled upon Dave's supply of Viagra. All she'd need was one and the women would be under the impression that Rogue was more than glad to be spending time with them.

In cabin #9, Rogue sat on the bed, waiting for Elijah to pick up the phone. He'd called the limo driver and told him he wouldn't be making his flight. Next, he'd called his mother and explained to her why he'd be missing their normal mid-week meal together. As her only child, he tried to see about her as often as possible. His impromptu trip to White-Wing had changed his plans in several areas.

"Where the hell are you?"

Rogue laughed. "Not in the land of Oz, I'm still in Kansas."

"Why? Why didn't you collect your pittance from Dusty and hightail it home? You know we have that meeting with Simmons Oil in a few days. If you can partner with them on this next well, you'll be sitting in high cotton."

"Oh, you could handle it, but I'll be there. As far as what's going on here - where do I start?" Rogue laughed. "First, it wasn't exactly a pittance. Dusty bequeathed me one quarter of a business valued at half a billion."

"Did you say billion?" Elijah repeated with disbelief.

"I did."

"Holy shit. Who got the rest, his wife?"

"No, my three half-brothers."

"What the hell?"

"Exactly. And the will requires that we each spend a week here learning the business. I don't know about the others, but I do this stuff for a living. It won't take long for me to get up to speed. Dusty, in his own way, was preparing me for this all of my life."

"Wait. Did you say three brothers?"

"Yea, I'll explain it to you when I see you. It's like something out of a damn soap opera...and get this—we look like four damn peas in a pod. No one could deny we're related. He even gave us all the same belt buckle, you know the longhorn one."

"Wow, just wow. Well, are you still dealing with the will or did you find a card game?" Eli knew him well.

"A card game." Rogue let out a long breath. "But it got complicated."

"How?" Eli snickered. "Don't tell me you lost your shirt."

"No, I was trying to corner Barnaby Miller. I wanted to challenge him to a showdown, but he ran out of steam. Instead, I got tangled up with a local rancher who didn't know if he was playing Texas Hold 'em or monopoly."

"So?" Elijah prodded Rogue to finish his story.

"I won a real estate note, amount owing on it is fifty grand."

"Great. You did well this trip."

"Oh yea, but that's not the problem." Rogue pushed his hand through his hair, wondering how best to explain his quandary.

"So, what is?"

"The ranch, White-Wing, is a former cattle ranch. Now it's more of a hunting resort, has a lodge and a pond. Nice place."

"So far I don't see a downside, Walker."

"The place belongs to Kit Ross and her mother. The man who bet the note is her stepfather."

"What? Repeat that."

"You heard me. Kit Ross."

"Roping, poison ivy, blow-job Kit Ross?"

"The same."

Eli laughed. Hard. "Oh, I bet that went over well. The woman hates your guts, or at least she used to."

"Still does."

"Well, unload it and come home. Get out of the line of fire."

Rogue paused. "Well…I don't want to, just yet."

"Why?" Eli waited for Rogue to stay something and when he didn't—it hit him. "Oh. Oh! She's still hot?"

Rogue groaned. "Elijah, if there was one time in my life when I did something truly stupid, that was it. I need to make amends."

"Love and business don't mix, Walker, you know that."

"Well, no one said anything about love. But I hear you."

"Keep me informed. Do you need me to come up there and protect you?"

With a snort, Rogue put his fears to rest. "I'm sure I can handle it."

"Considering how well you handled your last blind date with her, I'm not so sure."

"We're not dating—yet. Right now I'm just trying to keep her from killing me."

"Well, good luck. And stay close to your phone, I might need you. Between the two of us, I have the brains, but you have the charm. I might need you to help me prepare for the Simmons deal."

"Sure, let me know and thanks for the luck, I'm going to need it." He hung up and checked the clock on the wall. Rogue didn't wear a watch, and he wasn't married to his phone either. Knowing how slow women ate and how much they talked, he figured he would be early—but what the hell. He left his room, locked the door and went to put the first phase of his plan in motion. Project Learn. He was on a mission to learn as much about White-Wing and Kit as possible.

Knowledge is power.

In the dining room, Kit was torn between trying to impress the reps from the class of 2005 and watching for her arch enemy. She'd told them about the facilities and given them a list of some local bands Kit had made previous arrangements with to play for dances. Cook had prepared a luscious array of brunch food from eggs Benedict to croissant bread pudding. They'd also spread out samples of entrees that could be served at the banquet itself. The lodge or bunkhouse as she sometimes thought of it could sleep fourteen and the guest cabins could sleep another twenty, so she could handle a good-size party.

"How about swimming, do you have a pool?" Nina asked.

"Well...yes," Kit began.

"The reunion is in November, Nina, the temperature will be in the forties." Maureen rolled her eyes, and when she did, she saw Rogue coming across the room. "Oh, there you are, we've been waiting," she squealed.

Kit frowned. Maureen's voice was like fingernails on a chalkboard. "Sit, Rogue, let me get you a drink. Mimosa?"

She was waiting on him again? He smiled. "Ah, I'd rather not. Could I have some coffee instead?"

"Coming right up." This was better. The pill would dissolve in the hot liquid much quicker.

"Black." He threw over his shoulder.

"Sure thing." Kit tried to muster up some remorse or guilt at what she was about to do. She wasn't successful.

Rogue almost got a crick in his neck watching Kit as she moved across the room. God, he loved her hair. He knew he had a breast fetish, apparently he also had a thing for hair. Hers especially. It hung in big bouncy spiral curls to well past her waist. The night he'd fucked up, he could remember wondering how in the world she'd crammed it beneath that cowboy hat. And her eyes sparkled like diamonds, another feature she'd hidden behind those thick safety goggles. Not to mention her damn fine rack she'd covered up with a thick cowboy shirt and a blue jean jacket or her heart shaped ass…well, he had to admit, he hadn't looked very hard. All that gear was a smart choice for a rodeo contestant to wear to keep from getting hurt, but it sure as hell had blinded him to her beauty.

When she returned, she handed him the cup quite graciously, maybe a bit too graciously. "What did you do, poison me?" he asked.

Psychic? She thought. "Now, why would I do a thing like that?"

He smiled, shrugged and took a big sip. Other than being a bit warm, it was good. "Thanks."

"We've been going over the details of what White-Wing has to offer," Charlotte said, as she cast an adoring glance his way.

"Have you?" Rogue saw a folder in front of Kit labeled Proposal. "May I?" He held his hand out and saw the reticence on Kit's face before she handed it to him. As he looked over the information, he was surprised at the detail and the variety. She was very good and White-Wing had more going for it than he'd first thought if this was any indication. After looking at it, he didn't comment but sat back to listen.

"What's your refund policy?" Maureen asked Kit.

"I'll require a general deposit to hold a block of rooms and reserve the facility. Reservations need to be completed by October first so I can order food. Individuals may pay up until the day of the event, cancellations may be made up until one week in advance."

Rogue thought the terms were generous, perhaps too generous.

"What are we going to see today?" Nina enquired.

Kit cut her eyes at Rogue before she answered. "I want to show you our surroundings, including the lake, the reserve where the men will be hunting, the trails available for riding and the gun range for skeet shooting. We try to bring the great outdoors to those who don't often get to enjoy it."

Charlotte ate the last bite of her bread pudding and delicately licked her fingers. "Delicious. Well, I'm ready. How about the rest of you?"

"Sure." Kit stood and glanced at Rogue. "Coming?"

Right then, he vowed she'd say that same phrase to him again someday—except next time she'd be on her knees at his feet. "Wouldn't miss it."

She led them out to the parking lot and waved her hand at a double cab pickup. Rogue opened the driver's side door for Kit, then the back door on the same side, walked around and opened the other two doors. He'd intended to get in the front next to Kit, but Charlotte popped up and announced, "Sorry, I get car sick." Rogue graciously helped her in and joined the other two ladies in the backseat. Somehow, he ended up squished between them. Great.

Kit met his eyes in the rearview mirror. Was she laughing at him? Trying to convey his confidence, he met her gaze and fed her a devil-may-care grin. "Comfortable, Mr. Walker?"

He folded his hands in his lap and tried to make his shoulders not quite so wide. "Certainly, never better."

With a wry smile, she turned the vehicle's engine on and backed out. For a while they rode around and she talked about the ranch and the area. "I know you're from Kansas but I always love to tell people that our state is named after the Kansa Native American tribe and means 'people of the wind'."

"Whew, that sounds about right, when the north wind starts to blow there's nothing between us and the north pole except a strand of barbed wire," Charlotte said dryly.

"Our weather does get cold when the chinook winds begin to blow." She continued with her spiel. "The geodetic center of the United States is located just a few miles away on the Meades Ranch. Oil has recently been discovered in parts of the state, unfortunately not here." All of the ladies tittered. "We used to be known as the flattest state in the union, flatter than a pancake, they said, but we're actually number twenty-five or so. Tornado alley also begins here."

Rogue could tell she was losing them. Who knew she was a little Miss Fact-check? So, he started to talk, as if he was helping with the tour-director job. "The biggest ball of twine in the world is north of here in Cawker City. And the graham cracker was named after local pastor Reverend Sylvester Graham who died in the mid-1850s, he was a Presbyterian who strongly believed in eating whole wheat flour products." The way the women were staring at him with love-sick expressions, he absolutely believed he could've quoted the phone book to them and they would've sworn he was the most eloquent man in the world. "Did you know that at one time it was illegal to serve ice cream on cherry pie in Kansas?"

"No!" All the women except Kit chorused together.

Kit rolled her eyes. "How do you know all of this stuff, Mr. Texas?"

"My dad's from here, remember? He taught me more about this place than I realized, I guess." He was a little surprised himself.

Rogue's little tirade got Kit back on track. "White-Wing used to be just a cattle ranch, now it's much more. I raise horses and train them for team roping in the pro-rodeo circuit. We also keep horses for the guests to take for trail rides on the property. At one time we owned one of the premier stud horses in the country." She looked directly at the man in the backseat. "His name was Rogue Angel."

Rogue almost swallowed his tongue. "Was he named after me?"

Kit smirked. "No. My father named him and that was years before I met you."

"Stud." Nina giggled the word and Rogue tried to make himself smaller. "Does Mr. Walker give riding lessons?" She reached over and laid her hand on his knee and Rogue's eyes widened.

"No, Mr. Walker doesn't give riding lessons." Kit never missed a beat. "One of the main things White-Wing offers is spectacular hunting. This part of Kansas has always been known for its game, especially deer, pheasant, turkey and quail. We've gone a step farther and provided a perfect habitat for them, as well as offering guided hunts and game processing." She turned off the dirt road and drove slowly down a grassy lane, gradually coming to a stop. "Let's get out and I'll show you a place that's usually ripe with birds. Perhaps we'll see a few." Opening the trunk, she removed a small picnic basket filled with cool drinks for her clients.

Rogue was glad to get out of the car. His two traveling companions were getting a bit handsy for his tastes. Following Kit, they stepped out into tall grass and headed to a band of trees bordering a small creek. As they drew closer, they heard the sound of bushes rustling and then the flapping of wings as a covey of quail took flight. "Look! There they go! Bob-white quail are plentiful here."

The women began taking photos with their phones. Charlotte grabbed onto Rogue's arm. "Sorry, I wore the wrong shoes." She pointed down to her heels. Rogue wondered why a woman would make such a poor wardrobe decision, probably for this very reason, so she'd have an excuse to grab onto a man.

"Let's walk this way. Maybe we'll see some pheasant." Kit pointed ahead, but she let her gaze linger on Rogue. He gave her a smile and a slight rolling of his eyes as he glanced sideways at his recently acquired female appendage.

They strolled slowly through the underbrush. Kit was taking her time, the last thing she needed to do was stir up a snake and scare her guests. Furtively she kept glancing at Rogue, wondering how long it took that little blue pill to do its magic. Holding up a hand, she told them to stop, whispering, "I think I saw a pheasant, a ring-necked pheasant. They are majestically beautiful, watch." Sure enough, in a few moments a pair of large birds took flight and everyone watched in wonder.

"I don't think I could shoot one," Nina mused.

"I could," Rogue drawled. So far, he liked what he saw. This place had an immense amount of potential.

"Why don't we rest, enjoy the view down by the creek and have a drink." She raised the basket. They found a sloping area of grass and Kit spread a thin blanket for the ladies to sit down on. Rogue eased down also and found himself surrounded by females, just not the one he preferred to have close.

As soon as they were all settled and sipping on something cool, Kit asked, "Well, how do you like White-Wing so far? We still have to see the lake and check out the cabins." Trying not to be noticed, she kept taking surreptitious glances at Rouge. Surely, he was feeling something…

"Tell us about yourself, Mr. Walker."

Maureen leaned close, her perfume assailing his sense of smell. "Not much to tell. I work in the petroleum industry." Short and sweet. Rogue shifted, wishing he could escape.

Kit had taken Charlotte and walked down to the creek, which fed into the lake to show her some bass that had been stocked for game fishing. The shade was nice, but there wasn't any breeze. In fact, he was damn hot—and getting hotter. Stretching his leg out, he tried to make room in his pants for his growing...ERECTION! WTF? Where in the hell had that come from? Beyond admiring Kit from a distance, he wasn't even thinking a sexy thought. In an attempt to hide the growing bulge in his jeans, he sat straighter and jerked his leg upright. "Hell," he whispered, that was painful.

"My goodness." Nothing lost on her, Nina purred as she used one well-manicured hand to push her pale blonde hair over her shoulder. "You are quite a man." She ran a hand down his arm. "I do appreciate the...gesture."

"Sorry, I gotta walk around...I have a cramp." Shit. He stood up awkwardly, hampered by the hard-on that had risen up out of nowhere. He looked at Nina and then at Maureen, both of their eyes were glued on his crotch. Stepping backward, he hung his boot on the handle of the picnic basket and he would've landed flat of his ass if Kit hadn't placed a steadying hand on his back.

"Problems?" Kit asked, unable to ignore what the other women were finding so fascinating. Pressing her lips together tightly, she met his eyes. His expression was one of panic, totally unlike the cocky attitude he'd displayed in the park the night she had let him think she was going to go down on him.

"Nope! I can walk it off."

She couldn't help it, Kit had to hold herself tight around the middle to keep from laughing. The three stylish sorority women were staring at Rogue like he was a jar of honey and they were hungry baby bears. It was the funniest thing she'd ever seen. He kept backing up and they were stalking him like mindless zombies focused on their prey. If he didn't..."Rogue!"...stop..."You're going to back into the—"

SPLASH!

"Creek!"

By the time Rogue pulled his wet ass out of the water, he was royally pissed. The triple threat to his virtue were all trying to give him more assistance than he needed. And all the time his errant pecker had a seeming will of its own. Each woman thought his burgeoning, throbbing package, straining at the zipper was meant just for her.

Wrong.

"Excuse me, please." He stalked up the bank, dripping water.

"I guess you needed to cool off," Charlotte said, fanning herself with delight.

Kit handed him the blanket. "Here, use this as a towel."

"Thanks," he growled at her.

As he strode to the truck, his trio of admirers followed him. Kit tried to see if their tongues were actually hanging out but she couldn't tell from this distance.

"Kit!"

She pulled herself together and walked over. He had let down the tailgate and was sitting on it.

"You bellowed?" she asked.

"I'm riding back here. Do you think you could take me to the lodge to change clothes?" He emptied water out of first one boot and then the other.

"Sure." She hid a smirk and asked the ladies to load up. "We need to get Mr. Walker some dry clothes."

Something wasn't right, he had seen how women acted when they were pulling a fast one and Kit was showing all the signs—a half grin, too cooperative, a sexy twinkle in those amazing blue eyes. "Thanks," he murmured, whipping off his hat when he felt something brushing the hair on his head. "What the...? Hell!" He picked a little sun perch off the truck bed and carried it back to the water, its mouth gaping open and closed.

Loud laughter coming from the interior of the pick-up caused him to look at Kit Ross. She was having entirely too much fun. "Doesn't look like your dip did any good." She cast an eye down at his manhood. "If your problem persists for more than four hours you might need to consult your doctor."

At that moment he realized what she'd done. "Why, you little..." He narrowed his eyes and glared at her. "What did you give me? A damn Viagra pill?"

"Shush." She held her finger up to her lips. "Your fan club is going to offer assistance in dealing with your condition if you don't keep your voice down."

Rogue stomped to the back and he discovered Miss Smarty Pants had been right. Maureen met him. "Here's my room key, big boy." She winked at him, glancing at his ample assets, slipping the piece of hard plastic into his front jeans pocket. "Come up to see me later. I'll make it worth your while." Flabbergasted, he tried to give it back to her but she was gone, sneaking a peek at him through the back glass once she was settled in her seat.

Closing his eyes, Rogue settled back down on the tailgate, willing his dick to go down. Why had Kit done this? He winced. As a man he loved a hard cock, but a chemically induced one against his will sorta made him feel violated. Despite his irritation, he grinned. She had moxie, he had to give her that.

Seeming not to miss an opportunity to irritate him, she hit every pothole in the road and went the long way back by the lake, slowing down to let the women enjoy the view. The sun was so bright and hot that by the time they returned to the lodge, his clothes were beginning to dry. When he stood up, Rogue dusted off a bit of the caked mud. He frowned at his boots, he damn sure hoped they weren't damaged.

"Are you going to be okay?"

Rogue slowly raised his head and met Kit's gaze as she came near. One corner of her mouth lifted despite her apparent attempt to keep a straight face. "No thanks to you." He handed her Maureen's plastic key card. "Please return this, I won't be needing it." To his immense relief, the triple threat had found someone else to follow around. Another lone male guest was receiving the same flirtatious onslaught he'd been so unfortunate to experience. "So, you slipped me a sexual mickey. Is that it?"

"Just trying to give you a helping hand."

She tossed the quip at him and began walking off toward the

lodge. Rogue followed, noticing for the first time all of the care that had been taken with the plantings and landscaping. "I wouldn't have turned down a helping hand of another sort." She snorted and his ire rose again. "So, I guess you have to keep a supply of Viagra in your purse to ensure your own conquests?" The moment he said it, he knew he'd gone too far.

Kit wheeled on him, grabbing him by the arm and dragging him down the wide verandah to a secluded spot. He went willingly, he weighted too much for her to manhandle him—unless he allowed it. "How dare you?" she hissed when they were out of sight of anyone who might happen along.

Rogue crossed his arms over his chest. Looking at her rosy cheeks, flashing eyes and heaving chest, his hard-on was finally finding a place to focus its enthusiasm. "Look, it's you that seems to have an inordinate preoccupation with my cock. First you get me naked and make me think you can't wait to wrap your lips around it and now you drug me just so you and some desperate little hens can ogle the size of my package."

If he'd thought she was mad before, he learned a whole new meaning of feminine fury. Getting right in his face, she poked him in the chest—hard. "Listen to me, Rogue Walker. I know I'm not your type. You made that abundantly clear the night we were together. I'm aware a man of your age and appetite can…" she seemed to search for a word, "perform with very little outside stimulation, so I took advantage of that fact to show you how it felt to be stripped bare by someone else's cruelty. And since you've been here, you're still playing with me, pretending to be attracted to me, to have a crush. That's hogwash and we both know it! You're about as enamored of me as I am of you. The best gift we could give one another is to never lay eyes on the other one again! So please, let's put an end to this charade and go back to—"

Sometimes the only way you can effectively shut a woman up is to kiss her and so that's what he did. Rogue grasped Kit's shoulders and pulled her to him, crushing his mouth to hers, taking advantage of her shock to tangle their tongues together, eating at her mouth, pulling her close. For about three seconds she cooperated, but then she began to struggle, pushing against his arms, making noises of protest. "Stop!" she panted once she'd broken the kiss. "This doesn't help."

"I disagree, I think the only way we communicate effectively is with sex." His breathing was hard. "I propose a round of naked negotiations."

Kit opened her mouth to give him another piece of her mind when her mother stepped around the corner. "Mr. Walker, you have a phone call. A Mr. Elijah Bowman says it's an emergency, he hasn't been able to reach you on your cell."

"Damn, I bet it's waterlogged." He winked at Kit. "I propose we continue these exhilarating peace talks a little later, Kit-n-Kaboodle."

If frustration could kill, she'd already be knocking on the pearly gates. Kit threw her hands up as she watched Rogue saunter off, his ass looked amazing in his jeans – probably because they'd drawn up a bit in the water. She was at a loss. He didn't seem to be giving a bit on his ridiculous position. And he had to. She had to convince him to relent and give the note back to Dave. There was no telling what nefarious plan Rogue had for her and her ranch. It would be her luck that he'd raze all the buildings and dig the whole place up looking for gypsum to mine.

Oh well, she didn't have time to worry about that now, she had to get Maureen and the others to sign on the dotted line. She needed that deposit and about a hundred others just like it.

Chapter Four

As the plane landed, Kit stared out the window. She hadn't planned to ever return to Texas. When her dad died, she'd transferred from A&M to Kansas State to finish her degree in agriculture business. The reason she'd come to Texas in the first place was because the college at Bryan was one of the best in the nation for anything agriculture related. She didn't regret the time spent there. Because of her involvement in college rodeo, she'd discovered her calling. She'd loved team roping and raising horses trained specifically for that task was the next best thing.

In fact, she'd loved every aspect of the rodeo from the crowds, the animals, the lights—until the night Rogue's scathing comments had been broadcast to everyone who was anyone in the organization. Even if her father hadn't died, she probably would have quit. She could still remember the pitying glances she'd received, the titters, the snide comments. It was sad a woman's confidence was tied so closely with her looks. No matter what she had to offer, how good she was at what she did – people, especially men, were seldom able to see beyond their physical appearance to any worth they might possess.

Up to that point, Kit had dated rarely and had never shared more than a few chaste kisses with a man. And because of Rogue, she'd shunned contact with men since then. There were a couple of good ole' boys in Red Creek who'd asked her out, but she'd had no problem resisting. They were pale substitutes for a man like Rogue and even though what they'd shared had been a joke, an embarrassing episode that she should attempt to erase from her memory – she couldn't. He had ruined her for any other man in more ways than one.

And now here she was – flying in to throw herself upon his mercy. She was about to beard the lion in his own den. Using the information Rogue had provided at check-in, she'd shamelessly tracked him down and was about to arrive on his doorstep—unannounced and uninvited.

To Kit's surprise, she'd discovered Rogue raised horses also. He hadn't mentioned they had that in common, but their conversations had never been about friendly sharing. She'd figured that he lived in some fancy high rise off 6th Street, facing the river. Instead, she'd learned he had a place west of the Texas capitol near Johnson City. So as soon as the wheels touched the tarmac, she'd debarked and rented a car. Now she was heading west with a Texas sun so bright in her eyes, she had to pull down the visor to see the road clearly.

She was nervous, but she couldn't help it. After their confrontation on the porch, he'd left without saying word one to her. After she'd finished with the sorority girls and had gone to look for him to continue her appeal, she'd been surprised to find his room empty and his things gone. She had no assurance he would even contact her again unless he had to start foreclosure proceedings. The idea that her family could lose White-Wing, have to move – was unthinkable. She had to do something, had to convince Rogue. If only he would listen.

Thirty miles west, Rogue stood over his massive stone barbeque pit, basting a brisket. There was nothing in the world better than Texas BBQ, nothing. Placing a hand on his hip, he gazed out over his land. With a smile, he watched two horses frolicking across the pasture. It was a mare and a stallion, he nipped her butt and she pranced to the side—an age old dance of erotic play. As surely as if it was following road signs, Rogue's mind turned to Kit. He wondered what she was doing. A couple of times he'd been tempted to call, but at this point he didn't figure she'd answer the phone. As soon as he put this deal with Simmons to bed, he'd be heading back to Kansas and he didn't intend to wait for the last week in August when he was supposed to fulfill Dusty's request to spend a week at Walker Minerals.

He'd had his own lawyer, Zane Saucier, look into the White-

Wing matter while he was reviewing Dusty's will and his company's prospectus. From what Zane said, so far everything looked to be on the up and up. He was still waiting on the title search for White-Wing, but that was normal. Now he was having him look into his bothers—Dylan, Killian and Jackson. All he needed was to get involved with a crook and just because they were blood kin didn't mean squat. Look at what Dusty had done. The man had literally maintained and supported five different households, kept five women trapped in false hope and lies and sired four sons who'd had no inkling they had family.

It was Rogue's greatest fear that he would become his father. After all, he'd chosen to walk in his father's footsteps business wise. Who was to say he hadn't inherited Dusty's inability to have a normal family life? So he'd made some promises to himself— one, he'd never marry and two, he made damn sure he practiced safe sex. No child of his would ever have to wonder why he wasn't around, because Rogue never planned on becoming a father.

Bitter much?

"You're doing that all wrong." The feminine voice that had been torturing his dreams for the past week spoke up out of nowhere.

He wheeled around so hard and fast, he almost dropped his BBQ fork. "Kit!" He smiled, genuinely glad to see her. "To what do I owe this pleasure?"

She answered him with a perfectly beautiful but straight face. "I'm here to proposition you. You should be using hickory and your sauce is too thin." She leaned over to smell. "Might be worth eating, I'm not sure."

POW! She had a unique ability to knock him off his game. She looked gorgeous in a creamy yellow sleeveless sweater and a pair of linen slacks. He didn't know whether to focus on the tempting proposition or defend his meat. Why not do both? One thing at a time, he could multitask. "For your information, the best flavor comes from pecan or red oak. And my sauce has won six awards, reserve judgment till you get my meat…between your lips." He leered at her. "As far as your proposition, my room is upstairs, first door on your right. Head up there, strip, and I'll be with you as soon as I get this off the pit, which won't be much longer." He lifted up the slab of beef with his fork. "It's just about perfect now."

Kit gave him a patient smirk. "That's not the kind of proposition I was referring to and you know it."

"Pity." He took the platter from the sideboard and placed the juicy piece of beef on the white pottery. "Are you hungry?"

Actually she was starving. Knowing she was there to plead and not to argue, she decided to play nice. "I am, in fact. Would you mind if I joined you?"

"Not at all, grab the basting bottle, we'll use that as dipping sauce. I put jalapenos, root-beer, Jack Daniel's, red wine, and brown sugar in my recipe."

Behind his back, Kit made a gagging face but quickly erased it when he glanced at her over his shoulder.

"I saw that."

She giggled, then regretted acting like a foolish smitten teenager. Her eyes couldn't resist checking out his home. When she'd arrived, parking in the front circular drive, she'd followed her nose to where he'd been cooking on the pit. Truthfully, what he'd prepared looked amazing, and she was starving, her stomach was growling even now. What she'd seen of the backyard had been awe-inspiring, a pool, an outdoor kitchen and a comfortable patio faced a vast rolling green pasture where horses grazed.

The house itself made her think of the lodge at White-Wing, lots of wood and natural stone. In fact, she felt quite at home, which was dangerous. When they walked up to the back door, he held it open for her. "Welcome to my world, Kit-Kat. Who would have ever thought you'd be stepping into my house willingly?"

The idea of him bringing her in unwillingly caused a flash of heat to sweep over her. The last erotic romance she'd read bombarded her thoughts, all of that spanking and tying one another up had its own appeal. She smiled to herself, maybe it was their shared roping background, the possibilities were intriguing.

Rogue waited for her to go ahead. "This is the sun room, doubles as a breakfast room. I refuse to use the word nook. The kitchen is to the right, I've already made a green salad, some baked beans and I bought a chocolate pie at Royer's."

"Sounds good." And it did, her mouth was watering. When she stepped into his haven, she almost gasped. You can tell a lot about a person from their kitchen and his told her volumes. The man took his cooking seriously. She ran her hand over the thick granite countertop as she admired the stainless steel appliances, hardwood floors and state of the art—everything. Warm earth tones were accented with turquoise and he had a western/Texas theme going on. "I love your kitchen."

"Thank you." As Rogue cut up the brisket, he kept casting curious glances at Kit. He had no illusions as to why she was here—she hadn't flown five hundred fifty miles to have dinner with him. "Let's eat and enjoy one another's company before we…get down to business."

Kit sat down on a stool to watch him work. He really was incredibly hot. Even doing something innocuous as wielding a knife to slice their entree was tantalizing to watch. To cool herself off, she glanced away, taking in what she could see of the adjoining rooms, a big great room with vaulted ceilings and a spacious dining area with a long mahogany table. All of a sudden a thought hit her so hard she almost fell off the seat. These rooms were masculine but they also seemed refined enough to have had a woman's touch. "You aren't married, are you?"

With a chuckle, Rogue squirted some of the sauce into a small bowl and set it next to the platter of succulent beef. "Oh sure, I'm married. She's an understanding woman, I told her I kissed you and that I can't stop thinking about you. She's totally fine with it."

Kit's blood pressure jumped so high, it took her a couple of heartbeats before she realized he was kidding. "Oh, you!" She threw a dish towel at him. "Well, your house is too pretty to just be a man's domain."

"They're called interior decorators in Texas, Kit. I'm not sure if they have those in Kansas, though."

He was enjoying himself at her expense, she could tell. Kit was about to make some retaliatory remark when something wet nudged her leg and she squealed. "What in the world?" Grasping her chest, she looked down fully expecting to see a dog or a cat. Instead, she saw a small horse. A perfect doll-baby paint that was looking up at her with the biggest brown eyes she'd ever seen. "Rogue Walker! I'm in love!"

Kit didn't ask permission, she went to the floor, put her arms around the small animal, and started peppering his face and neck with kisses.

"You're making me jealous. Jester, what are you doing in the kitchen? Are you wanting a hand-out?" Rogue couldn't help but stop and look at the picture before him. His impromptu guest was sitting cross-legged and the small horse was in her lap, eating up the attention. He hadn't been lying, he was green with envy. Kit's face was animated, all of that glorious hair was hanging over one shoulder and she had such love on her face that she made him think of a beatific Madonna. Squatting down beside them, he offered his pet a piece of carrot. "Is this what you came in here for?"

Crunch. Crunch.

"I think you made him happy." Kit was still running her hands over the small horse. "He's wonderful and so unexpected. Does he stay in the house with you?"

"He comes and goes. There's a dog door big enough for him to get through off the laundry room. A neighbor bought him and decided she couldn't keep him, so he lives with me now. He's full grown and only twenty-five inches tall."

"And you call him Jester? Is he a clown?" She threaded her

fingers through his black mane.

"No, I named him after the dorm I lived in on UT campus, Jester Hall. It was a zoo." He grinned, captivated by her smile.

"Whatever, I have to say the name suits him." She stood, took another chunk of carrot from the salad and held it up to be eaten. She met Rogue's eyes, and Kit realized she was looking at him in a completely new way.

She liked him. He seemed to be a good man.

Which could only be explained if the man Kit had known had changed—grown up. And she supposed that was entirely possible.

"Come eat, he'll wander back outside." Rogue offered her a hand to rise. "Let's dig in while the food is warm." Taking plates, silverware, and glasses from their respective cabinets, he let her prepare a plate first. "Get more, you're not taking enough to feed a bird." He held the platter toward her until she took another slice.

"Thank you, it all looks good." She waited until he poured some wine, fixed his plate and began to eat. "Oh…" Kit started to compliment him on the meat, but it almost felt like a betrayal to the culinary reputation of Kansas.

"Taste better than you expected?" Rogue raised an eyebrow. "If you think this is good, wait for the pie. I like pie." He spoke the last three words with almost religious conviction.

Kit giggled. "I do too and I remember Royer's, there was one of those at Round Top, near to Brenham. I loved their pecan pie." She ate another bite of beans, then a bite of brisket. Before she knew it, he was passing her the dishes for seconds. Feeling content, she ventured to ask a question. "Where did you grow up, in Austin?"

"No," he shook his head, "out in West Texas, near Andrews. I came here for school and never left. My mother, Marian, still lives there. I've begged her to move here with me or let me buy her a place close by, but she won't have it. She stuck it out there when times were hard and people were cruel. It's not easy to be an unwed mother at any time, today people are more tolerant."

His voice faded off and Kit felt bad for him. "I'm sorry. You must love her a lot."

"I do." Rogue nodded. "That's one reason I'm having a hard time accepting what's going on in Red Creek. Dusty Walker made some decisions that hurt a lot of people and no amount of money is going to make up for what we've lost." Opening up, he told her what little he knew about his half-brothers. "I have no idea how this is going to work out. I never considered leaving Texas before."

She gazed around his home. "I don't blame you." Now seemed as good a time as any. "I guess you're wondering why I'm here."

Full, Rogue put down his fork. "I know exactly why you're here." He had to admire her determination. "Before we begin to hash this out, why don't we take a break? It's a beautiful evening and I'd love to show you around."

"Yes!" Kit brightened instantly. With a new sense of camaraderie, she helped him load the dishwasher and soon they were headed out the door. Jester met them and trailed their heels to the barn where they saddled the horses, even running along beside them as they took off in the moonlight. "You have a beautiful place," she conceded with a sigh. "How many head of horses do you have?"

"Not many, only twenty. My main business is oil. I'm not rich, not yet. I'm still in reinvestment mode."

Kit wanted to ask more questions, but she didn't. Their association wasn't one of friendship. They had an unfortunate past and an uncertain future—better to keep their soul-searching to a minimum. Instead, she threw her head back and took a big breath of fresh Texas air.

Rogue wasn't as hesitant. "Do you rope anymore?"

"Only when I'm training the horses for others. Since we don't raise cattle anymore, I buy a few steers every year then sell them when the season is over." While she was talking, her eyes were taking it all in. Rolling hills of green, limestone cliffs, and

469

tumbling creeks. She'd forgotten how beautiful this part of Texas could be. Kansas held her heart, but Texas was a close second.

Tipping his Stetson back, Rogue spoke sincerely. "You were damn good. I was jealous."

Hearing his admission, she didn't know if he was being sincere or playing some type of mind-game for advantage in their upcoming competition. "You had better form than I did, my header was a little faster, that's all."

With a chuckle, he wondered how Elijah would feel about her assessment. "I doubt that." He was glad Mariah knew her way around. He could give the mare her head and enjoy keeping his eyes on Kit.

"Do you still do any roping?" she asked, laughing when Jester ran ahead of them, bucking and prancing in the tall grass.

"No, my life is too busy." He raised his hand and waved it toward the horses. "I'm lucky to get out and ride with them, breed a few to sell," Rogue admitted with a sigh. "The best I can do sometimes is a video game."

"For team roping?" she asked incredulously.

"Yea, I guess they have them for everything—race car driving, fantasy football, tennis."

Kit nodded. "Soon virtual reality will take the place of living."

"I hope not. Some things just aren't the same unless you're actually there." He winked at her. "Like sex." She gave him a small smile. There was no way she was going to confess her experience or lack thereof.

They rode for a while in companionable silence. Finally, when she brought her mount to a standstill and stretched, the swell of her breasts had him salivating. The memory of what they'd looked like as she'd lain in the bed he thought was his was burned into his memory. Rogue wanted her, he admitted it. If he had his way, he'd have his hands all over her, molding that tender flesh and sucking on those big nipples. Reaching down, he adjusted his package. He was swollen and leaking—no Viagra needed. "Are you ready to go?"

"I am." She followed him back to the barn and helped him to unsaddle and tend to the horses. They even bedded Jester down for the night.

"I doubt he'll stay, he's short enough to get out of the stall. I had to install special fencing to keep him safe. Before morning, he'll be in the bed with me."

Kit laughed. "You're the only man I know who has a horse for a bedmate."

He loved to listen at her enjoy herself. "Anytime you're ready to kick him out, you won't get any argument from me."

His quiet, yet flirtatious words made shivers of awareness dance on Kit's skin. When they were finished, they returned to the house. "Okay, you didn't come all of this way to taste my brisket. Care to let me in on your thoughts?"

Taking a deep breath, Kit dropped her bomb. "I'm here to challenge you to a game."

"Really?" This certainly wasn't the answer he'd been expecting. Intrigued, he asked, "What kind of game?" He could think of several he wanted to play with her.

"Gin rummy." It was a game her father taught her, they'd played for jelly beans. As soon as she said it, she knew it sounded childish, but it was the only game she thought she could win.

Rogue hid a smile. Her reply was unexpected and adorable. God, he was losing his objectivity. Pouring her a glass of water, he handed it to her. "Here, cool off, you look flushed. This is still about White-Wing?"

"Of course." She gazed at him with big serious eyes. "I don't want to lose my home."

"You're not going to lose your home." Not if he had any say in the matter. There were a lot of things he could've said, but Rogue wanted to wait until Zane got back with him. Still, he couldn't ignore her. He didn't want to ignore her.

"White-Wing is more than a ranch, Rogue. My home is there.

All I have left of my father is there. It's my legacy." She hesitated to tell him that her father was buried on the land, that fact felt a little too personal to share.

Together they put up the leftovers and all of that time, Rogue had said nothing. He was assimilating his thoughts and weighing his words. Finally, he let out a long breath. "I wish you could trust me, Kit." Even as he said it, he knew she couldn't—not yet. Knowing he might be making a mistake, he agreed. "Okay, we'll play gin rummy. But remember, Kit, this is still cards and I'm very good at cards." He gave her a heated look. "I'm really good at several things."

Kit swallowed hard. The man was charming, no doubt about it. "Do you remember the rules?"

"Yea, I think so. We each get seven cards and we can draw and throw away from our hand. The object is to make spreads and melds, three or four of a kind and runs like straights of the same suit. Face cards and aces are worth ten points and the other cards are worth five. If you aren't the one who goes out first, you have to subtract the value of any cards left in your hand. Right?" He walked to a drawer and removed a deck of cards, a notepad, and a pen to keep score.

"Correct. We play until one of us gets five hundred points."

Facing her, he pushed a silky strand of hair over her shoulder. "It's obvious what I'm wagering. But what about you? What are you willing to forfeit if I win?"

Kit blanched. She hadn't thought about that. What did she have of value? She had very little money in her checking account. Maybe she could get a cash advance on her Visa. And how much would that be? As she worked through this process in her head, Kit realized what a harebrained scheme this was, what she was considering sounded like the reasoning of a desperate gambler, people who used one credit card to pay off another.

"You haven't thought this through, have you?" Rogue asked gently.

His voice was full of pity and that made her sick to her stomach. She put her hand to her throat, racking her brain. How much money did she have in savings? If she lost it, could she feed the horses through the coming winter? As she fretted, her fingers touched the necklace her grandmother had given her, a gold necklace with a diamond and ruby pendant, not terribly expensive but precious to her. Reaching up, she took it off. "Here, this isn't much, but it can be a down payment, I have more pieces at home." She did, she had the rest of what her father's mother left to her.

Rogue poured them both a cup of coffee, placing the cream and sugar between them. His heart hurt for her. "I'm not taking your jewelry, Kit." He had a choice, one option was that he could just give in and do what she asked. It wouldn't be any skin off his nose, not really, he didn't need the money. But when he did return the note to Dave Parker, there was a chance Kit could still lose her home. Kit was fighting this battle alone. There was no guarantee Dave wouldn't bet the ranch in another card game.

Kit fought down the tears. She refused to cry in front of him. "Okay, if not my jewelry, then one of my best horses."

Shaking his head, Rogue stated flatly, "Absolutely not. I'm not agreeing for you to bet something you can't afford to lose."

"I don't have anything else of value," she whispered. Unless...he probably wouldn't agree, but she had to try. Without thinking, she threw out an outrageous proposal. "How about sex?"

Chapter Five

Rogue was cutting them both a piece of pie and almost bit his tongue off. He covered his mouth to keep from yelping. "What did you say?" He had to make sure he'd heard right. When someone offered him exactly what he'd been wishing for, there was usually a catch.

"If you won't let me bet the jewelry or a horse, would you accept sex? That is, if you want me. I know how you feel—"

The pie lifter he'd been holding clattered where he dropped it. One second he was on his side of the table, the next he was on hers. "You don't seem to have a clue as to what I want or how I feel." This time, he picked her up and just sat down with her in his lap. His mouth was covering hers before she could make a peep. He kissed her as if his life depended on the nectar from her lips.

His reaction stunned her. Kit didn't know what to do with her hands, she wanted to latch onto him, cling, hold him so tight he had to cry uncle so she'd let him go. These kisses of his were becoming habit forming. Knowing they were at odds made this intimacy seem both forbidden and more exciting. Did this mean he agreed? Did this mean…hell, she couldn't think…it felt so good.

Rogue poured all of his hunger into the kiss. She was sweet - so sweet and the noises she made—he didn't even think she realized—were the hottest damn thing he'd ever heard. He kissed her slow, then deep, tracing the outline of her mouth with his tongue, sweeping his lips down her throat, feathering her skin with his hot breath, nipping and licking, getting off on every gasp and shiver she gave him. Gently he caressed her pulse point with the back of his fingers, letting them trail down her neck…lower.

Kit caught his hand. "You haven't won yet."

"I always win, Kit-Kat bar, you need to get used to that." His whisper fanned against her face and Kit jumped up, needing distance.

Almost shaking with anticipation, Rogue returned to get forks and hand Kit the chocolate pie. "Taste. I have a couple more questions about this game." As he took a bite, he didn't know what was better—the richness of the chocolate or watching the blissful look on Kit's face as she licked the sweetness from her fork. "Like it?"

"Better than sex." She sighed.

Rogue snorted. "I take that as a personal challenge." She blushed, and he couldn't help but think how beautiful she was. As they ate their pie, he broached the subject of their wagers. "Considering what you're putting up, are you going to be able to go through with it when the time comes?" He winked at her. "You'll be pretty pissed at me and that usually means a man doesn't get lucky."

Kit sat down at another place across from where he'd been sitting, tucking one leg underneath her and consumed the chocolate pastry, relishing every bite. "I am a woman of my word."

"Very well." Rogue set their empty plates out of the way. If they were going to go through with this, he had to have a plan. "Let's negotiate our terms. I think to make this really interesting, we need to have a prize for each hand and the one who reaches five-hundred points first wins the grand prize. I return the note and you give me…"

"All night in bed if you win. Sounds right?"

Rogue felt like he was probably going to hate himself tomorrow. "Why don't we say you give me only what you want to give?"

A wave of embarrassment flashed over her. He didn't want to sleep with her. Why did he keep kissing her? To throw her off her game? "Of course." She smiled weakly. "You're the one taking all the risk."

Tearing off a piece of paper, he began to write. "All right, let's see what I can come up with." In just a few seconds, he was done. "I plan on winning every hand, mind you. And I look forward to whatever we do together. But on the off-chance that you win a hand, here's my list."

Winking at her, he slid the paper forward. He'd written: Business advice to make White-Wing more profitable, mineral analysis of your property, promise that I will not foreclose on your property under any circumstances, and finally, Grand Prize, full relinquishment of note.

When she saw his offerings, her head jerked up and she met his gaze. "Do you mean all of this?"

He was a card shark—even if they were playing 'Go Fish', he'd have an advantage. But yes, he fully intended to honor his commitment. "I'm a man of my word too, Kit. And I'll put any of it in a legal document at any time. Are you ready?"

Kit shuddered. "Might as well get it over with."

Rogue let her lead. "I can promise you one thing, Miss Ross. No matter the outcome of the game, I can guarantee I will do my dead level best to satisfy you."

She didn't say so, but Kit had no doubt he was correct.

* * *

Kit patted her foot nervously as she studied her cards. Jester shuffled beneath the table, periodically pulling on the tip end of her shoe as if tempted to take a bite. To be on the safe side, she kept her toes scrunched up in her shoes. Looking up at Rogue through her lashes, she saw his eyes were on his cards also. She'd tried to determine what he was thinking but his face was like one of the heads on Mount Rushmore, he was made out of stone.

She squirmed, thinking of something else that could get equally hard.

Her hand wasn't bad. But it wasn't good. All she needed was one more card, a damn two of clubs and she could knock. She had a three and a four of clubs plus three sevens. Come on. Come on. She prayed as she drew a card from the deck between them. Damn.

"Gin!" Rogue yelled with a huge smile on his face.

An electric spike shot through her. She couldn't tell if it was excitement or terror. He'd taken round one. "You won." Kit wouldn't be getting the business advice but that wasn't what was bothering her. What did he expect from her?

Rogue growled, "Yea, I did. And I'm ready to claim my winnings." Feeling almost like a pillaging hero or a highwayman of old, he rose, took Kit by the hand and led her into the living room. "We need something more comfortable than a straight back chair."

"What will this be, like five minutes in heaven?"

She was nervous, he could tell. Knowing he was about to kiss those rosy lips, Rogue felt fire in his veins where his blood once flowed. He pulled her down to the couch until she was facing him on her knees. "We're adults, Kit. I think we deserve more than five minutes in heaven. Don't you?"

Her gaze was hung up on his sexy smile. She bit back a sultry sigh. Lord, he smelled incredible. "I'm ready. Let's get this over with." On second thought, this was something she'd never be ready for. He was more than she could handle. Just his smile made her weak in the knees, and a glimpse into those made-for-sin eyes made her tingle in places she hadn't known could tingle.

"Come here. You might've lost this round, but it's my job to make you feel so good you'll think you won." Rogue couldn't quit looking at her mouth, knowing he was about to taste her again was turning him inside out.

Damn, her lips were trembling. His overwhelming male essence swamped her in an erotic haze. Kit longed to launch herself into his arms and take what he offered. Her heart jumped in her chest as she went to him. Her skin was covered in frissons of pure anticipation. She went to him, allowing him to pick her up as if she weighed nothing, nestling her against his broad warm chest.

He brought his big palm to cup the side of her face. Locking their gazes, he lowered his head, canting his lips to hers, so close they could breathe the same air. So lightly, she thought she might be dreaming, he pressed his lips to hers, catching the tender flesh between his teeth—a nibble, a lick, a sigh of surrender. This wasn't their first kiss, but it was the first one that counted. "Open for me," he directed in a husky, commanding tone.

With a tiny gasp, she gave in and welcomed him, relishing his raw male taste. When Rogue's tongue found hers, Kit couldn't help but respond. Her heart pounded as he explored, making delicious tantalizing forays that almost had her swooning. He was right, five minutes wouldn't be enough—five days wouldn't be enough. Not thinking, she pressed herself against him, her moan of delight changing to a whispery protest when he broke the kiss.

"Are you really here?" he asked, his strong hands moving down to cup her breasts.

This time she didn't push him away and it didn't matter one whit who'd won the hand. She craved his touch. "I'm here, I want you." Her admission surprised even her, but it was the truth.

"Prove it," he growled, pushing her back to lie fully on the couch. Lying next to her, he crushed their mouths together, rubbing her nipples through her top with a steady stroking rhythm. Kit moaned, melting into him as she kissed him back, her lips scorching his.

Aching for him, Kit spread her legs farther apart, he moved a hard thigh against her pelvis and she tilted it up, lifting her hips while his mouth continued to destroy her. He was so far out of her league it wasn't even funny, but she wanted him so bad, she wanted them naked, skin to skin—no clothes and no barriers.

"Touch me, please touch me," she whispered. She held her breath as he pushed a big hand under her sweater, pushing it up all the way until her bra was exposed. "Oh yea, that's it," Kit panted.

Rogue stared at the thin scrap of lace that covered a pair of round, firm perfect tits. He was in breast heaven. "Beautiful," he murmured as he palmed them, the hard tips searing his impatient hands. Thanking God for a strapless bra, he unhooked it from its front clasp and the cups relaxed, baring her to his gaze. With a growl, he swirled his tongue over her sweet creamy mounds, lapping every exposed inch.

Kit thought she'd shatter if he didn't give her what she craved. Her nipples puckered, hard little nubs of absolute need. "Please," she whimpered. And when he buried his whole face between her firm globes, sucking the distended pink tip into his mouth, Kit felt a rush of pleasure so hot, she thought she'd explode. This was better than her fondest dreams. As he kneaded and suckled at her breasts, Kit moved her hips, pumping them up and down as tremors of hot bliss radiated from her pussy.

"Like this?" he asked. Her answer was to arch into him, her fingers clawing into his back, clasping the material of his shirt.

"God, yes!" she cried as he gorged himself, sucking on her tits, his mouth feasting as he branded her with his passion. The pleasure was so intense that Kit thought she'd lose her mind. As he flicked his tongue, nibbled and licked, using the edge of his teeth - she lost control - her whole body flashed in a rush of ecstasy. "Rogue!" she cried as she came, quaking with an orgasm so intense her hold on reality slipped, she had to clutch onto him to keep from drifting away.

Rogue was stunned, all he'd done was kiss her lips, caress her breasts with his hands and mouth and she'd given him the perfect gift. Lord-help, she was precious. He rubbed his face on her breasts, the rasp of his beard marking her. Raising his head, he joined their mouths, his tongue tangling with hers. He was still ravenous, but it was time to stop. "Thank you," he murmured as he buried his face in her neck, inhaling her feminine scent. She smelled like honeysuckle and sunshine.

Kit twisted her fingers into his hair. She wasn't ready to quit. What she wanted was to see his perfect nippable ass pumping between her legs.

"Time for round two." He stood up in one lithe move and held out his hand. There was no way he could hide the fact he was still painfully aroused. If he had a choice, he'd sweep her into his arms, carry her into his bedroom and fuck her till dawn.

"Round two," she repeated, still quivering from aftershocks. "I came." She announced as if he could possibly have missed it.

Rogue framed her face and kissed her slowly, completely, thoroughly. "Yes, you did. And if I have my way, I want you to come again and again."

Kit processed what he said, her natural insecurities rising to the surface. Did he mean he wanted to pleasure her within an inch of her life or did he mean he wanted her to lose the next three hands? As she straightened her top and bra, Kit was the first to admit that she had issues.

Over the next few minutes, she won round two with a forty-point advantage, three jacks, four tens, and two runs of royalty. "Ha!" She was stoked! "What did I win?"

Rogue checked the paper. "You won a full mineral analysis to see if you have treasure buried on your property."

Kit smiled. "Good." Although her nipples and clit weren't half as excited as she pretended to be. They wanted more one-on-one time with Rogue's hands and lips.

Round three went fast. Rogue drew an almost perfect hand and when he laid it out, he couldn't help but smile when she was out of her chair before he was, both heading back to the couch for more heaven. They were like teenagers making out in the dark. This time there weren't as many preliminaries. As soon as they were on the couch, he was tugging on her slacks, and she had her top and bra off and on the floor.

Kit had an odd sense of déjà vu as she unbuttoned his shirt. She was so turned on that she wanted to do to him now what she'd teased him with that night at the lake. But he had other ideas. "Not yet, baby. This is about you."

She was confused, she'd lost the hand. How could it be about her? "I want to touch you…" Kit was about to explain when she lost her will to argue—or talk—or do anything but… "Yes!" He'd pulled her into his lap where she sat completely naked, cradled against his hard body.

In a haze of pleasure, she turned her head to accept kisses, drugging kisses that made her boneless, malleable, completely at his mercy. She reached one hand behind her to touch his face while he nuzzled her neck, sucking on a bit of flesh while his hands were very, very busy. For an appetizer, he ran his hands over her, moving her legs apart. She hooked her feet around his calves and opened herself up to whatever he had in mind. What he was doing was amazing, and she knew he wanted her. Every move she made drew her attention to the immense erection rubbing against her bottom. "Ummm," she moaned as she scrubbed her pussy against his groin.

Rogue grinned. Nothing like rough denim to drive a girl wild. Hungry to have his hands on her, they roamed, skating the flat plane of her tummy. Up, up, he let his fingers dance until he reached her luscious breasts. After plumping and molding them while he kissed a path along her collarbone, he squeezed her nipples between his knuckles until she keened her approval. His erection grew even harder as she rocked her hips.

"Touch me, Rogue, oh god, touch me."

"Just tell me where you want me, baby." Like he was following a path to the Promised Land, he let his hand seek the sweet place between her thighs.

"That's it, that's it," she encouraged as her head fell back. She closed her eyes at his first intimate touch. She shuddered from her spiral curls to her dainty toes. His fingers had found her clit and were now stroking her wet pink folds.

"Look down, Kit." He playfully nipped her collarbone, one hand still on her breast, caressing, using it as the most erotic of hand holds. "See what I'm doing to you."

She did as he asked, almost unable to breathe. What they were doing was glorious. Rogue rubbed her slit up and down, teasing her clit until she was writhing in his arms. Placing his palm over the pad of her vagina, he massaged her pussy, using the end of his thumb to play with her clitoris until she began to moan, her bottom bucking to match his rhythm. And when he speared a finger deep inside of her to find the spongy G-spot, she arched her back and rode his hand.

"You are so hot. So sweet," he growled against her hair. Faster and faster he finger-fucked her—higher, harder—until she bowed her back and stretched her legs down to balance herself on her tiptoes.

"Rogue!" Her greedy little channel clamped down on his fingers as she flew apart. He held her as she trembled, his hand still slowly rubbing her drenched sex until the pulsing spasms came to an end.

"Thank you, that was amazing," he whispered into her delicate ear. When his own voice came out hoarse, he understood that she'd shaken him to the very core.

"We need to finish the game." She curled up against him. "Have you ever played like this before?"

Rogue chuckled. "Can't say I have. Although, I can guarantee Gin Rummy tournaments would far surpass the Super Bowl or the World Series in popularity if more people did." He helped her up and handed Kit her clothes. "You are one beautiful woman." Her skin was creamy, velvety smooth and her body was absolutely perfect, especially those breasts he couldn't get enough of.

Kit didn't know why she was blushing now, but she did. She also couldn't help noticing he was hugely erect. "You're hard."

This time Rogue laughed heartily. "Yea, I'm so hard, it's a mite hard to hide." At her look of dismay, he ran a caressing hand down her arm. "Don't worry. It won't kill me."

"Do you want me to..." she began, one hand reaching out toward him, then pulling back.

Rogue took her hand. "Like I said earlier, I don't want you to do anything you don't want to do. That's not what this is about."

Kit felt a fluttering in her chest. She was confused. Her heart didn't know if he was her hero or the enemy. "Thanks." Almost reluctantly she followed him back to the table, knowing the outcome was either going to push him out of her life, probably forever, or she might hate him if he won.

And she really didn't want either of those things to happen.

The score at this point was fairly close. She had a total of three hundred ninety-five and he had four hundred twenty-five. He'd bested her at three hands but she could still win if her cards and the fates would cooperate.

This time it was her deal. With hands that were shaking a bit, she handed out seven cards each, laid the deck in the middle and turned over one card, a three of diamonds. Casting her eyes on Rogue, she found he was looking at her, he hadn't even picked up his cards. "What's wrong?"

He covered his cards, pressed his lips together and spoke, "I want to say something before we begin. One of us is going to win, of course. If it's me, I want to promise you that all this game means is that I'm not handing you back the note tonight. It doesn't mean I'm going to abuse it or you. If I win, nothing will change, the payments will just be made to me rather than Dave."

Kit rubbed the wood grain of the table. "I'm sorry, maybe I have totally overreacted to all of this. Our past has colored our present."

Rogue knew she was right. "I know, so that's why I'm making a decision." He covered her hand with his. "If I win this game, I won't be collecting a prize. We shared some beautiful moments tonight, but so far it's just been fun and games. Once we play this hand, you are either going to be elated or disappointed, and I don't want to be the one who takes advantage of you under either of those circumstances."

A pang of disappointment hit Kit right between her breasts, those same breasts he'd worshipped just moments ago. Could she trust him? Was he her knight in shining armor or was he having fun at her expense? Sadly, she still wasn't completely sure. "Okay. I agree."

Slowly, hesitantly, Kit picked up her cards. It took all of her self-control not to stand up and shout! She was looking at four aces, two kings and a three. All she needed was another king and she'd have it made! Surely Rogue's hand couldn't compare to this.

"Your draw," Rogue said, pointing to the deck.

"Yes, okay." She drew the card, a queen. Drats. She discarded the three.

Rogue had been dealt a lot of good hands in his life, but even he had to admit this was one of the best. He couldn't draw. He didn't need to, he was holding a royal heart flush and three tens in his hand.

With an almost apologetic look, he announced, "Gin."

Chapter Six

All the way home Kit relived every moment she'd spent with Rogue. She'd gone there with the hope to beat him at his own game, instead she'd done everything but have sex with him. "Willpower, I have absolutely none." She had to admit the truth, the only thing that kept her from sleeping with Rogue – was Rogue. Why had he picked now to become a gentleman?

When her plane landed in Kansas, she'd gotten in her car and headed home.

When Kit set foot onto White-Wing property again, she knew something was wrong. The lodge looked abandoned. There was no one there at all. "What's going on?" Worried, she parked, tucked her hair behind her ear and climbed out. A flare of panic hit Kit in the gut. She'd had guests scheduled to arrive. But sure enough, once she'd bounded up the steps and grabbed the door handle, nothing budged. It was locked.

Racing back to the truck, she raced to her mother's house. It looked as dark and desolate as the lodge. Like a kid outside a candy store, she peered through the glass of the front door. "Mother! Mother!" She banged on the door. This didn't make any sense. Her mother wouldn't up and leave without letting her know. Her father had built their family this house when Kit had been small, a beautiful rambling house with high ceilings and big fireplaces. Then her mother had married Dave and he'd seen fit to push Sheila until they'd renovated every square inch of it. Not one floor board or wall had gone untouched. The changes had broken her heart. It's said that a spirit who haunts a house is disturbed by changes and will awaken when their home is in danger of being transformed into something they aren't familiar with—she knew the feeling. "Mother!" she called again. What if something had happened?

Digging in her purse for the key, she was about to insert it in

485

the lock when she heard a noise inside. Cupping her hand to the glass, she looked again. A feeling of relief swept through her when she saw her mother coming toward the door. She was crying. "Mama!" Hastily, she opened the door. "Mama, it's me, Kit. What's wrong?"

In half a second, she was in the foyer and had her mother in her arms. Sheila wasn't a fragile woman but she'd been protected to a certain degree. Will Ross had sheltered her. She'd never had to make a decision, pay a bill or wonder where anything she needed was going to come from. When their ranch had begun to fail, she'd relied heavily on Kit and then on Dave once he had stepped into the picture. It wasn't that her mother was simple. She, like many of her generation, was used to relying on a man for everything.

"He's gone! Dave's gone." She began to cry. "I don't know why he left me."

"I'm so sorry." Kit hugged her. "What did he say?"

Sheila cried harder. "He said something about that stupid note and that he wouldn't be liable and he didn't like people snooping around."

Kit's head was spinning. She opened a drawer in a side table and took out tissues to hand to her mother. "What people?"

"I don't know, but it's all because of the card game and that man, your friend, the one from Texas. It has to all be his fault."

Kit didn't argue. She didn't really know what to say. "Come on, let's go to the kitchen and get some tea." Maybe she could make sense of what her mother was saying.

Together they walked, her supporting Sheila, who was still crying. "He didn't take all of his clothes. Do you think that means he's coming back?"

Worry made Kit's stomach hurt. She wished he wouldn't come back. Her mother was blind to Dave's shortcomings – and he had plenty. "I'm sure he will." Bad pennies tend to keep turning up. Kit patted her hand. "Just rest and I'll be right back.

She sat her mother down at the breakfast table and went to put on a kettle in the kitchen. As she hurried around the country styled room, she remembered how warm and welcome Rogue's home had been. Kit still hadn't processed exactly what happened. Actually, she didn't know exactly what she'd been thinking—challenging a man like Rogue to a parlor game and then offering sexual favors as a wager. Color flamed in her face at the memory of all that had transpired.

She pushed the more erotic thoughts aside, this was no time to relive them, especially with her mother making accusations about Rogue. It was strange – but right now, she didn't feel that way. Rogue's only crime was winning a bet, he hadn't been the one to place the deed to her home at risk in the first place. That was all Dave.

As soon as the water boiled, she poured two mugs and filled a tray with cream, sugar, lemon and an assortment of flavored tea bags. This was one tradition her grandmother Ross had passed down to her along with her jewelry.

Rogue could have taken her jewelry. He could have taken her horse. He could have pressed her for sex, but he hadn't. And despite her insecurities, there was no denying he'd wanted her. He'd been hot and hard for her. A shiver of desire raced through her, making the china on the tray rattle. All of those thoughts and revelations made her seriously doubt that any of this was Rogue's fault.

When she rejoined her mother, she repeated her question. "Now tell me everything that happened, something must have set this argument off?" When her mother put her hand over her eyes, Kit grew suspicious. "Did he hit you? Did he hurt you?"

Sheila shook her head. "No, nothing like that." Her mother picked up her cup and chose a tea bag, dipping it into the water. "It was silly. We were about to have breakfast and I asked him to hand me a book I'd been reading. When he did a card fell out that I'd been using as a bookmark. It was an old birthday card your father had given me years ago. I'd found it one day stuck back in a drawer and slipped it into Nicholas Sparks' latest. Seeing that reminder of Will set him off."

Looking at her mom wasn't exactly like staring in a mirror, she'd taken more after her dad's side of the family—but the eyes were the same. She gazed into her mother's face and tried to read what she saw there. "I thought he and Dad were friends."

Giving Kit a small smile, she sipped her tea. "There was always rivalry between those two. I dated Dave first, he actually introduced me to your father. When I met Will, things faded with Dave quickly. Your father was quite a man."

"I agree with that assessment." Kit placed a hand on her mother's shoulder. "He loved us very much."

"Yes, he did." She nodded. "My father liked Will a lot more than he did Dave. He always said Dave was flighty and too willing to take risks." Sighing, she let her eyes wander to a window, seeing only their reflections in the darkened surface. "I guess he still is, he can't seem to stay away from those card games."

Kit took a drink of her own tea. "Games of chance have their appeal, I guess." She closed her eyes as she remembered being naked in Rogue's arms. Losing a bet wasn't always so pleasurable.

"My father gave us money when we married. I'm not sure what Will invested it in, but I know he and Dave fought over that too."

"But how was that any of Dave's business?" Kit realized there was a lot about her mother and father's early married life that she knew very little about. She'd always been close to her father, trying to make up for the fact that he'd never had the son he probably longed for.

Sheila shrugged. "Will always felt sorry for Dave. He seemed to have ill luck all of his life, his father drank too much and lost everything the family had. In his own way, your father tried to take care of Dave. He bought most of White-Wing from him." Sheila waved her hand around. "The land where this house sits and about a hundred acres surrounding it was mine, the rest Will bought from

Dave. He had Dave owner-finance the purchase so Dave would always have steady income coming in, or at least that's what he said."

Kit couldn't help it, she had to ask. "Knowing all of that, why would you marry him, Mother?"

Sheila blushed, she actually blushed. "I loved your father, don't ever think I didn't. But I always cared for Dave, too. He can be very charming and he cares about me." She ran her fingers over the wood grain of the table. "I need a man to take care of me."

Biting her tongue, Kit didn't say what she was thinking. Dave Parker didn't deserve her mother's loyalty. It was odd how women could overlook faults in the men they loved. "Okay, well, I'm sure he'll be back." As far as she knew the man didn't have any other place to go.

"I hope so." She wiped her eyes and took a last sip of tea. "He was acting strange. He kept asking me about some bonds. Do you know anything about any bonds?"

Her mother looked so lost. "No, I don't." Kit couldn't imagine Dave holding onto money long enough to buy bonds. She patted Sheila's hand. "Don't worry. Everything is going to be okay. Dave losing the note in the card game may not prove to be the disaster I first thought. Rogue isn't going to do anything crazy. I'll just make the payments to him." On to more pressing matters. "How about the guests and the staff?"

Sheila buried her face in her hands. "There was a cancellation, the group that was supposed to come rescheduled for the weekend. I sent the staff home because I wanted to be alone with Dave. We were yelling, I was crying. I was embarrassed."

Kit felt a bit of relief, at least they hadn't disappointed anyone. "It's okay. We'll get a handle on all of this. I promise." As they sipped their tea, Kit tried to make sense of the series of events. "What did Dave mean when he said he wouldn't be liable?" She wondered.

Her mother shook her head. "I guess he meant he wouldn't

pay the note for the ranch to Mr. Walker."

"I can't believe he kept the note alive. After you were married, why didn't he tear up the note or forgive it? Who ever heard of a husband making his wife pay back money?" Even as she enunciated the words, she knew Dave was that type of man. Now she found herself doubting any of Dave's motives when he married her mother. Would Rogue do something like that? For some reason she couldn't see that happening. Despite the accusations she'd railed at him, he'd assured her from the beginning that she had nothing to fear from him.

But he'd hurt her before. So, that was the question. She had to decide if she could trust Rogue Walker or not.

"I don't know." Sheila shrugged. "You know I don't like to think about things like that. I'd rather worry about what flowers we plant in the beds or what we're going to serve for dinner. After your father died in the accident, you managed things until Dave and I married. The few times we discussed anything like that, he showed me papers and I signed them, I let him take care of the details."

"What did you sign?" Kit asked, worried.

Sheila shook her head. "I don't know and all of the papers are gone. He took them when he left."

Kit didn't really understand what had gone on. "I'm sorry, Mother."

Sheila nodded. "I just never believed he'd leave me. I thought we were sharing our lives."

Okay, enough. "You need to get some rest." And she needed to think. As she helped her mother up the stairs, Kit's mind was whirling. Bottom line, she needed to make sure they weren't dependent on anyone else. To do that, she needed to raise money— fast. There were several horses she'd been planning on selling in a few months. They were ready, Kit had just wanted to hold on to them until the right buyer came along. Now, she didn't have the luxury of time. When they reached her mother's door, she kissed her on the cheek. "Have the staff come back in tomorrow. I need to make some calls and see if I can find anyone interested in buying my horses."

"Okay." Sheila hugged herself, looking into the darkened room that was now devoid of the husband who usually shared this space with her. "Is that where you were yesterday, seeing a man about a horse? Your father used to tell me that all the time."

Hearing her mother use the old idiom with a straight face made her laugh. Her father did always say he had to 'see a man about a horse' when he didn't really want his wife to know what he was doing. Kit now knew how he felt. She wasn't about to admit that she'd followed Rogue to Texas, much less confess that he'd had his hands all over her…and she'd loved every second of it.

* * *

Rogue stood next to the fence, watching Mariah frolic through the field. He'd put out some hay bales today. The heat had burned up the grass and he didn't want any of the animals doing without. Jester nudged his knee. He was tempted to pick the little horse up like a dog, but he didn't want to insult the little man's dignity. "Here." Rogue fed him a piece of apple. "You liked her, didn't you, fella?"

His answer was a soft whinny. Propping one foot up on a lower board, Rogue let his mind wander to Kit and what they'd done the night she visited him. It had been three whole days since he'd kissed her, since he'd rubbed the cream of her arousal all around her clit. "Fuck," he groaned. Rogue was hard again.

Twice he'd picked up the phone to call Kit and twice he'd laid it down. What he had to say would be better said face to face. After she'd left, he had called Zane and told him his concerns. Rogue had been prepared to hear his lawyer tell him he was crazy, but he hadn't. Zane Saucier had understood and Rogue knew part of that empathy was from his own relationship with his wife. Presley was a lawyer also and she'd handled some of Lone Wolf Oil's business.

When Rogue first met her, she'd been about to have surgery to repair a cleft lip. Not that she was unattractive, she was very pretty, but part of Rogue had wondered about her relationship with the dynamic lawyer. After he'd seen them together, there was no question. Zane adored Presley and when she looked at him with love in her eyes, she was beautiful. Zane had admitted that he hadn't really wanted his wife to have the surgery, he dreaded Presley going through one moment of discomfort. With tears in his eyes, the successful attorney had confided that he knew the surgery was for her, so she could feel as beautiful as he knew her to be. How different Zane's attitude was than his own had been. His shallow juvenile view of women almost cost him getting to know Kit—and that would've been a shame.

Hearing a car coming down the drive, Rogue looked up to see who was throwing up the cloud of dust. As if he'd conjured them, he was glad to see Zane and Presley pulling up. Rogue had known he'd hear from them today, but he hadn't expected a personal visit. "Over here!" he called, motioning them to come sit with him on the patio. He didn't have full time help, but the woman who cleaned his house bi-weekly had left him a big pitcher of lemonade to keep him cool.

Presley looked trim and crisp in a light blue linen suit with her hair pulled back into a pony-tail. Zane, on the other hand, looked like he'd just stepped off a horse, he was in full cowboy regalia like Rogue. When he drew near, he held out his hand to shake. "We were headed out to Kerrville to see the McCoys, I thought we'd drop these off."

Rogue greeted them both, offering a chair and something to drink. He noticed Presley looked a little flushed. "Would you rather go inside?"

"No, I'm fine," she answered graciously. "Just a bit queasy."

When Zane smiled a grin worthy of the Cheshire cat, Rogue caught on. "Are you two…?"

"Pregnant, yes," the proud father-to-be answered.

"Congratulations!" Rogue hugged Presley. "You two will

make wonderful parents."

"I hope so." Presley laid a protective hand on her middle.

"What did you find?" Rogue asked, knowing they had somewhere to be and the sun was beating down hotter by the moment.

Presley handed Zane a folder she'd been holding. He opened it up and took out the first sheaf of papers. "The Simmons oil deal is a go. I negotiated the best price I could per barrel. They've agreed to take as much as you can pump on this well and to give your next one every consideration." Zane smiled. "You're in business, my man."

"Excellent, I can't wait to tell Elijah and the other men." He paused to look at the bottom line. "Whew. That number looks good." He'd never been rich, he'd been comfortable. Once this money materialized, he had plans for his mother and a few other things he wanted to do, one of which he was about to bring up with Zane.

"We also checked your half-brothers," Presley interjected. She pulled out another folder. "I'll let you look at this when you have time, but we found nothing to be alarmed about. You have some interesting characters here—a guitar player, a rodeo cowboy and a ranch hand with the same dream of raising horses as you have."

"They seem to share some common characteristics with you." Zane laughed. "All three of them have a reputation of being rough and rowdy."

Rogue nodded his head, glancing at what they'd found. His emotions about this deal were all over the place. He didn't know if he had room in his life for a big family. And who knew if they would want to be his family? None of them had seemed overly excited by the prospect when they'd been at Benner's office in Red Creek. "How about Walker Minerals, is it on the up and up?"

Zane poured himself and Presley some more lemonade. "I contacted Dusty's lawyer myself and he was good enough to give me access to their financial statements." Slapping Rogue's shoulder, Zane grinned. "You've lucked out. Walker Minerals is solvent and has immense potential for growth."

"Well, I can't say I'm disappointed," Rogue admitted. "I'm relieved. Honestly, this all seemed a little too good to be true."

Presley shifted in her seat, making herself a bit more comfortable. Zane adjusted a pillow behind her back and she smiled at him. "I wish we had better news on the other item you had us look at, the White-Wing matter."

Jerking his head up, Rogue stared at his friends. "What's wrong?"

Zane handed him a piece of paper. "This note is just the tip of the iceberg. True, all that's owing Parker is about fifty-thousand, but there's another lien at Wichita Savings and Loan for a hundred grand with a balloon payment due in five months. Even if your friend paid this off, she's still got bigger problems hanging over her head."

Rogue was stunned. "Who made this loan?"

"The paperwork says Sheila Parker, she's the owner. Kit's name isn't on anything. She may be an heir but her name isn't on the deed or the note."

"Damn." He knew Kit didn't have that kind of money and he didn't trust Dave Parker as far as he could throw him.

"What are you going to do?" Presley asked.

Rogue pulled off his hat and held it by the brim. "Kit and I have a history. I owe her. And I am hoping we can mend some fences." He let out a long breath and gestured toward the paperwork they'd been going over. "All of this is future earnings. I know I don't have much money in the bank, but I want you to cancel this note and assign it to Kit and her mother."

"That's very generous of you." Zane studied Rogue's face, but he didn't ask any more questions.

"When you get ready, holler at me and I'll come into Austin and pick it up." He stood and so did they. "Thanks for all you did."

"Our pleasure," Presley said with a smile.

As he began to walk them to their car, Rogue held up his hand. "If you have any member of your staff that has time, have someone look into Dave Parker for me. Find out if he has any dealings that look odd and find out where he stays when he's not at White-Wing and who he hangs out with."

"All right," Zane agreed. "Do you suspect something in particular?"

"No." Rogue shrugged. "It's just a hunch."

"Okay, we'll see what we can find."

As they drove off, Rogue put the folders of information under his arm and headed back to his house. He had some good news, it was time to call his mother.

* * *

Three days later, Rogue winged his way north toward Kansas. This time he'd flown commercial, landing in Wichita and renting a pick-up. He didn't like to be without a set of wheels, and riding in a limo would never be his chosen form of transportation, no matter how much money he made.

Once he had the keys to a fairly new Ford, he headed northwest to Red Creek. All the way he rehearsed what he would say to Kit. He wondered how she would react when he gave her the paid note. What he really dreaded was telling her about the other note, but it was necessary. Hopefully she'd listen to him. He really wanted to help. Hell, he really wanted to spend more time with her. Last night he'd awoken hard and hungry, his cock swollen from dreaming about her. He could still feel her small body in his arms, him holding her tight, his fingers dipping deep into her pussy. God, she was perfect!

The miles passed swiftly as he daydreamed about what he wanted to do to her. Rogue was anxious to know what it felt like to be inside of her, to be joined with her. Even more, he wanted a chance to start over. To ask her out and take her to dinner. He wanted to get to know her and see if there was really something between them or if he was making all of this up in his head.

Soon, he arrived at White-Wing. To his pleasant surprise, there were guests. The place looked fairly busy. He parked and went inside, finding her mother behind the desk. "Hello, could I speak to Kit, please?"

The look she gave him this time was totally unlike the welcome he'd first received. "Rogue Walker!" She glared at him over her glasses. "Haven't you done enough?"

Rogue wasn't entirely surprised by her outburst. He knew Mrs. Parker would be ready to blame anyone other than her own husband. "I'm sorry, ma'am. I'm trying to make amends. I really need to see Kit. Could you tell her I'm here, please?"

"I would if I could." She slammed a drawer, then glanced around to make sure no guest had seen her outburst. "Kit's not here. I'm worried. She left Kansas City early this morning, she should have been here by now."

"When was the last time you talked to her?" Rogue was concerned also.

"About four hours ago. She's not answering her cell phone."

"Which way would she come, do you know?" He needed all the information he could get and then Rogue was going after her. A woman traveling alone just scared him to death. He knew how he felt every time his mother left the house.

"Kit would have come down I-15 as far as she could have, but then she would have cut down, probably on Richardson Ranch Road. There's a narrow farm-to-market road that forks off from it to link up to our road. She always called it a shortcut although I don't think it is, there's too many twists and turns and there's hardly any traffic..."

Her voice trailed off. Rogue could see she was worrying. He was beginning to imagine horrible things himself. "I'll find her."

Sheila Parker's face crumpled. "If you do that, I just might forgive you."

Rogue tipped his hat. "I'll hold you to that, ma'am." He didn't linger, instead he got back in his truck and pulled up the GPS.

Usually he just liked to drive, but this time he needed the help and he was going to take it. In a few minutes, he was on the road.

* * *

The sun was setting and Kit was hearing and seeing things. Every rustle in the bushes made her cringe. She'd recently read a story about a wolf being spotted in Kansas and she knew there were bobcats. Of course, none of those things were probably anywhere near, but her imagination was running away with her just the same. Shadows were lengthening and she was too afraid to hitchhike. Since her tires went flat about an hour ago, she was on the move to find the nearest gas station or even a house with a telephone. There was absolutely nothing on this road. Kit didn't remember it being so desolate. So here she was, walking in the ditches and hugging the tree line. Her stupid cell phone had died and there hadn't been a car pass in the last half hour, not one with a woman in it. Kit knew she was probably being foolish, but she was afraid to accept a ride from a strange man.

Vehicles didn't go by often, maybe one every quarter hour or so, but she hung back, unwilling to flag down a man alone. This hadn't been a productive trip. Art Hoffman had insulted her with his offer for the horses. She desperately needed the money but she wasn't willing to give them away.

Oncoming lights made her dash into the trees, but when a truck went by at a snail's pace with the window open, the lights from the dashboard illuminated what looked like a familiar face. "Rogue?" No, she shook her head. It couldn't be. But what if it was? Elation battled with caution, but there couldn't be two men who looked like him and wore a cowboy hat coupled with a leather vest. Dashing down into the road, she yelled his name as hard as she could, waving her arms in the air. "Rogue!"

For a few seconds, she didn't think he'd seen her. And then she saw the red brake lights come on. He pulled over to the side of the road and got out. A huge sigh of relief slipped from her lips and she didn't even think about it—she took off running. She didn't have to run all the way either, because he came toward her and when she launched herself at him, he caught her close. "I've got you."

"Rogue!" She hugged him tight and knew without a doubt that no matter what the vastness of space held, there was no safer place in the universe than in his arms. "What are you doing here?"

"Looking for you," he whispered against her hair. "I came through earlier searching for you, found your truck and I was making a second pass." His voice changed from thankful to stern. "Just in case you were foolhardy enough to be walking on the side of the road. I've called the sheriff's department, the hospitals, everyone I could think of. Your mother is scared and so was I."

Kit didn't argue. Walking was a foolish thing to do. Even in rural Kansas bad things could happen. "I didn't know you were coming back," she admitted breathlessly.

"Yea, you did," Rogue drawled. "You knew I couldn't stay away." At the doubtful look in her eyes, he added, "And it had nothing to do with the land or with Dusty. I would've come back if neither of those things existed. I came back to see you."

"Thank you for finding me."

Rogue's breathing still wasn't normal. "You're welcome, but I'm paddling your sweet ass the first chance I get."

"If you'll take me home, I'll let you do it tonight." Her offer surprised Kit herself, but she meant it. He'd come looking for her. She wasn't exactly sure what that meant – but it had to be good.

Chapter Seven

Standing on the side of the road in the middle of rural Kansas is an odd place to consider romantic, but that was exactly Kit's thought. The moon was bright, she was cradled in the arms of a sexy handsome hunk and he'd just suggested that he give her a spanking.

Rogue wasn't shy, he wanted clarification. "Did you just agree to let me put my hands all over your epic ass?"

"I think you already have," she whispered against his chest. "I'm just inviting you to do it again."

With a chuckle, Rogue lifted her hand and kissed her palm. "You must really be glad to see me." He didn't release her hand but pulled her nearer. "You'll never know how glad I am to see you." After brushing his lips gently over hers, he deepened the kiss.

Kit didn't struggle, she was right where she wanted to be. Her whole body rejoiced to be back in his arms. She could've kissed him all night, but the noise of an oncoming car had them moving over to safety. "Come on, let's go." He opened the truck and settled her in, fastening the seatbelt himself. "Here, call your mother and tell her you're alive." Rogue handed her his phone, then he went around to climb behind the steering wheel.

When he was settled, she relinquished the phone and he pressed a few numbers. "I'm calling for a tow truck and then I'll take you home. Did you run out of gas or was there some other trouble?"

"Flat tires, slow leak, I guess. I didn't have a blowout, the two front tires just seemed to deflate."

Rogue thought that sounded odd. When someone answered, he gave them directions and repeated his credit card number to pay for it. He heard Kit's gasp but he took no notice. When he was through, he hung up. "He'll get it fixed and deliver it to White-

499

Wing when he's done."

"You didn't have to do that," Kit protested. "I'll repay you."

"I'm not worried about that," he drawled, glancing at her in the moonlight filtering through the front windshield. "What were you doing in Kansas City?"

The radio was turned down low and Kit could hear Tim McGraw singing about riding and not worrying about the fall. She guessed he was right, it was the cowboy in them all that made them act like they had nothing to lose. "I was trying to find a buyer for my horses."

"No!" He hit the steering wheel with the palm of his hand. "There's another way, I'm sure of it."

Kit jumped and placed a hand on her throat. "I don't know what it could be."

He had planned on waiting, but there was no use. "Here. This is for you." Rogue took the note from his pocket and handed it to her.

"What's this?" Kit took the paper, never taking her eyes from his face.

Turning on the interior light, he said, "Read it."

She did and couldn't believe her eyes. The note her family had owed to Dave Parker and now to Rogue was paid in full. "How?" Kit stared at him until realization dawned. "You did this?"

"I never intended to profit from you, I just needed to check some things out."

Kit stared down at the piece of paper. "I can't let you do this."

Rogue divided his attention—one eye on the road, the other on her. "You've been asking me to return that note for two weeks."

He was right, she had. "I expected you to return it to Dave, not to release it yourself." She sounded ungrateful, but she wasn't. She was awed.

"Dave needed to be out of the picture," Rogue stated flatly.

"He may be," she confessed. "He left my mother, took all the money in their joint account and disappeared."

Rogue

"Damn." He looked over at her. "He's a piece of work."

"Yea and she said he kept asking her about some bonds but we didn't know what he was referring to." His hand was resting on the console between them and she couldn't resist, covering his hand with hers and entwining their fingers.

Rogue needed to tell her the rest. She had to know. Somehow, he couldn't spoil the moment. Finding out she'd been missing had just slain him, he was weak, his bones felt like water. "Where am I taking you?"

"My house. It's been airing out all day. I don't want to go to the lodge. I want to be alone with you." Kit couldn't believe she was saying this, but Rogue had proved himself. He'd come looking for her when no one else had. He cared.

"There's nothing I want more," he assured her.

As the truck ate up the miles, he rubbed her hand, every stroke of his fingers felt like he was petting her between the legs. "Um, how's Jester?" she asked, trying to maintain control.

"He's fine. My mother is staying at my house for a while. I had some good news on a business deal and I brought her over so she could do some shopping. She'll barely tolerate Jester, probably lock the horsey door." Rogue chuckled. "The first time she saw a horse in my house, you should have heard her carrying on. She kept expecting to find big dollops of horse sh—dookey all over the house."

Kit laughed out loud. "Well, it's not like you could sandbox train him."

"True, but Jester's smart. He's only made a couple of mistakes since I've had him—although they were some big mistakes."

Soon, he was pulling up to her place, a small farm house complete with a wrap-around porch. "Welcome," she said. "It's nothing fancy."

She was reaching for the door handle when he stopped her. "Stay put, let me be a gentleman."

His face was sincere, his eyes hooded and Kit froze,

completely willing to wait for him—for as long as it took. "Okay." In no time, he was at her side, taking her hand and together they covered the distance between his truck and her door.

"I know there's a lot between us that needs to be said," Rogue admitted. "But I have to tell you that talking isn't my highest priority right now." He wanted to taste her, take her in his arms and make all his dreams come true.

Kit quickly fumbled with the door, barely getting it open before they were in and he was pushing her against the wall. Rogue eased his head forward and she framed his face in her palms, loving the scruff of his beard. "You're so sexy. I've always thought so."

"I was a dick to you on the circuit. I couldn't see you for what you are and I'll always hate myself for it." He slid his fingers up her arms, over the curve of her shoulders until he cupped her throat just below her ears.

"Stop." She raised her face for his kiss. "The past is over. We're here now. Together. Let's celebrate." Her lips met his, a soft mingling of firm and tender.

Kiss and retreat. "Believe me, my whole body is up for a party." He nudged her with his erection. "I've wanted you for so long, I think my cock is petrified."

"Scared?" She giggled.

He laughed. "No, permanently hard like petrified wood."

The room was dark and Kit was hesitant to break the mood with light. Everything seemed so right, she wanted nothing to go wrong. "Kiss me again."

"Gladly." He sighed as he mated his lips to hers, his tongue darting out. Holding her still, he began a slow, sensual exploration. A sense of urgency teamed with a gentle seduction.

The reality of what was happening was almost more than Kit could take. "Are we going to make love?" she asked in wonder.

"If you'll let me," he whispered.

"Come." She took him by the hand and led him through her

home.

Rogue knew he wanted to explore her world. He wanted to know her, learn her secrets. First, he would start with her beautiful body. "Turn on the light," he requested, not wanting even one of his senses to miss a moment with her.

Flipping a switch, she illuminated her bedroom in a soft warm glow. So much of her life had been spent in the pursuit of activities not always suited to a girl. So here, in her inner sanctum, she had allowed her sensuality to emerge. A big bed was piled high with pillows, a chaise lounge was draped with a silk throw. Off to one side a deep Jacuzzi tub sat with candles arranged in groupings, just waiting for someone to relax and enjoy a fragrant soak. While all of these things brought her comfort, none of them seemed erotic until tonight. Kit began to tremble, realizing she was about to give herself to the one man who'd occupied her dreams for years. "I'm nervous," she confessed.

"Why?" Rogue asked. "I'll never hurt you again, I promise." He came to her, lifting the weight of hair so he could plant kisses on her neck. "You don't know how sexy I think you are. I love this tumble of curls." As he gazed into her eyes, his other hand was busy, hunting buttons and zippers, gradually and carefully undressing her.

"I've never…" How lame was this going to sound? Here she was in her mid-twenties in the year 2015 and had never been intimate with a man other than what she'd done with Rogue.

Rogue strained to hear what she said. "You've never…" When she raised her eyes to his, he had his answer. Shy. Uncertain. Hopeful. He understood. A powerful possessive pride swept over him. "I'm glad."

"You are?"

"I'd like to think you waited for me."

She would've liked to tell him she'd waited for him, but that would be a lie. This was totally unexpected and totally amazing. "We've run the gamut of emotions, haven't we?" Kit asked softly.

"Yea, but a few have dominated my thoughts." As Rogue pushed her blouse from her shoulders and she stepped from her jeans, her clothes weren't the only thing on the ground—his jaw dropped. "Desire. Need. Lust," he growled. "Woman, you are breathtaking." Before, on the couch during the card game, he'd seen her but the time had been rushed and the circumstances had been awkward. But now, there was no wager between them and their time together wasn't limited—heaven could take its time.

Almost reverently, Rogue let his eyes and hands rove over her. A perfectly feminine hour-glass figure flowed into long, slender legs. Placing one arm behind her knees and the other around her shoulders, he picked her up and walked the few steps to the bed. As he laid her down, he kissed her again. "Don't think I've forgotten the spanking," he muttered with a smile, "but I plan on loving you first."

Kit was trembling, but not from fear. She wanted him so much she ached. "Just don't forget, I'm looking forward to it." She wanted to do everything with Rogue. He made her want things, things she didn't fully understand, erotic play she'd only read about in books.

Her teasing made him laugh. "I don't think that's something I could ever forget." He knelt by the bed and stroked her hair, his thumb grazing her forehead. "I've wanted to be with you like this from the moment you drove away from me on that dirt road." His warm breath caressed her cheek as he bent his head near hers.

"I wanted you too. I've wanted you for so long," she admitted, watching him begin to undress. Almost hypnotized, she saw that his body was bigger and harder than she remembered, perfect in form and symmetry. The vest went first. Kit wondered how many he'd worn out over the years, this one looked exactly like the one he used to wear. Next went the shirt, this time a light blue one with snaps that he opened by holding the shirt at the neck and jerking it open. Kit groaned at the sound. What he revealed made her hot, she put her hand up to touch.

"Careful, I'm on a hair-trigger here, Kit-Kat," he cautioned her. "If that little hand wanders any lower, I won't be responsible for what you find."

Kit licked her lip nervously and met his eyes. He was undoing that belt buckle now, she could hear the rasp of the zipper. "I promise, you're in good hands." Kit knew she was displaying more bravado than she was feeling. "Would you kiss me?"

"Hell yes, baby." Helpless against the temptation, Rogue felt a desperate hunger rage through his body. "I dream about kissing you."

He came to her, stretching out beside her. They both still wore their underwear and Kit wondered if they were both preserving some last boundary to protect their feelings. Could he possibly feel as vulnerable as she did? Mesmerized, she stilled as his mouth lowered, felt his breath on her face, then moaned when the warm rough glide of his lips touched hers. Kit's breath hitched as the electric sensation sizzled over her skin. The pleasure was so intense it took her by surprise.

She whimpered and his hand tightened on her neck, his lips settled more firmly on her as she opened and let him in, her eyelashes fluttering closed as pleasure cascaded over her. Kit's heart was hammering in her chest as his tongue swirled against hers. She placed a hand on his chest, caressing the strength she found there and was surprised his heart was thundering as loudly as her own.

Wrapping her arm around his neck, Kit pressed closer to him, rubbing herself against the hard ridge of his erection. Rogue was incredible. Masterful. His kiss swamped her. But she knew it wasn't really his kiss that excited her—it was him. Rogue dominated her as he sated himself and she surrendered to anything he wanted. Liquid heat flowed through her body, pulsing through her sex.

Knowing this was her first time, Rogue was determined to take his time. "Anything you want," he muttered. Her answer was a little mewl of need that was almost his undoing. Fighting to breathe, he slipped one arm beneath her and lifted her closer. Her nipples bore into his chest and she slipped one leg over his and ground herself against him. Rogue didn't know if could hold out, this was unlike anything he'd experienced before.

"Rogue," she whispered, tearing her lips from his. "I'm burning up."

"I know, I know," he murmured, "me too." Every move she made, every little mewl from her lips were only fanning the flames higher.

For years, old insecurities had haunted her. She'd never been flirtatious or confident around men. Her one big experience had been with Rogue and after that she'd shunned any advance a man would make.

But this man…he was the only one who could free her. And now she was in his arms and he was tense and hard with arousal— for her. For a moment she opened her eyes and stared at him. His face was tight and flushed with excitement, his eyes were intense and gazing at her with what she could only term lust.

Rogue wanted her. This was no joke. A man couldn't fake something like this. "Help me," she said as she pushed at the waistband of his briefs. The last time she'd done this, she'd been wanting to hurt him and now all she wanted to do was please him.

"Are you sure?" The question sparked in his eyes, but he let her have her way, even raising up to make sure the cotton shorts slid down his hips and off his legs.

"I'm sure." She licked his lips, craving his kiss, but aching for even more. "I want to touch you."

Shaking with need, Rogue lay back as Kit began to make herself at home. Having her lying half on half off his body, her glorious tits were rubbing his chest and arm, making his mouth water to suck on them again. But this was her rodeo—for as long as he could stand it, then he'd take over and give her what they both needed.

Rogue

She began at his lips—one tender kiss, before moving down, leaving a path of licks and nibbles on his throat to his shoulder. When he felt the scrape of her teeth, shivers tore down his spine and his cock jerked with anticipation.

The many times she'd rehearsed this in her head, Kit hadn't been able to get past a certain point. As she kissed and explored his chest, running her hands and lips over every bulging muscle, Rogue encouraged, soothed, and praised her with whispers and touches. His hand was caressing her hip, slipping beneath her underpants, warming her flesh and making her wet.

"I don't want to be the only one naked," he said as his hand skated from the back to the front of her panties, making her jump. Would he notice? She held her breath as his fingers delved across her mound, a mound that was now as smooth as silk. "Jesus," he hissed. "You're bare."

"Yes." She didn't explain, didn't tell him that she had taken advantage of her trip in Kansas City to go to a spa. At the time, she hadn't even admitted to herself that she was doing it in the hopes she'd one day soon be in the place she was at the moment—in bed with Rogue. "Undress me," she requested and he wasted no time in ridding her of panties and bra. For a moment, she let him caress her – his hands lifting and molding her breasts. "You like my…" she hesitated, even saying the word to him seemed so erotic.

"God, yes, I love your tits. I can't get enough of them." He plumped them, pushed them together, raking his thumbs over the swollen tips. When he tried to suck on both nipples at one time, Kit lost her ability to breathe. "I want all of you." He confessed this as one hand left her chest to slip between her legs, giving her something to push against.

Kit didn't know how to process so much pleasure. He was pushing her past the brink of thought. Eagerly she rubbed against him. The feel of skin on skin was so luxuriously heady that she thought she might swoon. She rubbed her face against his softly furred chest, lavishing him with kisses, running her fingers over the silky hair, tracing the line that ran from between his pecs to a narrow trail that led to…

"Ah, God, yes, touch me – right there, please," Rogue groaned.

The idea that she could make him beg was euphoric. A niggle of memory pinched her, she'd made him beg before and look how that had ended up. But this time would be different. This was different. But what was it – really?

"No, no," she murmured to herself. This was now. This was tonight. Tomorrow might never come, but she wanted what he could give her—now.

"What is it?" he asked, whispering in her hair.

"Nothing," she answered. "I just want you so much." And so she showed him, letting her fingers acquaint themselves with his heated flesh, curling her fingers around his thick, heavy shaft. Her womb clenched and her pussy tightened, the cream of her need iced the bare folds of her femininity.

"Fuck, you're making me mad with wanting you." Rogue closed his eyes, bowing his neck as she began to slowly pump him – up and down, the thick crested head throbbing in her hand, the tip glistening with a pearly drop of liquid. A turbulent rush of pleasure crashed over him as she touched him. He arched off the bed, his whole body shaking.

Her hand stroked down the velvet steel, the sight of him loving what she gave him was something she never wanted to forget. "You're so big, so perfect," she whispered. The night of their regrettable fiasco, it had been too dark and she'd been too angry to really look. But now, they were here and things were different. He seemed to want her as much as she wanted him, so she could appreciate his male beauty and know he was responding to her. Heavy veins pulsed underneath the skin as his cock flexed in her palm, rock-hard and powerful.

"Can I?" she whispered.

A gasp of laughter slipped from his lips. "Anything, anything you want to do is welcome - just do it."

He sounded desperate, Kit marveled. The pure sensuality of the moment struck her. She knew what she wanted, she wanted her mouth on him—to taste him, to suck him. Moving over him, between his spread thighs, Kit leaned down and soothed her lips over the softer flesh just above his cock, gripping the stiff, heavy rod at the root.

Rogue wasn't missing a moment, he was propped up, watching her beautiful face as she took him in. He was nearly crazed with lust. It was all he could do not to wrap that waterfall of hair around his fist and take control. "Kit, please, honey, I'm dying here." She met his gaze, gave him a mischievous smile and lowered her head. Rogue held his breath. And when she finally gifted him with her lips, fitting them over the head of his cock and sucking it into her mouth, his hips bucked and he pulled the sheet loose from where it was tucked.

Her soft tongue was like a flame of fire flitting over the sensitive head of his cock. The grateful flesh jerked with ecstasy and she hesitated, looking back up at him to see if she had done something wrong.

"Don't stop, please don't stop," he pleaded. "I just want you so much, that's all." His reward was a smile and her return to him—he almost levitated from the bed when she took him between her lips, her tongue curling around and licking his shaft, teasing the sweet spot under the head. "God, it's good," he groaned. What was it about this woman? As before, she had him in the palm of her hand.

At his urging, Kit's confidence grew and soon she relaxed and did what she wanted, enjoying herself. It did her ego good when he panted and cursed as she licked and rubbed. Taking him deep, she began to suckle, her hand still rubbing and pumping the portion of his sizeable length she couldn't take into her mouth.

Rogue was fit to be tied. He didn't know if he'd survive the pleasure. He'd gone beyond fisting the sheet, if he hadn't torn a

hole in the material it would be a miracle. "Touch my balls, Kit."
Seeming to want to please him, she did as he asked. Cupping his
balls, Kit rolled them between her fingers, massaging the sac,
letting herself play as she continued to suck. The bliss was almost
too much, he was about to explode. Her sensual innocence was
pure erotica. Rogue tried to muster up some guilt, but he couldn't.
He was a bastard in more ways than one. "That's it, that's it."
When she looked up at him through those long lashes and hummed
her happiness, he had to clench his teeth and every muscle in his
body to keep from jetting his cum between her lips.

Women have no idea how gorgeous they look to a man with
their lips stretched around his cock. He couldn't be still to save his
life. His hips bucked helplessly and he threw his head back and
groaned. Sweat beaded on his body as he jerked, forcing his dick
deeper into her throat. She didn't flinch, she accommodated him
and kept sucking.

"Fuck!" Rogue hissed, reveling in her attention. Virgin she
might be, but she was turning him inside out. She was going to
have to stop or he was going to… "Kit." When he said her name,
she raised her eyes to his once more and the joy on her face and the
sparkle in her eye told him she was enjoying it as much as he
was—nah – impossible! He was loving every second, every lick,
every suck and there was no way in hell he was going to last.

Rogue arched his back, his hips thrusting upward, his balls
wound tighter than a top. White hot electric ecstasy radiated up his
body from his cock. "Baby, let go unless you want a mouth full
of…"

She didn't let go, if anything she concentrated more – holding
him tighter, sucking him harder, giving him incredible mind-
blowing pleasure. "Kit!" His hand shot out and gripped her hair,
his fingers threading in the curls, holding her tight. His resolve
shattered. Rogue could feel the climax rising from his sac, flowing
into his cock.

Whether he held her or not made no difference, she wasn't

letting go. She doubled her efforts—sucking, laving, tongue dancing on the end, slipping into the little slit so she could drink his very essence. Kit wanted him to cum, she wanted him to be blown away, she wanted to absorb everything about him into her very soul.

With a harsh cry, he exploded, his cock jerked, throbbed, then his release spurted into her mouth. Kit accepted it, the taste unlike anything she'd expected—sultry, salty, all man. She whimpered and tried to draw more from him, her lips and tongue massaging the head as she milked him dry of every drop.

Seeing him orgasm, watching Rogue lose himself in what she'd done was glorious. Her whole body was prickly with arousal and heat. She wanted to slide up his body and rub on him like a cat. Her clit was pulsing and her sex ached. Even though she'd never had it, Kit knew she was craving sex…and only Rogue could satisfy her.

Wanting more and not knowing what to do, Kit sat up, her hands moving over her own body – cupping her breasts and rubbing her swollen nipples. "Rogue, please," she begged.

"Down." He reversed their positions, covering her. He said nothing, but bowed his head to her breasts and began to suck the sensitive flesh—his mouth on one breast and his fingers on the other. Kit writhed beneath his touch. She threw a leg over his and canted her hips, desperately trying to rub her clit against him.

He was voracious, his mouth wide, devouring as much of her tit as he could take in his mouth—his tongue, teeth and lips giving her mindless ecstasy. "Rogue, yes, God yes!" Her arms went up and her hands moved over his back feverishly. Kit was enthralled, her whole body on fire.

Rogue was determined to gift her in equal measure. His hands moved to her ass and he lifted, burying his face between her thighs.

"Rogue!" she screamed as he feasted, licking a fiery path up her slit, teasing her clit before thrusting his tongue deep into the tight hot channel of her femininity. She tossed her head, her body floundering until he held her still, lifting one leg over his shoulder as he ate her out, fucking her deep with his tongue.

Kit was out of her mind. She couldn't be still. If Rogue didn't hold her, she was going to slip over the very edge of the world. Never had she known such ecstasy existed. What he'd done to her in Texas had been perfect…but this—this was beyond any rapture she could conceive. There was only one other thing she wanted…

"You," she panted. "I need you. Now. Please."

"Not yet," he murmured as his head moved high enough to capture her clit between his lips. And—God in heaven! - when he sucked on it, Kit's world exploded. She wanted to cry out, but she couldn't. Her whole world condensed down to that one euphoric point where his lips touched her body.

Rogue worked her clit with his tongue and held on. He could feel her thrashing, convulsing. Spasms shook her body and he lapped at her until she went limp. He moved up her body and began to kiss her. "Breathe, baby, breathe."

She tried. She'd almost blacked out from the sheer bliss he'd given her. Rolling into him, she clung, her hands caressing his shoulders and chest. "I still need you," Kit whispered. "I want to know what it's like…"

Rogue grabbed for his pants. "Condom."

Kit stopped him. "No, I want my first time to be just you. I'm safe. I'm on the pill, please."

He heard her. His cock voted yes and his brain wasn't working.

"I want to feel you, just you. I want to know what it's like when you fill me up."

Rogue looked into her pleading face. "I don't do commitment, Kit, and I never want kids. You've got to understand."

He hadn't said it before, but she'd always known. He was a Rogue, in name and in deed. He'd never be anything else. "I know. I understand. I still want you."

Groaning, Rogue gave in. "You'll be the death of me, Kit." He rose over her and she opened her legs wide. Pressing the head of his cock at her opening, he began to work his way in.

Kit gasped at the feeling. He was so big—hot, pulsing. Her heart almost stopped as he pushed in the tip. Fuck, he was big. Burning. Stretching. He pushed her legs up, spreading her wider and she raised her head so she could see the miracle of their joining.

Rogue closed his eyes and undulated his hips, gradually letting her pussy suck his cock up inside of her. It hurt. It felt good. She wanted to ask him to stop and beg him to continue. Years of just being female with her monthly flow and using a vibrator had left her only a technical virgin. Nothing had ever felt like this. Greedily she lifted her hips, worked her muscles and tried to ensure he went nowhere but deeper.

"Good?" Rogue chuckled. "You like fucking me, don't you?"

"Yes. More!" She was completely unashamed.

Putting his hands on her knees, he opened her up even farther. She was creaming, her juices coating his cock. "God, just look at you. I love this." He drew out, then thrust back in, making her gasp. "It feels so good."

The in and out motions were taking her higher. Each thrust bumped her clit and she found herself anticipating, countering her movements to match his. "Fuck me, Rogue," she encouraged. If this was all she'd have of him – she wanted as much as she could get. "Harder!"

Rogue let go. He drove into her as far as he could – pulled out – drove back. He fucked her hard and deep. Kit held on to his forearms, her nails marking him.

Tossing her head, she let the pleasure swamp her. Harder. Deeper. Relentlessly, Rogue took her. Pounding into her female flesh, giving her what she was born to accept. The need didn't let up, it grew. Wanting, needing more, she pressed up, begging him to impale her – bury his cock inside her aching, hungry pussy over and over again until it happened—a tightening, rippling, growing, consuming fire that froze her. Her pussy clamped down on him as her mind and soul tore from her body and she flew – free from the chains of uncertainty that had kept her bound to the past. Her cries mingled with his as he pushed himself deep and held there. Kit could feel the warm jets of his cum bathe her secret places and she quivered as a fresh release exploded from within.

Rogue was knocked on his ass. He was having a hard time comprehending what he was feeling. Whether it was coming inside of her – all that bare flesh sliding against one another – or if it was just Kit herself, he didn't know. He came down over her, wrapping his arms around her and holding her close, absorbing the echoes of her climax. "Easy, baby."

While he cradled Kit, offering her a safe haven to anchor after the storm of their passion, Rogue wondered at his own emotions. Confused. Flummoxed. He didn't know what he was feeling. This was different and he wasn't comfortable with different. He didn't bond, yet he refused to entertain the notion that this wouldn't happen again—and again.

"Thank you," she breathed, her lips warm against his skin.

"Rest," he urged. "We'll get up and talk in a bit, but we're worn out right now. Let me hold you. Rest."

She didn't need much convincing, Kit felt warmer and safer than she'd ever been. The chance to sleep in Rogue's arms wasn't something she was willing to pass up. So, she cuddled next to him while he pulled up the covers and in a few short moments, she knew no more.

Rogue's mind wouldn't let him sleep. He'd only told her half the story. When dawn came, he had the unsavory job of telling her there was another lien on the property. White-Wing was not in the free and clear. She wasn't going to be happy about it. And despite the self-knowledge of his limitations concerning relationships and commitment, he had no intention of letting her fight this battle alone.

While she needed him, Kit Ross had a champion.

Chapter Eight

Kit opened one eye. A beam of sunlight was filtering through her curtains. She buried her face in the pillow, rubbing her cheek against the fabric. It smelled good – different. In fact, she felt different. There were places on her body that felt tingly. Wiggling beneath the covers, her nipples rubbed against the sheet and her breath hitched. They were sore, a good kind of sore. Other places on her body felt…touched. An ache between her legs had her hand moving down to feel what might be different—and then it hit her.

Everything was different.

She was no longer a virgin. And…

Rogue had slept in her bed.

She sat straight up, eyes wide, taking in the wrinkled but empty bed. Was he gone? Had she dreamed it? Jumping from the bed, she hurried to the bathroom, took care of business and hastily pulled on jeans and a T-shirt.

Padding down the stairs, she frowned. If this was a hit and run, she'd track that handsome hunk down and kill him. But by the time she reached the bottom of the stairs, she could smell coffee. "Rogue?"

"In here."

She crept through the door a bit hesitantly. Mornings after weren't in her realm of experience.

Rogue hadn't been up long. He'd awakened with an angel nestled against him. All he'd wanted to do was kiss Kit awake and find solace for his aching cock between her sweet thighs.

But he'd refrained, getting up to take himself out of temptation's way.

Now that she was near, however, there was no way he was going to keep his hands to himself. She was dressed, but her face still held that 'dreamy just risen from sleep, well-fucked look'. As far as looks went, this one had to be his favorite. She'd just stepped through the door when he nabbed her, pulling her close and covering her mouth with his before she could make a hint of a protest.

Kit melted into his arms like butter on a warm biscuit. She hadn't realized how much she'd missed waking up without him until every inch of her responded in its own way—parts of her were tingling, others, like her nipples, were hardening, and yet others, like her sex and her lips, were softening and readying themselves for his possession.

Because that's what he'd done last night—he'd possessed her. He might not want to keep her, but she was his for the asking.

"Morning, sunshine." He hugged her. "Ready for some coffee?"

Coffee was a poor second for what she really wanted, but she wasn't sure enough of herself to start making demands from Rogue Walker. "Yes, you should have got me up. I would've cooked breakfast for you."

"Already done." He fanned his hand toward the table where a couple of plates of eggs and bacon sat waiting, still warm. "I drove into Red Creek and stopped in at the Creekside Café. I've got to get used to this place. Next week is my turn at Dusty's place."

She settled at her table and took a nibble of toast. "Are you excited?"

Rogue sat across from her, took a swig of orange juice and considered what she said. "Maybe. I have a lot of questions." He smiled. "I saw one of my brothers this morning. Killian's his name. He's originally from Montana."

"What did he say?" Kit was curious. She was trying not to stare. How did he look so good first thing in the morning? She probably had pillow creases on her face and puffy eyes. Rogue looked like sex on a stick in tight jeans, a tighter white western shirt and that sexy leather vest she wanted to rub up against.

Rogue laughed. "Oh, he didn't see me. I didn't stop, I just saw him heading into the Mineral office as I passed by on my way to the café." Shaking his head, he admitted, "I'm not much on family. It's been my mother and me for all of my life and adding to our small circle goes against my grain."

Kit smiled at him weakly. "Yea, so you said. No commitment. No children."

A little uncomfortable, he added, "I just don't want there to be any—"

Interjecting, Kit finished his sentence. "Misunderstanding, yea, me too." She shook her fork at him. "I know exactly how you feel. I have plans that don't include a white picket fence and baby diapers." Even as she spoke, Kit knew half of what she was saying was some type of defense mechanism.

"I see," Rogue said, a little surprised that her response didn't sit really well with him. But it did open the door for a topic change that he'd been dreading. Taking a deep breath, he pushed back his plate. "We need to talk."

Four words that never bode well. "Okay." Kit straightened up in her chair. "What's wrong?" Was it about last night? "If you're worried about the no condom thing, I'm on the pill. I have been for years."

Shaking his head, he stopped her. "No, it's about White-Wing and the note."

"Oh." Well, that stopped her in her tracks. "If you want it back, I could understand. Your gesture was too generous for words." Insecurities began to assault her. He'd given her a gift and she'd slept with him in return. What did that make her?

"No, no." Rogue took a paper out of his pocket. "This is something else entirely."

Kit wouldn't let it go. "I intend to pay you back. Just as soon as I get some advertising out and get my guest list built up, I should be fine. Since I don't have to sell the horses right away, I can pick and choose a buyer and not have to take a low-ball offer."

"Stop." Rogue felt like he was about to kick a puppy. She was so optimistic. "Before I show you this, I want to tell you that you aren't alone. We're friends now." Friends. Hell, he didn't feel like her friend. He felt like a heck of a lot more. "I will help you."

Help? Why did she need help? "I thought everything was okay." A sense of panic hit her. "What are you talking about?"

Not knowing anything else to do, Rogue just plunged in. "When my lawyer was checking into Dusty's affairs and some of my company's business, I also had him look at the note." He saw Kit swallow, like she was preparing herself for the worst. "He ran a title search on White-Wing and he found there was another lien against the property other than what I turned back over to you."

"How?" Kit's voice came out in a croak. "How much? Who?" She moved to the edge of her chair. "Dad never told me anything about another note."

"It wasn't your dad who borrowed money against the place. Again, it's not the homestead, it's the acreage. The note is in your mother's name, but I'm sure your stepfather is behind it."

Kit felt sick. "How much?" she asked again.

"What's owing on it is close to a hundred thousand. The payments are three months behind and there is a balloon payment due in five months."

Wham! She felt like she'd been run over by a freight train. "I can't believe Mother agreed to this." Covering her face in her hands, she remembered Sheila saying she'd signed papers not really knowing what they were. "How in the world can I survive?"

"Don't worry." Rogue covered her hand. "I'm going to help you. We'll go see the banker and try to come to terms. First, we'll look over your books and see what income you've got coming in and see what you have to do – then I'll help you do it."

Kit stared at him. She didn't understand. "Why would you be willing to help me?"

Rogue searched for words that could explain what he didn't fully understand himself. "My life hasn't necessarily been easy and I can understand feeling like you don't have control over your own destiny. Right now, I don't have a lot of cash. My assets aren't liquid and most of my worth is future instead of present, but that's going to change soon."

Suddenly the topic of conversation was making her uneasy. "I'm not going to accept anything else from you. I don't even want to accept what you've already given me."

Realizing he was losing her, he decided to talk fast. "I told you I'd come on your property and do an evaluation." Rogue held up his hand. "While I don't expect to find oil, maybe I can help you come up with a plan."

"Sorry, I can't think straight." With a frustrated huff, Kit got up and paced across the kitchen.

She was playing with the hem of her shirt, feeling the threads and every step she took, Rogue got a glimpse of her tanned firm midriff.

"You're thinking too hard. Come here." He reached out for her. "I told you, I'm going to help you."

A flash of anger hit Kit. "You don't owe me anything! Just because I heard you spouting off about my lack of looks and sex appeal doesn't mean you have to take care of me now!"

"Dammit!" Rogue's hand flashed out and took her arm, pulling Kit to him. "Are you ever going to let me forget that?"

She was right up in his face and the heat of their bodies drew them like charged magnets. "I don't accept charity and my favors…are not for sale!" Kit sputtered out the words, determined to make her point despite the way her traitorous body was reacting.

"Charity? Favors?" Rogue sat down in his chair and spun her across his lap.

By the time Kit realized what was happening, she was lying face down across his wide thighs, looking at the floor. "What in the hell do you think you're doing? Let me up!"

"Nope." Rogue's hand settled on her bottom and he rubbed sensuously, across both cheeks.

Kit felt her pussy flood with heat. "No! Let me up!"

"Can't do that." Rogue kept up his erotic exploration, even

dipping between her legs to rub her vagina. "Damn, you're hot. I can feel your wet heat through this denim."

Damn! Kit was humiliated. Here she was being manhandled with her ass in the air and she…liked it?

"That spanking you promised I could give you?" Rogue reminded her. "Well, its time. I'm not mad at you, in fact, I'm turned on, but this is a good time to point out that nothing between us is charity and any sexual favors you give me are…" He slapped her on the ass hard – POP! "…because we are hot as hell for another." POP! Her other cheek stung like it was on fire.

"Ow!" Kit cried. "I'm going to get even with you, Rogue Walker." She twisted and tried to struggle out of his grasp.

"Steady, baby. You know you like this." Instead of holding her across the back, he had slid his hand underneath her and down the front of her shirt.

Kit was about to embarrass herself. Much to her chagrin, she was getting off on this blatant male display of dominance. While he warmed her ass with his palm, his other hand was down her shirt, in her bra and massaging her breast. If she didn't get away from Rogue, she was going to orgasm and then – she'd never hear the end of it! "If you don't let me up, I'm going to…to…"

POP! "Do what?" He milked her nipple and she shook. "What you gonna do, little girl?"

"Let me up and I'll show you," she said it in the meekest, mildest, sweetest voice she had.

So, he did.

Kit was up and off his lap before Rogue could count to three. He halfway expected her to backhand him. Instead, she singed him with a heated glance, framed his face and claimed his lips, eating at his mouth like she was starving to death. Rogue was taken aback for about half a second before he wrapped his arms around her like bands of steel.

A whimper left her lips as she pressed against him. He stole her breath every time they kissed—every damn time. When his hand palmed her breasts, his fingers working the tender tip of her nipple, she started pulling at his clothes. She had no defense against this man—none. He was like a forbidden pleasure she knew would only be available to her for a short time and she had to make the most of every second.

Rogue was as turned on as Kit. "Let's get you out of these jeans." He worked on the buttons and zipper while she pulled her T-shirt over her head. The bra and panties were next and soon she was as naked as he was.

"Should we go to bed?" she asked, her eyes stuck on his huge erection.

Panting like a winded racehorse, Rogue pulled her to him and sat back down in the chair. "No, right here is fine. Straddle me." He held out his hand and she placed her small delicate one in his. The morning sun was shining through the kitchen window and he loved looking at the gentle curve of her waist, the soft coral of her nipples and the tempting triangle of her pussy.

Rogue settled Kit across his lap, her legs resting on his thighs. Reaching up, he curled his hand around her neck, urging her back into his kiss. "You taste so good," he cajoled, "like sweet, spicy woman."

"I can't believe you spanked me," she whispered. "I can't believe I liked it."

"You knew you would." He chuckled. "You promised me that out on the road."

"I was kidding," she admitted with a grin.

"I liked it too." Rogue liked everything about her. Sealing her mouth to his, he kissed her again, taking advantage of the bounty in front of him. She gasped when he slid his hand on her breast, pressing harder against him. Her fat sassy nipples were already hard. Rogue rubbed them between his thumbs and first fingers. They pebbled even more, begging for more of his touch. "And you like my hands on your tits, don't you?"

Kit nodded, pressing her nose into his cheek, easing herself forward on his legs. Her hair hung over one shoulder, an enticing curl looped around one nipple. Rogue picked it up, rubbing it over his lips before he pushed the silky strand over her shoulder. "I like your hands all over me," she admitted.

Rogue shivered when she traced his smile with the tip of her teasing tongue, making his skin break out in chill bumps. When she raised her head, she stole his breath when she cupped her breasts and lifted one of the firm globes to his mouth. He bent his head and teased her by rubbing his closed lips over the pouting nipple. She wasn't deterred from letting him know what she wanted, pushing the mound of female flesh closer to him and prodding his lips with the swollen tip.

"Kiss me?" she asked.

In answer, he opened his mouth and accepted her generous gift, twirling his tongue around the nipple and areola. "God, you're sweet," he murmured as he plumped her tit with his fingers, taking even more of her in his mouth, laving and sucking. When her head fell back and she let out an eager moan, the sexy sound was music to his ears. A woman with sensitive breasts was a blessing to a man and Kit loved her nipples to be stimulated. Her body was warm with arousal, her nipple hot against his tongue. Drawing her deeply into his mouth, he swept the crest, suckling with increasing pressure.

"Rogue!"

Her cry of delight turned to protest when he eased back. "Steady, honey. I just want to give the twins equal attention." With a sigh of relief, she slid to the right, giving him room to work.

His worship of her breasts was amazing, but Kit wanted more. "There seems to be something here that requires my attention."

His cock was hard and demanding. "I'm grateful you finally noticed," he whispered. Snaking his hand from her breast to her pussy, he was gratified to find her warm and wet. He let his fingers slip through her thick cream, parting Kit's silky folds and delving down toward her tender opening. As his fingers dipped in, she grasped his cock and began to pump him up and down.

Rogue clenched his teeth and moaned. He didn't know what he liked more—her fisting his dick or her pussy tightening down on his fingers like the sweetest vice. "Rise up," he instructed through clenched teeth. Kit didn't react immediately, she was so hazy with desire and loving the way he was touching her and the feel of his staff in her hand as she petted him.

"Up, up," he almost begged, his hands on her waist. The sensual glide of her fingers on his cock was almost his undoing.

She turned him loose, resting her palms on his shoulders while he put himself into position. "I've never done this before."

"Kit, you're a cowgirl, you'll ride me like a dream."

Holding his gaze, she held her breath as he placed the head of his cock at her entrance. She ached with a mindless need to be fucked. With exquisite care, she eased herself down, impaling inch by slow, delicious inch until he was fully seated in the tight glove of her pussy.

Rogue almost bellowed with the pleasure as his cock sank into her velvet sheath, her slick juices easing his way. "Perfect, fuckin' perfect."

Kit shuddered at the way he filled her. Tentatively she began to move, finding her rhythm. Looking up, she could see their images in the reflective surface of the stainless steel refrigerator. God, they looked hot. She'd never feel the same in this kitchen again. Nothing of her life would ever be the same. No matter how long she had with Rogue, he'd changed her world. He'd brought wildness and pleasure into her life.

Helpless moans escaped her lips as she moved up and down on his pole. He shifted his hips and flexed his cock inside of her. The look of absolute bliss on her face as she rose up then ground herself back down, a carnal conquering. Rogue had never known he'd be so pleased to have a woman in control.

Kit bit her lower lip, moving her hips in a circular motion, taking him as deep as she could. Rogue wasn't sitting idle, as she rode him, he played with her tits, sucking her nipples, making her want to weep with pleasure.

"Kitten," Rogue murmured as he drove deeper and deeper into the tightest little pussy he'd ever known. Her inner walls clung to his dick, fighting to keep him within her when he'd pull out only to push back in.

"Touch me," she begged, taking his hand and pushing it down to her smooth mound. A bolt of lightning flashed between her legs as the pads of his fingers played with her clit. He rubbed his fingers around the hard little nub. Swollen and needy, she closed her eyes in gratitude when he began to fuck her faster.

Rogue was about to blow. Juice was coating his fingers as her whimpers begged him to continue. "Cum for me," he demanded as he milked her clit, his fingers working in time with the motions of his cock.

That was all it took. Kit came hard, her orgasm overtaking her in a blinding rush. An explosion of pleasure shook her, shattering her focus until all she was aware of was where they were joined and how he made her feel. His hands held her, caressing her back as she came down and when she did, she realized he was still rock hard inside of her. "What can I do?" she asked.

Rogue smiled. "Squeeze me."

As if accepting a pleasurable challenge, Kit wrapped her arms around his neck and began to kiss his throat. "How hard?"

"Let's see what you got."

Kit longed for him to really see her—as beautiful, capable, someone worth having in his life. Despite all of his assurances and compliments, Kit was afraid he was missing the real her. The one who was perilously close to falling in love with him.

Whoa!

Her heart was running way ahead of her mind, and her body was the bridge. At this moment, she held Rogue close to her heart and she had the chance to show him how she felt. This wasn't sex.

They didn't call it making love for nothing.

With everything she had, Kit showed Rogue how she felt. She wound her fingers in his hair, kissing him on the face, neck and lips. Moving her hips, she massaged his cock, tightening and grasping, squeezing and milking – drawing him in and gripping him in the most intimate caress a woman can give a man. Harder. Faster. She loved him until he was growling, grazing her nipples with his teeth. Kit kept up a tantalizing, irresistible rhythm until he shuddered, pumping his hot seed into her welcoming channel. With a sigh, she buried her face in his neck and came too. For long moments after, they sat entwined, still joined – reluctant to let one another go.

* * *

"Okay, now where were we?" After they'd cleaned up the kitchen and showered together, which proved to be as fun as it was sexy, Rogue was determined they would come to some type of understanding.

Kit was still towel-drying her hair. She sat cross-legged on her bed and watched as Rogue fastened his belt, hooking the buckle. He'd had to put his same clothes back on, and for a moment she wondered what it would be like to live with him. It might be old-fashioned, but she'd iron his shirts and jeans. Taking care of a man like this would be a pleasure.

She knew what he was asking, but she chose to ignore it. Taking money for him felt wrong. "We got sidetracked when you went all Dom on me."

Rogue put his hands on his hips, narrowed his eyes and smirked at Kit. "I don't do the ropes and leather thing. I'm the real deal, Kit-Kat, I'm naturally dominant."

Her body flushed hot. "You let me make love to you today."

"I was still in control, every moment and don't you forget it."

His blunt words turned her on more than putting her off, but she pushed the inclination away. He was right, they had things to discuss. "I think I was in the process of explaining to you that I won't...can't accept charity from you." To emphasize her capping the topic, she got up to leave the room. "Let's go to the living room where we can talk without the distraction of a bed."

Behind her, Rogue laughed. "Don't think the absence of a bed is going to make you any less sexy. We just made love in a kitchen chair, for fuck's sake."

Again, she ignored him. While they were in one another's arms, she'd been able to forget her problems momentarily. But while she'd managed to push the note and Dave out of her mind for a while, that didn't mean the problems weren't real, pressing and...hers. Not Rogue's.

Rogue followed, trying to not look at her butt. God, she had a good butt. Round, firm and heart-shaped, he'd really enjoyed warming it up. The only thing he regretted was it hadn't been bare.

As he made his way down the hall behind Kit, his eye was caught by a series of photographs on the wall. "What's this?"

Wincing, she stopped in her tracks. The photographs! God, no! She'd completely forgotten about them. "Just some old pictures, nothing you'd be interested in." Turning, she grabbed his arm and tried to forcibly propel him forward. To no avail. It was like a kitten trying to move a Great Dane.

"I want to look." Rogue glanced behind him, saw a light switch and flipped it on. The paneled walls were golden oak and the framed photos were arranged in groupings of five. More intriguing than their artistic flair was their subject matter. Kit. "This is you roping." He folded his arms and leaned closer to study the images. "I like these, whoever took them understood action shots."

She hugged herself, waiting for some off-hand remark about how she looked. The girl portrayed in these keepsakes was the Kit that Rogue had seen, judged and rejected. The granny bun, thick glasses, plain face and boyish clothes hadn't been just camouflage. Red dress girl who had stripped Rogue of his clothes and his asshole attitude had been the imposter. Since that time she'd morphed into some combination of the two, and she hadn't done it all because of Rogue's reaction to her changed appearance—she'd done it in part because she longed to be pretty.

"I've told you this before, but you were great. You held the best time in the record books up until just a few months ago."

Don't let him see it. Don't let him see it. "Quit wasting time looking at those old things. Come on, let's go discuss…"

"Is this me?" Rogue bent closer. "Hell, it is me."

Kit shut her eyes tightly, wishing either she or Rogue would disappear in a poof of smoke.

"Why?" He turned to ask why, only to see her disappearing around the doorway. "Kit?" Rogue headed after her. "What's going on?" By the time he reached her, she was huddled in a corner of the couch, legs under her, head lying in her own lap.

Kit had made herself as small as possible. She was so embarrassed.

Rogue asked again, "What is my ugly mug doing on your wall?"

He knew. He had to know. She'd told him point-blank that she'd had a crush on him. Had he not heard her? "It's just a picture."

Instead of letting it go, the ego-maniac had put a hand on his chin and given her a sideways grin. "Did you stand in front of it and stare at me all googly-eyed?"

Googly-eyed? Picking up a sofa pillow, she whacked Rogue with it. "No, I forgot it was there, actually."

"Likely story." He smirked at her, appearing to fully enjoy the idea that she might have mooned over him, standing in the hallway and staring at his picture.

Kit wasn't about to explain it to him, but she'd had that photograph framed about six months before their blind date. True, she came close to destroying it after he'd hurt her so much. But she'd found it one day, years afterward, when the wound wasn't so fresh and she'd brought it back out, hanging it in its place when she'd moved into this house. "Hush," she tried to ignore him.

"So, you named your horse after me and hung pictures of me on your wall." Rogue was having a good time. He wasn't being mean…in his mind he was flirting.

Exasperated, Kit tried to explain. "We owned the horse before I ever met you on the circuit."

"Yea, likely story." He teased, sitting down beside her.

Realizing what was in front of her, Kit leaned over and picked up the heavy statue. It took a bit of hefting, she picked it partway up and Rogue hurried to help her. "This is Rogue Angel," she announced. "Dad bought him two years before I began college. I have no idea where he came up with the name. He doted on the horse and…" Kit pushed her hair over her shoulder. "He was worth doting on. Rogue was a champion. Every horse we have is descended from him. My father always said that Rogue Angel would take care of me." She ran her hand over the bronze. "He gave me this right before he died."

Rogue had sobered. He took the statue. "I can't vouch for the horse's name, but if he looked like this he was a beautiful animal."

Kit smiled, relieved he wasn't picking on her anymore. "I often wondered about the name. A rogue angel would be a fallen one, wouldn't it?"

A sad smiled shadowed Rogue's face. "Oddly enough, my name's Rogue Michael. Not exactly the angel the term 'rogue' would apply to, I believe."

"You're no devil, Rogue," Kit said, trying to make light.

Rogue was studying the statue. "Did you know this is an Aron McCoy?"

"A what?" She didn't have a clue what he was talking about.

"Aron McCoy is a talented sculptor from central Texas where I'm from. He's friends with my lawyer, Zane Saucier."

"The statue's value to me is because it's from my father, not who sculpted it," she stated, tracing the carving on the plaque. "He always said the Rogue Angel would take care of me. I guess he thought the money from the stud fees would always give us something to fall back on." She shrugged. "My father was pulling the stallion behind him when he hit that damn tree." Gesturing toward the statue. "Dad said this was my own personal Trojan horse, whatever that means."

"Hmmm, odd," Rogue murmured, turning the horse over and looking at it from all angles. The whole thing was about eighteen inches high and the stallion was standing on all fours wearing a bridle and a saddle. Setting it back down, he locked eyes with Kit. "I'm not an angel, Kit. But if you'll let me, I can help."

Kit's stomach clenched. "I don't know what to do." Even though she tried to stop them, the tears began to flow.

"Let me help. Do you have anything I can look at, financial information, insurance information?"

His sincerity shook her to her core. He really wanted to help – and God knows she needed it. "I can't let you do it for nothing." She let out a long breath. "Would you consider being an investor, a partner?"

"I'd be honored." He held out his hand. "Let's shake on it."

She let him enfold her hand in his. The contact felt solid, permanent, warm and safe. "Deal." Kit started to kiss him, but didn't think that was appropriate business deal behavior. "Come on. Let's go to my office, I'll give you what I have."

Rogue went with her, eager to see what she could show him. He had a lot going on with Dusty's company and his own, but he felt a sense of excitement knowing that he could help Kit. Standing back while she opened the door, she shocked him when she cried out.

"Rogue! Someone has been here." He stepped over the threshold and saw that her office was ransacked. Papers were everywhere and the file cabinet was on its side.

He pulled his phone out of his pocket and called the cops.

"Maybe being my partner isn't a wise decision." Kit sighed. Could things get any worse?

Chapter Nine

Dave Parker pulled into the motel and slammed out of his car. "Fuck!" The drive from Red Creek to Hutchinson had only given him more time to think. But so far, thinking had gotten him nowhere. Where in the hell could Will Ross have stashed those bearer bonds?

Glancing around the parking lot of the Shady Hill Motel, Dave made certain he saw no one who would recognize him. Not that he knew anyone in Hutchinson, but with his luck he had to be careful.

As he made his way into the office to rent a room, his mind was full of panic. He had no money and nothing to hock.

"Can I help you, sir?" the clerk asked, standing behind a counter with a bored expression on his face.

"Yea, give me a room, king-size bed, by the pool if you have it." Not that he felt like swimming. Maybe he'd drown himself.

Dave gave the clerk his last hundred dollar bill, then looked down at the meager change. He needed a card game. Taking the plastic key card he was given in exchange for the greenback, Dave turned, almost knocking down a woman in the process. "Excuse me," he grated, heading for the door. What was he going to do next, knock off a convenience store?

Frowning, he studied the sidewalk as he returned to his car. Everything had gone to hell in a handbasket. All of his carefully laid plans were crumbling around him. Almost blind with agitation, he climbed into his car and started the engine. He'd just backed out of the parking place and was easing across the parking lot toward the room he'd rented when his cell phone rang. Snatching it up, he looked at the caller I.D. "Barnaby Miller."

"Barnaby, what's up?" He knew what was always up with Barnaby. Texas Hold 'em.

"There's a game next week. Want in?"

Dave felt the familiar rise of lust. Some men got off on women and sex. He found his pleasure in fifty-two cards and the luck of the draw. "You bet." He found himself answering before his brain was engaged.

"Great. We'll be playing in the back room at the Red Rooster bar."

Even as Dave hung up, he was wondering what he could get his hands on to make that game happen. Maybe this time, his luck would change. Life owed him. Will Ross owed him. Nothing had been the same since Sheila had chosen Will instead of him. He'd taken everything that should have been Dave's, including the investment in the Rogue Angel Gas Field.

* * *

"I don't understand why someone broke in." Kit huffed, hands on her hips. "They didn't take anything." She and Rogue had spent three hours cleaning up the mess. After the cops had come and looked around, they'd determined there wasn't much they could do. There was no evidence of a break-in, it appeared that Kit had left the garage door open. Since nothing seemed to be missing, they told her to take more precautions next time.

"I think it was Dave," he announced out of the blue.

Kit whirled. "Why would you say that?"

Rogue shrugged. "I don' know, it's just a hunch. He gives off a funny vibe. Any man that will trick his wife into signing a note for a quarter of a million will break into your house. He's up to something."

"But what?" Kit asked. "I don't have anything worth stealing."

She had a point. "I don't know." Putting his hands on his hips, he took one last look around.

"I won't tell my mother that, not till I know more. The very idea would break her heart."

"Well, there's one thing we can do." He turned and walked out of her office.

"Where are you going?"

"Check your locks."

"They don't need checking." He didn't pay her any mind. Instead, he looked at her doors, fussed at the lack of deadbolts and made a list of things he'd need to fix it. "You don't have to do this." Even as she protested, Kit had to admit it felt good to have a man see to things like this. No one had taken care of her since her father died.

"I know I don't have to." He kissed her on the end of the nose. "I want to." Rogue gave her a wink. "You're my partner."

Kit felt a stab of regret. She knew the score. A partner was a good thing. Pity her poor heart wanted more. "We're more than that, Rogue." The little demon on her shoulder decided to tease him. Watching him stiffen didn't do a whole helluva lot for her ego.

"Sure we are." He gave her a swift grin. "We're friends."

"Yea, friends with benefits." With that emotional volley, she grabbed his hand. "One of the benefits is that you get the insider's tour of the ranch and get to sample some of Cook's meatloaf. Let's go, partner."

The sexual innuendo got his cock's attention. "Kit-Kat, what you've been doing to me surpasses benefits, I think this is more like friends who've hit the erotic lottery." He caught up with her, wrapped his arms around her waist and nudged her sweet ass with his swollen dick.

Part of her wanted to lead him back to the bedroom, but they had too much to do. "As much as I'd like to stop and play powerball with you, I would feel better if we worked out the details of our relationship—our business relationship."

Dang, she doesn't have to be so emphatic, Rogue thought. He knew what their relationship entailed, he'd set the damn boundaries himself.

During the next few hours, Rogue saw a whole new side of Katherine Ross. The day of the Viagra debacle, as he thought of it, Kit had been as concerned about one-upping him as she'd been about showcasing White-Wing. Today, she poured herself into telling him and showing him why she loved her home. They started in the lodge and she proudly carried him from room to room—kitchen, dining, the billiard room and out to what she called the dance hall, a large open room with hardwood floors where a band could play and people could celebrate in whatever manner they chose.

"This is great." Rogue looked around, checking out the facility.

"I think so." She ran her hand over the keys of an upright piano. "We've already had a couple of events here and I'm hoping to have a lot more."

Rogue crossed his arms. "We need a sound system in here." He pulled out his phone and made a note.

"Do you think so? Most bands have their own, don't they?"

"Sometimes, but if you have one installed, there's always a back-up, plus the regular guests can use them for their functions. It's a smart thing to do."

"I can't afford it." Kit sighed. "I have to make the most of what we have and try to get the funds coming in before adding on more debt."

"Not if your partner takes care of it." Rogue grinned.

"Rogue, before we go any further, let's hash this out." She grabbed him by the hand to lead him to a chair and he whirled her around, kissing her lips. "What are you doing?"

"It's a dance floor, I'm dancing." Rogue laughed, he was in a good mood. The stuff with Dusty seemed a million miles away.

"Be serious," Kit chided. "I want to talk to you about your investment. How does this sound? You get twenty-five percent of all the take, beginning today. What do you think?"

Rogue seemed to consider her words. "Fifteen and only after all expenses and only till the notes are paid in full. And I'll be responsible for the note payments until such time that you're caught up."

His generosity was a little overwhelming. "You know, you're

more like your father than you know."

Rogue froze. "How?"

Kit realized she'd offended him. "You're generous. There's hardly a family or a business that Dusty didn't step up and help or bail out. He's been our area's greatest philanthropist for years."

"You do know what he did, don't you? I told you about my brothers. But I didn't tell you they were by three other women—none of them his wife. He cheated on his wife with four women and sired a bastard by each one."

There was no way Kit could stop herself. She put her arms around his neck and hugged him. "I'm so sorry. I know how important a father is, I wish you could've had a childhood as good as mine." Kit sniffed, then giggled. "My father loved me dearly, but I knew he always wanted a boy. I did everything I could to make him not regret me. I don't think he did."

Rogue held her tight. "There's no way anyone could ever regret you."

Kit's heart dipped. "There's no way Dusty regretted you, either. Or you wouldn't be here today. Didn't you say he left you and your brothers his business?"

"Yes, he did. That's what I have to do next week, all week. I have to step into Dusty's boots and try to walk in his path."

"You're taking on a lot. With your own business and Walker Mineral, I don't know if you have time to take White-Wing on too."

Rogue kissed her on the temple. "I have time for White-Wing because I have time for you."

Kit felt feelings rise that stole her breath. She could not afford to get too attached to this guy. Rogue had made it very clear that he only wanted a casual friendly association. And her brain agreed, her heart and body were more difficult to convince. "Okay, shall we go on?"

"Sure, you lead the way."

For the next couple of hours, she carried him over the entire property. They toured several of the cabins and the grounds. Before heading out to the lake and woods, Kit ducked into the kitchen and picked up a picnic basket she'd had Cook put together. "I think you'll like this," she said, holding up the wicker container. "We're having some of my specialties."

"I'm sure I will, smells great. Allow me." Rogue took the container from her, following her outside.

"Let's take the horses. We can see everything better," she suggested.

"Perfect." A woman after his own heart. She escorted him to the barn where they led out two of the horses, saddled them up and started off. "Let's head over to that far ridge to the north." Kit pointed. "I want to tell you about the deer."

As they rode, he was struck again how graceful she sat her mount. "I have to confess something to you," he began. "When I hurt you back in college, when I said all of those things…"

Kit didn't want to hear it. She didn't want to be reminded of that time. Things weren't different, she felt different. "There's no need, please."

"Yes, there is." Rogue insisted. "You've got to know that the problem I had with you was never your looks. You might not have been as flashy as the girls I hung out with, but the reason I balked at spending time with you was because you were better than me. I resented you because you were a girl and you were more talented."

"That's debatable, I was lucky."

Rogue was beginning to think he was the lucky one. With her long hair streaming back behind her, she looked like a Native American princess. As they topped a hill, a movement caught his eyes. "Look, whitetail."

They brought their horses to a stop. "Yes, we have about two hundred head of deer here. A special ten foot fence keeps them on White-Wing."

Rogue leaned on the saddle horn, one arm crossed over the other. "Kansas whitetail are bigger than the ones we have down in

Texas. I know one guy that was going to bring some down to go on his ranch. There's a legal way to do it, but he didn't get the permits. This fella trapped them, tranquilized them and loaded these deer on a small plane." Grinning, Rogue finished his story. "The only problem was that about halfway there, they woke up." He laughed. "Talk about a problem. Once those deer started moving around, he had to make an emergency landing. He had to pay a big fine."

Kit giggled. "I guess deer on a plane was worse than snakes on a plane."

They laughed and rode on. Rogue asked intelligent questions. He wanted to know what services and guides they provided and what White-Wing charged. "Do you process the deer for the guests?"

"Yes and there's a cook provided for their overnight camping trips, if they choose to rough it rather than returning to the cabins." To Kit's surprise, he kept making notes on his phone. And when they rode across the fields to get nearer to where the pheasant nested, he took photos.

"We need to get a professional photographer out here. I think we need to make up some brochures and buy some advertising in Garden and Gun, maybe Southern Living or Texas Monthly." He named some well-known periodicals. When Kit looked skeptical, he eased her mind. "This is something else I'll take care of. Investments like these are what's going to make the difference between a full house and vacancies."

Kit knew he was right. "I guess I don't have the best head for business."

"Nonsense." Rogue shook his head as he looked around. "Your vision was spot on. All we need to do is let people know about it. Next we'll work on the website and some social media." When he saw her amazed look, he winked. "I don't know how to do this stuff. But when I got Lone Wolf off the ground, there was this young guy back in Austin who established an online platform for me. I'm sure the same type rules will apply."

For the first time in a long time, the knot in Kit's insides seemed to loosen. "I'm not sure how I can ever thank you. All of this is so unexpected. You didn't have to do any of it, you didn't owe me anything."

Reaching over, he took her horse's reins and tugged the mare closer. When he had her near, he leaned over and kissed her. "I never do anything I don't want to. And I want to do this." He captured her lips again and kissed her until the horse danced away, forcing their mouths apart.

Kit didn't say anything as they turned to ride toward the lake. Rogue took the lead on the trail and she hung back, the fingers of one hand covering her lips where he'd kissed her.

For the next hour, she showed him the docks and fish cleaning stations, the trail that led around the lake for horseback riding and the area far away from the livestock that had been designed for skeet and target shooting. Finally, they ended up at a shady area near the lake. Dismounting, she raised her arms over her head and stretched. The hem of her shirt rose where he could see a strip of tanned, smooth skin. As she flexed, her breasts were thrust out and Rogue felt his cock respond. This erection wasn't due to any oil beneath the ground, it was due to the sexy woman at his side

"Well, what do you think?" she finally asked.

"About what?" He teased, knowing full well what she meant.

Giving him a smirk, she expounded. "What do you think about the ranch, partner? Are you still willing to make the investment?"

"I am. I'll get Zane on the papers as soon as we get back to the lodge."

"Are you ready for a picnic?" She took the basket from behind her saddle.

"I'm hungry all right." As she spread out a blanket and sat down the wicker container, Rogue untied a length of rope from his saddle.

"Are you coming?" Kit asked as she bent over.

"Soon," Rogue whispered as he twirled the rope over his head and let it go, smiling as it gently settled over her shoulders. Before she knew it, he tightened the rope. "Gotcha."

"Rogue!" Kit squealed as he took her by surprise. "What are you doing?"

"Flirting with you, is it working?" he asked as he threw one leg over the horse, stepping down, never letting go of the rope.

"Maybe." She gave him a sly little smile. "You've caught me, now what are you going to do with me?"

Going to her, Rogue walked up behind her, wrapped her in his arms and pulled her back flush to his front. Pressing his cheek to hers, he answered, "That depends on how much privacy we have out here."

Kit smiled, all of her female parts perking up at the possibilities. "Almost total. No one has any reason to come anywhere close today."

Sliding his hand to her neck, he tilted her head back, brushing his thumb over her lower lips. "Good, because you're impossible to resist."

Kit's stomach bottomed out. She looked up at him, drowning in his eyes. Her heart was pounding. "Rogue..." she whispered, shocked at herself at what she wanted him to do. She wasn't certain if he truly cared for her or if he was still, in his own way, trying to make up for past mistakes. Did it really matter?

"Kiss me, Kit," he whispered. Collaring her throat, Rogue angled her head and began to devour her mouth. Taking command of the kiss, he ravished her with lips and tongue. His chest eclipsed her back, she felt small and helpless, at his mercy. Tremors of excitement shook her to the core as he crushed her mouth with his and left her with no question as to who was in charge of her pleasure.

Knowing he didn't need the rope to keep her in his arms, he gently removed it, turning her in his embrace. She tasted like sunshine, spring and desire. He rubbed his face on her skin, knowing he'd leave a mark – and liking it. "Lie with me," he instructed, guiding Kit to her back on the blanket. Taking her wrists, Rogue pulled them over her head, holding them securely in the grip of one hand.

"I love kissing you," she murmured just before he delved deep, taking complete possession of her mouth, laving and seducing her with his tongue. His other hand wasn't idle, he palmed her breast, flicked her nipple, then moved to grasp her hip, holding her still.

Beneath him Kit writhed, bucking upward, wishing she could get closer. Her head spun and her heart took flight. The only thing tethering her to the earth was Rogue, so she clung to him, wrapping her arms and legs around him, rubbing against his thick cock. He seemed to enjoy it, Rogue rode against her, humping the vee between her legs, causing her sex to vibrate with electric arousal.

"Open up," he moaned and she spread her legs wider, giving him more access. The noises of his appreciation made her shiver. Rogue knew how to please a woman, and Kit was grateful the woman was her. With a whimper she surrendered, tangling her tongue with his, arching against him and rubbing her breasts back and forth against the hard muscles of his chest, scrubbing and gyrating on the hard cock nudging between her legs.

"I need your hands on me," Kit begged.

Rogue raised his head, taking in air in harsh gasps. "I have to be careful of you, I have to protect you," he whispered, his eyes searching her face before he slanted his mouth over hers for another consuming kiss.

Kit couldn't wait, she slid her hands between them and started unbuttoning her shirt. "My nipples ache, Rogue." Her breath hitched as he rose up to help, spreading her shirt and pushing up her bra. As he did that, she worked below the waist, undoing her pants and wiggling her hips to get them down just enough and off.

"You have the sweetest nipples," he muttered, watching them

bead, harden and swell.

Kit never knew she could be so aroused. The way he stared at her, as if he had to have her, made her almost crazy with need. "Suck them." She made a demand of her own.

Licking his lips, he swooped down, latched onto her nipple and drew it deep into his mouth, suckling hard.

She couldn't keep quiet, it felt too good. Every tug he made on her nipple, she felt it directly on her clit. Rogue held her tight, grunting his enjoyment as he all but swallowed her tit. The intense pleasure made it impossible for her to think. She weaved her fingers in his hair and yanked him even closer. Like he couldn't get enough, Rogue moved to her other breast, licking and abrading it with his teeth before sucking it hard into his mouth.

Kit almost swooned. She never knew her nipples were so sensitive, but Rogue showed her she was capable of feeling so much more than she ever dreamed. She reveled in his attention and he didn't let up, Rogue kept coming back for more and more. He kissed, nuzzled and nursed, sucking at her tits until her nipples were red and throbbing. Her pussy was pulsing, her whole sex ached with hunger for him. "Rogue!"

"Ask me," he instructed. "Tell me what you want."

She started to say 'fuck me', but she couldn't get the words out. That's not what she wanted. Kit wanted it all. With a pang of loss, she knew she wasn't going to get it – but she could have this much. "Make love to me, Rogue. I need you."

Her entreaty inflamed him. His hand moved down to the tiny pair of panties covering her mound. He wound his fingers in the thin silk covering her crotch, twisted and ripped them from her body. "Now, let me see how much you want me." They both moaned when he dipped between her thighs and found the hot creamy center of her. She jerked at his touch. "Want me to make you cum?"

Kit felt shameless. "I want you inside me, please." In answer, he came over her, covering her mouth, pushing it wide with lips and tongue, claiming her whole body with one demanding kiss.

Rogue prepared her to accept him. His fingers rubbed her clit as his mouth glided from her mouth back to her nipple. He sucked at the hard crest as he massaged her pussy, the silkiness of her slit slick with cream. When he couldn't stand it one more moment, he took his rod in hand and stroked it. He was thicker and harder than he'd ever been. "You're killing me, Kit-Kat."

When she spread her legs wide, thrust up her hips and gazed up at him in wonder, he knew it was time. Situating himself between her legs, Rogue fit himself against her small hole. Just one touch and they both gasped with anticipation.

"Now!" she demanded.

Rogue growled, tossed his head back and bucked forward. Sliding into her tight heat, he immersed himself in ecstasy. He held still until the hunger became so wild, he lost control. With a savage grunt, he exploded. Rogue couldn't take her fast enough or fuck her hard enough, he wanted to be so deep inside of her that he couldn't tell where one of them began and the other ended. Shoving in and pulling out, he took them both on a wild ride. "Damn, baby," he whispered, every other woman he'd ever been with paled in comparison to this. She was his dream girl, his wet dream girl.

"More, more, more," she chanted as she pressed her body upward, her pussy tightening around him like a tiny fist. He plowed into her like this was the last fuck he'd ever have. Electric sensation raced through his body. Holding her tight, he set a desperate rhythm. Good God, she was destroying any self-control he pretended to have with her. Framing her face, he took her mouth again, finding out it was imperative to take her in every way possible. As his tongue speared into her mouth, his cock set the rhythm and she writhed beneath him—arching, moaning and blushing like a rose.

What drove Rogue crazy was that Kit didn't hide how she felt. With her fingers digging into his shoulders and her legs lifting to cradle his hips, her keening cries of ecstasy were as great a gift as the electric bliss sizzling through his own body.

"Rogue! I need to…"

"Come for me, Kit." She was writhing beneath him and he didn't let up even as she tightened around him. What he was feeling was more - the pleasure didn't just burn, it flamed, removing any memory of any other time, any other woman. His balls were heavy, tight with the need to explode.

"Yes!"

She screamed, bucking up and Rogue held her, the pressure inside him giving way. He plowed deeper, laying his face next to hers on the blanket, his breath coming in heaving pants. And then it happened—a release of ecstasy so powerful he couldn't contain it. "Kit, Kit, baby." Something inside him eased—an empty place filled and questions were answered. He couldn't comprehend it, all he knew was that holding Kit in his arms felt right.

When they'd recovered, Rogue rose and held out his hand. "Let me help you up."

Kit rose to her feet. They avoided one another's eyes as they straightened their clothes. "Thanks." She couldn't put her finger on it, but she could sense something had shifted. "Let me set the food out."

"I'll help." They sat down and spread out the goodies. "What did you make?"

"Steak sandwiches, German potato salad and Triple Chocolate Brownies."

Rogue was impressed. "Sounds great." He chuckled.

"What arc you laughing at?"

"I have to tell you, for a guy, a picnic is not something we normally look forward to."

"Oh, really." Kit held a bottle of lemonade, still partially frozen. For a moment she considered whacking him with it. "So, when I suggested we have a picnic, you dreaded it?"

"Well, yea." Rogue grinned. "Until I decided to rope you and have my way with you."

She shook her head. "Men."

"The steak and brownies help too."

"Well, I'm glad I could provide you with a modicum of entertainment," she said dryly. Searching for something else to say, Kit stared out onto the tall Kansas grass, their own version of amber waves of grain. She had no idea what caused the shift in his mood, but she did know what had changed for her.

Just what she'd been afraid of. Kit was in love.

With Rogue Walker.

"I'm going to put some of those things we talked about in motion while I'm here." Rogue began to remind her of what they'd talked about. "Get the agreement drawn up, order a sound system and get some advertising and a website started. The payoff on those things should be fairly immediate."

Her mind wasn't exactly on business, instead she latched onto the phrase 'while I'm here'. "How long will you be staying?" She did her best to keep all emotion out of her voice.

"I have to fly back to Texas tomorrow for a couple of days, then I'm coming back."

"You have to check on Jester." She smiled, hearing he had plans to return soon, but knowing she'd miss him.

Rogue nodded. "Yes, Jester, my mother and my business."

"When you come back, feel free to stay in one of the cabins," Kit said in a rush. "Or you could stay with me if you'd rather." She felt like a teenager offering to do a guy's homework.

Rogue's answer took a few moments before he voiced it. "Thanks, but I'll be staying at Dusty's house over on Osprey Lake. It's one of the stipulations of the will."

"Oh," Kit said flatly. "Good." She tried to brighten her tone and not let her disappointment show.

Rogue felt like he was on one of those amusement park rides where you're slung from the left to the right, then sent spinning around in circles, leaving you with your stomach clinging to your backbone for dear life. He wanted to run away from this woman as fast as his feet could carry him and he also wanted to grab Kit up and take her back to bed. "I'll call you," he offered.

Relief flooded her heart. "Okay."

"After all, we're partners," he said before taking the last bite of brownie.

"Right." Rogue had just burst her bubble and didn't even know it. "Partners."

Chapter Ten

"Is that all you can give me?" Dave Parker stood at the counter of a Wichita pawn shop with Will Ross's guns. He'd slipped back into the main house while Sheila had been asleep and lifted everything of value he could find. Knowing her, it'd be days till she noticed anything was missing. She was too caught up in her own little world to be very observant.

"Yep, what you have here is more functional than collectible." The clerk soothed a hand down the barrel of a Holland and Holland shotgun.

Dave felt like the man was pulling his leg, but he had no choice. "All right. I'll take it."

Seeing a gullible prospect, the clerk leaned forward and whispered, "If you're short of cash, you can talk to a friend of mine. He'd be willing to make you a short term loan?"

"Oh, yea?" Dave knew better, but he pressed on. "Who?"

"My cousin, here's his card. Give him a call."

Taking the card, Dave glanced at it. "Rex Ranford, Quick Cash, No Credit Checks." The very paper it was printed on felt greasy. "Thanks, I might do that."

Pocketing the money the pawn shop clerk gave him for the guns, he turned to go. Going to a loan shark wasn't the smartest idea, but beggars couldn't be choosers.

Once in his truck, he stared out the windshield. The weather was so hot, the concrete sidewalks might soon melt and buckle. Last night he'd dreamed about days long past, when he and Will Ross had been young. Dave had been the one who was courting Sheila, admittedly with dollar signs rather than stars in his eyes. When Sheila turned her roving eye to Will, Dave had begun to hate him. And when Will married Sheila, earning her devotion and her father's inheritance, that act proved to be the last straw as far as Dave was concerned.

545

Dusty Walker had also been their running buddy. When Dusty, like Will, had married for money, Will had been the first to tell him he'd be sorry. Hypocrite. And the word currently spreading through town proved that Ross had been right. Dusty had spread his seed around as liberally as a farmer planting corn. Four women and four sons. Dave had no idea if Theresa had known. Who knows? Maybe they had been arguing when the car crashed.

Slowly, he lifted the phone and slowly he dialed the number. Maybe this would be his lucky break. It was his turn. Over the years their fortunes had taken different directions. While Will and Dusty seemed to have the Midas touch, Dave's luck had soured. The more he gambled the more he lost. Will had even taken pity on him, buying his land and having Dave owner- finance it. Will had the audacity to tell Dave that he wanted to do it that way so Dave would always be assured of having money coming in every month.

"Ranford." The brusque voice sent chills down Dave's spine.

"Yea, this is Dave Parker. I'm calling about a loan."

"Good. How much?"

As Dave made the deal and arranged for pick-up, his mind went back to Will Ross. He hadn't proved to be Dave's friend. Their friendship had gone on the skids when Will and Dusty had pooled their funds to invest in Lucius Angelo's venture. Dave had told them there was no oil in that dry well. He had nothing to chip in but hard feelings. And Dave had been proved right, but not in the way he'd hoped. The field had no oil in it, but it turned out to be one of the biggest gas finds that the country had ever seen. Lucius had always had a sense of humor, he'd called the field Rogue Angel, a play on his name being so closer to Lucifer and his station before the fall. Now no one called the field by the name Lucius gave it, now they just affectionately called it 'Hell'.

And hell was what Dave had. Jealousy ate at him like a cancer, especially after he learned that Dusty and Will had cashed out of the operation, hiding their profits from Uncle Sam by taking bearer bonds, a half million dollars' worth of bearer bonds each. Everyone knew what Dusty did with his, he added it to Theresa's money and built Walker Mineral.

But Will...Will was a different story. The only thing he'd spent money on had been that damn horse he'd bought and named after the gas field. Even when he'd almost lost the ranch, had to sell his cattle, he'd been careful and conservative. Once Will had fathered that daughter, Katherine, he'd settled down.

But those bonds, those bonds existed. And Dave wanted them. He deserved them. Will had been in the way and Dave had gotten rid of him. It had been fairly easy. A little tampering with the brakes at just the right time and Will and that stupid horse had run off the road on Half Moon curve and plowed straight into a tree. After that, it had been fairly easy to reassert himself back into Sheila's life.

Cranking up his truck, Dave headed to where the loan shark had told him to go. This was his final shot and he knew it. Something had to work, the odds were in his favor. For the last three years he'd turned White-Wing upside down looking for those bearer bonds. He'd convinced Sheila to let him renovate the house, even getting her to sign a note for the funds. Dave had given her a sappy story how he wanted their marriage to be free of memories, make their own place. And as the workers had gone from phase to phase, he'd been there first, searching under every floor board and behind every wall.

Nothing. The bonds weren't in the main house. Now he knew where they had to be. That bitch of a daughter had to have them. The ironic thing was that she didn't know it. If she had, she would've used them to get herself and the ranch out of hock instead of scrimping and working herself to death with those stupid horses.

So, he had to get rid of Katherine. He hadn't been so lucky the night he'd stuck a sharp skewer in her tires, she should've had a blowout. Instead, she'd been rescued by Dusty Walker's bastard.

Next time she wouldn't be so lucky.

* * *

When Rogue got back to Texas, a few things surprised him. First, Elijah had stepped up and filled his shoes admirably. Second, Jester had thoroughly charmed his mother and last but not least...

He missed Kit.

He couldn't stop thinking about her.

Taking a break, he slipped off to his office and placed a call to her. It rang five times. Finally, she answered with a giggle. "Hello?"

"You sound happy. What's going on?"

"Rogue, hey!" She giggled again. "I'm so glad to hear from you."

"Sounds like it. What are you doing?"

"I'm showing Garth around." Another giggle.

"Who's Garth?" Rogue wasn't smiling.

"Oh, you know Garth Busch, running back for the Kansas City Chiefs." An additional giggle rang in his ear like tinkling bells. "He came to check out White-Wing, they're thinking of giving a hunt as part of an incentive program."

"Ah, yea." Okay, this sucked. "I talked to a friend of mine at a travel agency in Austin. He said he'd put it on some trip adviser sites. I'm sure that's where the recommendation came from." Great, he had tried to do a good deed and lured a damn football player in to hit on his girl.

Whoa! His girl? Rogue rubbed his head.

"Thank you, Rogue," she said sweetly. "Can I call you later? Garth and the guys are waiting on me."

"Sure thing," he said, so jealous he knew his skin matched his eyes. "Bye."

She said goodbye too, but it was fleeting and accompanied by male laughter.

Dammit.

Back in Kansas, Kit wasn't having nearly the good time she

548

pretended to be having. The players were nice enough, but they were asking for things she didn't know if she could provide. When Rogue called, she'd wanted to throw the whole weight on his shoulders and ask him to take care of it.

But she couldn't. He was putting in money and that's more than she could hope for. A few days ago, at the picnic, she'd presumed too much, offering to let him stay with her. Who was she kidding? She was really asking him into her bed—again.

And he'd said no. Rather easily and smoothly. No. Rogue had said there was a stipulation in Dusty's will that he had to stay at his father's house. Could that be true?

Maybe.

Either way, he wasn't here, he wouldn't be here and she had to stand on her own two feet.

Rogue Angel wouldn't be taking care of her.

Immediately a contrite feeling filled her. He'd done more for her than any other man other than her father. She was just greedy. After having a taste of life with Rogue, she wanted it all.

After she had escorted the committee from the Chiefs to the dining hall and seen that they were served, she had answered a call from her mother. One that she had ignored twice already. "Hello?"

"Katherine, your father's guns are gone. Did you take them?"

"No." Kit assured her. "I didn't. They're gone?"

"Yes." Sheila's voice rose. "Do you think I've been burglarized? There's no sign of a break-in."

Knowing how Rogue had seen that her locks were changed, she now felt guilty that her mother's might not be up to par. "Call the police and let them come check it out and I'll be over as soon as I can."

* * *

Rogue hung up the phone after talking to Zane. He was putting together his contract with Kit to invest in White-Wing. Pouring himself a cup of coffee, he pushed Jester out of the way to get to the refrigerator. "Do you mind?"

549

"He wants some apples," Marian announced.

"You spoiled him while I was gone." Rogue didn't mean to sound grumpy, but he couldn't help it. Kit hadn't called him back.

"What's wrong?" his mother asked. "Come sit down and talk to me."

Reluctantly he joined her at the kitchen table, watching as she fed Jester sugar cubes. His mother could read him like a book and he wasn't ready for her to know what was really bothering him. She would jump to conclusions, get all excited and be ordering a wedding cake if he wasn't careful. He'd never dated a woman more than twice and he'd seen Kit any number of…

A cold stab of reality knifed him. He'd never taken Kit on a date. They'd eaten together, slept together – had amazing sex, but he hadn't so much as bought her a cup of coffee. Not unless you counted the breakfast he'd bought and brought back to her house.

"Rogue," his mother said. "Are you listening to me?"

Jerking his head up, he answered with a smile. "Of course. What did you say?"

She swatted him with the end of a dishtowel. "This carousel horse pays better attention to me than you do." Her smile faded and she asked, "Is it your father? Are you worried about what you have to do?"

Covering her hand with his, he smiled sadly. "Can I honestly tell you how I feel about this?"

"Of course, you're my son." Marian looked at him with all the love in her heart shining in her face. "You're the light of my life. No matter what your father has done, he gave me you and that was worth it all."

Wow. The woman sure knew how to take the wind out of his sails. "I wish I could be so charitable." He took a deep breath. "When I think about those men who are my brothers and that company I'm supposed to want to help run, all I can see is what he took from you."

Marian rose and hugged him. "You can't look at it that way.

Dusty was a much better man than you're giving him credit for. He was generous and kind. He was good to me."

"Yes, but he cheated on you. He cheated on his wife. He lied to everybody." Rogue let the bitterness boil out.

Marian placed her hand on her son's heart. "Rogue, I was happy. Your father made me happy. He couldn't give us everything, but he did his best to provide for you."

"I used to watch those stupid sitcoms on television and imagine we could have a normal family." If money was how love was measured, Rogue was well-loved by his father. But that wasn't what he'd needed from his dad, he'd been hungry for attention. The ten or so weeks a year Dusty had seen fit to give Rogue hadn't been enough.

"I wish you could see how much you're like your father."

Rogue knew his mother meant well. But hearing the words repeated that Kit had said just made his stomach clench. "I'm nothing like my father." Maybe he should rephrase that. "I don't want to be anything like Dusty Walker." His mother had no idea how the idea scared him. He didn't want to make promises he couldn't keep. And he certainly didn't want to bring a baby into the world he couldn't make time for.

"Rogue, sweetheart..." His phone buzzed. "Who's that?"

Lifting the phone, he saw Katherine Ross on the screen and his heart bumped funny in his chest. "I've got to take this." He gave his mother a smile, but no information.

"If it's a woman, I need to know," Marian called out as he left the kitchen.

"When did you become a psychic?" Rogue yelled back at her, then laughed at her whoop of joy.

Answering, he lowered his voice. "Ralph's Mule Barn, Ralph speaking."

"Oh, sorry, wrong number. I was trying to reach Channing Tatum, we have a date tonight."

At the mention of her dating, he bristled. "Maybe you're

trying to reach Garth Busch?"

Was he jealous? "Don't be grumpy. Garth actually turned into a good thing, we booked three hunting excursions this fall."

"That's good." He breathed a little easier. What was wrong with him? "What else is going on?"

"My father's guns were stolen."

Her flat announcement made him stop in his tracks. "Another break-in?"

"Not really. I had them do fingerprints, but they didn't really want to. I told them I thought Dave took them and the local cops, some of them his friends, didn't seem to think that would be a crime."

"Hell." He let out a long breath. "How are you? Really?" Rogue lowered his voice, making their conversation seem more intimate.

Kit clenched her fist and took a risk. "When are you coming back?"

Rogue decided to tease her. "Why?"

"Why?" Kit repeated his question with a smile. "Maureen is coming back and she's asking for you."

With a snort Rogue smiled. "Is Maureen the only one who wants to see me?"

"No," Kit answered lowly. "I've noticed you were gone."

"Ha!" Rogue laughed. "You're mean."

"No, I'm sweet." She countered with a mischievous giggle.

"Yes, dammit, you sure are." Jamming his hand down in his front jeans pocket, he backed his ears and took the plunge. "How about if we take in a movie when I get back up there?"

Kit's heart thudded in her chest. "You're asking me out on a date?"

"Yea, I know we sorta got the cart before the horse, but – how about it?"

"Yes." She said too quickly and probably too loudly.

"Good. I'll call you when I get there."

"I'll be waiting, Rogue Walker." They lingered for a few more moments, listening to the other one breathe.

"Sleep well, Kit-n-Kaboodle."

Oh, she would. "Goodnight." And she knew exactly who'd be starring in her dreams.

* * *

This time, Rogue didn't fly. The drive took about eight and a half hours, but it would be worth it. He needed the time on the road to think and he wouldn't be beholden to Dusty Walker for a vehicle. Twice more he'd talked to Kit, not long conversations, just touching base. When she'd found out he was driving, she'd asked him to check in so she would know he hadn't fallen asleep behind the wheel.

Her worry made him smile. Kit was sweet.

When he drove into Red Creek, the whole thing hit him differently. This time it seemed everybody stopped on the street to look at him. He knew he was imagining things, the residents had no idea what he'd be driving. Hell, they probably weren't even thinking about Dusty Walker and his bastard sons. Still, he met the eyes of several people who smiled and waved—and what the heck—he waved back.

Sooner than he'd liked, Rogue pulled up in front of Walker Mineral. The whole place needed a face-lift. It certainly didn't look like a company worth a half billion. Parking, he climbed out, locked his doors and headed for the entrance. Right before he turned the knob, the door opened. Rogue jerked his hand back, raised his head and met two green eyes behind some tinted reading glasses. "Well, hello. There's no mistaking you for a traveling salesman."

"I suppose not," Rogue answered dryly. "I suspect the view's been a bit boring, having to look at different versions of the same face all month."

The woman threw back her head and laughed. "Hardly. At least it's a handsome face." She stepped back and opened the door wide. "Welcome, Rogue Walker. I'm Abby Hollister, the receptionist/bookkeeper. In other words, I keep this place going."

"Glad to meet you." He shook Abby's hand and followed her into his father's sanctum. She waved her hand around. "So, this is it. Your inheritance. Today, Elaine and I will be getting you up to speed. Would you rather sit at Dusty's desk?" Abby pointed in an office with a desk stacked and piled with papers. "Or a smaller..."

Rogue stepped into his father's former office. "This will do just fine. If I want a true feel for the place, I need to get right to the heart of the matter."

This seemed to surprise Abby, but she smiled. "Great. Elaine Dennis, one of our mineral and oil rights specialists will be here any moment and she'll give you the rundown, start teaching you the ropes."

Rogue sat down in the chair and began leafing through some of the folders. "I'll be up to speed in no time, I think." He waved his hand around. "This isn't new to me, the apple didn't fall very far from the tree."

"What do you mean?" another voice spoke up. Rogue looked toward the door. A pretty woman stood there, her dark hair streaked with silver.

Rogue looked from one woman to the other. Both were older than him, but he wouldn't hazard guessing their ages. And he wasn't about to ask, he wasn't dumb. "I have a small business back home, Lone Wolf Oil."

"Rogue, this is Elaine. Elaine, this is Rogue." Abby gestured, her blonde curls bobbing around her head.

Elaine crossed her arms and leaned against the door jamb. "I've heard of Lone Wolf, but I had no idea that was you." She grinned. "You have quite a reputation. I've heard some unusual things about you."

"Believe everything you hear," Rogue answered evenly, then gave Elaine a big smile. Standing, he shook her hand. "I'm sure there's a lot you can teach me."

"I doubt that," Elaine said, sitting down at one of the chairs in front of Rogue's desk.

"Let me get you two some coffee," Abby offered. "I don't usually do this, Rogue. So don't think it's going to be a habit."

"I understand, Abby," Rogue countered. "I'll get the next cup for all of us." Turning to Elaine, he tapped a folder in front of him. "I've studied the financial statements and the royalty reports already. If you'll show me the maps and charts of any ongoing work, I think I can catch up quickly."

"No problem. Vic and Walt should be in tomorrow and between the three of us, we'll make sure you get to visit several of the sites this week."

"Sounds perfect." Rogue accepted his coffee from Abby. "Thank you."

For the next three hours, Elaine and Abby briefed Rogue. He absorbed what they said and made copious notes. Finally, Elaine leaned back and looked Rogue square in the eye. "I haven't asked your brothers this, but since you're number four out of four, I'd like to know before I go any further."

Rogue leaned back in his chair. "Go ahead."

Casting a glance at Abby, Elaine placed her hand on the desk and asked, "Your brothers were no slouches, they're all intelligent guys. But you're different. You could step into Dusty's shoes tomorrow and fill them. You're way ahead of the learning curve."

"I realize that." This was no time for false modesty, Rogue knew.

"So, do you have any intention of staying, of working at Walker Mineral? Or are you just fulfilling the requirements of the will to cash in on its sale later?"

Rogue took off his Stetson and tossed it to his right where it landed on target, catching on a hat tree standing next to the wall. "I can't make any promises. My future plans were pretty much laid out before this bomb was thrown into my lap."

"This bomb is a damn fine company worth a helluva lot of

money." Elaine pinned him with a glare.

"Yes, it is." Rogue nodded. "But you have to look at this from my viewpoint. Dusty Walker wasn't my favorite person when he was alive. I had no idea about the clones…" He paused and thought. "Hell, I can't even remember their names. My business is based in Texas and who in their right mind would leave Texas to move to Kansas?"

"Depends on what kind of incentive you have," Abby chimed in, slapping a piece of paper on Rogue's desk. "Kit Ross just called. She says there's a special showing of Me Before You tonight and wants to know what time you'll pick her up."

Elaine raised her eyebrows and grinned. "I'll get someone to paint your name on one of the parking spots downstairs."

Chapter Eleven

"We could have been seeing Fantastic Four or The Man From U.N.C.L.E. but instead, we're seeing some chick flick." Rogue gave Kit a hard time. Frankly, he had to distract himself with something other than how fantastic she looked. Dressed in a halter top dress with a barely there skirt, all he wanted to do was take her to bed.

"I am a chick, in case you haven't noticed." Was her snappy comeback.

"Oh, I've definitely noticed." Rogue drove his truck into Red Creek's city limits. "Where's the theater?"

"Two blocks off Main, next to the Fire Department." She pointed and he turned at the light. "Look, there's a parking place."

Kit waited in her seat until Rogue came around to help her out. Her eyes followed him as he walked in front of the truck. Watching the handsome hunk coming to escort her into the theater, Kit pinched herself. They'd slept together several times. So why did this perfectly normal date seem so momentous? Before she could analyze the situation her door opened and there he was.

"Is this movie gonna make you cry?" he asked teasingly.

"No, but you might. It's a love story without guns. I don't even think anything gets blown up."

Rogue snorted. "You might be right."

She took his arm and noticed three or four other women pausing to look at her date. Her date. That's right. Kit gave the jealous females a cool gloating stare.

A bit of guilt ate at her. "There are other movies showing, we could see something else."

Rogue placed a hand on her lower back. He didn't know what was more fun to touch, her curls or her spankable ass. "You must have wanted to see this show, you chose it. It's a romance, isn't it?"

His touch was making her tremble a bit. "It's a love story, but not a romance. I read the book and I loved it." Yes, she loved the book and she had every intention of watching it when it came out on blu-ray. This date wasn't about the movie.

"Well, that's good enough for me." He kissed her on the cheek. "We'll just take turns, the next movie we see has to either be a horror or a bromance."

Kit laughed. "Deal." She waited while he purchased their tickets and then when they got inside he bought a giant box of popcorn, a large soda and a box of chocolate raisins for her. "We're going to get fat."

"Calories consumed on dates don't count." He winked at her as they went down the hall and turned into the darkened theater. "Where do you want to sit, down front?"

Was he kidding? "No. I don't like to sit too close. Let's go to the back."

Rogue glanced at Kit curiously. "Okay. Whatever you want."

Once they were settled, she ate a few grains of the popcorn and put her chocolate treat into her purse for later. Not many people came to the back and no one was in the last row where they were or two rows in front of them. For all intents and purposes, she and Rogue were alone...just the way she wanted it.

Once the lights were down, Kit sat there a moment while Rogue continued to eat popcorn. The show started out pretty slow and she saw her date fidget in his seat. He wasn't enjoying it, but he was doing it—for her. Well, it was time he was given a little reward.

Slowly...casually...oh so casually, Kit let her hand wander from her lap over to his. Holding her breath, too excited to inhale, she fit her palm over his cock.

Rogue had been about to put three or four grains of popcorn in his mouth when... "Fuucck," he whispered, tossing the entire bucket of buttered popcorn high into the air.

Kit had copped a feel.

Rogue

A hailstorm of small white fluffy goodness rained down on half the crowd. Dozens of people turned around to look at them. Rogue lifted his hands in apparent confused disbelief. He had to be the one to show his hands because one of hers was very busy.

Even now she was palming his cock, which was enthusiastically swelling at her touch.

"What do you think you're doing, Kit-Kat?" Rogue asked out of the corner of his mouth. "Are you trying to get us thrown out?"

Did he not want her to? Suddenly doubt hit her and she moved her hand so quickly one would think she'd been burned. "No."

Not the reaction he intended. Like lightning, he flashed out his hand and grabbed hers, returning it to its former position. "Don't you dare stop."

In the low light she studied his face and what she saw gave her confidence to continue. Rubbing. Caressing. She loved the growing ridge beneath her fingers. He was getting into it, his eyes never leaving hers, even lifting his hips slightly to encourage her to continue. Dare she?

Feeling brave, she began to undo his belt. But that damn longhorn belt buckle wouldn't cooperate. Turning to him, she doubled her efforts.

"Take two hands to handle a whopper?"

His whispered comment made her giggle so hard she snorted. "Watch the movie, I'm busy here."

"Hell, baby, I'd much rather watch you." When had he had so much fun? To his delight, she worked till she freed his cock and then all he could do was rest his head back and revel in her touch. There were moments when he closed his eyes and just felt – her palm gliding up and down his rock-hard shaft, her thumb swirling over the sensitive head, rubbing the pre-cum all around the flared crest. At other times, he couldn't take his eyes off of her, she sat there so innocent and demure with eyes on the screen while she blessed him with a hand-job so good his toes were curling in his boots.

Finally, he couldn't stand it. "Spread your legs." Two could play this game.

Kit didn't hesitate, she was so turned on she was about to faint. Thank God for dresses. With a sneaky little smile, she waited to see what he'd say when he found out...

He crossed his arm over hers so he could slip his hand up her skirt. All the time she never let go of his cock, continuing the up and down motion that was driving him crazy. Scooting the material up, he let his fingers dance on the silkiness of her thighs, up – up – until he could touch paradise. "My God, woman, you're commando!"

To Kit's chagrin, his voice carried and she sank down in the seat, which just served to give him better access. "Oh, my goodness," she whispered and when his fingers found her clit and began petting, she added another, "Oh, my goodness!"

Yea, this was a small town, her reputation was probably in tatters—but this very second, Kit didn't give a damn.

In all of Rogue's years of sexual adventures, he'd never done anything like this. It was risky, it was fun and it was exciting as fuck. He didn't know what he enjoyed more, her greedy little hand on his cock or the sweet wet heat of her pussy. She was aroused because of what she was doing to him and that was the single best head rush he'd ever felt.

On-screen Lou and Will struggled with their problems. Off-screen Rogue and Kit played, pleasuring one another with soft rhythmic touches designed to bring them release. And when it came, hers triggered his and he leaned over and captured her cries into his own mouth. The kiss grew and held, becoming a sweet lingering kiss of promise.

Rogue was reluctant to let her go. Even though this had been at her instigation, he wanted to protect her. So, he gently removed his hand and straightened her skirt, tucked his cock back in and zipped up his pants. Then, he pulled her close with an arm around her shoulder and tucked her head under his chin until the credits rolled.

"I'll buy you the DVD," he promised.

"It's a sad movie, at least what we did had a happy ending," she murmured as he led her from the theater.

"I'll say." Rogue chuckled. Escorting her to his truck, he kept his arm around her and anyone who appeared to be looking at them funny received a steely-eyed warning. "I thought we'd go to the Roadhouse and get a steak. As far as I can tell, that seems to be the best choice."

"Sounds good to me," Kit said, amazingly aware of his seemingly possessive arm around her waist. When they were in the truck and headed to the edge of town, she couldn't quell her curiosity. "So, how did your first day at Walker Minerals go?"

Rogue was a bit surprised at his own positive mood. "All in all, it went well. I still have to go to the house and meet the housekeeper and the caretaker later on tonight, but I don't foresee any problems."

"That's a relief." She'd known he dreaded it. "The sound system is supposed to be installed tomorrow and the woman you contacted about making the website called me today."

"Great." Rogue was pleased. "Tomorrow two of the geologists are taking me with them to check out some sites."

"Do they know you are more than qualified to run the whole business?" Kit couldn't keep the pride out of her voice.

"I hinted at it." He laughed. Quicker than he expected, they were at The Roadhouse.

This time Kit waited on him to come open her door. She could get used to this type of treatment. "They have good steaks here and a chicken Marsala that I'm fond of."

"What I need is something to drink. That movie took a lot out of me." He grinned, watching her blush. She was so adorable.

Once they were inside, the hostess led them into the restaurant and seated them at a corner table where they could have some privacy.

"This is nice, thank you." Kit smoothed her napkin. She'd been here before, but being here on a date with Rogue made everything seem better. The colors were warmer, the people more friendly and the food smelled delicious.

"Wine?" he asked. When she nodded yes, he motioned for the waiter and asked for their best merlot.

They'd no sooner ordered before a woman came to the table. Kit knew her face but it was a moment before she could remember her name. "Hello, Ms. Clark. Rogue, this is Ellen Clark. She owns the pharmacy in town. Ms. Clark, this is Rogue Walker."

"Nice to meet you." Rogue took her hand.

"It's very good to see you," she responded. "After seeing your brothers around town this month, there was no mistaking who you were. I've been hearing good things. It seems Rori, Lexie and Zoe have especially enjoyed meeting the Walker boys. Should we be expecting a double-double wedding?"

Kit felt her face flame. "No!" she answered quickly. "Rogue and I are just friends and business partners. He's advising me on some changes at White-Wing." Knowing how Rogue felt about commitment, she felt extremely uncomfortable.

"That's right." Rogue nodded. "I'm always looking for a good investment." He put a smile on his face but her declaration didn't sit well with him for some reason.

"I see." Ellen Clark put her nose in the air. "If what I hear about Dusty is true, that doesn't really surprise me."

"If you'll excuse us, Ms. Clark, we're trying to decide our next move." Rogue held the woman's gaze until she backed down and left them with a barely civil goodbye.

Kit was sure the next move he wanted to make was back to Texas. After the meddling woman had returned to her table, Kit apologized. "I'm sorry, but that's a small town for you. Everybody loves to know everybody else's business.

"No worries. You can't tell me anything about small places and smaller minds. My mother and I heard it all, believe me."

Not wanting their evening to be spoiled, Kit purposely brightened. "Let's not allow her to ruin our good time. Tell me about Jester."

Rogue followed her lead. "Well, Jester totally charmed my mother. I think she gave him his own shelf in the refrigerator. What have you been doing?" he asked as he pushed a strand of hair behind her ear.

"I've been working with a young horse. Her name is Diamond and she's showing potential. As you know, getting them to the point where they can anticipate what we want them to do is key."

"True, I admire you. Mariah was already trained when I bought her." Rogue picked up the pepper shaker and turned it around between his fingers. "Let me ask you this. If White-Wing comes into its own and you get all the business you can handle, which do you plan on focusing on? Running the lodge and the tours or training horses?"

Kit smiled. "I hope to have that problem someday, but if everything works out I'll hire someone to help my mother manage things so I can stick with the horses."

"I knew it." Rogue winked, seeming to be happy that he understood her. About that time the waiter brought their food. "This looks good. Dig in." As he ate it dawned on him how erotic it was to watch a woman eat. The glide of her lips on the fork, the delicate movement of her throat as she swallowed, the way her tongue came out to decadently lick her lips.

"What's wrong?" Kit asked.

"What?" Rogue blinked his eyes.

"You looked frozen with your hand in the air and your fork halfway to your mouth," she explained. "Are you hurting somewhere?"

"Ah, no." He took the bite, chewed, swallowed and repeated the process. She kept watching him curiously.

"Are you not having a good time? Do you want to go?"

Was she kidding? At her questioning stare, he let out a low

laugh as he sopped gravy from his plate with a piece of dinner roll. "I'm having the time of my life. There's just certain parts of my body that are behaving badly."

She didn't respond right away. Kit studied his handsome face as if trying to ascertain if he were serious. "Let's go," she announced quietly.

"No, really." Rogue assured her. "I'm enjoying myself."

"Get the check, you're about to enjoy yourself more." As he took care of the bill, she politely folded her napkin, retrieved her bag and stood.

"You've got my attention." Rogue followed her out of the well-appointed room, tipping his hat at a few people who smiled or waved. He didn't know who they were, perhaps they knew Kit or thought he was one of his brothers.

By the time she got to the door, he was there to hold it open for her. "Where are we off to in such a rush?"

"We're going parking," she announced. "No poison ivy this time, so don't worry." At his surprised expression, she continued, "You have someplace to be tonight and I won't be able to sleep without having felt you inside me. So, we're going to find a quiet dark place and—"

"Fuck," he breathed.

She realized what he said was more of an exclamation than an explanation – but it was correct all the same. "Exactly."

When they arrived at his truck, he helped her in, fastening her seatbelt. Needing to let her know how he felt, Rogue touched her cheek. "There's something about you that I can't resist. I don't pretend to know where this is going, but I do know I'd rather be with you than anywhere else in the world right now." He kissed her gently on the lips and tears welled in her eyes. Then she gifted him with the most dazzling smile Rogue had ever seen.

"I feel the same way. I know this is just casual, but I wouldn't trade our time together like this for anything."

He didn't say anything else, just gave her an intense look,

went to his side and crawled in. When they were underway, she gave him some directions. "Go out of town toward White-Wing but take the first left. There's an abandoned farmhouse down there, we won't be disturbed."

Rogue shook his head. He wasn't surprised at the sense of déjà vu he felt. "Why don't you think we'll be disturbed?"

"It's supposed to be haunted, most people stay away from the area."

Rogue threw his head back and roared with laughter. "Well, okay. Never let it be said that I let a ghost or two get in the way of making time with my favorite girl."

Kit smiled, she enjoyed the designation of 'favorite girl'. She gave him directions and in no time he had turned off onto a narrow dirt road where the trees and the undergrowth grew so tight on either side that it felt like they were driving into a tunnel. "Just keep going until you see the overgrown bungalow. We can park there."

He drove faster than he should have, he was just that turned on. And the woman beside him wasn't helping. The scent of her, the shape of her. He could see her in profile, gorgeous face, a delectable body. Wait…what was she doing?

Rogue almost ran off the road when he realized that Kit was cupping her own breasts, her eyes closed, head thrown back in ecstasy while she pulled at her own nipples. His cock went crazy, it would've stood up and shouted if it could have. "Turned on, baby?"

"Absolutely."

"Little nipples need to be sucked?"

"So bad," she whimpered, too horny to be inhibited.

"Do you want me to fuck you?"

"More than I want my next breath."

Rogue pulled in the drive, shut off the engine and reached for her. "Over here. Now." He gave instructions, but he didn't wait for her to follow them. He lifted her up and guided her over his lap to face him. As Kit straddled him, he lifted her skirt and thanked heaven she wore no underwear. There was simply no time. With one hand he probed her drenched opening and with the other he took out his cock, rubbing the end of it from the back of her slit to the front.

Kit whimpered and laid her head on his chest. She dug her fingers into his shoulders. "Rogue, my Rogue…"

"What do you want, Kit-Kat? It's yours."

"I want you hard." Her breath hitched. "I need you deep. The ache is more than I can stand."

He didn't speak, he just gave her what she needed. With one violent upward thrust, he filled her up, driving his cock to the hilt.

"Oh, my God!" she keened.

"Good?"

"Oh, yes!"

"Want more?" He flexed his cock inside of her and felt her grasp at him with her inner muscles.

"Please, please, please," she murmured.

Holding her by the waist, he pulled out and plowed back in with a mighty thrust. She gasped and moaned, her sugar walls tightening around him. Reaching between them, Rogue traced the bare mound of her pussy, letting his finger verify the place where they were joined. "You're stretched so tight. Does it burn, baby?"

"So good, so good," she wailed.

Her unfettered response ignited his blood. He was desperate to take her, to possess her. His fingers skating up her sides, he held her slight body high on her rib cage, his thumbs rubbing her nipples. With a slight lifting motion, he slid out and crashed back. "Ride me, baby."

"Yes." She understood. Placing her hands on his shoulders, she began to rise and fall – undulating up and slamming down on the pole of his erection, every move accompanied by little cries of feminine lust.

Rogue's eyes rolled to the back of his head. She was like

lightning in his arms, the rhythm she set was exquisite. Together they danced, her pussy milking his cock with every gyration. Faster and faster, tighter and tighter, Kit kissed his chest from his pecs to his throat, her teeth grazing his skin.

"I can't...I need..."

"Coming, love?" Complete pleasure overtook him, he panted, jackhammering into her over and over again.

"Yes!" she screamed, her fingers tearing through his hair as she convulsed in his arms. Rogue held her tight as she let go.

The perfect repeating grasp of her pussy around his cock set him off. He pounded into her once more, jetting a hot stream of his seed deep into her pussy.

Pure white hot bliss.

Rogue cradled her to him, the quivering tremors of her pussy massaging his cock. "Are you all right?"

"Yes." She sighed, going limp in his arms. They held one another for long minutes until Kit sat back, kissing him sweetly on the lips. "I guess you should take me home. You have places to be."

"And people to see," he agreed. Reluctantly he lifted her from his cock, then reached into his glove compartment to get a soft paper cloth to clean them up with. Once they were straight, he turned on his lights and the beams highlighted the spooky old house. "Dang, I wouldn't want to spend the night in there."

"No, there's a sad tale here. A girl killed herself over love. He broke up with her and she couldn't handle it, she took cyanide."

Rogue frowned as he started the truck. "Fair to say they must have had a one-sided affair."

Kit playfully slapped his arm. "Don't be mean."

"Never," he assured her. "Never would I be mean to you."

"Thank you."

Rogue pointed to the house. "Do you want to go ghost hunting before we leave?"

"No, it's getting late. Don't laugh, though, many people have seen her over the years, sometimes they say her mouth and lips look burned from the poison."

Rogue did an exaggerated mock shiver. "Woo-ooo."

"When are you coming out to White-Wing?" she asked, then hastily added. "To check things out, I mean."

"Soon." He sighed. Right now life was good. "I'll call you tomorrow when I know what my schedule will be."

"Okay." She wanted more, but pushing a man like Rogue would be a fruitless task.

"I had a good time tonight," Rogue said, his hand finding hers in the dark.

"Me too."

"Hey, look." Rogue pointed ahead. "Is that a girl walking on the side of the road? Something must be wrong." He stared. "What the heck?" The beams of the headlights seemed to go right through her.

"Don't stop," Kit said emphatically.

"Why?" he asked, glancing at her, an odd cold chill covering his body. "She might need help."

"We're too late to help her. That's the ghost."

When Rogue turned his face to look back down the road, the girl was gone.

They were quiet for a few minutes, seeing something unexplained made them both feel funny.

Suddenly, Kit felt something brush her leg. She squealed and jumped.

Rogue laughed. "Gotcha!"

"You wish."

She shot back, but she was the one who was wishing. She wanted Rogue with every breath in her body. But what did they say?

If wishes were horses, then dreamers would ride.

Chapter Twelve

Driving away from White-Wing had been hard. Rogue had felt the indeterminate pull to stay. It was the sex, it had to be.

He was addicted to sex with Kit.

Oh well, he grinned to himself, there were worse things to be addicted to.

The drive from White-Wing to Dusty's house on Osprey Lake took about a half hour. It was nearing midnight when he pulled up to the sprawling stone and wood structure. The place reminded him of the lodge at White-Wing, just more luxurious. Floor to ceiling glass windows reflected the high beams of the truck. As he pulled in next to the garage, he saw that somebody had left the lights on for him.

Climbing out, he closed the door and took his duffle from the trunk. Since he'd be staying here a day or two, he might even unpack. As he walked up toward the door, a chill passed over him. He'd already seen what could've been one ghost tonight, was he about to see another? Knowing that Dusty and his wife had lived here made Rogue uneasy. Taking a deep breath, he stopped and stared into the darkness. The moon was high in the sky and its reflection glittered on the lake. He hadn't realized this was waterfront property. Prime waterfront property. Glancing around, he could see that Dusty had spared no expense.

His mother's small house came to mind. They'd spent his lifetime in a structure small enough to fit in the front foyer of this grandiose barn. As his eyes adjusted to the darkness, he could see the manicured lawn and the sidewalks winding among landscaped flower beds. The whole place reeked of money. And while Rogue had nothing against money, this whole business made his stomach hurt. His reaction to the business hadn't been this visceral. Maybe it was because Dusty had lived with his wife here.

While his mother and the other women he'd duped lived

elsewhere. Far away with their children. The sons of Dusty Walker.

"Are you coming in or are you going to stand outside all night?"

Rogue whirled, seeing a motherly looking woman framed in the light flowing from an open door.

He didn't move.

"Rogue Walker, get your ass in here. It's getting late and I've been waiting up for you."

"Yes, ma'am." He was a Texas boy and Texas boys were polite to women, especially women old enough to be his mama.

His response brought a laugh from the woman's lips. "I'm gonna like you." She held the screen door open for him and he walked into a kitchen made warm by soft lights and great smells. "Cinnamon rolls?"

"And milk. Sit yourself down."

A man walked up from behind the pleasantly plump lady with the kind face. Who did he look like?

"Lou, this is Rogue. Rogue, this is my husband. He's a good man to have on your side. Do you want a roll, honey?"

Lou took Rogue's duffle. "No, save me one." He nodded to Rogue. "I'll put this in the room Marliss made up for you, second floor, west hall, last room on your right. You'll like it."

"Yes, sir." Arguing with Lou was probably fruitless.

"The keys to the vehicles are on the pegboard by the back door. Use what you need." Lou pointed behind him and to the left.

"I brought my own truck, thank you." He didn't want to drive anything that had belonged to Dusty. In fact, he wasn't going to do one damn thing he didn't have to. A new sense of rebellion was boiling up inside. What had brought this on? He'd been feeling relatively calm.

And then he realized. The pictures. It was the pictures that covered one solid wall. Dusty's image had been caught in a dozen different poses, some with fairly famous people. Many with an attractive woman he assumed to be his wife.

Marliss placed a warm fragrant cinnamon roll and a big glass of milk on the table. "Eat up."

"Couldn't I have coffee?" Rogue asked.

"No, it's too late. You need your rest. You've got a big day tomorrow." She puttered around and handed him a napkin.

Rogue drank his milk. "This is good." He didn't realize he'd been hungry. Dinner was cut short, he'd had other things on his mind.

"Of course they're good. Lou made them." When Rogue looked surprised, she laughed. "He and Cubby are always in competition about something. Which is good for me and Sherry. Cubby introduced some new cinnamon rolls at the Creekside Café, so Lou had to show him up."

"I think he did," Rogue said around a mouthful. "Did you sweeten up Dylan, Jackson and Killian this way?"

Marliss shook her head. "No, we saved the best for last." She winked at him. "I hear you're seeing Kit Ross."

Rogue stopped chewing. Marliss had gone from coddling to meddling pretty fast. "We're old friends." That was as good an explanation as any.

"That's not what Sheila said." She patted Rogue on the arm. "Never mind. We'll talk more about this tomorrow." She began to turn out the lights, then picked up his plate and glass. "If you'll be down here at seven, I'll have pancakes and bacon ready for you."

"I don't usually eat breakfast," Rogue muttered.

"I bet you did while you lived with your mama." She went to a closet and opened the door. "And you'll eat breakfast while you're staying with me." Marliss handed him a big thick book. "If you can't sleep, here's something for you to look at."

"What's this?" Rogue asked.

She took him by the arm and started walking him toward the stairs. "I'll show you around the place tomorrow."

"What's in this book?" he asked again.

Marliss smiled at him. "You. The topic of that book is you."

* * *

Rogue wiped the condensation off the side mirrors of his truck. His image was obscured by fog, much like his life. He felt as if he'd been living on the outskirts of something big that he hadn't even known was there, existing on the fringe and never realizing what he'd been missing. The scrapbook had been a revelation. He'd stayed up until three, staring at photograph after photograph of himself as a baby, a toddler – playing sports, riding horses, attending church, his whole life on display. His mother had to have sent Dusty the pictures, but Rogue had never known. The pages of the memory book were well worn as if someone had touched and stared at them repeatedly.

This morning, frankly, he didn't know how he felt. Marliss had sensed his mood and his restlessness. She'd plied him with strong coffee and blueberry pancakes. "I won't bother you this morning, but we'll talk when you're ready," she'd said.

Now he was on his way to the office to meet Walt Forester, another of Dusty's mineral and oil rights specialists. Today he was going out in the field. Rogue wondered how his brothers had reacted to this situation. It was second nature to him, and if he was going to be honest, Rogue was excited. Lone Wolf was young, his resources were limited. Not so with Walker Mineral. The idea that he could play in the big leagues of the oil business was exciting.

When he arrived at the office, a middle-aged man with a paunch and a fringe of grayish-brown hair was waiting on him out front. "Rogue?" he called as soon as he cut the truck's engine. "There's no use going in. We have a lot to do."

Before Rogue could agree or protest, Walt had opened the passenger door and joined him. "Hope you don't mind if we take your truck. Vic has the company vehicle and mine's in the shop."

"Not at all." Rogue shook his hand. "Nice to meet you."

"I've heard a lot about you. Elaine was telling me you're Lone Wolf out of Austin."

"I am. We're just starting but I signed a pretty lucrative deal a few days ago."

"Not surprised. You're Dusty's boy. I don't know what he told the others, not much I'm thinking, but he confided in me while we traveled. We're closer to the same age, been friends a long time. He was proud of you," Walt confided.

Rogue felt a knot form in his throat. He didn't really want to hear this. Trying to maintain the level of animosity that he'd harbored for his father for so long was beginning to be difficult. But he wasn't ready to turn loose of it—not yet. "So, what's on the agenda for today?"

Walt waited a few moments to reply, probably digesting the fact that Rogue didn't want to talk about his dad. "Well, we've got two places to visit. Let's drive north out of town and head west. There's a small farming community about an hour away that's fixing to give Kansas a few more millionaires. I think we've found something."

As they drove Walt talked and Rogue listened. "I've seen a lot in my time and Dusty saw even more. A few weeks before he was killed, we talked about the craze sweeping the prairies of Kansas. Your father built a good business buying up leases for oil drillers. Up until a few years ago, he was purchasing leases for around fifteen to twenty dollars an acre. Now those prices have shot up into the thousands of dollars."

"I know what you mean." Rogue nodded. "It's the same in Texas, Louisiana and Oklahoma. Horizontal drilling has made a big difference."

"It's almost like a gold rush," Walt noted, adjusting the air conditioner vent to blow more directly on him. "New technology is turning acreage once thought to be drained dry of oil and gas into huge untapped reserves that will produce for the next century."

"I agree." Rogue followed Walt's directions as he pointed which way to turn. "Hydraulic fracturing coupled with horizontal drilling has changed the complexion of the oil industry in our country. I've heard estimates that two trillion barrels of oil are waiting to be drilled, nearly twice what's available in the Middle East and North Africa."

"Dusty was in the middle of it all," Walt said. "Because of his foresight and optimism, thousands of jobs have been created in our state. Landowners are receiving huge payouts from leasing agreements and soon from royalty checks."

"Yea, Dusty was a saint," Rogue drawled.

"Well, no." Walt smiled. "He was a human being with all the requisite faults, but a keen sense of humanity. If he saw a need, he tried to meet it and that's a characteristic you don't find every day."

Rogue was so tired of people singing Dusty's praises that he didn't know what to do. So, he tried to change the subject. "You know what I envisioned us doing today?"

"What?" Walt asked.

"I figured you spent most of your days at local courthouses, searching through handwritten records scribbled in land books."

Walt chuckled, rubbing a hand over the smooth dome of his head. "Hey, you're not that far off. That's still the only way here to track down ownership of mineral rights to countless acres of wheat fields. Today we'll be meeting up with some landowners to see if we can get them to sign."

"A visit from you is like Ed McMahon stopping by with a big check from Publisher's Clearing house." Rogue slowed down as he came into a speed zone.

"I don't think he actually worked for them, that's an urban legend," Walt mused. "But you're right, we make people's dreams come true."

"Competition must be fierce."

"It is," Walt agreed, "that's why we're here today. We need to get this sewn up. We've been working on the Wright Field for months and losing your father could have set us back, so we've doubled our efforts to make sure that doesn't happen."

Rogue

"You know, I used to think of Kansas in terms of tornadoes and hot weather. Now, I'm seeing it in a whole new light." It wasn't just the opportunity that was changing his mind, Rogue knew it was Kit too. He just wasn't ready to consider what it all might mean. He didn't know if he'd ever be ready.

"Good. I brought you on purpose today. These folks need to see a Walker and that you already speak the language is a plus."

For the next few hours Rogue followed Walt's lead and they visited four farming families. Folks whose lives were about to be changed. When they were through, Rogue turned to Walt. "I wonder if they'll be buying yachts."

Walt laughed. "No, but they'll pay cash for their tractors from now on." As they headed back to Red Creek, Walt consulted his phone. "Look, I have to check on my car. I'm going to go out on a limb here and say you're ready to try some of this on your own. Why don't you take the Lear and fly to St. Joseph? We need to do one of those courthouse deed searches you were talking about. This will give you a hands-on opportunity to see how things work without me looking over your shoulder. Take your time, get some dinner, spend the night if you want. This is your company – act like it."

Rogue considered what Walt said. "All right," he agreed.

"Great." He handed Rogue a folder and a company tablet. "Here's all the information you'll need." When they got back to town, Walt asked to be let off at the garage. "You know where the airport is, Dusty had it built for his use a few years ago. I'll telephone the pilot and tell him to expect you."

Rogue thanked him. As he was pulling out, he had an idea. Walt was right. This was his company. He could take a guest with him if he wanted to. Picking up his phone, he gave Kit a call.

"Hello?" She answered after three rings.

"What you doing?"

"Paperwork. Yuck."

Rogue smiled. "Well, I'm your hero, here to save you from

boredom. Pack a bag and I'll be by after you in a few minutes."

"Where are we going?"

He could hear the happiness in her voice. "St. Joseph, work trip. We'll be mixing business with pleasure."

"I'm all for that. I'll be ready."

"Good." Once they'd hung up, he called Marliss and let her know. He sure didn't want to upset a woman who could make the lightest fluffiest pancakes he'd ever put in his mouth.

As he drove toward White-Wing, Rogue made two other phone calls. One to Elijah and one to his mother. After finding out everything was as it should be, he took a deep breath. He had no idea what the future held, but so far he was enjoying the journey.

* * *

Kit hadn't really known what to expect. She'd understood that Dusty Walker had been a wealthy man, but he'd never acted like it except for his generosity. The office in town wasn't fancy and she'd never been inside his house. A private jet was another matter altogether. "I like this." She touched the leather of the seats almost reverently.

"Yea, it's pretty nice, isn't it?" Rogue watched Kit lean back in her seat. The swell of her breasts was like a magnet to his eyes. He'd been busy on the trip up studying the files so he'd know what to look for when he got to the courthouse. Then he'd wined and dined Kit at the finest restaurant St. Joseph had to offer, the J C Wyatt house, a restored tour home with more Victorian ambience than Rogue was comfortable with. But that wasn't the issue. Kit had liked it, in fact, she'd loved it. They'd had pumpkin seed encrusted salmon with bacon and potato hash served with a pumpkin cream sauce. It wasn't Texas BBQ, but it had made his girl happy and that was all that mattered.

"It's amazing." She looked out the window. "The tops of the clouds look like cotton candy."

"You've flown before." He knew she had taken a jet back and forth to Texas several times.

"Yea, but I was always squished in between two people or on the aisle seat. This is entirely different." She sounded almost giddy as she stared out into the wild blue yonder.

"Okay, if that's how you want to spend your time." Rogue sighed. "Oh, well."

Almost immediately, Kit swiveled in her seat, her long hair swinging over her shoulder. "What else did you have in mind?"

He gave her a seductive grin. "I told the attendant we didn't want to be disturbed. And there's a couch behind us that looks really comfortable." The dreamy sensual look that came over Kit's face stroked his ego almost as well as her delicate hands had stroked his cock the last time they were together.

Unbuckling her safety belt, she rose to her feet and started undressing. "Doing it on an airplane is definitely on my list."

Rogue rose and began taking off his belt, then unbuttoning his shirt. He was mesmerized by the sight of Kit disrobing. She had lost most of her shyness with him, but it still turned him inside out when she would glance back over her shoulder and look at him through those long lashes, her pink tongue darting out to moisten her lips. "What else is on your list?"

Kit slipped out of her skirt and pulled her blouse over her head, leaving her in nothing but panties and a bra—a new purchase especially designed to drive one Rogue Walker around the bend. "All kinds of places and positions."

Rogue's eyes practically bugged at the sight of the tiny cream colored scraps of lace lovingly cupping her ass and tits. "Damn, baby." Coming up behind her, he gently pulled on a lock of her hair, winding it around his finger. He found he loved touching her, needing the connection. "You'll have to let me read it."

Kit couldn't help but laugh. "When I was writing it down, I made myself think of a child making a Christmas wish-list." Slipping off her heels, she faced him and once more she was almost knocked off balance by how incredibly sexy this man was.

"Rest easy, in my book you get extra points for being on the naughty list."

For a big man, he was graceful. Kit stared while he tugged off his jeans. "You know, if we had music, you could dance. Magic Mike has nothing on you." To her surprise, he spun around and finished with a hip thrust that made her clit throb. "Be still my heart." She teased him by placing her hand on her chest, then opening her front-clasp bra. There was no doubt about it, she loved to be with him. Kit couldn't imagine him not being a part of her life. A small voice in the back of her mind whispered that she was going to get hurt, there wasn't really any way around it. Was it worth it?

Hell yeah.

"You do know how to fire me up," he growled as he took her arm, tugged her close and melded his lips to hers.

The man kissed like a dream. Kit gave herself over to him, not wanting to think. She only wanted to feel. Rogue slid his hands down her arms and clasped her wrists. He was taking charge. Elation sparked in her veins, causing her blood to flow hot. Since she couldn't move her hands, she rubbed her tits back and forth across his chest, the nipples catching in the manly curls.

"God, what you do to me," he murmured, picking her up and laying her back on the couch. Before she could bat an eye, he ran a hungry hand up her leg and parted her thighs.

The plane hit a bit of turbulence and her breath hitched, but it wasn't because of the dip and sway of the jet riding the air currents. That's not what excited her. It was the man kneeling at her feet. With a hot hooded gaze, he bent his head to her pussy, licking and nibbling, flattening his tongue and passing it across the hard nub of her clit.

Slapping the leather of the couch, she moaned at the instantaneous bolt of pleasure. "Rogue, please..." She didn't know what she was begging for, but it certainly wasn't for him to stop.

Rogue didn't stop. Using his hands, he opened her wider and feasted on her like she was a banquet to a starving man. Kit whimpered loudly. There was nothing delicate about the way he ate at her. He did it with relish. No hesitation, no half-hearted effort. He knew exactly what he was doing and precisely how to please her.

She rose up, needing to see, needing the connection. Placing a hand on his head, massaging the scalp, she wordlessly let him know what this meant to her. At her touch, he looked up – never stopping, just holding her gaze. Shivers of excitement encompassed her. He was almost more than she could handle.

"Do what you did yesterday. Play with your tits for me," Rogue whispered as he planted a kiss above her mound.

Last time it had been dark, she hadn't been sure he was watching or could see that well. Now, he was here—right here. She blushed. Her breasts were so sensitive and when she masturbated, they were where she began and where she ended. Trembling, she did as he asked. With lazy motions, she circled her breasts – rubbing, caressing. Then, she cupped them, kneading and shaping, molding them between her fingers. He watched, his tongue busy on her clit.

"More," he demanded. "Touch your nipples."

His voice was like an aphrodisiac. As if hypnotized, she took her nipples between her fingers and began to rub – tweaking them, pulling them, squeezing, milking. The more she stimulated her nipples, the harder her clit began to throb.

Rogue was enthralled. The sight of her pleasuring her own tits made him crazy. He latched back on to the little bundle of nerves and sucked hard.

Kit squirmed, she couldn't be still. What he was doing to her was too much. The more she petted and played with her nipples, the more voraciously he sucked. "Rogue," she whispered his name. She was on fire. She needed…him. "Rogue, please!"

"Don't stop, I'm not through," he instructed, his voice hoarse. "Pull those sweet nipples, beg me to suck them."

Beg? Her whole body was begging. She was heated, blushing.

Her breasts were aching and her pussy was creamy wet. Kit tried to tell him, she wanted to tell him. "God, Rogue, I need you," she sobbed. As if she were caught up in an out of body experience, Kit seemed to rise above herself. All she could do was compare this wanton sexual creature to the one who had stood cringing as Rogue had judged her unworthy. How could she reconcile the two?

Rogue moved closer, his mouth closing tightly over her clit, his hands pushing hers out of the way. He gripped her nipples between his own fingers—tweaking, twisting, pulling, milking—while at the same time he sucked hard on her clit. So hard that she dissolved, she melted, pleasure flooding her loins. A need that had wound into a tight erotic knot suddenly unfurled and she splintered apart into the oblivion of a mind-blowing orgasm.

Before she could even think of coming down from the peak, Rogue stood, fisted his own cock and grasped her hips, thrusting home. Kit was lost in a haze of ecstasy. Her heartbeat thundered in her chest, she couldn't think, couldn't breathe. "Rogue!"

This woman would be the death of him. Rogue understood this. Never had he been so desperate to mate, so desperate to merge. He bellowed her name, "Kit, baby," even as he pumped inside of her, fucking her so hard that the couch was almost torn from the bolts holding it to the floor of the plane.

"Don't stop," she pleaded.

"Never," he hissed, pulling out and flipping her onto her belly, wrapping an arm around her body. Seeming to know what he wanted, she held herself up on hands and knees as he gave her support. With a possessive snarl, he pounded back inside of her, splitting her open like a ripe peach, thrusting deep.

Kit melted, she tilted her ass up and laid her head down on her forearms. "Fuck me, Rogue. Fuck me hard!"

Rogue covered her, molding himself to her body, one hand reaching up to palm her breasts. His touch spiked her need once more. She was at his mercy, an instrument for his playing. Looking back over her shoulder, she sought his eyes, needing to know what he was thinking.

"I'll never get enough of you," he whispered as he ground into her pussy, undulating his hips in luscious figure eights. "You're addictive. I want to fuck you all the time. I can't get you out of my head. Being inside of you is all I can think of."

Kit didn't know if it was the relentless pounding of her pussy, the filling, the stretching, the possessing. Or if it was his words, the idea that she held Rogue Walker in the palm of her hand that made her explode. She shook and trembled. Rogue wrapped her in his arms and kept her safe, even as he ravished her body. Kit didn't know where she ended and he began. She didn't want to know – she didn't want this to end. Clawing the couch, she pushed back against him—over and over—impaling herself on his cock, opening herself wider for him to plunge in and fill her to the brim.

Rogue was blind with pleasure. His cock sank into her again and again, deep into her lush hot pussy. As his whole body shook with pure unadulterated bliss, he felt Kit begin to quake. Beneath him, she was convulsing in a climax so hard he was afraid she'd shatter into a million pieces. And he followed her, right over the edge.

Long moments passed as he held her, kissing her smooth, silky back. "So good, you're so good, so beautiful." As he praised her, held her, letting her calm down and her breathing ease, Rogue realized they hadn't needed a plane to fly.

Chapter Thirteen

"You had a successful trip, I take it." Marliss sat a big bowl of chicken and dumplings in front of him.

"Yea, you could say that." In more ways than one. "How do you know all of my favorites—this, cinnamon rolls, blueberry pancakes?"

Marliss patted his shoulder. "Baby, I know everything about you. Everything about all of you boys. I cooked lasagna for Killian and chocolate cake for Jackson. And Dylan – the boy loves liver – go figure."

"So Dusty talked about us, I take it."

Marliss sat down beside him. "He sure did. Theresa had her own life. She traveled, she had clubs. But your dad, when he wasn't with one of you boys or traveling, he would spend time at this table and tell me everything." She smiled. "I know all about your mama and how much he loved both of you. Hell, all of you. If life had been perfect, he would've had all of you right here with him."

Rogue tried to process what Marliss was telling him, he tried to assimilate his feelings but decades of ill will were hard to push aside. "I don't see how you can think he loved us the way you say. How can a man love five women?"

"We love people in different ways, there were things about each one of your mamas that were dear to Dusty. He took pride in you."

"How can you say that? Look what he named me—Rogue. Have you ever looked up the definition of the word rogue?"

Instead of showing pity, Marliss threw back her head and laughed. "You don't know why Dusty named you Rogue, do you?"

"Because he didn't name me Sue?" Rogue snarled.

Marliss watched him clean his plate and then she reached behind him and brought over a chocolate meringue pie that was at least nine inches tall. Rogue's eyes widened. Another one of his favorites. "No, you were a celebration," she said as she sliced him a generous wedge of pie and handed it to him. "You can go look up the details in Dusty's journals and books, but there was a huge find, a gas field that was called Rogue Angel."

At the familiar name, Rogue almost fell out of his chair. "Seriously?"

"Yes, your father followed his own instincts and invested in something everyone else said was a dud. There wasn't any oil in the ground, but it was full of gas. I don't think they call it Rogue anymore, I think they call it Hell—and that's no joke, it's one of the biggest most profitable gas finds in the world. It made Dusty. He was able to pay Theresa and her father back the money they'd given him. Oh, he stayed with her, Dusty was a man of his word, but he was no longer beholden to her. And when you came along right after he received the good news that his instincts had paid off, he named you after that field."

Rogue's head was spinning. Something was clicking in his head, but he wasn't sure what it was. "Well, at least I'm glad it wasn't because he couldn't stand me."

"Not a chance. Did you look at that scrapbook?"

"Yes, I did."

Marliss went to the closet and brought out three more. "Here's some more light reading for you. I think it's time you got to know your brothers."

* * *

And get to know them he did. Rogue pored over the books and he was amazed at what they had in common. Oh, they were different—different mothers, raised in different parts of the country. But there was a common bond, a similar thread of interests and strengths. The greatest thing they all shared was the obvious fact that they were special, a huge part of Dusty Walker's life. A wave of remorse washed over Rogue. If things had been different, they could've been closer, all of them. What they'd lost, what they'd missed seemed like a huge chasm dividing the paths that each of the Walker boys walked. But what was also evident was that Dusty had been laying the groundwork for them to be united. It was as apparent as the nose on his face that Dusty had dreamed of the day when he and his brothers would know of one another and become close—become family.

It was just a shame that he had to die for that to happen.

All of this, coupled with Marliss's insight into how he got his name, Rogue couldn't sleep. So about three o'clock he got dressed and went into the office. He wanted to know more.

Once he'd let himself into Walker Mineral and got the lights turned on, he went about making himself at home. Rogue even made a pot of coffee, then he went upstairs to where the records were stored and carted back as much as his arms would hold. Then he made another trip and came back with a box filled to the brim. All of the ledgers and papers from several years before his birth to several years after now lay on and around the desk. Rogue intended to learn everything he could about Dusty Walker and what made him tick.

When Abby came in a little after seven she brought him another cup of coffee and offered to help. He waved her off and went back to work. Elaine's arrival forced him to stop and explain that he was after the big picture, he wanted to know how Walker Mineral came to be and the building blocks Dusty had used to amass a fortune and make himself a name in the industry.

Walt looked in on him and answered a few questions Rogue had and he stopped to meet and eat lunch with Vic Armasa, the other minerals analyst and then he was right back to it. Rogue made notes and looked things up on the computer. A lot of what he was seeing was no surprise, but he also began to see a pattern, places and people that had proved to be invaluable, the systematic way Dusty proceeded to get a tip, follow through and amass the leases, investors and contacts necessary to get big deals off the ground.

And then sometimes after three, he found it. In 1989, Dusty had signed a contract with Lucius Angelo to explore a site named Rogue Angel Field. Rogue stared at the name. His eyes quickly scanned down the information until he saw another familiar name, Will Ross.

Will Ross was Kit's father. Rogue could see where the two men had invested and the amount of money their investment brought. "Whew!" He let out a whistle at the amount. And there was another notation about a tax shelter and the pay-out being distributed in…bearer bonds.

Rogue sat up in his chair. Bearer bonds were bonds without any registered holder's name. They could literally be cashed in by whomever presented them without question or proof as to how the person presenting them acquired the bonds. This made them risky to own but easily transferred and you only paid taxes when they were cashed in.

Over and over again Rogue went over what Kit had told him. It was obvious Will named the horse after the mine. "Like my father did me." He huffed. Will had apparently used part of the bonds for that purchase, but according to the number he was looking at, there should be a helluva lot more money left. What had Ross done with the money? He wasn't the type to gamble it away like Parker. And he'd told Kit that the Rogue Angel would take care of her. And he gave her a statue and told her it was her own Trojan horse…

All of a sudden Rogue sat straight up. He grabbed the phone and placed a call to his lawyer, Zane Saucier. He needed to talk to him anyway, but now there was something special he wanted to ask. After he'd listened to his attorney update him on several matters, he asked what might seem to be an unusual question. "You know Aron McCoy, don't you?"

"Yes, I do. Quite well."

"He's a sculptor, I'm aware of that. And Kit has an original that her father gave her about five or six years ago. I may be crazy, but would you ask if he put a secret compartment in the bronze?"

Zane laughed. "This does sound a little odd. I'll be glad to ask but he might have a problem giving that information to anyone but Kit—if there is indeed a secret compartment."

"I could understand that. The issue is that her father may have put some bearer bonds in the compartment and died before he could tell her. Those bonds could save White-Wing."

"I see your point. Stay on the line, I'll be right back."

Normally Rogue didn't like to be put on hold, but this time he felt it might be worth it. And he didn't have long to wait, soon Zane was back. "Rogue, it's not in the statue itself, it's the wooden box the horse is sitting on. There's a spring in the bottom that opens a secret drawer."

"Thanks, buddy, I owe you," he said even as he was heading out the door – to White-Wing.

* * *

White-Wing had taken on a new life, or maybe it was her, she wasn't sure. But the world seemed brighter, the sky bluer. Everywhere she went, Kit hummed a tune. A bright smile was her gift to all she met. Even the more mundane chores she had to do around her house seemed full of joy. The mere act of cleaning out cabinets was something to be appreciated. "Where did all of this stuff come from?" She dragged box after box from the depths of the cabinet. Sitting back, she stared at the mess. "Whew!" With a hand, she pushed her hair from her forehead, she was tired and hot. A wave of dizziness made her sway. "Goodness," she mumbled. "What's wrong with me?"

Standing, she made her way to her bed to lie down for a few moments. And when she did, Kit became aware of a light cramping. Surely not. She was on the pill, this was weird. Forcing herself to her feet, she went to the restroom and pulled down her panties, adjusting herself on the porcelain seat. When she'd done her business, she wiped and something felt odd. Was she bleeding? This wasn't right. Maybe she needed to go to the doctor, she'd been on the pill for years because of her heavy cycle but never had she felt this way. Perhaps she needed to change the type of birth control pill she was taking.

A noise in the living room caused her to look up. "Mother?" she called out. No answer. "Hello?" Maybe it was one of the employees.

Another noise, this time something breaking. She stood, adjusted her clothing, quickly rinsed her hands and started toward the front part of the house. As she turned the corner, something jerked her back. A hand came over her mouth and she screamed, or tried to.

"Where are they?"

It was Dave, her stepfather. His grip on her arm tightened, bruising. Letting go of her face, he spun her around and shook her. "Where are the bonds?"

"I don't know what you're talking about." Kit was afraid, his eyes looked wild and his face was ruddy like he was about to have a heart attack.

"Of course you do, Will told you everything. He bought you that damn horse, I know he told you where he hid the bonds. I thought if he was out of the way I could find them."

"Out of the way?" Kit asked, not able to follow him. "You need to leave or I'm going to call the police." Dave was either drunk or high, she didn't know which.

"No, you're not. No police. I'll see to that. I tried to get rid of you once, punctured your tires. But you survived, unlike your idiot father. I took care of him so I could take back what was mine."

"Did you kill my dad?" she asked, stunned and horrified.

"He took everything from me—Sheila, my land, my luck." Dave was rambling now. He still gripped her hard, but he wasn't looking at her at all, he was staring outside.

"You jerk, you pompous murdering son-of-a-bitch. All of this has been you, you broke into my house, you took my father's guns. You killed him!" she screamed, pulling out of his grasp.

But she didn't get far.

Dave was on top of her. He grasped her around the throat, drew back his fist and hit her as hard as he could. "I have to have money. I lost another game. I took money from a loan shark and he'll kill me if I don't pay him back. Tell me where the bonds are hidden!"

"I don't know!" she screamed. "Let me go."

Kit struggled but there was no use. He was choking the very life from her body. Looking up into his enraged face, a terrible sense of loss enveloped her like a cloud. She'd never grow old, she'd never see Rogue again, she'd never have children…

Dave kept pressing on her throat and hope left Kit's body as quickly as her life would.

She closed her eyes, not willing to see the last moments of her life—and then, blessedly, air flowed in her lungs. Dave was gone. There was a scuffle. Kit was choking, a cruel hand was squeezing her throat. One second she was on the floor and the next she was lifted up.

"Kit, oh, baby, are you okay?"

Rogue. Rogue had come in time. He'd come to save her. Kit's arms crept around his neck. "You're here."

"I'm here."

"Just in time," she whispered against his rock-hard chest. "He killed my father, he punctured my tires, he took the guns."

"I know, baby, I know." Rogue rocked her. He held her close but kept an eye on Dave Parker, who was unconscious on the floor. "Let me call the cops." While she sobbed into his shirt, he called the law. "They'll be here in a few minutes."

"He kept talking about some bonds. I didn't know what he was talking about."

"I do," Rogue said. "And I'll show you as soon as we make sure the trash is taken out." He pointed at Dave.

Kit was almost in shock. She clung to Rogue and he never once let her go, holding her close until the man who'd tried to destroy her world was off her property. "I don't want to stay by myself."

"I'm here." He kissed her on the forehead. "Now, let me show you something that's going to cheer you up." Rogue hoped he was right. He hoped that when he found the hidden door that inside of it would be the answer to all of her problems. If not – maybe she would enjoy the notion that there was a secret hiding place in the work of art her father gave her. He led her over to the table where the horse statue sat.

"What are you doing?" Kit asked as he picked it up.

"You'll see." Gently he turned it over and probed with his finger on the bottom of the base until he felt something give and heard a slight pop.

"Rogue? What in the world?" She sat down close to him and looked over his shoulder as he removed some slips of paper.

Unfolding them, Rogue quickly verified that they were indeed what he expected. "Here, Kit. Your father was taking care of you. These are bearer bonds worth almost half of a million dollars issued by the Rogue Angel Gas Field."

She took them from his grasp, handling them like they were made of tissue paper. "I don't believe it. How?"

Rogue tried to explain. "All of my life, I've hated my name. I thought it was my father's way of ridiculing me, of hampering me with a name that would either make me stronger or do me in. When I made a comment about it to Dusty's housekeeper, she informed me that my name was a celebration of a huge profitable venture that my father had made, the Rogue Angel Gas Field. After talking to you, it hit me that all of this was just too weird to be a mere coincidence. So, I investigated the records in Walker Mineral's storage closet. Imagine my shock when I read that both my father and yours accepted bearer bonds to pay off their investment. I kept remembering what you said your father told you, how Rogue Angel would always take care of you and this horse," he patted it, "being a Trojan horse. So, I called my lawyer and had him ask Aron McCoy if there was a secret compartment—and here it is."

Kit was flabbergasted. "This solves everything, doesn't it?" She threw her arms around his neck and kissed him over and over again.

"Yea, I guess you won't be needing me anymore."

He said the words almost sadly and it hit Kit that it sounded an awful lot like he was telling her goodbye.

* * *

As promised, he had stayed with her. She'd slept in his arms and he'd made love to her gently. And it hit her that her Rogue Angel had taken care of her, in more ways than one. He had walked in at just the right moment to keep Dave Parker from killing her and it was Rogue who'd figured out what her father had meant and led her to the answer to her prayers.

But he'd gone home the next morning and she was left still not really knowing what the future held for them. Were they just friends? Were they still business partners? Did he want more from her than just sex? She knew what she wanted from Rogue—everything. But we don't always get what we want.

The hard part had come when she'd had to break it to her mother than the man she'd married was a liar, a cheat and a murderer. Her mother had wept in Kit's arms. She'd felt better when Kit informed her about their windfall and that their financial woes were over.

Everything would be perfect if it weren't for two things. She wasn't sure where she stood with the man she loved and two—Kit felt like crap. What she was going to do about Rogue, she didn't know. She'd thought about confronting him, just flat out asking. When he'd left this morning, he'd given her those words that could mean something or nothing. He'd said, "I'll call you." Didn't he know a woman needed more than that?

As far as her physical well-being was concerned, Kit was heading to the doctor. She had an eleven o'clock appointment and soon would know if she'd picked up a virus or just needed a big dose of vitamins.

Across town, Rogue sat at Dusty's desk and stared at the calendar. His week was almost over. Soon, his brothers would be coming to town. He'd received emails from each one of them. They were reaching out to him. What was he going to do?

Rising, he picked up his Stetson and walked out to where Abby was working at her desk. "I think I'm going to take a walk. Can I bring you anything?"

"No, I'm good," she told him with a smile. "Before your week is over, I want to tell you that I've enjoyed getting to know you. It's been a little strange getting to know all of you Walker boys and seeing how you're the same and how you're different. But I do know that this can work. You and the others can step into Dusty's shoes and make Walker Mineral even bigger and better."

"Thanks for saying that." Rogue tipped his hat to the lady and left the office. At the moment, he didn't really know what else to say. He set off down the street of the small town, taking it all in. The businesses were all family owned and operated. People knew one another, they spoke, they asked about their kin folk. There was a down-home, earthy feeling to the place. Nature seemed closer here. Red Creek ran right behind his father's office and there wasn't so much concrete that it made you feel claustrophobic with urban sprawl. Could he be happy here?

As Rogue meandered down the street, he saw families strolling, couples holding hands, people meeting and greeting one another with a smile on their face. For years, he'd kept to himself, running his company but staying aloof from everyone but Elijah. Even with Eli, he'd never really let him in. Only his mother had been his confidant.

Feeling like he needed to talk, Rogue made his way to a bench and sat down. First he phoned Elijah. "Hey, how's everything going?"

"Just fine. The oil should be flowing soon. I've got the crews working steadily and all of the contracts with the distributors and the refineries seem to be in order. Lone Wolf Oil is about to hit the big time."

"Sounds like you have everything in line," Rogue said, not knowing whether he was relieved or disappointed.

"When are you coming home?"

Ah, the question of the day. "I don't know. Soon."

Before Elijah could ask more questions, Rogue told him he had another call—and he did. Like always, his mother seemed to know when he needed her. "Hello?"

"How's my boy?"

Rogue had to smile. Her 'boy' was six-four, weighed two hundred-forty pounds, could grow a full beard and wrestle a bear if necessary. Still, he'd always be her 'boy', he knew that. "I'm good, Mom. How are you?"

"I'm great. When can I come to Kansas and see your new business?"

Her request shouldn't have surprised him, but it did. She didn't usually like to travel. "Well, I'm trying to decide if I'm going to get involved with Walker Mineral and my brothers or if I'm going to do just what I have to do to sell when the time comes."

"Oh, I don't think you should do that," his mother began. "This is your inheritance, it's your right, it's your connection to a big part of who you are."

She wasn't saying anything he didn't already know. "I just don't want to give up what I have."

"You aren't giving up anything, Rogue. You'll still have Lone Wolf and Elijah and God knows, you're not getting rid of me. If you settle part time in Kansas, I'll find my way up there part of the time too. You're not getting rid of me that easy."

"I can't let that happen."

"Rogue, listen." His mother's voice grew serious. "You've got to look at what you'd be gaining. Your heart and your life are big enough for more. Family isn't defined by a number. We've been a family of two, three sometimes when Dusty was around. But who's to say it can't be six with your brothers and even more when they marry and have children. And you, one day you're going to meet a woman who'll be everything to you, a woman you're going to want to have children with."

At the talk of family, a wife and children, Rogue felt all of his past insecurities and doubts come roaring to the forefront. "You and others have said that I'm more like Dusty than I realize. And I may be, I seem to have inherited some of his interests and talents. But what if I'm like him in other ways? What if I can't be true? What if I put other things in front of my family?"

Rogue heard his mother sigh. "Let me tell you something, something I should have said a long time ago. Yes, I wish things had been different, that it had been me, you and Dusty living together and being a family – but it wasn't. What I had of him, the time I spent with him was worth so much. I'd rather have had that than not have him at all. Your father was a good man and he loved you, he provided for you. Will you make the same choices he did? No, you'll make better choices – but there's one thing he did right. He gave me the most wonderful son in the world, and I wouldn't trade that for anything."

When his mother finished, Rogue got up and continued walking. Could he do it? Could he redraw the circle of his world and let more people in? He smiled. There was one thing for certain—whether he lived in Texas or Kansas, whether he ran Lone Wolf or Walker Mineral – there was one person he couldn't live without. When he'd seen Dave Parker choking the life out of Kit, he'd known she was more important to him than all of the other things in his life put together. He couldn't live without her, he didn't want to live without her. Being with her, making love to her, planning a future with her – that's what he wanted. He'd almost bared his soul last night, but he'd waited because he wanted to make sure what he could offer her. Rogue wanted to be able to tell her his plans and where they'd live and where they'd make their home. And now, now he felt like he had the answer.

Rogue wanted it all. He didn't have to choose. He could live in Texas and he could live in Kansas. He could be a part of Walker Mineral and keep Lone Wolf Oil. He could cherish his mother and still accept Dylan, Killian and Jackson as family. But most importantly—wherever he lived, no matter who he called brother—Rogue wanted Kit by his side.

And it was time to tell her. With that decision under his belt, he made his way to the jewelry store. He had a little shopping to do.

Chapter Fourteen

"You're pregnant."

At first the doctor's words didn't make sense. Kit was floored, shocked beyond words. "But I'm on the pill. There must be some mistake."

The doctor shrugged his shoulders. "Sometimes they don't work. No form of birth control is a hundred percent effective. It's rare, but sometimes your metabolism or your diet or some medication you take can cause the pill not to work."

He spoke so casually, but to Kit, the bottom had just fallen out of her world. She bent her head and covered her eyes, not knowing whether she wanted to laugh or cry. Complete and total elation filled her. She was going to have a baby! Rogue's baby! There was honestly no more wonderful thought in the whole world—unless it was the idea he could love her. That realization led her down another road where immense anxiety and despair lived. How was she going to tell him? He'd made no secret about his desire to stay unencumbered, uncommitted and single. She couldn't say she hadn't been warned.

"I see," Kit murmured, accepting his prescription for prenatal vitamins and a card for her next appointment.

Picking up on her confusion, Dr. Reed stared hard at her. He'd known her most of her life. "You don't intend to terminate this child, do you?" Obviously he knew of her unwed state, the whole town would know of her unwed state.

"No, no." Kit shook her head. Another wave of uncertainty nearly knocked her over. How could she stay here and be the constant subject of gossip and speculation? Even if she and Rogue came to some peaceful agreement about sharing custody, how could she subject him to the talk? Memories of what he'd said about his mother and their experience growing up in a small town without benefit of marriage came roiling back to her. "I'm just

595

surprised."

Dr. Reed helped her up. "I understand. Well, you'll be fine. Just think how happy you'll be when it comes."

Kit realized this was his standard speech, one he always gave to new, nervous mothers. "Thank you," she murmured as she left, avoiding the receptionist. She considered—for about a split second—going by Walker Mineral to see Rogue. But she quickly nixed that plan. Before she saw him—if she saw him—she had to do some thinking.

As she drove home, Kit played one scenario after another over in her mind. Should she leave? How could she do that? She hadn't even considered leaving when they'd almost lost the ranch or when her father had died. Been murdered, she now knew. Her life was here. Her mother, her home, her horses. Could she withstand the talk? Could she face Rogue and confess that her assurance she wouldn't get pregnant was false?

Good God! "What a mess." Immediately, she felt bad. Laying a protective hand across her middle, she mentally apologized to her child.

When she pulled up at White-Wing, she was momentarily distracted by the sight of all the cars and activity. Things were looking up. The ads Rogue had placed were working. Would he want to continue their partnership? "I have so many questions," she whined.

Parking, she got out of her car, straightened her skirt and went in search of her mother. There was no use keeping it a secret, they needed to clear the air about a few things anyway. On the way into the lodge, she stopped to speak to several people and to note how good the flower beds looked. Every step she took, she had to concentrate on not freaking out. All she could think was how wonderful this could be if Rogue were by her side and how scary it felt because he wasn't.

When she opened the big front doors and walked in, the difference in the temperature was startling. She rubbed her upper arms, it was too cool. Their electric bill would be astronomical. She stepped into the office and adjusted the thermostat, seeing that their part-time help was manning the desk. "Where's my mother?" she asked.

"She's setting up for a meeting in the...dance hall?" It was obvious the girl didn't know what to call the large room.

"Okay." She nodded and started that way. As she moved down the hall, she rehearsed what she was going to say. As usual with her mother, nothing went the way she planned. The moment she walked into the hall, it was to find her mother sitting behind the control board of the new sound system crying her eyes out. "What's wrong, Mother?"

"Nothing, I was just dusting." Sheila dried her eyes.

Her mother's sad mood didn't surprise her. "You've had quite a shock." Going to the older woman, she hugged her. "We're going to be okay, I promise. We're going to be better than okay."

"I know." Sheila stroked her daughter's hair.

Taking a deep breath, Kit unburdened her soul. "Mother, I'm going to have a baby."

As if she grabbed onto something else to focus on, her mother exploded. "What? A baby? Who's the father?"

Kit backed up. "You know who the father is, I haven't been with anyone else."

"Rogue Walker will never marry you! He'll be just like his father!"

Sometimes moments of clarity come unexpectedly. This was one of those moments for Kit. She stood straight and proud and spoke to her mother. "I'm not asking Rogue to marry me. Although, I believe if I did, he would. He's an honorable man. I promised him I wouldn't get pregnant. I don't know what happened. The doctor doesn't know what happened, it was just one of those unexplained things. I went into this relationship with my eyes open. He has just lost his father, his world has been turned upside down. Even then, there has been no one kinder or more supportive than him. He has been my protector. He saved me from your husband who was trying to take my life. I love him with my whole heart and I refuse to ask him for more than he would willingly give me."

"Ask me, Kit. See what I'm willing to give you."

The voice from behind her almost caused her to faint. She whirled around, then to her horror she realized they had come full circle. She'd overheard things he hadn't meant for her to hear, and now he had overheard her. "Oh my God." She turned and—too late—flipped off the speakers.

"I guess the cat's out of the bag now." Her mother sighed. "Hello, Rogue."

"Hello, Mrs. Parker. If you'll excuse us, I need to speak to your daughter. Alone."

Before she could protest, Rogue had Kit by the hand and he led her to the front desk.

"Why are we stopping here?"

"We need to be alone. Get the key to cabin #6 if it's free," he said, his touch gentle, one arm around her waist.

She followed his instruction and then let him guide her outside. "I'm sorry," was all she could think to say.

"I'm not," Rogue said flatly. When they were at the right cabin, he took the key from her and opened the door. Then before she could say a word, he backed her up against it and covered her mouth with his, stealing Kit's ability to think. Her eyelids fluttered closed. His lips were warm and demanding, moving slowly and gently. With a low moan, he moved closer, both hands framing her throat. She knew he could feel her heart pounding beneath his fingers. Kit whimpered and surrendered to his kiss, wrapping her arms around his neck. His tongue slipped in and teased her, stroking with a sensuality that sent frissons of desire dancing across her skin.

Kit knew they needed to talk, she wanted to talk. But this was too good. She felt cherished—and right now she could pretend this kiss meant they would be together forever. Her nipples tingled and puckered as he pressed his chest against her breasts. Finally, she had to breathe. "Rogue, please…"

"Please what, Kit-Kat?"" She was so tiny and helpless…and pregnant with his child. He wanted to pick her up, wrap her in cotton wool and keep her safe at all costs.

"We need to talk." She pulled from his grasp and turned away from him. "God, I can't believe you heard me."

"I'm glad I did, I'm not sure you were going to tell me." He stepped closer, placed his hand on her cheek and made her look at him. "Were you?"

"I don't know," Kit admitted. "This is too new."

"You said you loved me." Rogue pressed. "Do you? Love me?"

Kit hugged herself, powerful emotions rocking her body. Finally she whispered, "You know I do." To her utter amazement, big bold brash Rogue Walker sank to his knees.

"Marry me."

Kit gasped, staring at him in amazement, tears welling in her eyes. "What?" She placed her hands on his shoulders. "No. Not like this."

"Why?" Rogue asked, his face tender with feeling. "How do you want me to propose?"

"You don't mean it. You overheard me and now you're trying to do the right thing."

Rogue clasped her hand. "Listen to me." He turned it over in his and raised her hand to his mouth, gently kissing the palm. "When you overheard what I said that day at the rodeo arena that was me being jealous and petty. Now, let me tell you what I heard today. You defended me. You stood up for me. You gave me the two greatest gifts I'll ever receive."

"What?" she asked, her voice shaking. "What did I give you?"

"You said you loved me. And you told me about our baby." He leaned forward and pressed a kiss right over where their child lay beneath her heart. "Marry me, Kit-Kat."

Kit wanted to. It was like a child seeing a beautifully colored balloon and reaching out for it, only to find that it had drifted up and away beyond her reach. "You're proposing because I'm pregnant. I don't want that."

Rogue shook his head. "No, and I can prove it." Reaching down into his pants pocket, he pulled out a diamond engagement ring. "I bought this for you today. I came here for the express purpose of asking for your hand in marriage." He held out his hand. "May I?"

Someway, somehow Kit's dreams were coming true. She laid her hand into his and he slipped the ring on her finger. "I don't understand. Did you change your mind?"

Rogue rose to his feet. "Baby, I love you. I love you so much." He held her tight. "And let me tell you why. I love to be with you. You make me happy. You make me laugh." He kissed her long and hard. "And God knows you excite me, you turn me on. Touching you, making love with you is out of this world. And the crazy thing is that you make me feel safe."

"Are you sure?" She couldn't help but ask. "Because I'd live with you without being married. I know how you felt…because of Dusty."

Rogue ran his fingers through her hair, weaving them, binding her to him. "I am like Dusty in many ways. He was my father. But there's a difference…he kept searching for what I've already found. All I need is you."

Kit smiled and went up on tiptoe to kiss him. "And our baby."

"Yes," Rogue agreed. "And our baby." Sweeping her up, he carried Kit to the bed where he undressed her with great care. "The day I walked into this room and found you in my bed was the luckiest day of my life."

"Make love to me, Rogue," she whispered.

And he did. "With pleasure."

Epilogue

On the thirty-first of August, three private jets arrived at the small airport outside Red Creek, bringing Jackson, Dylan, and Killian Walker back to Kansas.

The four half-brothers met at Cubby's at noon as agreed via email.

"You're driving Dad's Caddy?" Dylan gestured to the champagne-colored land barge parked at the curb. He grinned at Rogue, who'd spent the last week in Kansas.

"Damn right." Rogue gestured to a table for four, and the brothers sat, one at each of the four sides. "The thing is smooth as sin."

Jackson fiddled with the fork that sat on a napkin in front of him. "You know, Dylan, when I got your email after that first week, I thought you'd gone crazy."

Rogue and Killian nodded.

Dylan had sent a note to his brothers telling them that the town had a lot to offer, the business was surprisingly interesting, and the people of Red Creek had accepted him like a born-and-raised Red Creekian.

"I was under the influence, I guess." Dylan scratched his cheek. "But damn if I don't feel exactly the same way being back here today."

"I figured that." Rogue hung one arm over the back of his chair. "Figured you'd found yourself a gal. But I agree, this place grows on a man." A smirk curved his lips.

Killian set his forearms on the table. "Sure does. I mean, who knew this dustbowl in the middle of fucking nowhere would leave an impression."

Jackson. "So we're all agreed? We're going to do this thing?"

The men looked at each other.

"I'm in." Dylan shrugged. "Got nothin' else going on."

Rogue nodded.

"We'll stay the week, the four of us getting to know each other, just like the old man wanted?" Jackson frowned. "Get the business sorted out between the four of us?"

"That's the plan." Killian curled his upper lip in a sneer. "Live in the house for a whole week and bond with each other." He snorted.

The guys laughed, but Rogue pointed at Killian. "From what I hear around town, you found yourself someone to help pass the time."

Killian grinned. "Sure did." He looked at Jackson and Dylan. "And rumors are spreading about you two. You both fell for a local gal?"

Jackson nodded. "Afraid so." He smiled to soften the words.

"Yep. Happy as a puppy with two tails." Dylan stared off, looking lost in thought.

"What about you, little brother?" Killian winked at Rogue. "Don't tell us you're the only Walker boy without a happy ending?"

Rogue sat quietly for a few seconds. "Well, I wouldn't want to be the one to ruin a perfect record." He tried to keep from grinning, but his brothers smacked him on the back, laughing, and he let go with a smile.

For the next hour, they ate burgers, fries, and pie a la mode, and talked about the ladies they'd found and claimed in Red Creek. They discussed the company and pondered out loud their prospects for the future.

Cubby's wife brought their bill to the table. "Well, you four are quite a sight, sittin' here all lookin' like peas in a pod." Sherry cocked her ample hip. "You all decide if you're stayin' or goin'?"

The brothers smiled.

"Hard to believe, but it looks like we'll be staying." Jackson pulled out his wallet.

"Yeah, but you three cowboys forgot about that damn

bonding." Dylan grabbed the bill and handed it back to Sherry with a couple twenties. "Come back and ask us that same question again in a week."

They all looked at each other, matching pleased expressions on their faces.

Killian tapped his belt buckle. "Damn if I don't feel that these tell people we're part of an exclusive club of some kind."

"We are," Jackson said. "The Walker brothers club."

Rogue shook the hands of the men whom he now realized would be his family for the rest of his days. "I can't wait to meet your ladies and for you to meet my Kit. Let's get together soon."

"You got it, Rogue." Killian slapped him on the back. "Drive carefully."

Rogue didn't have to be told to be careful. He had more to live for than he ever thought possible.

Kit was waiting when Rogue drove up from his meeting with his brothers. As soon as he was parked she was out the door and in his arms. "How did it go?"

"Great." He kissed her. "I think we're going to be fine. Tomorrow I'm going to order them a pair of boots to match their belt buckle."

"They'll like them, I'm sure." She took his hand and placed it on her belly. "Do you think he could make a really small pair of boots?"

Rogue laughed. "I'll special order them."

"I love you, Mr. Walker. You're my Rogue Angel."

He cradled her in his arms. "Just like your father promised, I'll always take care of you."

~~*~*

About Sable Hunter

Sable Hunter writes romance, some of it quite spicy. She writes what she likes to read and enjoys putting her fantasies on paper. Her stories are emotional reads where the heroine is faced with challenges, like one of her favorite songs - she's holding out for a hero - and boy, can she deliver a hero. Her aim is to write a story that will make you laugh, cry and sweat. If she can wring those emotions out of a reader, then she has done her job.

She combines the cultures of her two favorite states into many of her stories - from the mysterious bayous of Louisiana where the Spanish moss hangs thickly over the dark waters to the rolling hill country of central Texas. She is passionate about animals and has been known to charm creatures from a one ton bull to a family of raccoons. For fun, Sable has been known to haunt cemeteries and battlefields armed with night-vision cameras and digital recorders hunting proof that love survives beyond the grave.

She owns Beau Coup Publishing Company where she publishes her own work as well as many other fantastic authors. Join her in her world of magic, alpha heroes, sexy cowboys and hot, steamy, to-die-for sex. Step into the shoes of her heroines and escape to places where dreams can come true and orgasms only come in multiples

Visit Sable

Website: http://www.sablehunter.com
Amazon: http://www.amazon.com/author/sablehunter

Hell Yeah! Series
Cowboy Heat
Hot on Her Trail
Her Magic Touch
A Brown Eyed Handsome Man
Badass
Burning Love - Cajun Style
Forget Me Never - Cajun Style
I'll See You in My Dreams
Finding Dandi - Cajun Style
Skye Blue
I'll Remember You
True Love's Fire
Thunderbird – Equalizers
Welcome to My World
How to Rope a McCoy
One Man's Treasure - Equalizers

Texas Heat Series
T-R-O-U-B-L-E
My Aliyah - Heart In Chains

Hill Country Heart
Unchained Melody
Scarlet Fever
Bobby Does Dallas

Dixie Dreaming Series
Come With Me
Pretty Face

El Camino Real Series

A Breath of Heaven
Loving Justice

Moon Magick Series
A Wishing Moon
Sweet Evangeline

Green With Envy (with Ryan O'Leary)
For A Hero (with Jess Hunter)
Love's Magic Spell
Wolf Call

Audio Books
Cowboy Heat - Sweeter Version: Hell Yeah! Sweeter Version
Hot on Her Trail - Sweeter Version: Hell Yeah! Sweeter Version

Cookbook – SABLE DOES IT IN THE KITCHEN

20142563R00336

Printed in Great Britain
by Amazon